Freya's Flight

by

CRAIG P. MILLER

FREYA'S FLIGHT

by

Craig P. Miller

This is a work of fiction and events portrayed
in this book are fictitious, and any resemblance to real people
or events is purely coincidental.

Copyright © 2014
Published : July 2014
Vé Publishing

Paperback - ISBN: 978-0-6482622-0-6

Cover creation and design by
Dean Reynolds
www.dcreynolds.com

Chapter Icon :
spaceship by Jonas Nullens
from the Noun Project

DEDICATION

I'm not sure about dedications.
While I always received encouragement from those who knew
that I wrote, it was I who had to dedicate a large part of
what can be laughingly described as my free time to writing.
It was I that encouraged me every hour that was
spent writing and revising. It was I that helped me through
the format changes into an E-pub format and back again for
print-on-demand. But that's self-publication for you.
I'm not sure I should dedicate this book to me anyway.

If I'm going to dedicate this book to anyone,
it is the Science Fiction writers that inspired me:
Heinlein, Asimov and Clarke as well as Le Guin and McCaffrey,
Varley, Robinson, Brin, Niven, Zelazny
and all the writers I don't have space to acknowledge.

Thanks for the inspiration.

ACKNOWLEDGMENTS

I have worked for most of my life in film and television
and it is a recognized principle within the industry
that any project is a collaborative effort.
Although this book has been, for the most part, a solo project,
it has not been written in isolation.
I would like to thank Simon, Chris, and John
for their encouragement. They had ideas bounced off them
that helped me chart Freya's course.

Thanks to Dean for his enthusiastic work on the covers.

And thanks are due to my editor, Tina Shaw.
Your oversight and attention to editorial detail
was an essential element shaping this book.

A NOTE

While published as "Patty's Flight" and its sequel "Patty's War",
the story was originally conceived and written as one piece.
It brings me great pleasure to return this work to her natural
state.

Table Of Contents

Freya's Flight

Part One

Patty's Flight

by

CRAIG P. MILLER

CHAPTER ONE

Patty Balke floated smoothly down the center of a pale blue corridor. She was feeling a little blue too, despite the animated chatter of her two best friends, and despite winning her latest bout. Memories of the arena flashed into her mind. The padded fencing gear protected her from physical pain when Jas Rightson's blade scored again and again, but those strikes were seared into Patty's brain as if they drew blood, and she flinched at the memory of her coach's dressing down. *I'd still be sweating under his icy gaze if he didn't have to leave OASIS. He was right, one hundred percent. I was distracted, slow, uncoordinated, and damned lucky*, Patty admonished herself. Even so, it was hard to feel entirely down in zero-gee. Since joining The Lightning Strike, OASIS's zero-gee fencing team, flying filled Patty's dreams. Flying, free of gravity's restraint, made her soul feel alive. The micro-gee environment in Low Earth Orbit suited her perfectly.

"No, it was more like this," Tina Franks insisted as she kicked off from a wall stanchion and spun, her body following a sinuous path, corkscrewing down the passageway. Tina was blond and often described as petite, but Patty thought of her as distilled rather than just small. She was a jam-packed ball of energy, pure trit. "What do you think, Patty? Did I get it right?"

"No, no, no. There was more energy at the start," Hine interrupted. "She twisted around Jas' thrust before she delivered the kill-stroke." Hine Whiniata was as dark as Tina was light and as bold as she was buxom. Compared to her friends, Patty felt like a gangling filly, all knees, and elbows. Even Tina's tiny frame was rounded and beautifully proportioned.

"Knock it off, you guys." There was no way Patty could hide her embarrassment, so she did not even try. Tina and Hine enjoyed making her blush. She did take pleasure in hearing her friends praise her. *If only it didn't make something inside me twitch. What is that?* Patty wondered.

"Patty! You were so hot! I loved the way you spiraled in to make contact," Hine said as she thrust forward, mimicking Patty's winning strike, arm extended, wrist cocked just so. "I would never have been game enough to try that."

"I was desperate," Patty responded with a shrug. "Jas had two points on me, and the clock was running down. It was a Hail-Mary. You should have heard Coach tear strips off me afterward, and he was right, it was a crazy maneuver. If Jas had been a microsecond faster, she would have skewered me." She shook her head. "It was dumb." She was proud of her win, but it had been a near thing. Zero-Gee Fencing was more than just using your thrusters, buzzing around the arena, hacking at your opponent; it demanded balance, timing, quick reflexes, and an unruffled demeanor. Patty grimaced at how she let Jas' sly jibes get under her skin. Never again, she promised herself and meant it just like she had the last time. Impulsive, her coach had said, his focused disapproval almost disguising the pride her win brought to the team result. The Lightning Strike had almost won. Almost. And next comp we're up against L4's Fusion Thrust. They were a very tough crew.

"It was inspired," Tina said. "I'm gonna practice it."

"But don't use it in competition or Coach will pin a piece of your butt to the wall next to the chunk of mine he just chewed off." Patty rubbed her backside for emphasis.

"That may be so, but you didn't hear him cheer when you scored," Tina told Patty, her grin lighting up her face. "I knew you'd make a great addition to The Lightning Strike from the moment I saw you on The Bus." Tina was good at spotting prospective team members - four this year, not including Patty - and proud of it. Patty had been waiting to boost up to the Open Access Science Industrial Station, OASIS, for flight school and discovered a whole new reason to be where the speed of their flight countered Earth's gravity.

"Speaking of transport, I've gotta head home," Patty apologized as she descended to the Gecko-Grip flooring. Tina and Hine followed her down, alighting one on each side. The corridor had reached the crowded G5 thoroughfare, and the usual mix of floundering tourists and almost competent Corporates choked the broad passageway. Only a few were game enough to try flying free, so there was plenty of room above the heads of the masses. OASIS is getting crowded, Patty thought.

"Leaving? No! Say it's not so!" Tina exclaimed.

"L3's Starlight Tigers are holding a celebratory bash at Shadrach's," Hine said, grinning slyly at Tina. "Biff Ramos is going to be there," she added with a wink at Tina.

Patty blushed, again, and the two girls had another chuckle at her expense. Biff had a nicely shaped butt, which she had mentioned once, just once, in passing, and now her friends would not give up ribbing her about it. Biff was only an average swordsman who used brute strength to win his bouts. To top it off he believed he was the current incarnation of D'Artagnan. He did cut quite the dashing silhouette, but when he opened his mouth, the illusion was shattered; he was as ignorant as a stump and utterly unaware of it.

"Oh! Be still my beating heart," Patty responded, camping it up by fluttering her eyelashes, feigning weak knees, and placing her hands over her palpitating heart. She stopped the romantic pretense and frowned, hands-on-hips. "Did you see the way he stampeded over Danny? I can't wait until he comes up against LaRue. He's going to run Biff ragged." Anatole LaRue was captain of the Lightning Strike men's team. Now there was someone to moon over; his bright blue eyes did make Patty's knees go weak, but he was way out of her league.

"Oh yeah," Tina agreed. "He's going to make Biff work keeping that shapely butt of his intact."

"Do you really have to leave?" Hine asked. "Tina's only going so she can trip up one of the Tigers and add his skin to her collection." Tina laughed and wriggled her eyebrows suggestively.

Patty could not get over how relaxed her friends were about men. It was not that she did not like boys; they were interesting, in a strange kind of way. Patty understood the evolutionary impulse to procreate the species, and experienced hormonal surges a time or two, but she just did not feel the rampant urge that seemed to infect everyone else. Despite her mother telling her that she would bloom in her own time, Patty thought that something was missing inside her.

Patty sighed. "If I don't turn into Daddy's Courier Service..." She left it hanging and mimed being strangled. "I promised to have a delivery in his hands by morning. He was so pissed off I missed the last slot for SoCal he booked me an egress window." It was so humiliating. Only tourists booked their departure time.

"At least you have your own Curve," Hine whined, letting her genuine envy shine through. "We're still humpin' it up to OASIS on The Bus."

"You can't complain," Tina punctuated her words with a disgruntled huff. "You can just about walk to the port," she continued with a mocking voice. "The Bus only leaves from Darwin once a week. Most times I gotta use the 05 from Darwin to Sydney, three hours there and back."

"I've told you, you can hitch a lift with me," Patty offered, "I don't mind flying a semi-ballistic across to Darwin to pick you up."

Tina paled.

"Why, you big chicken!" Hine declared. "Patty's one of the best pilots around." Now it was Tina's turn to blush. Patty and Hine laughed at her discomfort. It did not happen very often.

"It's the pillion seat; way too small," Tina argued, desperately trying to find an excuse."

"For you?" Hine cracked up again. "I could pack you in my overnight bag, and there'd still be room for my fencing kit."

Patty's wrist comm sounded a countdown warning. "Sorry

gals. Gotta go. Ping me," she told them. Patty's shoulders slumped, and they gathered for a group goodbye hug.

CHAPTER TWO

Patty secured her helmet to her P-suit's collar and double-checked the seals. The telltale lights on her wrist comm flashed green, and she punched the big red airlock-cycle button. Despite being in zero-gee, a thousand boots had scuffed the deck, and the graffiti-covered the walls made the airlock leading out to OASIS's East Chandra docks look more decrepit than it was. Air whistled through the valves as pumps sucked it into storage. The light above the door flashed green then red, then green again. A groaning sound accompanied the inconstant light. OASIS was old but not infirm despite the need for running repairs. Patty sent a maintenance report. The integrity of the airlocks was always a high priority, and that meant that maintenance teams would be scurrying. The hissing faded as cold vacuum replaced the station's warm air. The heavy door emitted a grinding vibration Patty felt through her boots as it shuddered and withdrew into the wall.

Securing the parcel of golden monofilament to her belt, Patty pushed off the deck. As she rose above the array of safety lines, she pumped a blast of cold gas from her P-suit's thrusters and headed towards Freya. She had not used the safety lines since her first trip to OASIS. Only tourists would pull themselves hand over hand along the regularly spaced cords strung across the broad deck. Monofilament thread was stronger than anything known to man and finer than the hair on a newborn babe and only one of the exotic materials produced by the zero-gee factories in orbit. It was not the first time she had transported items for Balke-Spalding Enterprises. It was either be a part-time courier for her father, Christopher Balke, CEO of Balke-Spalding Enterprises or take The Bus. It was no choice. Most of the time, it was not much more than a folder of documents; this time it was a spool of monofilament.

Her CRV license made carrying a commercial product not precisely legal, but then again it was not exactly illegal either. As far as she was concerned, she was only transferring material from one branch of her father's business to another, minus expensive shipping charges and other things of which Patty preferred to remain ignorant. Running errands for her father was the price she paid for getting her Civilian Re-Entry Vehicle. To those that flew them, they were CRVs or *Curves*, the most exciting thing to happen since powered flight.

She was late. There were only five or six CRVs still docked at OASIS's East Chandra moorings. Everyone else who needed to make a California landing had gone. The orbit-return window for SoCal would expire in about ten minutes. After that, landing in San Francisco would be impossible. Waiting another eight hours up here for the North America return window would be bad, but having to land in Hawaii would be worse. She had already missed her scheduled flight by goofing off with her friends after the competition. The Lightning Strike was in an excellent position to reach the finals, and Patty took the regular contests between the teams seriously. On the other hand, hanging out with Tina and Hine was serious fun. She would be with them in Shadrach's Bar and Grille, but for her promise. Promises were important too.

Unperturbed by fifty kilos of precious monofilament slewing her off target, Patty made course corrections instinctively, cold gas firing from hip and shoulder. After another quick blast, Patty's boots skidded across the scorched deck, killing just enough of her momentum so that she did not injure herself when she collided with Freya, her red and gold striped CRV. An almost wingless lifting body - a design pioneered in the late twentieth century - Freya was five meters long, had a wingspan of nearly three meters and an engine powerful enough to achieve Low Earth Orbit. Not that she would ever consider using the fusion engine during lift-off, but if the Sabre launch engines failed Freya would keep her safe.

Patty's wrist comm pinged, and she opened the channel. "Cutting it a bit fine, aren't we?" She recognized Cian Kerr's hometown accent instantly and looked around the dock. Cian was two bays over. His canopy was up, and he was sliding inside his sleek machine. Cian's brand new Dragão 540 was nearly twice Freya's size and sported a garish pink and green paint job. It looked fast.

"Had to pick up this stuff for Dad. He calls me his On-The-Cheap delivery service." Patty opened the forward hatch and secured the monofilament inside. She checked the seal closely as she closed it.

"You gotta look after those old birds." Cian sounded almost wistful.

"Yeah," Patty agreed as she ran her hand over Freya's smooth prow, "but she flies so sweet." She gave the exterior a quick once-over. Everything looked in the green, so she detached the umbilical that kept Freya fueled and charged.

"I used to have an MC-150T. Launch phase was a bitch. Couldn't make orbit without the Sabres, but she cut some swe-e-et curves on re-entry. They haven't bettered that body shape in years. She won the inaugural Trans-Lunar, y'know. A bigger engine of course. So, what's sparking under your hood?" Cian was a good-natured fellow even if he was a bit of a goofball. He was not the best CRV pilot, but he could hold his own, on a good day.

"250 worked out to a 310." Patty was proud of her machine. She popped the canopy and slid into her custom-formed seat with a sigh.

"Swe-e-et. Cian Kerr to Tower. UA-6214T requests egress clearance, over." The flash from Cian's engines lit the dock, harsh and bright.

Patty strapped in. Freya was nothing fancy on the inside. A simple utilitarian layout of engine readouts and flight controls, almost flying seat-of-the-pants but that was the way Patty liked it. Freya had an adequate flight computer, but she only used it for launches and when in the clutches of Traffic Control. She ran her eyes over the instruments. Preflight was in the green. Her sleek machine was prepped and ready to go.

"Tower to UA-6214T, standby Cian. Tower to DH-1031C, Patty, your egress window expires in twenty seconds. Are you clear?" Jake Chowdhury's warm Texan drawl always made Patty smile. She unlocked the docking clamps and unleashed her engines. The acceleration snapped her back into her seat.

"Thanks, Tower. We are clear, Jake! Cian, last one down buys lunch for Large Marge! Over," Patty challenged as she left the docks on a pillar of fire.

"You're on!" Cain came back. "Tower?"

Jake's chuckle came over the comm. "Cian. You're in so much trouble. You're not gonna catch that one. UA-6214T you have egress clearance, over."

Cian's engines roared. "How much you wanna bet, Jake?" Cain asked. Patty laughed as she tweaked her heading, but Cian's craft was much more powerful than hers and with a new orbital computer to boot. It would take some fancy flying to keep him in her wake.

"You booked an egress window? You day-tripper!" Cian's voice came through her comm, dripping with disdain.

"My Dad did... after I missed the last one." That was embarrassing and made Patty squirm. She just hated it when her dad did things like that.

"Well, your father won't save you now!" Cain declared.

Patty took a bearing from Cian's transmission and painted him with her LADAR. The Laser Direction and Rangefinder was accurate to a few angstroms, and her display showed that Cian was close and getting closer. He would be right on her tail in thirty seconds or less. Patty pumped her thrusters and dropped to a lower, faster orbit. It would put her into the atmosphere sooner, but she trusted Freya's aerodynamics to counter anything Cian could throw at her, even with his extravagant new machine.

The proximity alarm gave a banshee wail. There had been a concerted effort since the war to clear away the debris accumulating in Low Earth Orbit. It was mostly successful, but you had to keep alert. Her reactions pumped her thrusters before she even thought about it and spun Freya's orientation, presenting the smallest possible cross-section to the approaching object. The outer fringes of Earth's atmosphere were approaching fast.

"Wha'cha up to Patty?" Cian's voice clashed with the proximity alarm. The alarm's pitch and frequency increased as, whatever it was, flashed closer. The warning signal peaked alarmingly, and Patty was sure she was going to feel a mighty crash as it pulped her tiny craft. To her relief, the piercing frequency and volume began to taper off.

Then there was a sound of disaster. It took Patty a moment to realize it was coming over the comm, not from her ship.

"Cian?" she asked.

The only comm return was profanity and then, "Mayday, mayday! I've been hit!" Cian shouted.

"Cian? Are you alright?" Patty demanded.

"I've lost my ship," Cian cried. "I've lost my ship! Spinning! Out of control! I'm ejecting! Repeat I'm ejecting!" The channel went dead. A chill rushed through Patty.

"Cian? Cian?" she called.

"I read you, Patty," Cian finally responded. "I'm clear. I'm out. Suit integrity... in the green." At their speed, Patty knew that it would not remain that way for very long. There was a big difference between doing a long drop from a balloon and entering the atmosphere with thirty thousand klicks up your sleeve.

"What happened?" Patty asked as she took a bearing, painting Cian with her LADAR. Two substantial returns appeared on her screen surrounded by an expanding volume of the wreckage. The most significant blip was what remained of Cian's ship, drifting into a higher orbit.

"Well," Cian began, "I seem to recall I was catching up with a cocky young woman in an obsolete hunk-a-junk when I noticed she had assumed a rather odd re-entry attitude."

"I had a proximity alarm...."

"Ha! Of course. I muted mine. My autopilot kept insisting we were too close," he grumbled. Patty listened to Cian breathing heavily. "Wish we'd been closer," he muttered under his breath. OASIS was almost out of sight and too far away to do anything useful anyway. They were on their own.

"Looks like I'm gonna have to renege on Large Marge's lunch," Cian remarked. Patty could hear the stress in his voice. "Been nice knowing you, Patty."

"Standby Cian." The instructors at flight school had told her of the handful of rescue attempts made in orbit, but there had never been a successful rescue during re-entry approach. One thing they did say: in the event of an emergency, keep clear of the debris field. Despite that warning, Patty fired Freya's maneuvering thrusters and edged closer.

You're going to be biting air real soon. I have to do something more than this! But what. It was infuriating!

Patty stamped her foot in frustration.

CHAPTER THREE

The firewall between the cockpit and the forward storage bay bowed under the stress of Patty's boot. An idea, or the hint of something similar, began to blossom. She did not clutch at it but let it drift through her subconscious, gathering strength and vitality as it developed. Patty focused on her frustration, and she stamped her foot. The firewall complained, emitting a low squeak. And then the penny dropped. There was a ten-thousand-kilometer reel of almost unbreakable, military-grade monofilament beyond the firewall. *Can I get one end to Cian? If I can't risk taking Freya to Cian, can I haul him clear of the wreckage?* It was a crazy plan, but at least it was something. Cian was a big geek and not what she would call a close friend, but she was not going to leave him to burn up on re-entry without trying something.

Patty checked the clock. She had a little time up her sleeve. She prayed it would be enough and dogged her visor down. Pumping her lateral thrusters, she spun Freya end for end. A warning light flashed as the air in her cockpit pumped into the holding tank.

"Cian? How's it hangin'?" she inquired casually.

"Funny you say that," Cian came back with a chortle. "The stars seem very bright. It's a beautiful night out here."

"How good are you at catching?" Patty asked. She opened her canopy and unbuckled herself. For a split second, she almost went ex-vehicle without a safety line and felt a flash of cold sweat. Buzzing around on-station while untethered was cool. It showed you were an old space hand, experienced. Climbing out of a CRV that was about to re-enter the atmosphere was foolhardy, but going EV without being tethered was madness. Snap, click, she was secure and on the move.

"Catching?" Cian answered. "Well, I was never the first choice for a pickup softball game, does that help?"

"Not really. What's your P-suit's thruster status?" Patty asked.

"I used a fair amount getting out of my CRV, but the cold-gas gauge reads seventy-four percent. Maximum delta-v, about ten kph," Cian replied. "I've done the calculations, Patty. I might be able to move in your direction, but I'd never be able to find you. Me ol' P-suit ain't got no radar." Patty could hear him sigh. "And ten kph ain't enough to change my re-entry profile either. Cian's gonna get crispy!"

"Don't panic!" Patty insisted. She floated smoothly, serenely, out of the cockpit and over Freya's smooth prow. The fact that she was traveling at nearly thirty thousand kilometers an hour seemed irrelevant.

"What me, worry?" Cian responded with a maniacal laugh. "My brand new Dragão 540 is a write-off, and in a little while, I'm gonna turn toasty. What have I got to worry about?"

"Just keep your chin up. I've got an idea," Patty told him. The forward hatch opened smoothly. She grabbed the parcel of monofilament and closed the hatch as gently as she could even though her mind was screaming for her to hurry. If that opening was not correctly sealed, Freya could get a lethal burn through. In a matter of minutes, the only thing that would stand between her and ionized gases was Freya's ablative shielding. She needed to get back inside as quickly as she could. Patty took a couple of deep slow breaths to calm herself. Thrashing around in zero-gee was a useless activity. She pulled herself carefully along Freya's smooth fuselage and back into the cockpit.

"What kind of idea?" Cian started chuckling. His voice held a panicked edge that gave Patty goosebumps. He better not lose it.

"Cian! Keep chilled. Patty's on your case. Get icy!" She demanded. The parcel ripped open easily once Patty's gloved fingers found the tab. She popped open the toolbox, stowed under her seat and pulled out an adjustable spanner. *That should mass enough*, she thought. Patty wrapped the monofilament around and around the chrome tool and secured it with a generous coating of gray duct tape. *Some days it's impossible to do anything without duct tape.* Unable to get a visual sighting on Cian, Patty painted him with her LADAR once more. The laser range finder showed Cian drifting slowly to port of her re-entry track, two hundred and fifty meters to stern.

Patty took a deep breath. This had better work. There was no time for second tries. She lined the spanner up as best she could and threw it; not too hard but with enough force to give it plenty of momentum. The monofilament paid out smoothly. Patty squeezed the line. The LADAR display showed the spanner gently arcing towards the tiny dot that represented Cian. A warning light flashed, and Freya bucked as an atmospheric shockwave began to form beneath her tiny ship. Patty strapped in and tried to balance Freya's tail first plummet, her left hand skipping across the controls, the right paying out the insubstantial golden strand.

"Patty?" Cain called plaintively. "You still there? Can you call my mother when you get..."

"Cian, just wait," she told him. "You've got a present coming!" The LADAR said the spanner was only ten meters away from Cian. Freya bucked and writhed under her, threatening to spin out of control. Maintaining Freya in a tail first attitude kept the building pressure from ripping her canopy off. She would be as dead as Cian if she could not keep her tiny craft controlled. Flying backward during re-entry wasn't something that was taught in flight school and making course corrections was harder than she imagined it would be. The spanner was five meters away from Cian.

"My present's getting pretty close. You should be able to see it by now," Patty advised.

"Stand by." A crackle of silence. "I see it. It's below me, about three meters to starboard. You, you sent me a spanner?" Cain asked with a chuckle.

"It's attached to some of Dad's monofilament," Patty told him.

"Hang on."

"No, you hang on Cian!" Patty joked, and Cian's chuckle sounded much more relaxed. Good.

"I've got it... I think," Cian replied.

"Hold on!" Patty cried.

"Oh, I will. I promise."

Patty hauled on the monofilament. It slipped through her fingers. Wrapping it around her glove, she pulled again. Once, twice she dragged an arm's length of the shimmering thread into the cockpit. On the third pull, it snapped tight. "Gotcha! Hold on tight!"

"Roger!" Cian replied smartly. Patty pulled again and again and painted Cian with her LADAR. He was closing at one point two meters per second.

"You should have your heading now Cian," she told him.

"Brilliant Patty, pure genius!" he responded with a shout.

Patty took up the slack as quickly as she could. LADAR had Cian approaching at five kph. His retro burn would leave his thrusters just about dry. It was a thin line between getting him to Freya quickly and being able to catch him when he arrived. She did not want Cian splattered across Freya's delicate prow. The buffeting increased and Freya almost unbalanced completely. Patty struggled with the controls. Her CRV bounced like a rock skimming over a pond. *Oh Freya, you poor girl. You were never meant to be flown like this. If Cian doesn't get here soon something's going to break.* The bright flare of ionized gases started to flicker around the stern. If she did not correct her re-entry attitude, she was going to burn up.

Cian was ten meters away, then five, flying towards her, cold gas blasting from his suit's thrusters. Freya bucked like an angry bull. Everything rattled and shook alarmingly. Then Cian was there, clinging grimly to the prow.

"Get in! Get in!" Patty shouted.

"I'm trying," Cian muttered. Freya's buffeting made the task more than a little awkward. Cian inched his way aft, turned and entered the small cabin feet first. He aimed for the rear of Patty's customized chair with only some success, his booted foot getting tangled in Patty's harness. He took what felt to Patty like an insane amount of time to free himself. With Freya bouncing around, it was almost impossible to maneuver into the confined space, but Cian managed it as quickly as he could.

"Hey! You've got a pillion seat back here!" Cian said as he strapped himself into the small rear seat. Most CRVs were solo craft.

"Once you're secured, get the filament hauled in. The canopy won't close with that thread hanging out there." Patty had her hands full maintaining Freya in a steady attitude. "My Dad had some alterations made when we bought Freya. I have to bring my little brother up here every other weekend so he can practice with his basketball team."

"Well, thank your dad for me," Cian told her.

"Do it yourself. Are we secure?" Patty asked.

"Almost." The last of the golden thread flipped over the edge and into the cockpit. "The thread's all in," Cian announced.

"Securing canopy," Patty said as she activated the control. It seemed to take forever for the canopy to caress and then sink securely into the seals. Returning Freya to the correct re-entry position was hellishly difficult. Every time Patty touched the attitude controls, her nimble craft threatened to roll over. That would mean instant death. If they rolled over now, the canopy would flare into non-existence, and the pressure wave would crush them both before they succumbed to the intense heat of the ionized atmospheric gases.

Warning lights flashed red, and their associated beeping and blatting was more an annoyance than assistance. Patty already knew they were in trouble. Freya bounced and bounced again like a skimming stone dancing over a lake. It gave Patty an idea. There were little bounces and big ones. If she could time her attitude burn to one of the more massive bounces, she might be able to turn them around, like a surfer doing an aerial stunt from the top of a wave. Bounce, shudder, bounce, BOUNCE...

With a burst from Freya's main engines to give a little extra lift, Patty fired her thrusters. Freya slammed around. BAM! The pressure wave hit hard. They bounced again. The shock wave caught at the leading edge of Freya's stubby wings and threatened to flip them over. Although the bounces began to reduce in intensity, her ship now had a horrifying Dutch Roll, the bane of lifting bodies like Freya. Her prow yawed back and forth, as they rolled from side to side. The hot ionized gasses were getting closer and closer, threatening to spill over the edges of the ablative shielding. At least she had managed to keep Freya's nose up. Patty's stomach, usually rock solid, tried to empty its contents with a violent contraction. She clenched her teeth and swallowed against the acidic flow. Throwing up in her helmet would surely sentence them to a fiery death.

Executing a swift rudder doublet, Patty flicked the foot controls ten degrees to port, back to the center, and then an equal flick to starboard and back. That helped a little. A quick rudder singlet to port and the nauseating yaw yielded some more, but there was still something that was throwing Freya off balance. Patty would have slapped her forehead if she had not been wearing her helmet. Of course, she's unbalanced.

"What do you mass?" Patty asked.

"One eighty-five," Cian groaned, "suited of course."

"Of course." Patty chuckled as she adjusted Freya's trim-tabs. The roll slowed, and the yaw all but vanished. One by one, the flashing red lights littering her control panel turned a constant reassuring green. Patty sat back panting, her hands shaking, hovering just off the controls. There was one blinking light, but Patty could not summon the concentration to deal with it. Suddenly her chair shuddered, and for an instant, Patty thought disaster had claimed them.

"Wooo Hooo! Wow!" Cian shouted. "Man oh, man! Damn it, girl, that's some pretty flyin'! You're the real deal girl! WOOO HOOO!"

Patty had to laugh. The shake that made her heart leap into her throat was Cian bouncing around in his restraints. "Keep it seemly in the cheap seats please," she told him.

"Aye, aye skipper. Wow, man. I thought we were goners." Cian broke into peals of laughter, and he pounded the back of the seat once more. "Wow! You're damn slick with a stick, Patty. There ain't no fancy onboard computer that could pull off a maneuver like that. What are ya gonna call it?"

"Call it? What do you mean?" she asked, puzzled.

"How 'bout Balke's Bounce?" Cian suggested.

"What are you on about?"

"Ya gotta put your moniker on a move like that girl!" Cian told her as he chuckled and flopped back in his seat with a sigh. "What do you think, Jake?" he asked.

"Jake? Who are you talking to?" Patty inquired.

"I've got OASIS Traffic Control on the Emergency Channel in my left ear and the P-suit channel in my right," Cain told her. "Jake's pitching for Patty's Pirouette. I think that's a bit of a mouthful."

That last blinking light on her control panel was the comm's Emergency Channel. Patty reached across the console and flicked a switch. "... got no sense of style, Cian." It was Jake, back at OASIS Traffic Control. "DH-1031C. Patty, I see you're online. How are you doing?" It was so reassuring to hear his relaxed drawl Patty felt her heart rate slow immediately.

"Pretty good, I think. Freya's in the green as far as I can tell." Patty took a deep breath. They would need a mid-course burn in a minute, but their re-entry track looked pretty good.

"OASIS Control confirms your telemetry DH-1031C. You're tracking five-by-five, Patty. Well done. Well done indeed." Patty could hear laughter from others in the control room over his open mike.

"Who's with you, Jake?" There was usually only one controller in there at this time of day.

"Oh, it's pretty crowded in here at the moment. Cap'n Burt's here," Burt Hanover was the OASIS manager. No one dared to call him Cap'n Burt to his face, but all Patty could hear through Jake's open mike was laughter, "Security Chief Randle, Todd Franks from The Interplanetary Chronicle, Jenny Northrop from The Times and a few others. You're famous, Patty. We've had a scope on you and Cian from his first mayday. Global News has been streaming it live." Jake laughed. "Chief Randle's pretty pissed it took you so long to turn on the Emergency Channel but then again if you'd listened to his advice, Cian would be crispy by now. You done good, girl."

More flashing lights demanded Patty's attention. The comm channels were lighting up.

"Err, thanks, Jake." Patty felt uncomfortable listening to Jake's praise. Her hands were still shaking. "My comm's lighting up, Jake. Traffic Control, are we clear? Over."

"OASIS Traffic Control to DH-1031C. Emergency protocols are rescinded. Err, before we go, Todd and Jenny want you to promise to listen to their offers before you sign up with anyone else, over."

"Sign up?" Patty asked. "Over."

"You're hot news, babe," Jake replied with a soft laugh. "You're gonna be in the middle of quite a media bidding war. Over." Jake's voice was full of good humor, but Patty shuddered anyway.

"Tell 'em to talk to my dad's lawyer," Patty responded with a groan. "Talking to flacks is the last thing I want to do right now. Over,"

"I understand. See ya next trip, Patty. OASIS Traffic Control, out."

Patty looked at the flashing comm and sighed. They could wait; she had a mid-course correction to calculate.

INTEGRATION

Er'men did her best not to stomp as she approached the concealed compartment in her bed head. *Genedalt doesn't deserve your anger*, she admonished herself. Her giant Hel'omi guard felt her frustration nonetheless, but he stood impassively beside the elaborately engraved doorway to her bedroom. During the journey across the depths of interstellar space, historians had painstakingly decorated the GreatMother's suite aboard Tal'anis with the pictorial history of her people. There was hardly a single surface in her rooms that had escaped her brothers' sharp records.

"No disturbances this time, no matter what RegentFirstMother Harrum'Bar wants," Er'men insisted, locking eyes with her giant Hel'omi protector to drive her point home. There was no need. Clan Bumurnam FirstSon Genedalt took her usually polite requests as battle-field instructions. *I wish Harrum'Bar were as compliant. I'm not a pouchling anymore!* Er'men grumbled silently.

Bowing low to acknowledge her command, Genedalt returned to his relaxed but alert pose. "Your will, GreatMother. Clan Bumurnam holds the GreatMother's suite. None may pass."

A wave of excitement lifted Er'men from the solemnity of the moment. "Thank you."

The RegentFirstMother's intentions seemed legitimate, but there was something about her that disturbed Er'men. The decision to attack without warning had precedent in Clan Lore, but it still felt wrong. She was sure they needed to know more about these people before embarking on such a venture, but there was nothing Er'men could do about it. *Not now. I need to learn more. I need the wisdom of my forebears.*

Propped on the edge of her bed Er'men's little fingers felt for the release mechanism that would reveal the hidden but not secret compartment. It was traditional for a GreatMother to keep her most precious possessions away from casual inspection. The sensitive tips of her fingers found the latch concealed as a scalloped rise below the edge of an angry thunderhead. A hidden mechanism whirred and clicked as a small door swung open. The scents that rolled through the opening made her stop for a moment as she absorbed the messages within them, signals that triggered subtle adjustments in her body chemistry. It was impossible to treat the contents of the hidden compartment with anything other than reverence, but the overpowering fragrances did not dampen her enthusiasm.

A dark-grained box made from a single piece of wood fitted neatly within the shadowed cavity. There were no latches or hinges; its surface was unadorned. No historian had charted its history, only gentle hands, over thousands of years, had softened the dark wooden edges and sharp corners until it was completely smooth, hard yet soft to the touch. Er'men's delicate hands were just as caring as she placed the box on her bed's embroidered quilt.

Instinct guided her long fingers, and the concealed catch released the lid. The intensity of the intoxicating aroma redoubled, and Er'men took another moment to bathe in its glorious embrace. She lifted the folded green-blue dappled Jahn fur pelt from the box and laid it on the quilt. Lifting away the soft pelt's top and side folds exposed fourteen tiny golden spheres of mel'andrin. They were more than the sparkling jewels they appeared to be; they contained Er'men's inheritance, the memories of her predecessors. It would take many years to integrate them all, and Er'men was keen to continue her education.

The offering spoon, as smoothed by use as the box itself,

detached from its recess in the lid and Er'men's hand hovered over the sparkling collection. There was little to differentiate one sphere of mel'andrin from another. GreatMother Pur'unnan's mel'andrin was the most recent and was the richest in coloration and shine. The next oldest sphere was only subtly paler, but the difference was enough for Er'men's keen eyes.

"GreatMothers guide me." Er'men felt the prayer come from deep within her, from a racial memory embedded in her very bones, as she coaxed the mel'andrin sphere into her spoon and raised it to her lips.

"GreatMothers, show me the way. Show me the path in the darkness."

Taking the fragrant ball into her mouth, Er'men slipped it under her tongue. She took a deep breath and relaxed, waiting for the memories to unpack, reinforcing the ones she had absorbed in her first session. This time she wanted to go back as far as she could and examine the oldest of her inherited memories.

The light brightened behind Er'men's closed eyelids, and the sound of a vast body of water lapped at the shore. She could taste the salt on Fe'ren's lips as her ancestor took one last look out across the inlet. Two sailboats leaned into the wind, and a light plane buzzed slowly overhead before disappearing beyond the lush forest that covered the hills on the far shore.

"Fe'ren?"

"Coming Mother." She picked up the woven reed bag filled to the brim with sweet whil'luw eggs and joined her parents on the picnic blanket. The hot sun felt good on her skin but that only brought to mind a news report that their star was dying. That frightened Fe'ren, and she could tell that her mother was scared too. *You can't hide that kind of thing*, she thought.

Father was more confident, reassuring them both that it might not happen for millions of years, that they were safe. "We are adaptable. That's why we're on the top of the food chain. Our sun's too small to explode; she's just going to deflate and get fat and red. That's going to take millions of years. We've plenty of time. Don't you worry yourself about it."

"What a beautiful world, Genedalt," Er'men sighed. The scan was not very detailed, but she could clearly see the blue of oceans and the greens and browns of continental landmasses. White, moisture-filled clouds joined with the brilliant polar ice caps to add a sense of pristine wilderness to the image. "And such a big moon," she added. The scan showed it as an over-exposed silvery blob. She wished Harrum'Bar had deigned to give her access to the real scans. There were lies in the RegentFirstMother's eyes, but Er'men did not have the status to call her on them.

"Go back to your memories, infant!"

Not that the RegentFirstMother had actually said infant, but she might as well have. *Leave us. This matter is for adults.*

Er'men hated it when Harrum'Bar was right. The faster she integrated those memories, the sooner she would be able to make the RegentFirstMother stand aside. *What is she hiding from me?*

Er'men sat back from the glossy image and relaxed her breathing as much as her twisted body would allow. It took almost nothing to bring the recall of her inherited memories into focus, and she sought out the earliest times once more, even though they held some of her people's darkest moments.

Fe'ren bit back a curse when the wayward trolley crashed into her ankle and hobbled over to the dusty concrete wall for support.

"Sorry doctor," the nurses' assistant apologized and bobbled a curtsy as she struggled to control the bed on the rough surface. An underground parking building was no place for the sick, but at least it was somewhere safe. Fe'ren steadied the leading edge and gave a quick glance at the patient's stats. Not good. *How were they supposed to care for these patients when there was no power? This patient needs a respirator for goodness' sake.*

"Take him over there to your left. Dirma'don will have ... some space for him." And some drugs to ease his passage. Maybe they had been right to send him to the upper levels. The depths of the hospital's underground shelter was no place to die. There was nowhere to dispose of a body down there either.

"Do you know what's happening, Doctor? I mean..."

"No, I'm sorry. We're lucky we had advanced warning," Fe'ren sighed. She knew much more than this poor child would want to hear. "It's not as bad as the sunstrike down south."

"Isn't our magnetical field thingy supposed to protect our planet?" she asked.

"Normally, yes," Fe'ren replied. "Look I'm a doctor, not an astrophysicist. I don't know much more than what they've been telling us; seek shelter underground. I've been told the coronal discharge will be over before nightfall. We just have to hold on until then."

"Yes, Doctor," the nurses' assistant trundled off with her charge.

Fe'ren could not draw her eyes away from the flickering light that found its way down the offset ramps of the parking structure. The Lights made for wonderful nighttime shows. She remembered how special it was when she was little more than a pouchling. There were magic curtains of light in the night sky. Her father's reassuring voice, telling her it only happened once or twice in a person's lifetime, that their sun had millions and millions of years before it would transition into a red giant. By the time she entered college, she had seen The Lights five times. Radical conservatives proclaimed it a judgment on modern profligate lifestyles, demanding that cities be dismantled and that everyone return to the swamps.

Ridiculous! The Arumpo'or are an adaptable species. We will survive. But Fe'ren could feel doubts sapping her confidence.

The Lights had become The Fire, and the primeval swamps were no refuge when The Fire touched the ground.

CHAPTER FOUR

"You're a freak!" Alan's snarl had a hint of a smile that barely diffused the venom of his words. Patty sighed and concentrated on eating her breakfast. Some mornings he would do almost anything to get a rise out of his big sister. She did not have the energy to combat his display of brotherly shove this morning. The day was brilliant with the sun streaming into the kitchen, bouncing off the blue-green wall tiles. Too bright, Patty complained. For all her parents' technological savvy it was a cluttered, chaotic space with hanging copper saucepans and knife and spice-racks, cupboards filled with crockery and a walk-in pantry. They even had a convection oven. It was the old-school late twentieth-century manual kitchen that had convinced her mother that this was the right house to buy. She could make anything in it though she hadn't cooked for a while. *I wish Mum would do more baking. Her brownie-cakes are way better than store-bought ones.*

"Just eat your breakfast, Alan, and stop hassling your sister," Dr. Cynthia Balke instructed her son. She did not usually interfere with Alan's sister baiting, believing a little ribbing promoted character. "Give her a break. She was up late last night." Patty gave her mother a grateful smile.

"It's not my fault she's the media's darling," Alan replied, fluttering his eyelashes.

"But you could be more considerate," Cynthia countered.

"My psych teacher says teenagers are notoriously inconsiderate," Alan argued and shoveled in another spoonful of muesli. Milk dripped from one corner of his mouth.

"Well, when you become a teenager, you can be

inconsiderate but until then..." Cynthia began.

"My birthday's only a month away," Alan interrupted.

"You can be inconsiderate then, but until that time, you can pull your horns in and give us both a bit of peace, okay?" Cynthia insisted as she sat at the dining table, a steaming mug of coffee in one hand, the first draft of her newest research paper in the other.

"If I have to," Alan complained but his grin was infectious, and Patty could not help but smile. He could be an annoying, pain in the butt, an irritant under her skin, but they got on surprisingly well most days. When he's asleep, Patty grumbled to herself. "Where's Dad?" Alan asked.

Cynthia sighed, frowning as she made a correction to the report and sipped her coffee. "Good question. He received a call at about three this morning and raced out. Another emergency at the plant, I guess. For the life of me, I can't understand why the over-paid managers he employs can't handle it." She frowned again and made another correction.

"Perhaps it has something to do with Tempelman," Alan proposed and scooped the last of his muesli onto his spoon.

"Unlikely," Patty countered. "Dad's business has nothing to do with the Tempelman-Frobisher asteroid." Patty sipped her juice and wondered just how distracted her mother was. "Though it'd sure be something to see first-hand." Her mother continued working, ignoring her daughter's not-so-subtle hint.

"My friend Drake says it's gonna crash into the Earth and we're all gonna die horrible deaths," Alan declared, looking almost gleeful at the thought.

"You know as well as I do that it's going to miss us by ten thousand kilometers," Patty insisted.

"Sure," Alan drew the word out sarcastically. "You been listening to gov'ment 'ganda again?"

Patty knew she should have been using her mouth for eating and not talking, but it annoyed her when the media was full of shrill fear-mongers. Don't people listen to scientists anymore? "No. I was talking to Doctor Wentreck who studies at the OASIS observatory. He's been tracking it for weeks. Get your facts straight, peabrain."

"Brainiac!" Alan poked out his tongue.

Urgh. There was still some masticated muesli in his mouth. Disgusting. "Paraplegic kicker!" Patty retorted.

"Poo brain."

"Proboscis face."

"Bum nibbler!"

"Please, children. Not this morning, please," Cynthia pleaded.

"Sorry, Mum." Patty snarled at her little brother. He grinned back at her and took a swig of his orange juice.

"Mum?" Patty asked.

"Yes, dear?" Cynthia replied without looking up.

"Since we're on the topic of the Tempelman-Frobisher asteroid I was wondering if..." Patty began.

"If you could watch it from OASIS," her mother cut her off. "Look, honey, we've been over this. It's the middle of the school week, and you can get as good a view from down here. In fact, UNET will be showing the same pictures down here as you would see up there."

"But..."

"I'm sorry" Cynthia replied. "Your father and I have talked it over, and with all the fuss the media is making over your little adventure, we're concerned that you are getting behind with your schoolwork. You have homework due this morning, yes?"

"Yeah," Patty conceded reluctantly.

"And I'll bet that appearing on The Late Show last night meant that you didn't finish it. Am I right?" Cynthia continued.

"Yeah." Her mother was right, but Patty thought she had a reasonable excuse. Ms. Mathews will give me an extension.

"Patty just wants to hook up with Cian the Barbarian again," Alan grinned cheekily.

"I don't think so," Patty declared angrily, realizing regretfully, the moment the words left her lips, that she had risen to her little brother's bait. That was the last thing she wanted this morning.

"He's too old for you Patty. He's what, twenty-two... twenty-three, and you're seventeen," her mother said, seemingly oblivious to Alan's taunt.

"Oh, I know that, Mother. I have no romantic interest in Cian at all, I swear." Patty put one hand to her heart and raised the other. Cian was tall and gangly and had the personality of someone half his age. *There are much better fish in the ocean, even if I haven't hooked one yet. I'm not going to settle for anything that just swims past. I'm not even sure if I want to go fishing.*

"Suuurrre," Alan's grin matched the laughter sparkling in his eyes. *Damn. He'd definitely won this round. How does he do that?*

"Okay, okay. Enough of this. It's almost time for you both to be out the door. Get goin' guys," Cynthia insisted.

"Okay, Mum," Patty replied, and quickly finished her muesli, chugged down her juice and trudged up to the upstairs bathroom. *There never seemed to be enough time for her just to stop and gather herself. Some days she felt like she was trying to run in zero-gee! All action, no traction.*

Patty looked in the mirror as she cleaned her teeth. *Is that another pimple?* Her shoulder-length mousy-brown hair was brushed, tidy and tied back; her white blouse, clean, her pants tight where they needed to be, flowing loosely down her long legs; conservative and practical. She was not a fashion plate. Despite the inclinations of her gender, fashion was a part of human culture that Patty did not quite get. She understood, intellectually, that it was about attracting a mate, gaining and holding social status, but she was more interested in having honest friends than a mate. *It sounds so ... so Darwinian, something built into my genes, a program running in the background ensuring the continuation of the species.*

Patty spat into the basin, rinsed, and leaned closer to the mirror. *Mum's right. Just a touch of foundation and you could hardly see the circles under my eyes. Appearing on The Late Show had been worthwhile, hadn't it?* Despite her misgivings about the media, she'd enjoyed the attention she received last night. She'd been ushered backstage, into the green room and there was Philip Shain! Oh, I've had a crush on him since I was nine when he starred in Vegan Holiday. He was there to promote his upcoming feature, of course. What a star! It was hard to keep focused. Was that the Darwinian urge kicking in or was I just star-struck? His eyes are so blue, Patty sighed. And then to sit on the couch next to him while Pete Rais interviewed them. It was great fun under those bright lights with cameras swooping around, the band playing and the audience laughing. And Philip had been so kind to her when the show was over. He seemed genuinely impressed with what she had done. They all were. Rescuing Cian did not fit into her idea of being brave. It had been foolish and reckless - and dangerous - and she broke into a sweat every time she remembered what she had done.

I don't want to be a hero. I don't want to be famous. Do I? Some days her head was so full of doubts and conflicting points of view she did not know what to think. Isn't it supposed to get better as I get older? It always felt like things would change next year when she was older, but it never did. Things just seemed to get more complicated. Her mother and father looked secure and confident. If genes win out over my environment, maybe there is hope for me after all. Last night's appearance on the long-running show was meant to be a sop to the slavering media hounds, but there were still a couple of broadcast vans parked outside the house. Why can't they leave me alone?

As Patty rinsed away the last of the toothpaste, she heard voices downstairs. Raised voices. Dad was home. "Patty! Get down here pronto!" Father sounded upset but not angry. What have I done this time? "Patty?"

"Coming, Dad," Patty called.

Christopher Balke looked disheveled, unshaven. That was most unusual. Patty stopped on the last step, unsure whether she should get any closer. Something was seriously wrong. She had never seen her father like this. There were rings under his eyes, darker than her own, and a frown creased his forehead as he paced the lounge room. Damon Triggs, her father's assistant, immaculately dressed in a conservative suit with a white flower in his lapel, stood patiently at the edge of the room beside the Pic-wall. The news was on, but the sound and the 3D projection were off.

"What's up?" Patty asked hesitantly.

"Good. You're here. Prep Freya. Your mother's packing some things for you." Christopher's frown deepened.

"What's happening?" Patty asked.

"It's just hit the newscasts, but I've been watching it all morning. Tempelman-Frobisher has changed course," her father told her.

"What?" Patty's mind tried to refute her father's assertion, but her brain did not seem to want to work this morning.

"Early this morning, it changed course," Christopher repeated.

"What? How? What have the research team said?" Patty asked as her thoughts spun. How was it possible for an asteroid to change course?

"We don't know," Christopher replied with a shrug. "We lost contact with both the mining and research teams on the 'roid. All we really know is what was going to be a certain miss is now a confirmed collision. Your mother and I want you and your brother up in OASIS as soon as possible. There's no time for more questions, just get Freya ready, okay?"

"But what about you and Mum?" Patty asked and took one step closer.

"Don't worry about us. We won't be more than an hour or so behind you, I promise," her father reassured her.

Alan came leaping down the stairs. He looked pale and afraid. Cynthia was close behind him, a bulging bag in each hand. "... but my pressure suit's not back from the service techs." Alan's voice had changed from its usual cocky bravado. He now sounded like the frightened twelve-year-old boy he was.

"There's an emergency Zip-Lok p-suit in Freya; you can use that," the tone of Christopher's voice brooked no argument.

"Aw, Dad," Alan complained.

"Shut it, son. You have no say in this. You're going up with your sister if I have to stuff you in that Zip-Lok myself. There's no time for arguments. Okay?" their father said gruffly.

"All right," Alan relented. His head dropped, and he shuffled on the spot.

"We'll get you a replacement suit when we get to OASIS," Cynthia said, and she began to hustle him outside. "We won't be too far behind you. I promise."

Patty ran over and hugged her father. His strong arms wrapped around her. It was small comfort, but it was better than nothing. She had never felt so scared. He squeezed her and kissed her forehead.

"You better get Freya ready. I've booked you a launch window." He glanced at his watch. "And you better hustle or traffic control will lock you out." He gave her another squeeze. "Go on. Time's tickin'." He sighed and looked deep into her eyes. "Try and keep your little brother out of trouble until we catch up?"

"I will, Dad, even if I have to lock him in Freya," Patty told him confidently.

Her father chuckled. "I wouldn't advise that. He'd probably hack through your lockouts and steal her the first moment your back's turned. Just keep an eye on him. He'll behave."

"He better."

CHAPTER FIVE

Patty was glad her father had gone to the expense of replacing the old helipad at the rear of the house with a launch ramp for Freya. It could take hours to queue and launch from San Diego. There were still signs of the old tennis court that preceded the helipad with its tall, overgrown link fence that ran down the south side of the yard. A post that had once supported one end of the net stood a meter in from the wall and now held a fire extinguisher. The neighbors were far enough away so that if they coped with the noise of a helicopter, they would have no complaints about Freya's Sabre launch engines. Christopher helped Patty load the bags into the forward hold while Cynthia assisted Alan into the emergency Zip-Lok pressure suit. Before she sealed it, she hugged him and kissed his cheek.

"Now you look after your big sister. Try not to give her too much trouble," Cynthia said as she helped Alan into the small rear seat. "We'll see you soon."

"Promise?" Alan asked.

"I promise," their mother reassured him. "I love you, son."

"Love you, Mum," Alan replied glumly.

Patty pulled on her gloves, sealing them to her pressure suit as her mother pulled her into a tight embrace from behind. Patty wriggled around and gave her a big hug of her own.

"You be careful, Patty." Cynthia's eyes were troubled even though she tried not to show it.

"I will, Mum. Cross my heart," Patty promised.

"Okay, scoot," Cynthia told her as she gave Patty one last squeeze and a quick kiss. "See you soon. Love you."

"Love you too," Patty responded.

Her father patted her on the shoulder. "Fly true, pumpkin. See you soon." He took Cynthia's hand and pulled her back towards the white, stucco house. "Come on, Cyn. We've got to scoot, too." They waved briefly before going inside.

Patty pulled on her helmet, climbed into her CRV and wondered if she would ever see her home again. *I wonder what Mum packed for me.* Despite her feelings of unease, she had confidence her parents would be safe; they had access to any number of corporate shuttles. Patty logged into Freya and sent a launch confirmation. The clock was ticking. There was no time for fussing. The last of Freya's preflights came up green. They were ready.

"DH-1031C to Traffic Control. Over," Patty called.

"Traffic Control to DH-1031C. You have clearance. Over." That sounds like Jake's Texan drawl. *What's he doing handling lift-off clearances?*

"Jake?"

"Hi, Patty," Jae replied. "Don't have time to chat, chum. Earth-side Traffic Control's got us doing overflow. Get your butt off the ground now! See ya soon, kiddo. Traffic Control, out." The comm channel cut into silence. Patty hit the Go button, and the launch sequence began counting down. Freya's cradle tilted up to the vertical and locked into place with a reassuring clunk.

"Ten seconds," the autopilot announced blandly.

"Patty?" Alan asked.

"Can it wait?" Patty dogged her visor down.

"Five seconds."

"I guess..." Alan replied.

Freya's Sabre launch engines spun up quickly and lifted her from the ground. Designed for much more substantial craft, the Sabres pushed Freya through the thousand-meter mark in less than a minute. The engines cycled into rocket mode and roared, pressing Patty back into her padded seat. Two-gees, three-gees, four; Freya built speed quickly. They passed a thin veil of high cirrus clouds in seconds. *Five-gees and holding.* Ten more seconds and the lift-off sequence throttled back to a much more comfortable two-gees, then after thirty seconds, it cut out altogether.

Boosting into orbit was something Patty never took for granted. Flying was always an exciting time for her, no matter what the maneuver. Lift off and boosting into orbit, changing orbits to rendezvous with OASIS, atmospheric re-entry, cutting through the ever-turbulent air, thick with moisture, bringing Freya into perfect three-point landings - it was awesome, every part. Flying made her feel alive. The sky faded from summertime blue to the deep black of space, sprinkled liberally with bright stars. *Freefall.*

The cradle with the launch engines fell away, and Patty made a quick check to confirm its rockets deployed correctly. They were self-landing, but no one wanted a launch assist rocket falling into their backyard. If they didn't fire the cradle would fall into the Atlantic Ocean. Nevertheless, since most of the Atlantic Ocean was someone's backyard, dropping your expensive launch engines on their heads was a practice to be avoided. The telemetry looked good. Now that Freya was above most of Earth's sweet atmosphere, her fusion engines ignited, lifting them into Low Earth Orbit.

"OASIS Traffic Control to DH-1031C. Over," Jake called.

"DH-1031C reading you five-by-five. Over," Patty responded.

"Hi, Patty. It's getting pretty crowded up here. Change your heading to 103.52, delta-v 63.034 KPH, in ten seconds, on my mark. Over," Jake instructed.

Patty smiled at Jake's Texan twang. She always felt safe with Jake watching over her. "Roger, Traffic Control. Course change laid in, Jake. Over."

"Five seconds," Jake began. "Three, two, one. Mark!" Patty's finger pressed home the control, but the autopilot beat her to it. Freya's engines fired for three seconds and then cut off. "Sorry 'bout the extra orbits, Patty. We'll have you safely ingressed as soon as we can. Catch ya soon. OASIS Traffic Control out."

Patty did not mind a few extra circuits. She only wished Freya had a bit more room to stretch out, but they would dock with OASIS soon enough.

"Patty?" Alan asked.

"What's up, li'l buddy?" Patty replied.

"I think I had too much for breakfast," Alan gulped. "I'm gonna be sick."

Patty shuddered. "Well, keep your Zip-Lok sealed. I don't want your half-digested breakfast floating around the cockpit."

"Err. Yuck!"

"Kidding," Patty responded with a laugh. "Unzip. Freya's sealed tight. You know where the barf bags are."

"I'll be okay, I think." Alan did not sound very confident.

"You'll be fine, ya old space hound," Patty told him as she heard her brother swallowing.

"Yeah," he swallowed again. "Right."

"Look, use the screen on the back of my seat. Turn on. Log in. Tune out. You know the drill," Patty instructed and tried to keep it light. She did not want to start this flight with a sick passenger. "Give your mind something to do, and it gives your inner ear a chance to remember that zero-gee is okay." Alan's usually so blasé about going to OASIS. *It's not like him to get queasy.* Crazy music and cartoon chatter drifted over from the back seat, and Patty relaxed. *He'll be fine.*

Patty scanned her favorite UNET channels. There was panicked chatter everywhere. The main media outlets were screaming doom, Doom, DOOM! Even the usually calm and well-reasoned Atlantic Observer had commentators spouting End-Of-The-World nonsense. *Was there no one out there keeping a level head on their shoulders?*

"Patty?" Alan asked again.

"How ya feeling?" Patty inquired.

"Err, a bit better, I guess. What's that? Port side..."

Patty adjusted Freya's attitude, rolling her gently to port. It was a launch – or, rather, lots of them. Two, three... Patty blinked. Four ships arced up from the North American continent and they were really moving, aiming for high orbit. It was a coordinated launch, and the ships were slowly moving closer to each other. *Now, why would you do that?* It did not look very safe. There was no point in getting together this early in the launch phase. You only attempted rendezvous once you were in orbit. *Unless they're not going into orbit.* One by one, first stage engines died and were discarded. Second stage engines fired and in seconds, they streaked above Freya, burning hot, arcing even higher. Patty rolled Freya, tracking them, as the bright exhausts faded into bright points. A chill spread across Patty's skin. That was a military launch.

"Oh no." Patty swallowed the lump in her throat. "They wouldn't..."

"Whoo wheee!" Alan shouted, "they're gonna blow up the asteroid!"

Her little brother was right. Patty felt sick, and it was not freefall-nausea. It was dread. *Why would they fire missiles at the asteroid?* The chance of deflecting it from its course was marginal at best. Tempelman-Frobisher was an irregular conglomerate with a long axis of nearly four hundred meters and an average diameter of two hundred and thirty meters. It was not a dinosaur killer, but four missiles would not be able to deflect it, not at this stage, it was too close. All they would do was fracture it; break it into hundreds, maybe thousands of pieces that would rain down on the Earth for weeks.

"Oh, this is bad. Very bad," Patty muttered.

"Whadda ya mean?" Alan asked.

"The missiles are going to break the asteroid into pieces, not push it out of the way," Patty told him.

"And that's bad?" he asked.

"Very," Patty added.

"DH-1031C this is OASIS Traffic Control. Over." *Whew, my Texan angel is still online.*

"DH-1031C receiving you. Jake, did you see that? What are they thinking? Over," Patty replied.

"Don't know, munchkin, but Cap'n Burt's pitchin' a fit. DH-1031C, how's your fuel supply? Over," Jake inquired.

"In the green. Freya was fully fueled at launch. Be prepared; I know the drill. Over."

Jake chuckled. "DH-1031C, I have a course correction for you. Heading 253.04, elevation 19.32 degrees, delta-v 503.29 kph. Over."

"Course laid in. Over." Patty confirmed. *Heading 253.04, elevation 19.32 degrees? Where is he sending us?*

"Ten seconds on my mark. Over." Jake told her.

"Jake! Where we going? This course is going to take us way out of LEO. Over."

"Are you ready? Over," Jake insisted.

"Of course. Over," Patty replied.

"Trust me. Five seconds, three, two, one, mark!" Freya began her internal count for ten seconds, then leaped forward.

"Jake?" Patty asked.

"DH-1031C, you're looking good. You are in the green. Expect mid-course corrections in twenty minutes. Over."

"Jake?" Patty asked again.

"Patty, I told you Cap'n Burt pitched a fit. We're going to L1," Jake told her.

"You're going to move OASIS?" Patty inquired, not quite believing him.

"Done it. We're boosting now. Gotta run. Catch ya. OASIS traffic Control, out." The comm went silent.

Patty was stunned. They were taking OASIS out of Low Earth Orbit. Wow. Didn't think the ol' tub still had the legs for a major boost like that. Bet she springs more leaks than the Titanic.

"What's happening? Where are they moving OASIS to?" Alan asked. He sounded distressed.

"L1. They're taking OASIS to Lagrange One," Patty told him.

"Where?"

"Lagrange One. It's an area of gravitational equilibrium in the Earth-Moon orbital system," Patty said.

"Huh?"

"Pea brain," Patty muttered.

"Brainiac!" Alan teased.

"You better believe it," Patty insisted. *Now how can I explain this so my mentally deficient brother can understand?* "Earth has a gravitational field, right?"

"Yeah." Alan's bravado barely disguised the uncertainty in his voice.

"A gravitational field just means that if you come near the Earth, you will fall towards it, okay?" Patty informed him.

"Sure. I know that."

"And the Moon has one too, right?" Patty prompted.

"Of course," Alan snorted.

"Well, there is a place, between the Earth and the Moon, where the opposing gravitational pulls cancel each other out. Sort of a gravitational flat spot," she told him.

"Oh, I get it. Hey, that's pretty cool. Why Lagrange One? How many are there?" he inquired.

"Five. L2 is on the opposite side of the moon to L1, L3 is in the Moon's orbital track, on the opposite side of the Earth, L4 is sixty degrees ahead of the Moon's orbital path, and L5 is sixty degrees behind."

Alan was silent for a moment or two. "What about the sun?"

"Hmm, maybe you do have some brain cells," Patty responded with a chuckle. "Good point. The Earth and the Sun have five Lagrange points as well. The sun's gravitational field does interfere with the Earth-Moon Lagrange points, but most orbits need occasional adjustments, station keeping, so it's not a major issue."

"Patty?"

"Yeah?" Patty replied.

"How are Mum and Dad going to find us?" Alan asked plaintively.

"What do you mean?"

"OASIS isn't going to be there," Alan said flatly.

"You don't think they're moving it without telling anyone, do you?" Patty chortled.

"I guess not."

But another thought chilled Patty. Most spacecraft used OASIS or one of the other orbital platforms in LEO as way stations if they were going on to the Moon, one of the Lagrange stations, or points even further afield. OASIS was relatively easy to get to, a perfect place to rest and refuel before going on. Public shuttles like The Bus were only able to reach Low Earth Orbit and, without OASIS, there would be no way for them to boost higher. Patty's heart beat faster. *Calm down, calm down. Mom and Dad won't be on The Bus. Dad will have organized something private, something corporate, something with much more grunt than The Bus. They'll make it. Of course, they will.*

Patty did not want to think about that anymore. She needed something to do. Working out the flight plan to rendezvous with OASIS instead of relying on Jake's friendly assistance would be just the ticket to keep her mind off those terrible what-could-be nightmares. She took a steadying breath and set up the problem on her computer. Slowly the numbers began to flow into a usable solution.

"DH-1031C, this is OASIS Traffic Control, I have your mid-course corrections. Over." Jake sounded stressed.

"Reading you, OASIS Traffic Control. I have my own calculations. Can you verify? Over," Patty replied.

"Of course, you have," Jake chuckled. "Fire them at me. But if you're off by more than quarter of a degree, and half a klick, you're buying dinner. Over."

"You're on." Patty transferred the result of her calculations and checked the time. "Burn in eleven minutes, thirty seconds on my mark." She waited until the clock ticked over. "Mark. Over."

It was good to hear Jake laugh. "On the money, honey. Looks like I'm gonna have to mooch dinner off one of the other freeloaders heading up here. Over."

"Oh, I'll buy you dinner. It would be my pleasure, sir," Patty told him.

"That's the best offer I've had all day. I'm off duty in an hour," he replied.

"Shall we say 2230 hours GMT, Shadrach's B&G?" she suggested.

"With bells on. Fly true, munchkin. OASIS Traffic Control will be monitoring your burn. Out," Jake finished.

Patty confirmed her settings and sat back. The autopilot would take care of the flying now. Freya's burn was flawless.

LEAVING HOME

The change in Genedalt's posture was minuscule; his head was a hair's breadth straighter, his broad shoulders cocked as if he had repelled a breeze. The RegentFirstMother had sent one of her functionaries in another attempt to distract her. They had not penetrated any further than the outer reception suites.

Er'men gave a nod of appreciation before returning to her contemplations. Something was wrong. *If this beautiful new world was everything the reports said it was, we should have landed by now.* The RegentFirstMother held the reins of power as tightly as she held the flow of information, but Er'men knew the solution was not to be found confronting Harrum'Bar in a frontal assault. *Well, not yet anyway. A GreatMother's strength is the wealth of her memories. My memories.*

One last look. Fe'ren set her pack down and gazed across the broken city while stretching the kinks out of her back. Old age was creeping up on her. Sunset painted the shattered towers blood-red, filled with soft dusty shadows. Survivors had picked the city clean years ago. They had to move while they still could, north, where there was fresh water.

"There's nothing left down there." Ter'illion laid his pack beside hers. He had been her strong right hand for so many years, backing her up in public and correcting her only when they were alone. A pang of grief echoed through Fe'ren. After all these years the fact their union was barren was a raw hole within her being. The knowledge that many other couples were infertile only scared her.

"Just memories," Fe'ren muttered and tried to remember the brightly colored signs advertising wares or shows or exhibits, but they were hard to recollect clearly, overlaid by the harrowing years of darkness, hiding in a powerless bunker. They had lost so much. *The benefits of civilization had been such a thin veneer.* She glanced up at Doronem. The closer of their two moons showed clear signs of habitation, but it had been years since they had heard from the colony. *What would future Arumpo'or generations think? Arumpo'or, The Risen Ones, risen from the swamps and wetlands. Risen so high only to fall so low.* She hoped the city in the sky would inspire them.

"Just death," Ter'illion growled and kicked at a rock. "Those of us that have survived so far have to stick together. You've heard the reports. They have power. Fusion power. And water."

"Yes, yes. I know," Fe'ren agreed. "We need to gather and share our talents while we still have them."

"You don't think Jar'eared's idea is going to work?" Ter'illion asked. "What does he call it?"

"Mel'andrin, gift-memory. It does work. The memory I tried was crystal clear; so clear it might have been my own."

"But for how long, one breath? Two?" Ter'illion was such a doubter. Fe'ren felt joy flow through her. *He has such a level head.*

"He is on the cusp of something that could save us all. We've lost our libraries and our universities, all the structures that kept us out of the swamps. We need to support him," Fe'ren insisted.

"I agree, but I'm not sure the Northern Council will," Ter'illion grumbled.

"Old men. They will support him after I get through with them," Fe'ren growled.

"I'm sure they will." Ter'illion kept his laughter at bay for as long as he could. "Come on, or we'll be walking in Hel'omi crap all the way." The big pack animals did not seem to mind the heat or the dust and had to be restrained from breeding, or they would consume all their precious supplies. Primitive but more robust than their so-called superior cousins, they had taken shelter during the worst of the sunstrikes and seemed no worse for it.

Fe'ren picked up her pack and shouldered it, bouncing it once or twice until it settled comfortably. She took Ter'illion's hand and turned away from the remnants of their bright city. *He's right. There's nothing but death down there.*

CHAPTER SIX

The East Chandra moorings were full or almost full. There was always room, even on race days, but there were CRVs and small ships of every size and design stacked up closer than regulations usually allowed. It was a tight squeeze, but Patty placed Freya in her assigned position, not a full bay, with barely ten centimeters between her and the craft to either side. One was a garishly painted Hammerhead-650 that looked fresh from the showroom floor, and the other, a scratched and beaten-up old Singer-125. Patty locked Freya down and sighed. Landing gently on the deck and squeezing into this tiny space while OASIS boosted to L1, had been challenging.

It felt strange, looking out across the East Chandra flight deck and experiencing weight pressing her into her seat. The acceleration was not great, about a fifth of a gee, but it seemed very foreign. OASIS had always been her land of perpetual flight, a zero-gee, somewhat scruffy, paradise.

"Alan, are you sealed?" Patty asked.

"Yeah. Do I need to take anything?" Alan responded.

"No, I've got your travel docs. We'll leave everything in Freya until we need it. With all these people here, it could be difficult getting accommodation. I don't want to have to herd bags around too."

"Roger that," Alan confirmed.

Patty depressurized Freya and opened the canopy before unbuckling her restraints. Alan was already halfway out of his cramped seat. "Tethers!" Patty insisted.

"What?" Alan objected.

"Use the safety lines," Patty told him. OASIS is boosting, and

I don't want you drifting away if they change headings. Mother would be so disappointed in me. Your Zip-Lok doesn't have thrusters, remember."

"Okay," he said reluctantly. "But only if you do."

"Oh, I will be. Don't worry about that." *I'm Safety-First-Girl now. No more adventures, not here, not if I can help it,* Patty thought. She climbed out behind her brother and secured the canopy. The CRVs were packed so closely together, Freya did not have its own umbilical. There was no way Patty was going to leave Freya without a full tank and a full charge. The umbilical on the dilapidated old Singer indicated it was charging, but the Hammerhead's was idling, so she hooked it up to Freya. Interfering with another ship was a punishable offense, but Patty did not care. *Not today.*

ID Control was chaos. It took them over an hour to get to the head of the queue. It would have been longer, but OASIS stopped boosting when they were halfway to the desk. Tourists and newbies of all shapes and sizes began tumbling and then vomiting all over the place. It was disgusting. *Don't they know how to put their face in a bag?* Alan laughed and kept his Zip-Lok sealed. Getting cleaned up by going through decontamination was unconventional but essential for both of them. They started a trend.

When they finally arrived at Shadrach's, Jake was already perched at the bar, floating at about a fifty-degree angle to the deck as he looked out the huge window. He would have been slowly turning, head-over-heels, if Shadrach's had not been so crowded. One of the handfuls of the long-term inhabitants of OASIS, Jake did not care which way was up. He had been a great pilot in his day and had spun long yarns that meant Patty had missed more than one egress window, listening to him. It usually took Patty a while to lose the Earth-bound instinct that relied on having a stable horizon. When she could, Patty stayed on station for a few days before a fencing competition just to make sure she acclimatized to a horizon-less orientation. The fencers that unconsciously relied on a horizon found themselves eliminated in the early rounds. It was one of the reasons Jake interested her. That and the fact that the old-timer deigned to notice her.

When she first met Jake, he had been in Shadrach's with a bubble of Jack Daniel's in one hand and a pair of binoculars in the other. Unlike everyone else in the room, he was turning sideways, slowly, head-over-heels, always staying oriented to the broad window where a sparkling blue Earth dominated the view. He never twitched with a careless thought or over-corrected when he took a swig on his bubble of booze. His rotation axis was centered somewhere near his navel, and his body was completely relaxed. Daichi, Patty's fencing coach, would have called his form near perfection. She could not help but stop and watch Jake slowly turning.

"You're never gonna learn by sittin' and watchin'," he'd said to her as he casually pivoted in place. "Ya gotta do." It had taken him less than a minute to notice she was watching him, not the view. He told Patty he'd seen her fencing, and they had talked before, of course. He was the calm voice of OASIS Traffic Control. He knew who she was and why she was watching. Jake invited her to join him, spinning slowly, watching the Earth roll around beneath them. He never taught her anything formally, but she picked up so many little things as he talked about flying and a million other things. Her flying and fencing had improved out of sight. Patty had no idea why the grizzled old veteran had struck up a friendship with a newbie pilot like her, but she was glad he did.

"What'll it be, Little Lady?" Jake exaggerated his natural drawl when Patty hooked her booted foot into the railing beside the tall but portly Texan.

"My usual. Thank you, kind sir." Patty enjoyed playing along.

"And you, young man?" Jake asked.

Alan's pout looked fixed. He still wore his Zip-Lok P-suit. There had been three emergency pressure warnings while they had moved through the crowds, and it would have been funny watching new arrivals as they struggled to get back into their P-suits if it had not been so scary. Patty had been sure they would have been able to pick up a replacement pressure suit for her brother, but the newbies had scoured the stores, and there wasn't even a half-decent second-hand one that would fit him.

"Beer," Alan replied with a straight face.

Jake roared with laughter. "I've half a mind to let you. It's been a trying day for everyone." He caught the barkeep's eye. "I'll have another double, one bitter lemon and lime," he looked at Alan and smiled, "and a Jango Juice for the young man." He pushed off from the bar and nodded at the concierge as he floated over the velvet rope, disdaining to use the Gecko-Grip floor. It was impolite to break the conventions of up and down in public, but an old hand like Jake had his own rules and kowtowing to newbies and tourists was not on his list. Alan pushed off the deck and followed him through the air. Patty pursued them.

Jake had his usual table reserved, positioned with one side pressed up against the window. If not for their subtle reflections in the laminated glass it felt as though you could fall out and tumble away into the darkness of space. Jake floated beside the table, looking out at the Earth. In a few minutes, the terminator would be visible as OASIS's expanding orbit took them over the daylight side, but for now, Earth was dark, city lights flickering in the night.

"Jake, have you heard from Hine or Tina?" Patty asked.

"Sorry?" Jake shook his head; he looked distracted. "Who?"

"Hine Whiniata and Tina Franks," Patty reminded him. "They're on my fencing team. I've tried to ping them, but OASIS's servers crashed again."

"Oh, of course. Sorry. Hine and Tina, no," Jake murmured as he shook his head. "They didn't pass through my board, but I was only one of three OASIS controllers on duty, and we were only handling the overflow."

"They would probably be on The Bus if they were here," Patty commented.

"What about Mum and Dad?" Alan asked, sounding worried,

and Patty could not blame him.

"Sorry kiddo. Was your father flying himself?" Jake asked.

"Dunno." Patty did not have any information about their parents' flight plans. It made finding them almost impossible.

"Sorry. Can't help you," Jake apologized. "But if anyone's got his act together, it'll be your Pa. Traffic Control was madness for a while, but it's calmed down now. I'm sure your parents are fine." Jake sighed and looked out the window once more. The waiter arrived with their drinks and menus. He waited patiently while they ordered, then jetted back to the bar.

"It's going to be bad, isn't it?" Alan asked. Jake looked down at him and frowned, nodding solemnly.

"We'll find out just how bad soon enough. One more orbit and we'll be able to see for ourselves."

"Have you heard about the missile strike?" Patty asked.

"Did they blow it up?" Alan chirped.

Jake nodded and put one hand on his wrinkled face, covering his eyes, massaging his temples.

"It was pretty much as we expected," Jake said as he looked out the window once more. "Tempelman's trajectory changed by not much more than a degree and there are at least five major fractures. It is going to be very messy. Damn! It took us twenty years to clean up all the orbiting detritus from the war."

"Not all of it," Alan added.

"No, not all of it," Jake acknowledged and smiled at Patty, who flushed with embarrassment. "But most of it. If it's as bad as I think it will be, we could be up here for some time. LEO is going to be littered with lethal crap."

When their food arrived, Jake floated down and sat at the table. It was one of the few times he was oriented to the local horizontal plane; sitting at a table was the only way he could get a good grip on his food. He looked strangely out of place as he cut into his steak. Alan began to devour his burger, but Patty just picked at her pasta. Although her stomach said it was empty, she did not have the heart to eat. A falling rock was about to shatter her whole world. *Thanks to the military, lots of rocks*, Patty grumbled.

"Eat up, Patty. Fuel up. It ain't over yet," Jake told her.

He's right. We still must find a place to stay. Patty checked her comm. The server was still down. *Overloaded by newbies I'll bet.* She felt lost. *How can I get anything done with the servers down?* She had been hoping to use the bulletin boards to locate a second-hand suit for Alan. *How will we find Mum and Dad?* She picked another fork-full from her plate. The adhesive base kept the plate on the table, and the thick creamy sauce kept her meal from floating away. *Fuel. Jake's right, as usual.* She ate quickly, not tasting it, stoking the furnace for what was to come.

The cluster of churning rocks that had once been the Tempelman-Frobisher asteroid came into view as OASIS crossed the terminator. It had already spread to over twice its previous size, a great mass of ice, pulverized stone and dust backlit by the sun. Flaming debris already carved sooty streaks through the atmosphere, precursors of the devastation following in their wake.

Alan pressed himself against the window, his eyes wide, and his mouth hanging open. "Wow!"

Patty tried to make a count of the larger pieces through the polarized glass. Jake had said the asteroid had fractured in five places, but Patty could see seven or eight large pieces and one very large dark shape bringing up the rear. It was difficult to see, looking towards the sun. Dust and millions of small fragments made sighting anything with any clarity impossible. One thing was for sure, instead of one big strike, there were going to be hundreds.

"Someone's made a mistake," Patty murmured. "It's too big." Her hands were sweating, and she began to regret taking Jake's advice. Her stomach churned. *Please, oh please, don't be down there. Dad. Mum. Please don't be down there.*

"The Pacific for sure, up North," Jake mumbled as he floated up from his chair. "Euro-Asia's gonna get a couple." He blinked. A tear spilled from one eye and bobbled away, splashing against the window.

"Patty?" Alan's hand slipped into hers.

"It's all right. Mom and Dad won't be down there." Patty was not certain of anything anymore, but she felt she had to reassure Alan. For once, he did not argue. She did not think she would be able to keep herself in one piece if he had. *I must be strong for him.*

A woman screamed, and Patty twisted around. Everyone was motionless; every eye glued to the window, except for Patty's and the man who attended to his distressed companion. Patty turned back, morbid curiosity making her feel ill.

"Patty." Jake slid close and whispered in her ear. "The sternmost piece. Take another look."

Patty blinked tears from her eyes and took a deep breath. The largest of the fragments cruised sedately behind the chaos. *Smoothly.* Patty blinked again. Everything was in turmoil, tumbling and bouncing as it traveled down Earth's gravity well, except for the last piece. A chill flashed through her, and her heart pounded. *That's wrong. Very wrong.*

"It's a ship." Jake's whisper sent a quake of fear through her.

"No. No! It's not possible. It's not!" she gasped and squeezed Alan's hand involuntarily. He squeezed back.

"It is. It has to be," Jake murmured. He glanced over his shoulder. "The only way Tempelman could have changed course was if someone changed it."

"Aliens?" Patty whispered aghast.

"Well, I'm sure we don't have anything that could move an asteroid of that size so quickly and keep it in one piece."

It felt like something spun loose in her head; she felt giddy. Aliens? Aliens attacking? No! That was something out of a science fiction feature, not real life. What did people do in a feature when aliens attacked? Run about. Scream and shout.

"You have to get out of here," Jake remarked; his voice was tight with fear.

"What?" Patty asked.

"OASIS has at least two more orbits before we transfer out to L1. OASIS is as slow as a pig and a sitting duck to boot. You don't think they'll let us stay up here unmolested, do you?" Jake asked. Patty had never heard Jake speak with such urgency. "And when this mob gets a whiff of *Them*," he nodded out the window, "there'll be riots. Get off now."

"But where will we go?" Patty asked, her mind was spinning.

"Boost straight for L1. You can be there in hours. Even if *They* allow us to swing clear, we're going to take days to get there," Jake advised.

"Can't." Patty's mind was whirling.

"Why not?" Jake inquired.

"Alan needs a P-suit," Patty replied. "Those Zip-Loks are okay for a quick hop, but he's been wearing it all day. If we're going to boost for L1, he'll need something more substantial, something with plumbing. And...." There was something else. *Oh, yeah.* "We're supposed to wait here. Dad'll be pissed if I go off gallivanting with Alan in tow."

"No, he won't, not now. Chris would be the first to say, run for it," Jake argued convincingly. He paused, looking at Alan, his eyes sizing him up, and he smiled. It was a relief to see the frown release its hold on Jake's face. "I think I know someone who has a P-suit that will fit him," he grinned, "but Alan won't like it."

Patty took a deep breath and another look at the alien spaceship. It was big. Bigger than OASIS. *How did everyone miss it? Jake was right. Staying here was foolish and dangerous. Run now!* It felt as though something cold solidified inside her. In the face of an overwhelming attack, the only logical choice was retreat; Patty could hear her coach's voice echoing in her ears. Even though she did not like it, she knew it was the truth.

"He'll adapt," Patty said firmly.

"Good. Come with me."

CHAPTER SEVEN

Jake turned on the spot, pushed off from the table, and headed towards the bar, ignoring the cluster of shocked tourists still staring through Shadrach's expansive windows.

"What's happening?" Alan watched Jake arc away from the table.

"No time to explain. Not now, just keep up, okay?" Patty pushed off, traveling over the heads of the gawping masses; more pressed into Shadrach's trying to catch a glimpse of Earth's doom. Getting out the main entrance would be impossible, but Jake was not making for the front door, and Patty gave her thrusters a tiny puff to correct her heading. It was against station regulations to use thrusters inside, but Patty did not care about that now. When she felt her brother's hand grip her boot's heel, she gave her thrusters another pump.

Over the bar and out through the 'Staff Only' door they flew, into the deserted kitchen, and out into a gray maintenance passageway. Jake was an economy of movement personified, and it took all of Patty's youthful skills to keep up as he sailed along the empty corridors.

"Where are we going?" Alan asked angrily.

"Jake knows someone who has a P-suit you can use," Patty informed her young brother.

"Okay," he responded hesitantly. "But there's something else. What was Jake whispering to you about?"

"I'll tell you, but you have to keep your mouth shut about it, at least for a while, okay?" Once word got out that there was an alien ship hiding behind Tempelman-Frobisher, there would be panic. "Promise?"

Alan frowned. "Okay, I promise."

"There's an alien ship pushing the asteroid. That's why it changed course. I know it sounds unbelievably corny, but Earth is under attack."

Alan grinned. "Earth's under attack. Right! Alligators in the sewers. Come on Brainiac. Ya gotta be able to come up with a better one than that."

"Believe it or leave it, I don't care, but we are getting you a proper pressure suit, and we are getting out of here," Patty insisted.

"What? We're leaving OASIS?" Alan asked.

"Yes," Patty confirmed.

"No way!" Alan shook his head. "We have to wait here for Mum and Dad." He stretched out his arm and slowed himself, pressing his fingers against the wall. He directed his feet to the Gecko-Grip floor and came to a halt. "I'm not leaving."

"Yes, you are. You're coming with me on Freya. We're going to L1, ahead of OASIS. We'll catch up with Mum and Dad there," Patty insisted and came to a halt, frustration boiling through her. *We don't have time for this.*

"Alan!" Jake's Texan accent boomed down the passage. "Why have you stopped?"

"Patty says we're leaving OASIS," Alan replied, his voice cracking with fear.

"You are." Jake approached slowly.

"No, we're waiting here for Mum and Dad," Alan asserted

"Don't do this, young man. What did your father tell you before you left the ground?" Jake inquired.

"What do you mean?" Alan pouted, not a good sign.

"Didn't he tell you to obey your sister? That she was in charge? How would he have put it? Her word is your command," Jake said calmly. Alan's eyes sprang wide, his jaw popped open, and he tried to do a little jig on the spot. Never really works in zero-gee. "Well?"

"Yeah," Alan conceded.

"Then what are you doing? Get the lead out! Patty's not just your big sister, she's your captain, and you're her crew. When she says jump, don't wait to ask how high. Get it?" Jake settled to the floor beside Patty. She had never heard him so angry.

"Yes, sir," Alan replied, looking at his feet.

"Good. Now get your ass down this corridor as fast as you can, left at the next crossing, then right, through the hatch, turn left. Fourth door on the left, room 2901. Got it?" Jake barked like a drill sergeant.

"Yes sir," Alan scrambled to get away.

Jake's cold expression melted into a sheepish grin. "That should last for a while. Make him call you captain when we catch up," he told her casually as he pushed off the floor and cruised down the corridor.

Patty followed, amazed. "How did you do that?" she asked.

"What, scare a small boy? It's easy really. All you need is a deep, loud voice and..."

"No. How did you know what Dad told him?" Patty clarified.

"Would you believe a wild guess?" he chuckled.

"No, I wouldn't," Patty answered.

"We flew on The Intrepid for a tour or two; he was the First Officer; I was a pilot. I heard him give that speech, with some variations, on more than one occasion." The frown on Jake's brow did not match the wry tilt to his smile.

"You flew together? Dad doesn't talk about the war. Old history. All done and dusted, he says," Patty remarked.

"He's right." Jake took the left turn, pushed off the corner, powering down the hall. Patty was pleased to see Alan waiting quietly outside the correct door. He was not very happy, but he was trying hard not to show it. Every angry thought that buzzed through his mind made his body twitch with repressed movement. Her coach had shown her what to look for - betraying thoughts that rose in an opponent's mind before they attacked - and now she saw them everywhere she looked; thoughts echoed in the body.

Jake hit the door comm's buttons. The light stayed red. Patty heard him chuckle. "Of course, of course. She was working late last night," He muttered and leaned closer to the keypad and tapped out a sequence. The comm blatted and the light stayed red. Jake laughed and tapped out another sequence.

"Welcome home, Maya," the comm declared in a warm contralto. The door hissed open, splitting down the center and retracting into the walls. Jake chuckled again and grinned at Patty, who was not sure about the ethics of breaking into someone's apartment.

"We're in." His face split in a broad boyish grin and he wiggled his overgrown eyebrows. "Don't look at me like that. We're old friends. She won't mind. Maya! You have visitors!" Jake called out as he pushed off into the apartment. Patty followed him somewhat reluctantly. What's Jake doing? He moved with such confidence it was hard not to follow him. The apartment was dark. The Pic-Wall at the far end projected a forest at night. Cool blue beams shone out from the full Moon, high above, painting the floor and the sparse furniture with pale light. Jake was already on the far side of the room leaning in through a doorway. Patty hung back when she heard Maya.

"Jake! You better have the fifty you own me, or you can get the f..." her voice was raw and angry.

"Maya. A thousand apologies. Code red. Real emergency," Jake told her.

"Anything less than an alien attack and you're dead meat old man!"

"Funny you should mention that. Tempelman's a 'Big Brick'," Jake replied.

"What? You're kidding. Someone's dropping a Big Brick? Aliens?" Maya let out a string of curses that made Patty's hair curl.

"Cross my heart," Jake confirmed.

"Shit!" Maya cursed again.

"Madeline's old P-suit. You still have it?" Jake asked.

"Yeah. It's in her room," Maya replied.

"Brilliant!" Jake declared.

Alan looked pretty in pink, bright iridescent pink. Chains of cartoon blue daisies danced, hand-in-hand, around the cuffs and up and down the seams; flocks of multicolored butterflies encircled his torso. Alan looked pretty as a picture, standing in the bright sunlight projected by the Pic-Wall that now displayed a sunny tropical beach.

Patty tried her best to keep the smile from her face. He looked so, so sweet, except for the brooding scowl. His expression said he hated the P-suit with every fiber of his being. A giggle bubbled up, catching Patty by surprise as it burst out. Jake started laughing, and Maya joined in too. Even Alan cracked a momentary smile.

"It's quite clever really. If a seal is compromised the butterflies turn red and flock to the problem area," Maya rubbed the OASIS t-shirt over her trim belly trying to ease the laughter-induced stitch.

"Don't worry, Alan. It's only until we get to L1. We'll get you a new suit then. Promise." Patty prayed he would agree.

"You can always put your helmet on with the visor down. No one will recognize you." Jake sipped on his coffee to try and bury his chuckles.

"You better believe it!" Alan immediately put the helmet on and slammed down the visor.

"Oh, I wish I had pictures of this," Patty whispered.

Maya grinned and winked. "I got you covered."

"Ping me some?"

"Sure thing."

"I need to get some things from my locker." Patty sailed down a back corridor beside Jake; the bright, self-illuminated Alan followed close behind, his dark, polarized visor firmly in place. "East Chandra, north side, level two." He nodded and took the next passageway to the left. Patty lost count of the times she had been to OASIS, but she had never seen half of these corridors. They had crossed only two crowded public thoroughfares. The people they passed seemed troubled but not panicked, which was good, it meant they still had some time up their sleeves.

The locker rooms were relatively quiet, and a young family had set up home in one corner. The mother was breastfeeding her youngest while the father played with a toddler. Patty wanted to tell them that aliens were coming but what good would it do? They were already homeless. Refugees. *Refugees in OASIS.* It was unthinkable. Then another unthinkable thought penetrated Patty. *I'm a refugee too.*

Patty only wanted one thing from her locker, and she breathed a sigh of relief when she pulled out her sports kit. She did not care about the unwashed socks and the stab-proof competition suit; it was her blades she reached for and one in particular, her rapier, Lady Estelle. The épée she used in competition was a fine sword, but Lady Estelle balanced beautifully four centimeters from the woven steel hilt, a perfect replica of an eighteenth-century French dueling sword. There was no way Patty was going to leave it for some aliens.

"Whaddya wanna bring that for?" Alan sneered.

"Beg pardon?" Jake snapped in his best sergeant major's voice.

"Sorry. Whaddya wanna bring that for ... Captain." Alan repeated a tiny bit more respectfully.

"Because she's beautiful. Captain's prerogative." Patty removed the sword case, stuffed the bag back into the locker, and secured it. *On second thoughts.* Patty unlocked the door and retrieved her kitbag. *Who knows, I might never return. Freya's got enough room.*

Jake stayed with them until they reached the airlock.

"Give your captain your full support. She will need it." He grinned and gave Alan a friendly slap on the back. "I'll keep an eye out for your folks, and I'll ping you the moment I hear anything."

"Thanks, Jake," Patty said. "Don't know what I would have done without your help."

"You're welcome. Fly true." He smiled and pushed off down the corridor before Patty had the chance to open the airlock.

A NEW PATH

A new urgency possessed Er'men. Even the RegentFirstMother could not disguise the sounds of war. Tal'anis reverberated with the fevered beat. A rising bloodlust filled the ship's warm air. Genedalt was not immune. His eager scent joined the consensus mingling through the air ducts. Er'men felt ill. *If we are fighting, that means this beautiful world is someone else's home. We are not welcome here.* Er'men steadied her breathing and relaxed into the flow of lives unfolding within her.

Mu'nruberra was split between watching the monitors, and standing beside the Hel'omi surrogate mother, feeling the sharp contractions with her own hands. Red'onothal cleared his throat nervously and fidgeted, but the other councilors stood quietly, intent on the action in the birthing room. His twitch ended with a whisper. "Are you sure?"

"You've seen the scans; she's perfect." *As perfect as anyone could possibly ask for.* "The Hel'omi make ideal surrogates. Our two species are very close genetically..."

"So you would have us believe." Councilor Wal'dren was dressed in gray; it matched his skin color and his tenor.

"My research is available if you cared to read it," Mu'nruberra replied confidently.

"I'm not sure I have the requisite background to understand it clearly," Red'onothal muttered.

Then why are you here? "But you understand clear method and reasoning." Mu'nruberra's eyes were drawn to the trembling needle as it drew inky arcs across the scrolling paper. That was the strongest contraction so far. The primitive conditions in this makeshift laboratory chafed. *I have better instruments at home.*

"We are not sure how clear your reasoning can be if you conclude that we should ... blend our species with that of the lower creatures," Wal'dren grumbled and grimaced, and Mu'nruberra had to hold back a chuckle. When word of her experiments had leaked, it had been his face used by the political cartoonists in their ribald creations.

"Your research has provided excellent results using the Hel'omi as surrogate mothers. That will continue." Red'onothal shook with barely restrained outrage, "but this ... this genetic tinkering must be discontinued. The venerable members of the Northern Science Directorate have issued an edict this very night barring your experiments."

Mu'nruberra did not expect to be shut down so soon but had guessed it would happen at some stage. She let an irritated shudder pass through her to disguise the disdain she felt for the Science Council. It would not take more than a handful of days to transfer what she required from her experiments to her workshop at home.

"We believe you risk polluting Arumpo'or bloodlines," Red'onothal continued.

"We must adapt or die out. The Hel'omi are vigorous, and we are lucky to have a species whose genetic code is so similar to our own. We must act while we still can," Mu'nruberra insisted. Eighty years after the first sunstrike, they clung desperately to their rapidly decaying technology. Exchanging mel'andrin was not enough. They needed to advance in all areas if they were to survive and not wallow in nostalgic memories of their species' marvelous past. They could not afford to let what knowledge they possessed slip away from lack of use. There were only two cities in the northern hemisphere with power and only one with a working fusion reactor, only one in the south, too. The southerners had the benefit of renewables, wind, and water. The north hadn't seen rain in any volume for years, and their sun was overdue for another bout of flatulence. *We are, at least, prepared for it this time. Time. There was never enough time.*

Mu'nruberra gritted her teeth and bowed to her collegial supervisors. "Of course, we will obey the council and have these experiments cleared away."

"Good." Red'onothal stamped, but that was more a reflex than a physical threat.

CHAPTER EIGHT

Patty passed the sword case to Alan who slipped it down inside the cockpit where a special mount held it securely. She stowed her sports kit in the forward compartment, detached the umbilical and reconnected it to the Hammerhead. A twinge of guilt flashed through her. She looked over the shiny new CRV once more and blinked. The sale yard's vehicle ID was still stuck to the inside of the canopy. Patty looked closer, Clifford Brothers, San Diego, the ID read. She laughed. *You got burned, man.* If the owner of this cycle could afford to lay down cash and fly it from the Clifford Brothers' showroom floor, they would not notice an extra fuel charge. Freya only took a moment or two to wake up from standby mode. Patty closed the canopy and by the time the cockpit was pressurized Freya was in the green and ready for flight.

Patty opened a comm link to Traffic Control as she strapped in. "DH-1031C to Egress Control. Under Flight Rule 0402 section 3b, we have an emergency clearance; the flight deck is empty. We are rolling. Over."

"OASIS Traffic to DH-1031C," the comm replied. Patty did not recognize the voice. She was not going to wait though and fired her thrusters, lifting them gently above the other CRV's. "Ah, most unusual, but it's been that kind of day. What flight rule was that? What emergency? Over."

"0402, 3b. Ask Jake. DH-1031C out," Patty responded. Not that Traffic Control could do much to stop her. *They could give me a citation.* Patty chuckled. She gave the thrusters another gentle nudge, and Freya moved away from the docks and out into open space. Earth's brilliant blue ball was marred with gray stripes.

The main body of Tempelman-Frobisher was still more than an hour away from making planet-fall but the smaller pieces, the advance guard, were leaving hundreds of fiery trails as they entered the atmosphere. Most would not hit the surface, but the ashes of their flaming descent left dark stains on Earth's clear blue skies. It would be a very cold winter this year. The ominous shape at the rear of Tempelman-Frobisher had separated from the asteroid, but it had not made any other moves.

Patty's heart beat faster. *Who were they? Why have they come to our world?* Patty wondered as she lit Freya's main drive and boosted gently away from OASIS. Would she ever see it again? Another home left behind. It was a lumbering old hulk that had seen better days but now OASIS was full-to-bursting with scared people, she was more precious than ever. *Fly true, old girl. Fly true.*

Patty calculated the fastest course to the L1 station, within the margins of safety. It was the first time she had plotted such a long journey, and she rechecked her figures twice before she was satisfied with the result. She loaded the course into the autopilot and sat back. The thrusters puffed, fractionally altering Freya's heading. The acceleration warning chimed. Thirty seconds.

"Patty! Look! Starboard side!" Alan shouted. Patty twisted around on her seat. Lights were flaring around the alien ship. Missiles twisted in towards the dark shape. Patty traced their path back to their points of origin. They were fired from orbit. *Naughty, naughty. Who's been maintaining secret orbital weapon platforms?* She wondered. Beam weapons of searing blue cut through the asteroid's debris field and struck the ship.

"Ten seconds," the autopilot calmly informed them. Patty settled back into her seat. *You go boys! Kick their butts!* Freya's engines opened with a mild half-gee kick.

"Oof!" exclaimed Alan as he dropped into his seat.

"Tighten your restraints!" Patty demanded.

"Aye, aye captain," Alan responded smartly.

The ten seconds of half-gee was just a warning. Freya opened up, one gee; two, three, four, five and she held it there, seemingly without end. After the relaxing almost-freefall of OASIS's environment, five-gees was pure torture. The burn seemed to last forever. Patty checked her actual course against what she had calculated and smiled; they were in the green. The engines cut at the preordained instant and Patty could breathe again.

"Patty has this bucket got a scope?" Alan asked.

"I beg your pardon crewman?" She was not sure if Alan would still play along, but it was worth a try.

"Sorry, Captain. Does Freya have a scope?" he asked again. She did have a small telescope designed for star sightings if there were no navigation beacons, but Patty had not used it since she sat her pilot exams.

"Good idea, crewman," she replied.

The autopilot had control of the ship, but Patty was not willing to disengage it just to get a view of the conflict. She fired up the camera and sent a feed to Alan's small screen on the back of her seat. The telescope had a pathetic lens, but it was stabilized and better than nothing. They could see the dark form of the alien's ship silhouetted against Earth's bright surface. Pale blue dots that indicated energy-weapon fire flickered on and off all over the mothership. Suddenly the screen flared white as a flash overloaded the camera's exposure settings.

"Wow! Hit 'em hard!" cried Alan. As if on cue, there was another flash and then another. "Whoa, go boys! Hit 'em!" Alan bounced around in his restraints.

The picture cleared and nothing seemed to have changed. Suddenly there was another flash, but it did not come from anywhere near the big ship.

"They've got birds of their own!" Alan declared. Patty looked closer. It seemed like there were hundreds of tiny dots, engine flares, flying about. *They're alien ships.* An explosion bloomed in the path of one of the tiny flares. The flare changed course. Another explosion erupted in front of it, and the flare turned again. One by one, the bright blue dots trying to penetrate the alien ship's hull winked out. Six more missiles detonated against the huge spacecraft, but they seemed to do no more damage than the others. The ship altered its trajectory and slid into a polar orbit. The battle was over. In a little over five minutes all the orbital weapons platforms, illegal or not, had either been destroyed or exhausted. Alan sat quietly.

The comm channels were all lit up. Patty decided to sample the chatter but switched the sound off when a piercing howl broke through her earphones. It was on all the comm channels, which puzzled Patty but only for a second or two. The aliens were blanketing the comm channels with interference. It was logical when she thought about it. *We're at war, aren't we?* Her mind felt like mush, and her heart pounded. *Is this what being in shock feels like?*

The autopilot began an urgent beeping. Data from the navigation beacons was missing. *How could that be?* The autopilot took readings from Earth's orbital navigation beacons one hundred and twenty-eight times a second. Patty ran some diagnostics on Freya's systems and broke out into a cold sweat. The beacons were not there. The signals that everyone relied on to navigate had been turned off or destroyed. The Lunar beacons were quiet, too. *Of course, they'd been turned off. Why supply vital navigation information to the aliens? How many things would change now that their world was at war?* Patty wondered. *Everything.*

"Patty, err, Captain, my UNET link dropped out." Alan's voice sounded worried. "Are we okay?"

"We are," Patty reassured him, "but the satellites keeping UNET running have either crashed or been silenced. The aliens are also broadcasting noise, so that's going to gum up the works too."

"Got nothing to do," he groused.

"Sorry, I've got plenty." *What can Alan do?* She thought. Patty's to-do-list was getting longer and yet her brother was crammed into the small seat with nothing to keep his mind from current events. "The manual for Freya's systems, you should give it a read if you're going to be my full-time crewman,"

Patty suggested. Alan groaned, but moments later she heard the introductory video begin playing.

Patty took control of the sighting camera and began astronomical observations. Polaris was visible and Alphecca and Vega. They would do for a start. When combined with readings before the beacons went quiet and the inertial data accumulating since then, Patty calculated they were ... *No, that's wrong.* She took another set of readings and got a different answer but one that agreed with the autopilot. She did it again and got yet another answer. *Which solution's correct? Our lives depend on getting the right answer, not four or five possible outcomes.* Patty pressed hard on her rising panic to keep it out of her calculations. *If all's good and true in the universe, the autopilot should still get us to L1; it doesn't need the beacons now that we're on our way. If only Jake was here to check my figures,* she complained and grimaced. *That's pathetic.* Jake would be able to find his way from OASIS to L1 with not much more than a compass and a slide rule! She took another reading and applied a different algorithm to solve it. Her answer agreed with her second set of calculations and the autopilot. *That's better.* She ran the figures once more, just to be sure, and when they agreed Patty felt much better. *L1! Here we come.*

"Captain?" Alan pipped up.

"Yes, number one." Patty smiled.

"We don't know that Mum and Dad got to safety, do we." Alan's inflection made his words more a statement than a question, and it took Patty's smile away.

"No, we don't, but I reckon it's a pretty safe bet," Patty reassured him.

"Really?"

"You know Dad. He's a force of nature when he's focused on something," Patty insisted.

"Yeah. I guess, but accidents happen," Alan mused.

"By their very nature, it seems, things do go wrong. You know, Murphy's Law: Whatever can go wrong, will ..." Patty began.

"... go wrong at the worst possible moment. Yeah, I think I get Murphy's Law now. That's why I was thinking; it could be just the two of us. It could be just us," he stated with a quiver in his voice.

Patty sighed. It was something that she had been trying to put out of her mind, but the possibility that her parents were dead was very real. "Yes. It could be just you and me, and Freya. But 'roid or no 'roid, aliens or no aliens, Mum and Dad will pull through, always have, always will. Count on it," Patty declared. "We've just gotta keep on our toes and stay alive. Give Dad a chance to do his thing. They're probably on OASIS right now. Jake'll have his eyes peeled. There's a message waiting for us at L1. I'd put money on it."

"You're probably right, but I just wanted to say sorry for pulling that hissy fit earlier," Alan confessed.

"That's ancient history as far as I'm concerned, forgotten. We're all square," Patty told him and breathed a silent sigh of relief. Battling with her brother was the last thing she wanted to do.

"Thanks, Patty."

"That's all right, li'l Bro'. We gotta stick together," Patty insisted.

"Yes, Captain!" Alan responded.

"Try and get some rest. Sleep, if you can. There's nothing to do, until turn-over, in about six hours," Patty said and tried to take her own advice, but her mind was flying faster than Freya.

The autopilot woke Patty with an annoying ping, ping, ping. It took a few moments before she could clear her head of the nightmares that had stampeded through her mind: alien creatures with slimy tentacles, little gray ones with big eyes and silvery probes, slavering beasts of all descriptions. It was as if her dreams had replayed every science fiction feature she had ever watched. Patty took a sip of juice from her P-suit's supply to clear her mouth and then peed. There was no point holding it in; her suit was designed to store urine until recycled or dumped. *Besides, you don't want to have a full bladder while you're under five gees of acceleration.* That was what the autopilot was warning her about; turnover was approaching.

"Alan?" Patty asked.

"Huh?" came Alan's sleepy reply.

"You should take a leak. We're just about at turn-over," she informed him.

"And?"

"Freya's about to give us a five gee kick in the backside. This is your captain speaking. Pee now or you'll regret it," she said sternly, trying to remember how Jake had sounded.

"Yes, ma'am."

The port thrusters fired, yawing Freya around one hundred and eighty degrees. *Damn, I should have taken a sighting. I should have been able to see L1 from here.* There was some additional firing to tweak the orientation and Freya responded smoothly to the preprogrammed instructions. *Oh well, we'll find out soon enough if I dropped a decimal place.*

"Burn in thirty seconds," the autopilot announced calmly.

"How's it going back there?" Patty asked.

"All peed out, Captain. Luggage stowed away, and my tray table is locked, in its upright position," Alan declared with a chuckle.

"Coach has tray tables? What luxury," she laughed softly with him.

"Ten seconds," the autopilot announced.

The half gee burn felt terrible compared to the luxury of zero-gee. Patty could hardly breathe, but when Freya's engines really kicked in, she was scared she would pass out. Her vision began to narrow as if she was looking down a long dark tunnel and then everything began to fade. Patty knew what was happening to her, but there was nothing she could do about it. She needed to breathe.

Suddenly, the elephant sitting on her chest, crushing her into her seat, moved off. Sweet, cool air poured into her lungs as she gasped and panted. Her head cleared quickly but left behind a thumping that would not quit.

"Burn complete. Manual control is now required." *Were we at Lagrange One?* Had she calculated correctly or were they lost? There was only one way to find out. Patty took manual control and slewed Freya around.

CHAPTER NINE

Lagrange One Station was all clean lines, sparkling white domes, and arches, tapering star-scrapers that looked as if they had been extruded as a single piece. It was very clean, very proprietary, and very Corporate. Patty was sure that before each new manufacturing plant or research center was constructed, it had to pass through a team of design consultants to make sure it was aesthetically synchronized with the rest of the station. Where OASIS was a wild and untamed combination of disparate shapes, L1 was a bland and desolate example of conservative Corporate culture. Patty hated it. It was too clean, too blended, over-planned.

At that moment, the L1 docks looked more like a beehive that had been kicked. There were ships, CRVs, unconventional broomsticks, and P-suits buzzing around the installations. It would take ages to go through Ingress Control, but Patty had other plans. Balke-Spalding had a research facility in amongst this corporate blandness. She had been there once before and knew they had their own landing dock. They were the first people she would check with to see if her parents had made contact. If Dad had reached out anyone at L1, it would be these people.

"Hey! You did it!" Alan announced, sounding genuinely surprised. Without seeing his face, Patty could not tell if he was kidding. She was not going to tell him she had had her doubts.

"L1 Traffic Control this is DH-1031C, over," Patty called. There was still some interference on the comm channels, but it was not as bad out here.

"DH-1031C this is L1 traffic. Take a number. Ingress times are at about an hour unless you have an emergency. Over." The woman answering her call sounded stressed.

"L1 traffic. Requesting a heading for the Balke-Spalding research center. Over."

"Sorry don't have time for that but you can hail them on this band." She rattled off a frequency outside the usual comm channels.

"Thanks, L1, over," Patty replied.

"Good luck DH-1031C. L1 traffic, out."

Patty adjusted her comm to the frequency specified and sent out a hail. "Balke-Spalding this is DH-1031C, requesting a heading." The comm was silent for a while, so Patty re-transmitted her message.

"DH-1031C this is Balke-Spalding. We are reading you. Transmit your ident codes. This is a secure facility. Repeat this is a secure facility, over." The voice was steely cold and had a very proper British accent.

"Balke-Spalding this is Patty and Alan Balke. We're looking for our parents. Over," Patty told him.

"Oh, Ms. Balke. We thought you might turn up." The cold steel was gone from his voice. "We have a message for you from your father..." Alan let out a whoop as he bounced around in his restraints. Patty released a sigh. She had been hoping against hope that there would be a message, something, anything that would indicate her parents were still alive. Relief flooded through her.

"Sorry, I missed the last part of your transmission. Can you repeat, over," Patty asked.

"All the nav beacons have been turned off, but I can switch ours back on for a second or two. Will that be sufficient? Over."

"That'll be just fine, over," Patty replied. A single navigation beacon blinked on, and Patty locked on in less than a second. "We have you five-by-five. Thanks, Balke-Spalding, over." The beacon went silent once more.

"Excellent. I'll put the kettle on. See you in a couple of minutes. Out," the voice answered.

The Balke-Spalding facility was a huge cylinder chamfered to a dome on one end. An array of communication dishes sprouted from the center of the dome pointing in all directions. A blinking red light spun above a bright square; the dock was open for them. Patty glided them in and gently eased Freya to the deck. The hatch closed behind them and air flooded in. We're safe! Patty sighed with relief as she popped the canopy.

"Oh, the pain! I'm stiff!" Alan complained as he climbed out.

"Ditto," Patty replied as she stretched. She spied an umbilical coiled up on a wall bracket. They won't mind if we refill. "Number One."

"Yes, Captain," Alan responded smartly.

"Grab that umbilical and charge Freya up," she told him.

"Err. I'm sorry Patty I'm not sure..."

"That's why I'm going to show you. Over there, hanging on the wall," Patty said, pointing to the coiled cables.

"Got it." Alan bounced over, his fluorescent pink suit lighting up the gray dock. Patty had to smile and was glad he had been sitting in the rear seat. That P-suit is a bit bright. Patty showed her younger brother how to open the small hatch just forward of Freya's engine bay and to connect the umbilical.

"You really should lock your ship down too." The voice with the very British accent frightened Patty, and she spun around. "Sorry, didn't mean to startle you." He extended his hand as he floated closer. "Kenneth Frobisher," he introduced himself. He looked not-at-all the way his voice suggested he might appear; he was short with jet-black hair, and his face was very brown with a large, hooked nose, a flying buttress for his face.

"Lock it down?" Patty shook his hand; it was warm and firm, and she introduced herself and Alan once more. "Frobisher as in Tempelman-Frobisher?"

"Yes and no, that's my brother Phillip. He's the astronomer in the family. I just manage this place," he told her.

"Lock it down?" Patty asked again.

"Yes, we have been given orders to scatter. We will disconnect from L1 in a short while. All essential manufacturing and research facilities have been ordered to go and hide." That made sense to Patty though it brought the fact that they were at war back into focus with a chill.

"No," Alan muttered under his breath. Patty had to agree with him. She did not want to do any more running now. Scattering would mean a major delay in finding their parents. Who knows where this facility will end up? Patty squeezed Alan's shoulder to calm him.

"I don't think we can go with you," Patty said hesitantly.

Kenneth shrugged. "Be that as it may, come inside. We have hot food and extra supplies you can have."

Patty looked down at the umbilical and back at Kenneth. "Hope you don't mind."

"No, not at all. I was going to suggest it. Come inside. The tea will get cold," Kenneth said with a broad smile as he pushed off towards an open hatch.

The research facility was pretty much as Patty remembered, gray and white corridors with wide windows looking into sealed, clean-room laboratories. Anonymous bodies in fully enclosed lab suits worked at strange machines or floated at Pic-Wall workstations. There were long passageways with numbered doors, crew quarters Patty guessed, and then the dining room. A broad Pic-Wall, displaying a sunny, thickly treed valley, made the small room appear much larger than it was.

Roast beef, with all the trimmings, sat on a broad white plate. Sweet baby peas, string beans, broccoli, roast potatoes, and pumpkin, all held in place by the steaming thick brown gravy. The smell alone was intoxicating. Patty had eaten all her pasta back at OASIS, but that seemed like days ago, so she set to, while Kenneth called up their father's message. Alan was way ahead of her; his fork was a blur.

"Here we go." Kenneth floated back, as the screen beside him flickered to life. Their parents were sitting close together. Christopher patted his wife's knee and leaned closer to the lens. Patty did not recognize the background.

"Patty. Alan. We've had a few delays but will be boosting in about fifteen minutes. Cyn thought it would be a good idea to tell you we are going to be a bit late. I'm going to send this to all our orbital facilities as well as your inbox just in case." Christopher looked pale and shaken, but his innate confidence still shone strongly. Her mother leaned closer to the camera.

"Kids. Stay safe. We've just heard that OASIS is boosting for L1 so I guess it could be a while before we can catch up," Cynthia said. Their mother looked worried.

"Make contact with Kenneth Frobisher at L1," her father continued, "he'll look after you." Someone called her father from off-screen.

"We've got to run," her mother said nervously. "Love you both." The message ended. Patty sat back and took a deep breath.

"What's the time stamp on that?" Alan asked between mouthfuls.

Kenneth looked at the file. "2143 GMT."

"That was before the aliens showed themselves," Patty said, almost to herself. Kenneth nodded solemnly. "So, I'm betting they don't know about the order to scatter," Patty said, her thoughts whirling.

"I wouldn't think so, not then," Kenneth said. "The order came from pretty high up the food chain. I would be certain that Mr. Balke would have had a say in the decision, even if they had to contact him during their launch."

"But he won't know where you're going, right?" Alan asked.

"Actually, I'm not sure where we're headed, so..." he left the obvious conclusion unspoken.

"Patty?" Alan had one thing in mind, and Patty did not need to hear him say it aloud. She knew what he wanted to do; he wanted to stay and wait for their parents.

"It's all right Alan; we're staying," she reassured him.

"Well, if that's your decision I'll call the Hilton and book you a room," Kenneth told them. "Finish your dinner. I'll be back in a jiffy."

Patty sat back and closed her eyes. It had been so good to see her parents' faces and hear their voices. The time stamp indicated they should have been off planet when Patty was with Jake at Shadrach's. She just hoped they were nowhere near the battle at Low Earth Orbit.

Alan had cleaned his plate and copied their parent's message to Freya's database by the time Kenneth returned. Patty had lost her appetite again and was pushing peas through the thick gravy. Waves of nauseating fear kept rolling through her. He led them back to the dock without a word. That suited Patty. She didn't feel like talking anyway. When they arrived, there was a man in a pressure suit disconnecting the umbilical.

Frobisher extended his hand, "Good luck. Your ship's fully fueled. I had the water tank topped up and the waste extracted. You're all ready to go. If we meet up with your parents before you do, I'll tell them your plans."

"Thanks for your help," Patty said and tried to sound as if she had more confidence than she felt as she shook his warm hand once more. "We'll be just fine. Fly true."

"Fly true," he returned with a smile and then pushed off.

Alan was already seated, his harness pulled tight. Freya would not need her main engines, so Patty ignored the red preflights littering her board. She sealed the canopy and waited calmly for the air to cycle out of the lock. The door slid aside, and Patty pumped the thrusters. Freya lifted slowly from the deck and drifted out into space.

"DH-1031C to Balke-Spalding, we are clear. Over," Patty told them.

"Yes, we see you. Chin up. Fly true. Catch you soon, I hope, in better circumstances. Balke-Spalding, out."

For a moment Patty thought Freya had picked up a strange vector because the research station began to slide past them, but then she realized Balke-Spalding was boosting away. Patty increased their separation and watched as it cleared the surrounding buildings.

"So, where's the Hilton?" Alan asked, sounding chirpy.

"Don't know. I guess we are going to have to go through

Ingress Control after all. I wonder how long the wait's going to be now?" Patty mused. The swarm of angry bees still surrounded the L1 docks. Three more facilities boosted away from the main structure as Balke-Spalding had done. Patty was tempted to wait a little longer. But then again, maybe it's better to join the queue sooner rather than later. A relatively small section of L1 boosted away, but it did not travel far, taking station about a kilometer away from the main docks.

Suddenly, three very hot energy beams impaled the small craft. Freya's canopy darkened in response. Patty shaded her eyes from the energy that poured out from the ship as it combined and focused the three beams onto one almost solid bar of light. Searing white energies speared Earthward.

"What's that?" Alan demanded. He did not really need an answer. Patty scanned the local comm channels, and despite the interference, found a camera feed. It showed the dark shape of the alien ship hastily maneuvering away from the intense beam. Yes! We have something that can hurt them! And from all the way out here. The beam flicked on and off for a second or two before shining brightly once more. Patty was surprised at just how quickly the aliens' ship changed course. The searing light could only strike the craft for moments before it slipped away.

"Go for it, boys! Hit 'em hard!" Alan cried enthusiastically.

The Balke-Spaulding station had been at some distance from the energy weapons, but that was too close for Patty's liking. The aliens are not going to sit still and take a pounding. She took care of those red lights littering her display and brought Freya's engine to full readiness while using the thrusters to give them even more separation.

Suddenly, the small station that focused the three beams exploded. I hate it when I'm right like that. A split-second later, the facilities producing those lethal green beams erupted in flames, and then, the main docks became an inferno, the center of an expanding wall of tumbling shards and burning gases. Patty played back her sensor readings as she flew Freya away. Something had struck L1. Missiles.

Patty did a quick radar sweep. Two ships rose from Earth's gravity well, fast. Too fast to stop at L1. She watched her screen as something detached and accelerated away from the lead ship. Patty did not wait. She knew what it was, another missile. She turned her radar off, spun Freya and accelerated. Where could they go now? Patty wondered desperately. Where would be safe? Should they go to the Moon... down to Tyco City? No, we'd be trapped down there. Then where? Is anywhere safe now?

Alan took control of the sighting camera and looked back towards L1 when the last missile hit home. L1's bland corporate construction shattered. "Patty? Captain?"

"Yes, number one?" Patty changed her display to the flight computer. The sight of explosive decompression on such a scale made her feel ill.

"I think the Hilton's gonna need some refurbishing," Alan remarked wryly.

Refurbishing! L1 was a broken mess. L1 would need a complete rebuild. Patty did not want to think about how many people had just died. A small fraction compared to those down on Earth, but still many hundreds, thousands of lives had just been snuffed out before her. What can we do? We're two kids in an over-powered rocket sled! We can't help those poor souls down there; we have to look after ourselves.

"I thought we could try L2," Alan concluded calmly.

L2 was on the far side of the Moon. Hey, Alan's thinking. There were some research stations there but no manufacturing plants. No one would be building weapons there. Activity at L2 centered on the huge radio telescope arrays. Orbiting on the far side of the Moon, sheltered from Earth's noisy transmissions, it was the perfect place to look deeply into the distant universe.

"Thank you, Alan. Good work," Patty praised him as she took some observations and began flight calculations. She loaded the course into the autopilot and activated it. There was nothing they could do here.

A NEW VECTOR

Mu'nruberra was ready for the brownout this time. The workshop's circuits switched over to her unregistered tap on the government barracks down the road without a hitch. The military never went without power. She was so close to a solution, finding the right vector to spread the changes had nearly broken her heart and her will. At first, she thought it would be a matter of months before she could announce her discovery and her plans. She had suffered setback after setback, both with her splicing and with her status at the university. Months turned into years. *And years! Tainted! They'd said my research was tainted when they took the surrogacy program away from me.* But it was politics. The same politics that built that barracks down the road, filled with ignorant soldiers ready to crush any dissent. *The same politics that would announce my breakthrough-suicide.* Times had changed since her early successes and not for the better.

Data began to assemble on her great grandfather's display. Despite the growing loss of pixels, it was far superior to the inky chart scratchings, and the oscilloscope bounces she had to put up with in her university lab. If the council knew her family hoarded old-tek - they were not the only ones - an example would have to be made. They would be turned out of the city. Her mother would not last more than a day or two outside. *Father's tougher.* He helped her with the Hel'omi. Finest breeding stock in five counties. *He'd last days, if not weeks. They both know what I'm doing.* Her mother loved looking after the little ones when they came.

The figures looked good. They looked better than good. It

was everything Mu'nruberra had hoped for, but she did not allow herself to get excited. What worked well in a laboratory did not always survive the rigors of real life. *And you've made so many changes. A compromise here, a compromise there. But it works!* The evidence was right there before her. It was going to be another successful birth. To the current testing regimes - quite inferior to her own - the child would be genetically indistinguishable from anyone born naturally.

Natural birth, Mu'nruberra scoffed. That was a horrible joke. No one was born *naturally* these days. Mu'nruberra was glad official eyes had not been drawn to her precinct. If they looked close enough, they would see the market for healthy children paralleled the trade in Hel'omi, a market filled with eager would-be parents, parents that would be discreet about the miracle of their blessing.

Everything, at last, seemed to have fallen into place. The virus had inserted the genes correctly into the Hel'omi rootstock and had been passed onto the first generation. When bred, the females, with the correct feeding regimen, birthed litters with both Hel'omi and Arumpo'or offspring. The modified Hel'omi males did not breed as successfully with unmodified females as their unmodified cousins but when pregnancy did occur, if the correct dietary routine as adhered to, the female produced the same result, perfect Arumpo'or babies. She was concerned that the males were not as successful breeding with the unmodified females, but they were much more biddable now they responded to voice commands. *They may even learn a language one day. And one day, after I release my vector, there will be no unmodified females at all. With the right dietary conditions, there can be an Arumpo'or resurgence.*

Collecting her data, Mu'nruberra copied it to the long-term crystalline storage and placed her latest mel'andrin in the small wooden box beside the filing cabinets. Whenever she had made significant progress, Mu'nruberra added another golden pearl of mel'andrin to her growing collection. Her notes and data might decay and fall to dust, but the record of her life and struggles would live on.

CHAPTER TEN

Northeasterly winds, warm and full of rain, lashed the windows. Sporadic flashes of lightning gave some definition to Rangitoto Island's dark conical shape squatting just offshore. Apart from the illumination provided by the occasional but intense forks, the night was black. Hine smiled as a muted flicker streaked through the clouds, and she began counting, *one thousand, two thousand, three...* Whoom! Thunder shook the old weatherboard house, and Hine's smile grew into a grin. She hugged her tiny niece tightly, rocking her gently as the contented baby suckled at her bottle. She did a quick check to be sure she was getting milk and not air.

"See, little Whetu, Whaitiri is busy making noise in the sky tonight. Boom," Hine cooed softly to her niece and kissed her warm forehead. She enjoyed helping her aunt care for Whetu, even if it meant having to get up in the very early hours. *That's what family's all about.* Her aunt and uncle led very busy lives, and until the next semester began Hine was only too happy to help out. *Whetu's such a cutie-pie.*

Forked lightning flickered over the horizon, far to the north. It was too distant to bother counting; she would never hear Whaitiri's booming voice. Unannounced, a wave of goosebumps rose and fell across Hine's arms. It was not cold. She flexed her shoulders and turned away from the window with a yawn. The antique Swiss clock on the mantelpiece chimed three o'clock. The Bus *will be landing in half an hour,* Hine thought. She loved the fact that she could see the landing zone from the lounge room window, and had spent countless hours watching the big ships swoop down from orbit, belly landing in an arc of spray only ten kilometers offshore and then slide elegantly to the docks at Caster Bay. *But with any luck, this sweet milky-breathed child will be sound asleep and so will I.*

Hine sat at the comm, rearranging the bottle and her suckling niece to free one arm and logged on to her UNET account. Someone pinged her almost immediately; it was Tina. Hine checked to make sure the volume was set to little more than a whisper and put it on the main screen.

"Hine, you're up late," Tina remarked. She looked as if she had been out partying; her hair was in a wild tangle and her electro-lurex top rippled with fat sparks. *Was that all Tina did?*

"Just helping out." Hine lifted Whetu towards the camera. "Been out dancing?"

"Yeah, Black Pump were playing at the Stock Yard. Big crowd. Is that my little Whetu? Give her a kiss for me. You look born to it Hine, EarthMother style," Tina complimented her.

"Thanks ... I guess."

"Hine, have you been in touch with Patty?" Tina asked.

"This morning? It's three AM," Hine objected.

"Yeah, but it's eight in the AM in the So-Cal. I've been trying to get through ever since I heard the news."

"News?" Hine asked.

"Temple-Frobisher changed course," Tina told her with a straight face.

"Huh?" Maybe it was because of the early hour, but Hine could not make sense of Tina's statement.

"The asteroid changed course. Gonna be a big splash in the northern hemisphere," Tina told her.

"It's going to hit?" Hine's goosebumps returned with vengeance.

"Gonna be nasty. Very nasty," Tina answered with a grimace.

"It changed course? How is that possible?" Hine mind flip-flopped about, trying to find a reason why that would happen.

"Dunno, it's got all the pointy heads in a real flap. I've been trying to get through to Patty, but there's all manner of dropouts on the net. I can't get a ping through. If anyone's got the skinny on what's going down, it'll be Patty," Tina reassured her.

"Hang on." Hine did a quick trace and pinged Patty. Tina was right. Even the old fiber optics were off-line. *How could that be?* She checked again and realized the cables were not dark; they were disconnected from the system. The hair on the back of Hine's neck stood to attention as those goosebumps returned. *Military.* The government was the only ones with the grunt to secure those links. That meant bad. Very bad.

"See what I mean?" Tina ran her fingers through her unruly hair, and it looked as though she had caught a whiff of her sweaty underarms, recoiling.

"Yeah, something big's sparking," Hine replied.

"My thoughts too. I'll be going out to the supermarket for some storable food. After I shower."

"Thanks for the heads-up. I'll see if I can steal some Corporate bandwidth. Keep you looped," Hine told her.

"Fly true." Tina winked out.

Hine sat back and rocked Whetu. She had finished her bottle, and Hine gently swung her up to her shoulder and began the rocking, patting ritual that always ended in a hearty burp. Whetu was such a good baby. She would sleep soon and not wake until seven or eight, but Tina's news had woken Hine, and she knew it would be hours before she would be able to sleep, if at all.

The day broke clear after last night's storm, and the ground was soft under Hine's feet, the grass was still damp although the sun rose hours ago. Mount Victoria was unusually quiet. On a bright morning like this, there would usually be joggers pounding the paths, and families with young children running around the old volcano. Her feet took her usual route without any conscious direction, south around to the Devonport side. The Waitematā Harbor was choppy, but that did not deter Auckland's sailors; they were out on the harbor in droves. Traffic across both bridges looked heavy. She went on, winding east. Tamaki Estuary, Browns Island, Waiheke Island, the Coromandel peaks were hazy in the distance. Around to the north, Rangitoto Island lay across the channel with Mototapu tucked up beside her. Cheltenham Beach curved west and north towards Takapuna's sprawl and further north, the spaceport docks at Castor Bay.

Hine sat in the damp and leaned back against a weathered stump. *The Bus* had not made it down last night. By dawn, she would have been refueled and ready to launch, but the docks were empty. *Completely empty.* None of the Corporate ships were berthed, not so much as a captain's gig. That was scary. *Add it to the list of scary-things-that-happened-in-the-last-twelve-hours: Nasty interference killing the Sat feeds. International fiber restricted to government data only. Local networks crashed. It was time for a walk anyway.*

It seemed that every generation went through a crisis of some sort. For her parents, it had been the Belter War. *Was this the Big One for my generation?* Whatever this one was. As if the wayward Templeman-Frobisher was not bad enough, the last flash Hine had scooped from UNET was either a fuzzy picture of a very large spaceship or a particularly grimy lens. Hine thought the worst. *There hasn't been this much fuss over a smudged lens since Galileo.*

A startled gasp from somewhere up the grass slope drew Hine's attention to the pale blue sky. Two fat sparks drifted southwest. *Comin' in too steep, boys.* A chill flashed over her. *Too steep by far.* It was a fiery re-entry but to Hine's practiced eye, the trajectory was good. Her mouth went dry. There was no point trying to hide.

The harpoons did not carry a warhead. The first struck to the north at the Castor Bay docks, delivering twenty megatons of clean kinetic energy. Half a second later, another strike to the south flattened busy Auckland. Hine had time for one prayer before the combined concussive waves scorched the grassy slopes of North Head and Mount Victoria down to the old lava flows.

CHAPTER ELEVEN

OASIS Traffic Control was not a significant workspace, hardly a breath more than sixty cubic meters. Two consoles dominated the control area in front of the holographic display, and two small auxiliary controls sat off to the right. With no inbound traffic, only the two main consoles were manned. Jake stood ready at Traffic Control, and Kashi Kaur hunched over Communications. Jake watched the holo-display; Earth and her Low Earth Orbit environment, though the position and velocity of all the orbital craft shone brighter in his mind than the updating annotated screens in front of him. Not that there was much to see.

The environment below two hundred kilometers was lethal over most of the Northern Hemisphere and would remain that way for weeks. Even without the patrolling alien ships, no one was stupid enough to launch into the orbiting remnants of an asteroid strike. Thanks to the short-sighted military, there was so much debris, chunks of ice and rock in eccentric orbits, that even a launch in the emptier skies to the south was a risky proposition. There was nothing he could do for anyone on Earth. There are going to be hard times down there. Very hard. He had to concentrate on the people he could help.

Six squadrons of twelve ships patrolled above the orbital chaos, but there had been as many as twelve squadrons at the height of the brief battle. Jake had been surprised at how hard the limited resources in orbit fought - considering they're not supposed to be there at all - and disappointed at how quickly it was all over.

The comm crackled, and Jake heard Burt Hanover's nervous

voice trickle into his ear. "Any change?" There were other voices in the background. Jake could not hear the words clearly, but he could discern the tone; panic. That was one admin meeting he was glad to avoid.

"Not so far. Mothership is on the far side, so I won't be able to tell if she changed orbit for another seventeen minutes," Jake told him.

"Any comm chatter?" Burt asked.

Jake looked across the room at Kashi huddled over the communication console, analyzing the interference, trying to clear away the noise so that they could reconnect to UNET. She was not having much luck. "Nothing so far."

"Keep us posted of any change. We keep boosting then..." The connection terminated abruptly. OASIS was boosting at nearly half a gee. Jake smiled. The ol' girl still has what it takes. He moved his weight from one sore foot to the other and wished he had been able to organize a chair. Who had chairs in a zero-gee environment? Newbies and tourists wanted them and the chairs at Shadrach's were bolted down. Traffic control was not built with gravity in mind. OASIS had been in the same orbit, give or take a few kilometers, for over forty years but she had been boosting on and off for over three hours, and Jake was feeling worse for wear. OASIS certainly was. Reports of seal failures flooded in continuously. None were critical, so far, but OASIS flexed under the continued stresses, waves flowed through the ungainly structure, an unremitting pressure test, exposing the old and infirm station.

"Yes!" Kashi stood straight and knuckled the small of her back. Jake smiled to himself; maybe it wasn't his advancing years that made the extended boost incessant torture. Kashi was young and fit, and she was feeling it. "I've got through, sort of. Bitrate's lousy." She flicked her head towards Jake, tossing her thick black plait over her shoulder and gave him a crooked smile. "I've got both high gain directionals focused on L1, and I'm only just picking up the server, what there is of it. There's no link through to the rest of UNET."

"Thanks," Jake replied, priority pinged Burt and waited. He'd only just opened an aux connection on his board to the UNET feed when Burt responded.

"You have news?" Burt demanded. Jake had not heard Burt sound quite this frazzled.

"We have UNET comm to L1, just. Low bandwidth," Jake informed him.

"Good, good. Make sure admin has priority access," Burt said.

"That is the protocol, sir."

"Yes. Of course, of cour..." Burt cut off the line.

"Jake, you got to see this. Oh god!" Shaking, Kashi had her hand pressed over her mouth.

"Put it on the holo-display," he told her. The annotated orbital projection collapsed into one small corner, and a flat, grainy security feed flickered and buzzed in its place. It took Jake a while to even comprehend the image. The clean corporate lines of the L1 docks were charred and broken. Jake felt his gorge rise as he pumped the feed as an override to Burt and he began to search for other camera feeds. By Murphy's black flabby heart, this is a right proper mess. It did not take long to assemble a broad picture of the strike on L1. Most of the damage was in three specific locations, but there were ruptures in most of the interconnected passageways. Jake stopped counting bodies when his informal toll reached triple figures.

The sound of running and panting preceded the arrival of a red-faced wheezing Burt Hanover to Traffic Control. The disheveled OASIS manager was frantic. Security Chief Randle was in better shape and was murmuring into his comm as he followed Burt.

"You have to make sure that none of this hits the LAN!" Burt commanded, swallowing convulsively.

Kashi sighed and cast an irritated frown at Jake. "Nothing has crossed into the local network, sir."

"There'll be panic, riots. We're not designed for riots," Burt muttered. Burt was not designed for crises either. He would be much better off managing this from his offices, but he insisted on being on the scene, hovering over their shoulders, micromanaging. Interfering. Jake returned his attention to the views of devastation. There were some good signs. He could see tiny skiffs and P-suited figures shuttling back and forth between the fractured structures.

"Damn! L1 was supposed to be our refuge," Burt growled as he paced back and forth.

"Instead, it will be brave old OASIS who rides to rescue the Corporates," Jake announced. He did not enjoy the irony. L1 certainly needed more help than OASIS did. They were short on consumables and OASIS was popping more seams than a fat man at a fashion boutique, but at least they were in better shape than L1.

"I don't know if I would go so far as rescue..." Burt mumbled.

A red flashing alert on his console dragged Jake's eyes down from the array of L1's destruction. He swept the camera feeds to one side and returned the orbital feed front and center. The big red dot with the annotated note, Alien-Alpha01, crept from behind Earth's sphere. It was early. The way that ship moved grated against the wealth of experience in Jake's mind; it ignored the basic rules of orbital mechanics, moving in straight lines from point to point, holding geosynchronous positions where it was not possible, moving as if Earth's gravitational field did not exist. That ship scared Jake more than the squadrons of fighters. They, at least, appeared to use conventional fusion powered engines, but the mothership moved in a manner that said they had technology far in advance of human abilities. Jake ignored the usual rules as he plotted the ship's vectors. It was not transferring from one orbit to another. Jake looked at his answer and did not like it.

"Shit! They're coming here," Jake announced.

Burt squeaked. "How long..."

"Current rate, about an hour." Jake could not blame Burt for his state of panic, but he wished the man would take it somewhere else.

"Can we talk to them?" Burt asked. He tried to hover over

Kashi's shoulder and inspect her console, but with the pseudo-gravity provided by OASIS's acceleration, he could do little more than hop on the spot. Kashi was a big girl, and Burt could fit snugly under her arm. He was never going to be able to see over her shoulder.

"Our high gain antennas are both aligned to L1," said Jake. "Without the error correction, we would not be able to get any signal at all."

"Communicating with L1 will have to wait. We need to tell these ... these aliens we mean them no harm, that I'm ... we are unarmed, carrying ... families, women, and children," Burt babbled.

Jake could not help but sniff with disgust. Burt, thinking about the refugees aboard OASIS? That'll be a first. He had wanted to close the docks and boost away at the first sign of trouble. The illegality of such an act did not faze Burt at all. "I'll handle it, Burt. Traffic Control comm systems should be able to cope." Jake closed his eyes and cleared his throat before opening his microphone. "Alien vessel, this is OASIS Traffic Control, I have you on an approach vector. Can we assist?" Jake waited for a beat to see if there was a reply before continuing. "Alien vessel on approach, this is OASIS Traffic Control. OASIS is an Open Access port, welcoming all visitors. We are unarmed. Repeat, we are unarmed."

Burt left Kashi's elbow and focused his attention on Jake. "Tell them we won't fight. Tell them..."

"Alien vessel on approach, this is OASIS Traffic Control, please respond." Jake ignored Burt and concentrated on monitoring the comm channels for the glimmer of a return signal.

"Alien vessel on approach..."

"I have something." Kashi patched the signal through to Jake's console.

"... Control," rumble, rumble, "Strike Leader," rum-rumble, "Would you," rumble, "parlay?" The voice was pitched very deep, and it took all Jake's concentration to understand it. The fact that they spoke a recognizable version of EngStand was a relief.

Jake spoke as slowly and clearly as his Texan drawl could muster. "Strike Leader, OASIS management would indeed like to parlay." Burt was nodding vigorously. "OASIS is unarmed. Repeat; OASIS is unarmed. Do you understand? Over." Traffic control hushed, waiting for the alien's response. Even Security Chief Randle stopped whispering into his comm.

"OASIS," rumble, "Tra ... affic Control, you," rum-rumble, "offer no," rumble, "resistance?"

Jake opened his microphone and opened his mouth to speak, but Burt leaped forward shouting. "We surrender! We surrender!" Jake closed the connection and pushed the little man off his shoulder. Burt sprawled to the floor, spluttering.

"Control yourself, you coward." Jake's shoulders shook, an involuntary flinch that might shake off Burt's taint.

Rum-rumble, "OASIS, Strike Leader," rumble-rum-rumble, "will," rumble, "your," rumble, "surrender is," rumble, "acceptable." The assertive reply from the Strike Leader cut through Jake's disgust like a knife. "Prepare to be," rumble, "boarded."

"What now, oh fearless leader?" Jake sneered at Burt as he picked himself up from the floor. "Randle, the upper Aldrin has the largest airlock."

"Yes, send them there," Burt told him as he climbed to his feet. He looked as if he saw a safe path before him. "I will meet with their leader. OASIS will survive this."

You will survive this, you mean. Jake held the words and the contempt back. It would not help. "Strike Leader," Jake did not even try to pronounce the rumbling name if that was what the rumbling was, "OASIS has no facility to dock with a ship of your," Jake searched for a sufficiently sycophantic word, "magnificence!" If Burt was that keen on surrendering then perhaps, he should lay it on a bit thick. Jake turned on the navigation beacon for Aldrin's upper dock.

"Strike Leader, I have set a beacon at 2210 hertz ... err ... 2210 cycles. This is our largest airlock. Do you read it? Over."

"OASIS, the," rumble-rum, "beacon," rumble, "is observed."

Jake waited for more, but the channel remained silent. On the display, the alien ship's vector was unchanged. In any other craft, the high-speed approach would be disastrous, the energy required to neutralize all that inertia would be impossible. The alien ship was a behemoth, and it would plow straight through OASIS without losing much more than a coat of paint. But Jake had witnessed that mammoth ship stop and jink about as if it had no mass at all. It would stop, or at least it could, but watching the speed of its approach gave him a chill. It was wrong.

"How much time do I have?" Burt asked.

Burt. Was he still here? "Too much, and not enough. Same as the rest of us." Jake did not like having the coward at his back.

"How long until the aliens get here?" he persisted.

"Twenty minutes plus however long it takes them to maneuver into place," Jake informed him. Burt turned and left, muttering to Randle.

"Urgh. What a creep!" Kashi shuddered. "Is he always like that?"

"You never know how someone is going to respond to a crisis. Burt's tenure has been pretty much stress-free, until now," Jake replied as he glanced at Kashi. She was usually a bright and cheerful young woman and good at her job, but she was somber now. "How are you holding up?"

"I have family in London and ... and I can't get through." Kashi's fear turned to frustration and anger. "It's just wrong. I can always get through."

"Well, keep trying. There's always hope. It'll be tough down there for some time. As near as I could tell London was not in line for a direct strike," Jake comforted her.

"But there was one in the Atlantic. That'll mean a tsunami, won't it?"

"Yeah. But London shouldn't face the full brunt of that," he suggested.

"But England will," Kashi countered.

"And Africa and the Americas, and Europe."

"Why would they do such a thing?" Kashi asked.

"Don't rightly know." Jake frowned and then rubbed at his creased forehead as if his fingers could ease away the deep lines. "Never thought a war was a good idea … and interstellar war? Didn't think it was possible. As to why? Why does anyone fight? For resources, or freedom." That was what the last human war had been fought over. That would be why this one would be fought. Humanity may have lost the opening rounds, but they were far from down for the count. Reeling from a sucker punch, yes, but not down, not yet.

AT THE FORGE

Le'ealani used the hem of her thick leather apron to grip the hilt and thrust the hot steel in and out of the glowing coals. *Just a little longer.* The day was bright, but not too bright. It brought her cheer instead of fear. The time of sunstrikes was long behind them or seemed that way. Some called it the *Age of The Second Rising.* Le'ealani hoped it was true. People still built their homes in a conservative style, below ground, but it had been years since anyone had even heard of a strike. The land was prosperous and food plentiful.

Trade grew, far beyond the three villages that were nearby. She could not help but think about the trader that brought in ore from the mines to the south and the news. *Darfelenornal,* the almost fabled city in the East, wanted people. *Steam!* They used steam power to drive great machines: machines that tilled the earth, machines that wove fine cloth. He said they had sent steam-powered boats to the Southlands, but Le'ealani was sure you could not believe all the tales.

The more she heard, the deeper her desire to learn what they were doing. The most common machine in her village was the lever, and that required no moving parts. The idea of using steam to create power made her mind spin wildly. *But how did they contain and control the steam?* Le'ealani had made many little models, but none of them worked the way she wanted them to. *What do they know?* Le'ealani could not wait to find out. It was rumored Darfelenornal had mel'andrin from before The Fall. *That's how they know how to do all that fantastical stuff.* It was so difficult to make improvements all by yourself. *I just don't know enough.* The itch to answer that City's call burned the soles of her feet as if they were held to the forge's heat.

She gave her huge Hel'omi brother a nod, and Tan gave the bellows another pump. Byn was just as large and waited for her nod before stepping in and drawing the radiant steel from the furnace. With careful supervision, Tan and Byn could turn that glowing steel into a lethal weapon. The power of their great bodies outmatched Le'ealani's tenfold, but her mind exceeded theirs to the same degree. They made a perfect team.

Byn paused, a great hammer in one hand. Tan had hold of the glowing steel, keeping it level on the great anvil.

"You don't have to wait for me. The steel will cool," Le'ealani laughed and shook her head. "You know what to do." She loved her big brothers; they were dim-witted but good-hearted.

Byn nodded and brought the hammer down sharply. THAWANG! The steel rang out as it was flattened. THAWANG! THAWANG! He paused again, and Tan turned the steel.

"See! You don't need me."

THAWANG! THAWANG! THAWANG!

When she left, her big brothers would travel with her. There was no way she could stop them even if she wanted to. Leaving home was going to be hard but leaving Tan and Byn would be impossible. Le'ealani stepped away from the forge and leaned out of the doorway. Dor'em, their closest moon, was still up, a bright sliver, hanging above the horizon and she wondered if the tales were right, if that really was a city up there, high in the sky. *I wonder if the Darfelenornal know how to fly there.* It was an exciting time to be alive.

The light flickered.

Green and red sun banners rippled across the sky. Le'ealani had heard her Pa talk of them, but she had never seen them for herself. *Sunstrike!* For a moment she could not believe her eyes. Her whole being wanted to deny their vivid existence - *No! Not now!* But she was no fool. Her Pa had told her the signs so many times she could recite them in her sleep. She rushed back into the forge.

"Inside! Tan! Byn! Put that down! Sunstrike! Go. Go!" she

shouted. They were good boys, and her brothers dropped their tools immediately. They waited, though, for her to enter the safety of their deep holding before following her down. *Pa will never let me go now. If there's anything left to go to now.* The cool darkness of her home should have felt comforting, but it did not. Le'ealani felt stifled, trapped.

Er'men wondered if Le'ealani ever managed to leave her father's holding. The GreatMother's suites, for all their magnificent splendor, were just as constraining. That forge-side memory was all she held from Le'ealani life. The uncountable years between the lives of Le'ealani and Mu'nruberra felt like a raw hole. She settled on her comfortable bed and returned to the task of integrating her ancestors' experiences into her own.

CHAPTER TWELVE

The mothership loomed over OASIS. Its rendezvous seemed effortless, and it did not change its orientation as it came to a halt relative to the accelerating station. Jake could not see any exhaust ports. *Do the aliens have a reactionless drive?* He was not a physics major, but as a pilot, he was not unfamiliar with the sciences, and the only way he knew of moving forward was to throw something very quickly out the back. Whether it was burning chemicals, hydrogen and oxygen or a fusion engine's plasma flare, Newton's Third Law meant that opposite and equal reactions moved you forward, but these aliens did not seem to need Newton's Third Law to drive their mothership. A squadron of smaller ships peeled away from the behemoth's port side dock. *The boarding party.* At least these ships behaved like regular spacecraft. Jake panned the camera to follow the approaching spacecraft. *Aliens. Aliens were here.* After centuries of speculation, he was going to be one of the first to see an alien from another solar system. True, it was not the way he would have liked to meet aliens, but it was somehow comforting that there was life out in the stars. *Looks like we live in a bit of a tough neighborhood*, he grumbled.

The squadron peeled into two groups, one splitting even further as three pairs of ships began to patrol around OASIS. The remaining six ships continued towards the Aldrin docks. Jake switched cameras and watched them enter and land. Doors slid open and large dark forms emerged. Jake zoomed the camera for a closer look. Bipedal, though they looked to be walking sideways. Their pressure suits disguised their bodies quite effectively. They wore netting vests that concealed a multitude of small packages, and they all carried white staffs about a meter long. There was no visible trigger or stock, but they held them as if they were weapons. The two airlocks on the upper deck opened, and the aliens crowded in.

Jake switched to a view of Aldrin Plaza. There was quite a crowd, and they did not sound pleased. Jake could not see Maya, but her comm was down there somewhere. He sent her a ping. The line opened almost immediately.

"Maya, how is it?" he asked.

"Not good Jake. My spidey-sense is tingling off the scale. There've been a few scuffles, but this is too close to what I would describe as a nascent ugly mob," Maya replied

"Where are you?" Jake asked.

"Post side, Concourse Gamma."

Jake panned the camera around and caught sight of Maya, stunstick held out before her, confronting the crowd with her back to the lock. More security guards stood to either side of her, in a curved line surrounding the airlocks.

"Gotcha," Jake told her.

"Perve."

"Someone's gotta watch your back."

"Jake, if this goes sour..." Maya began.

"Action Station One. I'll collect Madeline. You get yourself clear and meet us."

"Thanks. This has got me spooked," Maya confessed.

"Snap."

The locks opened and the aliens, with their pressure suits on and helmets still firmly in place, began to form an arc around the doors; their white staffs pointed at the crowd. The surging mob pressured the security team, but Jake kept his counsel. Maya had enough on her hands without him distracting her.

The locks cycled closed as Burt, and chief Randle approached the line of aliens to an accompanying chorus of boos and catcalls from the crowd. The aliens ignored Burt's bobbing and weaving, and he gesticulated in vain until the locks cycled open again. More large aliens poured out, reinforcing the line. The last to exit was smaller, much smaller. *Burt would be able to look eye to eye with that one.* Its richly decorated pressure suit and its stance mirrored that of the larger aliens. It did not carry a white staff, but something that looked suspiciously like a sword hung from its hip. The line of aliens parted, and Burt was allowed through, although Randle was excluded. Burt looked around fearfully but kept his focus on the smaller alien. He bowed, and the alien returned it, briefly, a shallow nod.

Suddenly Burt was screaming, engulfed in fire. Liquid flames splashed over the short alien. "A Molotov Cocktail," Jake gasped. Three more flaming bottles sailed through the air from the upper concourse, exploding into the line of aliens. They did not hesitate, firing their white staffs into the mob. Jake could not see what they were shooting - there seemed to be no recoil - but the effect was immediate and bloody. The first line of humans went down, and Jake scanned desperately for Maya. He could track her comm, but he could not see her in the scrimmage. It was time to go.

"Kashi, get to your quarters and lock yourself in," Jake commanded. "You have some supplies?"

"Yes, but..."

"No buts. Traffic Control is closing for the interim. Get ye gone. Now." Jake began shutting down the system.

"Yes, sir." Kashi reluctantly withdrew from her console.

"Keep safe. This might blow over," Jake offered.

"But you don't think so."

Jake pointed to the main display. There was open warfare on Aldrin Plaza. Despite the firepower of the aliens' staffs, people were still resisting. More Molotov cocktails fell around the invaders. An overloaded stunstick exploded amid the surging mob. Suddenly weightlessness returned, magnifying the chaos on show.

"Go somewhere safe and stay there," he added quickly.

Kashi nodded and fled. As the systems shut down, Traffic Control grew dark. *I've spent years in this room and never seen it quite like this.* He opened a panel beside the doors and removed the circuit breakers. Traffic Control was dead. His wrist comm pinged a text message AS1, Action Stations One. Jake breathed a sigh of relief; Maya was on her way.

Madeline waited at the rendezvous point in maintenance shaft four, wearing her brand-new P-suit, with a pack on her back and helmet under her arm. She was not alone. "This is Missy," she told him. "Her parents are Earthside." Missy was much younger than Madeline's fourteen years. She had been crying, her eyes were red, and her freckled cheeks showed dried tear lines.

"Hi, Missy," Jake greeted her cheerily. He did not want another child tagging along, but he would not turn her away. There was room in the skiff for this little one. "Pretty scary, eh." The little girl nodded, her lower lip quivering. "Do you have a P-suit?" She shook her head. "Well, don't worry, Uncle Jake'll find you a Zip-Lok. That'll keep you safe." Where they were going, a P-suit was essential. Keeping all of OASIS pressurized was too expensive for the shoestring station, and most of the maintenance areas were in a vacuum. It was an ideal way to get across the station unnoticed by anyone.

The emergency locker at the maintenance airlock held Zip-Loks in two sizes, too big and too small. While Madeline helped Missy into the over-sized P-suit, Jake pilfered the supplies, stacking water and rations into his pack and putting the spare oxygen cylinders beside the lock. He returned to the locker and pushed out the rear panel. Reaching into the cramped space, Jake's fingers wrapped around a stunstick. It was not half as good as whatever the aliens had, but it was better than nothing. *A fully charged stunstick could disable a crowd so it should have some effect on the aliens, even if I have to overload it.* Jake shuddered. *Last resort, that one.*

Missy stood patiently as Jake double-checked her seals and

dropped low so Madeline could check his. He connected an umbilical and safety line to Missy's Zip-Lok. "Ready?" he asked.

"Yeah," Missy replied, nodding gravely. "Been down here before. Playing hide-and-seek." She chewed on her lower lip and was surprised when Jake smiled.

"Playing hidey down here's pretty naughty, but it's just the ticket today," Jake told her. Knowing that Missy was not a helpless waif was reassuring. Jake had watched kids playing fearlessly around OASIS's orbiting structure. It was a constant nightmare for parents, the authorities and safety groups, but the kids always found ways around the tightest security.

"Do you know how to get to the central shaft?" Jake asked.

Missy grinned. "What junction?"

"Sub-five, quad four," Jake told her, and Missy thought for a second before nodding. "Good, that's our next rendezvous point. Madeline's Mum is meeting us there."

It was a squeeze fitting everyone and their supplies into the lock, but cycling twice would take too long. Green luminescent guide strips indicated the catwalks, but there was no other source of light. That suited Jake just fine. Anything carrying a torch was to be avoided. Insulated pipes and ducts ran in many different directions. Over the years, OASIS had undergone many refits, and often it was easier to leave the existing structure in place and lay the new over the old. What probably began as an interim measure, had become policy; OASIS's underbelly was a nightmarish tangle.

Jake took some joy watching Missy pirouette through the jungle of pipes. Within seconds of leaving the lock, it was apparent Missy did not need the tether; she was perfectly adapted to freefall. Her pantomime efforts at silent communication were remarkably efficient, and the two girls seemed happy enough nattering away as they moved through the dark snarl. Unencumbered, the girls went ahead. Jake was not in a hurry but was not moving slowly, just carefully, keeping their supplies in order.

Missy's worried face emerged from the darkness. She reached

for the coiled umbilical line and plugged in "Maddy says her Mum's not there yet."

Maya was stable, reliable, but anything could go wrong on a day like this. "She will be. Don't worry," Jake reassured her. Missy nodded although the frown did not leave her little round face. She disconnected the umbilicus, spun around and surged away once more.

The junction was a cramped enclosure of perforated plate with a cylindrical core with access to twelve crawlways. Madeline was relaxed, but Missy was trying to look in every direction at once. Jake secured the oxygen and the pack and took a sip from his P-suit's supply. The water tasted flat, but it had been a long time since he'd used bourbon in his suit. Now that he had a chance to catch his breath, the problem of where to go flared once more in Jake's mind. His skiff had good range, but it was far from being an interplanetary spacecraft. She could get them to the moon safely enough, but sitting down at the bottom of a gravity-well where aliens could drop rocks on their heads had proven to be a poor choice once today. Maya was sure to pitch for L3. *If anyone could hold off an alien attack the cantankerous bunch of independent misfits at L3 had the best chance.* It was still too close to the action for Jake's liking. *Ceres is the place to go or maybe Europa.* The skiff could make it, but they would be dead for a long time by the time it arrived.

A shadow moved, and Jake pounced, the stunstick glowing red, throwing fat sparks as the charge came on-line. Maya dodged away from the discharge. Madeline flew to her mother, and they hugged and bounced around, their helmets pressed together. Missy sidled up to Jake and plugged in the umbilical.

"How's it going sweety?" he asked.

"Bit thirsty," she replied.

"I can take care of that." Jake connected a bulb of water to the girl's Zip-Lok, and Missy took a big swig.

"Need to pee too."

"Well, I can't help you there. Can you hold it in for a bit? We're going down to J section. I have a skiff moored there.

Shouldn't take us too long," he said casually. Missy nodded, smiled, and looked uncomfortable at the same time. Maya and Madeline broke from their reunion hug and joined Jake and Missy beside the supplies. Umbilicals connected them.

"Looks like you've been pilfering an emergency locker. That's an offense you know," Maya remarked. She was in her official OASIS security P-suit, and she began to reach for her comm to write a citation. Missy giggled.

"It was an emergency, officer, honest," Jake continued the joke." Good to see you in one piece." Maya gave Jake a don't-go-there look that froze his tongue.

"Hi, Missy." Maya took the little girl's hand. "Good to see you. You okay?"

"Yeah, I guess. I'm gonna need to pee soon," Missy confessed with a squirm.

"We should move on then," Jake said and put his hand on Maya's, and Madeline put hers in the middle too. "All for one and one for all." Jake looked expectantly at Missy, but she just looked puzzled. Madeline knew what he was quoting and gave him a grin.

"Come on, you old pirate," Maya remarked and punched his shoulder with her free hand.

"Section J. Ultra-sneak mode," Jake told the young girls. They nodded. "Let's go." The two girls disconnected and pushed off into the dark. Maya grabbed the pack, Jake the improvised sling with the oxygen bottles, and they followed the girls but kept their umbilical connected.

"I was worried until I received your ping," Jake remarked now that the girls were out of earshot.

"It was truly ugly." Maya shuddered and shook her head, frowning. "Never seen anything like it. Their staff things, I think they shoot focused sound waves, nothing that hurts the decking or walls but does nasty stuff to people. We've got nothing like it." She nodded at the stunstick. "They were useless. Couldn't get close enough to use them."

"I saw one overload and explode," Jake noted.

"Yeah, but that's suicide. I didn't see who it was." Maya punched through the darkness as if it were aliens, wall to wall.

A light flashed bright, one layer above and some way behind, but moving closer. Another light joined it. *More speed. Less speech*, Jake thought, and they moved on as fast as they could. The girls waited at the hatch ten meters ahead as two beams of white light struck Jake and Maya. Jake flinched under the glare.

"Get them out of here," Maya commanded as she pushed the bag of supplies at him with one hand. She pulled a plastic bag from her hip; a pressure sealed Zip-Lok baggie with an antique handgun inside it. Calling it a handgun was to damn it with faint praise. That thing in Maya's hand was a small cannon, a revolver. He had seen it before, Smith & Wesson circa 2003, .500 caliber. The chrome barrel glinted in the torchlight. "Go!" Maya shouted. She ripped the umbilical free and aimed. Unless she'd treated the cartridges, there would only be enough air in the bag for a couple of shots.

Jake pushed off and sailed the last few meters at full speed, hitting the code locked door with a thump. His gloved fingers made no mistake on the keyboard. Something flashed brightly behind him. The door slid open. Another flash and another. Jake bundled Madeline and then Missy through the door. Another flash and Jake pushed through. He could see the skiff.

A white staff with a knobbly end swung towards his helmet. Jake turned. The girls were held securely. Aliens surrounded them. The white staff touched his helmet, and the lights flared very brightly before dying away altogether.

CHAPTER THIRTEEN

"You know, I really hate space flight," Alan said from his cramped back seat for the fourth time in the last half hour. "It's so boring."

"You're mad." Patty stared up at the moon, her eyes wide, and with a broad smile stretched across her face. Despite all that had happened in the last twenty-four hours she was pleased her heart could still feel wonder and awe. She had yawed her CRV until they were flying sideways. With Freya's smooth prow set at a low elevation, her cockpit pointed directly at the Moon. Tycho City was well below the horizon; most of the familiar craters, shining seas and rugged mountain ranges were either hidden around the Moon's curvature or distorted out of recognition. Although she had a globe of the Moon at home, this was the first time she had seen the Wyld crater or the Aitken Basin with her own eyes. In a little while, Daedalus would come into view. *How could you be bored with such a magnificent vista spread out before you?*

"Boring!" Alan complained.

"We could always play I-Spy," Patty suggested.

"Oh yeah, that'd be great. I spy with my little eye something beginning with, M. Err, Moon I think, or maybe something beginning with S that would be a hard one, err, space, no, stars. Thought you'd trick me, eh? I'm no fool," Alan ranted.

"Is that so," Patty replied dryly.

"How long until we get there?" he asked.

"Twenty minutes less than the last time you asked," Patty replied dryly as she checked the flight computer. "Only seven hours forty-three minutes till our next burn then there's another nine hours till the rendezvous burn."

"Why so long? I thought Freya was a hot little go-buggy," he whined.

"She is," Patty answered. She took a deep breath and tried to relax the knot that suddenly appeared in her belly. "But we can't go racing off at full speed anymore. Plotting a fast course to L1 was foolish, wasteful. I could have gotten us there almost as quickly and used half the fuel."

"But Tritium's cheap."

"We were lucky. Lucky that we found the Balke-Spalding center as quickly as we did, lucky they had fuel to spare. That may not happen anymore," Patty told him.

"We were lucky you boosted us there as quickly as you did," Alan argued. "If we'd taken too much longer, we would have missed them altogether and missed Mum and Dad's message too."

Alan was right; they had been oh-so-lucky. If they had arrived after Balke-Spalding had boosted they would have been waiting in an Ingress queue when the missiles ripped L1 to pieces. "We were fortunate in lots of ways, but we can't rely on luck. Jake would say, ya gotta check your seals *every* time, check 'em yourself, check 'em twice. There's no room for the blame game in space; either the seals are right, or you're dead. So, you reckon Tritium's cheap, do you? Pop quiz, crewman. Where does it come from and why is Tritium so cheap?"

"Ice mines on the Moon ... and the asteroids?" he answered hesitantly.

"Okay, half a point for the first part of my question, what about the second part?" she asked. Alan was quiet. Patty could almost hear the gears in his head grinding.

"I guess it may not be so cheap anymore," he eventually replied.

"Why?"

"Well, there's lots of ice down there but *Them*," he flicked his thumb over his shoulder, towards the half-lit Earth, "*They* ain't gonna let us keep it, are they?"

109

"No, I don't suppose *They* will. Humans could do all sorts of mischief up here with a plentiful fuel supply. If they choke it off, we're finished. Not much we'd be able to do then but, float around waiting for our oxygen to run out."

"We've got water. We could split that. We'd have oxygen to breathe and hydrogen for Freya," he suggested.

"Good thought. We *can* burn pale old hydrogen, and it might be enough to save us, in a pinch, but can you see why I've put us on a slow course now?" she offered.

"Yeah. I guess," Alan growled.

Patty went back to studying the Moon as it rolled beneath them.

"Space travel's BORING!"

"Quiet in the cheap seats."

Freya executed the rendezvous burn flawlessly, and Patty slewed her around once manual control resumed. She grinned. L2 was precisely where it was supposed to be.

"Hey, Sis. I think you blew it. There's nothing here," Allan announced.

"Yes, there is. Right there in front of us," Patty corrected him.

"You're kidding me," Alan snorted his disbelief. "That? It's tiny."

L2 was small, much smaller than OASIS, unless you included the array of radio antennas spread over hundreds of kilometers, dynamically locked to the station. The observatories peered into the heart of the universe, but they were too far away to see. In the center of the array's spider web of receivers was the station itself, only two or three times the size of the Balke-Spalding center, it was tiny for a space station.

"DH-1031C to L2 Traffic Control, over," Patty called. There was no reply. Patty waited another minute while Freya drifted closer. There were plenty of lights on, so someone was home.

"DH-1031C to L2 Traffic Control, over," Patty repeated.

The comm buzzed and crackled, then Patty heard a microphone turn on, a sudden profanity, and a bang so loud it made her ears ring.

"Sorry about that. Dropped the mike. L2 TC how ya doin'?"

Patty waited for a second or two; had they finished talking? "DH-1031C to L2 Traffic Control. Requesting ingress clearance. Over."

"Hey, Ma! Ya better kill dem chickens, we's got visitors!"

"Hey! Give me that!" Another voice came over the open mike and the sounds of what seemed to be a struggle for possession of it. "This is neither the time nor place for your games, Carl. Give it here!" The microphone cut off. *What's going on down there?*

"Unidentified vehicle this is Lagrange Two Traffic Control. Err, sorry about that. The guys down here get cabin fever pretty bad sometimes. Over."

"DH-1031C to L2 Traffic Control, I know what you mean." Patty glanced over her shoulder at her little brother. "We are requesting ingress clearance, over."

"Sure thing, come aboard, come aboard. Do you need a beacon? I can flash it for you. Over."

"Thanks, but I think I can see where to go. DH-1031C, out." Patty cut the line. Indeed, the landing platform was obvious. The closer Freya got, the more L2 reminded Patty of OASIS; it was just smaller and a little tidier. *A little.* L2 had undergone a series of alterations and additions over the years, but no design committee guided their hand. Buildings and extensions of many shapes and sizes jutted out at all angles. The only indication that there had once been a local horizontal plane was the landing pad. *Jake would like it here*, Patty thought. *Was he alright? Was anyone? Mum and Dad, Tina and Hine, they were all ... maybe not gone but...* Her heart wanted to break, but she put her needs to one side; she was flying Freya. Having a well-deserved nervous breakdown could wait.

There was plenty of room to land with just a small

maintenance sled and a twenty-seat emergency escape shuttle secured to the landing platform. Patty locked Freya down but kept her on standby just in case. Alan floated out and hooked Freya to an umbilical. Not that they needed much fuel, she'd used less than a tenth of their Tritium capacity getting to L2.

"Good job, crewman," Patty complimented Alan.

"Thanks, Captain."

CHAPTER FOURTEEN

There were no guidelines set for nervous tourists on L2'S dock, so Patty pumped her thrusters and glided to the airlock. Alan followed close behind. Formal ID control was nonexistent, but two men met them when they cycled through the lock. Both had beards, but only one was trimmed. They were wearing loose gray overalls with an embroidered patch bearing a mason's compass and the words 'Metire Universum' encircling it. Patty prayed they were not the emergency crew.

The one with the long straggly beard would take an age to get suited up. He held an arm up, shading his eyes. "Alert, alert!" he exclaimed. "This is a Bright Boy alert. This is not a drill. Repeat, Bright Boy alert!"

"Very funny," Alan muttered angrily.

"Keep your cool, crewman," Patty said.

"Aye, sir," Alan replied, but she could still hear him grumbling.

"Welcome to L2, I'm Joshua Sanchez..." the man with the trimmed beard had the voice of the sane traffic controller.

"And I'm ... pleased to meet ya." The man with the unkempt beard stuck out his hand. He was the mad one.

"... and this is Carl Hawk," Joshua continued. "You'll have to forgive him. We don't get many visitors out here."

"I'm Patty Balke, and this is..." Patty began.

"*The* Patty Balke?" Carl exclaimed. "Space pilot extraordinaire? Hey, Josh, we's got ourselves a real celebrity here."

"Knock it off, Carl," Joshua growled.

"But she was on *The Late Show* just the other night," Carl added.

"You watch too much crap media. It's rotting your brain," Joshua grumbled before turning to Patty. "Sorry, Patty, was it?"

"And Alan, my brother." Patty did not mind Carl's somewhat manic attitude; his warm smile offset the craziness in his eyes.

Carl frowned, and he turned to the control panel behind him. "Josh," said Carl.

"What is it?" Josh turned to him with a frown.

"We have a message for them," Carl remarked as he approached a control display mounted to the curved wall. He tapped it with one finger. "Two actually."

"Two?" Alan asked as he bounced over, his bad mood evaporating. "We caught one at L1."

"This one's been trickling in for hours. Even with ears like ours, the bitrates from Earth are abysmal," Carl remarked as he called up the file and floated out of the way so that Patty could get a closer look. "Gotta do something about that." He frowned; a finger tapped at his lip.

Alan logged in, and the message unpacked. The picture was terrible quality, but they could see their mother strapped in an acceleration chair. She was shaking so much it must have been recorded while they were boosting into orbit.

"Alan, Patty. We've just heard about the aliens. I can't quite believe it myself but your father's confirmed the integrity of the data, so I guess they're real. I hope this will reach you before OASIS gets to L1, if not it doesn't really matter, my message is still the same. Don't stay. I repeat, do not stay at L1. It would be a perfect refuge if it were just Tempelman-Frobisher falling on us, but with aliens giving it a nudge, certain black-ops military facilities are sure to tip their hand. L1 will be a target. Do not stay at L1 any longer than you absolutely must. We are..." The message ended in static.

"Is that all?" Alan demanded. Carl leaned closer and checked the file.

"Sorry, the file is definitely closed. There's no more on the server. That's all we've got." He frowned; all his manic levity had drained out of his body leaving him deflated and empty.

"Patty?" Alan sounded very worried. He had every right to be.

"What's the date stamp?" Patty asked.

"2238 UMT," Carl said.

"That was well before the battle in Low Earth Orbit. 2238 hours. We were still eating in Shadrach's."

"Hmm, Shadrach's Bar and Grille," Carl mumbled, "Been a while, been a while."

"They're safe, Alan. I just know it," Patty insisted. *If I want Alan to believe it, then I'll have to as well. We have no proof they're dead.* Patty's heart said they were alive. That was good enough for now.

"Then where are they?" he asked. Panic crept into Alan's voice.

"Not here," Carl added mournfully.

"No, that's obvious. They would have had time to get to L1 by now." *What's left of it.* Patty shuddered.

"They could be at L3, 4 or 5, I guess," Alan said slowly.

That sounded better. Alan could use his head when he needed to. "Could be," Patty encouraged.

"Patty?" Alan stretched his shoulders, and a swarm or butterflies flocked around his p-suit's seals, none of them turned red.

"Yes?"

"Do we have to leave right away? If I have to sit in that back seat for another long flight, I'll be as mad as him," Alan remarked as he pointed to Carl with his thumb. Carl smiled.

"Is there somewhere we can stay?" Patty asked Josh.

"Well, since you're a Balke I guess the FC research facility would be appropriate," Josh replied with a smile.

"Sorry?" Patty had heard that name before but for the moment could not place it.

"FC, Fermi-Cingolani, they do optics research, and help maintain our fifty-meter mirror, among other things," Josh told her.

Fermi-Cingolani, Fermi-Cingolani. It rang a bell in Patty's mind, but she could not pin the memory down. It had something to do with her father's business, she was sure, but for some reason, she kept seeing a glass of red wine, and a pale blue shirt stretched over a large belly, and then she remembered. "Fermi as in Giuseppe Fermi?" Patty asked.

"Yes. Do you know Joe? Your father does, I'm sure," Josh replied. "A big guy, especially 'round the middle. Loves his wine."

"You know our father?" Alan interjected.

"Only by reputation." Joshua smiled apologetically. "I don't move in those circles."

"I've met him," Patty muttered to herself. A smile spread across her face; her heart warmed as the memory unfolded. "He dragged Dad and me away from a sales yard when we were looking for a CRV and gave Dad a good telling off." *Oh yes, I remember Giuseppe all right.* "He found Freya for me. Is he here?" The delight in Giuseppe's eyes when he delivered her CRV to their home was electrifying. His booming laughter was contagious.

"Yes. Joe comes here every six months or so. Likes the peace and quiet, or so he says," Carl remarked, but he did not sound convinced.

Joshua turned to his colleague and patted him on the shoulder. "Don't you have a shift starting soon?"

"Yeah," Carl sighed, his face brightened a little, and his posture straightened. "Yes, I do." He turned to Patty. "Sorry I've been such a freak. It's been nice to meet you. Hope you find your folks. Good luck." He pushed off and swam down the corridor.

Joshua turned to the control panel and tapped a few keys. "I better call ahead."

"Hello?" an accented voice Patty recognized came back.

"Joe, it's Josh, down at the lock."

"I noticed we had visitors," Joe replied.

"It's me, Mr. Fermi, Patty Balke, and Alan," Patty called out. She was sure he would remember them.

116

"Patty? Patricia, my dear! How's your CRV, err, what did you call her?" Mister Fermi asked.

"Freya," Patty replied proudly.

"Yes, yes, Freya; how is she?" he asked. "Is that what you flew in on? My, my. Josh, bring them straight over."

"Will do, Joe." Joshua turned back to Patty with a smile. "This way." He pushed off and headed in the opposite direction to Carl. Patty followed with her brother at her side.

"Patty?" asked Alan. "You know this Joe... Giuseppe?"

"Yes! Don't you remember when I got Freya?" Patty reminded him.

Alan scrunched up his face. "Sort of. I remember when you got Freya. I was pretty pissed off, jealous, I guess. Didn't want anything to do with your little celebration. And you were off-planet as soon as you could."

"But you remember Giuseppe, don't you?" she asked.

"I think so, sort of, a fat guy with a funny accent, yes?" Alan asked. Patty nodded. "He dragged Dad into his office the moment you left the ground. Had him bailed up in there for hours."

"Relax. Giuseppe's a nice guy," Patty reassured him. At least that was how Patty remembered him, a big smile, and a generous face with laughing eyes. They followed Joshua down a set of winding corridors that upset whatever remained of Patty's sense of the horizontal. By the time they reached a pair of secure pressure doors Patty had no idea what direction was up, not that it mattered. The large man was waiting for them inside the second set of pressure doors. He looked like someone from an ancient period, wearing a long red silk jacket and a cravat. Green and gold embroidery spread up his sleeves like creeping ivy. Thinning hair, cut short, topped his round face and a well-trimmed beard graced the folds of his chin.

"Patricia!" He swept her up in a warm embrace. Then held her at arm's length, "You look tired. Have you eaten?" He turned to her brother. "And this is Alan? I must admit we didn't have a chance to meet properly, what was it, eight, nine months ago."

He extended his hand, but Alan did not shake it until he looked at Patty. Her minuscule nod encouraged him to be polite. "Come in, all of you. Josh, you too. If you don't mind, my dear, we're going to debrief you. We're starved for information. It's ironic really. I come out here to get away from it all, and now that our flow of information has been cut off it's all I want."

The Fermi-Cingolani facility's corridors spiraled around a substantial internal space. The white walls had pale green trim and were a relief from the endless gray of the rest of the station. Giuseppe led them through the curving corridor by pulling himself along by conveniently placed straps. The way Giuseppe floated through his domain reminded Patty of an African wildlife documentary she had seen about hippopotamuses. His graceful movements belied his bulk.

"Have you heard from your father?" Giuseppe asked over his shoulder. "Communication from Earth has been cut to a trickle. We've been getting most of our feed relayed through the deep space network, and that's taken major damage."

"We've had two messages, one before they took off," Patty told him, "And one from Mum that looked to have been recorded while they were boosting into orbit."

"But nothing since," Giuseppe frowned. "Nasty business. Nasty business." They arrived at another set of pressure doors and cycled inside. The lock was tiny, and the four of them made it quite a squeeze. A low-pitched humming vibrated through Patty's boots. It increased in volume when Giuseppe opened a sealed hatch.

"Lead the way, Josh," Giuseppe instructed as he floated his bulk to one side, and Joshua climbed into the narrow shaft. Patty and Alan followed with Giuseppe bringing up the rear, sealing the hatch behind him. It was a most unusual layout. Most facilities had broad corridors, not crowded little access ways.

Alan looked more than a bit concerned. "Patty, what is this place?" he whispered.

"You'll find out soon enough, young man. Soon enough,"

Giuseppe said, followed by a laugh that Patty remembered well. When they arrived at the end of the tunnel, Patty's eyes sprang wide. The small room they had entered was cylindrical and the curved wall, with four opposing hatches, rotated around them. The facility's unusual layout suddenly coalesced in Patty's mind.

"You have centrifugal gravity!" Patty cried out with astonishment.

"Yes, my dear. My body does not react well to the calcium replacement drugs, so I have to bring my gravity with me," Giuseppe told her. "We need the centrifugal gravity in part of our manufacturing process. It's a convenient combination of circumstances. Please continue. Don't forget to use the climbing rungs. It's only a quarter-gee down there, but it will be a rather nasty fall if you don't hang on." Once again, Joshua led the way. It was quite peculiar, slowly feeling her weight build as she climbed down the rungs; the tubular corridor was suddenly a vertical shaft. About halfway down, the shaft opened out, and the ladder turned into a wrought iron spiral staircase that led down into a sunny foyer. Pic-Walls displayed a balcony that looked out over a green alpine valley dotted with little farms. It made Patty feel a bit giddy.

Giuseppe stood for a moment staring out over the valley. "I was born down there," remarked as he pointed into the vale. "And I always wanted to build a home up here. That wasn't allowed of course, so I just have to make do with Pic-Walls." Patty was impressed; the outlook was incredibly realistic. Most Pic-Walls were impressionistic rather than photo-real; these gave an almost holographic feeling of depth.

Their hefty host turned from the grand vista, led them down a curving passageway, and into a book-lined library with an open fireplace on the far wall. Four leather wingback armchairs sat around a burled oak coffee table. Patty's mind spun with confusion. The room was not like anything she had experienced in space. *Why would someone fill a room with books?* The expense of moving all that mass into orbit must have been astronomical.

He uses a fireplace? Alan walked over to one of the walls and suddenly stepped back when his hand failed to reach one of the leather-bound covers. *Pic-Walls! The room was covered with Pic-Walls!*

Giuseppe laughed at their reactions. "I may be rich, but I'm not indulgent enough to bring real books up here. I must say, with some pride, that Fermi-Cingolani's Pic-Walls are superior to the average. Would you not agree?" He stood and waved them to the chairs. "Are you hungry?" He pressed a concealed panel beside the door, which turned, presenting a standard comm board. "Antonio! Refreshments for four please." He did not wait for a reply. "Come, sit. Tell us of your adventures."

Adventures, Patty grumbled. *That's the last thing I wanted, but Giuseppe's right. We are on an adventure, but one that I wouldn't have chosen for myself. Who would?* Patty began with their flight up to OASIS. That was routine enough except for the additional course correction required to catch the space platform as it boosted to L1. Joshua and Giuseppe leaned closer as she began to tell them about the battle in Low Earth Orbit.

"Were you recording?" Giuseppe asked.

"Yes. Freya has the video. It's not very good quality though."

"That doesn't matter. Josh, can we patch into her CRV?" Giuseppe asked.

"If she's hooked up to an umbilical," Josh replied. Patty nodded, and Giuseppe tapped an unseen control on the edge of the oak coffee table. A standard comm display projected from its polished surface. Patty logged into Freya, found the file and began the grainy playback. Giuseppe and Joshua had her play it back four times before allowing her to continue with her story. She told them about their rendezvous with the Balke-Spalding research facility and how it had disconnected from L1 and boosted out to places unknown. She played back the sensor data of the missile attack on L1 without explanation. There was none needed. The devastation was horrific. They played her recordings again and again. Alan sat quietly through it all, pale and unresponsive.

Giuseppe leaned back in his comfortable chair and stroked his double chin, deep in thought, while Joshua played Freya's sensor data once more. "Scattering," Giuseppe frowned. "It's not a stupid idea, not at all," he muttered.

"We're not going," Alan blurted out.

"Sorry?" Giuseppe turned to Alan with a frown.

"He's right," Patty added much to Alan's apparent relief. "We're going to find our parents, one way or another, and scattering to the far corners of the solar system won't be the quickest way of finding them."

"You're right my dear, you're right." Giuseppe's frown bloomed into a smile. "If you're sure you are going to stay then I think I have a few things here that will help you."

"Like?" Alan asked.

"How about some long-range fuel tanks?" The smile spread into a grin. "There're a few other things with which I might be able to assist you. Let me think about it some more. In the meantime, why don't you make yourselves at home?"

CHAPTER FIFTEEN

Patty enjoyed sleeping in a real bed almost as much as she enjoyed having a shower. The feeling of crisp sheets and warm blankets kept the ravening alien monsters from her dreams. They were still somewhere out there; out in the dark, watching and waiting for the right moment to strike, but for the time being, they were far away. When Patty woke, she had a vague recollection of being in Shadrach's with Jake. He had been drinking a fish milkshake. "Whale blubber flavor," he'd said with a wry smile. "It's an acquired taste." *That's just wrong*, Patty thought. She shook her head to try and shake free of the disturbing image.

Giuseppe's apartments had beds for three guests that shared one bathroom, but what a bathroom it was. Glided mirrors covered the walls; there was a shower with hot water! And the marble tub could easily fit three adults. It made her giddy to think of such extravagance. Patty was accustomed to using a sonic scrubber whenever she was in space. Conserving water was completely second nature to her. Sonic scrubbers got you clean, but it was not the same as luxuriating in hot water. She took the opportunity to wash her hair. *Who knows when I'll be able to do this again?* She sniffed the melon-scented shampoo and sighed.

While they slept, Giuseppe had moved Freya to his workshop, which peeved Patty, but she swallowed her anger when Freya showed a clean bill of health. Junk, of all descriptions, filled Giuseppe Fermi's workshop; all carefully secured to walls or in wire mesh bins stacked four or five high. Patty's first glance took in at least two CRVs in various states of disrepair, an ancient robo-arm with no manipulator on its extensor, and half a dozen small telescopes. There was even an old V-8 internal combustion engine sitting on one of the workbenches. The head was off on one side, exposing rusted pistons.

"It is a bit of a mess in here, but I have everything we'll need to fit those extra fuel tanks." He began to weave through the rows of bins. "Come with me," he whispered with his eyes twinkled. Patty trotted behind him, her excitement building. She recognized that twinkle. He had had it when he delivered Freya. In the far corner, an indistinct shape sat covered in a blue Mylar wrap. Giuseppe took hold of the cover's leading edge, whipping the blue film back, posing theatrically. The burnt and beaten shell of a CRV with two tanks mounted on the upper side of its stubby wings lay strapped down to the deck. Its undercarriage was gone, as were the canopy, the pilot's seat, and the engine.

"Do you not recognize it?" Giuseppe asked. The hair on the back of Patty's neck began to stand up and then she knew. Its body shape was nearly identical to Freya. "It is the original *Mercurio Cuore*, Mercury's Heart! She won the inaugural Trans-Lunar race in '27. She's seen better days. Been meaning to put her to rights but I guess that project is going to take even longer now." He chuckled and walked back to the tool rack. "Shouldn't take too long to strip the tanks off and mount them to your Freya but connecting them to your fuel lines will be impossible. We can use the loom from the old bird but purging the fuel lines is going to be painfully slow." They set to work.

Patty was surprised at how much Giuseppe seemed to be enjoying himself. For a man who had brought such luxury to an isolated place, he was having fun getting his hands dirty. When

Alan brought them lunch, they had dismantled the old ship's fuel system and made a good start pulling out Freya's. With any luck, they would have the tanks mounted in a couple of hours.

"Patty?" Alan asked with a mouth still full of a sandwich stuffed with salads and cold meats. He swallowed, "Carl wants to show me the fifty-meter telescope."

"You've discovered an interest in astronomy?" Patty asked.

Alan squirmed on the spot. "Actually, he said he might be able to hack into my P-suit's graphics." He took another bite.

"Giuseppe? Is Carl," *now can I say this without sounding offensive*, Patty wondered. "Is Carl ... err ... safe?"

Giuseppe laughed and scratched at the side of his face, leaving a greasy mark. "Carl's mad as a hatter, totally in love, married to that fifty-meter scope of his. Last two times he was scheduled to rotate out, he found excuses to stay on. Doesn't do his head any good, but he does good science." Giuseppe grinned. "But is he safe? I would say so. He may be mad as a fish, but he's gentle as a lamb."

"Okay then, but if you damage your P-suit, you'll have to cope with traveling in a Zip-Lok," Patty warned him. Alan grinned and bounced on the spot.

"Don't worry; we'll just be tinkering with the graphics." Alan turned and was gone in a flash.

Giuseppe's ever-present chuckle returned once more. "Where did you get that P-suit?"

"A friend of a friend on OASIS," Patty told him.

Giuseppe's grin faded.

"What's wrong?" she asked.

"OASIS. I guess you are not up-to-date." The large man sighed. "We only received a partial message. Aliens boarded last night before OASIS could complete their burn for L1. Reports are confused. There was a fight." He shook his head. "I can't imagine Burt taking that course. Two decks experienced explosive decompression. There are many dead."

Patty could not believe her ears. OASIS had been her home-away-from-home all year. It had been harrowing seeing it filled with strangers, refugees, but hearing that aliens had captured it, cut deep into her heart. *Mum, Dad, Jake, and maybe even Tina and Hine, I hope you all kept yourselves safe.*

"Come on, let's get these tanks mounted," Giuseppe encouraged. "Nothing like focusing on work to put your mind at ease." Giuseppe's smile was back. It looked forced, but it did lighten Patty's sinking heart, somewhat.

CHAPTER SIXTEEN

A discordant blaring from the comm panel gave Patty such a fright she barked her knuckles on the engine and dropped the recalcitrant nut she had been trying to thread onto the intake manifold. "Damn! What is that?" she exploded before sucking on her bleeding fingers.

Giuseppe had already moved to the comm. "Sì?" The comm spat a reply in Italian. Patty could not understand a word, but Giuseppe's body language was enough to make her afraid. Suddenly the workshop shook. What could do that? Giuseppe turned to her, his face pale. "They're here. The aliens are here," he told her. A chill flooded Patty. She had run as far and as fast as she could. The fuel loom was in place and would not need much to secure it, but they would have to purge the lines before Freya's engines could fire up. That could take hours.

"Patty!" Giuseppe was suddenly beside her, shaking her shoulder. "We have started to detach the FC complex from L2. It's going to take a while to lock everything down and spin down the labs. We have no weapons. We're scattering," he said. Patty looked up at him from the disarray in Freya's engine bay. Her thoughts were sluggish, caught in the invisible stuff that clings to you in a dream, slowing you, so the monsters could capture you, blocking your mouth, so even your screams were stifled. *The space monsters are here.*

"Patty, the comm link to the L2 station is down, we cannot reach anyone. We have to go and find your brother."

Alan! Suddenly the dream treacle was gone. Her heart pounded, and her knees shook, but she could move again. She pushed Giuseppe out of the way and reached into Freya's cockpit. She discarded the case and her competition épée without a thought. Patty ran through the workshop, Lady Estelle clasped in her steady left hand, before Giuseppe could protest. She could hear his panting calls and the sound of his leaden feet when she got to the spiral staircase, but she would not wait for him.

"Patty! We'll be ready to boost in half an hour!" Giuseppe called after her. "Be quick! Fly true!"

She flew up the shaft using the rungs to push off. It felt good to be back in zero-gee. It took an unearthly age to cycle through the pressure doors, and the spiraling corridor seemed to be without end. Patty pressed herself up against the wall when she cycled through the pressure doors that connected to the L2 station. There was no one to be seen or heard.

Rapier extended *en-garde*, Patty moved carefully down the gray corridor that led back to the reception area. She wanted to run and call for her brother. *Alan! Where are you?* But she dared not open her mouth. She sidled up to a corner and peeked around it. There were monsters! She pulled her head back, choking down a scream. *They're not monsters; they're not monsters. They're aliens, big, strange-looking aliens, but they're not monsters.* Patty took a deep breath and then another. *Right. Let's do this.*

There were three of them standing with their feet on the Gecko-Grip floor, their backs to her. They were misshapen creatures, their bodies twisted, and lopsided. And they were big, well over two meters in height. All wore dark brown pressure suits under webbing jackets that carried all manner of things, and they all held long white batons with a broad knobbly end. Patty did not like the look of the staffs, whatever they were. She felt a little foolish with her duelist's blade, but she would not be here without it. Five men in gray overalls lay bound, hand and foot, in front of the aliens. One of the prisoners had soiled himself. Patty did not recognize any of them. The vrip-vrip sound of someone walking on Gecko-Grip came down the corridor in front of her. She had never been to L2 before, but the fifty-meter telescope was to her right, on the other side of the main airlocks.

A misshapen alien approached, and Patty had barely a second to size it up. It moved oddly, as if it was walking sideways, like a fencer presenting the smallest possible target, little black eyes shone, protected beneath a prominent brow. Shiny, mottled yellow-brown skin covered its face. There were no fangs, but its mouth looked big enough to contain nightmares.

Without thinking, Patty pushed off and spiraled in, bringing her rapier down and attacking in *tierce*, high on the outside. She was not aiming at its head, though it did flinch most satisfyingly as it brought the knobbly staff to block her strike. The white baton shattered in sparks and shards and the alien retreated quickly. Patty lunged and punctured its P-suit near its shoulder. Her blade did not penetrate very far, and the creature let out a hooming cry. She used the solid mass of the extra-terrestrial to halt her momentum, and she gave it a kick to the chest as she pushed back up the corridor.

The three other aliens were only just reacting as Patty flashed past. She spun, her rapier was a blur. They were locked to the floor and slow to move as if covered in dream treacle. She disabled the white staffs of two aliens before the fourth lumbered, screaming, around the corner. It had a sword in his fist. It was not, in Patty's opinion, an elegant weapon. It looked like a long broad-bladed double-edged dagger. It was shorter than her rapier, but the big alien had long arms. Patty slashed wildly at the last white staff and pushed off the startled alien, retreating down the corridor.

"Where's Alan?" she yelled as she flew past the trussed-up scientists. She did not have time to listen to their replies. Their expressions were enough, *Alan who?*

The enraged alien with the enormous dagger pushed his fellows out of the way and charged up the corridor bellowing. Patty kept moving, keeping it in sight. She was looking for some space, and the central reception area had high ceilings. If she were caught on the ground, the alien's mass and its greater reach would defeat her for sure.

Patty surprised three more aliens standing guard at the airlock. They began to raise their staffs, but the cries of their enraged comrade charging down the corridor behind her stopped them. Instead of coming at her, they moved to the two other passages that opened into the foyer, cutting off her escape routes. Patty did not mind as long as they did not attack her. They all remained Gecko-Gripped to the floor.

The alien came to a stumbling halt, panting and groaning. The others Patty disarmed came thundering in behind him, hooting and booming. Patty backed away, towards the center of the room, floating in a relaxed posture a few centimeters from the floor. The alien followed brandishing his sword-sized dagger.

"Tell me where my brother is, and I'll let you live," Patty shouted at it.

The alien coughed as it brandished its blade. *Was that a laugh?* Patty tapped the point of her rapier against the broad tip of its weapon. The alien was right-handed from its thick rear boot to its shiny forehead. It returned her touch on her steady blade in a move telegraphed from its bent knees, though its twisted torso and out through its upper arm. Its wrist rotated not one degree. *Was it locked in place? That would be awkward.*

"One last chance. Where's my brother?" Patty asked.

It grunted. There were words in there somewhere. EngStand words. "Male sibling. Ours. Make study." Then it coughed. Patty was sure now it was laughing.

She flicked her wrist down; her slim blade slid down the broad dagger. A small crossguard gave scant protection to the alien's gloved hand. It was a weak attack, and any competent swordsman would flick it away, catching her blade with a flick of their wrist. The alien's response came from its shoulders. It was fast, but Patty ducked under its sweep. *You have to strike quickly, while he's wide open.* Her feet made contact with the floor, and she lunged. Razor sharp, Patty's rapier slid over the helmet seals of the alien's P-suit collar. Patty had seen it shift its head. The skin around its neck moved like thick leather. It cut like thick leather too.

Patty tried to pivot away from the cascade of blood exploding from the alien's neck, but she was not in her pressure suit and did not have thrusters. Red blood. A broad wave caught up with her as she pivoted in the air. Alien gore sprayed over her.

"Okay! Who's next?" Patty screamed as she pushed off from the ceiling, brandishing her dripping blade. She blinked blood out of her right eye and dived towards the closest alien. It held a knobbly staff but dropped it and fumbled for the sword at its hip. Patty cut at wrist and elbow, disabling him painfully if his hooming bellow had any earthly correlation. A kick to its head sent Patty back towards the remaining aliens who seemed to be trying to line up together. Patty flew over their heads, slashing inelegantly, breaking the aliens' attempt to work together. Rebounding from a wall, Patty screamed and met their uncoordinated charge skimming across the floor. She was able to make cuts at their ankles as she passed through their line, disabling two.

"Where is my brother!" Patty screamed. Patty pushed off, through a cloud of spinning blood droplets. The world was a red blur. One alien had fled through the airlock, leaving another holding the ominous white staff, protecting its comrade's retreat. *Why didn't it use its weapon?* Patty was on it in a heartbeat. It seemed stunned, so slow was it to react. She pressed the razor point of Lady Estelle into the same fold of skin she had pierced the first alien. It fell back and sank to one knee holding the staff in front of him, horizontal to the deck and growled.

Rumble-rum-rumble, "Oh mighty," rumble-rum, "we," rumble, "intruded," rumble-rum, "your domain," rumble, "paid," rum-rum, "honorable price." It sounded like something it had memorized; its body posture seemed submissive.

Patty checked the pressure of her thrust, withdrawing slightly. The alien moved not one hair if it had hair.

"I'm not interested in prices honorable or otherwise. Where's my brother?" She demanded and glanced over her shoulder. The aliens she had disabled groaned and writhed where they lay. The first dead alien was still upright, held in place by his Gecko-Grip boots. *They have red blood. Fancy that. I wonder what else we have in common?* "Where is he? Tell me, or you'll end up like that one."

"Oh, queen," rumble rumble-rum, "this one," rumble, "few words." It bowed meekly. "Seek male," rumble "sibling? Yes?"

"Yes. Alan's only twelve. He has a pink P-suit." *Or he used to have one.* "Where is he?"

Rumble, "Queen. This one," rumble, "not seen male sibling." Rumble, "Some gone. Not here."

"Gone? Where?" Patty leaned closer, tapping the keen edge of her rapier against the knobbly staff.

The alien said something that sounded like grmpfluugminks and then "Home, ship."

Patty wanted to scream. *Perhaps I will. Now's as good a time as any.*

Freya's Flight

Part Two

Patty's War

by

CRAIG P. MILLER

THE NEW CANDIDATE

Er'men gagged as she returned to her bedroom but managed to keep her meal down. Genedalt had disapproved of her dabbling in the human language when she should have been integrating her GreatMothers' memories. Although mel'andrin from her LeftLeading sons made her ill, it was worthwhile suffering the aftereffects. *Besides, if I use GreatMothers' mel'andrin, it settles my stomachs. Humans have a great wealth of knowledge for the taking,* Er'men marveled, although it puzzled her. *Just passing on words leaves so much room for misinterpretations.* It was vital that she understood the local inhabitants if she was to rule justly. She'd had a few books printed for her, and although the individual words were recognizable, their context seemed mailable and changeable from one book to the other. The dictionary reference helped, but sometimes it seemed she had to check every second word to make sure she understood what had been written, and then some words had multiple meanings.

What strange creatures these humans are, she pondered as she sat on the edge of her bed and opened the wooden box containing the golden drops of her inheritance. The rich scents rising from the mel'andrin had already begun to ease her discomfort. She took a slow breath and selected one of the golden spheres from the box with the engraved offering spoon secured under the lid and brought it to her lips. She rolled the ball around her mouth, and the memories contained within it began to fill her.

Bright Hope tried the door of her prison again, but it was immobile as the stone surrounding it, secured with straps of iron and an incomprehensible lock. She could not see the lock, but her hands had found it quick enough. *At least I think it's a lock. It's in the right place for a lock, and it has a handle*, she reasoned. But it had no keyhole, just rows of little boxes that moved when she pressed them.

She knew something was wrong when that old mother came to her papa's holding with all those soldiers. She had always thought no one paid her any attention, too small to be noticed. But someone had seen her, and they had come and taken her. *Papa treasured me. He paid attention to me and kept me safe. But Papa won't help me now. Can't help me. He couldn't stop them taking me and putting me in this dank hole.* The stench of rot pervaded the room, and Bright Hope stayed huddled against the door until her eyes adjusted to the dark. Curiosity drew her towards the clutter. Shelves were laden with strange objects coated in thick dust, glass-fronted cabinets were filled with jars filled with liquids and powders and small preserved animals, a long table with what looked to Bright Hope, like cooking equipment, stands, and racks, but there was no fireplace and no chimney. The walls were lined with books. Bright Hope had never seen so many.

Chinks of light filtered through a shuttered vent and Bright Hope edged towards it, past a large chair stacked with books and papers. The extra light would be welcome, but Bright Hope wished more air would circulate through the place. It was impossible to move without raising clouds of dust. She covered her face with her smock as the dust billowed about her. *It's difficult enough to breathe as it is. I don't want to suffocate in here.*

The shutters protested and groaned as she levered them from their resting place. The dim light from the Great Hall and fresh air from high above were a welcome relief. Bars behind the shutters were deeply embedded in the smooth stone and were as immovable as the door. She was small enough to wriggle through the duct if not for the bars. *I gotta get out, or I'll never see Papa again. That old mother said I would find a way out or die.* Bright Hope shuddered.

The increased light showed Bright Hope an arched doorway on the far side of the room, but it was the sound of dripping that drew her away from the fresh air. *Water.* Her mouth felt dust coated. Slipping past the table laden with strange equipment, Bright Hope paused at the doorway until her eyes adapted to the dark.

The corridor was short, splitting in two directions. The sound of water came from her left, while the scent of rot to her right was even stronger than in the first room, and yet it held a note that almost drew her in before her thirst overruled her curiosity. *Drink first then explore.*

The water closet held a deep trough for bathing, a waste hole, and a small hand basin. A dark scum grew in the basin fed by the dripping faucet. A bizarre mechanism perched beside the sink with an arm that looked to be able to pivot the end so it would sit beneath the faucet's outflow. Its purpose mystified Bright Hope, but that revelation could wait. She opened the flow, and brown water filled with scummy lumps splattered into the basin. It did not take very long for the water to clear and she took a long drink before splashing its delicious coolness over her face. For the moment it filled the aching emptiness in her belly.

CHAPTER ONE

"Please dear," implored Giuseppe, "have a shower. You're dripping blood on my rug."

Patty looked at the trail of bloody footprints behind her. Two figures in white were on their hands and knees scrubbing the spiral stairs. A bright moon lit up the remote Italian vale, the village's lights twinkling in the distance. The virtual vista from Giuseppe's foyer suddenly made Patty dizzy.

"Please give me that. We will talk when you're clean." Giuseppe reached for Patty's blade. For a second, Patty was tempted to give it to him, point first. *We're running away! Every second we're getting further and further away from Alan.* Killing Giuseppe would not get this facility turned around though. Besides, she liked the fat man. *Killing him won't make you feel any better either. On the other hand, can you feel any worse?*

Patty presented her blade to him, hilt first, and he bowed a little as he took it from her hand. "I'll have it cleaned." She grimaced at the thought of unknown hands touching her rapier. "I'll clean myself, my dear, now please." He gestured to the bathroom. *Yes. A shower would be good. I'll have to wash my hair, again.*

The soap smelled of lemons and basil. Hot water cascaded over her head pushing a wave of scented oils through her hair. It rolled over her forehead, dividing at her small nose, splashing over her cheekbones. Her throat closed, involuntarily. Patty gasped for breath, and a cry broke from her. *I've lost Alan! I've lost my little brother!* Her knees shook, and she sagged to the marble, sobbing. There was plenty of hot water, but she doubted any of it would get her clean.

The pale, segmented fillet was partially covered in a creamy sauce, beautifully presented on a delicate white porcelain plate with gold-embossed edges. White wine filled a fluted glass. Patty was not interested in any of it. The bookish library had been transformed into a patio perched on the hand of Christ the Redeemer, overlooking Rio De Janeiro. A glass-topped wrought-iron table sat on Jesus' palm, under a blue sky dotted with elegant cumulus clouds. It was the best simulation Patty had ever seen; a cool salt-laden breeze came from the ocean, she could feel the sun's warmth on her cheek, but she could also see the corners of the room. They broke the illusion of depth. She felt as flat as the walls; any depth was pure illusion.

"You must understand we had to leave when we could. My heart breaks at your pain, my dear. Please eat. It's fresh. I caught it myself." Giuseppe took a fork full of his food and slowly waved it under his nose, sampling its delicate aroma before slipping it gently into his mouth. He made blissful faces as he chewed and swallowed, then sipped his wine.

"I've had Francesco working on Freya. Trust me; he's a good man," he told her. "The fuel lines are purged, and he's tuning the firing sequences even as we speak. She'll be faster than ever. Eat, my dear. You'll need all your strength."

"You're not going to try and stop me?" Patty asked.

"Little old me?" Giuseppe asked, holding a hand to his chest. "No, no, my dear. I am Italian. I know the demands of blood, of family. Although your father, he would try and stop you if he were here."

"But he is not here," Patty replied, feeling another wave of loss flatten her.

"Just so, just so, but if he were, it would be he who would be planning to beard them in their den, not you, my young dear,"

Giuseppe told her.

"And for all I know, he might not even be alive," Patty murmured.

"This also is true," Giuseppe agreed sadly. "But I will not stop you. I promise. Now, will you eat before the trout gets cold? And the Chablis is very nice. I hate to force alcohol on a minor, but I think you could use a drink."

The fish was pleasant and the vegetables hot and crisp, and they filled an empty place inside her. She did not touch the wine.

"Giuseppe?" Patty asked softly.

"My dear?"

"Why did they let us go?"

"Oh, my dear. You have magical gifts, Patricia," Giuseppe replied with a broad smile. "The heathens bowed down before your majesty. They handed what remained of the observatory staff over to you, and then we left. Simple as that."

"But why?" Patty asked. It didn't make sense.

"Oh queen, this one does not know," Giuseppe answered with a bow. Patty snapped her eyes to Giuseppe. His warm smile eased her embarrassment.

"You heard? I thought the comm links were down." Queen, Patty thought. It must be a mistranslation.

"If there is no one to answer a hail," he shrugged. "We hacked into L2's security feed and watched it all from eight different directions. You look magnificent in all of them! Heroic!" he toasted her with his glass. "Would you like to see it? If we meet your father before you do, I will show it to him. It will make him proud."

"I don't feel heroic," Patty grumbled.

"Ah, but you are truly heroic, not a character strutting about in a fantasy feature, you are real with real pain," Giuseppe consoled her. "Your father was in the war. He will understand."

"You fought with my father?" Patty asked.

Giuseppe laughed. "Fought with Christopher, oh no my dear, I do not like fighting, but I do enjoy watching."

Everything in Giuseppe's workshop leaned. The slightly curved floor worked wonderfully while the laboratories were spinning, but the constant thrust of boosting meant 'down' was at an angle to the deck. Giuseppe had shown her the plans for his remarkable facility. It was an extreme solution for an extravagant man.

"My dear, this is Francesco." A small man in spotless white overalls smiled and nodded. He spoke a few words in Italian to Giuseppe and shrugged. Francesco talked some more and turned back to the small control panel.

"He doesn't speak EngStand, but he says he likes Freya," Giuseppe said.

"Tell him, thank you. What has he got there?" Patty asked as she looked at the small control panel in front of Francesco; a cable snaked away from it and into Freya's cockpit.

"It is a remote control. Francesco can call up all the engine functions remotely. The pit crew used this to set up *Mercurio Cuore*'s engines before the race," Giuseppe told her.

"How is she?" Patty asked.

"Francesco," Giuseppe spoke some Italian. The technician nodded, kissed the end of his fingers, and replied. He laughed, and Giuseppe joined in. "She is ready. Ready to roar like a lion, he says."

"Then I can go?" Patty asked.

"Yes, Freya is ready to fly, but before you roar off into the dark, I wanted to ask you something." Giuseppe chewed on his lower lip.

"What is it?"

"In the past, while your father was fighting honorably, I was doing ... other things, slipping through to needy people and getting them urgent ... supplies. I used a coating on my ship. It absorbs electromagnetic radiation, not just visible light, and converts it into electricity. Of late, I've been working with it as a sensor to extract some magnificent images with the big fifty-meter telescope. I think it would be a good idea to coat Freya in it."

"Why?" Patty asked; she wanted to leave if Freya was ready.

"Sweet lamb, she will absorb over ninety-nine percent of *all* EM radiation that strikes its surface. Shine LADAR on Freya, and I doubt you'd get a return," he informed her.

"Stealthy." Patty tried to picture Freya *jet-black.* Freya *in black. It echoed the darkness in her heart. Giuseppe's right; a frontal assault's suicide. If I have any hope of getting my brother back, I'll have to sneak in.*

"She would be tough to track," he continued. "The military has been after something like this for years, but they never progressed much beyond the laboratory. They could not get the meta-materials to work over a broad enough frequency range. I won't let my work be used for such things, not by them, but for you, I would make an exception. You took those aliens on L2 by surprise, oh my queen; I think it would help your cause if you could surprise them again. Yes?"

"Yes. I'm going to need all the help I can get but what's the catch?" Patty asked. *There's always a trade-off.*

"Ah, my dear, you cut to the heart of it. The coating is layered, and each layer takes time to, to stabilize."

"How long?" A part of her was screaming to put off this flight for as long as possible; it warred with another part that wanted to suit up and leave right now.

"Five, maybe six hours." He shrugged apologetically, "But we could use the time to fit baffles. They would have to be looking right down your exhaust ports to see you boosting." He grinned conspiratorially.

"Six hours?" Six more hours? Could she wait that long? *The aliens have taken Alan away to study. Whatever that means.* Goosebumps ran across her skin, and her stomach churned.

"I know, I know, you want to strike now while the fire inside you is still hot," Giuseppe said. "But you should rest and eat more. You are but a slip of a girl. Recover your strength. It will be a long flight, whether you leave now or in six hours. Do not strike when you are tired. Strike when you are ready, when you are strong. Appear where you are least expected; make them fear you. They will bow down before you, oh queen." His wicked smile was contagious even as her heart quaked with fear. *One girl with a sharp stick against the might of aliens able to cross the vast void between the stars; I'm going to get myself killed, or something worse.*

"Is that offer of alcohol still open?" she asked.

Giuseppe frowned comically and feigned thinking about it. "Well, my dear, that's cutting it a bit fine." His eyes sparkled. "It'll have to be a small one." He laughed and spoke to Francesco once more before turning back to Patty.

"Come with me, young lady. I've been saving a bottle for a special occasion. It's made from pears," he whispered conspiratorially.

"A fruit wine?"

Giuseppe smiled, "Not quite, but I'm sure you'll just love it."

A deep and mighty yawn combined with a luxurious stretch convinced Patty that she was indeed awake. Multicolored butterflies had filled her dreams, swirling and flocking in random directions. None of them turned the slightest bit red. Patty yawned again and rolled over.

"Excuse me, Patricia." The small comm panel beside her bed chirped. "I notice you're awake."

"Yes, I think so. Should I be?" she asked. Last night's farewell bash was still mixed in with the butterflies.

"Indeed, you should, young miss. You have a big day ahead of you. Hungry?" Giuseppe asked.

Patty did not have to think about it. Her stomach was already rumbling. "Yes."

"Good. Breakfast in five minutes."

"Can I shower?" Patty asked.

"Of course, my dear, breakfast in ten."

Patty looked down at her plate. To call it just eggs and bacon was to do her meal a disservice. The beautiful crockery, the sparkling cutlery, it was almost too lovely to disturb. Despite the fact her insides were alternately wobbling Jello and twisted spring steel, Patty set to with gusto. She was hungry.

"What was that stuff last night?" Patty asked between mouthfuls.

"My dear?" Giuseppe leaned on the breakfast bar, wiping his hands on the blue and white checkered apron that barely covered his girth. The room had been altered to present a functional kitchen nook with a gas range; copper pots and pans hung on a rack on one wall. A window opened onto a kitchen garden to Patty's right. It reminded her of her mother's kitchen; the layout was different, but the feeling was the same, warmth and generosity.

"What were we drinking?" Patty asked. "It wasn't fruit-wine."

"No, it wasn't," Giuseppe chuckled. "A family, friends of my grandmother, they make it. It's a brandy, of sorts." He poured dark aromatic coffee into a small thick-walled cup and set it beside her plate.

"Did I really challenge you to a duel?" she asked between bites. That was probably the least embarrassing thing she vaguely remembered doing last night.

"Indeed, you did. You said I put a nick in your rapier's debole.

You were wrong of course, but I couldn't convince you otherwise, not in your condition." Giuseppe chuckled as he sipped his coffee.

"I got pretty drunk, I guess," Patty mumbled.

"By the stars! My dear, you were smashed! Totally out of your tree. And when we stopped boosting, we couldn't get you down from the ceiling. Darling, you were so funny. It's a memory I'll treasure forever. I will watch it often."

"Sorry?" Patty asked with a fork-full paused before her lips.

"I record all my social interactions, my dear," Giuseppe told her. "And last night, well, I wouldn't want anyone to accuse me of taking advantage of you, now, would I?" His eyes sparkled with feigned innocence.

"You show it to anyone, and I will ... I will..." *What would I do?* "I'll come back and gut you." That sounded full of bravado, something Alan might have said. Her heart sagged again, but she did not want to show that to Giuseppe... and the cameras.

"My darling Patricia, you were, at all times, a complete lady. A lady under stress, for sure, but a lady none the less." Giuseppe sighed and leaned closer. "You needed to let a little piece of your anger go. Not all of it, for you, will need it all too soon. You had to let go of that anger, that frustration, the fear of not being in control. Self-hate is pure poison to your soul. Have no fear that anyone would think less of you if they saw it." Giuseppe's smile cut off when he saw the look on Patty's face. "Not that anyone will," he added quickly. "On my honor."

Patty looked down for another bite, but her plate was clean. The last of her coffee went down in one gulp. *Time to go.*

Freya was not much more than a silhouette, a black hole, a cutout suspended in front of the gray workshop wall. The baffles gave her an unfamiliar outline and Patty had to blink to make sure she was looking at her CRV.

"... and we've had the chance to upgrade some things I didn't talk to you about," Giuseppe remarked casually.

"Upgrade? What things?" Patty stretched out her hand as she crossed the workshop, not exactly sure where the silhouette ended, and her ship began. The black, black coating was smooth under her fingers, but that was just about all she could sense of her little CRV.

"For a start, we removed your transponder," he said, counting on his fingers.

"I should have thought of that one," Patty remarked as she carefully inspected the canopy seals.

"Your stellar tracking camera," Giuseppe said with a grimace as he raised another finger. "My dear, I would have had it replaced when I first found her, but alas, I had no time. Fermi-Cingolani makes some of the finest optical equipment in the solar system. I could not let you leave with that piece of ... of plastic."

"Thank you. What else have you done to her?" Patty asked as she walked around Freya, inspecting every surface, touching every line.

"Passive radar." Giuseppe was positively beaming. "It's my coating, you see. Freya can see in the dark. When electrons are liberated by the electromagnetic radiation the coating absorbs, their vector, energy, and frequency are recorded. Without a lens to focus the energy, it is a slow process, but over time, it should map your environment in magnificent detail. Of course, we had to upgrade your flight computer to handle the data."

Patty nodded, listening but not concentrating on what he was saying as she examined the baffle that surrounded her engine's exhaust port. It was solidly mounted with cross bracing keeping the black cylinder stiff.

"It won't survive re-entry." She shook them. They were solid, immovable.

"Naturally. See, in here. Explosive bolts." Giuseppe rubbed his hand over Freya's sleek tail fin. "And my wonderful coating will not survive re-entry either. "That's life!" he chuckled.

The forward hold opened smoothly, and the seals looked clean. Someone else's luggage was packed into the compartment; two Coté-Rousseau embossed overnight bags were secured beside a matching kitbag.

"What's this?" Patty asked.

"Ah, a little surprise. I could not send you out there with rags on your back. Relax, your things are all there. I've just added a few items that were ... lying around. You never know what you'll need." Matching luggage was not very high on Patty's list of necessities; she carefully closed the hatch.

"Come, I think you are ready. It is time to say our farewells." Giuseppe swept her up in a hug. "My dear, it breaks my heart to see you go, but it is for a family that you do this thing, for the honor." He put her down. Tears were running down his face. "I salute you! My queen." He bowed low and kissed her hand before helping her aboard.

Silly man. Patty could not stop the smile that pulled at the corners of her mouth. He stopped and solemnly held her hand. Something must have occurred to him that made his eyes widen and brought a smile to his lips.

"Momento, please wait. I have something else for you." He plucked a black gem from his dinner jacket and raced over to the workbench. He hovered over a panel for a moment or two and then dashed back to Patty waving the little gem between two fingers.

"Here. You must take this," Giuseppe insisted.

"Ah, thank you, but you've been generous enough," Patty replied.

"No, no you don't understand," Giuseppe said, waving away her objection. "It's pretty, yes but it is more, a sensor, recording pictures and sound, among many other things. It uses a sensor made from the same coating on Freya. I've just downloaded and wiped its memory so it will record up to forty-eight hours before the buffer is full. It has a standard interface, password, peek-a-boo." He grinned, leaned in, and pinned it on the flap covering her p-suit's front seal. "Magnifico!" he stood back, admiring her, "It is invisible." Giuseppe leaned on the canopy's sill and whispered conspiratorially, "I would deem it a great honor if you would let me have access to the recording when you have returned."

"There's confidence for you, I haven't left yet, and you've already laid plans for my return." Patty tried to be more jovial than she felt.

"I have every confidence in you. You made the aliens bow to you when everyone else was trussed up like chickens!" Giuseppe laughed and patted her arm. "You will do well, I know it."

SWEET DISCOVERIES

Usually, Bright Hope would have kept well away from anything that smelled as bad as the dim, dank room, but there was something else in the wafting scents, something that was not rotten, something that made her spine tingle. *If there's any logic to this suite of rooms, there should be another shutter on the far side,* although she could not see any light leaking through it. The room was pitch black, and she advanced cautiously, one hand out in front.

Surprisingly, Bright Hope made it across the dark room without colliding with anything except spinner webs, and her small fingers found the shutter exactly where she thought it would be. It resisted her efforts to move, groaning as she prized it open. Less light made its way through this duct than the first, but it was more than sufficient for Bright Hope to see that this was a bedroom. The spacious bed was a ruin of rotting covers over the padded base. A closet filled with the collapsed remains of decaying garments stood on the far side of the bed, and a soot-choked fireplace dominated the wall to her left.

Air moved quickly through the suite now, dragging the surfeit of dust Bright Hope had stirred up with it. It also brought that tantalizing hint of something ... something amazing. Though her belly was full of water, it still gurgled, and her mouth filled with saliva. *When did you eat last?* Papa was always concerned she had enough to eat. The OldMother and her men had been days traveling, and she had only been given a wet rag to suck on to subdue her thirst and nothing for the crippling pangs in her belly.

Again, the subtle hint of goodness wafted past Bright Hope's nose. *How can something so wonderful be buried in all this rot? Papa has shown you how careful you must be.* There were lots of things in this world that hurt you if you weren't careful. *Learned that the hard way when I gobbled down all those Thang berries, didn't I.* They were so, so sweet but had given her an upset stomach. Even so, she could not stop herself from following her nose.

Attracted by the clean aroma but repelled by the rancid decay Bright Hope edged closer to the bed. *It's coming from the far side.* She hoped she would not have to delve into the rot in that closet. It was too poisonous for the small animals that had taken up residence in the early years of the room's abandonment. *Probably Ninkers.* The little rodents were a pest, but if they could not live here, then it was too dangerous for her, too. Papa always made sure to treat any mildew and mold as soon as he spotted it. He had told her on many occasions how perilous rot could be, how she had nearly died from a bout of Black Lung Fever when she was a pouchling.

The bed, at least, shows signs of recent Ninker infestation. Bright Hope would rather brave the scary but relatively harmless spinners and their sticky webs than the dripping spore heads in the closet. *The good smell is stronger here.* Her nimble fingers traced a safe path in the dark.

The bed base was clean stone as smooth as the floor. How the makers of this holding had been able to fashion such a place out of the mountain's hard granite was beyond Bright Hope's understanding. Papa had toiled for season-after-season to carve a holding from the basalt caves they called home. The land was good and unaffected by taint. *Papa.* She could not remember a time when she had been away from him, not further than earshot.

The short wooden table at the bedside crumbled when she tried to push it to one side. The tantalizing scent was more powerful. Her eyes could not penetrate the gloom, but her fingers traced over the bed head and found something. The seam was not very large, tracing out a rectangle only a finger's width and a half in height; and Bright Hope's fingers were tiny. Flush with the surface of the bed head, she pushed at the mattress to make some room but only succeeded in tearing a hole in the fabric.

Leaning as close as she could to the engraving her fingers could feel, she still could not see the details, but the scent was stronger. Overbalancing, Bright Hope's fingers could feel grinding as the insignificant seam moved a hair's breadth into the bed head. The little rectangle slid out a finger's width. The accompanying wave of the incredible scent made Bright Hope more than a bit giddy. *What is it?* Her fingers pulled open the hidden drawer and reached inside. She discovered a warm wooden box unaffected by rot, carrying a scent that overwhelmed the decay around her and gave Bright Hope a sense that everything was all right. The smells were so akin to her feelings of home; she sat for a moment with the little box clutched to her chest.

Bright Hope could feel the lip's seam and what she guessed was the latch but could not figure out how to open it. *Maybe if I could see it.* She usually was good at solving puzzles. *Better than papa, anyway.* Ignoring the cloud of dust she produced, Bright Hope surged through the suite back to the first room where there was more light.

The box was both smooth by design and by constant handling. Chestnut wood with an even darker grain, the box had a weight that belied its small size, and it only took moments for Bright Hope to discover the secret of the clever latch. *Push it in, slide to the side, then down.* The lid popped open, and that amazing, overwhelming aroma engulfed her again.

Three golden spheres rolled about in the smooth interior of the box, throwing back the light so brightly she had to squint to see them. *Mel'andrin, gift-memories. Papa's mel'andrin is not like this. They gave me headaches and made me feel ill.* But these were different. She brought the box closer to examine the golden balls but pressed the box to her nostrils instead and breathed in something she had no words for; happiness and wonderment were poor substitutes for what engulfed her.

The urge to put one in her mouth caught Bright Hope by surprise with one of those golden orbs already on her lips before a cautious thought arose. *Well, they are tiny, and surely one can't hurt. It won't be much of a meal anyway.*

Expecting a sudden, painful rush, Bright Hope braced herself, but the tiny sphere refused to dissolve. It tasted as marvelous as it smelled, sweet one moment and then a savory base note. The feeling grew, building, slowly increasing. Bright Hope became overwhelmed by the wonder coursing through her, and she sagged back against the wall, sliding to the floor. *Remember to breathe!*

CHAPTER TWO

Freya performed beautifully. Her maneuvering thrusters had been quick before, but they were silky smooth now. Patty rolled her over and watched Daedalus, the far side's most prominent crater, slide over the lunar horizon. It had taken Alan and Patty over eighteen hours to get from the ruins of L1 station to the speck that was L2, but at her current speed, she would be in Low Earth Orbit in less than half that time. Patty missed her brother's presence. She would have given almost anything to hear one of his snipes or one of his complaints of boredom.

Giuseppe was right, the passive radar was slow in displaying returns, but over the last half hour, her flight computer had begun to build up a considerable amount of data. Freya could see in the dark. The sun and the brightest stars were already visible in the simulation on her new displays. *I won't need that beautiful new sighting camera.* Patty tracked and logged the identifiable stars into the flight computer then it began cross-referencing her input with data from her flight almanac. She was even getting the sun's light as reflected returns from the moon's surface, and there were smudges of radio transmissions from what Patty suspected to be the stations at L4 and L5. There was nothing from L3; both the Moon and Earth eclipsed that space station.

In moments, she would be over the Moon's north pole and would have a direct sight of Earth. Already the alien's radio interference was drowning out communications, but the intelligent software that Giuseppe's people installed was rapidly identifying and subtracting its noise from her display.

Earthrise brought a lump to her throat; so beautiful, so delicate, a blue and white pearl hung in the darkness.

Her display pinpointed the alien craft immediately, a speck against Earth's broad face. It was broadcasting radio noise on a full array of frequencies. Two other sources of the alien's interference appeared as bright dots. From their positions, Patty calculated that there would be another satellite on Earth's far side, in geosynchronous orbit completing the coverage.

The alien ship stood out on her display as a blazing red dot. Patty labeled it and took a sighting with her new camera. The image was rock solid, but even at maximum zoom, she could not see the invaders' ship. She locked the sighting coordinates to the radio signal location and then she saw it, a tiny dot flying high over India's brown plains. *A tiny pinpoint filled with hundreds maybe thousands of misshapen aliens.* Patty swallowed the sour taste spreading into the back of her mouth.

Is this what being brave feels like? Patty prepared for Freya's next burn. *If it is, then it feels pretty lousy.* Rescuing Cian had not been an act of bravery. She had not thought about it at all; she had done it without thinking it through. It was gallant but foolish. Now she was doing something that made saving Cian seem like a well thought out plan. There appeared to be no hope, but there was no other path before her, none that left her with any self-respect.

The first pass over the alien ship was at a relatively safe distance. Her heartbeat racing, Patty guided Freya ten kilometers above the great spacecraft. At any moment, she expected an energy beam to skewer her or to be blown into tiny pieces by an accelerating missile. However, nothing happened; it was as if she was not there at all. Giuseppe's new camera gave her unprecedented detail of the boxy alien craft. The top of the ship was divided into three rectangular regions, the center section that held a collection of radio dishes was higher by three of four meters. The surface was comprised of irregularly shaped metallic plates, possibly indicating something of the internal structures. Patty logged the shots for later retrieval. There were four docks, one in the center of each of the huge ship's four vertical sides. There was not a great deal of traffic, but patrolling ships entered and left the docks regularly.

As Freya's orbit took Patty further away from the enormous gray spacecraft, she took what felt to be her only breath in the last hour. *Thank you, Giuseppe. There is hope.* Once she was over the horizon, Patty fired up her engines to take her much closer on her next pass.

Earth's northern hemisphere's atmosphere was dark, filled with smoke and dust. It was challenging to get a clear view of the ground. Patty found that that was a relief; she did not want to be confronted with the pain and suffering of millions, billions. It would be as cold as winter down there. Although Patty scanned the comm channels, she did not find any chatter. The reason why Earth was so silent became apparent when a ham radio operator began transmitting from somewhere near Manchester. Within a minute, a patrolling spacecraft was over the British Isles. It released a single missile that speared down to the surface. The detonation's flash lit up those dark clouds for hundreds of kilometers around. The poor ham barely had a chance to utter a few CQs before his entire neighborhood was obliterated.

The Southern Hemisphere had fared much better from Tempelman-Frobisher's strike although they had suffered more visibly from the aliens' attention. There were columns of smoke rising from Jakarta, Sydney, and Melbourne. Wellington and Auckland burned, as well as Bogotá, Buenos Aires, Brasilia, Cape Town, Johannesburg and a dozen other major centers. Humanity was being bombed back to the Stone Age. Auckland was burning. *Hine lives there!* Patty's heart ached. *Are you still down there, Hine? Are you alive, did you escape your city's destruction?* Patty was tempted to use the camera to get a closer look, but there was no point. There was nothing she could do, and she was too far away to see what had happened. Patty choked back her rising bile. Her hands shook. *This rescue is a misguided, foolish irrelevancy.* Compared to the suffering down on the surface her problems were as nothing. *I shouldn't be attempting to sneak aboard to rescue my brother; I should be trying to blow the offensive thing to kingdom come!*

Freya's scans of the mothership had excellent resolution on most of the EM bands, and although Patty naturally gravitated to the visual frequencies at first, her examinations quickly moved to the other bands of radiation. The arrays of radio antenna were evident even in visible light, and Patty searched the infrared for any sign of exhaust ports or any sign of a drive. Her little CRV and the alien's patrolling ships used fusion engines, but nowhere on the mothership could she see anything that indicated a drive exhaust. They could be on the underside, but Patty doubted this. She was tempted to tighten Freya's orbit to pass beneath the alien ship, but that would mean getting too close to the Tempelman-Frobisher's remains still in orbit. *Stick with the plan girl; stick with the plan.*

The hot and somewhat inefficient flare of an alien's engines caught Patty's eye. It was flying in a higher orbit than she was, higher than its mothership. Patty locked her camera on its flare. *Most unusual? Where was it going?* The flight computer calculated its path very quickly. She panned the camera along the projected flight path, and the ship's destination became apparent, it was heading for OASIS. The space station was in a high eccentric orbit. The old girl would not be getting to L1 anytime soon, but she was safely above the debris in LEO. She would have loved to squirt a call to the station, but she knew that would only draw attention to her. *Jake, are you alright?* In other, saner, circumstances Patty would have thought Jake would not hurt a fly, but now? *He's been in the military; he'd fight if he had to. But could he? Oh Jake, stay safe.*

Safe. How can I keep safe while there's so much devastation all around me? Not that I'm helping; I just want to get Alan back. But then again, maybe I can do something. She had collected a lot of data. *Someone should be able to do something with it.* Patty did not hold out much hope that there would be anyone down under the smoke and haze that could do anything. The Moon seemed locked down and quiet. *Mars?* There was a fiercely independent colony on Mars. It was not large, but it was booming. They were far enough away not to be an immediate threat, but they would put up a fight if anyone could. And the Belters. *They'll help, won't they? The Belter War's been over for such a long time.*

It did not take too long to set up an automated routine that would send a tight-beam transmission to Mars if anything untoward happened to her. It would probably burn out her transmitter, but she was sure the signal would get through. The program was not precisely a dead man's switch, but it would do.

Her second fly-by was much closer. It would not have taken much to boost across the five-hundred-meter gap and land Freya on the massive ship. However, this was still, for the moment, a reconnaissance mission. Patty's hands sweated. *We're so close!* She was sure someone, or something, was watching her. She worked hard capturing scans of everything; she even had a quick look into the starboard docking-bay.

When the alien behemoth arced over the horizon, Patty started laughing. It began with a sigh, followed by a chuckle. *I did it!* She had waltzed right past their front door, and they had not noticed her. The chuckle became a full-throated laugh, and tears began to trickle down her cheeks. It was not the happiest laugh she had ever had, there was too much fear underlying it, but the relief she felt was palpable. *They didn't see us!*

There did not seem to be a way to enter the alien ship along the side she had scanned most closely unless you counted the main dock, and Patty didn't like the idea of just flying into that brightly lit maw. She could not make much sense of the three pictures she had managed to snap of the interior, except that it was well illuminated and crawling with activity.

The topside had a couple of candidates, and the best of them was close to the radio array; there were signs of an access port, hopefully, an airlock. If she could keep Freya out of the direct, line-of-sight of those big dishes she should be able to fly her right up to the recessed entrance.

CHAPTER THREE

With her heart in her mouth, Patty flew over the stern of the huge ship. She was instantly aware that something unexpected was altering her trajectory, drawing Freya down towards the gray surface. It was too powerful to counteract with just her thrusters: she was going to have to land much sooner than she expected.

Slewing Freya one hundred and eighty degrees, Patty fired the main engine, slowing them, then spun quickly back. There was no way she was going to try to land while flying backward! The undercarriage unfolded, and Patty fired her thrusters. Even so, Freya touched down heavily, bottoming out the shock absorbers. *Hope nothing's too bent out of shape.* She turned Freya before they arrived at a wall, over which she had planned to fly. If she was going to have to take off in a gravity field, she wanted to have as long a runway as possible. Freya rolled to a stop beside what looked to be the vanes of a massive heat-exchange unit.

This is weird. I'm experiencing gravity! She checked her flight computer and all her tracking data. No, the alien craft was not boosting into a higher orbit; it was continuing its projected path. *Then how is this gravity being generated?* She certainly was not being spun, so centripetal forces were out. There was only one conclusion. *The aliens have artificial gravity!* It was another science fiction tale made real before her eyes. *Amazing.* The gravity felt a little heavier than Earth standard. Patty checked her G-meter, 1.12503. *It is a bit heavier than home but not too bad.*

The flight computer showed that she had landed nearly two

hundred meters from where she had hoped to rendezvous. She would have to cross it on foot. Patty stretched. *A nice walk under the stars is just what I need. It'll be a good warm up.* She put Freya into standby mode, closed her visor, and double-checked her seals before cycling the atmosphere out of the cockpit. Her legs shook as her boots contacted the gray metal, and she took a couple of slow deep breaths to steady herself before reaching back inside for her rapier.

It had taken Giuseppe only minutes to devise a way to hang the scabbard from Patty's p-suit, but it was time well spent. Her rapier was an incongruous addition to her p-suit's accouterments, but it hung at the perfect height for a quick draw. Fighting in her suit's thick gloves would be awkward, but Patty hoped she would have a chance to take them off before things got that bad. The last thing she wanted was to fight in a vacuum. She checked the list of extras one more time: extra oxygen, trail mix and chocolate, water, torch, a sharp knife, her small tool kit, and a spool of microfilament. Patty did not know whether she would need half this stuff, but if she did not take it, she knew she was bound to need it.

One more slow deep breath and Patty checked her wrist comm. A little red dot flashed in the top right corner of her display; *this way*, it indicated. The gray metal sheets were uniformly flat for another ten meters then they stopped at the wall that separated the area surrounding the radar array. She had aimed to land on this upper section; her reconnaissance showed breaks in the wall; Patty hoped they were stairs.

The mothership orbited in darkness, but that would only last another twenty minutes. The Milky Way gave enough light for Patty to see her way to the sheer wall, over three meters in height. There was no way to climb it, and the smooth gray metal continued out of sight to the right. To the left, a dark shape cut across the gray uniformity and Patty headed in that direction. She found shallow steps that climbed to the next section of the alien ship's hull, shallow, but very deep, nearly a meter from step to step. *That makes sense.* From what she had seen of the aliens, their legs would not cross over the way human legs stepped; they walked, front foot, back foot, front foot, back foot, like one side of a four-legged animal.

The stairs opened onto the upper plane of flat gray metal sheets. The array of radio antennas stood directly in front of her, the hoped-for airlock somewhere further on. She felt very exposed walking across the plane of gray plates and almost drew her blade. The access port was easy to find; small yellow lights traced a path from the array straight to it. The circular door was unusual but was not unrecognizable. It was an airlock. The glyphs surrounding the controls were indecipherable, but the device seemed simple enough. Patty knelt and turned a blue handle. A small blue light flashed above it, and she felt machinery moving beneath her. The circular doorway dropped a centimeter or two and rolled open, a fine spray of white gases, back-lit by a warm golden light, jetted into space. Patty leaned over and looked in. A set of widely spaced rungs led down about three meters into a circular chamber large enough for half a dozen of those big, twisted aliens.

This is it. Patty took some slow breaths before she felt steady enough to climb into the airlock. Once she closed the hatch behind her, she trembled all the way down to the scuffed cream floor while, hopefully, warm, breathable air hissed in. The inner door had the same kind of blue handle, so Patty gave it a turn. She loosened Lady Estelle in her scabbard and continued her slow deep breaths. It was the way coach Daichi had her prepare before a fencing bout. Unruly thoughts were slowly quietened.

The inner door slid open, revealing another room. Patty cracked the seal on her visor and took a sniff. The air smelt *freshish* but was filled with strange scents. That was unsurprising; every station Patty visited smelled different. OASIS smelled of busy people, sealant and had a faint ozone tang; L2 had a taste of plastic while Giuseppe's quarters had a delicate undertone of gardenia. The air did not smell bad, just different, warm and a little humid. She took off her helmet and hooked it on her hip. Her gloves came off next, and she stowed them in a thigh pocket. Patty checked Lady Estelle once more and walked calmly out of the airlock.

HER TRUE HERITAGE

Seasons! Longer than that. Seasons of seasons if the memories in the mel'andrin were any indication. Bright Hope breathed through the waves of information that poured through her; lives in vivid overwhelming detail overrode her every thought. She had never concerned herself with the future, not further than the next season, usually no further than her next meal. Now, centuries upon centuries of broken history unfolded in her mind. Resisting the urge to swallow, Bright Hope returned the mel'andrin to its two companions in the box and closed the lid. *Maybe some of those awful gaps, chasms in the continuity, will be filled in if I sample the other mel'andrin.* But now was not the time to indulge her curiosity. She had more than enough information to proceed. Getting out of this suite and being fed was on the top of her list.

Bright Hope rose to her knees. She steadied herself against the wall as she struggled to her feet. Every movement felt foreign, especially the constriction her twisted torso imposed upon her breathing. *That had happened since the last Fall.* None of her gift-memories included living in a body like hers. *Disease.* Whatever it was. It had spread. Papa and all in his holdings had the same twisted deformity as she did, although her body mirrored their condition. Everyone that Bright Hope had ever met was the same. She fought off rising panic as she re-entered the water closet and tried to relax her breathing the way Papa had shown her.

The swinging arm refused, at first, to swing. *How long has it been since an Arumpo'or has been here? Can we even be called that anymore?* With a shudder, the arm rotated into position, and Bright Hope opened the faucet. The water cascaded around the beautifully machined vanes and sent the little turbine spinning. It would not provide much current, but it would be enough for what she needed. There would be time enough to check the circuits to the solar collectors later.

At the door, a bright blue light glowed above the keypad. *Well, that's working. I wonder what else is still running?* She tapped the code that presented itself to her from out of the cascade of memories inside her, and she was pleased when a satisfying clunk announced that the solenoid functioned as well. *They built it to last when they knew it had to survive not just years but centuries. Possibly centuries of neglect.*

As she expected, OldMother Hea'rat and her entourage filled the corridor. *Did the old witch really know what she's unleashed upon her clan? How long has it been since an Arumpo'or has been awakened?* The OldMother's motivations were now as apparent as her every breath, self-aggrandizement. She expects the GreatMother to be as easy to manipulate as an ignorant girl-child, alone and afraid. It would not do to let Hea'rat get a word in first.

"That was cruel and unnecessary. Take us to temporary accommodations while someone disinfects that suite. We need everything preserved in there if possible. Do not throw anything away without consulting us first. Is that clear?"

The entourage was either on their knees or halfway there before the OldMother knew what had happened.

"GreatMother's will." Her stiff neck bowed.

"Now!" Bright Hope felt a warm glow at the reactions her command produced. Even the OldMother scurried to escort her down the corridor. *Maybe Papa can come and live with me?* She knew that would never happen. He had too much to do keeping his holding together. *Well, he'll have to come for a visit.*

CHAPTER FOUR

Half a dozen misshapen white pressure suits hung below broad helmets on either side of the airlock door. They looked well used. The EV prep room had a chest-high control panel that sloped out from the cream-colored wall on the right. The monitor above the board had an insistently blinking icon, and a yellow button on the panel flashed in sync. Patty could not read the script, but the flashing button shouted *touch me,* and she quickly decided she was going to do no such thing. Above the monitor was a twelve-sided grille that had to be an air duct.

Perfect. Patty scrambled onto the control panel, carefully avoiding the flashing button. Her fingers slipped into the mesh, and she gave it a heave. The top left edge shifted a little. Patty pulled again. The grille popped out, and she nearly toppled to the floor. With a pounding heart, she scrambled into the duct and re-seated the grille behind her. The pipe was twelve-sided too and broader than the grill but not by much. There was room to move.

I'm in! Patty sagged to the conduit's floor and lay for a while, breathing slowly, waiting for her racing heart to resume its natural rhythm. She could hardly believe she had made it this far. The alien's airlock security was loose. *Perhaps they didn't expect anyone to be able to get close to their enormous ship without detection, let alone board them.* The task in front of her felt overwhelming, but she had already done the impossible. It was time to move on.

The door to the EV prep room opened, and an alien sidled in. Patty froze. It was not wearing a pressure suit; in fact, it was not wearing much at all, just a blue open-sided cloak. The tabard was decorated with orange embroidered stripes and draped from its shoulders to its knees. It wore brown, open-weave sandals on its broad feet. She held her breath as it moved closer, but the alien did not look up at the duct; the blinking display attracted all its attention.

The flashing stopped, and Patty heard the alien rumble something. *Is that alien speech?* She leaned a fraction closer to the grille as a rumbled reply came from the panel. The alien gave a stiff nod, counted all the p-suits, reported, and received another set of rumbled instructions. The alien cycled the airlock, checked that everything was in order, and made another report. It then turned and left the room. Patty took a deep breath as she collected her thoughts. *So far, the aliens were not that alien. They used breathable air, had pressure suits, pressure suits with Gecko-Grip soles for goodness' sake. They were not that different. Sure, they were big and funny looking, but they were not implacable monsters. I can do this.* Patty began to crawl down the narrow shaft.

With the help of the inertial tracker in her wrist comm, Patty began to methodically map the air ducts. At every grille, she took a quick look and added her discoveries to a fledgling database. There were aliens in almost every room doing not so alien things. In this quadrant, most places had sleeping accommodation for three, but every sixth room was a small recreation/physical training area with strangely configured weights and spring balanced resistance devices. Patty observed them eating, sleeping and watching what might have been entertainment on a large flat screen - the content was incomprehensible to Patty. They wore tabards of every hue with many different patterns embroidered upon them. Patty quickly gave up trying to make a note of the multiplicity of designs.

There were many opportunities to move down to the next level, but Patty ignored them for nearly an hour as she clambered through the ducts. Having found no trace of Alan or any other human for that matter, she decided it was time to delve deeper into the ship. There were no climbing rungs, but the vertical ducts had strong, machined joins approximately two meters apart that gave reasonable purchase. The shaft was a little more than a meter in diameter so Patty could wedge herself against the opposite wall if necessary. Apart from catching her utility belt on the edge when she first climbed over, the descent into the gloom was uneventful and gave her more confidence.

Aliens were just as numerous on the next level, but Patty saw a different kind of alien, smaller than the ones on the upper deck. They had a darker brown tone to their skin with mauve striations, but the same, twisted, sideways-walking body as the larger lighter colored ones. They seemed calmer, quieter and did not bluster and stomp around like the many larger ones. *Males and females?* she wondered.

Patty discovered it was more likely to find a group of the smaller, darker aliens quietly working on a project regardless of their different colored tabards, whereas the large ones rarely mixed with others not wearing their colors. She witnessed more than one fight between aliens wearing different colored tabards, and there was always blood. On the occasion of a death, a group of the smaller ones arrived and quietly removed the corpse. *Respectfully?* Patty wondered. She did not want to attribute human motivations or reactions to their behaviors. A group of aliens, with the same design tabard as the winner, congratulated it with a round of hoom-hoom-rumbling and vigorous backslapping. Patty felt chilled despite the heat.

On the next level down, Patty saw her first captive human and her heart gave a start. He was naked, wearing only a gray tabard with a simple blue circle in the center, but he seemed to be in good health. He carried a large brown box, following yet another type of alien. *Three genders?* This ET was smaller again and pale, almost gray, and it wore a red tabard more ornately patterned than anything she had previously seen. There was another difference between the light-colored alien and the larger ones. It was left-handed. Its smaller body mirrored that of the larger aliens, but it moved with a smoother gait.

Patty crawled after the pale alien and its human companion as they moved down a corridor, but she lost them when her duct came to a more substantial t-intersection. The next grille looked out over a much broader thoroughfare filled with aliens of all three types, moving about their business, and humans, all with pale attendants. Her Patty's stomach gave a rumble. It was reason enough to sit for a moment and eat some rations while she watched the aliens and their captive humans. They were all performing some routine chore, carrying boxes, or hauling trolleys stacked with parcels of different shapes and sizes. It was manual labor, but it was not humiliating or degrading, and the men and women did not seem to be complaining; they were obedient little slaves, and that gave Patty another chill. Humans were many things, but obedient slaves was not an attribute Patty had high on her list. *Where is the rebellion?* she wondered.

Whatever the aliens have done to make them so compliant, so quickly, I won't find out sitting on my butt. Patty stretched and began to move down the larger but still cramped duct, parallel to the broad passageway. At every grille, Patty took a brief survey of the moving aliens but did not see her brother. Seeing humans walking about, gave Patty hope that Alan was all right and she moved on with new vigor. Etchings decorated the wall on the far side of the broad thoroughfare below her. A strange parade of plants, four-winged birds, and animals strode beside the busy aliens. At first, Patty thought their shapes so misshapen that they only represented fanciful caricatures. *Maybe they are accurate.* The aliens were distorted, as if someone had grabbed their hips and twisted, making it impossible to walk forward, condemning them to travel forever sideways.

The duct came to another intersection. This one, thankfully, was large enough to allow Patty to stand upright. The air moving through this large conduit smelled fresher than some of the shafts she had crawled through, although it was warmer and damper than Patty enjoyed. She took the opportunity to stretch her aching body.

"If I have to stay cramped up in there much longer..." stretch,

"I'll end up as bent as them." Patty muffled her groans as she tried to work the kinks out of her back.

To her right, the big duct curved into near darkness. To the left, a grille five meters across, and three meters high looked out across a wide area. Patty hugged the wall and edged closer to the opening. The broad thoroughfare had joined something much more significant. She felt her jaw go slack. A dome shone bright, warm light into an atrium nearly big enough to fit OASIS inside it. From her vantage point, Patty was above the highest of six promenades that swept sinuously around the cavernous interior. Over two hundred meters long and one hundred wide, Patty had shopped in bigger malls, but there was nothing as big as this in human space. The alien ship forced Patty, once again, to redefine what was possible. This place was huge. Sinuous walkways carried aliens hither and yon, spiraling up from lower floors or arching across to a spacious plinth that occupied the very center of the atrium.

Puffs of white gas rose from an unidentifiable contraption mounted on a series of risers in the center of that platform. Something was happening down there; aliens thronged around it. Patty cursed her decision to leave her binoculars behind. *Who needs binoculars inside a spaceship? Murphy's Law strikes again!* She noticed large grilles at regular intervals around the atrium, and one directly opposite the area with the most activity. She knew she would have next to no understanding of what was happening down there, but she had to have a look. Guilt strummed at her heartstrings as Patty strode off into the large air duct. There was little chance that Alan would be the center of all that alien activity. But then again, it would be just like him to cause such a commotion. *You're departing from your mission, girl. I'm not here to study aliens; I'm here to find my brother and get out.*

As Patty moved closer towards the atrium's short axis, the grilles showed her glimpses of the strange, steam-emitting device - Patty decided it was steam, not some noxious gas, because of the *chuff-chuff* sounds that drifted up to her. Why the aliens needed a steam engine, Patty had no idea. On the right side, she was sure she recognized a tokamak fusion reactor, but it looked like something built last century. Two pale aliens in red tabards hovered nervously over an antiquated control panel.

The object beside the reactor could only be a steam engine's boiler. The atmosphere was wet enough without an engine puffing out great white sighs of waste steam. Spread over a large area, a complicated array of gears and drive shafts connected to the large pistons. Two left-handed aliens in yellow directed a team of large right-handed aliens crawling amongst the cogs and shafts. The focus of the bizarre mechanism was a small object mounted to the side of a transparent box.

Patty took extra care to stay out of sight at the next opening, but she made sure Giuseppe's pin got a good view. The large white panel which sent control rods into the tangle of gears had six circular dials with a large lever beside each one. Two large aliens in purple stood at relaxed attention in front of the dials. Three pale aliens, also in purple conferred and made small adjustments to a spherical device with three narrow cylinders projecting through its ornately carved surface. Patty immediately thought of Freya's flight computer; it had a similar display for describing her attitude, three controllers projecting from the center of a sphere. Patty preferred to fly stick-and-rudder, but when programming a burn, the controllers were an interactive method to set Freya's orientation. *Is this the flight control system for the alien ship? If the sphere is attitude control, how did the six circular controls function? Thrust?* The dials connected to the steam-driven gears and the gears terminated at the object beside the transparent box. Patty decided that she had no chance of understanding how the bizarre concatenation of technologies functioned, and she hoped that Giuseppe's little scanner had recorded enough to analyze later.

In front of the transparent box stood a line of six huge aliens much bigger than any she had seen before. They wore multicolored tabards and had their long daggers drawn. *Four genders? Maybe they're not different genders. Who knows how they breed.* Patty shuddered at the thought of these ETs having sex. In front of the guards, a brown alien sat wearing the most ornate red tabard she had seen. The brown one seemed to be the center of attention as a disciplined line of aliens, large and small, passed before her. Patty had the impression whatever it was she held in her arms was the real focus of interest. From this distance, it could be anything wrapped in a multi-colored cloth. And then it moved. Patty jumped.

The brown alien folded the cloth back a little and revealed a tiny golden alien. *Was this an alien child?* It sat up and moved its prominent left arm. It did not seem to be as helpless as a human baby; its head turned smoothly as it watched the procession pass. Patty was sure she was mistaken, but she thought she saw the tiny alien make a nodding acknowledgment to some of those before it.

Whatever was happening down there, it was important; the processional queues stretched over the filigreed arches to either side of the atrium. But there were no humans down there. That fact brought Patty back into focus. It was interesting watching the alien ritual, town meeting, or whatever it was they were doing, it would not help her find Alan.

CHAPTER FIVE

Returning to the cramped ducts where she last saw humans, Patty was rewarded to see more pale aliens and their human workhorses. She lay down and watched as one directed its human, a woman with tangled, dirty blond hair, to unload some boxes from the trolley she pulled. It checked off each parcel against a list as she stacked them against the wall and then followed the woman as she turned and pulled the trolley back in the direction from which they had come. A portly balding man with a pale attendant approached the boxes. Without apparent instruction, the man sorted through the boxes, selected one, and carefully removed it from the stack. He hefted it in his arms and walked off, the note-taking alien sidling along behind him. Patty drank and ate some more rations as she watched a series of drop-offs and pick-ups. The packages were of different shapes and sizes, but none were big enough to trouble any who carried them. The left-handed aliens hovered about the humans, making notes and checking the boxes but they did not interfere.

Two pale aliens, with six attendant humans arrayed in two columns, arrived at the pick-up location. They waited patiently until another two aliens approached with six more humans in tow. The newly arrived humans joined the ranks of the waiting men and women, making three columns of four, as the aliens deliberated. After comparing notes, they headed off down the passageway with the humans following. Patty scrambled to pack her food and water away before chasing after them. When she caught up, they turned left and then right, marching the humans down a set of steps. Patty checked her comm for the closest shaft and set off in pursuit. The duct she chose was close to the stairwell, and even though Patty could not see the men and women, she could hear their marching feet. One level, and then another, down and around they went, and Patty slowed her scramble. One unguarded moment and she could slip from the over-engineered joins in the ducting and fall. It was impossible to tell how far down the shaft went.

While she did lose sight of the aliens with the twelve humans, there were many humans on this level, and Patty settled into an almost comfortable nook to rest her aching limbs and sip some water. The grille, placed at the corner of two wide thoroughfares, gave her a good view of the traffic. *If I'm lucky, I might even catch sight of Alan.* It was a slim hope. The idea of Alan as a domesticated zombie-child made Patty feel ill. She watched at least two hundred men and women pass beneath her observer's perch, but she had yet to see one human child, every human in a tabard was at least in their late teens. *They must be holding the children separately, somewhere else.*

Patty began to search methodically, spiraling out from the shaft, but it was over an hour before she hit pay dirt. A child's cry for reassurance made Patty realize she had not heard any of the people below her speak. It was challenging to triangulate on the child's voice, heartbreaking to listen to it cry out and frustrating when it fell quiet. The child stopped weeping before Patty was close, but she did find a room with two babies in portable cribs. Four left-handers in red hovered over their charges. Patty moved on.

The next two rooms were in darkness, but the third shone light into the confined duct, and hushed chatter filled her ears. By the time Patty reached the vent, the chatter had evaporated, and Patty could see why. A pale alien with two right-handed warriors at its side with their weapons drawn patrolled the aisle between six beds.

"Be quiet." Rumble, Rumble-rum, "Rest," the pale one pronounced the words carefully. It turned and left the room. The two soldiers turned but only went as far as the door. The place went black. A little light leaked in from the junction ahead, so Patty crept forward. She was tired, and the enclosing darkness made sleep a tempting idea. *One more corridor and I'll take a nap. If all the rooms are in darkness, I might pass Alan and not realize it.* She reached the dimly lit intersection. Her comm indicated she had searched the corridors on the right, so she turned left. She crawled past the second grille when a voice echoed from somewhere behind her.

"You pox ridden animal! You're gonna pay! Big time!"

The hairs all over her body stood to attention. *That's Alan!*

"You and your whole species of twisted degenerate bootlickers are gonna regret coming here!" The waves of profanity that washed down the corridor made Patty both blush and feel exalted. *Alan's alive and giving the aliens hell!* She wriggled as fast as she could towards the tumult, chuckling beneath her breath at each outrageous insult. She particularly liked "demented son of a praying mantis and a congenitally deformed baboon." She turned left into a large conduit and heard Alan cry out from just ahead.

"Get your stinking paws off me you damn dirty ape!" A gasp, and then nothing. Patty reached the grille in time to see six beds, the silhouette of two soldiers and their glinting weapons, as the light died and the duct was plunged into darkness. She had found Alan, she was sure, but he still felt so far away. It was only a grille and five or six meters, but with two soldiers in the room, Alan may as well have been miles away. *Just be patient. You've done the impossible and found your brother. Don't blow it.* Patty felt her racing heart slow with every breath. *They won't keep the guards in there all night.*

But it was difficult to stay awake in the cramped, dark space. It made little difference if Patty had her eyes open or not. Darkness on darkness, she blinked her eyes, it didn't have much effect; they still felt full of sand. Swirling, pulsing mandalas overlaid the dark. Her father's voice spilled into her ears about taking care when working with machined parts.

"Don't put too much tension on it or you will strip the nut," he whispered. *Strip the nut?*

"Slow and steady wins the race." Patty could almost feel his warms arms surrounding her. Her heart ached to be in his confident presence.

"Now you listen to your father. He's very good with his hands," her mother said.

"Yes Mom, I know." Cynthia's beaming smile held Patty in its warm light.

"That's good dear, just clear those things off the table, and we can all sit down and have dinner," Cynthia told her.

Patty reached for the nuts and bolts littering the kitchen table, but for some reason, there were always more small parts than she could pick up. Her mother put a steaming plate of rhododendrons and bicycle spokes in the middle of her blueprints.

"Come on Patty. You're gumming up the works. I'm hungry," Alan said with a scowl. "You spend too much time thinking and not enough time doing!" he shouted at her. *Alan!*

Patty sat up with a start, blinking, and her head smacked into the duct.

A DELICATE BALANCE

I fell asleep twice during Del'bidion, Er'men thought as she lay on
her soft bed and shook her head to clear it. *What is it about
Harrum'Bar that makes me feel ill?* That was not quite right, not
ill, dopey. Del'bidion, the Meeting-Of-The-Water, had been
Er'men's first real opportunity to experience for herself the size
of their great ship and those that traveled within her. Moving
from her ornate quarters to the central plinth at the heart of
Tal'anis put the memories of the ship's plans into context;
having all aboard come before her, focused her bright mind on
Tal'anis' precious payload. For the first time, she was able to
sample the mood of those aboard directly and was heartened to
discover not all blindly followed the RegentFirstMother.

Thousands of tiny pearl spheres of mel'andrin gave off a
mixture of scents that overflowed from the blue and silver glass
urn, each one a gift from Del'bidion. Er'men was not sure how
the aromas helped clear her head, but they did. She sat up and
wriggled to the edge of her bed where she could get a more
concentrated dose from the urn on her bedside table. She leaned
over the container and drew in a deep breath. *I think
RegentFirstMother Harrum'Bar achieved more from that procession
than I did. Dozing off like that made me appear immature and weak.*

Still, it was not without some benefits. Er'men sat back and
let her mind engage with the scents, decoding the nuanced and
subtle meanings contained within the aromas. All were happy
to have a GreatMother's guidance - *that's nice* - but there was an
undertone that cast doubt on the RegentFirstMother's status.
That will upset Harrum'Bar. As RegentFirstMother, head of the

Great Council, and Clan Bar'Durrunnan FirstMother, Harrum'Bar was the focus of every slight and annoyance. It was not surprising that there was dissatisfaction with her leadership. But Clan Bar'Durrunnan strutted their purported superiority at every opportunity, causing increasing inter-Clan violence. *If Harrum'Bar doesn't rein in her sons, they could shatter our Clans' fragile alliance.*

CHAPTER SIX

Patty took a deep breath and tried to steady herself. Alan's short-cropped haircut leaped into view as she peered through the grille. Her heart raced, and her fingers gripped the wire mesh. He was one of six children that lay quietly under gray blankets. Monitors stood at the head of each bed, displaying the occupants' physiological details. The smell of urine rose from below, and an insistent bleating came from one of the devices monitoring the bed-ridden girls. Patty withdrew her fingers from the mesh as a pale alien hurried in. It checked the little girl's vital signs while rum-rumbling to itself, turned off the monitoring equipment, and left the room.

Before the doors had a chance to close correctly, a group of Browns entered and clustered around the girl. They rumbled a low and mournful tune. The hair on the back of Patty's neck rose. *Was the girl dead?* Before the Browns finished disconnecting the medical sensors from the girl, another monitor began an urgent bleeping, and then another. The pale alien returned on the run. It inspected the two failing boys, turned off their monitors and left as quickly as it had arrived. The Browns took their time, singing to the dead girl, then carefully wrapping the limp body in the blanket. They gently lifted her and carried her slowly from the room. Unchecked tears flowed from Patty's eyes; a painful breath racked her body. *Alan, oh Alan, hang on. Patty's here to take you home.* Two groups of Browns entered and repeated the ritual with the two boys, their low harmonies blending. Patty's heart raced. *Alan, oh, be strong. Whatever they've done to you, fight it. Live!*

When the doors hissed shut behind the Browns, Patty counted to five and started working the grille free. She tossed it onto the vacant bench below her, where it struck with a not-so-gentle clatter. Patty slid her feet through, twisted over onto her stomach, and wriggled out of the vent. She dropped onto the floor and hid behind the vacant bench. The doors remained closed. The grille lay in front of her. There seemed no way she would be able to scale the wall to fit the mesh back in the duct; the bench was secured to the floor. She had hoped to drag it to the wall and climb back that way. *Oh well, there's always Plan B.* She wondered what that might be as she tiptoed across the room to her supine brother.

Patty held Alan's cold hand as she examined the medical display. She did not recognize any of the text, but one rhythmic readout had to be his heartbeat. It seemed regular, but Patty pressed her fingers to Alan's throat and checked for herself; his pulse was strong and steady. She leaned over him and shook his shoulders.

"Wake up!" she hissed urgently. "Oh Alan, please wake up. I won't be able to carry you. I need you to help me get you out of here." She straightened and looked at his pale face. His eyes were still; he was not dreaming. She took a thick pinch of skin on the back of Alan's wrist and gave it a firm twist. Alan's face twitched, so Patty gave it another wrench.

"Alan! Please wake up!" she whispered as she gave the skin on his wrist another violent turn. A deep breath moved Alan's chest, and his eyes fluttered open. Patty's heart leaped, and she could not help but grin. Her brother was alive and awake! "Alan, sit up. We don't have much time." She crossed to the sliding doors and looked through the small windows. A hallway stretched out before, intersecting the main corridor. It was empty except at the far end where a man walked with two children in single file before him.

Patty rushed back to Alan and pulled the blanket from him. He was naked. Patty blinked, surprised; of course he was naked. Everyone she had seen had been nude under their tabards. Patty turned to the monitor and pressed the yellow light Patty saw the Gray use; the monitor died. She stripped the sensors from Alan's chest. Patty wrapped her arms around her brother and slowly sat him up. *He'll need something to wear even if it was one of those horrible tabards.* An idea began spiraling through her mind, an idea that made her gut squirm. She looked deeply into Alan's eyes hoping for some response. They were vacant; his face was relaxed. "Oh Alan, please come back to me. I can't do this alone." He blinked and seemed stable enough sitting up, but that was all.

Frantically, her gaze spun around the room. A glass-fronted cabinet, flush mounted to the wall, held bottles of colored compounds. There were shelves along the wall with labeled boxes stacked neatly in them. The boxes had the feel of cardboard and the look of plastic. It opened easily. Gray blankets. Patty slammed it back on the shelf and opened the next, more blankets. The following box held more gray shapes, and she thrust it away. *Stop! Grey with a blue spot! Tabards!* There were a dozen or more folded cloaks inside. Patty flicked the first one out and blushed. It was small. Very small. Her idea now demanded center stage. Patty looked at the tabard and sighed. It was madness. *I'll have to be naked under that thing.* Well, maybe not that one; it was too small for even Alan to wear. She found a tabard of suitable size in the fourth box, but she still could not help but blush uncontrollably. *Get over it, girl,* she berated herself fiercely. *You haven't seen any of the passive slaves out there blushing, have you?*

She crammed the carefully folded tabards into one box, and then Patty cleared another. She put her boots and helmet into one and her pressure-suit into the other. Her p-suit packed pretty small but even so, it was quite a squeeze getting it into the box. Her underwear and her auxiliary supplies went in with her helmet and boots. Her sword was a problem and then she broke out into a cold sweat. *How am I going to find my way out of here with my wrist comm packed in a box?* The corner of a gray blanket stuck out from the edge of a box. Patty whipped it out and swirled it around her arm. *Yes! That would do nicely.* She wrapped the blanket around Lady Estelle and used a little gray duct tape to mount her wrist comm. She brought her booty back to Alan's bench and helped her brother to stand. He was a little wobbly at first, but he quickly improved. Patty covered his innocent nakedness with a gray cloak, and slipped a tabard over her head, breathing slowly, willing her body's embarrassed heat to subside. The tickle of warm air sliding over her skin was a distraction.

We're almost ready. What else do we need? Patty examined Alan. *You can stand but can you walk?* She gently wrapped her arm around his shoulders and led him forward. Once again, Alan was hesitant and uncertain; his muscles felt firm, but he was a little uncoordinated.

"Alan, please come back to me. I need you to help me," she whispered again. Her brother did not respond; his eyes did not acknowledge her words or her presence. She walked him to the door and back again. The smell of urine snapped Patty's attention to the little blond girl on the bench beside Alan's. She was flushed, and her body quaked, shivering and shaking. The monitor began chiming. *No, not now!* Patty grabbed a box and thrust it at Alan. Too much, too quickly. She had to slow down and show him how to hold it. Patty grabbed the other box and her blanket-covered sword and peeked through the window. No one was about, yet. That would not last. She caught Alan and pushed him out in front of her. He stumbled but steadied and walked on.

The urge to look left and right, as she followed Alan through the door, tested her will. I am an obedient slave without two thoughts to rub together. *Don't notice us. We are not even here.* There was a patter of feet, and she heard the doors to Alan's room open, but Patty resisted the urge to glance over her shoulder. The wailing monitor cut off, and Patty kept strolling. The end of the corridor arrived, and Patty urged Alan to the right. An alcove opened into a stairwell on her left. Patty nudged Alan, and he turned and began to climb. According to Patty's comm, they had six levels to ascend before they could access the airlock, and using the stairs was much easier than scaling a series of cramped shafts. Alan would never cope with climbing up the air ducts.

There was little traffic on the stairs; they walked past a few Browns, many more soldiers, and only the occasional pale alien. The pale ones stared at them as they sidled down the stairs. Patty kept her head down, concentrating on the next step and then the next one. If she did not, she found herself blushing. She felt so exposed. Another left-handed alien went past them. *Feel for the step before putting your weight down. Kick out just a little more. Good. He's gone. One more step, four more floors.* Patty slowed and deepened her breathing, letting the monotony of the climb wash over her. Her thighs burned, her back ached, but if Alan wasn't lagging, she would not either.

As they climbed higher, Patty stopped seeing the pale aliens. That worried her. If there were no pale ones on these levels, why would two of their charges be up here? Her heart beat faster, and it was not just from the climb; fear's cold fingers ran through the sweat dripping down her back. Alan slowed as he took the last step and stopped at the alcove. The corridor was not particularly busy; soldiers in colored clusters walked together, rumbling their alien speech, an occasional Brown and one pale alien went past. Two humans entered the passageway. *So, it's permissible for humans to be up here.* She checked her comm. *So, which way do we go? Left is closer to the airlock.* Patty waited for a group of green tabards to pass before nudging Alan, and they fell in behind the boisterous soldiers. The cream corridor began to fill with more noisy aliens as waves of excited hooming echoed towards them. The green tabards broke into a run, and Patty held Alan close giving another rushing group plenty of clearance. If there were a passage to the left Patty would have taken it. She did not like the idea of being swept up in whatever was happening in front of them.

The passageway entered an open area filled with soldiers, and Patty made sure Alan stayed close to the left wall. The roaring presence of excited aliens was overwhelming. The room was crowded, and still more poured in. Suddenly a single voice boomed out, and everybody in the room dropped to one knee. Alan also stopped and knelt as if he understood that booming voice. Patty copied him. A large alien in a blue and gold tabard of intricate design stood between two groups of warriors, red tabards faced green, remonstrating at the factions, expressing what appeared to Patty as anger and disapproval. Neither of the parties gave way before its tirade, and their aggressive shouts and posturing grew. The blue and gold alien gestured to them with his left hand and paced to one side.

The two factions faced off and drew their dagger-swords. They stepped forward or back and aligned themselves with their closest companion. The two groups coalesced into two lines, bristling with bright-edged weapons. The two lines struck, blades flashing. Patty gasped, and the kneeling crowd roared and raised their distinctive right arms in the air. Patty could not see the action through the forest of yellow-brown arms, but she saw a splash of blood arc through the air, and the mob surged to their feet.

Patty flung out her left arm to keep Alan in place, safe against the wall. She glanced to her right, and there was Jake. The man held a box high in his arms as he squeezed through the jostling mass. Patty's heart leaped as she tried to think of a reason that would let her cross the deck and intercept him. *Jake, I don't want to leave you here.* The man turned, and she saw his face clearly, it wasn't Jake. Patty closed her eyes and sagged back against the wall. There was no way she could have taken Jake even if she were able to persuade him to come; Freya was crowded with just the two of them.

Although Patty felt her heartbreak, she could feel her resolve harden. I'm going to get Alan out if it's the last thing I do. I'm sorry I can't help anyone else. I can't help you all, but I can help my brother. I hope.

CHAPTER SEVEN

Pressed against the etched cream wall by chanting, hooming aliens, Patty picked up her parcels and gestured to Alan to do the same. This time Patty took the lead, forging a route along the wall. The soldiers ignored them as they progressed along the wall behind them. The first exit was jammed with a jumping, cheering mob of aliens but, with a glance to make sure Alan was behind her, Patty pushed on through. The next exit was just as choked, but it led in the right direction; she pushed into the crowd. With bows and mumbled apologies, Patty pressed against the hooming soldiers. Surprisingly, they did their best to give them room to pass. After ten meters of shoehorned aliens, there was room to walk freely, and Patty double-checked her map; ahead was a corridor that linked with the hallway outside the EV prep room.

The door to the prep room was no different to the others they past, and Patty would not have recognized it except for her comm. Patty hustled Alan in and quickly followed. No pressure suits were hanging on hooks. The door closed behind her, and a right-handed alien stepped into the prep room from the airlock. It coughed. Rumble. It coughed again and rumbled some more. Patty dropped her box and drew Lady Estelle from the blankets before the alien finished speaking.

It stumbled back, looking to either side while reaching for the blade beneath its tabard. *Was it confused? Good.* Patty rushed forward, driving the point of her rapier into its right shoulder. The alien screamed and whipped out its sword. Patty could not afford to have a prolonged fight in the enclosed space of the airlock. Her opponent was bigger and stronger. She had to get a kill shot in, and quickly. The thought both sickened and excited her, adrenaline flooded through her with every beat of her racing heart.

The alien held back as their blades crossed again and again. Whether it was because of its dripping wound or because it was waiting for reinforcements, Patty knew she could not afford to keep circling. The alien was quick. Its right-handed stance and the confined space made it difficult to attack its inside line. The thick skin protected it somewhat from her rapier's needle-sharp point, and it didn't seem to be tiring. She had to do something to break this stalemate.

Alan stepped to the airlock door, and Patty's heart leaped to her throat. "No! Go back. Don't come in here," Patty shouted. The alien caught a glimpse of something and twitched to its right. It was just the opening Patty needed, and she thrust high and on its inside. The alien skull's heavy bones guided her point through its eye and into its brain. The alien sagged to its knees and fell on its side, blood flowing over the cream floor.

Although her stomach gave a heave, Patty clenched her jaw against the hot surge. *Not now*, she desperately told her quaking gut, *later, when we're safe, then you can heave to your heart's content.* Patty did not want to think about what had just happened. *I have killed again.* In her seventeen years, she had never slain anything more advanced than an insect, and in the last two days, she had slaughtered - *how many?* - living breathing aliens. Patty tried not to think about it as she cleaned her rapier on the alien's tabard.

Leaving the dead ET where it lay, she moved back to the prep room. *There're no pressure suits, damn! Surely, they have emergency suits somewhere nearby.* There were inset cupboards beside the racks and Patty opened the first, finding medical supplies, the second held five semi-transparent parcels. Patty grabbed one and prayed it was what she thought it was. She pulled it from its bag and sighed with relief. It was distorted, over-sized, and lacked the happy, smiley-face logo, but it was a Zip-Lok in

everything but name. Patty bundled Alan into the alien
emergency pressure-suit and began to seal him up. The boots
were well insulated, but the rest of him was going to get cold.
Patty unwrapped Lady Estelle's scabbard and draped the blanket
around her brother and finished closing his seals. The p-suit
looked ghastly, and when it hit vacuum, it would balloon
horribly. Patty unpacked her duct tape and began to rein in the
excess material. It was still going to puff out, but she hoped she
confined the worst of it.

Throwing her hated tabard to the floor, Patty donned her
clothes and p-suit as quickly as possible, reconnected her comm
to the wrist mount and put on her helmet. A red light flashed as
her p-suit pressurized - there was a leak. Patty prayed it was not
on her back; Alan would be no help finding it. Her left knee and
right elbow had worn spots from her climb through the air
ducts, so Patty applied duct tape there first. The pressure test
was still in the red until she remembered to put her gloves back
on and she tried to breathe slowly while she waited for it to turn
green. It did.

Patty grabbed Alan and walked him into the airlock. She
turned the blue handle, and the door sighed as it closed tight.
When Patty turned back to her brother, he had picked up the
alien's sword and was examining the blade.

"Don't hole your suit with that," she said, but Alan could not
hear her over the cycling airlock. She tried to pry it out of his
hand, but he did not want to let it go. As happy as Patty was to
see some form of life in Alan, she did not want him running
around with a sharp implement. Patty quickly checked the body
at her feet and removed the woven belt holding the scabbard.
She improvised the loops around Alan and showed him how to
sheath the dangerous blade. He seemed happy enough.

Patty drew Lady Estelle and started to climb the rungs. She
was determined to be at the top when the lock opened. If the
aliens had posted a guard in the airlock, they might have one
outside as well. Sure enough, when the circular hatch slid aside,
a guard in a p-suit leaned over and looked down. Patty slashed,

and Lady Estelle's point shaved a transparent peeling from the alien's visor. She scrambled up and out of the lock as the alien reeled back, drawing its blade. There was very little light; the alien ship was once again in Earth's shadow, and it took precious seconds for Patty's eyes to adjust. She hacked at the antenna that rose from its helmet and was pleased to see it spin away, but she gasped as she only just managed to dodge the alien's return thrust. Patty took a couple of steps back, keeping the alien at bay by pricking tiny holes in its suit. The minute leaks sprayed plumes of precious air into the cold vacuum. It was not enough to harm the alien, not yet anyway, but it did give it pause.

Alan's head appeared from the lock; Patty circled to her right so the hatch was behind the alien and fell back a few paces. The alien began a thrusting, slashing attack but something felt wrong, it was too slow. *The alien was lightning on defense, so what's holding him back?* The fights Patty had witnessed told her that these were fighters, not fencers. *It's playing for time.* Patty attacked low, ducking under its sweeping blade and making a substantial cut along its thigh. A jet of gas and blood billowed from the gash. The alien staggered back, clutching its leg. A blade, accompanied by a spray of boiling blood, suddenly burst from the center of its chest. Patty saw its eyes widen as blood poured from its mouth, splattering across its visor. It dropped to its knees, revealing Alan, gripping a long hilt in both hands. He was expressionless as he tried to wipe the blade on the alien's p-suit. He slashed the p-suit open, pulled the tabard out, and cleaned his weapon on that, and then sheathed the sword.

Where did he learn to do that? Patty thought as she grabbed Alan's arm and headed for Freya. *It's not polite to leave the airlock open but leaving two dead guards in our wake wasn't exactly well-mannered either. If someone wants to follow it will take extra time to cycle the air into the lock, time we can use to get out of sight.* Alan stumbled. The taped-up alien Zip-Lok ballooned out all over the place, making it difficult for Alan to walk let alone run. Even at a brisk walk, he nearly fell every third or fourth step. Patty wrapped an arm around him and kept them moving. They had traveled barely twenty meters when the airlock hatch closed. Patty did a quick calculation as she hurried on: fifteen seconds to fill with air, thirty seconds to pack the lock with aliens, forty seconds to cycle the air out again. They had no time at all. Patty scooped her little brother into her arms and ran.

The broad stairs caught Patty by surprise; only her quick reflexes brought them to a skidding halt, centimeters from the top step. Light from the newly reopened hatch spilled out. Patty settled Alan in her arms and moved carefully down the broad steps. They reached the bottom just as a bright beam shone above their heads.

Patty carefully put Alan down. He seemed none the worse, but her back was screaming. She stopped, took a deep breath, and crept back up the stairs. Three aliens swept the surrounding area with bright torches. Two of them headed directly for the stairs. *Time to go!* As Patty turned, she nearly fell over Alan who had crept up behind her, mirroring her stealthy pose. She pressed her helmet to Alan's head and shouted, "Let's go."

Alan's eyes looked at her but other than that, he did not respond. She turned him around, helped him down the steps, and turned left along the dividing wall, the blinking green light on her wrist comm leading the way. She picked him up once more, ignoring her complaining back, and ran.

Her comm said that Freya was three meters in front of her, but as hard as she tried, Patty could not see her CRV. She put Alan down and approached slowly, hands outstretched. When Patty's gloved fingers touched the curved edge of the stubby winglet, it felt like her hand rubbed against a substantial nothing, an invisible curve in space. Suddenly she saw stars, distorted through Freya's canopy. Her heart skipped a joyful beat. *We're home!*

Patty untied Alan's scabbard and helped him into the cramped rear seat of the ship. With his ballooning p-suit, it was no easy task to stuff him in back there, but somehow, she did it. She placed Lady Estelle back in the case with her competition épée, promising to give her a good clean as soon as she could.

Just as Patty scrambled aboard, a torch's light splashed across Freya. Patty's heart raced; although Freya was in standby mode, she still took maddening moments to warm up, minutes that felt like hours. The bright beam of light moved on, and Patty breathed again. When Freya refilled with air, Patty leaned over her seat to make sure Alan was safe and secure. Now that his p-suit was in a pressurized environment it hung loosely upon him, and he seemed much more comfortable. She tightened his safety belts but kept his Zip-Lok sealed, just in case.

One-by-one the flight computer's tell-tales turned green. Navigation showed that they had unobstructed space, so Patty lit the main engine. She held her breath, hoping the rough landing had not damaged the undercarriage. Freya rolled on smoothly. To counteract the artificial gravity, she forced one hundred and ten percent through the nose thrusters, and when Freya's nose-wheel lifted, she opened the main engine throttle wide. Five-gees slammed her back into her seat. *Five seconds*, Patty counted... *ten seconds*, they were clear. The flight computer terminated the main engine burn, and Patty sighed with relief.

Suddenly, navigation pinged for her attention; there were ships everywhere. It took Patty a while to understand the display. Six spacecraft, in two flights, had thundered out of each of the alien ship's four docks and had peeled away, making circular sweeps around the enormous alien craft. Their search patterns widened, but Freya was already high above them. As a precaution, Patty powered down everything she could.

Freya stayed that way for over an hour. Giuseppe's brilliant coating absorbed radar transmitted on every band, and twice LADAR swept right over them. Freya was invisible.

And then Alan threw up in his p-suit. There was little Patty could do except unseal him and wipe his face. Poor Alan was a sticky, stinking mess. She had spare Zip-Lok suits but climbing out of the alien one, washing, dressing and getting into a fresh Zip-Lok would be hard enough to do if Alan was his old self. It was an impossible task in his current state. From the compartment beside her knee, Patty retrieved a soft bottle of chilled water. She gave it to her brother, and he looked at it as if he had never seen packaged water before. It did not seem to mean anything to him. Patty squeezed the bottle, and a rotating bubble of water splashed into his face. Enough of it leaked into his mouth for Alan to understand what she was trying to do. Patty was pleased when he brought the bottle to his lips and drank by himself. His eyes and face remained unresponsive as if the aliens had erased his thoughts.

"Come home, Alan," Patty prayed wistfully. "We're safe on Freya. We'll go and find Mom and Dad now." Alan blinked. "I'll find Mom, don't you worry. She'll know what to do. Dad always says, give Mom a half decent lab and she could cure anything. Just hang on, Alan. We'll get you fixed up."

When the alien mothership dropped below the horizon, Patty was ready with a course correction loaded into the flight computer. She did not want to waste the energy her unplanned escape vector had created; it had given them a very eccentric orbit. Freya's burn would put them into a transfer orbit that would intersect with the closest branch of humanity, at the L3 station, the only Lagrange point out of sight of the moon. Freya's engines fired.

IN HER EYRIE

Bright Hope felt more like a captive in her Eyrie than the
GreatMother of the most significant Southern Clan. *Del'armorun,
they call me, Light Bringer, the Guide in the Dark.* One Arumpo'or
amongst so many Hel'omi. *Except they aren't Hel'omi anymore.
They have language and tribes and clans and war. I'm not sure I'm
wholly Arumpo'or either.* Somewhere, someone had changed or
altered the Arumpo'or genome. The fact that Hel'omi could birth
an Arumpo'or was proof of that, even if she did not have the
equipment to prove that guess or the tools to make the
laboratory equipment. *Or the tools to make the tools.*

She had hoped the two other mel'andrin she had recovered
from that abandoned apartment would bridge the gaps, but they
did not. So much had changed. The rate of live Arumpo'or births
had been plummeting for years. Hel'omi giving birth to
Arumpo'or had been seen as a miracle lifeline, and for a while,
Arumpo'or culture blossomed again. Del'armorun had one
memory that held a clue to what happened next. A report about
a disease that struck the Hel'omi in the north causing birth
defects was all she had to go on.

The Arumpo'or were now functionally extinct. Del'armorun
was sure her birth had something to do with her mother's diet
while she gestated. She had had some success getting the hybrid
Hel'omi-Arumpo'or mothers to produce male Arumpo'or, or
what were almost male Arumpo'or. They were smaller, and
much to Del'armorun's distress, they had lost some of the
sparks of individuality just as the Hel'omi had gained some. And
birthing males was still hit and miss; they all inherited the

twisted body forms of their parents. Her research was ongoing, but the results were slow.

The Eyrie was cold, drafty and would be exposed to a sunstrike, but its height gave her antenna extra reach, and it was not too far from the workrooms where she taught, and the court where she sat in judgment. Climbing the stairs kept her trim. Leaving OldMother Hea'rat to attend to most of the Clan's day-to-day details was not a good idea in the long run, but it suited the needs of the day. Hea'rat's nepotistic urge was impossible for her to resist for more than a day or two. *I need to get away, to have time just to think.* The Eyrie was as much a prison as a refuge, and it gave her the opportunity to scan the radio frequencies for herself. Static roared and squeaked from the circular diaphragm connected to the hand-wound coil she had built herself. She had created all the components of her transmitter. Recovering enough technology to blow the glass for the valves had resulted in an explosion of wealth for her clan.

The clan had had little infrastructure when she first received GreatMothers' mel'andrin. Except for the little village forges that kept a supply of bright-edged swords flowing, in the two hundred orbits since the last GreatMother the Clan's level of technology had been reduced to wood and stone. *Papa relied on stone implements.* Two hundred years where the Hel'omi muddled on by themselves. *The Hel'omi are not Hel'omi anymore. Should I be calling them Hel'Arumpo'or?*

A garbled series of pops and squeals from the speaker made Del'armorun focus on the speaker, but the sounds drifted into noise once more. *Is there anyone out there?*

The clan's wealth was hers, and she had spent it as wisely as she could. *Papa wouldn't recognize his little Bright Hope now.* The wealth of knowledge the mel'andrin brought her would not allow her to waste their precious resources, and the GreatMothers' memories of mistakes and successes provided her with inspiration and guidance. Bright Hope would have had no chance of leading this clan forward, but Del'armorun could. The change was slow because there was only one of her to instruct those stubborn clansmen in her new techniques. The old ways were best, they said, even when she taught them how to work better, faster, and be more productive.

A sigh racked Del'armorun's twisted body as she strained to find coherence in the static. Nearly half an orbit had past since the speaker had last vibrated with Tel'sars' excited voice. Tel'sars was her breeding program's most significant success - one of the few left-handed sons that understood the principles behind her radio.

His ship had been facing a great storm when last they spoke. It was not the first storm their mission to the Northlands had bested, and it wasn't the largest either, but something had gone wrong. One of her most enthusiastic supporters, Tel'sars knew the importance of this mission and would not have anyone go in his place. She missed his lively manner and his astute observations. The wind howled, making Del'armorun clutch at her warm robe, but she kept monitoring the static for his signal.

CHAPTER EIGHT

The smell of urine frightened Patty. Her mind immediately flashed back to the cramped ducts of the alien ship, watching the Browns as they wrapped a dead little girl in a gray blanket. Patty spun around and leaned over her seat.

"Alan! Are you okay?" Her brother did not respond, he sat, constrained by the safety harness, with his eyes closed, breathing slowly. "Alan!" Patty reached forward and grabbed Alan by his chin. "Alan!" She shook his head gently. Alan's eyes opened slowly. "Alan, are you okay?" Her eyes scanned him hoping for a reaction. "You've peed yourself." The nightmare of Alan dying in her back seat receded. Patty sighed. *Of course, he peed himself.* Alan did not seem to be worried about it, but anger boiled inside her. Sitting in a suit with half a liter of urine slopping around in it was humiliating whether Alan knew it or not. It was not his fault. *Those aliens!* Patty ground her teeth together. They held the upper hand for now, but soon, soon there was going to be payback, she promised herself. Frustration burned her gut. Patty hated leaving her brother in such a state. The urine and the vomit were just going to have to mix until she could find somewhere to get him cleaned up.

There were over two hours until the turnover maneuver killed Freya's motion relative to L3. She scanned ahead using the fantastic telescope Giuseppe had installed. It was almost impossible for Patty to locate L3 manually, but powerful transmissions cutting through the alien's interference pinpointed its location.

L3 had once been five independent stations. One was a long

cigar shape, another a collection of honeycomb structures. There was one squat pentagonal structure and two very similar cylinders, built at different times for different reasons. The five stations had amalgamated at the start of the Belter war, and now a crisscross collection of broad and narrow corridors linked the once-isolated space stations into one unit. They had held a fiercely independent stance during the war and once stood off an attack by thirty ships. They seemed to be holding their own against the aliens too. Six of the aliens' tough fighters circled L3, firing a volley of rockets every minute or so. Patty's eyes locked to the screen the first time she saw four missiles spiraling inward. She had witnessed L1 disintegrating and had no desire to watch L3 succumb to the same fate, but she could not drag her eyes away. One missile burst into flames, then a second. The last two blew up in quick succession. Patty breathed a sigh of relief as she realized that the station must have faced down more than that one volley. There was no way for her to know just how long the attack had been going on.

As good as the optics were on Freya's *new camera, Patty could not see how L3 was defending itself, but she was mighty glad it was. And surprised. Who would have thought that L3 had kept its old defensive array in working order? Independent and paranoid. Sounds like they're just the kind of friends I need.*

Patty chuckled and realized as a chill writhed down her spine that she needed to alter her heading. There was no way Patty was going to put Freya in the line of fire. *Was it worthwhile hanging out near the action at L3? Mom, Dad, did you find refuge here?*

"You okay back there?" Patty asked as she pulled herself from her seat to check on her brother. He looked at her when her head rose above the seat-back. That was a good sign. "Are you all right, Alan?" she asked again. He looked all right; his color was healthy. The bottle of water was still in his hand; he had drunk over a third of it by himself. *Good.* Patty wished he could communicate with her. She checked his restraints and tightened them; it was best to be held down nice and snug during maneuvers.

"We're going to be doing some course corrections," she told him, even though he gave no sign of understanding her. "Ready?" Nothing. She smiled and gave him the thumbs-up sign. Still nothing. Patty sighed and strapped in. She aborted the two-hour countdown and activated the turnover burn. Freya slewed around, and her engines fired, bringing her to all-stop, relative to L3.

Patty unbuckled and turned around to face Alan again. "You okay?" she asked giving him thumbs-up and nodding her head up and down. Alan's eyes tracked her head and glanced at her hand. He looked down at his right hand and back at her. His hand rose hesitantly into the thumbs-up gesture, and he gave one small nod.

"Oh, yes!" Patty shouted. "My brother's a smart boy!" She grabbed her seatback and shook it, laughing. "I knew you were in there, Alan!" The tension and fear in her heart eased. She leaned over and released his restraints. He watched her movements intently.

Patty refastened the restraints and looked Alan in the eyes. "Now you do it." She dropped her eyes to the buckle and tapped it before looking back at her brother. His face showed no sign of comprehension. Patty touched the clasp once more and wiggled the release clip. Alan's hand met hers at the buckle. He gripped the release firmly and pulled.

"Good work," Patty enthused. She nodded her head and gave the thumbs-up. Alan responded with a small nod. "Oh, that's my brother, smart as a whip!" Patty gestured with her hands and mimed pushing the buckle back together. "Buckle up! Put it back." Alan nodded and pushed the clip back into the buckle. Patty felt so happy she grabbed her brother and kissed his forehead. His hair was greasy and smelt rank. She added an extra line under the get-Alan-clean item on her mental list of must-do things.

Patty turned back to her flight computer. The program was having difficulty removing all the interference broadcast by the alien ships as they circled L3, but it was easy to see that she was not the only ship hovering on the outskirts of the siege. There were at least a dozen transponder signals nearby; three of them had automated emergency prefixes. That only happened if the ship's systems detected life support or engine problems. The closest ship was about twenty kilometers to port, but even at that range, Patty was unwilling to try transmitting a comm link. *What was the point of having an invisible ship if you made enough noise for the aliens to find you?* She maneuvered closer using Freya's thrusters.

Hugo-1350-HCs were big CRVs, but they were not large enough for three adults. Two of the occupants were not even wearing p-suits. *How deranged did you need to be, to open the cockpit thinking there was fresh air outside? Or did they suicide deliberately? There had to be a better way to go than explosive decompression.* Patty felt her stomach rebel, and she had to fight for control. She knew what had made them pack themselves into the Hugo. She knew the fear and desperation the aliens provoked.

Patty locked onto the next closest transponder broadcasting the emergency prefix and boosted over. She was angry with the aliens, but she was also peeved at the dozen or so ships sitting, out of the firing line, waiting for something to happen. Those people in the Hugo might have lived if one of them had moved off their lazy butts and done something. An emergency prefix on a transponder *was* a distress call. The Law of Space was the same as the Law of the Sea. You do not stand idly by.

When Freya arrived at the next coordinates, Patty recognized the ship. She had seen it docked at OASIS many times, though she did not know the owner. The spacecraft was a strange old bus, part Winnebago, part umbrella. It was not equipped for atmospheric flight of any kind. It reminded Patty of an ancient cottage haphazardly extended with each generation. Like OASIS, it was an assemblage of odd shapes, but this was writ small. Patty was sure she could park Freya in just one of its compartments.

Lights were on, but Patty could not see anyone through the

small portholes. She continued Freya's slide down the odd ship's port side until they reached the blunt prow. Patty killed her momentum, swung Freya around, and crabbed sideways until the two ships were almost nose-to-nose.

The cockpit was not well lit and appeared to be empty. Patty flashed her landing lights on and off and a young man, wearing a gray and blue shipsuit, popped up from below the console. He looked a little older than Alan, and his face was familiar. He picked up an old-fashioned microphone and Patty waved her hands trying to signal she did not want to use the comm. A large woman loomed up behind him and snatched the microphone from his hand. Her face was even more familiar, though Patty could not remember her name. She had seen this woman many times on OASIS, wearing the same grease-stained overalls.

She waved to Patty and pointed to their starboard side, mouthing the word, airlock. Patty gave her thumbs-up and maneuvered around the oddball ship. Sure enough, an ungainly industrial airlock was hand-welded onto the outside of a slab-sided compartment.

"We're going to depressurize, Alan," Patty said as she began sealing his Zip-Lok. He watched the procedure impassively. She double-checked his seals. "Are you okay?" she tried not to show her high expectations. Alan nodded and gave thumbs-up.

His response made her heart leap. If there had been a brighter day, explosively decompressed corpses aside, Patty was not aware of it. The barely restrained smile splashed across her face, and she returned his thumbs-up. "Good."

Her helmet clicked into place; she snapped her gloves' wrist seals closed and looked at the duct tape repair on her elbow. The gray tape still appeared to be firmly attached, but that did not stop a chill washing over her. As if she needed another reminder, *vacuum never forgives*. She closed her visor with a sigh and ran her integrity checks. All green. The air cycled into the holding tanks, and Patty opened the cockpit.

Far below, Earth looked so small and fragile. Bright stars littered the sky. *Which one did you come from? And what do we have to do to send you back?*

CHAPTER NINE

The strange ship's airlock would have been big enough for two, but with Alan's ballooned Zip-Lok it was a squeeze until the pressure rose, and Alan's p-suit deflated. The inner door creaked open onto a narrow corridor and the two people Patty saw on the bridge.

"I know you," the tall brown woman said with surprise. "Seen you on OASIS." She flicked away strands of thick black hair loosened from the knotted piece of brown string that held back the rest of her mane. A smear of grease accented her strong chin. "Welcome aboard the Jaswinder. I'm Madhur, and this is my nephew, Jai. How can we help you?"

"You're Patty Balke!" the youth exclaimed. "I watched your last bout. You were lucky. Lucky. Lucky." He laughed as he twisted into a three-sixty spin, his body spiraling in place. He pulled out smoothly. "I'm Strike Leader for *The Starlight Tigers*, Under-16s." He bowed.

Patty smiled as the memory of Jai's face clicked into place; she had seen him at a competition. She returned his bow. "You're right. I was very lucky."

"You look like you've had it a bit rough," Madhur said looking at her patched p-suit and her brother.

"This is my brother, Alan, and yeah, we've had our share of problems, but that's not why we're here," Patty replied. "Your transponder is broadcasting an emergency prefix. I came over to see if you were okay."

Madhur looked past her at Alan in his tape-wrapped p-suit and lifted one eyebrow. "Transponder." She nodded. "I've had problems with my fuel lines. That'll be why the stupid thing set off its alarm. Should rip the bloody thing out."

"With the new neighbors, that might be a wise choice," Patty agreed, "So you are okay? There's another distress beacon out there."

"Yeah, as soon as I can bleed my lines we'll be up and running again," Madhur said brightly. "Jaswinder's never out of action for long, not for fifty years."

"Well, if you're okay, it might be best if we chased down that emergency beacon," Patty replied.

Madhur looked at Alan once more. "I got a spare Zip-Lok and some space where your brother can get cleaned up," Madhur remarked as she examined Patty's patched p-suit once more, "and some Donegal's Suit-Sealer. If you're going on a rescue mission, you should make sure you don't need rescuing as well. We've been here for over a day; another few minutes won't hurt them."

"I suppose you're right," Patty said with a sigh. She tugged at the shoulder strap of her pack. "Thanks for the Zip-Lok offer but I have everything we need here. I just don't have enough space to clean him up on Freya."

"Freya!" Madhur shook her head vigorously. "Freya, Balke. I'm sorry. Heard about you saving Kerr's butt. That was ballsy. Come in, come in." She chuckled and gestured to Patty's left. "Jai, why don't you get that transponder off-line while I help Patty."

"Aye, aye skipper," Jai answered smartly as he pushed off to the right, sailing into the bridge.

"This way." Madhur spiraled down a passage that had doorways on every side, left, right, top and bottom. A paint-splattered aluminum extension ladder, spot welded into position across one corner, ran the length of the passage. Sections of safety harness that appeared to have been hacked from a dozen different restraints were in easy reach. Patty smiled. This ship had no floors, but who needed defined decks when there was no gravity?

Patty checked to see that Alan was following and moved aft. The walls were plastered with snapshots: smiling faces from family gatherings, sports functions, weddings, and engines surrounded her. There were ships and engines everywhere Patty looked. It was a messy collection of pictures from a range of years; some were even flat, fading 2D pictures.

The lounge had four acceleration couches mounted to the far wall, though only two seemed to be in working order and the layout gave Patty the impression she was emerging from the ceiling. Family pictures covered most of the walls except for one large painting of a jungle; rays of light partially illuminated the green gloom, and a pair of bright eyes peered out from the darkness. It made Patty feel those eyes were watching her.

Madhur was on the far side of the room beside a door. "Bathroom's in here. We have a water recycler, but not much in reserve."

"I'll be economical. Thanks," Patty replied gratefully as she crossed the room.

"So, what's your story?" Madhur asked when they began to strip the soiled p-suit from the silent and compliant Alan. "Your brother, does he have the aut? My uncle has a touch of Asperger's."

"The aliens," Patty began, but she did not know how to explain why her brother was in such a state; everything in the past day or so was almost dream-like, or rather, nightmare-like, endless tight beige tunnels, filled with thousands of monstrous, threatening aliens. Patty knew her dreams would be full of them when, if, she had the chance to sleep. "The aliens took Alan and did something to him."

"You've seen them?" Madhur asked. "We got off OASIS just before they attacked."

"The big ones are over two meters tall. If we can get that thing off Alan in one piece, you can see for yourself." Patty opened the last seal and carefully peeled it away from her brother, making sure the stinking contents did not escape.

"Where did you get this p-suit from? It looks like a Zip-Lok but..." Madhur's brow grew furrowed.

"It's one of theirs," Patty sealed up the deformed p-suit.

"It is?" Madhur asked. "Give that here. I'll look after it. There's the sonic scrubber, and it wouldn't hurt to shampoo his hair. I'll be back in a couple of minutes." She took the twisted Zip-Lok from Patty and left.

Peeling the sodden tabard from her brother, Patty began to wash him down with a little water and the scrubber. Alan was still and biddable throughout. She washed him from top to toe and then back again just to be sure and shampooed his hair twice as if cleansing his exterior would wash away his internal taint.

"Do you remember these?" Patty asked as she dressed her brother in his red, dragon-scale printed shipsuit. It was one of Alan's favorites. "These are yours too," she held up his blue and green striped gecko-grip soled, slip-on sneakers. They clashed horribly with the shipsuit, just as Alan liked it. "Do you remember them?" His eyes glanced at the shoes and back to her. "Nod for yes, shake for no. Do you remember them?"

Alan looked at the sneakers impassively for one slow breath and then another, before returning his gaze to Patty. He shook his head.

"How about the smell?" Patty asked. Alan had worn these shoes just about all summer. She took an exaggerated sniff - they did not smell too bad - and moved them to Alan's nose. He sniffed and blinked, and his eyes darted back and forth across the shoes. "Do you remember anything?" For the first time, Patty was aware of, Alan's brow creased with thought. He nodded, shook his head, and nodded once more.

"It's all right. Relax. Don't worry about it. Your memories will come back to you in their own time," she promised him, although it was more for herself. Despite the conflict in Alan's demeanor, Patty's hopes for Alan's recovery soared. *I'll get my annoying little brother back, and then I'll regret it.* She finished dressing Alan and began to unpack a nice new, smiley-faced Zip-Lok. Alan turned and retrieved the alien's sword. Patty felt fear wash over her. He was dangerous with that blade, and a part of Patty did not trust him with it.

Alan switched on the sonic scrubber and began to clean the bright blade and then the scabbard. Patty relaxed. She was pleased that he was showing some self-motivation although she would have been happier if it had manifested itself in a different area. He was definitely attached to that heavy blade. She kept an eye on Alan as she unpacked the p-suit and waited until he had finished before securing it around him. She sealed most of it up, leaving the visor flap open.

Madhur and Jai were cautiously removing the gray duct tape from the cleaned alien p-suit when Patty led Alan into the lounge room.

"Man, this is weird!" Jai exclaimed when he saw them. "Mad told me you've seen them. What are they like?"

"Well, if you can download the video from this," Patty detached the jeweled pin from her p-suit, "you'll see what I saw."

Jai's eyes lit up, and he glanced at his aunt, who nodded. "Just keep it well sandboxed, okay?" Madhur insisted.

"Sure thing." Jai took the pin and bounced out of the lounge, up through the passageway to the bridge.

"What are your plans then?" Madhur asked.

"Depends on what shape the next ship is in," Patty replied. "I was hoping to come back here before I had to decide what to do next. We want to find our parents. We know they left Earth before the fighting started but not much more." As much as she loved Freya, it was nice to have room to stretch out. "What about you?"

"I was bringing Jai to his family at L3, but since the Bugs seemed to have the station locked up tight, I was thinking of heading home to L4," Madhur told her, and her frown deepened. "I think L4's got a snowball's chance on Mercury of keeping the aliens out, but I gotta check it for myself. Look, you're most welcome to rendez back here with whoever you can rescue, and we can go together if you like." Madhur stopped talking as a thought occurred to her. "Hang on. I've got something in the workshop that might help." She spun around and left the lounge, moving aft. Madhur was back in less than a minute, brandishing a coiled umbilical and a well-used tube of Donegal's Suit Sealer. "You can use this to plug into most ships, siphon them some fuel, power or oxygen and make a comm link without broadcasting. Now, let's have a look at your suit."

Madhur's repairs were quick and messy, but the sight of orange blobs fused to her p-suit was much more comforting than the gray duct tape.

TEL'SARS' REPORT

The quiet isolation of her Eyrie gave Del'armorun the time she needed to think and plan. Well used to the cold, she actually enjoyed feeling the southerly blasts numb her extremities on clear nights like this. Her mountaintop retreat was the perfect place to test her newest telescope. The optics caused some rainbow-fringing, but that was only around the edges. The lens was much improved. She could see the broad boulevards on both moons' cities though no one strode them. She could see the quiet shipyards and ached to lay her hands on just one of those ships. Fusion power would revolutionize her world. Her experiments had failed. With a working model, things would be so much easier.

A burp in the static caught her attention. It had been so long since Tel'sars had been in touch she wondered why she stood vigil at all. But the results from the quiet time in her lab had produced more than enough results to keep even Old Mother Hea'rat quiet.

"Shhhwert - pop!" the speaker blurted, "Testing. Yes, it should be working. Testing on three, oh, nine, nine, three cycles." The sound phased in and out, and it was scratchy and thin, but it was Tel'sars.

Del'armorun nearly dropped her cup of tea as she scrambled to the microphone. "Tel'sars! We read you! This is Del'armorun at Eyrie Station."

"Bright Hope! It is *good* to hear your voice!" Tel'sars replied.

Only Tel'sars called her that. *Not since Papa died.* "Tel'sars, where have you been!" She remembered to turn on the recorder and grabbed a pad and pencil to make notes.

"Long-story-short, a storm wrecked us and most of our equipment. Bright Hope, you should see the patchwork board I'm using to transmit this. I'm glad I learned how to blow the glass for valves!" He chuckled. "We reached the north continent, or most of us did. We lost a lot of good people on the journey, but we made it. The short-range radios we brought with us mostly survived and has impressed the locals who rely on various forms of semaphore."

She listened intently, hardly daring to interrupt her long-lost friend's adventurous tale: shipwrecks and privation, adrift in storm-tossed seas. Tel'sars and barely two hands of the crew were rescued by a fishing boat and nurtured back to health. And then the journey north to the great city of *Darfelenornal*: deserts and snow-filled mountain passes where five died in an avalanche. His voice was a balm that eased her loneliness.

"Bright Hope, things are better and worse than we hoped. Steel they have in plenty and steam power though they don't use it to generate electricity. Raw steam power. But their ships! They make ours look like the matchwood they ended up as. They are marshaling the resources to send a return mission, and with the charts we've given them, they expect the journey will only take thirty or forty days! Can you believe it?"

Del'armorun did not know what to say. *How many orbits had he been gone?* "That is exciting news. And are they interested in trade?" she asked.

"Yes. Timber, wool, curiosities. The land is quite prosperous, green and rich. It has been many years since they have suffered a sunstrike. There is grain aplenty with many willing sellers."

"That would be a blessing. We thought the drought had broken last solstice, but it rained for three three-days and two. The floods damaged so much."

"Then this one is honored to say help is at hand GreatMother Del'armorun."

CHAPTER TEN

Patty leaned over her pilot's seat and gave Alan one last check. He looked so much better in his favorite clothes, and the Zip-Lok logo gave her a reassuring smile. Alan's finger ran under the safety harness to show he was tightly confined, and he gave her a thumbs-up. Patty returned the gesture with a smile and strapped herself into her cushioned seat. Entering the coordinates of the next emergency beacon on her list, Patty examined her potential flightpaths. She added a waypoint to keep away from the besieging alien ships.

One hour to get there, Patty calculated, using the least amount of fuel she could manage. *Hopefully, it won't take more than an hour to fix whatever's wrong, and an hour to get back. Madhur said she would be ready to leave in four hours. That gives us plenty of time, doesn't it?* She was tempted to increase her velocity, but even with the long-range tanks, she did not want to waste a drop; the port side tank was at 46 percent. Patty activated the program, and the autopilot spun Freya's smooth prow to the correct orientation and fired the main engines.

It felt good to know that Madhur and her crazy ship were near at hand. Everyone else who had helped her had departed as soon as possible, or in Giuseppe's case, had fled even before Patty left. Madhur was a woman with a rough and ready manner. Her solid reliability resonated with Patty's feelings. She did not like fussing about with irrelevances. Plot a course and fly true.

The fear of finding another ship with dead occupants made bile flood into the back of Patty's throat. She took a mouthful from her suit's sipper as she coaxed Freya into a slow approach. The distressed ship was a high-powered racing CRV with sponsors' logos splashed all over it. Patty knew the ship and the pilot by reputation only. Ken Underwood - if he was aboard - was part of the young and handsome set, a pilot for the G.A.V. racing team and always accompanied by a bevy of PAs, flunkies and assorted hangers-on. She had glimpsed that lifestyle in *The Tonight Show's* green room and had enjoyed being waited on, but it was not something she would cope well with every day.

The racing CRV's cockpit lights were on, but there was no movement inside. Patty brought Freya to All Stop relative to the sleek machine and turned on her landing lights. The reflective racing stripes made Patty blink and shade her eyes; she dropped the light's intensity to one-tenth.

A small figure waved. It was a young girl, backlit by the cockpit lights with her blond bangs drifting ethereally around her head. Beside her in the pilot's chair, there was another equally small figure, though it did not move. Behind them, crammed into a space that was more suited to carrying an overnight bag than a person was an adult-sized p-suit emblazoned with corporate logos that matched the ship. He did not move either.

Patty unbuckled and turned to her brother. "I'm going EV. I want you to stay here," she told him as she sealed his Zip-Lok. "Microphone check," Patty said and tapped her ear. "Do you hear me? Here, with the earpiece?" Alan nodded and gave a thumbs-up. Although Alan had a microphone, he had not uttered a grunt let alone a word. Patty had seen his jaw move behind closed lips and held hope that his breakthrough would be soon. He seemed to want to talk but could not find the controls. However, the changes he had gone through, from the blank slate she had woken on the slab, to the responsive, aware person he was now, was remarkable. *Talking will come when he's ready*, Patty reassured herself.

Madhur's umbilical was six meters long, a little short as far as Patty was concerned. Instead of putting Freya into standby, she kept her hot with a solid lock on the racer's transponder. The six-meter umbilical was barely long enough to reach the racing CRV; less than a meter slop and only ten centimeters clearance between Freya's stubby wing and the stricken CRV. Any sudden moves and the hearts of both ships would be ripped out.

A login request was already flashing when Patty returned to Freya's cockpit. Patty granted guest privileges and opened a window in her flight computer's display as she re-pressurized the cockpit. The blond girl was on the right side of the screen. A boy with close-cropped blond hair sat beside her. His eyes were open but showed only milky white orbs. He gave Patty the shivers, yet she smiled at her comm's camera anyway.

"Hi," the girl said in a relaxed, playful manner. "I'm Cicely, and this is my twin, Egbert." Her eyelids popped wide, and she looked at her brother. "I will not say that; you just behave." She turned back to the camera with a sweet smile. "Don't mind him. Boys. Urgh." She giggled, and Patty felt vaguely ill. Egbert had not moved or spoken at all.

"Err, hi, Cicely. How are things over there? Do you have enough oxygen?" *Was her behavior the result of CO2 poisoning?* Patty wondered. "Can you let me log into your systems?" Patty glanced across the gap between the two ships, to the crumpled form squeezed into the back. "And what about your passenger in the back? Is he all right?"

Cicely's bright performance dimmed. She looked over her shoulder and back to the lens. "That's Kenny. He's our big brother." She sighed and bit her lip. "He's hurt. The ET's shot him with something, knocked him into a wall, and he banged his head and broke his arm." She glanced over her shoulder again. "I checked him a little while ago; he seems to be breathing okay. He showed me how to program Griffin when we left OASIS so that we could get home, to L3 but..."

"The aliens were here first." Patty interrupted. "Cicely, can I log in please?"

"Oh sure, I think," she looked at her twin and then tapped at the controls. "Eg says you'll need full access to Griffin, hang on."

It took a moment or two for Patty's software to interface with the racer and then she began to get an overview of the ship's condition. Griffin was in pretty good shape, all things considered. It was low on oxygen, but not critically. At their current rate of consumption, they had five or six hours before the situation became dangerous. Patty made a quick check through all of Griffin's systems, and none of them appeared to have triggered their beacon's emergency prefix. There was no need to figure out why it activated; these kids were in trouble.

Patty inspected the settings in Griffin's flight computer and discovered a course already loaded into its memory. "What were you trying to do here?"

"We were trying to get to L5," Cicely answered brightly. "Eg says our uncle's there. I've never tried to solve a problem in orbital mechanics before." She pouted. "Eg helped."

"I'm sure he did." Patty looked at the equations. They were laid out in a most unorthodox manner, and she could not understand them until she rearranged them into a more conventional form. "Err, good try," *It's better than a good try.* For a girl, who couldn't be much older than ten, her solution was simple and quite elegant. "You haven't quite got a handle on the two-body problem for the orbital transfer, but the rest is, well, very tidy."

"We had to guess Earth's mass," Cicely said a little defensively.

"Actually, you didn't," Patty called up the almanac on Griffin's display and showed her how to find the appropriate entries. "Plug these values into here, and here, and voilà, there's your transfer orbit." Patty looked at the figures. "You wouldn't have made it, even with the right solution; you're too low on oxygen. Even with an extended five-gee burn, your flight time would be over seven hours, and I don't think Kenny would have coped with a burn like that."

"Yeah, I guess." Cicely looked quite disheartened.

"Don't be like that, sweetheart. You did... quite astonishing work. It was well worth the effort," Patty encouraged her. *If she pulled that out of her hat, the girl's a prodigy.*

Cicely perked up. "Yeah, that's what I told Eg. Better to try something than sitting here waiting for things to run out."

"Absolutely. And speaking of doing something." Patty cleared Griffin's flight computer and began transferring data from Freya. The return track to Jaswinder was simple to program into the racer's systems.

"Where are we going then?" Cicely asked as Patty finalized the program.

"Not too far. It's a ship called Jaswinder. We'll be able to help Kenny there," Patty informed her.

"Oh, good."

Patty maintained Freya's locked reference to Griffin's transponder and slaved her controls to the racer's. Theoretically, the two ships could fly back to Jaswinder as if they were one. *Theoretically.* Any engine stutters while boosting or during the retro burn would tear the two CRVs to pieces.

"Okay, I think we're ready," Patty remarked as calmly as she could manage. "Now, I want to have a quick test so seal up your suits just in case something goes wrong, okay?"

"Is something going to go wrong?" Cicely asked innocently.

"Best to prepare for the worst," Patty said and turned to Alan. "Tighten up," she said and mimed tightening his restraints. Alan nodded and secured himself. Patty smiled and gave him a thumbs-up.

"You should both get into that harness too," Patty suggested to Cicely, who nodded and slipped the safety harness over her brother's shoulder and pulled it tight. "Good. I just have to test Freya's offsets."

Patty began the racer's first orientation change, rotating along one axis only. Freya was a little slow responding to the racer's movement, and she overshot the cut-off by nearly a tenth of a second. Patty adjusted the slave program's offsets and swung Griffin's sharp prow to the correct heading. Freya slewed to the left and thrust back to accommodate the turn. It was the most uncomfortable feeling, but Freya performed flawlessly.

With a sigh and a deep breath, Patty engaged the autopilot. Both ships' thrusters fired synchronously, correcting their orientation by half a degree. The main engines idled for ten seconds before hot plasma flared; point zero one gee gradually increased to point seven five gees. They held that thrust for ten seconds and then cut it to nothing. Another sigh coursed through Patty. Her hands had been hovering over the manual overrides waiting for the worst to happen. She shook out the tension in her arms and hands and took another slow deep breath.

"Was that it?" Cicely sounded disappointed.

"Well, we do have one mid-course correction in about half an hour, and then there's the retro burn when we get to Jaswinder."

"Geez, the way you had us seal up and strap down, Eg thought we was gonna, like, blast away." Cicely made a whooshing noise, as her hand made a swooping arc. Patty could not stifle the laugh that bubbled up.

"Better to be safe than sorry," Patty said. "Ships only whoosh away like that in the features." Cicely was disappointed and made a cute little pout. "Caution's served me well, so far."

"I guess," Cicely sighed.

Patty could not help but be on edge for the mid-course correction and the turnover maneuver that spun both ships one hundred and eighty degrees. She could not relax, not until the umbilical was disconnected and Freya was independent once more.

CHAPTER ELEVEN

Jaswinder was just where she was supposed to be. Jai was waiting for them on the hull above the ship's bridge, performing a weightless kata - more martial art than fencing. He thrust the practice blade into his belt and signaled them to follow. Cold gas burst from his suit and Jai spiraled down Jaswinder's irregular hull. Patty swung wide and saw a large opening on the ship's side. Inside were racks of tools and a workbench. Madhur slowly extended a landing platform.

Jai floated up beside Freya and pressed his visor to the canopy. "Dock her to the platform, and I'll unplug you," he shouted. Patty could only hear a thin trickle of sound, but it was enough. "We'll bring the CRV in on a cradle; then you can dock over there and board through the workshop with the rest of us. Okay?" Patty gave him a thumbs-up. He jetted up and away, superhero-style, one arm extended. Patty had to smile. For now, Jai's adventure was fun. She hoped it would stay that way.

Landing the Griffin took care, but it was not too complicated. The display showed that the landing gear had a clean lock, so Patty shut Griffin's flight computer down and logged out.

"Cicely, that is Jai and his aunt, Madhur," she told them. "They're going to bring Griffin into the workshop, and then I'll dock Freya and join you. Okay?"

"Sure," Cicely frowned at the oddly built ship.

"Now log off, and Jai will disconnect the umbilical. I'll see you inside."

"Bye," Cicely chirped and logged out.

Patty waited until Jai floated into view, coiling the umbilical. A gentle puff from Freya's thrusters lifted them slowly away, and Patty rolled Freya over so she could watch Madhur and Jai load Griffin into the workshop. The stress Patty carried in her shoulders slowly ebbed away. Although she was usually relaxed about flying Freya, the joined craft linked by just the umbilical and some intelligent software, was an accident waiting to happen.

"Okay, li'l bro', all sealed up?" Patty asked as she cast a quick eye over Alan. He nodded, and Patty brought Freya onto the extended platform in one swift maneuver. The landing gear locked into place and Patty cycled to vacuum.

The cluttered workshop took long minutes to pressurize, and there was little to do but wait until it was breathable. Patty watched Madhur examining Griffin. She went over the racing CRV centimeter-by-centimeter with reverence, her gloved hands caressing the flashy racer. The red flashing light over the workshop's external door changed to a constant green, so Patty removed her gloves and opened her visor. Griffin's canopy opened, and Cicely floated up from the pilot's seat with her brother's hand clasped firmly in hers.

"Thanks, Patty," she chirped, "and thank you Madhur."

"Madhur, Jai, this is Cicely and her twin, Egbert," Patty introduced them. "And this is my brother, Alan."

"Pleased to meet you. Glad we could help," Madhur replied. "Now let's get Ken out."

"You know our brother?" Cicely asked.

"Only by reputation," Madhur replied with a wink. "Ken's one hot pilot. Let's get him into the lounge." Madhur gripped one of Ken's arms and glanced at Patty. "Gizza hand." Ken was stuck tight, compressed in the small rear section and it took some firm but gentle persuasion to release him. Once freed, Madhur took the lead, floating the unconscious pilot from the workshop, through an internal airlock, a corridor with sealed doors on all sides, and into the lounge.

"Jai, get the first aid kit," Madhur told her nephew, and Patty helped her strip the gaudy p-suit from the unconscious pilot. The left side of his face was one ugly purple bruise, and his right arm bent in too many places.

"That's nasty," Patty muttered. The way it moved made her feel queasy.

"What happened?" Madhur asked Cicely as they strapped Ken into one of the functioning acceleration couches. Cicely, with Egbert in hand, slid to the side of the seat and brushed Ken's long brown fringe back from his eyes.

"We were on OASIS visiting," Cicely began. "Mom and Dad are so proud of Ken; we try to see him before his races. There was supposed to be one this weekend." Her lower lip quivered, and she blinked tears away. "When we heard there were aliens on OASIS, everyone thought it was a joke. Someone turned on the Pic-Wall, and there was their ship. Dad and Ken decided we should get out of there, to try and get home." She sighed again. "The corridors were ... really scary. People were shouting, and screaming, and trying to run and lifting off the floor, floating free."

"Yeah, I was there," Madhur comforted her. "It was a bloody nightmare." Jai jetted in and handed her the first aid kit. "I'm not a trained medic, but I'll be able to secure his arm for the moment. He'll need a doctor to set it properly," she added and began to bandage Ken's arm.

"We were heading for the team workshops," Cicely continued, "so Kenny could get his p-suit and aliens appeared. They used these long white lumpy staffs. Eg says they're using focused sonic pulses. Whatever it was, if someone got shot, they went down and stayed down. The man next to Dad got shot. Mom and Dad got tangled up with him. Dad shouted to Kenny to get us out, and that was the last we saw of them." Tears spilled from her eyes, drifting away as tiny undulating bubbles. Patty floated to her side and wrapped her arms around the little girl. And they both began to sob. Patty had been holding her tears at bay for so long, and Cicely's distress cracked her emotional discipline.

"I know, I've lost my parents too." Patty gasped for breath and cried - for her brother, for her parents, for her friends, for her life that had been stripped away.

Cicely took a deep breath and wiped at her eyes. "Anyway, we got to the workshop, well, just outside, when an alien shot Kenny. We dragged him inside and locked the door. He woke up, and we got him into his p-suit, and to the garage. He kept drifting in and out, but we got Griffin fueled and ready. Kenny flew out of the garage with me and Eg in the back. We went real fast, but Kenny couldn't fly properly with his arm and his head aching, so once we were clear, he started to program our flight home, to L3. He kept drifting off, so we swapped over and Eg and I finished it off for him," she hiccupped. "Is he going to be okay?"

"I hope so, honey. We need to get him to a doctor," Madhur frowned. "The closest doctor's on L3, but they're buttoned up tight."

"Eg and I were going to go to L5. Uncle Stan's going to be there," Cicely insisted. "Eg says we can get help there."

"Yes, well, I'm planning to head for L4," Madhur countered. "I doubt it's held up better than L3, but it's my home, and I must check it out, and the trip to L4 is shorter. Patty? What do you think?"

"Well, I want to find my folks, and I know they were boosting into orbit before the aliens arrived, they could be anywhere," Patty answered. "They could be at L3," she added with a sigh.

"Yeah, but I doubt even your ship could get close enough to find out," Madhur replied. "Come with us. I can secure Freya to this ol' tub. You're a good pilot with a level head on your shoulders. We should stick together."

"We should go to L5," Cicely insisted again. Madhur nodded, but her expression said she had not changed her mind. "No really, they've got supplies and everything there."

"They've got all that and more at L4," Madhur said firmly.

L4, L5, Patty did not know which was the better choice, but she knew she wanted to stay with Madhur and Jai, at least for a while. As much as Patty loved Freya, the small ship was cramped. "Sorry Cicely, but I think it's best if we stay with Madhur," Patty told her, and the young girl pouted, and wriggled her shoulders, breaking free from Patty's embrace.

"It's all right, Eg," she said to her brother, "adults never listen to us kids. We can't make rational decisions," she complained. "We're too young to know what's going on."

"We'll be safer together," Patty said, trying to sound convincing. "Besides, if we can't rendezvous with L4, we will have to try L5."

"It'll be too late by then," Cicely said.

"Why?" Patty asked.

"Dunno. That's just what Eg says," Cicely replied with a shrug

Patty looked at Madhur and shrugged too. "Well Egbert, I'm sorry we have to go the long way around, but we do need to check out what's happening at L4."

"If you have to, I guess you have to." Cicely was noticeably unhappy with the decision but seemed resigned to it.

"Well then, let's get Freya locked down," Madhur enthused and smiled at the little blond, ruffling her hair, "then you can help me plot a course."

ONE LAST MOMENT

"Do you have my mel'andrin in a safe place?" Del'armorun asked. It was getting harder for her to breathe but she had to be sure before the end came.

"Yes, GreatMother. Your will, GreatMother," someone reassured her. It was Tel'sars' words, but it was not Tel'sars' voice. The striations on his face were different. Del'armorun knew who it was now. Dan'thel had received mel'andrin from Tel'sars and recently.

"He is well?" she asked.

"GreatMother, Tel'sars is well, but not strong enough to travel. This one feels the anguish of Tel'sars' separation, GreatMother."

"Diets! Mothers must have a good diet" she insisted. "They must be strong and bare strong children, and then another GreatMother will come. Do you understand?" *Have I made enough changes? Will they last?* Bright Hope struggled for another breath. "Do you understand?" It was too late to do anymore even though so much was left undone.

"You've done enough, GreatMother." The memory of Tel'sars' croaking voice and his bright eyes helped Bright Hope let go and embrace the gentle dark. It was time to rest.

CHAPTER TWELVE

The last piece of poached salmon nestled against half a cherry tomato. The cracked plate did not detract from their beauty. Patty toyed with them, coating them in the last of the mustard sauce. Everyone else had gulped down their dinner and was most of the way through dessert, but Patty wanted to savor hers. *Salmon. Will I ever have the chance to eat salmon again? And strawberries.* Half a strawberry sat atop a tablespoon of vanilla ice cream, scooped into a plastic mug. She was going to make her dessert last too. *Thank you again, Giuseppe.*

"Are you sure you're going to eat that?" Jai asked again as if she was going to change her mind between bites.

"Most certainly. Get your eyes off it. Don't even think about it young man," Patty berated him lightly. His cheeky attitude reminded her of the old Alan. Jai blushed and looked down while he wiped the last of his ice cream from his cup with his index finger. He brought his finger to his mouth and sucked it clean.

"Oh please!" Madhur laughed. "You've got such a crush!"

Jai stiffened, and his flushed face grew redder. "Have not."

"Have too," Madhur teased. Patty enjoyed the feeling of family even if she was the center of Jai's discomfort.

"Have not. It's ... it's just a bit of hero worship." Jai could hold his own with his aunt. He looked across at Ken strapped in the acceleration couch. "At least my hero's awake," he teased. Now it was Madhur's turn to blush.

"You know why we were ready for you?" Jai asked, but he didn't wait for an answer. "My mad auntie Mad recognized Griffin's transponder ID. Big fan. Didn't you see the G.A.V.

posters in the workshop? At least my hero's a dyed-in-the-wool, bona fide, save-you-in-the-nick-of-time hero, not some overpaid, glorified sky jockey with quick reflexes."

"Don't knock quick reflexes, Jai," Patty chuckled even as she felt herself blush too. "Hero? No, not me."

"Oh, you are, even putting your rescue of Kerr to one side, getting your brother out of the clutches of the evil aliens," Jai emphasized the last phrase as if it were the pitch line for a science fiction feature, "was damned heroic on anyone's scale. And I've downloaded so much stuff from your pin/camera/scanner thingy. Getting that much intel on the aliens is a coup and a half. I mean, take that machine thingy in the center of the shopping mall."

"Didn't see much actual shopping if I recall," Patty said.

Jai continued, waving away her interruption, "The scanner picked up some odd extra stuff." He turned from the table and sprang over to an old display mounted to one wall.

Cicely looked up from the sticky remains of her ice cream, pouted, and looked at Patty's dessert enviously for a second before grinning. "That was nice. Are you sure there isn't anymore?"

"I mean, look here," Jai said jabbing at the screen as he displayed a sequence. The pictures were jerky, but Patty could see the brown alien with the golden one in its arms and the mass of dark and light bodies parading past. Jai slowed the flow of images, stepping them forward until he had a clear frame. "This is the visible light, the default display, but there is a whole mess of data that can be overlaid." Jai did something to the display, and it changed to a green-hued monochromic picture. "Infrared." The steam boiler stood out brighter than anything else in the image, and hidden details from the aliens' shadowed features became visible. Jai flicked through a few more display variations, ultraviolet, microwave, radio, and there was even a display mode that showed a small gamma-ray leak from the tokamak.

"This is what I can't figure out," Jai said as he reconfigured the display once more. A horizontal slash of light appeared on the screen emanating from the device encased in the transparent box. The beam cut through aliens, supporting columns, everything as if they were not there.

"Phased gravitons," Cicely said. Patty turned and looked at the girl. She was poised with her hand hovering over Patty's dessert, one finger laden with ice cream. *At least she left me the strawberry.* Cicely blinked and stared at her twin. Egbert stood away from the table, pulling Cicely with him. She stuffed the ice cream into her mouth as her brother dragged her to the screen.

"I think twins can be pretty weird, but these two take the cake," Madhur whispered. She glanced down at Patty's pilfered dessert and chuckled. "I reckon she sees for him. I watched him eating; didn't miss a speck, his plate's as clean as mine. Telepathic twins." She shook her head in wonder.

"I'm not so sure," Patty replied. "They could be using some kind of sign language; subtle signals transferred from hand to hand."

"I guess that would be easier," Madhur smiled crookedly. "So. You still thinking of scooting past L4 for a recce?" Madhur asked.

"Fuel's at a premium, you know it. I can get in, find out if it's safe, or not, and get back without being noticed, I'm sure. Jaswinder, well, she's slow and sticks out like a sore thumb."

"I was hoping to see her with my own eyes, but you're right," Madhur admitted with a frown. "You should get some sack time before your flight."

"I can doze pretty well in Freya, but I wouldn't mind stretching out for a bit," Patty replied. Just thinking about sleep brought a realm of confined spaces and twisted creatures bubbling through Patty's mind. She was going to have nightmares again, but the chance to sleep was still precious.

A pain-filled groan from the acceleration couch brought Patty and Madhur to their feet. The pilot's eyes flickered open. "Where..." Kenny groaned again and then cried out when he tried to move his broken arm. "Oh crap. What's happ..." Patty pushed away from the floor but was cut off by the twins.

Cicely squealed with delight. "Kenny! Kenny, you're awake! You're awake!"

"Whoa, li'l pumpkin, tone it down a notch. My head's still thumping," Ken replied with a grimace.

"This is Madhur and Patty and Jai and Alan. Patty rescued us," Cicely toned it down to a loud stage whisper. "This is Madhur's ship."

"How are you feeling?" Madhur asked. "Your arm's busted up pretty good, don't know about your head though." Patty floated back to the table, picked up a bulb of water, and brought it to their patient. Cicely took it from Patty and slipped the sipper into Ken's mouth.

"Thanks," he said wearily after draining half of the bulb. For the first time, his blue eyes swept around the room acknowledging those gathered around him. "Thanks to all of you."

"Couldn't very well let you hang out there," Patty told him. "These two were plotting a course to Achernar." Patty gave Cicely a nudge and a smile. Ken was a handsome man, but that was a given. You could not get within hailing distance of a racing team like G.A.V. without passing inspection by the ugly police.

"Were not," Cicely poked the tip of her tongue out at Patty. "We were going to take Griffin to L5 to find Uncle Stan, and we would have got there too."

"Yeah, but we'd be dead when we arrived. Not enough oxygen," said Ken wearily. "Griffin's a racer, not much more than an engine and a seat. No room for frivolous extras like oxygen." Ken's chuckle turned into a racking cough and a groan as he moved his arm again. "Where are we headed then?" he asked when he regained his breath.

"We've programmed a wide pass of L4, and Patty's going to take her CRV in close for a peek," Madhur replied.

Ken's eyes snapped to Patty. "I thought I recognized you," he said. "They bumped me from *The Tonight Show* for you." He did not look offended, but Patty felt she had to apologize anyway.

"Sorry." She could feel her color rise.

"No need, no need. I've done my fair share of talk shows. And it gave Ma, Pa, and these two little freaks the chance to catch up with me." Ken turned a worried face to Madhur. "Is it bad out there?"

"Couldn't be much worse," Madhur replied with a frown of her own. "L1 is trashed, Tycho City is locked down, same goes for the Tritium mines. OASIS, well I guess you know about OASIS. L3 is still holding out."

"And I always thought funding gun maintenance was a waste of money," Ken sighed.

"Yeah," Madhur agreed. "Who knew."

"The paranoid old timers knew. Bless 'em." Ken kept his chuckle deliberately restrained to a quiet chuff, chuff.

CHAPTER THIRTEEN

After navigating through four hours of claustrophobic dreams, Patty felt surprisingly refreshed and stretched against her seat's restraints. Freya's controls were all in the green, and the stars were bright. *Ken called me Patta-Hari before we left. Super Spy!* Patty chortled and had to admit Griffin's pilot was not just a winning smile for Corporates to hang their logos on. He had watched Jai's bookmarked highlights of her journey through the alien ship. *I don't know about being a spy. I like being a scout though.* He helped Patty plot Freya's course to avoid occluding the brightest areas of the Milky Way and had grinned with that perfect smile and those blue eyes while telling her that he stole the idea from one of his father's old science fiction books. While it was unlikely the aliens' radar would find her, there was still a chance Freya's silhouette might be seen occluding the stars.

Now two new factors influenced Patty flight path: there were two transponder beacons with emergency prefixes, one on the near side of L4 and one over five kilometers away on the far side. Two distressed ships so close to the station was not a good sign.

Patty slowed Freya as she approached the coordinates of the first transponder. She had difficulty spotting the ship even with her new camera, and as she flew closer, it became clearer that there was little of the ship remaining. Patty had to maneuver Freya around an expanding debris field. The transponder still signaled, probably from its internal power supply, but there was not enough structure remaining around it to be called a ship. Patty was glad she could not recognize any of the debris as bodies, though she was sure they were out there, tumbling through the cold vacuum.

Encrypted chatter with the alien's formatting leaked from the space station and the closer Patty came to L4 the clearer it was that the invaders were in control. *Madhur's going to be disappointed.* The planar space station spread out in five wings, radiating from a central hub. L4 had many industries, but the core business was shipbuilding. Freya had been built on L4. Slipways and docking arms dominated L4's outline. From a distance, it bristled.

Focusing her sighting camera on the space station, Patty began recording the disposition of the alien spacecraft. It was not worthwhile getting closer. A dozen fighters held defensive positions around L4, although who they were defending against was anyone's guess. Humanity had nothing to strike back with. Blocky transport ships crowded around the docks and aliens with their distinctive sideways shuffle scurried over the spacecraft under construction in the brightly lit shipyards. Two new keels were being laid out in vacant slipways.

Don't waste any time, do they? Patty made a slight course adjustment that would rendezvous Freya with the second emergency beacon. She did not hold much hope that there would be survivors, but as much as she wanted to rejoin Jaswinder, she could not ignore the signal.

The hair on the back of Patty's neck stood up when she recognized the ship; it was the dilapidated old Singer she had docked next to on OASIS. Lights were on in the cockpit, but she could not see any movement within. Patty spun Freya around and fired her main engines to bring her to a complete stop relative to the Singer. It did not look good; the CRV's canopy was open. Patty flashed her landing lights, and the Singer's pilot nearly leaped from the seat.

"Looks like we got a live one, Alan," Patty chuckled. "Seal up, crewman." She unbuckled her restraints and checked on her brother. He sealed his Zip-Lok and gave her a nod and a thumbs-up. Patty gave his seals a quick check and returned his bow before cycling the air from the cockpit.

By the time vacuum replaced air, the Singer's pilot had jetted over. Patty's comm lit up, but she did not respond to the transmission. She opened the canopy and blinked as she recognized the person clinging to her ship, Cian Kerr. A laugh percolated up her throat as Patty waved to him. She could see his mouth moving, and she held up her hands urging him to wait a moment. In one compartment, Patty found an umbilical that could connect Cian directly to Freya's comm.

"Patty Balke! Fancy meeting you here!" Cian's excited voice broke through the moment he plugged in.

"Fancy," Patty replied with as much sarcasm as she could muster. "The Singer's a bit of a comedown for you, isn't it?"

"Best I could get at the time." Cian shrugged and had to correct his rotation with a burst from his thruster as he floated off Freya's starboard side.

"Your transponder's broadcasting an emergency prefix. Are you okay?" Patty asked.

"Well, if your interpretation of okay means being almost out of fuel and down to an hour of oxygen then sure, I'm okay," Cian replied with a silly grin. "Damn, it's good to see you." He looked over Freya. "Got yourself a new paint job, I see. It's a little ... somber."

"EM absorbent. Keeps the aliens off my back," Patty replied casually. "So, what are you doing out here?"

"Long story, but the short version is I was waiting for the last moment before heading in to surrender," he confessed.

"Well, I think you should avoid that if you can," Patty advised.

"That was my hope. Looks like your back seat's taken," he noted dryly. "Is that your brother? Hi Alan." Alan did not reply, but Cian did not seem to care.

"I've an umbilical I can use to transfer some fuel and O^2 to your ship, and we can get out of here, but first you've got to get rid of that transponder," Patty instructed

"Err, good idea." Cian nodded. "Gizz the cable and I'll hook us up." He took the umbilical Patty passed to him and set about linking the two ships together. While Cian worked on extracting the transponder, Patty logged into the Singer's systems and began calculating how much Tritium he would need.

"So, Patty, where we off to?" Cian asked via the umbilical link.

"Jaswinder's making a wide pass of L4," Patty began.

"Sanjaya's Jaswinder?" Cian cut Patty off.

"Is there another Jaswinder?" she inquired.

"Not that I'm aware of."

"Do you have a problem with Madhur?" Patty asked.

"Not as such, she has a problem with me," Cian grumbled. "Thinks I'm a useless pilot who's not serious about flying. She's probably right."

"Don't worry. You're not Madhur's only guest." Patty sent the command to Freya's fuel pumps, and they began transferring Tritium to the Singer's tank.

"She won't like it," Cian muttered.

"She'll cope," Patty told him and set-up the rendezvous course on the Singer's version of a flight computer if you could call it that. If Freya was seat-of-the-pants flying, the Singer was completely bare bones.

"She's a bit primitive," Patty commented.

"What you talking about?" Cian protested. "Hunter's a gem."

"Hunter? Is that her name?" Hunter. Patty had to chuckle; the CRV was in such poor shape she was more prey than Hunter.

"Yeah, Hunter, as in Alberta Hunter. She was a twentieth-century jazz singer," Cian said with a straight face. Patty groaned. "She's not as bad as she looks," Cian added. "She leaks like a sieve, and I doubt she'd cope with a re-entry without a burn-through or two, but her engine is top shelf. Cian extracted himself from his head-down-feet-up orientation in Hunter's cockpit and steadied himself on the canopy before throwing a small device towards the sun.

"I'll take your word on that," Patty said, disbelief colored her reply.

"Just you watch; she won't miss a beat. Guaranteed," Cian insisted.

"It's your life."

"Patty?" Cain asked.

"Yeah?"

"That's two I owe you," he told her.

"Well, you just keep your skin intact so you can pay off, I'm bound to need rescuing any day now." The fuel transfer finished. "We should get going. Remember, radio silence, especially when we rendez with Jaswinder."

"Yes, ma'am," Cian replied. He disconnected the two ships, flew back with the umbilical and saluted her smartly.

Patty maneuvered Freya to hide Hunter's plasma flare as they boosted away from the alien-occupied L4 station. *Are our parents there?* Patty wished she had a deity she could pray to. The closest thing to a god in Patty's life was her observance of Murphy's Law. With all her heart, she prayed to the hostile universe that her parents were not down there.

THE INVADER

The pictures were grainy, but the two humans were recognizable in every shot, one small, a child, and the other, almost at maturity, or so Er'men had been told. Their bloody exit from Tal'anis both excited and disturbed her. To have a human enter and leave Tal'anis almost without detection sent RegentFirstMother Harrum'Bar into a spiteful frenzy as she hunted for someone to blame. *I blame your complacency, FirstMother. The reports from the listening station beyond the moon should have warned you.*

She stacked the pictures into a neat pile on the hand-carved and gilded side table and turned to the video monitor and its unwieldy playback equipment. The hard lines and looping wires of these technologies looked incongruous alongside the ornately carved decorations in the foyer of the GreatMother's suite, but the customized power and data cables would reach no further. *The GreatMother's accommodations are long overdue for a refit.*

"She fights well. Don't you think, Genedalt?" Er'men prodded her companion. The footage from the security camera played on a loop from the moment the door opened, and the two humans entered the preparatory room, to when they fought their way out of the airlock. *That's not quite without detection, but how she arrived on* Tal'anis, *and how they left are still a mystery.*

The video had her chief protector's complete attention. Genedalt, Bumurnam Sept's FirstSon, was almost stationary, but Er'men could see minute movements in his shoulders and arms as he followed the action on the screen. The recording had the focus of most of the Hel'omi gathered around them. The foyer was not the ideal place to watch the screen, and her Hel'omi guards could not resist looking at the moving pictures. Few Hel'omi ever entered the security/maintenance control rooms and had rarely witnessed the playback technologies. Er'men did not mind them gawping; the Hel'omi led insular lives when there was no GreatMother for them to nurture. The vestibule was abuzz with excitement.

Genedalt pulled back from the screen. "GreatMother, that one is quick. The human blade is fast and subtle, dangerous where it appears weak." He gave an involuntary bow to the human's prowess. "That one moves with the grace of a GreatMother."

The human was LeftLeading and anatomically female, but her advisers said humans did not have GreatMothers. Human LeftLeaders, while in the minority, were not appreciably different to their RightLeading cousins. *Or were they?* Er'men was so excited she danced on the spot. *Oh, I wish I could meet her.*

CHAPTER FOURTEEN

Pounding, pounding, pounding. Jake choked on his dry mouth and cringed away from the bright lights. He was restrained. The bonds wrapped around him held him immobile, and helpless. If this was to be an interrogation, Jake knew he was in a bad way right from the very start; he would tell them whatever they wanted. There were voices, but Jake could not understand a word. A hand fell on his shoulder, and Jake flinched.

"Would you like some water?" The voice was familiar, a woman's voice. Jake tried to open his eyes, but a warm hand with soft skin swept gently down over his forehead and kept them closed. "No, no, just stay still. Drink." A water bulb's sipper touched Jake's lips, and he sucked it into his mouth. The water tasted flat, recycled, but Jake could feel his whole body respond. The pounding receded a little. Jake drained the bulb.

"That's better. What do you remember today?" she asked.

Remember? Today? Jake struggled with his pounding head. There were memories in there, but they were disjointed. His father waving from the ground as Jake flew overhead in his first ultralight was mashed together with his first atmospheric re-entry in a Mark Four shuttle. Running OASIS Traffic control on a busy day was blended with landing The Tennyson while he was crammed into the service locker because the cockpit was breached and sealed off. The sweet smell of the sea and the friendly faces gathered around The Tennyson, aground on Takapuna Beach, mixed with the angry mob in Aldrin Plaza. Crowded corridors aboard OASIS vied with dark crawl spaces. A revolver in a Zip-Lok bag spat fire.

"Maya!" Jake tried to sit up. The Velcro holding the sleep sack closed gave a little.

"She's not here. Neither are Madeline or Missy," the woman told him.

Jake blinked open his eyes. The sun shone through thick palm tree leaves. Someone had drawn a smiley-face on it. *A Pic-Wall.* Jake tried to focus on the woman with mousy-brown hair, cut short, kneeling beside him. She had a bruise on her left eye and a split lip. A name circulated through his head but refused to alight on his tongue. Jake squinted against the bright room. People were moving, and the sound of children buffeted his over-sensitive ears.

"Eva, Eva Trent, I work at Shadrak's, or used to," she introduced herself.

Suddenly Jake's memories slammed back into some order, his head reverberating with pain: OASIS, asteroids, aliens, a failed escape attempt. "How long?" Jake wormed an arm out of the constricting blanket and rubbed his chin.

"Don't know exactly. We don't have access to much information here, but it's probably about three days since the aliens came," Eva informed him. The stubble on his chin confirmed Eva's estimation.

"Where's here?" Jake asked.

"We're in the East Wing hostel. They put the injured men with expectant women and women with infants." Eva rubbed the barely noticeable bulge of her belly. "Not that we can do much with them, they haven't given us any medical supplies."

"You're a nurse?"

"I did a little training but flunked out. We have two women in here with their certificates. Jeana said you had a concussion and had to be watched. You've woken up three or four times before but not for long. Stay put. I'll be back in a second." Eva pushed off and sailed along the row of hammocks, getting the attention of a dark-haired woman breastfeeding a baby. They spoke for a moment or two before Eva moved away and out of sight.

Jake closed his eyes. *Oh Maya, what did I lead you into? Where did you get that canon of a sidearm? And Madeline and Missy.* He shuddered to think about what they were enduring. *What do you do when you're taken prisoner by alien invaders?* It was not something a rational person made plans for. Securing a ship was the critical step and getting out from underfoot. *An officer has a duty to escape. You're not an officer now but leaving sounds like a bloody good idea.* Jake tried to remember the layout of the East Wing hostel, but his pounding brain would not let him sort his thoughts.

"Awake again, are we?" he was asked. Jake smelt milk and blinked his eyes open. The brunette Eva had spoken to floated beside his hammock, her baby tucked in close, sleeping in a papoose strung across her chest. Her warm but firm hand grabbed his chin. "Hold still." A light flashed into his right eye and away, back again, and then the left. "Better. How's the head?"

"About Richter scale 9 with a force five hurricane thrown in for good measure," Jake replied with a wince.

"Name?" she asked.

"Jacob Aloysius Chowdhury, age sixty-two, SoCred 05-20539-0622," Jake responded.

"Good to meet you, Jacob, I'm Gale, and this is Tobias. I think you're back with us," she said but did not look too happy about that.

"What's the matter? You'd prefer I stayed unconscious?" Jake teased. He did not like seeing unhappy women. The universe was a much nicer place when women smiled. His line did not provoke even a flicker.

"They take the men that get better," Gale replied. "You're not the only one I've seen with head injuries, but they singled you out. You're a wanted man. A Gray came in yesterday and compared your face to a printout. They want *you*." A grin flickered across her face. "What you do to piss 'em off?" Gale asked.

"Sorry, can't help you there. I was busy trying to get off OASIS and caught a dose from some kind of magic wand."

"White? 'Bout this long?" Gale's hands spread about a meter

apart. She frowned, "Been a lot of that about."

"I was trying to help Maya Swati and her daughter escape."

Gale shook her head. "Sorry, you were here when I arrived. I haven't seen them." She looked over her shoulder at the security camera in the corner and back to him. "Now that you're awake it shouldn't be too long until they come for you. I'm sorry, I can't do much more. Don't fight them when they come. It always ends badly."

"Thanks for the heads up," Jake told her and put on his best understanding smile. "I'm an old dog with more than a few good bites left in him, but I don't feel like cracking my teeth against armor. When you're up against a big guy, you use your head not your fists."

Eva came over with a steaming bulb cradled in a hand towel. "Don't know what's in it but it will fill the gap if you're feeling hungry."

Jake took a second to see if he felt hungry; his pounding head was drowning out his body's other complaints. He needed the bathroom, but that could wait. "Yes please." Jake caught hold of the sleep sack's tab and ripped it open to free his left arm. The covering flipped back, exposing him to the knees. "Oh! Sorry ladies." Jake could feel his face radiating as he struggled to cover his nakedness. Gale and Eva looked at each other and exchanged smirks.

"You *are* better. Stay that way," Gale told him before she floated off. Eva kept her smirk and extended the steaming bulb when he was presentable once more. Jake took a cautious sip; it was an anonymous broth that needed salt.

"They took all our clothes, but we found these shipsuits in a locker and kicked up a fuss when they tried it again." Eva looked proud. "The solidarity of sisterhood stood toe to toe with the Galactic Overlords and prevailed." Her smirk took on a rueful attitude. "Gale told you about the Gray picking you out?" she asked. Now she was serious, even afraid.

"Yeah, but I'm not sure what she meant. Gray?" he inquired.

"There're two types, ones with mottled light brown hides,

and pale, almost gray ones. The Grays are shorter and are in charge; the brown ones are muscle, lots of it."

Jake's mind flashed back to the security cam images of Aldrin Plaza and the short p-suited alien, the last to cycle through the lock. No telling what it looked like under its p-suit, let alone the color of its skin.

"What do you think they want?" she asked.

"With me? No idea. Perhaps they want Traffic Control turned on. I didn't do a very good job of sabotage when I shut it down. It shouldn't take too long to get it running again. Apart from that, I can't imagine why they'd want me." Jake sucked up the last of the broth and handed the bulb back to Eva. "Is there a spare shipsuit? I do need the bathroom."

"Nah, but they did leave these. Hang on." Eva reached below his hammock, pulled out a folded gray cloth and shook it free. It was oblong with a hole cut from the center and a large blue dot printed in the middle of one side, a poncho of sorts. "They're a bit revealing," she said with her smirk returning, "but better than nothing." Eva helped him extricate himself from the sleep sack and into the poncho; his head added a nauseating swirl that threatened to have him revisit the broth. Jake clamped his jaw shut as she showed him to where he could freshen up.

Hygienic bathroom facilities are the hallmark of a civilized society. Jake felt clean and almost fresh except for the stubble on his chin. Handling his body's excretory requirements had priority; five minutes with a sonic scrubber came next. The essentials completed, Jake felt almost human. Now his cheeks itched. He resisted the urge to scratch. Just.

Jake was halfway through a second bulb of broth when the aliens came. Eva's simple description of big browns and small grays did not do them justice. Despite their sideways walk and twisted, lopsided bodies, they moved with purpose and not a little grace. The big guards especially made no false moves. They came straight for him, a flying wedge protecting the Gray from defenseless women and children. Jake kept his eyes down and attempted to finish his broth.

"O-A-SIS Tra," rumble, "fic Control." The Gray had a face squashed sideways; its black eyes sparkled.

Jake tried to look unconcerned as he finished the broth and looked up. "Clever," he muttered. They knew who he was. Jake tried to ignore the looming pair and their white staffs and concentrated on the Gray. Earth's diverse biosphere had evolved some strange creatures, but the asymmetry of these beings offended even Jake's eclectic tastes.

The Gray's poncho was another thing altogether. It was a hand-stitched work of art. Intricate embroidery graced the pale blue embossed material. Symbols and stylized creatures flowed across the garment in waves. From beneath the poncho, the Gray produced a flat picture in his smaller, right hand. Jake took the proffered image. It was grainy, but Jake could recognize his face and the face of his companion.

"OASIS Traaafic control," rumble, "knows this one." Its gray finger tapped on the face of the young woman. Of course, he knew who she was. He also knew where the picture had been taken, the East Chandra docks, barely twenty minutes before the brief battle in LEO. Patty Balke. Her brother was a bright blur in the background. *Why do they want to know about Patty?*

"This one has other," rumble, "pictures."

"Hope they're better than this one. It's not my good side." Jake kept a straight face.

The Gray bobbed a little. *Did that mean he was confused?* His right hand made a couple of hesitant gestures. "OASIS Traaaaffic Control," rum-rumble, "comes with this one." It turned on the spot. Half its escort turned as one and followed it from the room. Six soldiers remained.

"Mo-ove hu-uman," the one to Jake's left boomed. The white staff rose. Jake examined the arm that wielded the weapon. It was polished shiny brown interrupted by pale yellow and purple, a perfect camouflage for the open planes. What drew Jake's eyes were the etchings carved into the burnished surface of its forearms. *Much more intricate than its simple poncho. Self-decoration?* Jake wondered. *Someone has time on their hands.* And there were nicks and scrapes. This forearm had seen more action than just an engraver's needle.

"Yes. Of course." Jake stood, avoiding the alien's grasping hand. "After you."

"Move." The knobbly tip of its white staff jabbed, and Jake skipped forward.

"You know that's so clichéd," Jake complained. He caught Eva's eye and winked as he pushed off towards the door. Her lips said, "good luck" but he did not hear her. The guards grabbed his shoulders and pressed him down to the deck. A pair of gecko-grip stick-ons was thrust at him.

"Don't like flying, eh boys?" he asked, but there was no response as Jake stuck a pad to his left foot. "Like to keep your feet on the ground?" and then his right. Walking in zero-gee was stupid.

The white staff swung towards him again. "Move!"

CHAPTER FIFTEEN

OASIS's broad rose and slate hallways were quiet and looked distinctly shabby. The usual flow of tourists, Corporates and residents hid the stains and the scuffed and chipped surfaces. Jake had never seen OASIS like this. She looked tatty; the cafes were empty, and the shops were deserted. It was a ghost town. Between the hostel and OASIS HQ, Jake saw only a handful of humans, in gray ponchos like his, being shepherded towards the docks. The guard behind Jake prodded him with its staff. The jolt kept Jake moving, but it did not stop him observing. *Where was everyone? OASIS had been packed to the gunnels with refugees. Were they all locked away or had they been led off like those poor sods?*

Soldiers stood guard at every intersection and approximately every five meters along the corridor, outnumbering the Grays by a factor of ten or more to one. There were maintenance panels off everywhere with the smaller aliens examining everything inside. The Grays behaved more like scientists or engineers, and the big aliens were all soldiers. *Have they been bred for their roles?* Jake pondered as they marched on.

OASIS HQ dominated one corner of Central Square, which was neither the center of OASIS's irregular sprawl nor particularly square. It was more a flattened octagonal with four major and four minor corridors opening out into the two-story plaza. It was ominously quiet. Two humongous aliens, nearly half the size again of the regularly over-large invaders, stood guard at OASIS HQ's revolving doors. Their ponchos displayed elements of all the hues and were the most sophisticated of the alien designs, though not quite at the level of the Grays. *Hierarchical layers?* Given enough time, Jake was sure he would be able to categorize the aliens into different tribes or castes, or however they split themselves up. *Know your enemy*, Jake thought. He would have to confirm it, but he was pretty sure his escort had a simplified design reminiscent of the Gray that spoke to him. *Rank and phylum.* The colored ponchos were designed to be seen over large distances. *The same reason humans have flags - identification on the battlefield. The aliens are strange, but not that strange.*

Inside, the brown-soldier to gray-technocrat ratio shifted significantly; two to one at best. Suddenly a pattern popped into Jake's head. Colors. There were six distinct groups, one for each of the visible hues, violet/purple, blue, green, yellow, and red. *What were the chances that aliens used the same section of the electromagnetic spectrum to see with?* Jake wondered. Perhaps it was the best set of frequencies with which to observe the world. The saturation of the colors ranged from almost black to the palest of pastels, but the hues remained constant. *Where there are divisions, there will be tensions, but will we be able to exploit them?*

Jake's escort led him to an interview room. The lead soldier opened the door but did not enter. No one else was there, and the door closed solidly behind him. Three large cameras were mounted to the walls and provided overlapping coverage. *Someone - or should that be something - was watching.* He glanced at OASIS's unobtrusive security cameras tucked into the room's high corners and tried not to smile. *The invaders haven't managed to tap into OASIS's systems otherwise they would not need these clunky things.* A large table dominated the center of the room. There was no other furniture. *Where did they get the table? And why? These aliens cling tightly to their horizon and behave as if gravity is the norm. Is this the way a space-faring race acts?* Humans embraced zero-gee, modifying their bodies and lifestyles to adapt to an environment far more extensive than those at the bottom of a gravity-well.

Spread across the table was a collection of flat printouts. Most were from OASIS's security cameras. *Why were the aliens printing out pictures? Do they think paper grows on trees?* There was a Pic-Wall occupying one side of the room with the controls discreetly concealed behind a small panel. It looked undisturbed. *If the aliens had access to OASIS's security records, surely, they'd be able to pipe the feed into this room rather than wasting precious resources. Oh well.* Jake smiled to himself. He wasn't going to help them with OASIS's systems.

The printout pictures were why he was here, but they had nothing to do with OASIS's traffic control. Patty Balke was in every frame. *What have you done to get them riled up, sweety?* Jake wondered. There were two groups of pictures. The first collection was from OASIS's cameras, the second had a very different look-and-feel, the lenses were wider, and the colors were oddly muted. Jake was keen to examine them more closely, but because there were observers, he treated all the pictures with an equal amount of disinterest. One brief glance was all he allowed himself. *Patty! You've got 'em in a real twist.*

Jake had been surprised when Cynthia Balke pinged him last year. He'd never met her before, but she knew about him from the wartime propaganda, and from her husband. She was a smart lady but concerned about her daughter and her hot-off-the-press civilian re-entry license.

"Christopher recognized your voice while Patty was taking her examination," she told him. "I think he now understands a little better about what motivated you to resign. But..."

"But he couldn't bring himself to say it to my face," Jake responded with more venom than he intended.

"It was a hectic day. I'm sure he has plans to contact you... after all these years," Cynthia apologized.

All these years - since the war. Even after Jake's appeal had overturned his dishonorable discharge, it had been almost impossible to get a job. He had been the United Space Force's recruitment poster boy, but the Corporates wanted their revenge. He'd been blacklisted by the Corporations for having the audacity to resign in the middle of their war. *You don't go to war over an industrial dispute,* Jake grumbled. History had shown he had made the right decision, but being right did not help his job prospects; the Belters hated him, and he'd been lucky to get any work in orbit. Jake did not deny Christopher Balke was a hard worker, but it was easy when you have friends. *Corporate friends with deep pockets can be of enormous help.*

Despite her mother's concern, Patty had not needed any nursemaiding, not that he could see. She'd been the quietest of her boisterous teammates, she had a quick mind and was a good pilot who would only get better. If not for this invasion, he was sure she would have been tapped by one of the CRV racing teams, or the USF. After rescuing Cian in LEO, she would make a great poster girl at the recruiting stations. *Just like me when I landed The Tennyson.* Nightmares still pincered him between those equipment shelves as he piloted the ship remotely.

Jake peeled off the stick-ons and gently pushed away from the floor. With a subtle twist, he began to turn, revolving slowly. The gentle motion set Jake's mind at ease, and he could feel waves of relaxation roll through the tension in his neck and shoulders. It was not as good as a massage, but floating free in zero-gee was better than nothing. He flexed, adding a tumble to his rotation, presenting his feet, rather than his head, to the approaching wall. He landed and pushed off again, making a slow pirouette back across the room.

What do they want from me? There was only one answer, information. They want to know about Patty. Disinformation. How much truth and how much spin can I afford to use? Jake wondered. Who do they think she is? That depends on what she's done, I guess. Jake was busting to tell them a huge old hometown Texan whopper. His only concern was how it might backfire on Patty. If the aliens are on your sweet tail, Patty, the last thing you need is me sharpening their focus. I wonder if these guys have wild geese? Do they chase them? Jake prepared to rebound the far wall. The door opened before he arrived.

Rumble. "Traaaaffic Control! Why do you do this?" Rumble.

Jake was sure it was the same gray alien from earlier; his poncho was the same hue and saturation, pale blue. *Details.* The tabard's intricate embroidery was as distinctive as the alien's pale striated coloring. *Details.* Jake concentrated on memorizing both patterns.

"It relaxes me," Jake answered casually as he absorbed his momentum and rebounded, vectoring toward the table. The Gray looked uncertain, hesitant. *Good.*

"See," rumble, "there are more pictures." The Gray straightened, if that was possible with such a twisted frame, and strode to the table. "Traaaaffic Control is seen many times with this one." He stood with one hand gesturing to the OASIS security images, leaning over the table, obscuring the other set of pictures with his richly embroidered garment.

Jake took a discreet glance when the poncho swung open. The alien's skin looked like it was a combination of heavy leather and armor plating. The Gray's body was slim and wiry. He would be quick. A long knife in a jeweled scabbard hung from an embroidered utility belt. It had the look of something ceremonial, but Jake had the feeling this gray knew how to use it.

"What do you want to know about her? She's a nobody," Jake commented as his sliding grip on the table's edge brought Jake to a halt, hovering over the pictures.

"Traaaffic Control knows this one!" Rum-rumble.

"I'd look stupid denying it. What do you want her for? What's she done this time?" Jake asked. *Come on buddy, feed me something.*

"She! Yes!" the alien rumbled to itself for a moment, and Jake felt as if he had spilled his guts. *Didn't they know Patty was female?* Jake reached out and swept the pictures from under the poncho towards him. Maybe they would tell him something.

The first picture was of a broad spiral staircase. Patty was in a gray poncho carrying an armful of boxes with a rolled blanket balanced on top. *Where was that taken? Not on OASIS, that's for sure.* Part of the next image was blurred by a stream of dark forms. On the left side, Patty was pressed up against a wall, still with her arms full. Alan stood passively behind her. The hair stood up on the back of Jake's neck. *No, she wouldn't, she couldn't. Patty was on the mothership?*

The next picture confirmed it. Behind Patty and Alan, aliens were packed wall to wall. They ignored the two small humans. *She's been on the aliens' mothership!* The fact that the aliens wanted to know about her gave Jake hope she had slipped away from their leathery grasp. His heart surged, and he worked hard to repress the smile that tried to possess his face. *You go, girl!*

The next three pictures were taken with the same camera. The topmost image showed Patty in the first of two adjoining rooms with the boxes around her feet and her sword in her hand. The next showed Patty fighting the alien in the far room. In the last image, the alien was dead, and she was dressing Alana in an emergency p-suit.

Oh, you poor child. Why were you there? Jake's heart broke and felt elated at the same time. He had watched her practice fencing and cheered her on in the arena, but he never expected to see her putting her prized possession to its ultimate use. He knew from hard experience that killing took a toll, even if it was a case of kill or be killed. Jake pushed back from the pictures and waited for the Gray to do something, hoping against hope Patty was still alive. It all hinged on what happened next. *What do you want, you enigmatic bastard?*

"This one is," rum-rumble, "LeftLeading." The Gray flexed its leading arm.

"Yeah..." *Come on buddy, spill it.*

"A," rumble, "special individual." It tilted its head and leaned closer, its black eyes shining. "Not," rumble, "nobody."

That's it, buddy. You got me. I lied. Jake dropped his shoulders and his head but not his eyes. The Gray straightened. "No, she is no one special," Jake stated.

"A lie!" It coughed, and its right hand did an intricate dance. "Hu-uman," rumble, "tribe is not differ-er-ent. You lie to protect this one. She is," rumble, "precious!"

"Yes," Jake reluctantly confessed.

"LeftLeading, she is rare, yes."

Was that a question? How many left-handed women do I know? It was not an issue. A few. Rare? Maybe not so much, but definitely special. Jake gave an affirmative nod. "Yeah, rare as hen's teeth," he exaggerated.

The Gray bobbed about with excited little steps. "Again, our tribes," rumble, "parallel."

"How?" Jake asked. Come on, talk to me.

"Our," rumble, "researchers ... no ... our scientists tell us that something," rum-rumble, "special is," rumble, "expressed with the LeftLeading."

Were those bobbles and tiny bows a gesture of pride? It was a southpaw, of course, that meant it was special too. "Yes," Jake replied trying to sound knowledgeable, "the brain is rewired in interesting and novel ways."

"Yes! New," rumble, "connections unthought of. Traaaffic Control understands. The," rumble, "Great Council said humans were different, unblessed, but this one sees," rumble, "parallels where they see," rumble, "divergence." His left arm gestured broadly; his right hand danced a sliding jig. "This one sees the connections."

"What connections?" Jake asked. Come on. Gimme some more to work with.

"Traaaaffic Control would need to know much of our," rumble, "society, the blending," rumble, "ordering of our," rum-rumble, "tribes ... clans."

"Yes?" Jake tried to be attentive and submissive, speaking softly.

"There was a time," rumble, "LeftLeading were considered deficient," rum-rumble, "inferior in size and ability, most were," rumble, "exposed to the elements at birth. When mothers did not, and," rumble, "nourished them and the tribe was repaid," rum-rumble, "a thousand-fold."

It sounded to Jake as if the Gray was reading from a religious text. But it did answer one question; the Gray was male, and if that account was valid, he had a mother. *Were there just two sexes?* There seemed to be at least three varieties of aliens. *Could they be tri-gendered?* If there were three different types of aliens, were there any more hidden away? *A gender for every color of the rainbow?*

"We are always so few, barely one in," rumble, "thousand are LeftLeading and female," rum-rumble, "rare."

As bizarre as the Gray's behavior was, Jake had a feeling he was getting a bead on him. When he talked about the slim chance of being a left-handed alien girl, Jake was sure he heard awe in the alien's voice. *Is this why he's interested in Patty?*

"And they are special too?" Jake inquired.

"Very. Just as LeftLeading brothers surpass in mental acuity, our bigger brothers, the golden ones surpass us." Rumble, "GreatMother," the alien rumbled again. Jake could not sort out his words, but the alien was very enthusiastic, "... that united our tribes and brought us across the stars." Jake listened to the Gray as he talked about the "GreatMother" as if she were some demigod and, the idea that the aliens looked for similar manifestations of brilliance in the human population solidified in his mind. Once again, Jake wondered if he should feed that fire.

"She invaded our," rumble, "home. The," rum-rumble, "Grand Council was horrified that a human could infiltrate and leave undetected," the Gray told him.

"And that is why you seek her?" Jake smiled inwardly. *Patty's still alive! And out of their grasp.*

"Of course. This," rum-rumble, "conflict will be as nothing when our tribes unite, and the quickest way for that to happen is for the true leaders to," rumble, "join together, to align and bring peace," the Gray said solemnly.

"You want peace?" Jake asked, scratching his head. "Starting a war is a strange way of achieving it."

"The tribes will unite," the alien replied with great confidence. "It has always been so, and this one sees no major problem uniting the human tribes with those of their superiors. There will be," rum-rumble, "conflicts, there always are between tribes, but the strength of a united tribe will prevail."

Superiors, eh? Ya reckon? "And you just want to talk to her?" he asked.

"She shows all the," rumble, "signs of leadership. She is a," rumble, "queen, isn't she?"

Queen? Did I hear that correctly? Could he trust the fractured, rumbled EngStand this Gray spoke? Queen Patty. Jake tried to keep the laughter building inside from exploding. "Queen? We don't have queens." *Jake turned away. I'm hiding something.*

"So, this one believed. Your electronic repositories are filled with information about the," rumble, "demise of the," rum-rumble, "inherited rulers, but there is abundant evidence your," rum-rumble, "aristocracy became," rumble, "covert, hidden, still holding power, and controlling events from behind the veil, from the," rum-rumble, "boardroom. Is that not so?" he asked in return.

Jake took a moment to let the Gray's words sink in. It was true, all of it. There was an aristocracy of sorts. Powerful families had for generations wielded a disproportionate influence over the world's affairs. *Hell, some Corporations were more like fiefdoms.* They did take good care of their people and enjoyed considerable loyalty in return. They enforced their own laws amongst their citizens/employees with their own police/security forces and occasionally fought small wars with their rivals, with their own military forces. They were not countries, but they operated like feudal aristocracies. And Patty was undeniably a daughter of the industrial aristocracy. New blood and new money for sure; Patty's father had made some very astute decisions after the war, building a small but innovative manufacturing and distribution network, while Jake, the hot pilot, had bummed around living from one day to the next. He had given up berating himself over his choices after the war many years ago.

"She is a," rumble, "queen, isn't she?" the Gray leaned closer, staring intently.

"She is now," Jake confessed.

The Gray pulled back, his right hand aquiver with tiny movements; it was an elaborate language, Jake was sure. *What's that hand saying?* There was little that moved on the Gray's solid face with nothing to interpret or misinterpret. *Was he surprised?*

"What does Traaaffic Control mean? Your," rumble, "language is," rum-rumble, "difficult to interpret correctly," the Gray asked.

"You do a pretty good job," Jake complimented his and gave a respectful bow.

"It is the," rumble, "duty of the," rum-rumble, "collecting force in tribal," rumble, "unions. How can there be union if," rumble, "communication cannot be achieved?" the Gray demanded.

"You have a point," Jake agreed.

"So, this one asks again, what does Traaaffic Control mean. 'She is now?' Was she not a queen? This one does not understand," he confessed.

Jake tried to relax and let a story bubble out all by itself. The narrative would have to be knocked into shape on the fly, but that was what Jake liked, flying by the seat of his pants. "Well ... our special ones, there is no formal name for them, they flower irregularly. In time, she would have blossomed in unexpected ways, a shining example of humankind, but now. Well ... I fear you may have forced her."

"Forced?" the Gray asked.

Forced? Where am I going with this? "Forced! Your attack on our people has, without a doubt, forced the manifestation of her expanded abilities into fruition before their natural time." Jake tried to look worried and wondered if it was a waste of effort. *Could the alien read his body language?* He decided to play it for all he was worth, frowning and shaking his head.

"And this is bad?" the Gray crept closer.

"It can be," Jake replied, "both for the rapidly maturing youth and ... the cause of her stress. A traumatic event, such as your invasion precipitated, will cause her expanding powers to focus on those who brought this calamity into her life. You!"

The alien stepped back at Jake's last venomous exclamation.

"Yes, you. Be afraid. Be very afraid. You might have awakened a sleeping giant, someone who could manifest powers that would crush you like a bug." Jake looked at the pictures of Patty fighting the alien and shook his head. "Does your queen get angry? How would she react? Would you like to be the cause of your queen's grief and pain?"

The Gray bowed. His whole body quivered for a moment before he took a deep breath and returned to the table. "That would be an event this one could not survive."

"We take great care in the education and upbringing of our special children," Jake elaborated. "We know that if they are hurt or maltreated their talents can be twisted. Great harm can result. Only the Great Murphy knows what you have done, tearing this vulnerable child's life apart. It could signal the end of both our peoples. You must tell me. What has she done?" Jake demanded.

The Gray leaned forward and slid the picture of Patty fighting the alien toward him. "She defeated our," rumble, "queen's captain at," rum-rumble-rumble, "this one does not have the word for it. The station in orbit on the far side of your moon."

"Lagrange two. The place of gravitational equilibrium?" Jake inquired.

"Yes. That is the place. So ferocious, our reports say, she forced the surrender of the force sent to claim it," he told Jake. The alien sounded astonished.

Jake tut-tutted and shook his head. "This is bad. When violence is the first manifestation, the child's talents can be skewed totally in that direction. Every action creates an opposite and equal reaction. Beware of the events you have brought upon yourselves. We have a word for it, Karma. If she is angered, then it'll be more like Instant Karma." Jake hoped he was not laying it on a bit thick, but the Gray seemed to be lapping it up. "And then?"

The alien looked down at the picture once more. "She retrieved her younger male sibling from our mothership. Why would she do that?" he asked.

"You had her brother?" Jake responded with a question of his own

"Yes, he was gathered from your La ... Lagrange station."

"This is bad." Jake shook his head and frowned. "Very bad. You took her brother. Dear, dear, dear. Very bad. This is very bad."

"Please explain. Why is the male sibling important?" the Gray demanded. "This one has many, too many."

Was the gray worried? He seemed agitated. "You separated and probably killed a budding wunderkind's parents and kidnapped her one and only brother," Jake tut-tutted again. "We do not breed as you do." *Apparently.* "Her one-and-only brother is an essential part of her growth, aiding her stability. It is from her brother that her maternal nurturing instincts are developed, and you tore him away from her. Do you stand between a mother and her offspring? The relationship is different, but she is his protector. Do you understand the danger? I fear you haven't woken a giant but roused a demon."

"She appeared and disappeared without a trace," the Gray said. "Our ship is safe, guarded, strong." The Gray insisted with his right-hand dancing.

"Is it? Really?" Jake asked and laughed. "Huh! You could not stop her when she came to reclaim her brother, do you think you will be able to stop her when she comes for revenge?"

"Stop her? We could not find her!" The Gray was stock still, except for his darting right hand that looked to be reaching for something.

"Nor will you. She will appear wherever she wills it and leave just as easily. Your underbelly is exposed." *Do the aliens have underbellies?* The Gray seemed to get the gist.

"How can we stop this? We do not want to fight this," rumble, "emergent queen."

Jake held back as long as he could, feigning deep thought, drawing the Gray closer. "Appeasement. It might work."

"Sorry, this one does not understand."

"Make it worth her while. Do you hold her parents?" Jake inquired. "If they are unhurt, set them free." Jake shook his head, trying to express doubt. "Shower her with gifts. Draw her focus away from the conflict. If you truly desire peace, then tell her so. Show her you have made mistakes but are willing to make amends." Jake scratched at his bristly chin. "It might work ... if you're lucky."

"This one's tribe says, Fortune rides with the Uniter." The Gray turned away for a second before returning his direct gaze to Jake. "And, The Uniter's path may be difficult but," rumble, "success is assured."

Was that pride? Jake wondered. "One. Don't count your chickens before they've hatched," he fired back, raising his impudent middle finger in the time-honored fashion. "Two," he lifted his index finger converting his gesture to the two-fingered salute. "Heaven has no rage like love to hatred turned, nor hell a fury like a woman scorned." Jake did not try for another insulting gesture. There was not anything remotely suitable that used three fingers.

CENSUS DAY

Little Star scampered out of the way of her younger brothers as they wrestled at the grassy edge of the forecourt. She was too small and weak to tussle with them. Even the smallest of her brothers could break her in two without effort. They all grew so quickly. All except her. It was best to keep out of their way, so she climbed the bare earthworks that surrounded her father's holding. The day was bright despite the comforting cover of the clouds. The sun was cool again this season, and the crops had more than enough water. Papa was happier than Little Star could remember. He had not hit her and cursed her as a useless-mouth-to-feed in weeks. Mama was just happy there was going to be enough food for her new pups. They were due in a handful of days.

Stone Son was already there when Little Star reached the top of the earthworks, looking over the wrestling match with more than a little envy. Just as Little Star was too small to join in, he was too large. Stone Son was freakishly big. He was so big his pa, who held a place to the south, hired him out to the other holdings when hard work was needed. Stone Son lifted his powerful right arm, and Little Star clambered eagerly into his lap. He never said much, but she felt safer there than just about anywhere.

CHAPTER SIXTEEN

It did not take too much persuasion from Jake for the Gray to assign him to his apartment while the alien reported to his superiors. Jake was a very important prisoner and was not going to return to the hostel. *I'm getting a read on this Gray; smooth movements with his body and gliding swoops with his right hand indicated confidence, faster changes could show happiness, choppy and staccato might be fear or anger.* It was not much to go on, but it was a start. *Know your enemy.*

After a slow sonic scrub and a close-as-you-can-get shave that should last a couple of days, Jake slipped on a skin-tight sealed suit. It was not much good without a helmet ring, but it would provide some protection if there were a sudden decompression. Over that he wore his sharpest, brightest long-sleeved Hawaiian shirt and some loose gray slacks over comfortable but sturdy black boots. While arguing that he would be just as secure in his apartment, Jake took the opportunity to make a frank plea for something more to wear than only the gray poncho, sweeping aside his scant covering, displaying just how vulnerable his body was. Jake was sure he had managed to embarrass the Gray and chalked up another success.

There was not much in his small two-roomed home he could use as a weapon. There was an excellent collection of knives in his kitchenette, but they were too obvious. Jake had one thing that would be easily hidden and turned into a handy short-range weapon, a short-end reel of monofilament. It took only a few minutes for the improvised chemical bath mixed in a drinking bulb to sever a one-meter length from the roll. As a garrote, there was nothing better. The tricky part was securing the loose ends. If he wrapped the monofilament around his hands, he was sure to lose at least a finger. In the end, Jake settled for a pair of steel buttons from a fancy-dress costume. Rolled up, they sat discretely behind his belt. It wasn't much, but Jake felt much better.

And then he waited. There was no UNET access, no connection to anywhere on OASIS. His terminal displayed a "Sorry ... waiting to connect..." graphic. *Coffee and a decent breakfast then.* There was not a great deal of food in his tiny fridge: an egg, a little ham, and a slightly wilted piece of red capsicum. *Omelet.*

Nearly nine hours later, Jake contemplated the bottle of JD in his meager liquor collection for the fifth time and once again decided it was better to be sober and on his toes. The door slid open, and two soldiers in pale blue took up station inside.

"Stand!"

Jake ignored the emphatic guard, "Well, howdy pardner. Can I fix you a drink?"

"Drink?" the Gray twitched.

"Just bein' hospitable."

"There is no," rumble, "time for re ... freshments." The alien stopped, took a second look at Jake and twitched again. *Yes, that was agitation.* "Your garment is ... bright."

"You like?" Jake asked as he twirled. The gray poncho lifted, revealing the true splendor of his Hawaiian shirt; the blue of sky and surf battled with vibrant tropical flowers and colorful cocktails decorated with tiny paper umbrellas. "It brings out the blue in my eyes, or so I'm told."

"It," rumble, "offends."

Really? Maybe our two species have more in common than I thought. The Gray's right: this shirt is offensive. "So, what's up doc?"

"Doc?" the Gray looked up at the ceiling.

"Just an expression, a cultural thing. I gotta call you something," Jake replied. The Gray twitched again, definitely agitated with something else mixed in, confusion? "You know me, Jake, Traffic Control, and you are called?"

"Ah yes, names. Our tribe is not so ... free with the names our mothers give us, especially..." The Gray shuffled on the spot, and Jake caught the hint of a bow. *Regret? Shame?*

"Especially with a lowly scum human like me?" Jake asked.

The Gray relaxed and nodded, mirroring Jake's posture. He turned to the two guards and rumbled at them. They bowed and withdrew into the corridor. The door hissed shut. "Something like that." The Gray straightened. "But since Traaaaffic Control is an adviser to his queen you have high," rum-rumble, "status."

"For a lowly scum human," Jake added.

"Yes." The Gray bowed formally, not deeply but with grace. "This one is," rum-rumble-rum, "honored to make your," rumble, "acquaintance. This one was named..." the Gray began rumbling. When the Gray took a breath and continued, Jake had to stop him.

"Whoa there, pale face. It might be the low frequencies, but I was lost at the first rumbly bit. Please forgive me." Jake stood and bowed a hair's breadth deeper than the Gray although much less gracefully. "I need something shorter. I'll never remember all that."

"Shorter?"

"Your name," Jake told him.

"This one had not arrived at this one's name. It is customary to tell of one's forebears, to show one standing in history's roll," the Gray said.

"I apologize again." Jake bowed. "I'm just an ignorant Texan slob. Please continue."

The Gray did and needed another three breaths to complete the task. Jake waited patiently while the alien recited his ancestry and then bowed. "You honor me." The gray bowed again. "But I'm still not sure what to call you."

"Pum." He bowed again.

"Pleased to meet you, Pum. What's on the agenda for today?" Jake asked.

"We have an audience, with your queen," Pum told him. Jake

did not know how to react, but he felt as if an unseen hand had crushed his diaphragm; he could not breathe.

"There was much," rumble, "discussion and many on the," rum-rumble," Great Council discounted your," rumble, "testimony." Pum bowed, and his right hand made an elegant swirl. "My," rum-rumble-rum, "queen held out against such counsel and is quite eager to meet your," rumble, "special one. It is her ... ardent wish that there is peace between our two," rumble, "powerful and august rulers."

"You have her?" Jake had to ask but dreaded hearing the answer.

"Oh no," Pum replied, and the air came back into the room. "We go to where we expect her to," rumble, "visit. Come, we must depart." Pum opened the door and gestured for Jake to precede him. Jake bowed and walked into the hallway. Pum joined him and their escort wrapped around them as they moved through the empty corridors heading towards the Aldrin docks.

"So, you think you know where..." Jake swallowed, he had nearly said Patty's name. If the aliens were particularly precious about names that would have been a mistake. "... her divine majesty is going to appear."

"Yes. It is a," rumble, "process of elimination. Your queen has been to your Lagrange Two station, to our," rum-rumble, "mothership. There was an ... an incident at the station that orbits in the," rum-rumble, "gravitational eddy opposite your moon."

"Lagrange Three." Jake drew a little picture of the Earth-Moon system with his fingers naming the Lagrange Points.

"Yes, Lagrange Three, a most," rumble "unfortunate occurrence, though your queen was not sighted. The same on your L4. There were many deaths."

"So, we're going to L5?" Jake inquired.

"Indeed. Our gracious," rum-rumble, "Queen hopes to begin talks that would bring peace to the High Reaches," Pum answered.

"Really? Peace? That would be useful." Jake bit his lip. *Was Pum's sarcasm detector working?*

"Indeed. Peace will come, with your queen or without her. The tribes will unite," Pum declared confidently. Whether it was knowledge of just how dominant his race's position was or the security blanket of dogma, Jake did not know, but Pum's serenity disturbed him.

"Our glorious," rum-mumble-rum, "Queen has taken your warning most seriously and is willing to," rumble, "secede the station L2, and L5 if there can be peace. Search parties will be sent to learn the fate of your queen's parents."

"You don't have them," Jake asked.

"Not that this one knows. In truth, Traaaffic Control," rum-rumble, "your systems have proved to be more," rum-rum, "inscrutable than was expected. In ... formation is scarce." Pum walked on, his eyes almost closed, his right hand danced in interrupted swirls, darting from one path to another mid-arc as if he was changing his mind. His hand completed an elegant sweep. "But all that will change when there is peace between our," rum-rumble, "gracious Queens."

Yeah right, buddy. In your dreams.

CHAPTER SEVENTEEN

The corridor opened out onto Aldrin Plaza. Dried blood and scorch marks still desecrated the lobby. An ungainly lump of hardening ash marked Captain Burt's last resting place. *He wasn't the bravest man, but he didn't deserve that.* OASIS had never seen violence beyond a drunken punch or two. It shocked Jake all over again. Soldiers with deep red ponchos stopped their escorts well before the airlocks. There was much humming, hooming, and rum-rumbling. The lock cycled open, and a gray with a most impressive red poncho stepped out and strode towards them. Two guards of the really big kind in their multicolored ponchos attended him. Jake felt his neck creak as he gazed up at the monsters. He expected the big guys to be slow and clumsy, but they held themselves with a killer's grace. The new alien's heavily embroidered cloak held eye-slamming reds of a most intricate design. Pum and his entourage bowed deeply. A white staff's shock brought Jake to his knees. Rum-hooming-rumbles poured out of this newcomer. He was important, and everyone listened, especially Pum, who bowed and bowed again.

Suddenly their pale-blue garbed escort peeled back to be replaced by the red variety. When the two giant aliens took up posts behind him, Jake was allowed off his knees. *Was that a growl?* Pum approached with a transparent parcel; a Zip-Lok.

"Traaaffic Control," Pum bowed, "this one has been paid a great honor." As far as Jake could tell, it did not look like it. Pum was excited, but something cut at that gentle confidence Jake witnessed earlier. "Our most," rum-rumble, "wise regent," rumble-rum, "has seen the importance of this," rumble, "mission and so, has sent," rumble-rum-rumble, "as her," rumble, "most honored emissary."

Jake looked the new Gray over once more. If Pum's body language was any guide, the new boy exuded confidence. *And something else. The regent? Royalty. A prince?* Maybe it was his independent Texan nature, but there was something that disturbed Jake about the Prince.

"You're still coming with us, aren't you?" Jake asked.

"Alas. This one is," rum-hurumble-rum, "not of..." Pum rumbled incoherently. "This one is to continue with," rumble, "research, here." Pum's energy was flat, and even his right hand moved listlessly. *Poor guy.*

"Ain't it the way. You hit pay dirt, and the big boys swoop in and steal your thunder," Jake muttered.

"You must ... prepare for," rumble, "vacuum," Pum told him.

"No, no, no. This is no good! You must come. I insist," Jake declared. He had no desire to become a baton in a diplomatic relay. Besides, he had begun to open a rapport with Pum and did not want to start all over again with the prince-in-red. Jake's spine shivered. *There's that pesky instinct again.* Jake gave a small bow to Pum and stepped around him.

"Hey, err, Prince," Jake began and gave a half-hearted bow. "I think you need..." was as far as he got before one of his over-sized guards threw him to the floor.

"Hey, watch it, buddy!" Jake twisted in the air, catching himself with his left hand, rebounding to his feet. "If you think maltreating my Queen's representative is a good way to begin negotiations then think again!" he growled. Jake's shoulder ached, but he did not stretch. Catching the floor with one hand had been a near thing, a fraction late and it would have been his head hitting the deck. He was getting too old for gymnastics and was far too old to be picking a fight with this neck-straining guard, but he stepped up to the huge alien and locked gaze with his black-in-black eyes. "Back off, bub," Jake bluffed. Staring into the unbroken gaze of his giant escort was like looking into the unforgiving heart of a black hole; nothing good came out of it.

"Traaaffic Control!" Pum emitted a short high-pitched sigh. "Please!"

Jake held his pose and heard a rumbling exchange behind him. *Was Pum winning the argument?* The guard blinked, bowed to the prince and stepped back. Stretching his neck and shoulders, Jake took the opportunity to take a deep breath. His heart raced. *Any landing you walk away from. Any landing you walk away from.* That guard was rock solid, and Jake knew if his bluff had been called, he would have been dead before he knew it.

"Traaaffic Control, come. This one will," rumble, "introduce you," Pum said and struggled to find his footing.

Jake reached out and laid a settling hand on Pum's shoulder. "Thank you." Jake withdrew his hand and gave a brief bow. "I am honored." That seemed to settle Pum. Protocol, that was something the alien could embrace. *Almost as good as dogma.* Pum bowed in return and led him three steps to the prince who stood with a retinue of guards at his back. Pum bowed deeply, and Jake thought it appropriate to follow suit, although his bow was shallower. After a small hesitation, the prince gave a shallow bow in return.

"Grand Prince," rum-rumble-bum-rum, Pum began and continued rum-hoom-rumbling for some time. Jake took the opportunity to take a closer look at the prince. He was still. Not even the slightest movement of his right hand betrayed an internal monologue. Pum's hand was rarely still. "... this one has the distinct," rum-rumble, "honor to introduce, Traaaffic Control. It was this one that greeted Strike Leader," Pum rumbled for a bit, "so politely. Traaaffic Control is close adviser to their esteemed," rum-rumble, "queen." Pum bowed to the prince and then to Jake and stepped back.

The prince rumbled for a second before stopping suddenly and continuing in EngStand. "Traaaffic Control, this one listened to the exchange, it was conducted with," rumble, "integrity." The bow that followed was minuscule.

"Prince," Jake replied and gave a bow that was barely a nod. *Two can play that game, bub.* "I hope this venture will be of benefit to both our peoples." *In your dreams. I'm going to wild goose this thing so hard you won't know who or what you're chasing.* The prince twitched. It was a minute movement, but Jake was sure it was an involuntary act. *What did it mean?* Jake took a breath. *Disgust. Did the Prince just flash disgust?* Jake filed the gesture away.

"Our Queen has high hopes for this ... excursion." The prince turned away slightly, his eyes briefly inspecting the guard at his side.

"Well then, maybe we should make tracks," Jake said with a big smile, flashing his teeth. The prince did not respond. "We should leave, embark upon this great venture. That is why you're here, isn't it?" Jake did not wait for an answer, turning to Pum. "Where's that Zip-Lok? And you should ... prepare for vacuum." Jake held Pum's gaze until the Gray nodded a bow and scurried off. The prince was looking closely at Jake when he turned back, studying him. "See anything ya like?"

Prince began with a rumble-hum before switching to EngStand. "This one is not sure what happened. Perhaps you have come by that ... blue honestly."

"I'm sorry?" Jake asked.

The prince rumbled, and Jake caught a bit that was an extended portion of Pum's name, "... is of, I do not have a word for it, he is from a different stream, class." His thicker, stronger left hand caressed his bright colors, lingering on the eye-searing reds. "That does not mean he is without honor." The prince's right hand reinforced his words.

"Every society has its A-Listers. Pum is a good fellow," Jake agreed.

"Pum. Yes, Pum. It will suffice. Pum is a leader in Sky Blue, a place of high honor indeed. Without the ... knowledge ... the wisdom of this caste ... it does not matter. Pum has earned a place of high regard or his ... scheme would not have reached our," rumble, "Queen's ears."

"Well, that's good," Jake replied. "Good for Pum. Looks like a hard worker." *Scheme, eh?* Both Pum and the prince were cautious in their choice of words. *Scheme, eh?*

"This one just witnessed a captive .... human, order one of the highest of Sky Blue to fetch his pressure suit." The prince moved a little to one side and looked Jake up and down once more. "How is this possible? Traaaffic Control disrupts the order of things, and yet, it is the purpose of Sky Blue to be the bridge across the rifts of conflict. Your actions strengthen this mission. Perhaps this one has been mistaken." The prince bowed. It was shallow and brief but more honest than his previous efforts. "Is it certain that Traaaffic Control is RightLeading? You have the ... air of a maker of things."

"I don't know how long you guys have been studying us, but you will be surprised every day," Jake informed the prince. "It's what we're good at, for good or ill."

"For ill. There are many that doubt, missing the," rumble, "patterns that Pum sees. This one has always known that your tribe was dangerous. It is the ... core of," rumble, "to guard against dangerous forces." He gave another short bow. "Traaaffic Control, you are ... dangerous." The prince gave Jake a feeling his name had been added to a list of those to be eliminated: soonest. Jake just smiled and gave a little bow. "And by ... extension, your Queen, if she exists, represents considerable danger." The prince stood straighter. "This one feared to be chasing ... an illusion."

Oh please, be an illusion, Jake prayed. Patty, wherever you are, be somewhere else. There's a lot of space out there, girl. Stick out your thumb. Someone'll give you a lift.

THE TAKER COMES

Little Star had no idea what a Census was or what a Census Taker did. Mama said they came from a great city in the south. There had not been a Census Day since long before Little Star was born and she had no idea what a city was, let alone a great city. On such a mild day it was the perfect opportunity for all the local holdings to gather. Papa's holding was the biggest and one of the oldest in their valley, so it was logical to have the Census here. There was plenty of room for the tents spread out beside the tal'ee fields and plenty of room inside if things went bad. Tiny golden tal'ee ears waved gently in the warm breeze. There was water in the air. *More rain?* Little Star thought. Papa was right. It was going to be a bumper crop, third in a row.

An excited shout drifted up from the camp. One of Stone Son's much littler brothers raced into the forecourt with the news; the Taker was coming! The Taker was here! He pointed to the south.

Stone Son stood, lifting Little Star as he rose. She clambered up onto his shoulder. Bright green pennons broke through the thick foliage covering the southern trail. One, two, three, six, twelve, more! Little Star quickly ran out of fingers and toes.

Disciplined lines appeared below the trees, long spears with bright bronze heads leaning against broad shoulders. Helmets and breastplates of polished bronze shone in the dappled light as the company marched closer. *More bronze!* Pa had a bronze knife although Cook was more likely to be using it than Pa. Excited pouchlings from a dozen holdings mixed as they jumped and marched beside the track.

As the center of the column came into view Little Star gasped and so did Stone Son. Two lines of guards surrounded a litter of some sort, curtained in blue and white. It was not the blue and sparkling white of the litter that surprised Little Star, although she had never seen white quite that white, except in the clouds. The guards surrounding the litter were all as big as Stone Son. Some were even bigger.

CHAPTER EIGHTEEN

"Why don't you just shut up, Kerr," Madhur growled; her rancor dripped with disdain. "You're suckin' down our air and leaching the energy from the room. Air ain't free ya know." She ground her teeth together, glanced at Patty and calmed down a little. Patty wondered what Cian had done to get Madhur's back up. He had been copping it from Madhur for hours for being a useless pilot, for sponging off good-natured folk, and for being too tall. Cian looked at times, as if he were leaning into a strong wind, holding fast, lest he was blown over by her invective. It did not seem to bother him too much; when he got the chance he would slip away and talk to the twins, but he always came back.

"We know there's not much at Lagrange Five, but that's the fact we're hoping to exploit. Hestia's Hearth's construction site is too small for the aliens to pay much attention to," Patty remarked. "Why would they need a half-built generational starship? They've something much better." Flying reconnaissance was becoming Patty's specialty. *Then why do I feel on edge about this flight? You trust your skills, and you trust Freya. What's the problem?* Patty took a slow deep breath and stretched the cramped muscles in her neck.

Cicely and her inseparable twin floated over, and she laid a hand on Patty's shoulder. "Eg says it's a trap," she said gently.

"Thanks. I needed to hear that," Patty replied with a grimace and shuddered.

"I know, that's why we told you," Cicely smiled and pushed off with her brother, back to the console and the playback of Patty's journey through the alien ship.

"Does he ever talk?" Madhur asked as she watched the twins

depart.

"Egbert talks all the time, to Cicely," Ken replied, "and she constantly talks to Eg; she's his eyes. Even she didn't vocalize until she was six, Mom taught them Sign before they could walk. Cicely's much more ... social now, but a few years ago she never talked to anyone except Ma and Eg." Ken looked over Patty's shoulder at Alan. He seemed content just to be with Patty. "And speaking of talking, do you think he could learn sign? You seem to communicate well with gestures; I think you'd both be able to pick up some basic vocab. Luckily you only need one hand to use International Sign," Ken wiggled the fingers on his one usable hand.

"Do you think?" Patty asked. The cloud of fear shadowing Patty began to lift. She would love to do something more to help Alan's recovery, something that would take her mind off aliens and spaceships and confined spaces. They had practiced fighting along with Jai, but Patty was not comfortable seeing that big blade in her little brother's hands. *But if he's going to hang onto it, he better be able to use it.* She was surprised at how good her brother was with that heavy blade. They had over twelve hours until Jaswinder made the course corrections needed to slip around the far side of the moon. *Putting our hands to another use would be nice.*

"Bring your brother over here, and we can leave Madhur and Cian to get on each other's wicks in peace," Ken said with mock seriousness. Madhur gave him a dirty look and left to check on her nephew, standing watch on the bridge.

Patty scoured Freya's navigation display for any signs of lurking ships. Giuseppe's coating took a while to collect enough data to give a result, but space looked clear all the way to the shining crescent Earth. She could detect activity around L3 but nothing between the station under siege and the partially completed generational ship moored at L5. It still did not feel right, but that was not a sufficient reason for Patty to change her flight vector.

The accommodation wing, attached to the construction facilities, was a dark boxy shape. No windows were lit. It appeared deserted. Pairs of blinking red navigation warning lights lit the scaffolding surrounding what would have been Hestia's Hearth. Only one alien ship stood guard, five hundred meters from the partially completed starship. There was no movement anywhere. She tweaked her course to interpose Hestia's skeletal framework between Freya and the alien fighter. The bottom third of Hestia's two-hundred-meter length appeared to be complete; the rest was a tangle of half-finished bulkheads spreading out from its central core. Cian's exuberant description of the ship held true. When completed, she would have been a magnificent ship.

Freya slipped behind Hestia's Hearth, edging closer to the huge ship. Although aliens were obviously aboard, Patty could not resist the chance to see if her parents were there. If she could sneak onto the alien mothership, she could sneak aboard a human ship. Docked in the shadows where she planned to hide Freya, there was a stubby ship with a massive girth and enormous engines. By conventional standards, it was a big ship, but Hestia's Hearth completely dwarfed it. She had seen ships of this design many times; it was a tug, though they did not *tug* anything, they pushed, snowballs. Thousands of tonnes of heavy-water ice mined in the asteroid belt and covered in a silvered Mylar wrap to avoid sublimation made a comet's plunge into the inner solar system where the tugs caught them. Crack the water's oxygen bond, and you had Tritium, the hottest of the hydrogen isotopes.

The tug was hard docked to Hestia, and that suggested to Patty a way to board the starship that would not require her to open one of Hestia's airlocks. Anyone on Hestia's bridge would be instantly aware of a lock opening, but Patty doubted the aliens would be monitoring the tug's airlocks. The scaffolding was broad enough, in places, for Patty to set Freya down and get a decent lock. It would not hold if Hestia boosted away, but the partially completed generational ship would not be going anywhere.

"How are you, Alan?" Patty asked verbally and signed at the same time. She needed to practice. Alan took to signing almost instinctively and was much more proficient at the hand signals than Patty. Ken said it was odd that Alan used his left hand since he was right-handed, but Patty was just happy to be able to talk to her brother.

"Feel okay. Will need to urinate soon," Alan replied. It was not his usual banter, but it made Patty smile.

"Soon Alan, soon. We're going EV. Are you sealed?" she asked.

"Check once, check twice. You tell ... this one ... you tell this one, check twice. You check now?" he inquired.

"No. You know what to do." Despite telling Alan she was not checking on him, she could not help but have a quick look.

"You *do* check," Alan signed. Patty expected to see a smile on his face.

"Yes, I check. Help keep you safe," she answered. Although sneaking aboard Hestia was hardly safe, he would not be left behind.

"Keep you safe." His right hand sought the hilt of his sword.

"Yes, thank you," Patty thanked him. *Alan protecting me? It's supposed to be the other way 'round.* The thought chilled Patty and comforted her at the same time. "Work together, team. Protect each other."

"Team," Alan signed, and Patty nodded in agreement, closed her visor, and cycled Freya's air.

CHAPTER NINETEEN

The tug was a squat beast of a ship but hard-docked to Hestia's Hearth's immensity it looked like a fat tick on an animal's behind. There was a logo, and some writing below the bridge's starboard windows, but it was too dark to decipher. There was no sign of life. Near the ship's over-sized engine nozzles was a small port, a one-man airlock, although, with a squeeze, they should both be able to fit inside it. Patty found the manual mechanism, opened the flap and turned the handle mounted inside. The door slowly slid open, venting the airlock's contents into space. Patty replaced the flap and gestured to Alan for him to board. He nodded, checked to see that his sword was free in its scabbard, and climbed into the lock. Patty swarmed in after him.

It was cramped, but Patty did not want to enter the tug one at a time. Through the interior window, Patty could see a partially illuminated passageway but no movement. She used the manual winder to close the outer door and cycled in the air. Patty cracked open her visor. The lock smelled of human bodies and machines; compared to the atmosphere aboard the alien ship it was cool and dry. Alan followed her cue and unsealed his Zip-Lok.

The inner door opened silently, and Patty poked her head out of the airlock. An iron bar swung towards her face and Patty squealed as she snapped her head back.

"Shite!" The bar of twisted iron stopped centimeters from her nose. "By Murphy's crooked dice! What are you doing here, girly?" It was a gruff voice with an inflection broader than Tina's Australian accent. The man wielding the bar was nearly as large as an alien but was pale. Bright ginger hair seemed to grow all over him; his forearms were particularly hairy, and his thick but well-trimmed beard continued under his chin, down his neck, meeting up with curls that sprouted from the top of his white and blue ship suit.

Patty heard Alan begin to draw his sword. She reached back and placed her hand over the pommel. "Sneaking," she replied with a smile.

"Sneaking's damned right. Thought the bloody aliens had found us." He sighed as he dropped the bar to his side. "Well, come in. How did you get off Hestia? Thought they had you guys locked away."

"We didn't come from Hestia; we flew in on my CRV. I'm Patty Balke, and this is my brother Alan," Patty answered as she floated from the airlock. Alan examined the man before joining Patty.

"Welcome to The Ice Princess. I'm Chief Petty Officer Brennan; call me Stan," he introduced himself, extending his hand. Patty returned his firm grip. Stan's bloodshot eyes peered out from beneath a deeply creased brow. Although he was tired, those eyes did not miss the blades they wore at their hips, especially Alan's, suspended from an alien's belt, and shoulder harness made from assorted lengths and colors of restraint webbing. He tightened his grip on the bar. His eyes were steely. "Swords?" his jaw tightened. "Those bastards cut my brother down in seconds. Where'd you get swords?"

Patty raised her hands. "Please, we don't want to be any trouble. In the last few days, well, we've needed them. I'm on the OASIS fencing team and Alan," Patty swallowed at the memory of blood, "he took his from the one I ... I killed."

"Mixing it with the bastards, eh?" Stan's shaggy eyebrows rose. "And lived to tell the tale." His surprise softened, and then his frown returned. "I can't believe how quickly they carved up Carson." One shaggy brow raised, and he looked her over once more. His eyes lingered on her p-suit's fresh repairs. "Look like you came off pretty well. D'ya give lessons?" He hefted the bar and smiled. It was not a happy smile. His eyes were cold.

Patty looked at the iron bar and found a smirk sliding across her face. "It takes practice, but I think I can give a few pointers."

"Good." He waved the bar back and forth. "Sorry about tryin' to take your head off; wasn't expecting guests." His arm holding the bar twitched, and he stared into the middle distance. His eyes suddenly snapped back into focus. "I guess you're scrounging for supplies. Come with me. Have to take you to see the captain." He turned and pushed off down the corridor without giving them a backward glance.

Patty checked on her brother. He looked tense, and his hand still rested on his hilt. "Alan, these are friends. No sword, okay?" Patty signed. Alan took a few moments before he replied with a tiny nod. "We're okay. Safe."

Alan shook his head. "Not safe," he signed.

"Safe for now. Come on." Patty waited for Alan's nod before following the burly crewman.

The interior of The Ice Princess was gray with blue piping and the octagonal corridor arced around the massive engine room that dominated the ship. Stan led them into a side passageway and then stopped at a wall panel no different to any other. He did something, and the wall slid to one side, opening into a small room nearly filled with boxes stacked on shelves or held secure behind netting. They crowded in while Stan closed the sliding panel behind them. He twisted the recessed light fitting in the ceiling, and the back wall slid open. He pulled some netting aside and removed a box from the center of the stack, creating a tunnel to the hidden room.

"After you," he gestured with the bar. Patty wriggled through followed closely by her brother who kept a close eye on Stan and that iron bar. The room was narrow and had supplies held fast in every available corner. Five more crew huddled in the remaining space.

"Lookee what I found, captain!" Stan announced as he presented Patty and Alan. "We got visitors."

A young man with an ensign's stripes on his shipsuit's

epaulets moved to the front of the assembled crewmen. "How did they get aboard?" he asked Stan as he cast an eye over them.

"Stern, starboard side lock, sir. This is Patty and Alan Balke. Say they flew in on a CRV; although how they slipped past the alien guard ship is anybody's guess. She also says she can use that sword. Promised me lessons, she has." He grinned wickedly.

"Is that so?" the ensign-captain replied with a smirk. "I think there'll be more signing up for that class. Thank you, Stan. We'll look after them now."

"And I'll get back to me rounds." Stan nodded and left.

"I'm Lirsín Delaney, captain of what's left of The Ice Princess." His wry smile was a thin veneer over a tired face. He looked very young to be in charge, but he exuded warm confidence. His speech had the same broad accent as Stan's but with a slight British overtone. Patty liked him immediately. "You flew in on your CRV. Where from? We're well stocked; we have food and drink and…"

"My brother's more interested in finding a toilet at the moment," Patty replied. "Zip-Loks; they're fine for a short hop but," Patty left the notion dangling.

"Of course, excuse me," Lirsín's smile turned into a restrained grin. "Thrane," he addressed the crewman to his left, "please show, Alan, was it? Please show Alan to the head."

"It might be easier if I looked after him. He's mute and a little, nervous around strangers," Patty told them.

"Certainly, please, follow crewman Thrane," Lirsín said and moved to one side. The toilet facilities were tiny but functional, built into a bulkhead, and Patty took the opportunity to purge her p-suit and top up her water reserves when Alan was finished.

When they returned to the room, Lirsín offered them tea and something to eat, but he yearned for whatever news Patty carried. "We've been stuck in our hidey-holes for days. A little more than one watch was able to conceal themselves when the aliens boarded. One of us goes EV to check up on the guard ship every hour or so. We've almost hacked into Hestia's internal net so we can monitor some of the alien patrols, but as to what's happening out in the rest of the system, we're in the dark."

Patty tried to be as concise as she could in re-telling their story but her second mug of tea was drained, and her dry throat wished for a third before she finished. "If I'd moored Freya closer, we could run an umbilical, and I could show you the files. Hestia could fit in one corner of the aliens' ship," Patty said and picked up her empty mug.

"And what are your plans?" Patty asked.

"We've been trying to figure a way to break free and get out of here, but all our simulations tell us that before we've decoupled and maneuvered clear that alien guard ship would be on us," Lirsín replied with a frown. "They took all the bridge crew. I can pilot, in a pinch, but... We're just hanging tight hoping that something might change."

"How many aliens are on board?" Patty asked.

"On The Princess? None," Lirsín answered. "They cast a cursory glance through her a couple of times a day. There are at least a dozen big ones and a couple of smaller grays. They change out the guard ship's crew every six hours or so. The rest monitor what's left of Hestia's crew."

"There are people on Hestia?" Patty asked.

"Yeah. About a dozen or so, just to keep the systems ticking over, I think," he replied.

"Where are they being held? With your combined crews, we could take back Hestia, maybe not permanently, but long enough to evacuate and make a get-away. You'll be heading back to the Belt?" Patty surmised.

"Yes, of course."

"What do Hestia's crew think?" she asked.

"Well, actually..." Lirsín looked embarrassed, "It's high on the to-do list. The aliens keep a close eye on the comm. Rogers is working on a procedure to subvert the system, but it's slow going."

"I'm sure Hestia's crew would be able to help you. If you're serious about getting out of here, then we're going to need everyone working together." The hairs on the back of Patty's neck stood up, and she hoped that someone aboard the Jaswinder could come up with a plan. "We'll have to work with Hestia's people if you are going to get home."

"We?" He smiled, and that felt indescribably nice. "You're right, of course. Rogers?"

A young man with a straggly beard turned from a control panel, "Yes, sir?"

"How's it going?"

"We can make a call if we're quick. Hestia's crew have been quartered for the night, and the alien on watch is talking to a Gray. As I say, if we're quick..."

"Good, then patch us through," Lirsín ordered. Rogers opened an encrypted channel and moved to one side so Patty and Lirsín could approach the comm. The picture was dark, but Patty could see a woman in a white shipsuit. There were other dark shapes that suggested more people were there.

"Err, excuse me," Lirsín said in a quiet voice. The woman still jumped with fright. "Sorry about that, this is Captain Delaney, aboard The Ice Princess." He turned to Rogers. "Do they have a picture?"

"Not yet sir. I'm trying to keep the bandwidth low," Rogers reported. Lirsín nodded and spoke to the woman again. "We're trying to plan an escape and need to coordinate a few things. Don't look at the comm. Hopefully, we have this signal masked, but just in case, pretend that we aren't talking." The woman nodded. She looked away but moved closer.

"I hear you," she said quietly. "Daichi, come here." A shadowy form in the dim room moved closer. *Daichi?* Patty thought. Her heart skipped. *There can't be too many men named Daichi, can there?* Daichi Wakahisa, her fencing coach, moved into the light. If he was on-board, then they would stand a much better chance of taking Hestia.

"Give them a picture, Rogers," Lirsín said.

"Aye, aye, sir."

The man glanced up at the comm and away again. Short-cropped salt-and-pepper hair framed a face that bore deep lines revealing an age that his slender physique denied. He crouched down beside the woman as if he were talking to her. It *was* Daichi. Patty's heart leaped.

"Patty Balke. It's good to see you," Daichi said, his smile blossoming into a grin. "I've been praying for a change of luck."

"Let's hope it turns out to be good luck," Patty replied, and she could not help smiling too. Daichi was good news indeed, and it was great to see a familiar face.

"We make our luck by being in balance, staying flexible and finding the right moment to strike," Daichi instructed. "You have good balance, Patty. You know your center. Patty, this is Lily, she's the only qualified engineer on Hestia, a contractor from the Belt," Daichi introduced the woman. Lily was tall, easily over two meters, but she looked to be half Patty's mass. Some of the Belters were positively ethereal; Lily looked as if she would not be able to cope with the moon's gravity, let alone Earth's massive pull. Her platinum-blond hair, cut short, stuck out in every direction like soft bristles.

"Pleased to meet you, Patty," Lily said. "Delaney, I know that name well. My cousin Selene married a Delaney, round Ceres way," Lily said in a relaxed and friendly manner. She sounded like a country girl with time on her hands.

"Cousin!" Lirsín exclaimed. "My uncle Michael was that lucky man."

"Don't suppose you have room on your ship for one more? These Terrans have the strangest customs. I wanna go home," Lily drawl was laden with dry humor.

"That's the plan," Lirsín said.

"I have to confer with everyone back on Jaswinder," Patty told them, trying to steer the conversation away from social exchanges, "but I'm sure we will be able to disable the guard ship. Lirsín says that there is only a dozen or so aliens on Hestia at any one time. Lily, how operational is Hestia's Hearth?"

Lily sighed and slumped down. "They've been making me

decommission system after system. Only today, I had to take the Winterberg off-line. We're running on one tokamak that's just barely ticking over. It would take weeks to put Hestia back into the green, even if I had a full crew."

"Winterberg?" Patty asked.

"An offshoot of the old Orion program. It's the engine that gets Hestia up to speed by dropping little nukes under her tail." Lily looked proud of the technology.

"Is there any point in trying to take Hestia back?" Patty inquired. It seemed such a waste to leave her there. Lily shook her head. Patty had secretly hoped that it would be possible to free this ship, but if freeing her crew was the only option then that was what they needed to focus upon. "So, we need to get Hestia's crew to The Ice Princess."

"We've charted the quickest route from where you're quartered to the airlock," Lirsín said and turned to Rogers, "bring up the map." The display showed a wire-frame 3D view of Hestia with the route marked in a snaking red line. "Can you get access to welding gear? If we seal these junctions as we go, we can make a reasonably secure escape route. Where do you suppose we should aim to meet up?" Daichi and Lily moved closer to the comm. They could not help but look at the screen to examine the map.

"Here," Daichi said pointing to the map, "D4. I should be able to get our people to D4. Is that okay?"

"That should be fine," Lirsín said. Patty counted the junctions they would have to take and seal, two major ones and a couple of little ones, it should be doable as long as they didn't have to fight for every meter. *Fighting.* Patty repressed a shudder. *There was going to be fighting.* Daichi was speaking, and she had missed his first words.

"...shame to leave Hestia in their hands though," Daichi added. "Lily and I have been discussing Hestia's fate," he frowned, "as a last resort."

"I'm sure I can rig the Winterberg to fire one last time, even in its current state," Lily's smile held no joy. "The far side of the accommodation wing should provide enough protection from the blast if we can get there."

"What about hand weapons?" Patty realized she held Lady Estelle's hilt.

"There's not much we can lay our hands on larger than a kitchen knife," Daichi smiled, "but for all their size I think I can relieve one or two of them of their blades."

"What about their white, knobbly staff things? I'm told they fire a focused pulse of sound," Patty added.

"We saw some when they first arrived, but they don't carry them now," Lily told them. "They seem to like threatening us with their swords. Any excuse." She seemed more disgusted than scared.

"We have some ideas about putting together an electro-shock weapon, and we have enough spare steel to knock together a few swords," Lirsín added.

"Having a sword and being able to use one is a kilt of a different color. I've fought the aliens, and they know how to use those blades," Patty said solemnly. She did not like to remember what she had done.

"I know we're short on time, but you said you've fought them?" Daichi asked. "I won't ask why or how, but do they have any weakness I can exploit?"

Patty closed her eyes for a breath and tried to put her thoughts in order. "As you've probably noticed, their bodies are specialized right-handers. I don't know if you've seen it, but they can interlock their bodies and fight in unison as a phalanx wall." Patty swallowed and tried to subtract her emotions from her memories. "Their wrist is almost completely locked; you can read their next movement from their hips half a second before it reaches their blade. Vulnerable down the outside line, they lock at about ten degrees and can't rotate further than that. I guess that's so their partner can protect that side." Patty's mind boggled at the evolutionary path that produced an adaptation like that. Their ancestors must have fought, hand-to-hand, nearly every day for generations.

After a few more minutes they broke the connection. There was nothing more to discuss. They had a plan, and they had Daichi. His presence drew a mighty weight from Patty's shoulders.

Twenty minutes later Patty and Alan were suited up and ready to leave.

"Wait!" Patty turned her eyes from Stan's hand on the airlock release to the young captain in his p-suit as he hurried down the corridor, helmet in one hand and what appeared to be a data wafer in the other. "The footage!" he cried. "Your trip through the alien ship!" He came to a slightly inelegant halt behind Alan and grinned. His gloved hand slipped the wafer into his wrist comm and patted it. "Thought I'd accompany you to your CRV and catch a copy if that's all right with you."

Stan chuckled; Lirsín blushed and shot a momentary frown at the bear of a man. The chuckle transformed into a cough. Stan and Lirsín looked like two schoolboys sharing a joke. *What's going on here?* It was clear something had been exchanged between the two men. It seemed good-natured like the ribbing she gave and received from Tina and Hine. Her initial warmth at the shipmates' camaraderie hit a sour note when she thought of her girlfriends. *Are they still alive?*

"That's a good idea, Captain. Didn't Daichi say he wanted a look at how the aliens fought?" Stan pressed home the large red button, and the airlock door slid open. "Wouldn't mind a look myself."

Patty snapped out of her reverie and gave Alan a quick once-over; yes, he was ready. "Of course. I can give you copies of all my data." *I wish I had an edited copy.* She had not realized she talked to herself quite as much as the little device revealed. It was embarrassing, but she could not refuse. *Besides, it's nice that*

Lirsín came himself.

Stan double checked her p-suit's seals and helped her on with her helmet. She followed Alan into the lock. There was enough room them both but not for Lirsín. He waved as the door slid shut.

"I was wondering if you'd find an excuse..." The rest of Stan's words were smothered by the air pumps and vacuum. She could see Lirsín laugh and throw a punch at Stan's beefy shoulder. Though she did not know what they were laughing about, she felt a contagious tickle of mirth rise inside.

Hestia's bulk hid Earth, the sun, and the moon, leaving the Milky Way to blaze unchallenged. Before Patty realized she had been star-gathering, Lirsín, in his smart p-suit with an Ice Princess motif on his breast pocket, was beside her. He leaned closely and pressed his helmet to hers, his arm comfortingly on her shoulder.

"So, what's our heading?" Lirsín's voice was thin, but his eyes were bright.

"Sorry?"

"Where have you parked?" he asked.

Parked? Freya! Patty could feel her color rising. *Those damn blue eyes!* "Yes. This way." She felt for Alan's hand on her belt. *Yes, he's ready. Why am I in such a spin?* She breathed a small sigh of relief when she found Freya on her first pass. She had to hold Lirsín back from blundering into the exhaust baffles.

Alan stowed himself into his rear seat, and then Patty slipped aboard, passing Lirsín an umbilical. It was clumsy but safer than using the radio. Patty set up the transfer, and the data began to flow. "She's not much to look at..." Patty had to join Lirsín's burst of laughter.

"In this light, she's hard to see at all. She's a sneakship!" Lirsín floated back a little, his eyes darting about, trying to trace Freya's outline. "Brings back stories Dad and Granpa used to tell about the war." His face transformed from wonder to concern. "Have you had any more thoughts about how we will disable the guard ship?"

"A couple." Patty's mind whirled as she tried to force it back into gear. "I plan on taking a closer look on my way back to Jaswinder."

Lirsín edged closer. "You be careful. We are working on an explosive device..."

"Don't worry. I'll always be careful ... double-arm distance. I promise. Freya has a good camera. I won't have to get too close." It felt warm and tingly that he showed so much concern. An indicator light told Patty the data transfer was complete. *How long has that been blinking?*

"Make sure you do, and that's an order," he commanded.

"You're not the captain when you're on my ship," Patty fired back.

Lirsín grinned and let go of Freya. "I'm not sure I'm actually on your ship. It's more like a rendezvous, surely."

ROUND LEGS

Little Star gaped as the litter breasted the gates of her father's holding. A team of Stone Son's cousins wore thick leather harnesses and pulled the polished, intricately carved framework of the litter along the track. It was not being carried but glided forward on four legs, four round legs. *Round legs!* It was an obvious idea once she thought about it. Little Star was awestruck by the mind that had thought of it first. *Did the Taker discover round legs? Do they have something to do with the Census? Whatever that is.* Little Star could not see past the blue and white drapes even though the curtains were open on her side. She damped down the curiosity that burned so brightly inside her; it wasn't safe to be too inquisitive when Papa had strangers at his hearth.

Papa and FirstSon hurried out and bade them welcome, showed the company where they could set up camp before escorting the litter and its guards up to his holding's flagged forecourt. Little Star climbed down from her perch. Even if Papa was occupied, it was best not to be noticed and standing up here on the ridge on Stone Son's shoulder she more than stood out. She was lucky Pa had not seen her already and sent her to the sheds. There was always something mucky to do in the sheds.

"You should go and say hello to your cousins," she said. Little Star swung from Stone Son's big finger when her feet touched the damp ground. He looked down, not saying anything but expressing lots. "Oh, don't be a big duffer. They won't bite, I'm sure."

CHAPTER TWENTY

Patty tried to swallow the lump in her throat as she edged Freya closer to the alien spaceship. She had witnessed fighters like this move with incredible speed and agility, their plasma flares lighting up the sky. And here she was, creeping up on its stern, staring into the blackened maw of that large exhaust port. If it fired now, Freya would be crisped, but Lirsín said they did not use the main engine to move the ship, so Patty knew she was safe unless something disturbed the aliens' routine. That would happen later.

Patty checked the time and hoped she could remember Madhur's instructions correctly.

Madhur had been shocked at the engine's size when she first scanned the images Patty returned with, but then she started laughing.

"You've got to be kidding me!" Madhur exclaimed, shaking her head with wonder. "I haven't seen an engine configuration like that since I was an apprentice. Man, did we have to work on some clunkers, but this thing takes the biscuit. It must be a complete fuel hog. Even poor old Jaswinder's engines are more efficient by a factor of five or six."

"But how are we going to get rid of it?" Cian muttered.

"We should pack Hunter with explosives and fly it up its butt!" Jai pitched in, his eyes bright. Jai's excitement level was through the roof, and Madhur had to threaten him with a duty watch on the bridge to keep him still.

"Only if Kerr's on it," Madhur smirked.

Cian looked past her without batting an eyelid, studying the images. *Something's different between you two.* Patty doubted that they had kissed and made up, but the atmosphere felt noticeably clearer. Madhur still threw insults at him, but there was a noticeable lack of venom in the delivery. Now and then, Patty would catch him smiling at one of Madhur's barbs.

Madhur zoomed in on one image, spun it around, and re-centered it. She turned to Patty. "So, just how close do you think you can get?"

This close. Patty sent one last puff through Freya's thrusters, and her smooth prow came to a halt one meter from the blunt stern of the alien ship. *It's time to go.* If they stayed too long, they were sure to be discovered. Patty took another slow deep breath while Freya's canopy opened. It did not stop her heart from racing. She took a sip from her p-suit's water supply to get a little moisture into her mouth. Her gloved finger caught in the buckle of her restraint, and she cursed. *You can't afford to have a case of butterfingers right now.* One more slow breath and Patty popped the release, rising slowly from her seat. She undogged the toolbox and pushed away from Freya. Alan followed, unlit torch in his hand. Patty wished her racing pulse would ease; it made her hands shake.

Slow and steady wins the race and any other platitudes that will get me through this. Patty floated above the engine. Madhur was right about its configuration. "A fusion engine is a magnetic bottle," she had said. "Screw with the polarity controls and the plasma drive could point just about anywhere."

The control leads were where she said they would be. Two

leads at six junctions. Patty could not stop herself from timing how long it took to uncouple the first; thirty seconds. A quick calculation spiraled through Patty's mind as she worked; twelve minutes, not counting travel time between junctions. Say, fifteen minutes tops. *Work faster hands, work faster.*

Ten minutes later Patty eased away from the fighter, Alan at her back, eager to return to the relative safety of Freya's cockpit. His quiet presence at her side, with the torch, pointed precisely where she needed it, kept her calm. Patty did not want to think about the consequences of her actions; she had put the wheels in motion that would kill the aliens on this ship. In the last week she had killed in self-defense, but this time it was premeditated. *Was it murder? Terrorism? War? Does it really make a difference what you call it? I'm a killer.* That thought did not sit well with her conscience.

Patty slipped into the cockpit and buckled in. It felt good to be back in Freya, but it did not quell Patty's fears. She mentally reviewed Madhur's instructions. She was sure she had completed everything Madhur had asked her to do, but Patty still felt as if she'd forgotten something. Alan tapped her shoulder; he was secure in the rear seat. It was too late to do anymore. They had to leave.

Patty gave Freya's thrusters the gentlest of nudges, and they began to slowly pull away from the blackened cavity of the ship's exhaust port. She did not bother to close Freya's canopy, flight time to their next stop was only minutes. Stars lit the dark as they retreated, and Earth was a brilliant blue and white gem. As the distance between the spacecraft increased, Patty's heartbeat returned to its normal lub-lub, but her apprehension continued to rise despite their evident success. She gave a short burst to the nose thrusters, slewing Freya around to starboard. Hestia's Hearth rolled into view.

The next step was up to Madhur and Cian. Could they present a viable threat and create a reason for the fighter to use its main engines? Then, with the alien ship destroyed, Hestia's crew could break out, join The Ice Princess and leave, heading far, far away. *Far away from aliens and fighting and ... my parents.* That was the point that kept sticking in Patty's craw. If she left with The Ice Princess, she would be giving up any chance of finding them. Everyone aboard Jaswinder had been keen on a rendezvous with The Ice Princess. They all agreed that it was too dangerous to stay. It was time to leave for The Belt. *We should have gone with Mr. Frobisher and the R&D station when they scattered.*

Patty edged Freya around The Ice Princess's prodigious aft and slipped into her ample dock. The ship's runabout was secured beside an area marked out for Freya. Stan waved her in, his gloved hand resting on the door's controls. *This is it. Goodbye Earth. Goodbye Mom and Dad.*

Freya settled onto the deck, and the landing gear made the connection with a reassuring clunk. "Okay; everybody out!" Patty said with mock exuberance. Alan released his safety harness and pushed out of the cramped seat. Patty helped him up and followed, closing the canopy behind her. She secured Lady Estelle's scabbard to her belt and gave Alan their overnight bag. "Let's go see if we did a good job."

"Ship disabled," he signed.

"Yes. Ship go boom." The outer doors slid closed, and Stan helped her secure Freya. When The Ice Princess escaped, there was bound to be some radical maneuvering; she had better be locked down tight.

"Ship go boom, good?" Alan asked as they crossed the deck to the internal lock. There was plenty of room for them all in the lock. Stan worked the controls and warm air cycled in.

"Normally no, but in this instance, yes. Ship go boom, good." It was not enough to disable the engines; the guard ship still had thrusters and weapons. It had to be eliminated.

Alan nodded. His face was relaxed, but tiny movements throughout his whole body suggested that he was thinking and then his left hand moved. "And then we fight," he signed. He loosened his blade in its scabbard.

"Probably, yes, we will fight," Patty agreed.

"Who?" Alan asked.

"Aliens. The ones that took you and changed you," Patty told him. Alan hesitated and then nodded. "You know they changed you, don't you?" Alan gave no response. "Before they took you... before they changed you, you were ... you were like Jai. Do you remember being Alan?" *Am I pushing him too hard? He's been doing so well.*

"This one," Alan paused, his fingers flexed and closed as if he was reaching for something, "this one knows of ... of the *Alan.* Some things, this one knows. Patty says this one is the *Alan.* This one does not know that."

"Don't worry, when we find Mom, she'll put things to rights," she told him. That sounded hollow to Patty, the chances of finding their parents were getting slimmer by the hour.

"Welcome aboard, once more." Stan secured the lock and stowed his helmet. "Captain said you'd be about nine hours and you're right on time. You can use these lockers for now." He stripped off his p-suit and slipped into his white shipsuit with blue piping. He grinned and rubbed his hands together. "Been workin' on some things. The captain will fill you in." He collected the iron bar from his locker and gave it a wave. "Been practicing too." He waggled the bar again. "Got me one more patrol to do. I'll see you soon."

He pushed off, sailing up the curved passageway. Patty liked Stan, despite his apparent hunger for battle. She would be more than happy if they could pull this off without confronting the aliens aboard Hestia. It felt good to be out of her p-suit; it was beginning to reek. That meant she did too. *Oh, for a quick freshener, five minutes with a sonic scrubber would do.* Patty glanced at her comm; there was no time for luxuries. The air felt cool and dry as they proceeded to the smuggler's room. Patty squinted against the harsh light as her fingers gripped and twisted the light fitting. The back wall slid open.

"Patty! Alan! Welcome!" Lirsín floated beside Rogers who was still crouched over the control panel. Lirsín wore the same white and blue Ice Princess shipsuit, but he had captain's stripes on his epaulets, and a short sword hung from his hip. He looked quite dashing, and her smile echoed his. Patty cast her eyes over the other crewmembers and noticed they all sported short swords; someone had been very busy. None looked particularly comfortable with them.

"We've been finalizing the explosive, but the delivery mechanism's going to take more time," Lirsín said as he sailed across the room with the economy of motion of someone who lived their life in zero-gee.

"I'm afraid you won't need them." Patty returned his smile, not to be polite, it grew all by itself as Lirsín moved closer. "The guard ship's primed and ready to blow."

"How? You've been there?" Lirsín asked hesitantly, worry diminishing his smile. Patty nodded. "Really? You said you were going to keep your distance." His smile broadened again. "Double-arm if I recall correctly."

"That was on the way out. I didn't say anything about our return journey." Patty enjoyed throwing a cheeky line at him. It seemed like ages since she had felt like having fun.

"So, you boarded the guard ship by yourself?" he inquired.

"No. Alan was with me. Couldn't have done it without him," Patty replied.

Lirsín sighed, concern and relief combined. "Rogers has kept his eyes peeled and didn't see a thing, or so he says. You haven't been sleeping on the job have you, Rogers?" Lirsín taunted the young man, but there was a note of seriousness underlying it. Rogers looked tired, with dark rings under his eyes, they all did. Patty felt lucky she'd been able to nap on the flight. It was not as refreshing as an uninterrupted eight hours, but the less Patty slept, the fewer nightmares she had to endure.

The monitor displayed two images of the alien fighter: a wide shot, with the ship not much more than a bright dot with the curve of Hestia's Hearth's hull out of focus in the foreground, and a close-up, showing enough detail to see movement in the cockpit. Patty was surprised and quietly pleased they had not seen her. She leaned closer. "I came in from the far side. It's not your fault you missed us," Patty reassured him. Rogers still blushed.

"Hunter should be coming from that quadrant," Patty indicated the top left corner of the wide shot. The big question she had been suppressing floated insistently to the surface of her mind: were Madhur and Cian able to modify Hunter enough to create a credible threat?

"What is Hunter?" Lirsín posed the question, but the faces of the crew around her asked as well.

"A spark. Something to kick-start the fireworks," Patty told them.

CHAPTER TWENTY-ONE

The view from Hestia's Hearth as she orbited the LaGrange Five's gravitational eddy was awe-inspiring. Heavy ash clouds in the northern hemisphere tarnished Earth's splendor, but she was still the most beautiful thing in the sky. The Moon, shining with silvery brilliance, had its own glory but it was cold and dead. Jake felt cramped in the observation bubble; there was not enough room to slip into his usual meditative head-over-heels roll.

There was not enough room aboard Hestia's Hearth at all. Engineering and a section of the onboard accommodations were off-limits, and soldiers packed the rest of her pressurized cabins. Jake could not help but chuckle at the thought. So many resources were tied up in this goose-chase. At least a dozen fighters and three of the blocky transport vessels loaded to capacity with soldiers, escorted their ship for the trip to L5. Their escort had taken up positions all around the half-built generational ship.

A movement of lights outside in the dark told Jake that the single visible guard ship had returned to its post after rotating its crew. He could have set his watch on the regularity of the shift. *Three days so far.* That was Jake's nearest guess. *Three days, waiting for Patty to arrive at* Hestia's Hearth. *I wonder how long these guys are willing to keep this up? Wherever you are, girl, stay far away from L5.*

Of course, he continued to protest at the presence of so many soldiers. *Was this to be a formal negotiation?* It was more like a trap. Which it was, without a doubt. Prince Rumble-Bum was not available, ever; so poor Pum was the recipient of Jake's protests. Although his caste was the bridge-makers, not all were skilled at negotiations, some, like Pum, were researchers, data-gatherers. While Pum held high regard, his social status, vis-à-vis Prince Rumble-Bum, was woefully inadequate. This placed Pum in an awkward position as Jake pressed him to confront the prince directly instead of through the caste's channels. Watching Pum squirm was not particularly pleasant. *But war is hell.* Jake chuckled again.

As if summoned by the thought, Pum walked into the observation bubble and took up a position beside Jake although he kept his feet anchored to the floor. The short, sharp movements in his right hand indicated he was tense even though the rest of Pum's body moved serenely.

"She is a good world." Pum reached out and touched the insulated glass of the observation port as if he could caress Earth across the velvety darkness. "There are few so full of," rumble, "life in the ... the vicinity."

"She was until you started lobbing rocks around. Dropping a rock on our heads was not a very neighborly act," Jake complained.

"Surprise was a," rumble, "stratagem that could not be discarded," Pum replied with what seemed to be an apologetic gesture.

"If you're looking for a fight," Jake argued.

"We were looking for a new home."

"Well, I hate to be the one to tell you, mate, we were here first. You must have known," Jake insisted.

"I'm sorry Traaaffic Control, our probes, and observations did not," rum-rumble, "indicate your presence."

"But hell, we've been broadcasting EM for hundreds of years, you must have heard our signals," Jake grumbled.

"That is true, but they were not recognized as such until we were committed to coming to your system. Our ship can travel very fast, but three generations have been born aboard her. The signals were," rum-bum-rumble, "compressed, shifted along the electromagnetic band. We did not recognize them until we slowed to velocities suitable for interplanetary flight."

"There's still plenty of real estate out there, plenty of places for you to set up shop. Making a grab for the one warm wet world sure blew any goodwill we humans might have had for weary travelers," he told Pum.

"There were many," rumble, "discussions in high chambers, but when news came that we were to have a new," rumble, "queen, many took it as a," rum-rumble, "sign ... omen, especially the ... err ... military," Pum replied.

"A new queen?" Jake asked as casually as he could.

"Did I not tell you they are rare?" Pum asked in return. "Very rare. With such a small," rumble, "population we are very fortunate to have her glory guiding us."

"Sorry?" Jake shook his head. "Your queen, she is young, a child?"

"Oh yes." Pum agreed.

"I see," Jake replied, but he did not. "If your queen is an infant, how did she convince your council to have this meeting?"

"Our young are not like yours, true they are small and need extra care, but they do not lack for intelligence or the ability to express their will. All can walk and run on their first day, within hours," rum-rumble, "We know of no other species whose young are so helpless as yours," Pum added.

"Yes, our young are helpless for many years, perhaps that's why humans protect them so fiercely," Jake growled. It was time to change the subject and get Pum squirming again. "And speaking of protection, the place is packed to overflowing with soldiers. I know *your* intentions are honorable, but I will have to warn my Queen that this meeting place is unsafe, that this is a trap."

"Please Traaaffic Control, you know I communicated your concerns to," Pum rumbled for a bit. Jake could not catch the nuances; the frequency was too low for his aged ears to hear clearly.

"And what did Prince Rumble-bum have to say?" Jake asked.

"Well, this one was not able to," Pum began.

"Fobbed off again? Pum, this is not good. Not at all. As the emissary for my Queen, I must protest most strongly. If Rumble-Bum is unavailable, then you must use other channels. You *can* get word to your queen. Please convey to her my fears."

Pum gave a tiny bow, a whole-body nod. "It is," rumble, "err ... outside the usual bounds of ... protocol, but I will send a message immediately."

Suddenly the flare of a high-powered engine burned brightly in the star-strewn darkness, and it began spiraling toward them. Jake grabbed the window frame and slid to one side. There was not much parallax, but it was enough to confirm his initial thoughts; Hestia's Hearth was not the target. The guard ship sitting five hundred meters away was. It spun around to face the attack.

Judging by the speed of the incoming flare, it was not a missile, and it moved too slowly to be a military device. *It's a broomstick with its engine on overdrive. It'll be fast enough, but targeting is the real issue.* If it could lock on and make contact, it would not need a warhead. Collisions at orbital velocities were always spectacularly violent. Not that Jake expected the guardship just to sit there. *What are they doing?*

Stuttering light leaked from the engine bay, and Jake started grinning. *Engine trouble, eh boys? Better do something about it, quick smart.* The engine fired, and Jake's eyes popped wide as it flared in the wrong direction, through the bow, tearing the ship apart. Just as Jake recovered from his initial surprise, the relatively slow missile completed the demolition of the sentry ship spectacularly.

"Whoa!" Jake flinched. Hestia's Hearth would be lucky to escape unscathed from the flying debris.

"Oh." Pum rumbled some more. "What just happened, Traaaffic Control? Did this one see our ship explode before the," rumble, "projectile hit?"

"That's the way it looked to me. Your maintenance Grays need a good talking to," Jake said with a laugh.

"What do you mean?" Pum asked.

"Well, I've heard stories, with first generation ships, old ones, where the engineer screwed up and reversed the polarity of the engine's containment field. I mean, you'd have to be drunk or stupid to get something so radically wrong, but you'd know better than I."

"But the ... missile, striking now, at this time, can it be a," rum-rumble, "coincidence?"

Jake fought hard to keep from smiling, and then a chill blasted through him. *What if Pum's right? What if this is a sign that Patty's here?* "Seems to be a bit showy. Didn't you say my Queen slips in and out unnoticed? You've made a whole solar system of enemies. But with the ship's engine failing like that, surely, it's an inside job."

Rumble. "An inside job?" Pum asked, twisting around as he tried to parse the concept. "This one does not understand."

"Someone wants this meeting to fail, and they sabotaged the ship's engine," Jake told him.

"No, no." Pum backed away, his right hand making hesitant dabs. "That is not possible. No."

One of the huge guards stooped as he entered the small observation bubble and began to rumble. Pum's demeanor changed immediately, from uncertain to self-assured, his right hand swirled a confident dance. The guard bowed and withdrew.

"Your queen is here!" Pum boom-rumbled another few phrases. "Come. We must go."

Fear overwhelmed Jake's feelings of delight at seeing the alien ship taken out. "My queen is here?"

"Yes," rumble, "security cameras have shown her," Pum told him.

"*Aboard* Hestia's Hearth?"

"Oh yes. Come we must meet with," rum-rumble, "the prince's delegation."

There was nothing Jake could think of that would delay Pum. His mind felt blank, a soggy unresponsive lump. *What's Patty doing on Hestia's Hearth? Oh, please. I hope they've made a mistake.*

A SMALL BONE

Little Star was an expert at staying out of the way, but that did not keep her from getting a little meat with her stew that night. Mama tried to feed her a little piece whenever she could, despite Papa's objections. He always said that meat was wasted on a runt like her. But she got a taste almost regularly once she learned even Papa turned a blind eye if the theft was artfully done.

When Mama came to get her, Little Star thought she was in trouble for stealing her treat and tried to pretend she was asleep, tucking the evidence under her thin pillow. *Surely Pa hadn't missed such a small bone.* It was hard not to shake; she was already on edge. The angry shouts echoing up from the Great Hall earlier in the evening scared her, even if it had not been Pa doing the shouting. It was Stone Son's Pa by the sound of it. Ma shook her and held her face in her warm hands until Little Star opened her eyes. She hoped the grease did not show on her chin or her pillow, but Mama did not notice anything out of order. Little Star held little hope of returning to find the bone with all its juicy marrow still under her pillow, one of her greedy brothers always checked. Mama did not say anything but pushed her out in front of her all the way down to the Great Hall.

CHAPTER TWENTY-TWO

Three beeps. Patty's wrist comm chimed a ten-second warning, and she scanned Roger's display. *There!* An engine flare moved against the stars bright as a newborn sun. It was moving quickly. Patty's heart skipped a beat. Her gut-estimate had Hunter accelerating at over eight-gees! The flare jinked to one side and began a sliding, offset roll. It blazed brighter, flying faster. Patty couldn't suppress her grin.

"The old Singer's probably pushing fifteen-gees," Patty whispered under her breath. *Incredible.* It jinked again, reducing the offset and spiraling tighter. The tiny engine's plume blazed brighter and brighter, kicking it forward faster and faster. Patty could feel The Ice Princess's crew crowd closer. She edged sideways a little so they could see. It didn't hurt that she had to press closer to Lirsín. He gave her a quick grin before his eyes snapped back to the screen.

The alien guard ship spun slowly around. Its main engine gave one flickering burst, then stalled. The cameras tracked the ship as it drifted. Frantic motion filled the cockpit.

Suddenly a bright spear of plasma burst out, overloading the cameras. It flared, not out from the stern but forward, through the center of the ship, rupturing aft to bow, searing a growing hole in the sharp prow. A fireball erupted from the fuel tank on the port side, followed seconds later, by its starboard counterpart. Lirsín and his crew let out a cheer. Patty sighed and swallowed a rising tide of bile; she had killed again. And it was not over yet.

Hunter smashed into the burning remains of the alien ship, detonating spectacularly. Broken and burning machine parts, bulkheads, and pieces of fuselage spiraled away in all directions. Patty wished she had not watched. *Blood and flames, burning debris, are more nightmare fodder*, she thought with a shudder.

"Well done, well done!" Lirsín congratulated her, beaming, his hand resting on her shoulder. For a moment Patty wondered what it would feel like to have his arms wrapped around her.

"Ship go boom," Alan signed.

Patty laughed, partially in surprise at her brother's understatement and in part to join in with the crew's elation. She did not feel excited; she felt dread. "Yes, indeed. Ship go boom." Patty scanned the wide shot, wondering where Jaswinder was. *Don't be tempted to come in closer, Madhur, stay on course. We'll come to you. Just like we planned.* Patty was afraid it was going to get bloody before it got better.

"Now we fight," Alan signed calmly.

"Yes. Are you ready?" Patty asked, and Alan nodded. Patty turned and came face to face with Stan's bright eyes and excited grin.

"You're a clever girl, Ms. Balke," he said.

"With talented friends. That wasn't all my work, you know," Patty told him and could feel herself blushing; she did not want the credit, not at all. Madhur and Cian had modified Hunter. She had worked with Ken to plot the best flight plan and had sabotaged the alien vessel. No, it was not all her work.

"And modest too," Stan chuckled. He shook his head and looked at his captain. "I hope you've got a contract written up for this one. She's a keeper." He laughed.

Lirsín chuckled, his eyes sparkling. "I have to admit I'm a bit behind on the paperwork." His smile warmed something inside Patty. It was pleasant but distracting. *Concentrate, girl. You are Kali, Bringer of Death!* Patty reminded herself. Lirsín focused on his comm officer, "Do we have a link to Daichi?"

"Yes, sir," Rogers reported and slid the camera images to one side, bringing up a grainy comm feed. Daichi was waiting; his face was grave but calm.

"We are ready," Daichi said. "We caught the feed. Best strike while the iron is hot." He glanced over his shoulder at the remains of Hestia's crew; over a dozen men and women crowded behind him. A buzz of excitement rippled through them. "Lily's still in engineering. If she hasn't joined us by the time we get to junction C3, I'm going to," he frowned, "see what's detaining her. If not, I'll meet you at D4 as planned."

"We're all go on our side," Lirsín confirmed briskly. "We should have a secured evac route for you from D4 to our airlock."

"See you soon," Daichi replied and closed the connection.

Lirsín turned to face his crew. "Nanna, Tamir, Chao, Myung, you're with the Chief. Go, get your gear. The rest of you, we have to get The Princess prepped for flight in record time, so let's get to it. This is our one chance to get home. Call in if you are having problems; we can't afford any mistakes." He clapped his hands together. "Let's go. Let's go."

Patty was impressed with the way the crew responded to Lirsín, most were older than the young captain, but they snapped to attention. In seconds, the hidey-hole emptied as the ship's crew scattered to their duties. Patty, with Alan at her side, followed Lirsín and Stan, with the rest of his team close behind. Lirsín stopped at the airlock. "Nanna, Tamir, I know you're scared, but Stan, Myung, and Chao have your backs."

A sickening flush of confusion rolled through Patty as she opened her overnight bag and pulled out her fencing gear. Lirsín had not included her. Nanna and Tamir carried small hand torches, not big enough to seal the doors permanently but good enough for a few quick tacks.

"Get in, get Hestia's crew, and get out. Quick as you can. Stay safe," Lirsín told them.

Patty wanted to say something, but her tongue felt like rubber. "I have to go, too." It came out more like a whisper than the shout her gut demanded. She shook out her padded vest and wished she had one for Alan.

Lirsín looked at Patty with concern in his deep blue eyes. "No, you've done enough."

"Aye, the captain's right, young lass," Stan agreed and swung his iron bar. "We've got their measure. Don't you worry."

Patty knew when she was being patronized, and for a moment she nearly gave in to her fears. *Protect me!* "No! No, you don't!" Patty was not sure if she should be angry with Lirsín, but it was a good place to start. "I've fought them. You're strong but too slow." Patty took a breath. They were listening to her; she was glad she had not yelled; when her voice was stressed it had a squeak that even annoyed Patty. Stan frowned as he smacked his muscular thigh with that iron bar.

"Hestia's crew have Daichi," Patty continued. "He coached my fencing team and has more Olympic gold than all the other coaches combined. If anyone can take on the aliens and win, I'd bet on Daichi every time." Patty focused on Stan. "I know you're eager to face them, but that will only get you killed." That iron bar of his gave her a chill and hoped it would have the same effect on the aliens. "You need your most experienced team on point." Patty held her gaze until Lirsín wilted.

"But you're such a wee thing, and your brother," Stan objected.

"You've watched my recordings?" Patty asked.

"Yeah..." Stan backed off a little. He sighed and looked across at his captain. "She's right. We do need her."

Lirsín frowned. He took a breath and growled softly. "I'm sorry, Patty. I did not want this." His warm hands took hers, and Patty's heart raced.

"Captain, we gotta make tracks," Stan announced and looked at each of his team members. He received a nod from each of them and took the lead, pushing off down the corridor.

Lirsín's eyes followed them for a moment before returning to Patty. "I want to keep you ... safe." His fingers tightened.

"I don't want this either, but none of us will be safe until we're millions of kilometers from here," Patty said, trying to sound confident. "You have your job. I have mine. Get The Princess prepped." Despite her words, Patty held onto Lirsín's warm hands.

Lirsín's comm buzzed. "Stay safe." His beautiful eyes locked to hers for one second before he squeezed her hands. He turned and raced back through the airlock.

Alan drew his blade. Patty took a breath, swallowed and drew Lady Estelle. She knew she needed to clear her head of the giddy emotions coursing through her. She pushed Lady Estelle's lethal tip through a pair of tight spirals and felt her body respond. The muscles she used for fencing awoke, and her mind settled and focused. *Yes, we can do this.*

It only took a couple of seconds to catch up with the rest of the team. Myung and Chao had short swords at their hips, but they also sported what appeared to be a pair of kludged together crossbows with heavy-duty power leads running to a backpack. They looked nervous. Patty didn't blame them.

Hestia's corridor was pastel-pink with white trim, scuffed and sorely abused by the construction crew. More importantly, it was empty. The first doorway they needed to seal was starboard of the airlock. All the other doors were on the port side of The Ice Princess's lock. Sealing this one meant their backs were safe.

"What are they?" Patty asked Stan, looking at the strange crossbow in Chao's arms.

"Since guns are out of the question, muzzle velocity of a twenty-two could punch a hole in Hestia's delicate skin; I thought a crossbow might be a good delivery mechanism for an electro-shock weapon. The dart velocity isn't high enough to penetrate the hull, but it should penetrate the aliens. Just a little is enough, eighty thousand volts should get them twitching, don't you think?" Stan asked, wiggling his bushy eyebrows. "They've a limited range, but I promise they carry a huge kick." Stan looked inordinately proud as if he had hand-assembled each one.

They reached a section bulkhead, and Stan dogged the door closed. The bulkhead doors would close and seal the corridor automatically in the event of a hull breach but activating them would surely send an alert to the bridge. Nana and Tamir set to work on opposite corners sealing this end of the corridor. It would not be long before there would be a secure pathway, sealed off from the rest of Hestia, through which they could evacuate her skeleton crew. And then they could all leave.

"We should take the lead, Stan," Patty said brandishing Lady Estelle and he acquiesced with a smile and a theatrical bow.

"Of course, Ms. Balke," his gravelly voice replied, and he gestured back down the corridor with the twisted iron bar. "After you."

Patty pushed off, her heart racing. She did not want a confrontation with these aliens. If they could slip in and out without them noticing, Patty would be overjoyed, but she doubted that things would go that smoothly.

CHAPTER TWENTY-THREE

The first major junction they approached was empty. Stan dogged the pressure door on the right while Patty closed the one leading straight ahead. Nana and Tamir quickly made sure they stayed that way.

"Let's hope they're all like this," Patty whispered. The passageway to the left was unobstructed, but it curved to the right, and there was no telling who or what was around the slow corner. There was room for two to move abreast, but there was not much headroom. If they met an armed party, they would have to fight from the floor; there was no room for aerobatics.

The next small junction seemed clear, one corridor leading off to the right until Patty and Alan entered it. Patty's dream of an encounter-free journey evaporated. Two aliens with their blades drawn approached from the center of the ship at speed. Two more were hard on their heels. Patty did not want Nana and Tamir to get caught tinkering with the door controls when they arrived. She took a deep breath and stood en-garde in the doorway. Alan readied himself beside her. He appeared emotionless but bright-eyed and alert.

"I'll go high, you go low, just like we practiced," Patty signed with her right hand. She flexed her left wrist, and Lady Estelle's bright blade whistled as it cut through the air.

Everything seemed to move in slow motion; the two aliens in dark red striped tabards paused for a heartbeat. Patty was sure she heard one of them cough. *Well, cough on this, buster.* Patty stretched, her blade extended in front. *This is not a competition. There were more than team points at stake.* Adrenaline flooded through her, and her heart raced. She slashed the tip of her blade in a tight figure eight.

"It doesn't have to be like this you know," Patty called out trying to sound sounded defiant, hoping they could not hear the fear in her heart. It looked like the invaders were not interested in conversation. The leading aliens slowed their charge again and moved closer, their twisted bodies interlocking just as Patty had witnessed on the mothership. Two bright-edged blades moved as one, and they resumed their charge.

It was one thing to plan a coordinated offense and another to put it into practice. Patty and Alan had to retreat before the powerful attack, backing into the corridor, and fading back to the right. The aliens were fast and very strong. Patty felt uncoordinated fighting with Alan at her side. Despite their practice sessions her first instinct was to protect him. Every blade raised was a threat *she* had to counter.

Patty heard gasps from The Princess's crew, and urgent whispers under the clash of blades, but Stan kept them back and out of the way. Patty had pinked the alien confronting her nearly a dozen times before it realized it was bleeding. Alan had kept the other at bay but had not penetrated its defenses. Patty glanced into the corridor as she took another step back, retreating before a flurry of head cuts. The second pair of aliens had just entered the passage. *I'd better find a hole in this one's defenses soon; reinforcements are getting close.* The alien Patty faced was fast, but it suffered from something Patty witnessed many times in competition, it had never fought a southpaw.

The reinforcements arrived, and twangs sounded from behind Patty. Two twin-barbed projectiles, trailing monofilament wires, flew through the air. One hit the wall, knocked aside by a hastily raised blade as the locked-together pair came to a halt. The second dart struck its target, and that alien went down screaming and convulsing, pulling the other to the floor with it.

With a blood-curdling scream, Stan bulled his way over Patty and Alan, whipping that iron bar from side to side. The alien facing Patty flinched and was seconds behind when its partner attacked high, to Alan's inside. Patty faded to her left and let Alan deal with it. Her opponent attempted the same attack. Patty was already low, compressed, under his guard. She lunged, exploding forward. Lady Estelle's point parted the light body armor under the tabard, parted the tough skin and muscle, slid against bone, and emerged from the alien's back. She managed to grab the alien's head and turn it before blood exploded from its mouth. Patty felt her stomach spasm, but she savagely suppressed the urge to vomit as she pushed the body away, freeing her blade.

She whipped around to help Alan, but he had already dispatched his opponent, as had Stan. She had not witnessed much of Stan's fight except for the rise and fall of that iron bar as he hacked at the back-peddling alien. He was covered in blood from head to toe, roaring his glorious victory at the top of his lungs, a challenge that gave Patty a chill.

"Are you okay?" Patty asked Alan, her eyes darting over her brother's body. It was impossible to tell if that was his blood or the aliens'. He stood straight and took a deep breath, then flashed her a thumbs-up.

"This one is uninjured," he signed as he tried to catch his breath.

"I'm sorry," Patty apologized and paused to suck in a breath or two herself. "I was getting in your way."

"We learn. We live," Alan signed as his eyes scanned the junction. It remained clear. He took a long look at Patty and moved closer. His hand touched Patty's shoulder, and she flinched.

"Ouch!" Some of the blood covering her tracksuit was her own; her padded vest had two cuts. *When did that happen?* While Myung and Chao stood watch, Stan pulled a bandage from his belt pouch and dressed her wound. It was not deep.

"That will have it sealed in less than ten minutes if ya don't stress it," Stan chuckled. "As if that's going to happen."

"Stan, I really think you would do better if you put an edge on that thing," Patty told him. She looked down at the gore covered iron bar and shuddered.

Stan moved back, closed his pouch and picked up his dripping bludgeon. "Yeah maybe, but it wouldn't be as much fun." He gave his weapon a casual flick, sending a spray of gore across a wall. "I saw fear in its eyes." Stan laughed heartily. "Oh, that was good to see." He looked up. "That one's for you, Carson," he whispered.

As Nanna and Tamir sealed the door, Patty could hear either Myung or Chao vomiting at the sights and smells of the bloody carnage. She did not wish to compound their misery, so she turned away and continued down the corridor. They had done well to hold their nerve and fire their weapons.

Six aliens guarded the next major junction, and Stan pushed past Patty to meet them at high speed, flailing about him with a berserker's rage, sowing chaos amongst the alien's regimented lines. Once again, Myung and Chao fired into the row of aliens; two went down this time. Their phalanx was in tatters.

Patty and Alan advanced, quickly backing up Stan's reckless charge and met a pair of alien blades before they could flank Stan. Alan began the routine they had practiced back on Jaswinder, except about three times faster. Patty struggled for a moment to match his pace. The rumbles multiplied as the aliens retreated before their onslaught, tangling with the still twitching, electrocuted aliens beside them.

Stan screamed his war cry once more as he slashed with his iron bar and an alien went down. Patty's opponent shuddered visibly and tried to press forward, attacking in desperation, trying to keep away from the maniac and his bloody staff.

Alan held his ground and lunged low, his blade passing most of the way through his opponent's knee. The alien howled and began to collapse. Patty thrust high, across the line, blocking her adversary's hurried blow and piercing the other's throat. Blood sprayed. Alan attacked diagonally as well, stabbing upwards, through the armor and into the alien's warped belly.

Stan's twisted iron bar tore the remaining alien's head from its shoulders. It was very bloody; most of it spurted over Stan's the grinning face, turning into a nebula of churning particles. He frowned as he looked at the bodies. "Four at the last junction and six here," he shook his head, and droplets of blood sprayed from his hair. "There can't be many of the buggers left."

"I guess not," Patty replied and moved further down the corridor so that the door could be closed and sealed, but she had the feeling that things were far from over.

"And there's that other Gray. We haven't seen that one yet," Stan muttered.

"Best keep on our toes then," Patty said as she caught her breath. Her shoulder and wrist ached fiercely, and she tried to work the tension from her shoulders and neck. With the door welded closed, they continued down the corridor, trailing drops of gore.

Patty felt numb, in shock; she recognized the symptoms, her heart was racing, she felt cold and clammy, dizzy. She tried to take slow deep breaths. Her hands shook, her whole body shook. *Blood. I'm covered in blood. Again.*

EXPOSED

The Great Hall looked so different, filled with people sitting at table, and with the long trestles laden with food. Little Star had only been in the Great Hall to help with cleaning. It kept her close to Ma even if she was not much help. Pa would be sitting at the center of the high table with the honored Taker to his right, Little Star guessed. She was not brave enough to lift her head and look.

"Council wants it?" Papa asked with a laugh. "The runt? Sure, take it. Ha!" The sound of Pa's meaty paws smacking together as he laughed was such a relief that Little Star missed what happened next, but Mama was hugging her and crying as she hustled Little Star from the Great Hall. She could not miss that.

"Be brave, Little Star," Ma told her.

"What's happening, Ma?" Little Star asked, but Ma did not answer. She bustled Little Star out into the forecourt, pushing her towards the strange litter and the guards surrounding it. The night was crisp and refreshing compared to her stuffy attic space. Torches burned above the holding's broad doorway and at intervals around the forecourt. The Taker's guards stood around in relaxed groups, drinking or eating from the trestle tables. Little Star had never seen so much food.

"The Census Taker ... take ... Little Star," Ma stopped and gave her little daughter a last hug. "Said Little Star was special. I always knew, my bright little star."

And then she was gone, leaving Little Star not quite across the yard but far from the Taker's men. Little Star stood nervously, exposed.

CHAPTER TWENTY-FOUR

"Right, we're clear to D4." Stan grinned at Patty and saw her distress for the first time. "How you doing lassie? Sorry about doubtin' you before. Goes against the grain to see someone so young fighting like this." Stan glanced at Alan and shook his head. "We would have been mincemeat without ya."

"I'll ... I'll be okay in a minute ... when I catch my breath," Patty replied with a grimace. *I will master my fear. I will.*

Suddenly Stan's eyes glazed over, and his head dropped. He released the bloody bar. Patty rushed to him as Alan stood warily on guard. Stan had one deep cut on his arm, numerous small ones all over him and one deep wound to his belly. Patty grabbed a bandage from her waist pack, ripped open Stan's shipsuit and pressed it against the bloody flow. Bandages were great at re-knitting torn flesh but that wound needed surgery.

"Nanna, Tamir. Your help, please. More bandages, quickly," Patty commanded. She looked in Stan's eyes; they were open and a little glassy. "Stan! Stay with us. Why didn't you say anything?"

"What? Why have we stopped?" Stan blinked as if only just waking, and then his face contorted in pain.

"Lie easy, soldier," Patty told him and checked the bandage's readings; it was nearly full; she pressed firmly. Stan groaned. Tamir dressed the wound on Stan's arm as Patty thought about what to do. She wanted to pick Stan up and hurry back to The Ice Princess, but there was more than just her wishes to consider. Patty knew she would have to go on. But she could not live with the thought of abandoning Daichi and Hestia's crew. Patty took a slow breath and examined the bandage; it was full. She squeezed it out and wiped down the wound. The skin was almost sealed, but that just meant Stan was bleeding internally. He looked terribly pale.

"You need to get him back to The Princess, Tamir," Patty stated calmly. "Now. Give your torch to Nanna."

"You're going on?" Tamir asked as he began to lift Stan from the floor. He writhed and groaned under Tamir's hands.

"Of course. Now hurry, Stan's in serious trouble. Go," Patty said, trying to sound calm but urgent. Tamir got the message and pushed off, taking Stan under tow. They disappeared up the corridor.

"I don't know how you do it," Nanna told her. "Those aliens scare me witless." She looked pale, and her hands were shaking, "but I'm bloody glad you're here."

"We've only got one shot each," Myung told her. "We didn't think we would meet so many. Do you think we can do it?"

"We have to try," Patty replied firmly, setting her doubts aside. *You know what you need to do. Don't think about it too much.* "Ready?" Her team - *it's my team now* - nodded and she led them onward. They moved as quickly as they could down the curved corridor.

Aliens approached the D4 junction from the other direction, and two of the super-sized aliens moved quickly to take possession of space. They stood head-and-shoulders taller than the soldiers, nearly filling the intersection. Aliens in red hurried down the corridor behind the enormous pair.

Patty spoke over her shoulder to Chao and Myung as they continued down the corridor, "They're yours. Last shot. Make 'em count."

A familiar human face leaned out from the crowd of regular-sized warriors that were supporting the two huge ones, and he waved. Patty could not believe her eyes; surprise did not cover it. She raised her arm, slowing their charge. The familiar face was Jake's, and he wore a maniacal grin. Patty blinked and refocused on the dozen or so aliens confronting them. It was impossible. For the moment, the two huge ones held their ground.

Jake collected a pale left-handed alien with an intricate light blue tabard and pressed through the soldiers. The two giants had to squeeze out of the way to let them through into the junction.

"Hi ya, kiddo!" Jake remarked as he strode towards her. His eyes were bright, but he looked worried. And then he bowed extravagantly. The urge to throw her arms around her dear friend was almost overwhelming. *What are you up to, Jake?* The huge guards focused on Jake's flamboyant posturing. *We don't have time for this.*

"Go!" Patty commanded her troops. She elbowed the small alien in the face. Jake caught the stumbling alien, dragging it out of the way. A twang sounded from behind her. Alan feinted to his left, distracting the guard from noticing the barbed projectile. It struck home. The colossal alien's thrashing body pitched backward through the doorway.

Patty's thrust snaked around the other alien's guard and pierced its heavily protected wrist. It screamed as its fingers released its sword. Alan attacked low, severing the tendons in its forward leg. It hobbled backward as Patty smacked her palm into the emergency-close button. Pressure doors slammed shut from their recessed positions, or at least they tried to. They caught the big alien, as it stumbled backward, crushing its one good leg in a vice-like grip. The foot twitched. Screams and hooming came from beyond the partially closed door. It was not sealed, but it was closed sufficiently for Nanna to tack it in place. *They won't get through there in a hurry.*

Patty blinked and took a deep breath. *They'd done it! D4 was theirs.* Patty checked Alan; he gave her a thumbs-up. And then she remembered. "Jake! How in Murphy's Twisted Universe did you get here? Are you okay?" She reached out and grabbed his bristly chin and stared into his eyes; they looked clear. She could not get over the fact he was here. *How long has it been since we fled OASIS?*

"Oh, Patty my dear, don't worry about me. We gotta get outa

here," Jake urged as he ripped the tabard from his shoulders. "Prince Rumble-Bum has packed Hestia's Hearth to the rafters with soldiers. You've caused quite a stir. I don't know what you're after but..."

"The remaining crew of Hestia's Hearth," Patty told him. Noises echoed down the passageway to her left. "That should be them now." She gripped Lady Estelle and readied herself in case the aliens had found another way through. *Please Murphy, no more aliens.* Her experience of calm clarity during the engagement ebbed away. Patty could feel her hands start shaking again. A young woman poked her head around the corner and quickly ducked back.

"It's okay," Patty called out as relief flooded through her. "We have the junction, now move!" The face popped back into view. "Quickly!" The young woman pushed away from the floor and flew towards her, smiling. Others followed.

"Thank you," she said as she floated past.

"That's okay. Just keep moving," Patty told her as she kept her eyes peeled for Daichi.

"Patty, what should we do with this one?" Chao bluffed the cowering alien, keeping it his empty crossbow's sights.

"Jake? Is it an important ... alien?" Patty asked.

"You could say that, yes," Jake replied with a chuckle. "He's here to negotiate a treaty with you, my queen."

A part of Patty relaxed, hearing his Texan drawl. He was someone she trusted implicitly, but his words took some digestion. "A treaty? With me? What have they been feeding you?"

Jake laughed. "I embellished your status with the aliens, but only a little, oh queen. You were doing a fine job all by yourself. By defeating their queen's captain on L2 and making his subordinates surrender ... they recognize the station as your domain ... sort of. In their eyes, well some of them, you are royalty. You seem to be able to appear and disappear at will. Your visit to their mothership scared them spitless, and they've been blaming every mishap and rebellion on you. Pum, here, was going to offer you L5 as well if you would cease hostilities against them. Quite reasonable, I thought."

"Hostilities? Me against them?" Patty asked, her mind was spinning. "You've got to be kidding." *Were those fireworks going off in my brain?* It felt good to laugh.

The last of Hestia's crew - an older man with thinning hair - entered the D4 junction. He brandished a handheld welder like Nanna's. "The doors behind us won't be opening anytime soon. Daichi went to fetch Lily. Told us not to wait."

"Thanks. Go on. We'll be on your heels," Patty said and gave one last glance down the empty corridor.

"Yes, sir. And thank you." He smiled, gave Patty a salute, and pushed off strongly. *Sir?*

Patty looked at the alien once more. "Bring it along. It might be useful. Let's go." *I own L2? That's ludicrous. It's one of Jake's shaggy-dog stories, for sure.* Patty let Chao take charge of their prisoner and waited for them to get clear before following Jake and Alan. "A treaty? That's madness."

"Well, as I said, I did embellish your status somewhat. They've been jumping at shadows and were only too willing to accept you as a queen, or at least a queen in the making. I warned them of the terrible wrath of young Earther queens. You being a southpaw sold it."

Patty's mind flashed back to the mothership and swarm of aliens filing past the tiny golden one. *Was that their queen?* she wondered. "They think I'm like that? Great, Jake. Good joke. This time the shadow they jumped at landed them in my lap. We wanted to sneak in and out. No mess, no fuss, no paperwork."

"I'm afraid they would have been here in any case. I think they hoped to catch you by yourself. Having allies surprised them. Where did they come from? Where did you come from?" Jake asked.

"They are what's left of The Ice Princess's crew. They have ... err ... hiding places," Patty told him.

Jake laughed. "They don't flaunt it, but most Belters have secure bolt holes on their ships. Smuggling is in their blood."

"So, some of the crew managed to hide. I've been," Patty glanced at Alan, hovering at her side, "we've been everywhere." She gave Jake a quick rundown of their travels as they hurried down the corridor, finding Jaswinder with Madhur and Jai and Griffin with Eg, Cicely, and Ken and Cian. "By the time we get back, The Ice Princess should be powered up and ready to go. We took out the ship on guard. The Princess has more than enough grunt to get us far away and quickly."

Jake's eyes sparkled. "I saw the guard ship go up. Nice work. You must tell me how you pulled that one off." He frowned. "I think you'll find that there's a damn sight more ships out there than that one, but you're right, The Princess, without a load, could leave just about anything in its wake." He smiled. "Maybe we do have a chance."

A moving shadow flickered behind them. Patty turned and faced the rear as they flew back to the airlock. A broad blade edged around the corner they had just flown past. Patty rotated, her sneakers gripping the floor. A glance told her that Alan was beside her. As much as she wanted the old Alan back, she was glad his steady hand held another blade beside her. Jake kept well away but showed no sign of leaving.

Once again, relief poured through Patty when she saw Daichi's worried face behind the probing blade. A smile replaced his expression of firm resolve.

"Patty! It is good to see you." Daichi looked over Patty's shoulder. "Jake Chowdhury? Where did *you* come from?"

"Hitched a ride and thought I might take up Patty's invitation for a tour of the Outlands. Speaking of which." He pointed down the corridor.

"Yes." Patty looked over Daichi's shoulder. "Where's Lily?"

Daichi's frown returned. "I couldn't get through to her," he said. "There were just too many of them. She's been so keen on getting Hestia's Hearth prepped for her big send-off."

"Send off?" Patty asked. "Well, we better keep moving." Patty turned and led them through the corridors while Daichi watched their rear. Lirsín, Chao and the alien were waiting impatiently at the airlock.

"Oh good! You're here," Lirsín said as he hustled Chao and the alien through the airlock. "I just received a message from Lily. We have twenty minutes."

CHAPTER TWENTY-FIVE

"Twenty minutes 'till what?" Jake asked Patty.

Daichi answered before Patty had the chance to open her mouth. "Lily has been rigging the Winterberg for a parting gift. We didn't want to leave it for them." Daichi glared at the prisoner. "Is she still in engineering?"

Lirsín nodded leading them into the airlock. "We must make ready to depart; come aboard." He looked askance at the pale alien under Chao's steady eye. "Take it to the brig." Lirsín adjusted the settings on the control panel beside the lock after they boarded The Ice Princess and the outer doors slid shut, followed quickly by the inner doors. The ship shuddered, and a comm light flashed by the control panel. Lirsín leaned across and opened the connection. "Captain to the bridge. Hard lock disconnected," he reported.

"Reading in the green here, sir."

"We'll be there in a couple of minutes, Rogers." Lirsín turned back to Patty, wearing a frown. "I have a dilemma." He rubbed his face. His eyes looked red. Patty was tired too, but finding Jake had given her a second wind. "A cold start takes time for a ship of this size. We will be able to get clear in time but not if we have to maneuver around to Hestia's engineering lock."

Patty knew what he wanted; there was one last crewmember to save. "I'll get her. Freya can be ready in no time flat." She looked at her brother. He would insist on coming, and Patty did not want to be separated from him either.

"Thank you, Patty. But that means *we* are short one pilot. I'd use Stan, but he's injured." Lirsín's brows drew close together.

"Thanks for the vote of confidence, but I've never flown

anything this big," Patty told him. The thought was tantalizing. Patty had often wondered what it would be like to fly something bigger than her little CRV. She looked at Jake. The solution was obvious. *Why is he keeping silent?*

"Lirsín, this is Jake Chowdhury, ex OASIS traffic control, ex-pilot," Patty introduced them. "Jake, you've flown big birds before." Jake nodded, and Patty noticed Lirsín's frown intensify rather than relax.

"Chowdhury, eh. Yeah, he's ... known." Lirsín replied. His face was suddenly stiff and a little flushed. *What's going on? What's he angry about?*

"The war was a long time ago, young man," Daichi intervened and moved to intercept Lirsín's icy gaze. Jake just waited silently in his usual nonchalant stance.

Patty knew that some Belters held grudges but now was not the time for bickering. "I won't tell you what you must do on your ship Lirsín, and I don't know why you're angry with Jake, but if you're short a pilot, then you don't have much choice," she barked. Patty grabbed Jake's arm. "I'll meet you on the far side of the accommodation block."

"Sure thing," Jake replied. He was so laid back; sometimes she could not read if he was happy or upset. His hand covered his face as he pushed his hair back, but there was that smile. "Fly True, sweetheart." He glanced at the clock readout at the comm station. "See you in ten. Better scoot!"

Patty did not wait and heard Lirsín cry her name from around the curved corridor. She caught Alan's eye as they hurried to the down the passage. "Get ready for space," Patty told him in sign and speech. Alan nodded as they moved to the portside locks. She stripped off her torn and bloody vest, wishing once again she had time to get clean before climbing into her p-suit. *I won't need to plot a fancy flight path,* she thought as she checked Alan's Zip-Lok. *I wonder if The* Ice Princess *has a p-suit to fit Alan.* They cycled into the dock and climbed aboard Freya. The outer door retracted, and Patty released Freya's landing gear. Her only concern was how she was going to fit a third person aboard

Freya.

Patty left the canopy up as Freya lifted from The Ice Princess's flight deck. It was only the second time she had flown Freya with the top up, and she was beginning to like it; it shaved precious minutes off their flight time. She did not need her main engine but warmed it up on principle. *Murphy's law.* If the main engine was not available, she was sure to need it.

As Freya slipped down and away from the big tug, Patty saw The Ice Princess shudder and begin to move away from Hestia's giant cylindrical shape. Patty pumped her thrusters, and Freya sped forward. The engineering lock was on the far side, three decks up. Patty rolled Freya as she continued to adjust their heading. *Up and around. And up and around. Where's that airlock? Ah! There you are.* A p-suited figure clung to the side of the ship.

Lily was looking for them but did not see the CRV approach, until Patty bathed her in Freya's landing lights. Lily nearly jumped out of her Zip-Lok. She held an oxygen cylinder in one hand, a bulging bag in the other, and did not wait for Freya to come to a halt. She sprang from the airlock straight to Freya's cockpit.

She gave the little CRV the once-over, and her smile told Patty she was grateful to see them. They could not communicate, Zip-Loks did not have radios, but Lily seemed to know what she had to do. She gave her bag to Patty - it massed more than Patty expected and she took extra precautions as she stowed it under her legs - and her oxygen bottle to Alan. She then climbed onto Freya, placing her feet on either side of Alan's head, lying belly down on Patty's headrest, her hands braced on the cockpit's sill. Alan reached up and gripped Lily's ankles while Patty secured a tether around Lily's tiny waist. *It wasn't much, but it would have to do.*

Patty looked up and saw Lily say, "Go." Glad someone knows what's going on. Looks like she's done this before.

Patty carefully slewed Freya around and dived into the shadows below the rectangular accommodation block. She could not use too much power on the turns for fear Lily would lose her grip, but with her feet resting on the bulkhead Patty could use some straight-ahead power. It had taken longer to pick up Lily than Patty had hoped. They were late for their rendezvous.

As Freya slid clear of the nondescript gray accommodation unit, the navigation computer chimed for attention. Patty guessed that it was registering The Ice Princess's position; it was ahead and above them, moving slowly down to place the accommodation and workshops between it and Hestia's Hearth. Patty checked the time as she opened the display: twenty-five seconds. Navigation was alive with colors. There were ships out there, moving in from their hidden positions, a net surrounding L5. *Where did they come from?* The comm lit up.

"Freya, this is The Ice Princess, do you read? Over." That sounded like Rogers.

"Ice Princess, we read you. It looks like we have company. Over," Patty told him.

"We do?" he inquired.

"Yes!" Patty squirted the data stream from her navigation computer to him as she gunned Freya towards the tug.

"Thanks, we've been flying blind."

Suddenly the stars paled behind them as a brilliant flash, and then another and another came into being. Patty glanced around, but Lily's grinning face obscured her view; her parting gift had activated. Patty expected the flash to die off fairly quickly, but it continued, moving away from them, firing irregularly. Lily had tears in her eyes, but Patty could tell she was laughing. *Why do I feel cold?* A fusion engineer with a taste for practical jokes was dangerous to have around. *What's happening?*

Patty's navigation display gave her the answers; Hestia's Hearth was moving. The irregular flashes propelled it in spiraling stuttering arcs. Patty flinched at every explosion. Nukes gave her the chills.

Navigation showed red glowing dots with long tails indicating velocity and vector. They swept around, in pursuit of the accelerating white dot. *Where was it going?* The Winterberg continued to fire, and the aliens chased it away from L5. Three red dots did not change their heading: they were focused on The Ice Princess, and they were closing fast. Patty could make rendezvous, but by the time she secured Freya, those aliens ships would be upon them. Check and mate.

"Patty." Lirsín was on the comm. He sounded worried. "We have a problem. Jack says we must go, now."

"He's right. Don't wait. Go!" Patty squirted the algorithm that would provide them with the solution for rendezvous with Jaswinder's eccentric orbit. "Get lost. Meet here later."

The glare from The Ice Princess's five huge engines made Patty flinch, and she rolled Freya belly-on to the exuberant exhaust. *WOW! Hot stuff!*

While moving on just thrusters, The Ice Princess looked heavy, slow, and clumsy to maneuver but those massive engines were designed to caress a giant snowball's trajectory, guiding it gently to one of the many distribution sites. Without that load, the squat tug squirted away. It took a moment to confirm; The Ice Princess was pushing eight gees! That would hurt.

Patty rolled Freya around and followed the chase by eye. The bright engine flares made sighting the ships easy. The three enclosing spacecraft were slow to respond and slow to change their vectors. The Princess flashed through their loose cordon.

The distinctive five-plumed flare changed its vector, and then it turned again, jinking from one heading to another. The alien ships were fast, but The Ice Princess left them in its wake. *Fly True, Jake.* She wished she had had a chance to talk to him. He seemed to know what was going on. *There would be time later, fingers crossed.*

Lily gestured urgently. She pointed to the clock and then over her shoulder, miming a roll with her hands and then sheltering her head under her arms. Patty pumped Freya's thrusters and rolled her over.

A new sun bloomed.

Of Hestia's Hearth's nine attendants, only the tardiest ship survived. Its occupants were dead although they did not know it yet. The violent birth pangs consumed her most ardent suitors immediately; explosions cascaded through the rest of the squadron.

TRUSTED FRIEND

One of the giant guards, one of Stone Son's cousins Little Star
supposed, crossed the yard, marching directly towards her. She
froze, ready to duck out of the way at the last minute. Stone Son
was big and strong, but he was not particularly quick unless he
had a chance to get up some speed and then he was as fast as
anyone, faster. If Stone Son was any guide, Little Star reckoned
she could get away before she got snatched.

"Star."

Little Star stumbled back a step or two. *No one calls me Star
except for Stone Son.* The Taker's guard began to chuckle. Little
Star blinked and blinked again. *It was Stone Son! And he's wearing
all the fancy clothes the other guards have.* He even had sandals
with laces that crisscrossed up his legs and a sword at his hip.
Stone Son with a sword! He was so gentle. *What would he do with a
sword?*

"What's going on?" Little Star whispered.

"Been taken."

"I can understand why the Taker would want you, but me?
Who'd want me?" she asked.

"Taker angry."

Little Star did not expect Stone Son to know why, but it felt
so much better knowing he would be with her when the Taker
took them. She had never been much further from Pa's holding
than you could walk in a morning. *And with my little legs, that's
not very far.* She was never going to be able to keep up with those
soldiers.

"Glad Star friend. Glad Star come too." Stone Son did his
happy dance as he held out his arms. Little Star did not think

twice and scampered aboard.

"I'm glad you're my friend, Stone Son," Little Star cried softly as she hugged him.

"Little Star," Stone Son purred her name as he ambled back towards the strange litter. There was a fire and roasting meat suspended above it. And hot rolls. And tarts! Little Star gorged herself but did not forget to fill her pockets for later. Stone Son found her a blanket, a place by the fire, and sleep enveloped her quickly. In the deep of the night, when they tried to move her to a comfortable bed, she growled, clutching at her bulging pockets, so they left her cuddled up against her trusted friend.

CHAPTER TWENTY-SIX

L5 was deserted except for Freya, hidden in the accommodation block's shadow. Lily laughed, holding her side, tears filling her eyes. Patty opened a small compartment beside her right knee. Packed tight beside a spare Zip-Lok was a p-suit umbilical. She plugged one end into an outlet beside her seat and swapped it for the one connecting the oxygen cylinder. Lily's peals broke through as the connector snapped home.

"Gonna sew me a new shirt. An' writ across the front - Nine with One Blow!" Lily's voice cracked and rasped.

"It's ten if you count Hestia's Hearth. According to Jake, she was packed full of aliens," Patty told her passenger.

"I wasn't going to count her." Lily's grin cooled to just a faint smile then it snapped back into place. "'Ten With One Blow!' it is then." She stuck out her hand. "Lily Siskin, assistant fusion engineer, second class, glad to meet you in the flesh." Her hand was delicate, but she had a firm grip.

"Good to have you aboard, Lily. Though I'm afraid the accommodations are..."

"Hey, don't sweat it." Lily waved her arms around. "It's a beautiful night." She took an exaggerated breath and thumped her chest. "Hmm... fresh air. Nothin' like it." And then she cracked up, laughing. "Don't worry. I've ridden on some of the most precarious looking broomsticks. This, my dear, is the lap of luxury." She loosened the tether and twisted around to greet Alan. "Howdy shipmate." To Patty's surprise, Alan acknowledged Lily with a tiny smile and a nod.

"Quiet one, eh?" Lily asked.

"He's getting better, slowly," Patty replied. That tiny smile meant so much to Patty; her heart lifted.

"So, do we have a flight plan? Don't think it's a good idea to hang around here. Someone's going to notice us," Lily remarked.

"I wouldn't worry about that too much, Freya cuts a pretty low profile," Patty said.

"Yeah, I noticed the paint job." Lily looked over the edge of the cockpit, her head moving from side to side, as she tried to see Freya's light-absorbent body. "You'll have to tell me about it sometime."

"And I do have a flight plan, although I'll have to make a few adjustments. I've never flown her three-up before. What do you mass?" Patty asked as she loaded Jaswinder's rendezvous program into the flight computer.

"About seventy-five on a good day, maybe seventy-six this time of the month. Oh, those nodes mass about fifty kilos."

"Nodes?" Patty asked as she added the extra mass to the formula.

"Yeah, in the bag," Lily said casually. "There's a dozen of 'em. Winterberg firing nodes, a kiloton each."

Patty's eyes snapped down to the bag sitting uncomfortably close to her thighs and broke out into a cold sweat. "You're kidding!"

"Yeah ... err ... no. It was all I could get at the time," she apologized.

"I'm sitting on a dozen nukes?" Patty asked. She wanted to claw her way out of her own ship.

"Oh, don't worry about it, Sis. You've got more chance of a burn-through from that fancy fusion engine of yours than one of those li'l puppies going off," she chuckled.

Chuckling! A captain should know if her passengers were carrying dangerous goods! Patty shivered and tried to concentrate on adjusting the flight program, but the thought of all those bombs made her feel a little ill. The returns from her program did not make her feel any better; they were low on oxygen.

"I hate to ask but, how strong are you?" Patty looked up at her guest.

"Hey, we Belters can hold our own. I may not like standing down at the bottom of a gravity-well, but it doesn't mean I can't take acceleration. What's the problem?"

Patty showed Lily her flight solution. If it were just herself and Alan they would have no problem, a quick blast, four or five gees and then coast, but there was no way Lily could survive that. The program displayed a sliding scale; lower gee boosts meant longer transit times, correlating with three people consuming their available air. The lowest boost they could afford was one point two gee, twice the Moon's gravity. Any slower and they would run out of air. *Even with the oxygen topped up when Freya was docked to The Princess.* Patty concentrated on their problem.

"The cylinder!" Lily cried. "I brought air with me. Dad always said I would forget my head if it wasn't attached." Lily spun around and retrieved the oxygen bottle from Alan. She tapped the pressure gauge. "Should be four or five hours in there."

That would help. Patty adjusted the program to include the extra oxygen. It gave them a little leeway, but Lily was still going to have to cope with some heavy gees.

"Don't worry yourself about me. It's been a while, but I can cope with one gee ... well, I used to ... spent six months living down in that hellhole." Lily pointed down to Earth's marred globe. She looked at the program and frowned. "Let's do this thing." She settled herself back onto Patty's seat top. Alan held her ankles as Patty took up the slack on the tether around her waist.

"Ready, Alan?" Patty twisted around to check on her brother. He gave a small nod. "Lily?"

"Sure. Ready as I'll ever be. Fire up this go-buggy!" Lily gripped the edge of the cockpit.

Patty engaged the autopilot and sat back, tightening her own restraints, not that a one-gee boost would bother her. The engines fired, barely ticking over, providing acceleration not much greater than the maneuvering thrusters as they slid away from the abandoned accommodation block. The sun's bright face peeked out from behind Earth's silhouette. For over two minutes, Freya acceleration built to a little more than one-gee and then she held it. Patty felt quite comfortable, but she could see that Lily was already having difficulties. She checked the clock.

"Two minutes Lily. How ya doing?"

"Oh, this sucks." Lily gasped for breath. "Don't know how humans evolved down there, under this load." She looked pale, and her arms shook.

"Sixty seconds. You're doing good," Patty encouraged. The engines shut off on the button and weightlessness returned. They were on their way to Jaswinder's eccentric polar orbit. Lily sagged and floated. Patty loosened her restraints and manhandled Lily's limp body around so she could get a good look at her face. Her color was returning, a little.

Lily's eyes flickered open. "Are we there yet?" she asked.

"Not quite," Patty replied.

Lily withstood the second burn without fainting. "But I do have a problem. I gotta pee."

Patty had been considering that problem herself for a while. She had taken the opportunity to relieve herself before the burn. A p-suit with plumbing was a wonderful thing. "Since we are coasting for the next few hours, I don't see why we can't shuffle things around a bit. I'll slide out and then you can close the hatch and pressurize her. You should eat, but I've only some emergency rations," Patty apologized and turned to Alan. "Stay here. Pee. Eat, drink. I'll be outside. Okay?" He nodded and gave a thumbs-up. And there was that smile again. Not on his lips but in his eyes. Patty could not have been happier.

A few minutes later Patty floated outside the pressurized cabin, discreetly not watching as Lily and her brother relieved themselves. The Earth was mostly in darkness; the terminator caressed the right edge, illuminating the thick clouds covering the northern hemisphere. There were no lights to be seen anywhere below them. *Will I ever be back this way?*

Patty glanced back into the cabin and Lily, having finished

satisfying one aspect of her body's requirements, was busy fulfilling another. She held a bulb of juice in one hand and had ripped the *heat-me* tab from an emergency ration pack with the other.

Patty took a sip of water from her suit's supply and swallowed. *Emergency rations.* An involuntary shudder coursed through Patty's body. She was sure the tasteless horrors were invented in some dark laboratory. They had to be designed to taste so bad they would only be eaten in an emergency. She shuddered again. Having sampled one in flight school, she vowed never to be in a situation where she would be tempted to eat one. Giuseppe had stowed little snacks throughout Freya's many compartments, so Patty had not stooped to eat the emergency rations. Morbid curiosity drew her eyes. *How could Lily do it?* Lily was plowing through the ration pack with gusto. Patty felt a little nauseous and turned away.

CHAPTER TWENTY-SEVEN

"You have to try one, Patty," Lily told her as she floated off Freya's starboard side. She was connected to the little ship by just the umbilical that carried fresh air and the comm connection.

"I don't think I can," Patty replied. She could not suppress her shudder. "I've been scarred. Even the thought of opening one makes me feel ill."

"I tell you, I've eaten in some fancy restaurants, but that meal put only the five stars' to shame. Mine was fish, so moist and delicate it melted in my mouth, and vegetables ... still crisp. The tastes! Oh, and Alan's was chicken. The divine aromas will cure any psychological hang-ups, I guarantee it." Lily's enthusiastic endorsement made Patty's stomach rumble. "You gotta give me the name of your chandler."

My chandler? Suddenly she knew what had happened. *Did Giuseppe restock Freya's entire inventory?* "It's the same dear man who found Freya for me, a business colleague of my father's. We crossed paths on L2. He has a research facility there ... or did. Gone scattering. He could be anywhere by now." She was sure that wherever Giuseppe was, he was ensconced in the lap of luxury. "He gave Freya her special paint job too. We wouldn't be here without it. When we escaped from the mothership, they sent out a comprehensive search party. We were hit by LADAR a couple of times, and she didn't give us away."

Lily spun around, looking over Freya once more, but this time her eyes were wide with surprise and then awe. "Oh my ... you've got a Slippery Ship!" She floundered for balance, thrashing her arms and legs about for a second before grabbing the edge of the cockpit to steady herself. "Foxy Fermi. Catch-Me-If-You-Can-Fermi! Joe Fermi?"

What was Lily talking about? "I was introduced to him as Giuseppe Fermi. He's a ... big man. Likes his wine. He ... I guess he wanted to do a deal with my Dad. We were out, going through the used CRV yards, and Giuseppe blew in, claiming that Dad had insulted him and all his family because we hadn't come to him first. He came around with Freya. She had a different paint job then, red with gold stripes and trim."

"Yes. Yes! Slippery Joe Fermi!" Lily agreed. "He was a notorious smuggler in his day. Guns, drugs, you name it, he'd get it for you, if you could pay. He kept many Belters alive, and his smuggling probably kept the war going for twelve months longer than it would have otherwise, but it was time well bought." She shook her head with wonder. "A Slippery Ship. Wow. They were legendary back in the day. Dad told me they could breeze through the tightest cordon. I'm impressed."

Patty did not know what to say. I can't imagine Giuseppe as a smuggler, maybe a pirate.

Freya's engines shut off, and their well-baffled flare died as the flight computer completed the last instruction set. Patty checked their position. Unless something was drastically wrong, they were where they were supposed to be, an unremarkable piece of space, high above the North Pole. Space was a vacuum, and by non-quantum definition, empty. It was especially empty of Jaswinder. Patty swallowed a large lump in her throat. They were low on oxygen, very low.

A cold sweat washed over Patty as she reset the problem, took fresh sightings, and worked it again. She could feel Lily watching over her shoulder, but the fusion engineer said nothing. By the third sighting, Patty knew her navigation had been accurate to thirty-two decimal places. They were in the right place at the right time. No one else had made it. Jaswinder! *Madhur! Where are you? Jake? Lirsín?*

"Looks pretty clean to me." Lily sounded as lively and confident as ever. "Bang on the money, honey. You can pilot my boat anytime, Patty."

It was not much consolation to know she had flown Freya to the correct coordinates if no one else had. With only fifty minutes of air left, they were too far from ... from anywhere unless they landed.

"You know what my brother would do at a time like this?" Lily asked as she pushed forward a little and reoriented herself so Patty could see her face. "Sleep. It uses less air. Your brother has the right idea." Patty turned in her seat and checked on Alan. He was sleeping; his chest slowly rose and fell. "I'm gonna stack some Z's," Lily told her. She smiled and pushed out of the cockpit, halting her gentle flight by catching the canopy sill. "Wake me when your tardy friends arrive."

"Sure thing," Patty replied. There was not much for her to do, but going to sleep was not an option. *If ... when Jaswinder arrives, they won't be able to find us.* She looked at the comm. *Do the aliens really want me? Will they come to capture me if they know where I am?* Surrender wasn't an option. *We're so far from anywhere.* But that was why they chose this polar orbit.

Despite the pall of gray clouds, Earth and her barren silver companion looked particularly beautiful with a backdrop of unblinking stars set in black satin. *Gazing out into space will not help.* Patty poured over the navigation display, searching for movement. Jaswinder would be running as dark as possible with few emissions. Without active radar, Madhur's angular craft would be tricky to spot, and Freya would be impossible for them to find. It was up to her to make their rendezvous happen.

Patty tried to keep alert and took a sip from her suit. It had been a long day. She envied, only briefly, her passengers' privileged position. As captain of her little ship, she had responsibilities and keeping her passengers safe was her number one priority.

It was hard to stay awake without Lily's chatter. Patty could feel the beginnings of a yawn rise and became concerned she might doze off. *Keep alert girl, or you'll miss all the fun.* The memories of the overloaded ship at L3 flashed into Patty's mind, cold flesh gasping for air in a harsh vacuum, and that horror doused, for a moment, her growing fatigue. She set up a proximity alarm. If a ship approached, she would know it. With everything set in place, Patty decided to put Lily's advice to good use and closed her eyes.

An extended yawn made Patty's jaw crack. An annoying beep drilled a sound wedge into her ears. Her eyes flickered open. There was light in the darkness. Patty blinked and tried to focus. *What an ugly thing it was, all angles and patches. And far too close.* Patty looked at her control panel but could not find her landing lights to warn them off. Her mind felt like sludge. *What are all these buttons for?* The control she really wanted to find was the one to turn off that horrible alarm. She slapped at some of the more obvious buttons, but the annoying bleating continued. In the end, Patty decided that she could cope with the noise, snuggled down to snooze for a bit longer. *I'll get up in a minute, Mom, promise.*

SECONDS!

The Taker's company rose early. Bowls of hot, thick porridge and great mugs of sweet black tea were passed around. The cook did not blink when Stone Son fetched her a second helping. Little Star could not believe her eyes; it was bigger than her first and had half a red tart pressed into the top. Stone Son got seconds too. He did not get any tart, but she was happy to share hers with him. If she had been able to figure out a way of keeping some of the porridge or tea for later - her feet felt sore at the thought of marching all day - she would have.

Much to Little Star's relief, no one asked her to clean anything or lift anything or even told her to get out of the way. Stone Son kept her by his side, and all he was asked to do was stand near the litter with a great spear planted between his feet. A green pennant flapped high above. No one paid her any attention at all except for Stone Son's gigantic cousins; they all smiled at her and gave her little bows. Once they discovered she was not so shy if they had some food, she began receiving little tidbits that enticed her out from behind Stone Son's cloak.

When the Taker's column formed up, Stone Son was relieved of his spear and was sent to the rear of the litter. *Round legs!* It had to be better than lifting a wooden litter. Little Star chuckled again at the concept. Stone Son did not have to carry anything either - perhaps the Taker wanted him to pull later - so Little Star climbed into his arms and hid under his cloak when Papa waved them off. She tried to catch one last glimpse of Ma, but they were down the path and gone before she had the chance.

CHAPTER TWENTY-EIGHT

Her pounding head roused Patty enough to know she was no longer aboard Freya, but the moment she opened her eyes the intense light bounced around in her head, amplifying the pain. She felt restraints holding her on a padded couch, that frightened her at first, but the air smelled like Jaswinder. It smelled like home.

"She's awake! She's awake!" Cicely's yell combined with the light that continued to cascade through her head - even with her eyes shut - adding spikes to the boots that were trying to kick their way out. The pressure around her right hand became crushing for a moment. Familiar voices surrounded her. *Too many.* She could not sort one from the other. Suddenly the talking stopped. The sudden absence of sound was almost as painful as its overwhelming presence.

"Patty, are you with us?" Madhur's whisper inspired Patty to peek through one eye. Jaswinder's all-purpose lounge was intolerably bright. *I'm strapped in an acceleration couch.* She snapped her eyelid shut and heard movement. The lights dimmed.

"Yeah, maybe," Patty mumbled. At least that was what she tried to say; her mouth was dry. Her tongue was a thick unmoving slab. A straw parted her lips, and she sucked down fresh lemon-flavored water and felt it suffuse through her body.

"How are you feeling?" Madhur's whisper was close to her ear.

"My head wants to explode."

"Hang on a sec," Madhur whispered her reply.

Patty did not even try to open her eyes until Madhur

returned with a bitter tasting pill. She washed it down with more water and the football team in her head called timeout. Her hands felt a little numb, and there was a sharp tingling at the back of her neck, but the fog of pain dissipated. She cracked one eye open. Smiling faces surrounded her: Cicely, still holding tight to her right hand, Madhur squeezed in beside her, Eg was on Cicely's other side. Cian, Jai, and Ken, his arm in a sling, were at her feet.

Alan was on her left, smiling. His left hand flashed sign. "This one is pleased to see you awake." He looked more relieved than pleased, but that was splitting hairs. *He's smiling!* Then it slipped into a frown. His face was alive with thought, although for the moment, they seemed unhappy ones. Patty reached out to take his hand. She wanted to wrap him in her arms.

Strapped to a couch behind Alan, Patty saw another figure who had to be Lily. The chair was barely long enough for her slender body; an IV drip was mounted beside her.

"Lily." Patty turned back to Madhur. "What happened?"

Madhur glanced at Cian and frowned. "We were late. I'm sorry. We flew past L3 and, well ..."

"There was a big fight at L3." Jai looked both excited and grim. "We had to slow down and see if anyone got through the cordon." His expression told her that no one had escaped.

"The aliens knocked out one of the guns that were keeping them at bay and landed an assault team." Cian took up the story. "*Te Waka* and *Taylor Station* tried to separate from the other stations. It was a huge mess, and they didn't get far anyway. There was a handful of smaller craft that tried to slip through in the chaos, but no one made it." Cicely squeezed her hand. Patty felt numb. They had all lost so much. Cicely and Jai had family on L3. *And for all I know, my parents are there too.*

"Anyway, we were late to rendezvous," Ken apologized, "but as far as we could tell you hadn't arrived either. It was Jai who spotted your landing lights." He slapped the young man on the back. "But it took us longer than it should've to realize you were in trouble."

"Madhur and I suited up and got you aboard as soon as we could. Lily," Cian glanced at her comatose body, "she'd disconnected her umbilical. Surprised she was still alive."

"Breed 'em tough in the Belt," Madhur added grimly.

"Yeah, she's still hanging in there, and now that you're awake, well, maybe there is hope," Cian shrugged.

Lily disconnected her umbilical? When did she do that? The thought shocked and humbled Patty. She did that to save me?

"It was her choice," Madhur said. She looked stern but proud. "Air ain't free. She saved your life, and we'll probably face similar challenges in the not-so-near future. I mean, we went to L5 in the hope of getting some supplies. I'm not saying rescuing The Ice Princess was a bad idea, but we used a lot of fuel to power Hunter's flight, and well, we're no better off. Not yet."

"No sign of The Ice Princess, then." Patty felt despair creep up on her. The Ice Princess was so precious, well stocked and fully fueled, not to mention Jake, Lirsín, Daichi, Stan and the rest of the crew aboard her. *The fighting, the blood, was it all for nothing?*

"We have some time up our sleeves." Madhur looked at Cian and gave a wry smile. "Your friend's done a pretty good job of getting the best from Jaswinder's enviro systems, so we're not going to run out of air and water anytime soon, but it will take a while for the expanded hydroponics to produce anything edible."

"I still have some emergency ration packs aboard Freya," Patty told them. Everyone grimaced, and Patty decided to keep the fact that these were not regular emergency rations a secret. It would be a pleasant surprise for later. A burning pressure inside her told Patty she needed to pee. She was still wearing her p-suit so she could just relax and let her suit's plumbing take care of it - they didn't call it a p-suit for nothing - but the desire to get clean made Patty want to sit up. She wriggled a bit.

"I need to get up. Get clean."

"Hang on." Madhur carefully extracted the IV line from her forearm and undid the strap holding her securely to the couch. "I'll get your bag."

When she was free, Patty wrapped Cicely and Eg in a hug. "Thanks for looking after me."

"You're welcome. You saved us after all." Cicely gave her a sloppy kiss on the cheek. Surprisingly, Eg gave her a peck on the cheek too and an extra squeeze. By the time she had extricated herself from the twins, Jai, Cian, and Ken had disappeared. Patty wanted to thank them too, but that could wait.

You could not luxuriate under a sonic scrubber, but feeling clean was infinitely better than the build-up of living in a p-suit for days. *And wearing soft, warm clothes.* Patty relaxed as she brushed out her hair. Her knots had knots. She wished her mother were here to help her. It had been a long time since Patty had sat in front of her mother, feeling the bristles on her scalp and the gentle pull of the hairbrush. The memory was bittersweet.

Despite my two-day coma - or maybe because of it - I feel better now than I have for a long while. The burning need to find her parents had damped down, overshadowed by all the other events that billowed around her. A thousand and one paths seemed to spread out before her. *What to do now? If* The Ice Princess *has not turned up by now, the chances were bleak she ever would.* L1 was probably a good choice though the memories of its destruction gave her a chill.

The lounge was empty except for Alan who stood guard at the bathroom door. Patty could not resist hugging him. His body was initially stiff as a board, but he began to relax, a little. "So, how was it for you? How long have you been up and about?" He stiffened a little as he freed his left arm for speech and Patty unwrapped him to give him space. He gave a nod-like bow and frowned.

"This one is dishonored," Alan signed. "This one slept until ... until the ... the Cian and ... the Madhur came to our ship and then this one was of no help. Sleep held this one, but that is no ... excuse. This one ... apologizes and ... begs forgiveness." Alan bowed low, chin to his chest. Patty grabbed that chin and lifted his head, or tried to. Stiff-necked, Patty lifted and spun Alan rather than raising his head, but she met his eyes, and that was the main thing.

"You have nothing to be ashamed of. I have nothing to forgive you for," Patty insisted. "If anything, it is I who should be the one apologizing, to you." Alan's eyes were troubled as if he did not understand. "I was in command of Freya. I was responsible for taking her out, not you." Alan still frowned. "You are in *my* care."

"This one's duty is to ... to protect you. This one failed." There was a certain logic to Alan's words that was not-Alan, not her brother of old. This rewritten Alan had simple, almost hard-wired responses. Patty did not want to be anything but a sister to him, but that was not what he needed now. He needed something he could comprehend.

"No, you didn't. You did not fail," Patty told him. "Not for a second do I believe that. You have been at my side, defended my back; you have done all I have asked and more. Alan, you have not failed, not for one second," she repeated. "You have fought with courage and honor beyond my expectations." Patty drew apart and bowed as deeply to her brother as he had to her. When she rose, Alan was still stiff, but the pain in his eyes was gone, and Patty wrapped him in a hug once more. "You're my brother, not my servant or my bodyguard. We're a team. Yes?" Alan gave a hesitant nod. "Good. Let's see what's happening aboard this old girl." She gave him one gentle squeeze and waited for his response.

"The Cian and the two ... small ones are aft. The Madhur, the Jai and the Ken are on the bridge." Alan's eyes waited for her lead. Patty crossed the room to check on Lily.

Her chest rose and fell regularly. She was pale but not deathly. Patty checked her pulse. It was strong and regular. She held Lily's hand. "I didn't know you very well, Lily, but it was a pleasure having you aboard Freya. You're with friends on Jaswinder. We made rendez. I don't know why you did it but thank you for saving Alan and me. Wake up soon, or I don't know what I'll tell Lirsín. I know he was looking forward to meeting his cousin in the flesh."

Lily lay there unmoving. *There's nothing I can do here.* Patty gave Lily's slender hand one more gentle squeeze and headed for the bridge.

CHAPTER TWENTY-NINE

Jaswinder's central corridor was Madhur's Hall of Fame comprising of family, friends, loved ones, and rigs. All the *Special Projects* Madhur had ever been involved with were on these walls, somewhere. There was no apparent order to it; a sepia-toned 2D print of newlyweds from the twentieth century was partially covered by a 2D GIF-pic of two girls running down a grassy hill, and a 3D Pic-Flick of Madhur dwarfed by an enormous engine array. Somewhere on these walls, there was a Pic of Patty, Alan, and Freya's mysterious black silhouette. Patty did spot one new edition to the collection, a Pic of Ken, Madhur, and Cian, standing beside the remnants of Hunter, Cian's stripped-down old Singer. She was not much more than the central chassis, engines, fuel tank, and a control system. *They did a good job, but was it all for nothing? Are you still out there, Jake?* Patty pushed on to the control room.

There was not much space on the bridge if you stayed bound to the horizontal layout. Five tapered windows followed the flat curve of Jaswinder's prow. The controls and the acceleration couch were packed tightly together, but there was plenty of headroom, so Patty coasted up over the seat's back. For such an irregular ship, Jaswinder's bridge had a practical and straightforward layout although the controls had been salvaged from a dozen different sources. The portside console held the comm, the center piloting/navigation and to starboard was life support/engineering. The acceleration couch was covered in brown leather (or a reasonable facsimile) and stretched from one side of the bridge to the other. The bench seat could be configured to seat up to four people. Right now, there were only three, Jai, Madhur, and Ken.

"...would only take another day or so," Jai spoke in his adamant mode. Madhur was not listening as she concentrated on the navigation computer with Ken. "Patty! What do you reckon we swing past L2 before rendez with L1? Marginally higher fuel consumption, but if what Jake said was true, L2 might be abandoned, empty. Left for you. Won by the rite of combat, my queen." The imp grinned from ear to ear.

"Queen! Huh!" Patty gave a sour laugh. "Don't start something you won't be able to finish." Watched the new set of the gem's recordings, have we? Of course, he has. Jake did say something about the aliens seceding L2 to me, but the concept was too ridiculous to be true. "L2's most likely another trap waiting to be sprung. That's what L5 was." A trap for me. All those aliens, all those ships were there to catch me. A shiver of fear rattled through her.

"He does have a point." Ken's smile let out just enough mirth to stop himself from laughing. "He's going to make a fine flight officer one day. You should listen to your XO, Madhur."

"One day?" Jai rose, indignant, but Patty waved him down before he could open his mouth and put his foot in it.

"Cool it. Ken's pitching for you," Patty told him. Her voice was not much more than a whisper, but it caught Madhur's attention. She twisted around from the console and gave Patty a warm smile while her eyes surveyed her closely.

"Gangin' up on the Captain, are we?"

Patty threw up her arms. "I have no opinion on the matter, apart from my initial thoughts. First I've heard of swinging past L2. I know we can't stay in this orbit forever. I haven't put much thought into what comes next. The Ice Princess was supposed to be here, the answer to all our problems. No Plan B." Patty shrugged. "Sorry."

"No battle plan survives contact with the enemy." Jai nodded and frowned, trying to appear wise. Ken started chuckling, but Madhur just harrumphed.

"Thanks a heap, oh wise one." Madhur flicked a finger towards the comm station. "Back in yer box. You're monitoring the comm."

Jai grinned, sighed, looked put-upon, rebelled, and surrendered in the space of half a second before turning away and focusing on a screen full of text.

"The comm? We have communications?" Patty asked.

"Sort of." Jai pointed at the display. "UNET's back up." He laughed. "Sort of. You won't believe this, but someone hacked into the aliens' satellites and is piggybacking encrypted UNET into the noise. Bitrate's abysmal, but we can send text messages." Jai squirmed on the spot. "You've got mail."

"I do?" Patty inquired, raising an eyebrow.

"Err yeah, I sorta noticed that when I uploaded your videos to your account. Didn't look. Promise." Jai still looked embarrassed.

"You uploaded the data from the recorder?" *Probably half the solar system is witness to my every grunt, fart and mutter.* Patty was concerned about her muttering. She remembered losing it bad when she had fallen asleep in the duct outside Alan's holding cell.

"Yeah well, Eg's been making some," Jai went from cheerful to reticent, "err ... interesting discoveries."

"Dangerous," Madhur growled.

"Exciting," Kenny corrected. He did not look at Madhur, but he heard her. "I think Eg's figured out the aliens' stardrive, but with more minds on the job I'm sure they can get the bugs out."

"It bloody well holed my ship!" Madhur grumbled at Ken. It had the feeling of an old argument, warmed up once more. "Fixin' the recycler addressed the balance, I know, but I don't want him..."

"He won't, I promise." Ken was quick to defend his little brother. "The broomstick's nearly ready. We're going to float it far enough away before we fire it up so Jaswinder's safe."

"You're not serious about L2, are you?" Madhur asked as she turned from snarling at Ken and fixed her attention to the computer.

"It's worth thinking about. It was evacuated, right?" Ken

smiled up at Patty, and she had to refocus quickly. He was attractive. You did not get to be a hot racing pilot on looks alone, but in a world of ten percent racing, ninety percent promotions, Ken's smooth, good looks, and shining eyes were money in the bank, but they were distracting.

"L2 ... err ... yeah, right," Patty stammered. "Giuseppe said he got everyone out."

"It could be a larder just waiting for us," Ken argued. "It would be silly not to take a look. We know what the situation is at L1, chaos, and ruination; hundreds of people, cut off from each other and in pure survival mode. According to our comm officer, L2 is off the map. Not a peep. We should do a fly-by if only to know who's at our back door." Ken glanced across to Madhur and back to Patty. "And if our daring recon, saboteur, and all-around hero is up to it, Jaswinder could stay safely out of harm's way just like we did at L4."

"I've always wanted to lose a few kilos," Madhur mumbled.

"I've got some emergency rations," Patty added grimly, hoping she could hold back her enthusiastic grin.

Madhur turned away, looking a shade of green. "Stop that. You're still unwell. That's obvious."

"Guys." Jai waved an arm, but neither Madhur nor Ken noticed. He looked at Patty, his face bereft of a smile. "Captain Auntie! Ma'am! Urgent message on the comm!"

Madhur twisted around in a flash. "Sorry, Jai. What is it?"

"The blip's back, and it's closer," Jai reported. Gone was the banter, Jai looked afraid.

"Blip?" Patty asked.

Madhur glanced at her nephew and smiled, "Jai picked it up a day or so ago. It looks like leakage around a tight beam transmission. Someone's following us. How close are they?"

"They're almost exactly in our path, about twenty-five minutes behind us. They're gaining on us. It was thirty-five minutes yesterday."

"You don't think it's The Ice Princess?" Patty asked.

"The signal has the alien formatting," Jai countered.

"I would just love to drop something out the door for him to run into," Madhur growled. "I got so much stuff aboard but nothing that can make a big bang."

Patty cleared her throat and frowned, "Well actually..."

"What?" three voices asked almost as one.

"Lily brought some Winterberg firing nodes with her. They're in Freya. 'Bout a dozen of them. A kiloton each."

Madhur rubbed her hands together, a cold smile in her eyes. "That should do the trick."

ON THE ROAD

The path from Pa's holding wound through the undulating hills, and they had not traveled for more than half a day's twelfth when they came upon another group of the Taker's men with another litter on wheels. The Taker did not stop, and the extra men joined the rear of the company. The path slowly became wider and more traveled as other tracks joined it, but forest and fields continued to surround them. The team hauling the litter changed mid-morning and cold drinks, and bread stuffed with relish and cold meats were passed up the line. Little Star hardly felt the need to refill her pockets, but she did so on principle.

The path joined a road, and the hills seemed to deflate into rolling plains. That was when Little Star saw her first house. It was stone, to be sure, but it was above the ground. Even the old stuffy attic space that was not hers anymore had three or four hands of solid rock above her head. The above-ground house did not seem right, and the sight made her wonder where they would be sleeping that night.

They marched until around noon when the company came upon a grassy patch near a meandering stream. For the first time all day Little Star heard something from behind the blue and white curtains.

"Picnic!" The voice coming from within the litter had a higher pitch than Ma's and a pale face poked out from concealment, sweeping the curtains to either side. The Taker leaned against the sill and expressed his approval. "Yes. Lovely. Over there would be just fine by those trees. Thank you, Fel'eron." He turned and examined Little Star perched in Stone Son's arms. Somehow, Little Star resisted the urge to hide behind the folds of Stone Son's cloak. The Taker's finger called them closer, and Stone Son approached the curtained window as the litter rocked to a halt.

"Well, little sister, it is a surprise and a delight to have made this discovery. We came for your companion never thinking a GreatMother was there as well." The door opened, and the palest brother she had ever seen stepped out and performed an ornate bow. "Such a surprise, this one was unsure how to approach the subject." He turned and gestured towards the stream. "Shall we walk?"

Little Star was dumbfounded. No one had ever shown her deference to her. She looked up into Stone Son's eyes but knew he was always happy to follow her lead. "Umm. Yeah. Suppose that's alright."

The Taker stretched and began a leisurely stroll towards the tree-lined bank, making sure Stone Son walked beside him. *What a strange person he is. Who would want to talk to me?*

"This must seem very strange, GreatMother, but this one hopes it will not be long before understanding comes. Clan Tol'edranna has long held sway over this land..."

Little Star listened as well as she could, but the Taker spoke so quickly, and with such an odd accent she found herself lost as he talked about the history of this region. At least that was what Little Star thought he was talking about.

"This one had almost forgotten there was one in the supplies," Taker paused beside the stream and reached beneath his blue Clan cloak. "GreatMother, this one is honored to be able to offer you mel'andrin." His bow was exquisitely formal, and Little Star felt the urge to respond, even if it meant leaving the safety of Stone Son's arms. Without her prompt Stone Son lowered her gently to the ground.

"Umm, Taker, sir. We ... I mean ... thank you ... um but I'd rather not. Umm .... Even Ma's makes me feel ill. So, I ... we know you... err... it means a lot but..." Little Star's words choked off when the Taker lifted the lid on the tiny gray container. *What was that smell?* She found herself drawn to him. The ornate offering-spoon held something that struck golden sparkles in the dappled light beneath the sheltering trees.

This is the strangest of days. I've eaten better in the last day than ... than ever before. I've never been not-hungry before any meal, and I still have supplies in my pockets. Is this really mel'andrin? All the other gift-memories I've seen are pearly and much smaller. She repressed the nauseous reaction to the memory. *It smells so wonderful, so different.* She would have to try it even if it made her sick afterward.

CHAPTER THIRTY

Although Lily said they were perfectly safe, Patty treated the Winterberg firing nodes with the utmost respect. Madhur was much more matter of fact. She reached into the bag and pulled out a fat metal ovoid no more than ten centimeters long with a cubic extrusion at one end and placed it on the stick-em pad on her workbench.

Flicking her thick braid over her shoulder, Madhur flexed her arms and leaned in close. "Give a professional a little elbow room, if you please." Patty eased back but made sure she did not bump into Griffin, secured to the far end of the workshop. That would only distract Madhur. She was more protective of the racing CRV than its pilot.

Suddenly Madhur's right hand snapped out, "The Fisher." Cian placed the tool in Madhur's steady grasp. With great care, she placed the tip against an indent in the flattened end. A small panel opened. She set the firing node on its nose and inspected the interior.

"Oh, this is a tidy set up." Madhur lifted her head with a smile, "Now all we need is the delivery mechanism, and I think I know exactly what to use."

The bomb was not pretty although Patty was not sure what a pretty bomb might look like. The firing node was strapped to a small gas canister that supplied the reaction mass for p-suit thrusters. The sensor and control package were duct-taped in the center. The monofilament control cable flapped in the cold gas as she tested the systems. They did not dare use radio control to pilot the mine for fear their tail would detect it. The thruster was not correctly balanced, but it would do.

"Are you sure you have enough cable?" Patty asked and sipped from her p-suit's supply as she waited for the gas vapor to clear. Alan waited patiently beside her. She leaned out the open workshop door and looked aft. Freya's silhouette blocked out the sun, but she could not see the pursuing craft.

"Plenty," Madhur answered. "There's a good three thousand kilometers on that reel." She picked up the coil and floated out the workshop's wide doorway. Cian unlocked the bomb from the testing rack and flew it out of the workroom while Madhur set the reel on Jaswinder's hull and pulled out a couple of meters of thread. Patty breathed a relieved sigh as Madhur pressed the button. With a spray of cold gas, the bomb quickly disappeared into the darkness. The golden filament swirled and danced in their p-suit's lights as it played out from the reel.

"The sensor package is already picking up the alien's transmissions," Patty noted and showed the control display to Madhur; Cian pushed off the deck and peered over her shoulder.

"Jai, do you have a distance to target for us?" Madhur asked as she patched the feed from Jaswinder's bridge into the control's display. A second dot appeared. It had gained on them while they constructed their bomb. Madhur gave the thruster another burst.

"Can you monitor this, Patty? Cian, give me a hand with the next one." Madhur left Patty to pilot the bomb to the target and went back to the workbench. While one weapon should be enough, Madhur, like Patty, did not like leaving things to chance. If ... when something went wrong, they had to be prepared. Patty was glad her nervous sweat did not transfer through her p-suit's gloves.

When the bomb was one thousand kilometers behind them, Patty relaxed a little more. According to Ken, they were out of the bomb's lethal radius. Patty shuddered. They had been much closer to the exploding firing nodes when Lily's surprise package began boosting Hestia's Hearth away from its mooring at L5, but those had been directional blasts, with the fierce output focused away from them. This bomb would spray its energies in every direction.

"How we doin'?" Cain asked. Patty jumped. She had been concentrating on the display and had not noticed Cian's approach.

"Over three-quarters of the way there," Patty told him. "The ... target has not deviated. They haven't seen it, I guess... I hope." Patty's heart raced. *I'm doing it again. Patty Balke, bringer of death.*

"I wouldn't expect so," Cain replied. "They're not using proximity radar; it would give them away. They're flying as blind as we are." No one else seemed worried about blowing up their tail. *They haven't seen death close up, blood squirting, bodies screaming and begging for one more moment of life.*

Suddenly the flowing monofilament cable billowing out of the reel snapped tautly. The feedback from the flying bomb disappeared from the display.

"No! The reel!" Patty tossed the controller to Alan as she dived for the reel. There was plenty more monofilament wrapped around the spool, but a twist had developed and caught on the bail.

"What did you do, you useless ground slug?" Madhur growled as her hand fell on Patty's shoulder, and she leaned away so Madhur could get a look.

"I didn't go anywhere near it," Cian defended himself, backing away with his hands raised.

"It's not his fault," Patty told her. "The reel snarled."

"Yeah. Probably 'cause he looked at it," Madhur grumbled. "I tell you, ground-huggers are dangerous to have aboard, they..."

A small sun blossomed in the sky behind Madhur, followed a fraction of a second later by an even larger explosion. Cian whooped as did Jai through his open mike on the bridge. Madhur spun around and caught sight of the expanding fireball and joined in the cheer. Patty was not sure what she felt. She was glad the proximity circuits had worked. *You must have a Plan B.* Any thought of staying near their warm wet world quickly drained away. It was just too dangerous.

Jai's excited shout lifted Patty's heart more than the exploding ship. "The Ice Princess is online!"

Madhur harrumphed, but she did not have a more attractive alternative. Patty floated beside Lily's acceleration couch, held her hand, and kept quiet. Sometimes Madhur seemed to need space to move while she thought, room to swing her arms.

"The margins are ... nonexistent I agree, but what are our choices? If we're able to rendezvous with The Ice Princess, then we won't need any fuel reserves," Ken argued. "There is nothing for us here. It's time to cut the ties."

"*If* we're able to rendezvous with them. *If,*" Madhur grumbled. "I don't like ifs. We are going to have to drain Freya and Griffin just to get there." Madhur sounded more scared than worried about technical details. "I've never been this low on fuel. Never. We have safety margins for a reason."

"You know I don't mind. One in, all in. Suck her dry. I won't be flying her anywhere, not for a while anyway," Ken said and flapped his sling-wrapped arm. "We're fine for oxygen and water. I'm for a rendez with The Ice Princess. Not that I want off your fine ship, Captain."

"Don't worry. I wouldn't mind a change of scenery. It's just..." Madhur look as though she wanted to stamp her foot.

"As a ship's captain, I understand," Patty added. She knew the doubts flowing through Madhur's mind. "You can take us anywhere from OASIS to L3, but to make this rendezvous, you will need to take us beyond the point of no return, no safety margins. If we miss The Ice Princess again, that'll be it for us. No refund, no return."

"You're right. You're all right. I just hate going past PONR. It scares me. I'm sorry." Madhur turned and would have stormed back to the monitor if they had been experiencing gravity, as it was, she had to wait until she arrived at Lily's bedside before pushing off. She took the time to calm herself.

"Okay. If we're all agreed then," she said. "Let's do it."

Siphoning off the last of Freya's fuel was more traumatic than Patty thought it would be. *I thought I'd been through this when I decided we were going to leave on The* Ice Princess, Patty thought. It meant the end of her time as an independent agent. When this fuel was gone, it would mean more work than just filling her tanks. Priming the fuel lines could take hours. She was well and truly tied to Jaswinder's fate, although that was not a bad thing. She felt lucky to be with such a good crew, but it was like leaving home, again.

Low Earth Orbit's been my backyard, The Moon, and the LaGrange stations, my friendly neighborhood. As much as Patty rejected the sly propaganda that lingered after The Belter War, she could not help but think of the outer solar system as a primitive place, a rowdy frontier. It was exciting and scary but not as frightening as staying and facing the aliens. *Especially since they're looking for me.* She wanted to blame Jake for stirring the pot, but they had been seeking her before he added his unique selection of truth and half-truths to the mix. *I'm not special, just lucky.* That thought gave Patty a chill. Relying on luck got you killed.

While Freya's fuel transferred to Jaswinder, Patty took the opportunity to strip Freya of anything they might need. She collected the last of their luggage and the emergency ration packs. Sealing the canopy gave Patty severe pangs. *When am I going to be able to fly you again?* She handed Alan her bag of goodies and gave Freya's rounded prow a lingering hug.

"Be a good girl. Mommy'll be back as soon as she can."

Patty lingered outside Jaswinder's airlock for one last look at Earth's blemished but still beautiful presence. She did not like the idea of being a hero, but she hated feeling like a coward. Running away to Ceres felt like that, but it was the right thing to do. *We should have left with Dad's R&D station. Would have, should have, could have. But we're here now. Not in one piece but not broken. We will adapt.* Alan waited patiently in the airlock, their meager possessions all around him. It was not much, but it was enough. Patty squeezed into the lock and started the cycle. The doors slid shut. *Goodbye Mom, Dad. Goodbye, everyone.*

The raucous squawk of the acceleration all-clear sounded, and Patty relaxed. *That was it, the last burn.* They still had fuel, but in eighteen hours, it would not do them any good, they would not have enough to return to any of the orbital platforms. Despite her doubts, it felt good to be underway. *Rendezvous with The* Ice Princess *and then on to Ceres.* It was exciting. *The further away I can get from sword-wielding aliens the better. The closer I get to Lirsín, the better.* For a moment, the sweet smile and blue eyes of The Ice Princess's captain made all her fears dissolve. It would take over one hundred days to reach Ceres. Patty smiled. One slap and the harness fell away. She hugged Alan, and he returned a tiny smile. "Hungry pardner?" she asked, imitating Jake's Texan drawl.

"Yes. This one would like to eat. It would be good," Alan signed as he lifted away from the couch, his smile broadening. Patty pointed to the stash of emergency ration packs stowed in the corner of the lounge. Alan nodded and went to collect a pair while Patty checked on Lily; she was pale, but she had a strong pulse.

"You're not serious, are you?" Cian shook his head when he saw Alan collecting a pair of ration packs.

"Of course I am," Patty replied enthusiastically. "Everything a growing girl needs."

"Glad I'm not a growing girl," Cian gulped. He looked at the stack of ration packs and shuddered.

"I am, and I don't think it's a good idea," Cicely added. She and Eg unstrapped but stayed cuddled together on the couch.

"All the more for you and me, eh Alan?" Patty asked. She unfolded the table from its wall mount as Alan arrived with their meals.

"Is she really going to eat one?" Ken asked as he sailed into the lounge from the bridge. He grabbed a ladder's rung to halt his momentum.

"I think so," Cian replied. He looked a little green. "And she's going to inflict one on her little brother too." Cian turned away as Patty and Alan seated themselves at the table. She tried hard to keep a grin from erupting as she tore off the self-heat strips. She slid one pack down to her brother and sat quietly waiting for it to ping.

"That's just cruel. Come on Eg. I can't watch." Cicely grabbed her brother and began to fly up to the bridge, but Ken blocked their retreat.

"I can. I think it's fascinating," Ken remarked with a chortle.

"I think someone should tell Madhur. A captain should know when one of her crew is endangering herself," Cian added as he joined Ken and the twins.

"Did someone call for the captain?" Madhur asked as she poked her head into the room. She was not happy but appeared to be putting a good face on it.

"You have to talk sense into Patty," Cian said. "This space-survivor thing has gone to her head. Even a groundhog like me can see that something is seriously wrong with her."

"The rations?" Madhur cocked one eyebrow.

"Yes. What's next, cannibalism?" Cian asked nervously.

"Now you are going too far," Madhur chuckled and slid past

Ken. She reached out to Cian to bring herself to a halt. "I've seen stranger reactions to stress, but emergency rations shouldn't hurt them too much."

The flat, dull green box in front of Patty beeped three times, and a bright green light flashed. She lifted the corner tab and had to let it go in a hurry. *Hot!* She took another try and peeled back the top layer. An intoxicating and delicate aroma surrounded Patty. Her meal was trout in a creamy white wine sauce, garnished with fresh parsley and a range of roast vegetables, potato, pumpkin, onion, and steamed peas, broccoli, capsicum and sweet baby carrots. *Heaven!* A chilled bulb of Chablis sat in an isolated compartment alongside a small tub of gelato.

Patty had time to notice Alan had roast beef in a creamy brown sauce before she was mobbed. Everyone, except for Eg, was yelling, demanding a taste. She couldn't hold back her laughter any longer.

"Ha! Get your own!" Patty shouted. She grabbed her ration pack, tore out the fork, and fended Cicely away with a lunge, and a slap to the back of her hand. She laughed again as the tiny blond dived across the room for a ration pack of her own. Patty glanced over at Lily and wished she were awake. She would have enjoyed the joke. In seconds, everyone had one and gathered eagerly at the table waiting for them to heat. Patty did not wait for them, but she did not rush her meal. *Giuseppe will want me to savor it.* She took a sip from the Chablis; she was not sure if she would call it flinty, but it was delicious.

Cicely wolfed her roast chicken breasts down in record time followed by her dessert, grumbling over the fact that Ken had removed her bulb of wine. She tried, mostly unsuccessfully, to steal from everyone else's meal except for Eg's. Ken succumbed to her predation with good grace, but Madhur threatened to space her if she approached her plate one more time.

Having a full belly made Patty sleepy. *But Jai said he'd show you the stripped down UNET access. I have mail.* She headed to the bridge with Alan at her heels, chuckling at Cian and Cicely fighting over lick-the-bowl rights. She so hoped there would be something from her parents or Hine or Tina. *Maybe The* Ice Princess *is online.* Lirsín's bright blue eyes danced before her again, and her heart raced.

FRESH AIR

A warm, wet breeze, rich with uncountable aromas, blew across Darwin's harbor. *Dar'win.* The city's name reminded Er'men of *dar'nar whe'en,* an old-tongue phrase that meant rich pastures, fertile soils. It also carried connotations of easy pickings. *That's probably why Harrum'Bar chose it for the first landing site.* Er'men's frustration with the RegentFirstMother almost grew with each breath. *The last Great Council meeting was a disaster.* She was still unsure how Harrum'Bar had skewed the reports of failure at the human's generation ship to dump the blame on her. *With my mind full of GreatMother memories, it's difficult to keep track of what was happening right in front of me. That's why I have a regent,* Er'men growled. *They won't listen to me. Taking Darwin will be bloody. The humans will fight us every step of the way.* She could not blame the locals. It was what any Hel'Arumpo'or clan would do if their territory were invaded.

Er'men curled her left foot's toes over the edge of Tal'anis' flight deck and gazed out towards the southwest. The air felt wild and alive compared to the reconditioned and recycled air in the immense mothership. *Is this really going to be our new home after crossing the great desert between the stars?* There was life everywhere, in and around the harbor. Feathered creatures flew the blue sky. Some dived into the warm waters, rising with a wriggling catch clutched in their beaks. Small aquatic forms were easily visible in the clear water below her, and she ached to go swimming. *Genedalt would not like that.* Her towering protector stood close on her right side as she gazed out from the flight deck.

"You don't think I would just jump in, do you?" Er'men asked, leaning over the edge of the deck just a little more. Genedalt replied with a growling grunt that asked how much she wanted to annoy the RegentFirstMother. He gave every indication of following her in if she did decide to jump.

"I hadn't thought about her at all," Er'men replied. "The water looks most inviting, don't you think?"

"Dangerous for little pouchlings," he noted, pointing to the wake of a large reptile, swimming across the channel. He did not laugh but held his amusement at bay.

"Don't 'pouchling' me." Er'men groused. She could not stop her genuine anger leaking through, although he did not deserve it. Genedalt meant his teasing as play. RegentFirstMother treated her as though she was freshly born. *It's so frustrating!* Despite being only six earth-months old, Er'men was not a child. She held her race's most precious heirloom in her mind, the memories and wisdom of generations of GreatMothers that came before her.

"I want to go ashore." Er'men had seen pictures but could hardly believe all the houses built above ground. The tall buildings all had windows to let in the light. *They have a benevolent sun.* Genedalt had insisted she come to the side of Tal'anis that faced away from the city.

"Dangerous there too. Human hunters lie in wait. Tal'anis draws them," Genedalt grumbled his discontent. He did not like being down on the planet's surface. The full blue sky was too big; it made him feel exposed and vulnerable. And if he felt vulnerable then his precious charge was in danger too. "This landing was..." he struggled to find the correct words and shrugged at his failure.

Er'men could not blame him. "Premature." She sighed, turned away from the harbor and began to walk back across the scorched flight deck toward the airlocks. "We should not be here at all. Not like this," Er'men added, but there was nothing she could do to change the course RegentFirstMother Harrum'Bar had charted. *The only thing I can do is the task all GreatMothers must do: integrate my inheritance.* Er'men hoped that she would find some nugget of knowledge that would help turn her people from this invasion. *There's so much to learn.*

Genedalt swept her up in his comfortable arms and waded through the LeftLeading advisers the Great Council had assigned to her, returning to her apartments where she could meditate quietly.

CHAPTER THIRTY-ONE

The sounds of Cicely and Cian arguing over lick-the-bowl rights made a chuckle bubble out of Patty as she pulled herself down Jaswinder's central corridor on her way to the bridge. Jaswinder was, by anyone's standards, a strange beast of a ship. Madhur had built Jaswinder out of spare parts and salvage, and Patty was sure there were not two panels, compartments or doors from the same ship. Nothing matched but everything worked.

As Patty glided up the shaft, she felt a tap on her boot. It was Alan, in his usual position just behind her. She caught hold of a bulkhead and came to a halt. He looked as though he was trying to make an utterance, but he abandoned the effort in frustration and instead used his quick hands to make himself understood. Patty greeted his every attempt to communicate with delight. *Somewhere in there is my annoying little brother. I can't believe I miss the brat.*

"The Freya," Alan signed, pointing to a picture tacked to the wall. Pushing off the stanchion, Patty floated back to her brother, catching hold of his shoulder to kill her momentum. She took the opportunity to turn her grasp into a hug, slipping her arm around his waist and pulling him close. Alan stiffened but only briefly.

Pictures of family and friends covered the walls of Jaswinder's central shaft; old, flat 2D pics, GIF-pics and stereo pics formed overlapping layers in no apparent order. Many were skite-shots featuring Madhur next to the fusion engine or ship she was working on. There were tiny single-seat broomsticks - nothing but propulsion and navigation - multi-engine inter-planetary craft, and everything else in between.

Freya's super-absorbent jet-black coating drank in every photon that touched it, radio waves through to x-rays, and that made her a problematic ship to photograph. Madhur had backlit the CRV in her workshop, but even so, it was hard to interpret the silhouette. Madhur stood proudly on the left of the frame pointing to the dark outline, Alan, and Patty on the right. Madhur was an excellent and exacting engineer and had Freya in her workshop before each of Patty's reconnaissance flights. *She's so careful. Freya's special coating hasn't received so much as an oily thumbprint.*

"Yes, that's Freya and Madhur and us." Patty squeezed him.

He nodded, pointing to Madhur and then to the picture beside it and the one beside that. "The Captain Madhur," Alan signed, "is everywhere."

"Of course she is. Jaswinder is her ship. She shares it with us." Patty hated the thought of achieving anything through luck, but she had to admit that finding Jaswinder and Madhur near the L3 station was lucky. Tough and resourceful, Madhur had kept them all together.

"And the Cian." Alan pointed to another picture and another ship. Patty was not sure what had happened between Madhur and Cian before the aliens came - he had put up with earfuls of vitriolic insults when he came aboard at L4 - but they settled their differences while working on Hunter, Cian's CRV. Cian had sacrificed his ship at L5, giving The Ice Princess, docked to humanity's partial completed generational starship, the chance to escape. They were on the way to a rendezvous with her.

Alan pointed to two pics, before and after shots of Hunter. The first picture had them floating to either side of the old CRV; the second, they were almost touching. Almost. Madhur and Cian had stripped Hunter down to guidance and propulsion, turning a barely flight-worthy CRV into a deadly kinetic missile. Something had changed between them while working on Hunter. Cian was not a bad sort, for a gangly geek. *At least he's aware of his faults.* Patty chuckled. Madhur had lists of them. She still burned him, but she delivered the jibes with an amused glint in her eyes instead of cold contempt.

A sick shudder took hold of Patty. She had fought aliens at L5, blade-to-blade. Instinct had her reaching for the place where her rapier, Lady Estelle, customarily hung. Although L5 had not been a complete nightmare, Patty had been able to unite the crews of Hestia's Hearth and The Ice Princess and free them from captivity. It should have been a joyful memory, but the aliens she had killed lingered in her dreams, still bleeding, still burning.

If you hadn't gone to L5, you wouldn't have met Lirsín. Surely, that's worth a few nightmare images, and you saved your friends, Jake and your fencing coach Daichi. It was Lirsín's smile and his bright eyes that counter-balanced the bloody fight through The Ice Princess's corridors. Her thoughts were tossed about whenever she thought about Lirsín. The anticipation vied with her doubts to see which would disturb her the most. *He's a Belter. He probably doesn't even like fat Earther girls.*

"Patty. I was just coming to get you." Jai's voice jarred Patty from her tangled thoughts. Madhur's fifteen-year-old nephew floated at the far end of the shaft with one hand on a bulkhead. He looked as though he had tasted something sour, but that did not mute his exuberance. *I wish a bit more of that would rub off on Alan.*

"A Colonel - Lieutenant-Colonel actually - Saab has logged into Jaswinder's Yak Space, and he wants to," Jai tried not to look too guilty, "debrief you." He grimaced. "Sorry. I should have set up an anon account when I posted those videos."

Those videos. The little scanner-camera pinned onto her p-suit recorded everything. Having every mutter and burp posted for the solar system's perusal was a total embarrassment. All that 'life-cam' stuff was so last-gen, but Jai was right. Crowd-sourced analysis would discover more than she had, crawling through the alien mothership's air ducts while hunting for her brother. *Many hands make light work, don't they? And you did find your brother. The lack of privacy's a small price to pay.*

"That's okay, Jai." Patty squeezed Alan affectionately and

pushed off, gliding up the corridor. She could almost feel Alan, her shadow, follow her. "My dad flew for the United Space Force. I'm sure they're not as bad as you all make out."

"You reckon I've got a bit of L3 prejudice, eh?" Jai challenged playfully, his hand dropping to his hip where a blade might hang. He had been in L3's age-grade fencing team. The three of them, Patty, Alan, and Jai, regularly practiced together. Before the aliens came, zero-gee fencing had been a minority interest sport; now it was a serious vocation.

Patty smiled. "I don't know. You're the one that doesn't like them. Examine your feelings, grasshopper," she teased. "Do you feel prejudiced?"

Jai's thick black eyebrows bounced up and down as he thought about it, but his grin did not leave. "Yeah ... definitely ... with good reason." He nodded vigorously, agreeing with himself. He turned and pushed forward into the bridge.

The long curved red leather bench-seat dominated Jaswinder's bridge, stretching across the control room. It could be configured to seat five under acceleration, but Patty had never seen more than three strapped into its padded embrace. Madhur's ever-practical design ethic - if it worked, use it - was evident in the bridge controls; none of the control stations, comms, navigation, engineering, and life-support, were from the same ship, and most were customized with replacement controls or displays.

Jai swarmed over the back of the seat and secured a belt around his lap as he took his station at the comm. He smiled over his shoulder and patted the seat beside him. He tapped at a few keys and a page full of text filled the main screen.

"What is this?" Patty eyed the old keyboard sitting on the console as she strapped down. "You don't mean I have to type, do you?" she asked. Alan remained floating behind the curved seat as if guarding the doorway.

"Yeah, UNET is now F-UNET, and it's prim-it-ive." Jai swapped the screen for the usual UNET login page, but it was not quite the usual page. Someone had hacked it, adding a spray-painted F before the UNET header and a low-res animated character giving a single-finger salute, leaned up against the logo's T. Patty laughed as she logged in.

"I've never actually witnessed bitrates quite so low, but it's such a cool hack encrypting UNET into the interference-noise the aliens are broadcasting!" Jai laughed.

The screen changed back to the 'Yak Space' program that Jai had shown before with the names of those logged into the system - Jai, Patty, and Lt_Col_Saab - a record of the session, and an area to type messages.

Patty slowly pecked at the keyboard. "Saab, Can I help?" and waited for his reply. It took nearly thirty seconds before text began scrolling onto the screen.

"Capt. Balke good 2 make contact. Recording caused an uproar with analysts. Little hard intelligence. Bravery impressed all. Have mission 4 U. USF commission."

Patty sat back and considered her reply before typing. This time-lagged text communication has some advantages.

"A mission?" she asked.

"Not dangerous, or not as dangerous as invading the mothership. Need data from Darwin. Mission is recon. Freya stealthy, yes? Intel vital."

Darwin. Patty's hands began sweating. The alien mothership had landed in Darwin. She itched to find out what was happening down there. One of her best friends, Tina, another member of the OASIS fencing team, lived in Darwin. Patty had a personal interest in keeping on top of events, and her heart ached, knowing she could not help.

"Sorry Saab. Committed 2 rendez. Expended reserves," Patty typed.

Jai's hand hovered over the keyboard, preventing her from hitting the send button. "What if you put Eg's stardrive in Freya?" he asked.

"I thought it was only good for putting holes in Madhur's workshop," she countered. Patty had not fathomed the mystery that was Cicely's blind-mute twin brother. Cicely and Eg were more like symbionts than conventional human twins. Eg never did anything without his sister to guide him, and yet Cicely and Cian were certain Eg had discovered how the aliens' reactionless space drive worked.

"Cian says Jaswinder masses too much for the drive's current configuration, but Freya might fit the bill," Jai told her. "You could get her flying again."

"Really?" Patty's heart skipped a beat. She had volunteered to drain Freya's fuel so they could rendezvous with The Ice Princess, but losing her independence hurt. Jaswinder had to make that rendezvous. The Ice Princess would take them all far, far away from aliens and wars of conquest, out to Ceres and the Belt. She felt torn, wanting to go but wanting to stay.

"May I?" Jai selected her reply's text, and his finger hovered over the delete key.

"Ah ... sure. I guess," Patty relented.

Jai slid the keyboard closer to him and began typing. "Saab. Maybe possible. Need time." Jai cocked an eyebrow at Patty for her approval before hitting the send button.

"Understand," Saab replied. "Contact soonest if able. Contract info attached."

"Is the drive really going to be able to power Freya?" Patty asked.

"Let's find out," Jai replied as he opened the intercom channel to the lounge. "Cian?"

"Yeah?" Cian's So-Cal accent sounded thin as if he was on the far side of the room.

"How much mass can Eg's do-hicky push?" Jai asked.

"Is that a theoretical question?" It sounded as though Cian moved closer to the comm as he spoke.

"We were wondering if it might drive Freya," Jai answered.

"Jai?" Madhur cut in. "What are you up to?"

Jai grimaced, and then his grin popped back into place, "Nothing Auntie Mad." He shook his head and whispered even though the microphone was off, "She won't like this. She thinks the USF is Corporate spawn."

"Don't you 'Auntie Mad' me, young man!"

CHAPTER THIRTY-TWO

"Don't you dare sign that contract!" Madhur growled. Her eyes sparkled with fire. She settled herself deeper into the long acceleration couch that spanned Jaswinder's bridge. Patty opened her mouth to reply, but Madhur flicked her long braid over her shoulder and waved her down. "Don't deny it. I know you and your naïve, cockeyed opinion of the United Space Force but you've got to look at contracts with an eye for detail and hidden pitfalls even with," Madhur ground her teeth, "especially with the USF." She pointed to the contact displayed on the main console. "This rate wouldn't pay for a garbage scow!"

"That *is* why I asked you to have a look at it, Madhur," Patty answered, trying to keep her reply even-toned to hide her frustration. "I've never had to negotiate a contract, with the USF or anyone else for that matter."

The scowl on Madhur's face slowly turned into a grin, and that fiery spark in her eyes changed into a sparkle. "Is Sergeant Ford still online?"

"Colonel Saab." Patty corrected her and smiled as she relaxed. *I don't want to fight with Madhur but if I can help the USF, I will.* A thousand and one things would have to go right if Patty was going to successfully unmothball Freya and return to Earth. "No. I told him that Freya might be available for this mission and that I would have to get back to him. He sent through the contract anyway."

"That's a mighty big 'might' if you're contemplating using that so-called, stardrive of Eg's." Madhur shook her head, and that growl returned to her voice. "Holed the workshop, they did! Did I tell you that it came *this* close to hitting Griffin?" she held her finger and thumb millimeters apart.

Patty had heard the story and had hoped to avoid the hearing about it again. It had been one of the reasons she had asked Madhur to look at the contract while Jai conferred with Eg, Cicely, and Cian about the drive.

"I know Cian should have watched him more closely," Patty answered. "It won't happen again. Eg is only ten after all. If, and I agree, it *is* a big if, but if they can get that dimensional-probe-thing to work then I must help. My friend Tina lives in Darwin. The city and suburbs took quite a pounding before the mothership landed." Patty had been to her friend's house on many occasions. They had a well-stocked storm cellar, as did most homes. Cyclones were not frequent, but the citizens of Darwin had learned hard lessons from past weather events and were not complacent about such things. There would be plenty of places for Tina to hide out. *But she won't be hiding, she's pure Trit, and she'll be out there giving the invaders hell.*

Madhur nodded and began editing the contract. "It's Freya they're interested in, not you," Madhur groused. "It's not every day one of Fermi's Slippery-ships is available."

Giuseppe Fermi had found Freya for Patty when she had been looking for a good, second-hand CRV. He had used Freya to talk to Patty's father about a business deal. Enraptured by Freya's sleek, lifting-body design, Patty had not paid any attention to her father's business dealings as she admired her smooth lines and the gold and red paintwork. Patty remembered that day as if it were yesterday, not eighteen months ago.

It had only been a little more than two weeks since the aliens invaded and that felt like forever. Without Freya, she would have been stuck down on Earth when the asteroid, the aliens diverted, came crashing down. *Maybe. Maybe you would have been with Mom and Dad, wherever they are.*

Fleeing the invasion, Patty and her younger brother Alan had ended up at L2 where Giuseppe had taken them in. Patty tried not to think about the bloodshed on L2. She had lost a piece of her sanity when the aliens took her little brother. Giuseppe's workshop had provided Freya with long-range fuel tanks and the special coating that made her exceptionally stealthy. The Belter War history syllabus at Patty's high school did not mention the notorious smuggler, Joe Fermi, and his Slippery-ships, but the Belters all knew of Slippery Joe. He had warned her about the USF, too, and had not wanted them to get their hands on Freya's special coating.

"The United Space Force and a local strike force have assembled," Patty told Madhur. "They're going in whether I'm there or not but..."

"But they lack an asset in the High Frontier," Madhur sneered. "Not much space in that *United Space*," she paused before spitting out her last word, "*Farce.*"

"That's why I need to be there. No one else can do it," Patty insisted. The aliens had firm control of everything from the asteroid debris field in Low Earth Orbit to the Moon and all the LaGrange stations. *What was left of them.* The only way Freya would be able to fly back to Earth was if - *as Madhur put it* - that do-hicky worked. Cian had already admitted that the device was flawed. It could not move Jaswinder and had holed the workshop. Patty was glad she had not been aboard. Cicely had whispered to her that Madhur had been ready to space Cian.

Madhur gave a low harrumph, "This was an as-is-where-is contract. They're lucky a ship of Freya's capabilities is available at all." She began making changes to the contract. "That base rate's just insulting." She multiplied it by ten, added a fifty percent surcharge for hazardous duty and a two hundred percent performance bonus. Patty's eyes bugged out, and she tried to keep her jaw from flapping. She knew shipping was expensive, but those figures beggared her imagination. They were big-corporation numbers. *No wonder Daddy had me make small deliveries from OASIS.* She could buy a ship twice Freya's size with half what she could earn in a week at just the base rate.

"And they'll pay that?" Patty tried to keep her incredulity from her voice.

"They'll pay it and think they've found a bargain." She

changed the duration of the contract from open-ended to one of a limited duration, forty-eight hours, renewable on an hour-by-hour basis and made it dissolvable by either party for any reason at any time, beyond the initial forty-eight hours. "The bastards were trying to sign you up for a lifetime of indentured bloody servitude!"

A NEW NAME

Er'men settled down onto the deep cushions and tried to slow her breathing. She could feel the river of lives within her. The turbulent memories of her heritage were filled with loss and pain. Precious memories. She slowly let go of the rush and bustle of the landing and reports of the fighting outside in the city and dove into the multitudes within. Little Star was a GreatMother that began with few resources, caught out in the open during a sunstrike. The memories, gifted to the GreatMother from the ancestral mel'andrin, saved her life and those close to her. Er'men let go of the demands of the moment. *Perhaps I'll find what I need with Little Star.*

Little Star was glad Telanor did not insist that she travel with him into the town. *All those buildings are above the ground.* They made her feel unsafe even though mel'andrin's gifts had shown her the building could be safe if they were built properly, and if the sunstrike was not too strong or for too long. *That's a whole lot of ifs, if you're asking me.*

Bor'enop. Telanor keeps calling me Bor'enop. And all the Hel'omi guards call me GreatMother Bor'enop. All, except for one. Her mind automatically translated Bor'enop from the GreatMother's dialect to the tongue her mother had impressed upon her as a pouchling. Little Star. It was one of Telanor's little lessons that brought all those memories, all those lives from the golden mel'andrin sphere to the surface of her mind, but Little Star had had more than enough lessons for today.

The campsite was outside the town walls but somehow felt more secure. *I bet this was an old Holding.* Little Star felt patterns from her own memories mesh with those gifted to her. *The main door would be right where that shadow is.* "Come on Stone Son," Little Star said with a skip. "Let's take a look."

Taking Stone Son's hand, Little Star dragged her big friend forward. She could not believe how different Stone Son looked in his Clan Bumurnam livery. It was not just the smart uniform; he had received mel'andrin from his brothers. The gift-memories had changed the set of his shoulders, and his eyes looked at the world as if it were all new and yet old. *Do my eyes look like that?* A part of her wanted to recapture some of the simplicity of yesterday; the world had been smaller, and her limited understanding no worse than anyone else's. Now every little thing reminded her of something else, the shape of a hill, the sound of a river turning the rocks in its bed evoked a GreatMother's memory from long ago. *What am I supposed to do with all this stuff filling my head?*

Telanor said it would get better when she had integrated them into herself, that it would happen slowly over an orbit or two. *ORBITS!* One of her predecessors had flown orbits around their homeworld. The sight of her planet's brown-green arc filling the spaceship's viewport was as vibrant in Little Star's mind as if the memory was her own. *It is mine .... now.*

"GreatMother Bor'enop's will," Stone Son bowed. He had never done that before yesterday, and Little Star felt lost. "Come, Little Star," his rumbling purr progressed into a cough of deep mirth. "Stone Son still here. Never leave Little Star." Once his strong arms wrapped around her, the world righted once more.

CHAPTER THIRTY-THREE

"I should show you this," Cian told Patty as he unpacked himself from Freya's cramped rear seat, pushing her to one side of Freya's small cockpit as he climbed over her and opened a command-line screen. "It's an under-the-hood hack, but it's worth knowing." Another auxiliary window opened, displaying controls for the artificial gravity vector, arrays of numbers scrolling down a window and a three-axis chart showed rolling curves, billowing changes of hue and amplitude.

"Over here." Cian's finger pointed to an array of numbers in the left corner.

For nearly two hours they had been testing Freya with the stardrive Eg and Cian reverse engineered. Patty's back ached. Freya did not feel the same with the constant one-third-gee artificial gravity. Cian described the device as a trans-dimensional probe, but Cicely called it the Sprocket Drive. Somehow, it isolated Freya from the universe, moving her from one coordinate set to another. Even though it was limited to a ship of Freya's stripped-down mass, it was exciting to fly humanity's first reactionless space drive.

"I'm sorry Cian. What was that?" Patty asked.

"It's a little batch file that should zero out Freya's position to the local calibration point, a hundred meters outside Jaswinder's workshop."

"Zero out?" she inquired.

"Our local offset. These numbers over here." Cian pointed to an array of numbers in the top left corner. "Don't worry about the top set; they're the global offsets for this sector of the Milky Way. The next set down is the local quaternion vector. It corresponds to the coordinates one hundred meters off Jaswinder's workshop, so," he waggled his fingers over the controls, "if they haven't maneuvered, zeroing out this vector," Cian's finger stabbed at the last set of alphanumerics, "will bring us home."

Patty did not know how the 'trans-dimensional probe' worked, not like she knew Freya's old fusion engine - Eg's math was daunting - but it did work. So far, it had been worth the heartache caused by watching Madhur remove Freya's fusion drive. Despite Madhur's concerns and Patty's fears, the drive performed exactly as Cian, Cicely, and Eg promised. It seemed robust. Cian had re-booted the device five times and each time 'probe insertion' - whatever that was - proceeded without a hitch. *Freya flies!* Without the Sprocket Drive, Freya would be completely dead in space. She did not even have orientation thrusters anymore. They were all gone to get Freya under the drive's mass limitations.

On the control panel, the readouts that displayed Freya's fusion engine stats were gone too, but in their place was a line of toggled registers limiting Freya's velocity relative to a designated vector in the external universe. The lowest register range was from 'All Stop' to ten centimeters per second. The second register's range went between 10cm/s and 10m/s, the third between 10m/s and 10km/s. *That's nearly Earth's escape velocity.* The fourth and fifth registers made Patty's palms sweat. The fourth's range was from 10km/s to 10,000km/s. 10K km/s was seriously fast. *Thirty-six million kilometers an hour fast! At the touch of a button!* Nothing in the solar system was that fast. *Nothing human-made.*

The last register was grayed-out and inaccessible, which pleased Patty no end. It controlled Freya's velocity between ten thousand km/s and ten million km/s! *TEN MILLION KILOMETERS PER SECOND! That's just not possible!* Light, the universe's Ol' Faithful, clocked in two hundred and ninety-nine thousand kilometers per second and nothing was supposed to be able to top that.

For most of the last two hours, they had tested Freya within easy hailing distance of Madhur's ungainly ship, in case they broke down. However, on this run, they had put on a burst of speed and traveled all the way to Earth-Sun's Lagrange Two to calibrate the Sprocket Drive against Freya's internal navigational almanac. The positions of the satellite observatories, parked in the eternal eclipse of L2, provided excellent external references. However, the little black box worked - *Are these things always little black boxes?* - it meshed seamlessly with Freya's navigation and piloting systems. Patty could fly Freya from waypoint to waypoint on a detailed course or fly stick-and-rudder the way she liked, but it had taken a while for the little kinks to be worked out of the system. Patty was more than ready for a break.

"See?" Cian moved out of the way, and Patty dodged his elbow as he retreated.

"What?" she grumbled.

"I've written a little batch file that should 'zero out' Freya's position." Cian typed "Execute jas_home.bat" and hit the enter key.

Freya did not move - or did not seem to - but with a bright flash, the universe twitched around them. Jaswinder glinted in the sun off Freya's port side.

"Oh! Err ... that shouldn't have happened." Cian leaned back and scratched his head. "Or maybe..."

Patty struggled out from under Cian and gave him a taste of her elbow to hurry him back to his rear seat.

"What have you done?!" The hackles on the back of Patty's neck stood to attention, and she felt a little nauseated. She opened the flight logs. There was a discontinuity, a transitionless-transition between two points. If there was duration between the two readings, it was beyond Freya's sensors to perceive it.

Cian's long face contorted as he tried to explain, his eyebrows bobbing up and down in a twitchy dance. "I didn't realize this command level would bypass the lockouts but..."

"So, we traveled back here at the speed of light?"

"Faster, I guess. Have to look at the raw sensor data. I'm sure there was some duration. We just weren't looking. Wow!" Cian stopped and sighed. "You know? We were just the fastest humans ever. I'll have to send a note to the Guinness people."

Patty choked back her rage and checked in with Jai. "Jaswinder, we're back for a bit."

"Err... gotcha there, Patty." Jai sounded a bit unsure of himself. "You popped out of range, and I lost you. Snuck up on us, eh?"

"Something like that. Cian uncovered some controls that a pilot should have access to and he's going to do a little more UI tinkering before we have another run. Apart from that, everything is really smooth." *Smooth in a cocked hat!*

"Good to hear it," Jai replied. "Alan's been a bit worked up, but Ken's been talking to him. They're with me, on the bridge."

"Alan, please relax. I won't be too much longer. I promise," Patty told her brother and hoped he would keep calm. Even when he moved as her shadow, his apparent composure masked a burning inner tension. He had not wanted to be left aboard Jaswinder for this test flight, but there was not enough room aboard Freya for Alan and Cian.

"He says, cannot serve, cannot protect." Ken's voice was relaxed and sure but did not hide his concern.

"Alan, you can best serve me by waiting until I return. Do you understand, Alan?" She wished they had the bandwidth to include video; most of what she read from Alan was from his body language.

"Err, I think he understands, he just gave us a thumbs-up and seems ... less agitated." Jai sounded relieved.

"Can you show him the telemetry so that he can track us?" A yawn suddenly cracked Patty's jaw. She checked Freya's gas mix. No, it was not the ship's systems; she was tired. "We won't be too much longer."

CHAPTER THIRTY-FOUR

Dream treacle smothered Patty; she could not even move her chin to activate her p-suit's emergency beacon. *Not that it will do me any good, although someone might register my passing.* Falling. Faster and faster. Not that she noticed the increase in speed except for a voice in the back of her mind that kept working out the velocity of a body falling to the surface of the moon. *One-sixth the attraction of the Earth but that's powerful enough. Am I going to bounce or splat?*

She could see the crater-strewn surface where she was going to impact and felt vaguely disappointed it was not going to be near a populated area. *Maybe that's a good thing. Better to crash into some anonymous place on the far side than taking out an innocent.* She was on the far side, she was sure. It was all so familiar and eerily different. *So bright and dark. Too bright. Too fast. Too close.* Despite her rising terror and her frantic attempts to move, she could not look away or even blink. The surface arrived. Brilliant.

Patty recoiled, and her eyes snapped open - *Bright. Too bright* - and just as quickly closed them.

"Sorry, Patty. Madhur says it's time to rouse you," Jai told her from the door to her small quarters; his hand still hovered over the light switch. "Breakfast's almost ready." His apologetic smile sagged. "Sort of. Cian's cooking." He grimaced, turned, and shot away. The door slid shut behind him.

Patty sighed and tried to relax. It never helped to struggle when embedded in a sleeping sack's Gordian entanglement. A flash of fear pulsed through her, the fear of falling. It had been a long, long time since she had felt that, but it still had the power to make her heart stop and then race uncontrollably. Alan moved from his position, floating by the door to help extricate her sweating body from the sack. Dream sweat. Cold sweat.

"Breakfast now? Then fly?" he signed, his face was composed, but Patty could see the excitement in his eyes. He had improved so much from the state he had been in when she had rescued him from the aliens. *He'll be vocalizing again, one day, soon.* Before food, Patty had a much greater need; to get clean. Cold water, preferably. That usually cleared the dream treacle away.

"Yes ... no." Patty rubbed her face. "Yes. You go and eat. I need to wash. Are you ready for space?" Alan nodded. *Eagerly? Yes, he was keen to be off once more.*

"Checked over Zip-Lok with," Alan's signing paused, his eyes darting, "with ... the Ken. It was worn. There is a new Zip-Lok for this one. The Freya is stocked and ... the Captain Madhur says she shows full charge."

"And have you slept?" Patty held his eyes. He blinked and gave a little bow.

"This one has not." Alan's face looked remorseful, but Patty was certain she caught a glimmer of deceit, a flash of something that reminded Patty of her brother of old, "but there will be time when the Freya flies."

"There should be, but if there is an emergency? Mistakes happen when we're tired." Patty did not want to discourage his enthusiasm, but space was a dangerous place. Mistakes could kill you in a heartbeat. Alan bowed, and when he looked up - Patty was glad he did - his eyes and brow looked thoughtful. That was good; she could almost see thoughts passing through his mind. Anything was better than when he had been impassive. His vacant state had scared her more than she had wanted to admit.

Breakfast went by in a blur. Patty was surprised at finding her p-suit cleaned and delicately scented with sandalwood and gardenia. Everyone hugged her except Ken, who stood watch on the bridge; he sent his best wishes via the comm. Eg gave her a deft peck on the cheek as she was sandwiched between the twins.

"Eg says you have to keep feeding us telemetry bursts over the F-UNET." Cicely leaned in for a peck as well. "You promise to come back in one piece this time?"

"I promise, cross my heart." Patty smiled as Cicely seemed to consider her trustworthiness for a moment before accepting her word.

Jai leaned in and scored an extra hug as he pinned the jewel pin-camera to its regular position on her p-suit. "You've got a big fan base out there now, Patty. Gotta keep the episodes coming," he encouraged her.

Alan scrambled into Freya's cramped rear seat after having his Zip-Lok's seals checked and was belted in and ready before Patty had her helmet sealed. Patty took her time; there was no real rush. Freya could be in geosync orbit in minutes, but Patty wanted her to behave like an ordinary fusion powered CRV and not a spacecraft capable of traveling a sizable percentage of the speed of light. Cicely was adamant that Eg did not want the USF to know about the drive, not until he had determined why his version had a severe mass limitation. Patty still was not willing to believe the fifth velocity register would enable Freya to travel at the speed of light or faster. Some conceptual boundaries were too difficult to cross.

"Keep safe," Madhur said. "Remember, Captain Balke; hazardous duty doesn't mean letting yourself get shot at." Madhur pushed herself back from Freya's cockpit. She gave a cockeyed smile and a salute before herding everyone out of the workshop. Patty went through the steps for securing Freya for flight, carefully and deliberately, as the workshop depressurized. As much as she loved living on Jaswinder and loved her motley crew as though they were family, she was excited Freya was flight worthy once more. *We're free again!*

They were ready. "Freya to Jaswinder, we are set for departure." Everything that could be checked was checked. Even the Sprocket Drive was in the green, idling below a perceivable threshold.

"Gotcha there, Patty." Ken's reply was dry and matter-of-fact. "Oh, Eg just asked if you could send a test telemetry burst through F-UNET."

"Sure. Hang on." Patty opened the engine logs and sent a data packet to Eg's account. "Burst, away." It was only a small packet, but it had to travel to the servers in Earth orbit and back to Jaswinder. Depending on the traffic, it could take a long time to return.

"How are we doing, back there?" Patty threw the question over her shoulder.

An auxiliary window opened on her display, and Alan's reply began to appear slowly. "Ready, bladder empty, suit sealed." He could sign proficiently, but the human alphabet meant nothing to him. Ken had found a sign-to-text interface, buried in the operating system for Alan.

"Good to hear. We'll be departing in a second or two," Patty told him.

"Waiting easy."

"You are cleared," Ken began, but he was overwhelmed by cheers, and good wishes from all of Jaswinder's family gathered on the bridge.

"Thanks, guys. I'll keep you updated," Patty replied and nudged Freya from the deck. Freya glided slowly through the doorway, out into the dark. It was only dark by comparison to the brightly lit workshop; billions of bright pinpricks shone in the deep black. Patty threw Freya into a tight turn, rising above Jaswinder's shadow. Earth was mostly in darkness, but the sliver of daylight was bright enough to make Patty wince a little. The sun's massive outpouring quickly dimmed to an orange dot, masked by the canopy's optics.

"Freya to Jaswinder, we are clear. Thanks for all the help. Fly true. Freya out." Patty rolled Freya to take one last look at Jaswinder's irregular shape. Every panel, every extension looked like it was cobbled together from junk that should have been recycled as scrap. She looked dangerous and ready to fall apart at the slightest prod, but Patty felt as if she was leaving home.

"Fly true." The multi-voiced reply made Patty smile as she rolled Freya away and hit the throttle. Jaswinder's asymmetrical brightness dwindled quickly behind them.

Freya had less than fifteen minutes to hit the right coordinates for radio contact with the USF. With Freya's old flight profile, it would have taken a continuous and expensive burn to return to Earth orbit, but now Patty could guide Freya to just about anywhere in the Earth-Moon system in minutes, seconds if she really pushed it.

Her only regret leaving Jaswinder *was missing the rendezvous with* The Ice Princess. *Thoughts of Lirsín's smile sent shivers through her. Don't be a silly girl. He's a Belter. They breed them skinny like Lily. He won't be interested in a fat Earther-girl.*

THE STORM COMES

With doors this wide, and with such a broad terrace, Little Star knew this had been a Holding of some note when it had been in use. If the state of the overgrown entryway was any indication, the Holding had suffered generations of neglect. Stone Son let her climb down and put his shoulder to the iron-bound doors. The hinges groaned, then suddenly screamed as they twisted and gave way. The great iron-shod door crashed into the dark entryway.

"Oops," Stone Son mumbled.

"You don't know your own strength, Stone Son!" Little Star could not repress the bubbling chuckle. Stone Son shrugged and poked his head inside the Holding, before backing away, his strong right hand waving the dust filled air away from his face. "Bad. Rot!"

As mean and lazy as Pa was, he would not tolerate any rot in his Holding and actively encouraged others to be equally vigilant. Rot killed more people than sunstrikes. *Maybe that's why the Holding was abandoned.*

Disappointed, Little Star kicked at the flowering head of a shale-weed and the world flickered as if lightning had coursed through the sky above the clouds. But there was no accompanying clap of thunder, no tag-along rumble. A chill flooded through her.

"Did you see that?" she asked.

"What, Little Star?" Stone Son sank down beside her.

"Sunstrike!" She had never witnessed one herself, but the memories she carried within her recognized the signs. "Sunstrike! We have to get under cover!" She took in the bustle of their camp. "We *all* must get under cover. Stone Son, back to the camp, quickly!" The interval between a flash and a strike could be only moments. Stone Son swept her up and ran.

"Sunstrike! Sunstrike!" Little Star shouted and waved. The part of Little Star, the part that was still the frightened little misfit, was surprised at how quickly the great soldiers rushed to obey her. Perched atop Stone Son's shoulder, she took one last look at the commotion she'd caused before spurring her mount back towards the Holding. Telanor had taken a small honor guard but not his litter as it was 'a good distance to stretch his legs.' Six Hel'omi had the larger supply wagon moving. The litter was not far from rolling, too.

"Rot, or not, we're going in, Stone Son," Little Star told him, letting his protective hands bring her down from her perch, and he hit the remaining door at the charge. It crashed open and, surprisingly, remained attached to its hinges. The clouds were perceptibly brighter when the wagon bounced up the steps and into the foyer.

"Deeper! Go deeper," Little Star shouted, waving them past, and she gave one quick look at the clouds. They were roiling, boiling away. *This is going to be bad. I hope Telanor can find shelter in one of those stone houses.* She did not trust that they were any good, but hand stacked stone had to be better than nothing at all. *Didn't it?*

The litter, with Telanor's precious far-talking radio inside, rumbled over the portico and Stone Son followed it in.

"Deep as you can go!" Little Star shouted again. The world flashed brightly behind them as they ran deeper into the Holding, scattering into darkened side corridors as soon as they were found. They all followed her as if she knew where she was going. The funny thing was, the Holding did remind her of her old home.

"Down here and to the left," she ordered.

The air was cool and free from rot. Thick doors opened into a grand Great Hall. *This is much bigger than Pa's Holding.* Light flickered down the mirrored light traps. *Sunstrike!*

The Hel'omi gathered around her rumbling a low chant. "GreatMother guide us. GreatMother keep us."

Until today Little Star had not felt like one of the fabled GreatMothers of old, but now the memories lined up inside her, showing her the ways to survive a sunstrike, how they could survive and flourish. She could not remain as Little Star, not now. For the first time, she truly embraced her heritage and let go of the simple life that could no longer be hers.

"I am Bor'enop. The paths are dark beneath the ground, filled with hidden falls and traps. The GreatMothers' gifts light our way."

The Hel'omi chanted their reply. "GreatMother guide us. GreatMother keep us."

"There's water somewhere below us," Bor'enop told her Hel'omi. She could feel the rush and rumble transmitted through solid rock beneath her feet. "It is still too dangerous to go outside." The clicking radiation counter from the Telanor's collection of equipment did not click; it emitted warning tones when they ventured towards the entryway. She hoped Telanor was safe but did not think he was. The sunstrike had lasted for hours, well into the night. *The lush, fertile land they had traveled through will be burned to its roots. Ma will be all right. Pa will have put away plenty. He was an ignorant barbarian, but he knows how to manage a holding.* The radio spat static. That did not surprise Bor'enop at all.

"We'll need water soon. We'll take three," Bor'enop told Stone Son. She did not think she would *need* three guards as well as Stone Son, but the Hel'omi fretted. *Especially now that Telanor's gone. They need me.*

As they traveled through the winding corridors, the question why this Holding had been abandoned gnawed at Bor'enop. It was old. They were deep within the holding's safe surrounds, and the corridors were machine made. There was a little rot where dampness pooled, but the Holding was sound. Bor'enop was sure it could have housed the town above it.

Behind doors that resisted Stone Son's strength but not the power of all four of her entourage, she found what she was looking for and more. It took a while before a sympathetic memory surfaced to tell Bor'enop what she was looking at: a generator control room. The top of a great turbine protruded through the floor in the space beyond.

As Stone Son opened the sluice, Bor'enop tried not to hold her breath. *How well have the builders built? How long has it been since these systems ran?* Needles rose from their lower stops. *Power! Electricity!* Bor'enop danced on the spot.

Bor'enop was glad her memories helped them find the Holding's circuit breakers; they were close by or had been. Someone had dismantled them many years ago. They had not left it in ruins though. They had patched the generator's output into a newer conduit that led out into the corridor instead of using the internal ducts. It was, at least, easy to follow, although the reason why it had been done was not. *What did they need this power for?* The cables traveled up to the vulnerable regions near the surface. Bor'enop knew it was only her imagination, but she could feel the radiation seeping in through the ground above her and wished she had brought the radiation counter with her.

A corroded metal door sealed the end of the corridor with the conduit passing through an armored flange above its lintel. A tiny blue light glowed above the keypad beside the door. *Code-locked. That door would resist the muscular efforts of everyone. Brains will get us in there, not brawn.*

But it was the sensitivity of her fingers and not the acuity of her mind that unlocked the door. Etched into the surface above the keys, so finely her eyes could only catch a hint of it, was the word *primes*. Without thinking, Bor'enop's fingers began to enter prime numbers into the keyboard. The first few were easy: 2, 3, 5, 7, Ɛ, but then she had to think about it: 11, 15, 19, 1Ɛ, 23, 25, 27 - Bor'enop scratched her head - 31. A solenoid engaged; the heavy thunk reverberated through the walls. It still took Stone Son's best efforts to open the door.

After two steps Bor'enop concluded there was something very different about these corridors. The crunch of grit her boots tracked in made her realize that the passages were clean. Really clean. Only her oldest memories held recollections of such places. She backed out slowly and had everyone brush themselves down and clean the dirt from their footwear.

"Be careful. We must proceed slowly in case we damage anything."

It took more than a few seconds for Bor'enop to recognize the object sitting on the workbench. Even when the memory surfaced, she could not believe it, but the device could not be anything else: a fusion toroid. It was small and did not have a fuel injection assembly, but it was most of a fusion reactor. And on a heavy-duty trolley, fitted with an exhaust manifold, was a fusion engine, a rocket motor. Her pulse raced, and she felt Stone Son's hand steady her.

"It's all right. I'm excited, that's all." Bor'enop took a pair of deep, careful breaths, and gave Stone Son's finger a squeeze before moving on. He took his cues from her, and the other Hel'omi looked to him. They all moved carefully through the room, disturbing nothing.

The far wall moved stiffly at first when her Hel'omi escorts put their shoulders into it but then seemed to remember it was on rollers and glided quickly away to the side, revealing two things that took Bor'enop's focus away. The toroid looked intact although the loom would need careful examination before she tried to start the engine. And she would try. She had to at least try. The second item excited her as much as it broke her heart. A spaceship - a fast one by the look, designed for atmospheric flight - lay in pieces on the floor. *One thing at a time. One thing at a time.*

"IEEEEHHAAAAA! Stone Son! This is so exciting!"

It wouldn't have taken quite so long to prepare an engine for its test firing if Bor'enop had an assistant who had some idea what she was doing. Stone Son, as always, did his best. He was good at passing her the tools she needed, but that was only because he watched her intently. She did not mind the time spent working by herself. It was still too dangerous outside, although the sunstrike had died away days ago.

The engine sat in a custom-built bay, with all the fuel and control lines connected. Bor'enop skipped back to the control room. Stone Son rumbled his pleasure when she swung on his finger just as she used to do when she was only Little Star.

With the fuel lines purged and filled with hydrogen[2], Bor'enop opened the intake valve, waited until the pressure built and turned on the laser pumps. DRRRRBBMMMRRMRMMDDDRRRMMMM! The pillar of plasma sputtered, roaring. Stone Son groaned and held his hands against his ears. Bor'enop laughed as she leaned closer to the control panel and began tweaking the laser pump's timing.

The sputtering slowly died, and the plasma burn became constant, brighter than ever before, stronger. LOUDER! The whole room shook. *I wonder how long it's going to take to mount it to the ship?* Bor'enop coughed a chuckle as she throttled down the engine.

I'm going to have to declare a Gathering. *I can't do all this by myself.*

Bor'enop watched the launch with a mixture of pride and frustration. Pride, because it was only their third launch. The mission was to land at the docks on Doronem. There were ships there, big ships. Frustration, because she knew she would never be able to fly. That memory from her long-dead predecessor would be her only experience of space flight. But there was so much to do and so little time.

Clan Darf'ornal's help with metallurgy would continue to flow even though they did not like her alliance with Clan Durrunnan. *Well, they can just chew on it. Durrunnan has good doctors, and I need them more than I need your forges. Politics,* Bor'enop grumbled. It was difficult starting a new clan, but once word spread she had power, people came. *Even out here in the middle of the blasted lands. The* Gathering *was almost ceremonial.* They had clean water and clean energy. It had not stopped her from falling ill. *I actually thought I was getting better for a while.* But the tumors were coming back. There was so much to do to establish a stable space-faring economy. *One that would last and give our race the chance to escape the fate of this toasted world.*

Stone Son grumbled at her.

"Yes, I know, Dangaron, FirstSon of Clan Bumurnam; it's time for my medicine. Bring it here for me, please." She could not help teasing Stone Son with his official title. A gentle chuff in response relaxed Bor'enop. *He's not actually angry with me. Good. I do neglect him so.*

The telemetry from the *New Dawn* was excellent. The backup gyroscope worked perfectly when the primary gimbal-locked. She was sure that was *the* mission malfunction. There was always one. *At least one.*

Stone Son knelt beside her and brought the pale green medicine to her lips. It smelled as bad as it tasted, but it gave her more energy and more clarity. She was sure she was just burning her limited resources faster, but the tonic allowed her to get things done. She drank the concoction and leaned against her companion's hand while she struggled to keep the medicine down.

Stone Son's warm, reassuring presence had accompanied her life. She could not understand the attraction they felt for each other, but together they were complete. He would not live more than a few hours when she passed. Already, he grieved for her.

"It's all right my big brother. There's lots to do, and I'm only getting started," she reassured him.

Stone Son wrapped his arms around her and purred, "Star." He always knew when she lied to him or tried.

CHAPTER THIRTY-FIVE

Music blossomed from behind Patty. She knew this tune; it was one of *Drogo and the Danny*'s songs. They were old-boys from her school and had played there regularly until they became big. "Reece Fleecin'" was a pretty zap number; Patty's foot tapped in time all by itself. *Music!* With UNET down, she had missed her playlists, something chronic.

"Whatcha got there, Alan?" she asked.

"Sorry will vol-dwn" Alan's text appeared on her screen.

"No, no. It's fine. Keep playing it. I was wondering where you got it from?"

"The Jai loaded to local from central server as parting gift. The Jai is good."

"Yes, Jai is very good. They all are. Good friends," Patty replied. *Local storage, of course. Smart boy.* She set a note to remind herself to download some things from her archives, things she had not thought she would need until her doddering old age, pics, and vid from when she was younger, and anything with her Mom and Dad. *Freya doesn't have enough room for a gallery like Madhur's, but a picture of Mom and Dad would be nice. Maybe I can pull a frame from the video they sent before they left the ground. Dad's not in the one Mom sent as they boosted into orbit.*

Earth grew large very quickly. To go from something small enough to be hidden behind her thumb to an enormous presence that blacked out half the sky, in less than five minutes, was startling. Science Fiction Features often had animated zooms through space, flashing from one planet to another, so the concept did not surprise her; the actuality did. During the test flights, Freya was far from anything that indicated how fast they traveled, but seeing Earth expand so rapidly scared Patty. Her mouth went dry, and a cold sweat flashed over her body.

All her experience said speed equaled inertia, going fast meant working very hard to stop. She knew in her brain that Freya could literally stop on the head of a pin, but in her gut, Freya was either going to crash - the memory of her dream rose in Patty's mind - or she would be squashed to jelly by the gee forces required to avert disaster. It was only by monitoring the flight program and the navigational data that Patty was able to maintain her nerve and keep her hands away from the controls.

The gentle surge programmed into the artificial gravity that indicated braking was not enough for Patty to require the safety harness securing her to her seat, Freya inserted into the predetermined path that led to an orbit above Darwin. She flew as if she was using her old fusion engine, sliding from one orbital trajectory to the next. For the next few days, or until Eg and Cian decided otherwise, Freya had to behave as if she was just an ordinary ship, following the customary laws of physics.

Even with those restrictions, it felt good to be flying Freya. All her worries seemed to fade into the starry background as she waltzed the gravitational dance, dance steps that everybody had to obey, everybody except for her. The aliens' mothership enjoyed the same license, but she was anchored to the surface and so did not count. Not at the moment, anyway.

"Alan, you're going to have to turn the music down a bit, I have to get in touch with Saab." *Stressed On Sunday*'s 'Sonic Boom' became barely a rattle as Patty aligned Freya's directional antenna to the specified coordinates. *How did I cope all this time, flying without music?* From the faintest of tickles, flickering through the noise broadcast from the aliens' satellites, Patty coaxed a signal strong enough to lock onto and sent the coded return signal Saab had assigned her.

Earth-Sol L1 was nearly one and a half million kilometers from Earth, with a round-trip transmission lag of around ten seconds, so Patty did not hold her breath waiting for a response but scouted her flight path for other ships and debris in Earth's crowded skies. Her almanac accounted for the known inhabitants of the primary geosync orbital path, forty-two thousand kilometers above the equator, but it was the unknowns that concerned her. Far above the debris left by the broken Tempelman-Frobisher asteroid, geosync was the principal orbit for communication satellites. The site above Ambon Island, almost directly north of Darwin, was crowded with alien ships patrolling around their noisy satellite. A large column of space, tapering to a single point on the surface, swarmed with ships flying to and from the mothership parked in Darwin Harbor.

When the feeble analog handshake returned from a point hidden in the glare of the sun, Patty instituted the protocols Saab had provided her with and watched as the signal transformed into a secure digital communication stream far up the EHF band. There would be bandwidth aplenty up there.

A comm channel opened, and Patty slid the window to the far-right side of her displays. According to her flight plan, she had enough to do, flying Freya, to give him much more than her peripheral awareness. This mission was her first real interaction with the military, and a wave of confusion swept over her. *Dad's ex-USF. They can't be the bad guys.* But she found her guard was up, primed by the warnings and old grudges from her shipmates. An older man, in the dark blue USF uniform with silver oak leaves on his collar, and red and white piping down the seams, appeared on the screen. His face and eyes were dark, and his scalp was shiny. His right ear had a piece missing from the lobe; deep crow's feet framed and concentrated his eyes. He looked capable of smiling, in his youth. That ability seemed to have atrophied from lack of use.

"Captain Balke, you're early." He did not sound happy about it. "We like that. I am Lieutenant Colonel Saab. It's good to make contact with you."

Really? Patty felt more excitement from him when reading his text messages than she saw in his emotionless demeanor. *Did he have a ghost-writer?*

"You're welcome, sir. I'm glad to be of service." Patty gave the camera a brief smile but quickly returned her attention to finding a quiet spot with good line-of-sight over Darwin. That time lag seemed an eternity to wait for a reply.

"Our intel says it's quite busy up there. Are you going to be able to find an appropriate orbit?" Saab inquired.

"That's what I'm looking for now. Equatorial geosync is fully occupied; up and down range of Darwin has too much traffic arriving and departing. South of Darwin looks viable though it will need continual station keeping." The navigation system alerted Patty to a piece of debris. It was not exactly in her flight path, but she tagged it anyway. She had logged twenty-two pieces of debris large enough for Freya's passive systems to detect. The longer she could track them the better chance she stood of missing them the next time they were in the neighborhood.

"You have enough fuel?" Saab asked.

Was that concern? Patty kept a straight face and even managed to flash a worried frown. Freya could fly to Mars and back using less energy for her propulsion than the actuators used keeping the tight-beam antenna array locked on its target. "I have more than enough for the period of our contract if that's what you're worried about."

"And then? You would be welcome here if you could make it," Saab offered. *Madhur said they would offer you the world for a chance to dissect your ship.*

"Thank you. The future is uncertain. I might take you up on that," Patty told him. *There! An eyebrow moved.*

"We could make your commission a permanent appointment," he said.

"Hmm ... tempting. You'll have to excuse me. I have a burn to attend to." If Freya had to make a correction with her old fusion-powered configuration, she had to make one now. The Sprocket Drive flew in straight lines, a complete anomaly in Newtonian or Einsteinian space, but Ken had helped her plot a reasonable facsimile that Freya followed as if she were boosting and gliding, boosting and gliding. There were too many ships flying at too many different vectors for her to rely on the preset course, but it was a useful guide. She needed to stay clear of anyone's attention. Freya peeled gently towards the southern hemisphere. The tight-beam signals were uninterrupted as the enclosed dish in Freya's belly gimbaled around, tracking a point less than an arcsecond away from the sun.

When the flight computer signaled that the maneuver was completed, Patty returned her attention to Saab. "We should commence the system checks. Do you have access to my cameras?" Patty stayed alert as she waited for Saab's reply.

"Ah, yes, I can confirm that. We have good pictures and positive control. We were hoping you would allow us to use your ship in another role as well. It is somewhat more dangerous. The likelihood of discovery by the enemy is increased."

Madhur said they would change the mission. This will be the real reason they want you here. That did not scare Patty. She was not here because she wanted to play safe. "Barring going down there and picking a fight with the aliens, I'm willing to do what I can to help. What do you want?"

"We would like to use you as a communication link between us and the surface," he informed her. "It's imperative we deny the aliens a secure beachhead. You would be a vital junction in our communication network."

Was that emotion in his voice? "Colonel Saab, you don't have to convince me," Patty replied.

"Lieutenant-Colonel," Saab corrected her. "Excellent. Your father would be proud."

"You know my father?" Patty asked. Her long-term goal blossomed into her awareness. *Where are my parents?* With the F-UNET operating, it shouldn't have been too difficult to find them. Patty had left links everywhere, in all the refugee hubs and with her father's Corporate presence, but there had been nothing. No trace, no sign since that last message Mother sent while they were boosting into orbit. A chill flashed through

Patty. *Did they even make it into orbit?*

"I did not know your father personally, but I have read his record, a fine officer," Saab said.

"Do you know where he is?" Patty asked. "I'm sure my parents made it off-world, but I haven't been able to trace them."

"I'm afraid I don't, but I can certainly put the word out."

There, that was helpful, even if he didn't sound sincere. "That would be most appreciated," Patty replied.

"You are welcome, Captain. For this extended aspect of the mission, we will need to reconfigure your comm. We have some extra software you will need to run. We will aggregate the low powered ground traffic into a dozen or so high bandwidth targeted transmissions, targeted on you, of course. Therein lies the added danger. The signal will be disguised similarly to the way this civilian guerrilla network operates, broadcasting encrypted messages hidden in noise."

"That is an acceptable risk as far as I'm concerned," Patty answered. "And if we are discovered, well, Freya is faster than any of those antiques. I have back-ups of all my comm systems; you are welcome to reconfigure them to suit your needs. I will still require access to the, as you put it, civilian guerrilla network."

"Yes, that can be arranged," Saab confirmed. "Regarding the alien attack ships, I believe that, once again, you have provided a key piece of intelligence. Our weapons research boys have pored over all the pictures you uploaded. They have been invaluable. I have the software you will need to install and... err... an addendum to your contract acknowledging your consent to the changed mission parameters."

The downloads proceeded smoothly. Patty tried not to look like a rookie as she acknowledged the contract's changes that included a clause that doubled her hazard pay. She initiated the installation routines when all the software arrived. The warm boot did not even interrupt the hot communication lock with Earth-Sol L1, but Freya's multi-channel comm returned to operational status as a server focused on efficiency and throughput; a dozen dedicated high bandwidth channels replaced seventy-two independent links. Patty lost her direct feed to the F-UNET, but her system found a feed amongst the data stream pouring from the military station, and with a smile at the new animated logo, she logged in once more; there were no new messages which was a little odd. There should be one from Jai. And still nothing from Tina. Patty re-opened Lt Colonel Saab's window.

"The comm systems seem to be operating glitch free. When can I expect contact from the ground?" Patty asked.

"Any time now. We are initiating a scan, and there should be a signal from Alice Springs as well." Patty re-examined the interface and discovered some results in the lower left corner. The first hits were in, and secure lines established to the Red Center as well as two in Darwin itself.

Stressed voices came through the comm on the general channel. "I have communications, sir."

"'Bout bloody time! We need air support, now!"

"There are roos loose in the top paddock. I repeat; there are roos loose in the top paddock!"

Patty called up a window showing the output from her camera. Dawn was still over an hour away from Darwin, and the ground was dark. The angle was still quite oblique, but Patty could see the flares of alien ships through the atmospheric haze, darting over the city. A Surface-To-Air missile arced into the sky from a suburban street, tracked a ship and exploded on target with little effect other than to cause the bright flame to swoop around and begin pummeling the launch site with return fire. Patty stepped up the magnification to its maximum. Suddenly three more SAMs, at very close range, slammed into the alien fighter's vulnerable engine and the ship disintegrated into a churning fireball.

As quickly as she could, Patty poured on the speed in what would have been a very fuel-expensive maneuver. Freya needed to be in position now, not half an hour from now, and it chafed Patty to have to keep to normal flight parameters. Freya *could be, should be there now.*

CHAPTER THIRTY-SIX

Navigation showed two squadrons of fighters breaking away from their parking orbits. They began spiraling descents. Two more coalesced from their scattered patrols and converged on Darwin.

"Lieutenant Colonel Saab, you need to see this." Patty patched a link from her navigation computer's output into a comm channel. "I don't know what other assets you have up here, but I think you would like access to all I can see."

Ten seconds later Patty saw the faintest glimmer of surprise cross Saab's features. "Your ship's published specifications did not include mention of military grade radar. The added data will aid us significantly."

"You're welcome." Patty slowed Freya, bringing her to a halt, relative to the ground, over Litchfield National Park - at least that was what it said on the map - a mottled patch of red, dull green, and brown indistinguishable from the surrounding countryside. Even with Freya's enhanced spacedrive, staying parked above Australia would require continuous monitoring so that she did not drift out of sync with Earth's revolving surface far below.

There was a noisy beacon parked in stationary geosync orbit over the equator. Patty glanced at Cian's checklist before adjusting the settings of Freya's new drive. Having everything work properly during a test run, and getting it to work in the field, was another thing. That was when Murphy's Law came into play. Patty only knew one way to combat Murphy, and that was to do a job correctly the first time. Even that did not work every time. She carefully saved the current local offset, one hundred meters off Jaswinder's port side, into memory and transferred the coordinates of the geosync satellite into a buffer before initiating the transition. She held her breath and her hands hovered over the manual controls should something go wrong. If Freya slid anywhere when the transformation was completed, the change was imperceptible to Patty. Even if the satellite's transmissions died, Freya would remain locked to its vector. It was time for another breath.

There was little for Patty to do now but keep alert for approaching ships and or debris and watch the conflict below her. The multiplexed incoming comm channels were running at about eighty-five percent capacity, and Patty scanned through them. Some were A/V feeds from individual soldiers; others were from cameras mounted to low-flying drones. Patty did not have enough screen space for a quarter of the feeds, and without knowing who was sending what, they presented a very confused picture of the events on the ground.

Freya's telescope gave her a better overview through the dense tropical air but few details. Patty could see flashes in the predawn gloom, evidence of fighting south of the city proper, south of where Tina lived. Her heart went out to her feisty friend. *Keep your head down, girly.* That was a vain hope, and Patty knew it.

The heavily armored alien ships did not have it all their way. Patty saw another fighter explode from the focused efforts of four SAMs. It was still not enough to protect the ground forces. The alien ships flew with virtual impunity, poring ordinance into the streets.

Suddenly four squadrons of atmospheric fighters flashed into the skies over Darwin challenging the alien's dominance, two from the north, one from the southwest and one from the southeast. Patty checked the navigation display; it would be several minutes before alien reinforcements arrived from orbit, and for the moment, the aliens were outnumbered. Patty let out a small cheer. It was impossible to follow the chaotic dogfight, and the aliens were hardly defenseless - twice as many aircraft fell as alien ships - but sooner than Patty expected, the airspace above Darwin was free of the flares of those powerful alien ships. The chaotic flight paths of the dogfight turned into spirals and barrel rolls of joy.

The atmospheric fighters regrouped into two squadrons and began bombing runs against one point at the edge of Darwin's coastline. Freya's cameras were not powerful enough to sight the mothership from space, but it was the point from which encrypted alien radio signals were pouring. *A blind man with a dowsing rod could find it.* The two groups of bright dots, the aircrafts' engine exhausts, swept in from the north but before they could even get close, powerful energy beams shot out from that unsighted position and wiped the skies clear. Patty blinked and could not quite believe her eyes. The planes were gone. All of them. Dark blurred patches were all Patty could sight of the burning debris. Her heart sank.

Nothing flew in the skies above Darwin apart from the hedgehopping drones used by Earth's ground forces as they scouted enemy positions. They showed a mixture of artillery strikes, rifle and high caliber machine gun battles and some bloody hand-to-hand fighting on the ground. The aliens on the ground had their versions of machine guns. They were not very portable and appeared to be steam-powered, operated by a mixture of alien types, the hulking soldiers aiming and firing, the smaller left-handers, servicing the bulky equipment. Strategically placed at geographic choke points, their machine guns looked archaic, but they were well defended and lethal.

The aliens also had a few large versions of the knobbly white staff carried by the soldiers. The strange white machines stood over three meters tall, attended by a crew of dozens, continuously adjusting the device and the accompanying fusion power plant. When that weapon fired, it struck with devastating consequences, reducing whole structures to rubble with one shot and it could strike rapidly, demolishing a row of buildings in seconds.

The number of transmissions began to dwindle. The big alien

soldiers overwhelmed them all. Patty groaned as she watched human soldiers struggling to defend themselves against the lines of flashing blades; small arms fire seemed to have little effect on the aliens. Repeatedly, when groups of soldiers made contact with the aliens, there would be a round of gunfire that would seem to hold the aliens off, and then suddenly, there would be pairs of aliens in amongst the human lines with their swords cutting and slicing. Patty could feel her wrist flex in response to the bloody attacks. A part of her wanted to be down there, showing them how their blades could be parried but another part was glad she was far from the front lines. The aliens had little difficulty eliminating the human forces arrayed against them.

The one advantage humans held was the drones, and they began to change the tide. For the moment, the aliens seemed unaware of the little remote copters. Their covert observations helped make the artillery strikes on the big white devices pinpoint accurate. They had to be. A stray shell could cause the supporting tokamak fusion reactor to explode, devastating the whole area. Despite the risk, one by one, the heavy-weapon installations were silenced in a rain of ordinance. Added to that, the drone operators became better at spotting the alien pairs as they roamed the streets. These aliens took only seconds to flank any human contacts, slicing through them with ease. Human hand weapons were far superior to the aliens. If the ground forces had a warning, they could more than just hold their own, and once the alien scouts were dealt with, larger formations of aliens were pinned down and assaulted from afar, artillery pounding their positions.

An explosion on the monitor tapping into Freya's scope coincided with another flare from a feed from the ground. The main conflict was moving north. There was fighting all through the broad peninsula, but the focus was at the airport that acted as a bottleneck to the relatively slender cape that held downtown Darwin. Taking the airport would cut off the remaining alien ground forces. Patty flicked between the feeds;

the aliens were taking heavy losses. The airport terminal was ablaze, but the heavily armored machine gun emplacements still fired across the runways, pinning down the human forces. A barrage of mortar rounds silenced one gun, and just as soldiers were lifting their heads, an order - unheard by Patty - had them running for cover once more, looking fearfully at the sky.

Patty had not been watching her navigation output, but someone in the military had: the first squadron from geosync orbit arrived over Darwin in a formation and began the first of many strafing runs. The second squadron scorched past and flattened anything the first wave missed. The third flight joined in the mopping up. In minutes, all the heroic gains were wiped from the map, and the data streams from the surface winked out one by one.

The feeling of uselessness overwhelmed Patty. *There's nothing we can do. So many lives are lost, and for what?* The aliens were still heavily entrenched down there. Humans would have to hit the aliens with something more potent if they were going to dislodge them.

Navigation peeled an alarm and Patty's attention snapped to its display. Two rockets had launched; one rose from off the east coast of the United Republic of Papua, the other from west of Singapore, climbing ballistic paths into the sky. Patty shook her head with wonder. *Where are all these missiles coming from?* National Disarmament was supposed to have dismantled all those weapons long before she was born. *Have the USF been maintaining the old stockpiles or were these new and improved?* Patty did not know which scenario was worse and crossed her fingers. It was a futile gesture against Murphy, but it was all humanity had against the whimsical universe, that and careful, hard work.

Alien fighters scrambled from orbit, some chasing the rising rockets, others pursuing the maritime launch sites. Patty did a quick calculation and smiled. They would be late; the missiles were already reaching the highest point of their flight paths. First one missile then the other broke into an impenetrable mix of independent warheads and radar-reflective chaff. It was quite apparent that the aliens had no idea where the warheads were amongst the expanding spheres of noise, but that did not stop them flying through the field, hunting. *Too slow, too late.* The missiles were impossible to find. Patty's hopes and fears rose once more.

The alien ships suddenly sped from the expanding chaff, and the mothership let loose with a blinding screen of energy fire, dissecting the sky in quartering patterns that left no approach untouched. Nothing of a lethal nature emerged from the dissipating cloud. A groan escaped Patty even though the thought of using nuclear weapons on Earth's fragile surface gave her chills. She savagely suppressed the part of her that cheered for the aliens. *Should the security of Earth's biosphere be above such squabbles for possession? Haven't the aliens done enough damage? Do we have to wreck it some more?*

Although the sky above Darwin was abuzz with alien fighters, there was no fighting. Patty checked her clock and the position of the sun; it was nearly noon down there. Thick black smoke rose in forbidding plumes from countless sites. Patty sent a futile prayer for all those lost this morning. She knew Murphy did not listen, but it made her feel a little better. *And you had better have kept your hands off Tina, or I'll find some way of kicking your butt!*

"What now, sir?" Hiring Freya for two days had obviously been optimistic overkill.

"Please remain on station." Saab turned his head to check something, and then returned to his neutral stance, waiting silently.

Patty watched the alien ships quarter and search in an expanding and deadly pattern. Any active forces remaining on the ground were punished. In half an hour, they began to return to the mothership, stacked in holding patterns, queued up waiting for entry.

"Captain Balke. Do not look at the flash. I repeat. Do not look at the flash."

DISTURBANCE

Er'men did not like being right. Being right meant that many brothers had died. *And still, the Great Council won't listen to me. Oh, they listened and nodded their heads, and then they ignored me!* The folly of the Great Council bewildered her. She paced around her apartments, the oldest and most heavily decorated place aboard Tal'anis. Filled with the most precious relics from their homeworld, it was not the most relaxing environment. Mementos of the past cluttered the rooms, a blown blue vase from the First Rising sat ensconced in a niche next to a heavily bound gray tome from the Second. Banners and colors from long defunct Septs hung from every available perch. It was more a museum than a home. The clash of hues made Er'men's eyes ache.

The world shook.

Er'men slid across the polished floor as if she were one of the trophies and mementos flying across the room. She had never experienced anything like it. Tal'anis did not move like that, ever. *What's happening?* She scrambled out of the way of an ornate low table and jumped onto a padded seat a moment before they both hit the far wall. She was shaken but unhurt when Genedalt crashed through the doors.

"Harrum'Bar has to give the order to leave now," Er'men said from her position atop the pile of broken relics. Tal'anis would survive because of GreatMother Pur'unnan's plans and Darf'ornal's construction expertise. Despite Harrum'Bar's protestations, she would be much diminished in the eyes of everyone, not on the Great Council. Somehow, she managed to keep the clan FirstMothers firmly in tow - *for now* - but the air within Tal'anis was changing. It felt almost ripe, expectant. *I wish I were old enough to take advantage of this. I could call a* Gathering *just like Little Star did; I could form a new clan that would sweep up half the brothers on board.*

CHAPTER THIRTY-SEVEN

Patty did not need the second warning, and she rolled Freya, so her canopy was pointed away from the red continent. She did not see the flash, but Freya's sensitive skin recorded the birth of the micro-sun in Darwin harbor. Patty scanned the base of the expanding mushroom cloud with her scope on maximum magnification, but there was too much dust and flying debris for her to see much. And then, rising above and away from the center of destruction, a speck appeared. The radio transmissions confirmed that it was the mothership, slowly gaining altitude. *It was still in one piece and flying!* Patty marveled. *Had it taken any damage? Could anything stop it?*

As the swarm of the alien fighters crowded close, queuing up to re-enter the enormous spacecraft, a single SAM rose from the burning suburbs. The powerful ships ignored it. The lone missile detonated wanly between two fighters, and they both exploded, tearing themselves apart. *What was that?* Patty looked at the profile of the explosion's flash and wanted to scratch her head. The detonation was smaller than the usual payload; it missed those two ships, yet it still managed to take them out.

A second, and then a third SAM left billowing trails from their launch sites. Patty felt a surge of pride for the battered fighters down there. The city was flattened and ablaze, they had their butts scorched and flayed, and they were still fighting. Suddenly there were dozens of SAMs spearing up from Darwin's ruins. *They must have found deep holes to hide in.* Most of the houses in Darwin had some hurricane shelter. She grinned. There would be plenty of places to hide.

The alien ships broke from their congested holding patterns

and scattered but the SAMs were too fast, and even a near miss was inevitably fatal. Patty saw half a dozen spacecraft try and make orbit, but she doubted they would have enough fuel to reach the edge of the atmosphere. She tagged them in the navigation computer but did not expect them to survive.

Whatever powered the SAMs' warheads, they decimated the alien forces, and less than one squadron regained safety aboard the rising mothership. Patty gave a cheer. They had done it! Earth's forces had prized the invaders from the surface when all her hopes had dried up.

The speck slowly became a dot and then something that had depth. It did not blast its way out of Earth's atmosphere, but the mothership rose with increasing speed. Much slower than a ballistic launch, its rise had the feel of ominous inevitability. That ship scared her, and she encouraged Freya to slip further to the south. Patrolling fighters and alien vessels of all types converged on the mothership as she entered the vacuum of space. *Are you leaving?* Patty wondered.

"Keep tracking it." Saab's dry voice startled Patty. She had almost forgotten he was on the line. Patty did not bother to glance at the camera. *Really? Stupid man.* The mothership slowed to allow a squadron of ships to dock but continued to sail serenely away from Earth. The mothership began to alter her flight path, spiraling out towards - Patty did a quick calculation - she was heading toward L4. Of all the Lagrange stations, L4 was the aliens' strongest outpost. L5 was abandoned, L1 and L3 were broken, and L2? Patty smirked. *L2's supposed to be mine, secured by the right of combat or some such nonsense. They wouldn't go there, would they? Strange creatures.*

"Looks like Lagrange four," Patty told Saab and continued sliding south, breaking free of her position over Australia and converting Freya's path into a polar orbit. *Hope you kept your head down, Tina. Using a nuke to force the aliens from Earth was probably a good thing.* She remembered Tina finding a tick on her mother's terrier and wincing when she used a burning match to force the parasite to release its grip. One nuke should not hurt too much in the larger picture, but her gut told her otherwise. It reminded her of the feeling she had when the flight of warheads flew past her on the way to destroy the Templeman-Frobisher asteroid. Something about it stank even if Patty could not put her finger on what it was. Second thoughts and doubts began to spoil Patty's joy at the unexpected victory.

The noise-generating satellites the aliens had placed in geosync orbit still functioned, but no ships danced attendance upon them. Earth's busy skies were suddenly quiet. It was as if the alien mothership had scooped up all her baby ships as she swept through the system.

"What happened down there?" Patty asked. She almost did not expect Saab to reply.

"From this end, it was a perfectly executed plan," Saab replied without enthusiasm.

A perfectly executed plan. The hair on the back of Patty's neck stood up. The statement was up there with *Military Intelligence* as a watchword for be-very-careful. Murphy always had his hooks in *a perfectly executed plan.*

"A great many dead," Patty muttered, concentrating on flying.

"But the goal has been achieved," Saab said with a hint of pride.

"For now," Patty grumbled to herself.

"Excising that ship and its inhabitants from Earth's biosphere was imperative. It was what we were charged to do, from the highest councils."

But at what cost? A chill flowed through Patty as she guided Freya south. The surface was anonymous beneath the thick clouds. According to her instruments, she was over the Great Australian Bight. In twenty minutes, Freya would be over the South Pole, maintaining line-of-sight observation with the mothership and the comm link with the USF station at Earth-Sol L1. As fast as the alien ship was, it would still take hours at its current velocity to rendezvous with the space station at L4.

"Captain Balke, are you able to pursue? According to our

information, your navigational data says you have an L4 departure window approaching," Saab noted.

"That's just tidy flying, sir. Yes, I can pursue, although I won't be able to get too close."

"We understand how fuel-conservative you will need to be. Continuing intelligence is always required, a task you seem to excel at." Saab signed off and a formal set of orders, along with a modified contract for her to acknowledge, arrived in her comm. *Maybe two days wasn't such an overestimation of how long they'd need us. Do they have any assets in orbit at all?* Patty wondered. Her stomach gave a rumble. She had been so concentrated on her duties she had not thought of food or drink or anything but the drama unfolding below her. On the heels of her own needs came concern about her brother.

"Alan? How's it going back there?" Patty asked. It was quiet, and she could not quite remember when she had stopped hearing music. Patty wriggled out of her loose restraints to check on her brother. Alan was unresponsive, head back, eyes closed, with his mouth open. A line of saliva escaped the right corner of his slack lips. He swallowed and sighed. Patty chuckled to herself as she returned to Freya's controls. *The most significant battle in Earth's history and Alan sleeps through it. Oh, well, he'll have plenty of time to study it when school starts again.* She sipped from her p-suit's supply and reached into a compartment for a snack.

CHAPTER THIRTY-EIGHT

A flurry of activity surrounded the mothership as she approached the L4 station. Saab was not pleased by her definition of not-too-close, but Freya's camera could see supplies and personnel shuttle back and forth while the colossal craft sailed past. It never actually stopped although the mothership slowed as it continued along its flight path, on a trajectory that would take them out of the system. That sounded good at first, but it was apparent the mothership was not leaving permanently; squadrons of fighters left the mothership's brightly lit docks and either flew down to the station or returned to patrol in Low Earth Orbit. The mothership might be headed away from Earth, but she had left a heavily defended contingent.

The gigantic spacecraft was not a quick ship, not compared to a sprite like Freya, but she could move, building speed like no other ship Patty had seen, and now that the exchanges with L4 were finalized, she began to move very quickly. *Where were they going?* They could reach nearly anywhere in the solar system in a matter of days.

It only took a few moments for Patty to calculate the most probable destination: the Asteroid Belt. There were no planets along the flight path although it did intersect a patch of the Belt. *Why would they go there?* The answer blossomed in her mind without prompting; Earth was going to get another rock. Patty broke into a cold sweat. Nukes and energy beams, guns and blades were weapons that she could comprehend but dropping asteroids on a defenseless populace was unfathomable. *Why destroy the planet where you hope to live?*

A red light blinked for attention for a moment before dying away. Patty traced the momentary fault. It was in the link from the comm to the navigation computer. Data was trying to flow the wrong way. Her firewall was breached. Something was trying to infect her systems.

"There's no need to be alarmed, Ms. Balke." Saab did not sound reassuring at all.

Patty's mouth went dry, and she dived under her console. If she was quick, she could isolate the comm. Pings, blatts and all types of warning sounds rose and fell as she struggled into position. *If Freya's cockpit were in zero-g, this would be easy.*

"With the authority vested in The United Space Force by the Council of Nations, we are commandeering your ship," Saab intoned.

"You could have asked," Patty growled. It was dark and cramped, but she knew exactly where the data buses met. A multi-pin plug tore at her fingernail as she pulled the connector free, but the alarms continued. She yanked at the data-bus connecting the navigation computer to Freya's new drive, but the plug refused to separate. As a particularly noxious wail sounded, Patty saw Alan shoot up from his cramped seat, blinking and wiping the drool from his chin. Patty had to chuckle and returned her attention to the Murphy-cursed connector. She avoided screaming at it and took a breath before trying again.

Barely a whimper escaped her pent-up breath as her knuckle slammed into a hidden sharp corner when the plug slipped free as if coated in lubricant. She sucked at her knuckle's torn skin as she wriggled back to her seat. Alan looked worried and was in the process of making his Zip-Lok sealed and secure. That earned him a big smile and a thumbs-up.

"I don't think it will come to that, but full marks; good idea," Patty told her brother, and he gave a tiny nod and the hint of a smile in reply.

"We thought you would resist the idea of coming to our base. We believe you have technologies aboard your ship that are vital to the war effort." Saab had been talking for some time, but Patty was not listening to his droning voice. She killed the audio warnings. The silence was a gentle balm to her nerves.

"They're not mine to share, Saab. What have you done to my ship?" Red lights flickered everywhere. Patty began to triage Freya's systems.

"It's just a program to isolate the flight controls. According to our specifications..."

"Well, it's screwing up everything. I told you Freya no longer conforms to her previously published specifications. I consider this to be a hostile act on your part, Saab, you and your United Space Farce. I don't care if the Council of Nannies has given you permission, you are endangering my ship, my crew and myself and I think that voids our contract. Good luck with your war." Patty powered down the comm, and Saab's window blinked out. She waited for a count of three and turned it on again. The boot cycle was fast, and Patty could tell that things were not correct before Saab's window reappeared. Patty counted to ten and reached for her system backup files.

"Don't be alarmed. We anticipated your ship would be disabled. We have a craft on a rendezvous path that should arrive at your location in less than five hours."

"Go soak it, buster!" Patty growled and turned off Freya's comm, replaced the operating system with the backup, reinitialized it, but the comm came up in the military's configuration once more. Patty turned it off again before Saab could say anything and sat back.

Why are they doing this to us? She knew why; Freya was an extraordinary ship. But trying to snatch her out from under me is not the way you get a look under her hood. She was disappointed more than anything else. Why can't we work together? Cian and Eg are reasonable people. Talk to them.

Patty put aside the problem of communication and focused on her schizophrenic navigation computer. One section was convinced Freya flew towards the Earth-Sol L1 military station, another showed they were approaching the overlapping domes of L4, following the alien mothership, and another was frantically trying to marry Freya's apparent flight path with the data pouring in from her absorbent skin. The sophisticated software Giuseppe installed when he gave Freya her special coating was infected and having fits. Reluctantly, Patty powered it down too.

Space was mighty big, and losing your place in it was just another way of losing your life. The cold sweat that covered Patty when the navigation computer refused to boot up synchronized with nausea in her belly. Freya was mute and blind.

CHAPTER THIRTY-NINE

The Earth looked so close and L4 even closer. Patty was confident she could fly there by the seat of her pants, but L4 was packed to the gunnels with aliens. *Not the best place to pop in and make repairs. At least* Freya *can still fly.* The artificial gravity had not wavered, therefore - Patty crossed her fingers - the Sprocket drive still functioned. Patty hardly dared to make a wish. Without the navigation computer directing the Sprocket drive, the controls were in their last configuration. Theoretically, they were still following the mothership's flight path, although where she was now was anybody's guess. As far as Patty could see, the mothership was just another speck in the darkness. There was a lot of darkness and many specks.

Manual attitude controls responded smoothly to her hesitant touch; Freya rolled and turned effortlessly. Translating Freya was another matter. With only Earth's colossal presence and the reflected highlights from the Lagrange station as a guide, Patty could not tell if Freya was moving at all.

Only one display gave any indication they were moving, the hexadecimal readouts linked to the drive's Local Offset values. Although they had lost communication with the satellite, its vector and Freya's increasing offset from it, updated continuously. She could not comprehend the notation Cian and Eg used; Cian's explanation had been not much more than a shrug.

"Think of it as quaternions with a couple of extra dimensions thrown in for laughs," Cian had told her. "For practical purposes, we only tweak the last few decimal places, any more than that and you would be referencing something outside our solar system. I don't worry about the numbers; I just push them through Eg's math."

Patty's eyes flashed to the Local Offset and the memory buffer beside it. Freya's vector referred locally to a geosynchronous satellite orbiting somewhere below. In the memory buffer was another set of numbers, not a set of coordinates in space, but a vector describing Jaswinder's last known flight path. *Home!*

Just to be sure, Patty copied the current offset into a memory slot before transitioning into Jaswinder's reference space. Freya's current offset display adjusted, the numbers leaping to another register and the velocity controls moved in sync, showing the new values for Freya's current state. *Or that should be what's happened.* Freya had not bucked, swayed, or dived. Apart from her controls' changed configuration, altering the Local Offset reference seemed to have made no difference to Freya's attitude at all.

Theoretically, all I need to do is reduce the Local offset to zero, and we'll be home, coasting alongside Jaswinder. Unfortunately, Patty could not think of a way to fly Freya manually and reduce the offset quickly. The changing hexadecimal readout made little sense; Freya's vector was too complicated to be understood by the handful of numbers on display. She was slowly reducing the distance but finding the perfect return-vector was hit or miss. There was no way to display the different closure rates between one heading and another.

Cian didn't use any of the manual controls. He had opened a command-line window and written the instructions directly to the drive. Patty did not like the idea of using a direct command-line interface to fly Freya. *My fat fingers are sure to send us to another galaxy.* She opened the command-line window anyway with its simple flashing cursor and took a deep breath. Suddenly, a second window, filled with text, opened beside the dark command window.

"Patty, I hope you won't need to get in here, but since you've opened this up, I'm guessing you do. What follows are the drive properties and interface commands.

BE CAREFUL!!!

Be VERY careful.

Have fun.

Cian."

What followed was impenetrable techno-jargon mated with Quantum/String Theory, with links to peer-reviewed reference material - not included - procedures and properties that made no sense to Patty at all. It was like reading a different language, and then a veil of non-comprehension parted, at least a little. It was a different language with syntax and grammar rules. Her heart sagged - *How can I ever learn enough to make a useful attempt work?* - but she stuck to it, poring through the manual despite her spinning head.

By the time Patty reached the end of the voluminous document, she was equally confused and impressed. Cian was much more than a helping hand, an extensor Eg used to influence the real world. Although the math escaped her, the paper's logical layout was impressive, only someone with a significant academic background could have written such extensive footnotes and references; she had glanced over enough of her mother's research papers to know how they looked.

Patty was glad she took the time to work her way through the document, not that she understood much more about how the drive worked except for the section, barely two thousand words long, prefaced by a heading: Tips and Tricks - Some Useful Examples.

It took three careful read-throughs before Patty realized what she needed was the very first example; the Header did not help much: Translating Vector Equivalents. *Useful, huh! Useful if you were a programmer.* Still, it gave her a glimmer of hope.

Her fingers sweated, her hands shook, she typed where she had to and cut'n'pasted the rest straight from the manual. She looked the code over and made another line-by-line inspection. Theoretically, the program would align Freya along the vector before engaging the drive at register three's maximum velocity - Patty smiled at the comment Cian had added to this section of the example code giving her credit for this parameter.

"How's it going back there?" Patty asked as she sat back from the console and took a sip from her p-suit's supply before twisting around and kneeling on her seat. Alan, sealed into his Zip-Lok, looked to be quite comfortable in the cramped space. His eyes flicked open, and his fingers flashed into action.

"This one is rested and ready."

"Good. We've suffered a system failure with the comm and navigation, but I think I have a way to get us back to Jaswinder in one piece." Alan showed no sign he understood, but he indicated his acceptance of her statement with a brief nod. It both annoyed and pleased Patty; Alan accepted her words as if handed down from on high. He would follow her anywhere. *Grow some backbone, brother. I wouldn't follow me anywhere.*

Patty settled herself back into her custom-formed seat, sealed her p-suit and fitted her helmet over her head once more. This was going to be a straight-line flight without the means to avoid obstacles. A collision with anything more significant than a paint chip would be disastrous.

Rather than executing the complete program, Patty thought it prudent to run each section independently. The first should align Freya along the vector that would return them to Jaswinder. She marked the part and ran it. Nothing happened. She looked again at the piece of code and added another line to her marked section. This time Freya's nose slewed around to port. Her heartbeat lifted, and the hair on her head stood up. If she used this heading and ran the whole program, Freya would have flown straight toward Earth. Something was very wrong. She opened her visor, pulled off her gloves and set to work once more.

She found a '+' where there should have been a '-' and Patty reran the code. Freya slewed around. She was not sure Freya had aligned to the correct vector, but it was the closest to her earlier attempts to align Freya manually. Patty was, at least, becoming more adept at seeing a wrong answer. She slid the command-line window to another monitor; she pushed her finger along the throttle. Freya powered away with a programmed surge that gave only a hint of her actual speed. Patty felt she had some chance of avoiding anything big enough to see with the naked eye. If she had to maneuver around anything, she would have to run the realignment program once more before continuing their flight. Once they were clear of Earth's relatively cluttered space, Patty was quite willing to use the fourth register. The faster she could find the safety of Jaswinder, the happier she would be. She glanced at the locked-out fifth register and recoiled. *It'll be a very cold day before I open that can of worms.* Getting to safety was more important than experimenting with the laws of physics.

The first flash, close in on the starboard side, frightened Patty and she brought Freya to All Stop. Despite the quick response of the canopy's polarizing filters, the actinic burst caused swirling blobs to obscure half of Patty's vision. When she could see again, there was nothing to look at. Freya had not deviated from her course and had not reacted at all to the event. *How much did the artificial gravity disguise?* Patty wondered. Without the navigation computer's interface to Freya's sensitive skin, Patty could not even look at the flash's energy signature. As they seemed to be undamaged, Patty continued on their course.

The next time they collided with a piece of debris Patty saw a glint of reflected sunlight that gave her a moment to flinch but not enough time to do anything about it. The flash she saw behind her closed eyelids did not herald a catastrophic end to their flight. Her eyes ventured open. *Where was the screeching of torn metal? The howling of escaping air? Where was the broken section of a ship's bulkhead that flashed toward them out of the dark?* Freya had not bounced, recoiled, or reacted at all to the high-speed collision. She still flew along that straight line, unperturbed.

What happened? Patty tried to go over it in her mind. One moment they had clear space before them and the next, a curved bulkhead, close to twenty meters long, tumbled across their

path. She did not even have time to let out the involuntary
screech she now released with barely a sound.

She did not see what they hit the next time there was a flash,
but she did catch an impression of the cascade of sparks that
spread from a point meters in front of Freya's smooth prow. She
itched to analyze the burst but had to console herself with the
knowledge she did not have to keep such an alert watch.
Avoiding debris was the part of their flight she had the least
control over and worried her the most.

On the flight from Jaswinder to Earth's orbit, she had tracked
and logged dozens of dangerous objects spiraling in and out of
Earth's gravity well. For every object she recorded she knew
there were hundreds, maybe thousands more, following their
eccentric paths around Earth's gravitational knot of space-time.
The skies above Earth used to be a place where you were free to
soar, within safe local traffic conditions of course, but now you
would need military grade tracking and avoidance programs
just to get to Low Earth Orbit.

*Who are you to come here and despoil our garden? A lump filled
Patty's throat. She was green in places that hadn't sprouted anything
but dust for centuries. How DARE you! Patty resisted the urge to give
her controls an indignant yank.*

With L4, finally, far behind her and over an hour since the
last flash, Patty unlocked register four. If her programming were
correct, if they were heading along the right vector, then a little
turn of straight-line speed would have them home. She felt
surprised at just how fast Jaswinder had displaced her family's
home in So-Cal as *Home* in her heart but was happy she had one.

Her rough calculations had their flight time at her self-
imposed maximum speed - two-thirds of register four's
maximum - at a little over five minutes. Suddenly the desire to
be with her friends, to hear their voices and catch the sparks in
their eyes became overwhelming. *What am I doing, playing
soldier? Can't trust the USF. I should have listened to Madhur. I should
be heading for the safest place in the solar system and stay there.*

With one eye on the reducing hexadecimal numbers and one

eye quartering the sky for a glimpse of Jaswinder, Patty slowed Freya to a relative crawl but there was nothing. When the offset numbers zeroed out, and Freya came to All Stop, she still could not believe her eyes.

Jaswinder was not there.

Freya's Flight

Part Three

Patty's Peace

by

CRAIG P. MILLER

REFLECTIONS

Waiting for the heaviness that accompanied her morning meal to pass, Er'men paced slowly back and forth in her drawing room and wished she had more of Little Star's life memories within her. How so much had been lost was a mystery to her. There had not been any major catastrophes since that GreatMother had established her clan. She should have had all of Bor'enop's memories but those she had, had given her hope that once she had integrated her inheritance, she would be able to call a Gathering that would turn everything around.

But will it be too late? Harrum'Bar had the clans in her control. *But not my clan.* The Hel'omi had always been the GreatMothers' source of support throughout the ages. *Two genetic throwbacks, clinging together.* Er'men growled as she paced. *We can do more than just cling together.*

"Genedalt!"

The ornate door opened at her shout, and Bumurnam Clan's FirstSon entered, cautiously radiating his concern. Er'men stopped her anxious steps and tried to compose herself so she could apologize to him formally. She had behaved poorly in banishing him from her rooms, but with all the GreatMothers' memories cascading through her, sometimes it was difficult to remember who and where she was.

I am Er'men, Star Born.

CHAPTER ONE

Patty did not know whether to laugh or cry. *You've stuffed this one up good and proper.* She looked at her program and then back to the drive's display. According to the readouts, Freya was stationary with a zero offset from the local coordinates. No matter how bad her programming skills were, you could not arrive at this vector without being one hundred meters off Jaswinder's workshop.

A hand waved at the edge of her vision, and Patty turned. Alan was partly out of his seat, and he bowed a little. "This one is ... there is discomfort. The muscle in this one's leg. It spasms."

"Let me cycle the air, and you can stand up and stretch. I've got some thinking to do. Is there anything else you need? Hungry? Thirsty?"

Alan shook his head. "No. This one's bladder is evacuated hygienically and is ready for vacuum."

Patty smiled and saw to her own p-suit's seals before cycling Freya's air into their tanks. When she opened Freya's canopy, she took the opportunity to stand and stretch as well. As much as she loved flying Freya, having artificial gravity made her cockpit feel cramped. *Internal gravity controls need to be added to the UI.*

The stars were bright, and the Earth and Moon looked particularly beautiful, backlit by the sun, but the remarkable vista surrounding her did little to lift Patty's spirits. *What am I going to do now? This is one of only two places I know with any certainty, and the other is in geosync orbit. Should I fly back and try to deorbit? Land in Darwin, find Tina?* The idea of trying to land without instruments was beyond harebrained even with Freya's new drive. *If push comes to shove, I can find L1 by willpower alone.*

Alan's hand tapped at her wrist. He was not using an umbilical so nothing Patty said would reach his ears, but her attention was sufficient; his fingers did the rest.

"This one sees ... something. There." Alan pointed over her shoulder, and she turned. A tiny red light blinked in the darkness a few meters from the tip of Freya's stubby winglet.

Patty dropped into her seat, her feet slipping onto the pedals, her hands to Freya's joystick. She lowered Freya, sliding away from the blinking light, slewing around until the beacon was above and in front. Patty flew Freya forward, and then when the light was above her, she came to All Stop and slowly translated up. Suddenly a bright flashing light atop a little black box with a red ribbon wrapped around it dropped into the open cockpit and onto her lap. She felt Alan lean over her shoulder to look.

"Let's secure the ship first." Patty waved her thick gloves. "I don't think I can open our present with these on." Alan nodded and sat back. The wait for Freya's cabin to become breathable was interminable. As soon as the telltale showed Freya was tight, Patty opened her visor and ripped off her gloves.

The black ribbon-wrapped box was vacuum-sealed and, after she carefully unpicked the bow and stowed the ribbon, she unlocked the fastenings and flipped open the lid. A white sheet of paper, folded in two, covered a sealed baggie containing several cookies and two small soft-paks of white liquid. *Is that milk? Where did they get milk?*

Cicely's bold handwriting filled the page.

"Eg thinks you're in trouble. He is probably right. We were all worried when you dropped off the comm.

The Ice Princess arrived not long after you left. They got here early 'cos someone's on their tail. Captain Delaney is very worried about you too, so is Uncle Stan.

P.S. I think Captain Delaney likes you.

P.P.S. Cian says you might need this."

Patty lifted the paper away and looked around for whatever *this* was. Tucked into one corner was a memory wafer. Patty loaded it into her wrist comm. One file played immediately, although there were many voices in the background Cicely's voice dominated.

"Hi, Patty and Alan. Hope you enjoy the milk and cookies. We miss you and Eg is worried you dropped offline so early. Cian says he has mapped our flight path into a vector offset, but he hopes you don't have to use it. Between you and me, I don't think he reckons you'll know how to use it." The message began to repeat.

Patty checked the other files on the wafer. The text file was not very large, but it was filled with the peculiar contextual language that was slowly becoming familiar. By the look of it, the text appeared to be a program, ready to be uploaded directly into the drive but Patty had no way to do that. The drive controls were isolated from any of Freya's systems and the comm, the nexus of Freya's systems was dead. A particular pattern in the program caught Patty's eye, a sequence that she knew was a multi-dimensional vector. *I can do this.*

Patty uncoupled her wrist comm and placed it beside the drive controls and slowly, carefully, character-by-character, transferred the data across. Once the hexadecimal number was in her drive's system, it was a simple matter to substitute the new vector and realign Freya to Jaswinder and The Ice Princess's current flight path. Without hesitation, she executed the code, and Freya pointed her prow to a new heading.

With no idea how far ahead Jaswinder was, Patty kept Freya's speed in register four's lower ranges - it was impossible to tell with any certainty just how fast Freya moved - and in less than a minute a tiny point of light appeared dead ahead. She pressed the throttle forward, and the dot grew into an engine flare, and when they were closer the single flare divided into five. The Ice Princess's squat shape remained hidden behind the bright exhaust plumes until Patty translated Freya to port. Approaching an accelerating ship from directly astern was hazardous to your health.

Patty began to call via the tiny transmitter in her p-suit,

"Freya to Ice Princess. Do you read me?" No one responded. P-Suits used a band of frequencies most ships did not usually monitor. Unless someone was wearing a pressure suit, she could shout herself hoarse, and no one would hear her. *Well, if no one can hear me I'll just have to make sure they can see us.* Patty turned on Freya's landing lights. This was no time to be invisible.

A spontaneous chuckle broached Patty's reserve as she boosted Freya past the thickset tug. The Ice Princess was not what Patty would call a pretty ship, squat and powerful but not pretty and Jaswinder was an oddball concatenation of spare parts. Together they made the strangest ship Patty had ever seen but one that filled her heart with joy. *We're home.* They were safe. *Almost.*

Jaswinder's gangly form was balanced perfectly on the specially reinforced pusher plate that usually guided tones of tritium ice sent from mines in The Belt. Jaswinder was a fraction of the tonnage of a Mylar covered snowball and looked to be securely tied down, with rigid lines crisscrossing the junction between the ships.

Freya's landing lights had the bridge crew ducking for cover. Patty turned Freya and sidled her up to the main viewport. An unfamiliar face pressed up to the window, and Patty waved, pointing at her wrist comm.

With a crackle, Patty heard the beautiful hiss of a carrier wave. "Ice Princess to Freya. Having some comm trouble, are we?" Rogers' voice was a very welcome sound.

Three more faces gathered at the port. One was short with her honey-blond hair tied back and she waved so enthusiastically she kept drifting away from the window. *Cicely.* She waved once more before she ducked away.

"Yeah, you could say that," Patty grumbled. "Tell Madhur I owe her an apology; the USF did try to take Freya out from under me. Any chance you have a little corner where I can get my CRV back to spec?" she asked.

"You know you have carte blanche with The Princess,

Captain Balke." That was Lirsín's voice, and Patty felt something turn over inside her, something warm and soft and yet urgent. She had to take a sip from her p-suit before she felt game enough to answer. She could not see him at the window, but she could see him in her mind's eye, broad shoulders, long legs, tight...

"Err, thank you, Captain Delaney," was all Patty could manage without stammering. The image of Lirsín's bright eyes kept overwhelming her.

"We're cycling the dock now, Patty. Your comm is down. How are the rest of your systems? Do you need any assistance?" Lirsín asked. Patty saw his slim silhouette at the port and returned his wave.

"Navigation is down too, but I think I'll be able to find my way. Thank you." Patty turned away from the window, away from Lirsín, and had to stop and reorient her brain before flying Freya the short distance to the dock. *Concentrate, girl, or you'll mess up in front of him.* Patty took a breath and steadied her hands against the console. They shook until Freya was underway, then they were rock solid once more.

CHAPTER TWO

A red light flashed forward of The Ice Princess's main engines. The pressure door beneath it began to slide open, and a suited figure inside the dock waved her in.

"Again, welcome aboard, Captain Balke. Park her over there, if you please." The p-suited figure pointed to the docking bay she used last time, next to The Ice Princess's skiff.

"Is that you, Stan? How are you?" Patty asked as she flew Freya over the threshold, extended her landing gear, and settled into place. The release of built-up tension inside Patty rushed out in a gasp. *Oh, it's good to be here.* Flying Freya was fun, but it took its toll. *Especially this last trip.* Patty felt ready for a good night's sleep. Her wrist comm read 19:47, but it felt more like 03:00. Now the pressure of captaining Freya was gone she began to feel a host of complaints from her body; her eyes were full of grit, and she had a pain in her back she had never experienced when flying Freya in zero-gee.

"I've still got some hurt, but we have a pretty good medico when we can keep her sober," Stan replied as he turned back from securing the door and bounded over to Freya as cold atmospheric gasses began filling the dock. Patty powered down the drive and felt The Ice Princess's boost take over. At a rough guess, The Princess was accelerating at one-tenth gee. After Freya's one-third gee, it felt enlivening.

"Damn, it's good to see you, girly," Stan said with a laugh. "Our young Captain was more than a tad peeved we missed you. Here, let me help you." Stan had been the first of The Ice Princess's crew she met when she was on the hunt for supplies at L5. He was a great bear of a man. His large hands steadied

Patty as she climbed from the cockpit. He hugged her before relaxing, and then he squeezed her close once more before setting her free.

"And that's for Cicely, Eg and Kenny boy." Stan looked her up and down and shook his head. "Medico had to break the poor Kenny's arm and reset it, but it's a miracle they're here at all. You're a bloody marvel. You know that don't you?"

"What are you on Stan? Sounds like your medico's been sharing it around," Patty joked.

"Patty!" A ferocious blond girl leaped through the air and knocked Patty onto the deck. "Eg was very worried when you went offline." She looked comically severe, with brow furrowed and pout. It didn't really work, and Patty struggled to hold back a grin.

"Well, you can tell him that his message saved my life," Patty told her. "And the milk and cookies were delicious too, thank you."

Stan, having removed his helmet, swooped in and lifted Cicely away, tickling her mercilessly. "Now that's no way to treat a returning hero."

"Stop, stop, stop, Uncle Stan. Stop!" Cicely screamed and kicked and wriggled and laughed, but Stan tossed her around as if she were a doll, laughing with her. *Uncle? Was Stan her uncle? The solar system's a small place.* Alan reached out and helped Patty to her feet. He looked at Stan, playing with his niece, with a slightly puzzled expression.

"Questions?"

Alan's fingers moved quickly. "The little one, the Cicely, cries in distress and then laughs."

"They're playing. Having a moment of fun." Patty could see that Alan still did not understand. "If she were in trouble, it would feel very different." Patty tapped her chest, and that seemed to satisfy Alan though he still looked at the playful pair askance. She popped the forward hold open and retrieved their bags. She itched in all the awkward places. P-Suits kept you safe, but the manufacturers still did not have a solution that would allow you to scratch in any meaningful way. *The sooner I can get out of this p-suit and clean, the better.*

Suddenly voices and a crowd of joyful people surrounded her. Jaswinder's crew jostled for position and fired inquiries at her from all sides. Patty ignored the questions until she had finished hugging everyone. Even Eg seemed keen on a hug, and Cicely joined him for another energetic squeeze. Patty unclipped the jewel camera from her p-suit's lapel and tossed it to Jai who grinned appreciatively.

"It's all on there if you're really interested," she said, although it was not sufficient to slake their curiosity.

"We caught some info about the battle, but it was pretty thin," Cian muttered. Patty smiled to see him with one hand on Madhur's shoulder; they looked comfortable together.

"It was nasty, brutish and relatively short," Patty told them. "All over in a couple of hours. The upshot was the aliens got moved."

"Where to? Are they going to make another landing?" Jai asked. It looked as if the jewel camera was burning a hole in his hand. He wanted to hear Patty's report, but he wanted to watch what she had seen. Instead of dividing in two, he hopped on the spot.

"You don't know? The mothership left orbit, heading for The Belt," Patty added. That shocked everyone and brought all activity to a standstill.

"Where?"

"Not sure exactly," Patty said. "About forty degrees aft of Ceres, the last I looked. If we can get Freya's navigation systems up and running again..."

"You found us without navigation?" Cian asked. He separated from Madhur and walked over to Freya, running his hand over the smooth prow.

"Yeah, thanks to the "tips and tricks" chapter," Patty answered, "and the vector information you left for me. I think we're all square on the life-saving front, Cian."

"You're welcome." Cian smiled and gave a little bow. "So, Eg and I are pretty keen to get our hands on your flight data." He rubbed his hands together. "Shouldn't take too long to get your other systems up and running."

"Oh, Patty," Madhur interrupted, "I found that pressure door I told you about. Refitting Freya's interior would be a nice project to work on during the flight."

"All modifications on *this* ship must be approved by the chief engineer, and that's me." Stan tapped Madhur on the shoulder. "And I think that there should be another bidder if Freya needs a refit."

Madhur tried to ignore him. "Look, I have the door. It won't take more than a couple of hours…"

Patty stopped listening. The only person from Jaswinder's roster she did not expect to see entered the dock. Lily looked pale, paler than usual if that were possible, and a little unsteady on her feet but the fact she was even standing made Patty's head spin. When they left L5 after setting The Ice Princess free, they had been three up on Freya and short on oxygen. They had made the rendezvous, but Jaswinder had been late. Lily had been in a coma ever since. Patty muttered an 'excuse me' to everyone - not that Stan or Madhur noticed, they were on the verge of shouting at each other, each laying claim to the right to revamp Freya - and ran across the scorched deck, a laugh building inside her.

"Patty!" Lily wrapped her up in a warm embrace.

"You're awake!" A painful knot inside Patty burned as its tension ebbed a little. Having someone in her care come to harm had shaken Patty's confidence.

"Yeah, tough as leather, me. Burned through a few brain cells, but I've still got more than enough to tell me hirin' out to the USF was a bad idea." Lily grinned and thumped her on the bicep. "I hear you had some trouble. I won't say you got what you deserve but…"

The knot of tension, buried because she had to go on while Lily lay unresponsive, burst in relief. A twinge of pain in her shoulder triggered tears she did not know lurked so close to the surface. "I'm so sorry I screwed the rendez with Jaswinder," Patty began, but Lily would not hear of it.

"Don't say that. Madhur told me what happened. It wasn't your fault. I'll call you on it if I think you screwed up," Lily grinned, "or if you're about to. Girl, you pulled off a stunt that had Murphy's head spinning. Don't go all false modesty on me now. How many people did you lose on that caper?"

"I..." Patty hadn't thought about it. "I don't know."

"I do. None. Not one."

"But I nearly lost you. You were my charge, on my ship," Patty insisted.

"Yeah, but ya didn't. It was my decision to disconnect my umbilical, not yours. It's not the first time I've been caught short. Dad used to have a weekly competition, with prizes for which of us kids used the least oxygen." Lily gave her a sly wink. "Personally, I think it was just a ploy to keep us quiet. We all take risks out here, and we all stretched the boundaries that day. I've been stretchin' them for a lot longer than you. I know the risks. You did your best, and that's all anybody can ask." Lily wrapped Patty up in another hug that confirmed to Patty that Lily was well; the squeeze drove the breath from her.

Suddenly Patty felt as if there should be warning sirens; all the air had mysteriously disappeared. *Was this the onset of hypoxia?* The extremities of Patty's vision faded. All she saw was a pair of shining eyes and Lirsín's broad smile. She felt entangled in dream-treacle or was that just Lily's arms?

Lily released her and swirled to one side, the connection between Patty and Lirsín's eyes snapped, and the world crashed in. Stan and Madhur were nearly at blows and Eg, Cian and Cicely had already clambered aboard Freya. Everything seemed to be conspiring to draw her attention away from the one place she wanted to let it rest, with Lirsín. Patty knew, in a rational corner of her being, what was happening to her: hormones were being released, and a cascading series of reactions were pouring through her body. She felt giddy, her usually serene orbital path was disturbed by Lirsín's approach. Knowing that 'up' was only relative did not help. 'Up' was changing from moment to moment.

"Brennan, I hope that is just a heated discussion between colleagues. Captain Sanjaya is a guest, remember." Lirsín's tone had more than a hint of command mixed with gentle humor that stopped Stan with his mouth open; his finger, in mid-wag, dropped to his side.

"Of course, Captain, we were just..."

"Your Chief Engineer doesn't consider me qualified to..." Madhur began.

"Lift tools or carry them," Lirsín finished for her.

"I'll have you know I've worked on more ships than you've set foot on. I've a list of clients longer than your knuckle-dragging arm!" Madhur eyeballed Stan, her fists clenched.

Lirsín sidled up to Patty. She could feel the hair on her arms stand up. "I think you are going to have to step in and settle this. It's your ship they want to strip down and rebuild." He chuckled and touched her arm. Patty could feel the spark through her p-suit.

"Oh, yeah, I guess. Freya's software's a write-off but a re-fit?" Patty asked.

"We're going for a hard-burn transfer, but there'll be more than enough idle hours," Lirsín noted.

Idle hours. Idle hours with you. That sounds nice.

"Patty?" Lily's eyes bounced between Patty and Lirsín and her smile broadened. "They want to dismantle Freya."

"That's probably not a good idea, not tonight anyway." Patty's attention drifted back to its natural resting place, with Lirsín. He blinked but did not look away. A hot sweat pulsed through Patty. *In a heartbeat, he'll be close enough to kiss.* A hesitant breath paused on her lips, and she leaned closer.

Alarms rang through the air. *Damn!* Patty stood at alert.

"This is the five-minute warning on my mark." Jake's Texan drawl boomed over the internal comm. "Mark! All hands to acceleration stations." The comm on Lirsín's wrist chimed an open channel. "Has that flatfooted, saggy-assed refugee from the

431

bottom of a gravity-well docked or will we be delayed once more by this tardy, ill-disciplined reprobate!"

"Captain Balke is at my side, as we speak." Lirsín tried to growl but could not muster the gravel through his chuckle.

"Thought she might be." Jake's deep voice squeezed out of the Lirsín's comm. "Hi, Your Royal Majesty, Queen Patty. Welcome aboard. We've got a lurker not a half hour behind us. It's well past time we were not here. Sorry to break up the welcoming party."

It was good to hear Jake's voice. He had worked as the OASIS station's traffic control officer, and despite their age differences, he was a close friend. His voice had often guided her along safe paths. If home was truly where her heart lay, then she was home already. Most of the people she cared about were right here. *Mom and Dad are going to turn up. It's only a matter of time.*

"Jake, I'm just about to take Patty to her quarters," Lirsín said. "I'll be on the bridge in a minute."

"Aye, aye, skipper. See ya soon, Patty. Bridge out."

CHAPTER THREE

"Come on. Let's get you settled in," Lirsín remarked. He picked up one of their bags and moved to the airlock, Patty at his side. "Stan! Get these guests to their stations. Jake has the con. You know he's not afraid to use it." Cicely, Eg, and Cian still pawed over Freya. Lirsín groaned. "We were black and blue by the time he shook our pursuers from L5, well most of them anyway. This last one's persistent; I'll give him that." Patty was glad she detected pride in Lirsín's voice. He was impressed with Jake's piloting skills. The last time she had seen him talking to the ex-USF pilot, it was with barely restrained anger. That was nowhere to be seen now.

"A lurker? I thought you said Jake lost your pursuers. I didn't see anyone on my way in," Patty told him as they left the dock. Under acceleration, the layout of The Ice Princess was unfamiliar, but Patty was not too concerned about where Lirsín led her if she could keep her arm wrapped around his. *When did that happen? Feels nice. Not as nice as a kiss but...*

"The lurker has a low-profile, a single-ship, like a CRV only bigger. Not as stealthy as Freya, but if Jake hadn't been able to pump Pum for information we would not have spotted it. We had the resources to burn harder and longer than they did, but we did not actually lose them."

A door slid open. Patty suddenly realized it was not a small room but a lift. On most ships, you strapped down and waited for the boost to finish, but when operating as a tug, the Princess ran her engines continuously. They needed lifts to get from floor to floor.

"Pum?" Oh, the alien that had been taken aboard The Ice Princess when they escaped from L5. *"Has it been making trouble?"*

"No. Jake's been filling its head with fairy dust. Seems content, although quite disappointed to have missed you when we rendezed with Jaswinder."

"Just Pum?" Patty asked, feeling a little guilty fishing for a compliment.

Lirsín blushed and stammered, "Pum... well no, I..." He blinked and shook his head as the lift doors opened. "Patty, I..." Lirsín stammered, blushing. Patty had to let a chuckle escape. He was sweet. "Of course I was disappointed. *And* you'd gone on a mission for the USF. Doubly disappointed." Lirsín almost looked serious, except for the laughter in his eyes.

The acceleration warning chimed again, and Lirsín frowned. "I've got to get to the bridge." He looked around to take his bearings, almost as if he had never been on this deck and made a dash for the second door on the left. It slid open at his touch. He looked a little worried as he put the bag down inside the threshold. "You won't have to strap down, the bed's designed for acceleration. You and Alan should have no problems. Just stay put until you get the all clear."

Alan! Patty glanced around; he was at her hip, where he always was. She breathed a small sigh of relief. *How could you have forgotten about Alan?* "Of course, but how bad can it be?" Patty put her bag inside the room.

"Three gees."

"That's not so bad. Freya used to top out at over seven," Patty mentioned.

"For half an hour?" Lirsín asked.

"Oh. Urgh, that's terrible. Half an hour?" Patty's head spun with numbers.

"Jake says we'll be in Ceres in around one hundred days. I'm sorry, duty calls. Please make yourself as comfortable as you can," Lirsín apologized.

He looked like he was about to turn and leave. *Don't let him go, not just yet.* Patty grabbed a handful of his collar and drew him down to her. It was not a long kiss, but Patty would remember the surprise, relief, and delight in Lirsín's eyes forever.

"I hope I'm not being too forward..." Patty stammered.

"No! No. I've been unable to take my eyes from you since you first appeared with Stan." Lirsín sighed. "I just couldn't get the time to... Time! I've gotta run."

"Go keep Jake in his place," Patty told him. "It sounds like we will have some time after the burn. Go!" She resisted the urge to pat his butt as he turned and dashed off and then regretted it. *One hundred days. There will be time enough for butt patting.*

"This is your thirty-second warning." Jake's drawl echoed throughout the ship. *Time!* Patty grabbed Alan and thrust him into the room. There was a double bed in the left corner.

"Onto the bed," Patty said and signed. "Acceleration." Alan knew what to do; Patty quickly followed him. There was plenty of room.

"I know I gave most of you folks a rough ride," Jake's drawl broke over the ship's comm, "but we're going to ease on up to our max so just relax. Don't forget to breathe. Ten seconds..."

Patty cast her eyes around the room. It was more than just a cabin; it was a small suite. At the far end was a large porthole, a writing desk beside it. Behind the desk and, Patty hoped, firmly attached to the wall was a sizeable gold-framed painting, a family portrait in oils, a ship's captain sitting straight, smart uniform brushed lightly with stars and gold braid, her husband/pilot at her shoulder, her son perched on her knee. Patty's jaw dropped open. *Is that Lirsín? He looks so cute!*

The acceleration was brutal. The five-gees she had experienced at lift-off was terrible, but it was all over in a matter of minutes, while the three-gee boost went on and on and on. Patty cast a weary eye toward her brother and would have snorted if she had the spare breath - breathing had never been such hard work. *He's sleeping!* Patty joined him, but only after the herd of animals stopped sitting on her chest. Exhaustion overwhelmed her, and she sank into the warm dark.

Alan stood by the door dressed in fresh clothes when Patty's eyelids fluttered open. Her bladder was calling for attention, but that was her sole discomfort. The Ice Princess still boosted but only enough to make the bed feel as though it was stuffed with down. He pointed to the interior door and began to sign, "Is bathroom. Am evacuated and clean. Ready." He finished with a thumbs-up.

"Good, good." *A bathroom?* Patty expected the door to be a wardrobe at best. She rose carefully - the boost was only one-tenth of a gee, and it would take her a little while to acclimate herself to moving in low-gee - grabbed her bag and headed to clean up. The bathroom was not much bigger than thirty-six cubic meters, but it was more than enough. It had a shower! Patty stripped quickly. There was not much pressure, but the water was hot! *Clean again! Heaven.*

Dark blue slacks, white blouse, light blue pullover, hair brushed, shiny and held back by a blue static-thong. Patty looked in the mirror and tried to recognize the reflection. *It is you, sort of.* So much had happened since she had stopped to look at herself in a mirror. Her face and bearing reflected such change, Patty had difficulty recognizing herself. *Who are you now?*

Alan still stood guard at the door. *Must get him a hobby or something to concentrate on.* Patty was keen to find Lirsín, or Jake, or someone. Her empty stomach also drew her out of her quarters, but that could wait for a bit.

STUDIES

With the sons of Clan Bumurnam circulating through Tal'anis, they spread the message of their GreatMother's concern without saying a word. Their very presence would fire memories of past Gatherings. Little Star's successes, building her clan, had inspired Er'men. It was not a direct attack upon Harrum'Bar or The Great Council. *How could they protest at something that was in the natural order of things?* But the RegentFirstMother would see it for what it was, a challenge to her position and power.

It would take time for the atmosphere within Tal'anis to reflect the changes she set in motion, and Er'men closed her eyes to the ornate decorations in her room and settled down on her broad, comfortable bed to review the life of her direct predecessor GreatMother Pur'unnan. She had designed the almost miraculous drive that powered Tal'anis, a ship she also designed to cross between the stars. She was the GreatMother that had succeeded where Little Star had failed; she had given her people the chance to survive their dying sun. Er'men let the memories unpack and wash over her.

"The GreatMother is, of course, free to leave," Nor'Harrum, Clan Bar'Durrunnan's FirstMother, leaned closer, feigning an intimacy that did not exist, "but if there is anything this one can do to persuade the GreatMother to stay."

The day was bright, and Pur'unnan and her entourage of

437

Hel'omi were able to join a merchant's train journeying north, out of the Bar'Durrunnan badlands. Their departure had been well signposted. It should not have been a surprise, and yet the FirstMother had come at the last moment, to dissuade her. The bricked forecourt of the original Bar'Durrunnan Holding picked at Little Star's memories within Pur'unnan. The Badlands had been lush, with a great river flowing through it before the sunstrike drove Little Star and her Hel'omi underground.

Pur'unnan was eager to leave and did her best not to reel back as the FirstMother encroached upon her space. *There's something ... something very not-right about Bar'Durrunnan's FirstMother.* It made her stomachs churn. Nor'Harrum's eyes burned with a hunger that disturbed the young GreatMother. *Power.* The FirstMother craved power like no one Pur'unnan knew. She was like someone her forebear knew. Their features and the patina of their flesh were dissimilar, but there were moments when their mannerisms were almost identical. *It's not possible is it, that two FirstMothers, separated by so many years, would be so alike?*

"It is our affliction, our melancholia that would have us leave," Pur'unnan told her. It took careful preparation to maintain her air of dejection. It was not hard to let her genuine feelings of despair rise and dominate her speech patterns. *You should never have trusted her.* Pur'unnan was truly horrified to see her research stolen and turned to destructive ends. *She's going to try to make weapons. It was obvious what they were testing. But it's going to take them a while to get it working.* Bar'Durrunnan had some good technicians, but they had to be led to a solution and had difficulty finding one by themselves.

"We are most grateful for Bar'Durrunnan's hospitality and the use of your excellent workshops. We are not sure if we have the skills to be an experimentalist. Maybe one of the theoretical fields will attract us," Pur'unnan said as glumly as she could.

"Yes, perhaps when integration is more advanced the GreatMother will find what eludes her now," Nor'Harrum replied. "A GreatMother should be properly prepared with wide experiences. Know Bar'Durrunnan is ever willing to give of its plenty to serve the GreatMother. If the GreatMother has need of our technical assistance, the GreatMother has but to call."

It had been integrating Little Star's memories that had inspired Pur'unnan to study with Clan Bar'Durrunnan, to bring her aspiration to fruition, helping her people escape their aging sun. They were so close to being able to leave this solar system to find a newer younger world. It was painfully ironic that Clan Bar'Durrunnan had used their position in the high frontier to gain more power and control in this world. They did not look outward to where the future lay.

It had been integrating more of Little Star's memories that had been the turning point for Pur'unnan when the myriads of unconnected events began to coalesce into a pattern. Whether it was real or just a construct of her imagination was yet to be proved. There were doubts about the authenticity of GreatMother Durrunnan. She was not included in any of the mel'andrin that Pur'unnan had integrated, but that was inconclusive; there were more gaps than contiguous sections. Little Star's mel'andrin fascinated her even though her last days were the most difficult to integrate. It took days to recover from the sympathetic pain and nausea they brought her.

Durrunnan FirstMother Tarrun'Bar had often attended GreatMother Bor'enop personally when she first needed treatments. The way they moved their heads, the false start when they spoke, the feigning humility. Bor'enop had seen Tarrun'Bar hold a cup of tea just as Nor'Harrum held hers now. It was common to see a reflection of the mel'andrin gifter in the recipient, but only for a day or so. *No, it wasn't that. It's as if Tarrun'Bar was Nor'Harrum. Or the other way around.*

When tracking down the perpetrator of her theft, she had uncovered more than she wanted to know. Bar'Durrunnan had good doctors, but that was a veneer that veiled their *Cleansing* operations. That gave Pur'unnan a sick chill. A dirty tool used by all the Clans to recycle their unwanted. The thought of having her memories, her heritage stripped from her made her feel physically ill. *There's a lot that's wrong with Bar'Durrunnan from their FirstMother down.*

Nor'Harrum had made it clear enough that she would tolerate no deviation from her interpretation of Bor'enop's will. Bor'enop's end years were not within her, so it was a mystery why the two clans had merged. *Another gap in my understanding.* A GreatMother's mel'andrin was full of gaps, but it was not difficult to see the sweep of history. Nor'Harrum was set on a course. Pur'unnan would have to overthrow her and take charge of Clan Bar'Durrunnan herself to effect change. She would not be the first GreatMother to unseat a clan's FirstMother, but Bumurnam swords were no match for Bar'Durrunnan's fusion power. Nor'Harrum was almost untouchable.

"We thank you for your generosity and promise to call on Bar'Durrunnan when need arises," Pur'unnan replied. *And you won't like that one bit. If my theory holds true, fusion power will become as obsolete as steam.* It had been impossible for her to make even a few notes about her idea. Bar'Durrunnan's surveillance was total. Nothing she said or did went unrecorded. *But they can't get at anything inside my head. Not yet anyway.* The impossible sweeping curves her equations produced haunted her dreams and her unguarded moments. She had found herself doodling the curves on numerous occasions and carefully destroyed the pages as soon as she was able. Her inner vision burned to be released. *Soon, soon. As soon as I can get away from this hideous FirstMother.*

CHAPTER FOUR

The bridge was a couple of doors down the corridor, but when Patty entered there were only three people on watch: Stark, a junior crewman she had met only briefly, a woman Patty recognized as a member of Hestia's Hearth's crew and Chao Zhang. Chao had backed her up with one of Stan's jury-rigged crossbows during the fight at L5. The bridge had a conventional semi-circular layout with the captain's chair rear-center and the various stations in a continuous arc in front. A large display covered the center windows, but the two to either side showed starless black.

"Captain Balke." Chao stood at attention and gave her a snappy salute. He looked worn down. They all looked tired. "How are you?"

"Good. Rested and wondering where everybody is?" Patty asked.

"We've all been running heel-to-toe watches since L5. I wouldn't expect to see the Captain or Mr. Chowdhury 'til first watch tomorrow, ma'am. The mess is open. That's where the crew hangs out, Captain Balke."

"Chao, it's Patty."

"Yes, ma' ... Patty." His smile seemed to brush aside his tiredness.

"Um ... so where's the mess?" Patty's stomach rumbled to add a little emphasis, and Chao displayed the ship's layout on the big screen. Patty's previous forays from the stern lock to the smuggler's hideout - not shown on the diagram much to Patty's amusement - had taken her through a small fraction of The Ice Princess's bulk. The two paramount considerations for a design like this tug were anchoring and driving a mountain of mass; everything else was secondary, spread around the massive engines and the triple-reinforced pusher-plate. Although not designed to haul freight, there was ample space for crew quarters and cargo. No corner was wasted, even if it was not on display. The mess was two decks down and forty degrees to starboard.

"Can I get you anything?" Patty asked.

"No thanks, m... Patty." Chao blinked and gave a nod of respect anyway. "If we need anything we can ping them. We'll last until watch-end." The ubiquitous corner clock displayed 03:32. *How long did I sleep? Damn.* Her Earth-bound home in So-Cal was eight hours off UMT. She was used to being out of sync with the rest of the solar system. She did not like it, but she was used to it.

"Fly True, Chao." *There would be someone up. Or maybe I can find a terminal and log-on.* The need to discover if Tina had survived the Battle of Darwin suddenly burned hot.

The mess was large enough to hold a formal ball, occupying nearly one-third of the deck. Twelve expansive windows looked out into the depths. Even with the lights set to dim Patty could not see out, the internal reflections from the kitchen/bar and the games corner overwhelmed the subtle glories of the beyond. Woven rugs in all manner of intricate patterns covered the floor and some of the walls. A power loom, the source of the mats and hangings, stood in one corner. Handcrafted carvings and paintings covered the rest of the walls. A small man was attending to something in a glass-fronted cabinet behind the counter. Two other crewmen sat at tables eating; one had an F-UNET connection showing on a terminal beside his plate. *Excellent.*

"Patty Balke! I am so glad you caught up with us." Daichi snagged the cloth in his hand to a stick-em and floated around the counter; at one-tenth of a gee, even a small push could send you flying.

"Daichi!" Patty cried. "Not as glad as I am. Getting here was seat-of-the-pants. Very scary." Patty had had only the briefest reunion with her sprightly fencing coach back at L5. He had left with The Ice Princess while Patty had flown Freya to pick up Lily. It was good to see him.

"Are you hungry?" Daichi touched down in front of Patty, his hands extended. Patty reached out and steadied him as Gecko-grip pads on his feet contacted the deck. Daichi seemed to have planned for that as he took the opportunity to look her over with a calculating eye. "Have you been eating properly?" His concerned expression eased. "Lily told me about Freya's special emergency rations. I can't quite offer that level of cuisine but..."

"Thanks for the fret but I'm doing okay. I am hungry but not..."

"I have some fresh rolls, still warm, Soy-synth but tasty enough and miso soup. It will earth you." He turned and smiled at Alan. His eyes analyzed her brother's state. "And for your brother?"

"I'm not sure he has a preference yet."

"You took him back from the aliens," Daichi said.

"But they had been treating him with something, something that pacified him, wiped out the Alan I knew," Patty told him.

"I saw the recordings. I'm sorry for your loss." Daichi frowned for a moment, and Patty could feel her heart echoing his sentiment. They had all lost friends and family. Retrieving Alan, what she had of him, was a victory of sorts. He was getting better.

"Come, sit." Daichi turned and showed them to a table near the counter. The lights brightened slightly as Patty sat down.

"Is there a terminal I can use?" she asked.

"Yes, but food first," Daichi insisted. He was back in moments with a covered tray. Crusty rolls with a thick dab of It-Sure-*Looks*-Like-Butter on one side sat on a plate beside two steaming bulbs of soup. At one-tenth gee an open container of hot liquid was dangerous. Alan tucked in without encouragement. Eating with Cicely had taught him to protect his food. *There were more important things for him to learn before table etiquette.*

Patty sipped at her soup; it tasted earthy and nutritious. "They've got you slaving in the kitchens?" Patty broke open a roll and took a bite. It was breadish, sort of.

"An honored position, keeping the health of the crew in balance," Daichi bowed. "I also have a dojo on deck two. I am hoping you will attend." He glanced at Alan. "Your brother, too. Physical therapy can assist in uncovering lost mental pathways. He fights well. Why have we not seen him at competitions?"

"I don't think he knew a riposte from a retreat before the aliens changed him," Patty said glumly.

"Really?" Daichi's brows sank in thought as Patty drank more soup. She did not particularly like Japanese food, but hunger made this soup taste very good.

"So, why were you on Hestia's Hearth?" Patty asked. "I was so glad there was someone else who could face the aliens. We wouldn't have made it if you hadn't been clearing the path from your side."

Daichi closed his eyes as he took a slow breath.

"I'm sorry." Patty winced. *No, I've opened a wound.*

"It's all right." He gave a pained smile; his deep brown eyes were forgiving. "I thought I had lost Haruto but seeing Alan, even as he is, gives me hope. Haruto is my niece. She had been selected for Hestia's crew, deploying and maintaining the life-support systems on the generational ship. It was an important position. We, my family, were so proud." Daichi still beamed. Losing his niece to the aliens did not diminish her achievements. "I was taking a flight to L3 and stopped over to visit with her and to see the ship that would take her to the stars. I don't remember much beyond experiencing a pressure emergency. I awoke with Lily and the remains of Hestia's crew; my niece was gone." He shrugged. "Some events are beyond our control."

"I'm sorry. And L3 ... you had family there..." Patty shut her mouth. *Of course, he had family there, stupid girl.*

"It is war. There is tragedy enough for everyone." Daichi closed his eyes. A moment of silence reached out, and even Alan

444

stopped eating. "I will get you a terminal."

For the next hour, Patty read her mail wishing there was something from her parents or Tina. She wanted to tell her friend what she had witnessed from orbit and confide to her about stealing a kiss with Lirsín. She had a flash of guilt at how happy she felt but dismissed it. *You must catch what happiness you could, on the fly.* She'd heard that old saw but had never really understood it until now.

She answered greetings from those who had seen her recordings. Many messages conveyed considerable anger at the way the USF had treated her - Jai had obviously made another upload - which gave Patty a warm feeling of support even as she regretted distributing evidence of Earth's divided effort. *We have to work together! But I'll be damned if I'll let them take my ship!*

CHAPTER FIVE

"I'll be damned if I'll let you or anyone else take my ship!" Patty growled. "If it's Freya's mission, it's my mission." *Were all Belters as parochial, blockheaded, and patronizing as Lirsín? No!* It wasn't possible. His mother captained The Ice Princess, a dangerous and difficult job by anyone's account. "You're a Belter, Lirsín. I've always heard a Belter's ship was their castle. How could you even think such a thing?" Patty tried to calm herself so she wouldn't accidentally push herself away from the briefing room table. Alan was reacting to her anger; his hand gripped his sword's hilt.

"That's ... I mean that's not what I meant..." Lirsín stammered.

Patty was too angry to let Lirsín finish. "You think the USF is awful for wanting to take my ship, but you think I should just give up Freya to someone else because she has a dangerous mission." The idea of attempting to sabotage the aliens' mothership scared Patty spitless, but the USF was right. Freya was the only ship that could get close. The Belter fleet would probably be able to hold their own against the alien fighters, but against the mothership, they were merely an inconvenience.

Patty was surprised that there even was such a thing as a Belter fleet - ships mothballed since The Belter War - but Lirsín did not even blink at the news. I probably shouldn't be surprised, what with the nukes sent to pulverize Tempelman-Frobisher, all those WMDs in orbit and those used in the Battle of Darwin. Were those hard-fought disarmament treaties just a sham? But all that's beside the point. I'm really seeing Lirsín's true colors now. The thought made Patty a little ill.

"You wouldn't give up The Ice Princess, why do you expect

me to step aside?" Patty asked, and Lirsín blanched. He opened his mouth to reply, but she would not give him a chance. Angry words that Patty knew Lirsín did not deserve rushed out. "It's because I'm a woman. It's because I'm young. It doesn't matter what your polite rationalization is; you don't think I'm capable."

Lirsín leaned back frowning, "No, no you're wrong..."

Jake, sitting on her left, placed his hand on Patty's wrist. She shook him off. "No one thinks you're incapable of anything," Jake said. "In fact, most of the crew think there's not much you can't do. If you asked any of them to jump, they wouldn't wait to ask how high. I include myself in that group, and I'm sure Lirsín does too." Jake's words penetrated enough for Patty to let go of her anger, at least enough to take a slow breath. She swallowed. Fear and anger pulsed and fed off each other.

"I hate to have to correct my captain but since we are not in public," Jake said to Lirsín, "Patty's right, and you know it. Freya is the only ship that will make this mission work, and I cannot, for the life of me, imagine anyone else piloting her." Jake patted her hand again and slouched back in his seat. Patty trusted Jake implicitly; having to obey him exactly was a natural response. His role as OASIS Traffic Control probably gave him a more direct route to her attention than anyone else

"But just because you're piloting does not mean you have to do everything," Jake added. Patty opened her mouth but stopped when Jake raised his hand. "You're a pilot and a damned good one but are you a demolition expert? A trained saboteur? The USF is right, but the only reason they've pitched this plan is to get you to fly to their base at Earth-Sol-L1, to get their hands on Freya. They're probably right about sabotage being the only way to stop the mothership too, but that doesn't mean you have to do it personally." Jake's smile eased Patty's fears a little. *Jake can spit a better plan the USF.* "We have some time up our sleeves."

"You've got an idea?" Lirsín lifted his chin from his chest.

"Not so much, but I can feel something ... percolating." Jake slipped out of his chair and floated up to the ceiling, and he nearly made it before The Ice Princess began to catch up with him and he dropped back to the floor. "Or maybe I need another coffee. I know I need a little time to think." Jake suddenly took a formal pose. "May I be relieved for the rest of my watch, Captain?" Jake waited for Lirsín's nod before pushing off the floor once more, heading for the briefing-room door.

"I'm sorry I hurt you, Patty." Lirsín leaned close, and Patty felt inclined to move into his warmth, but his words had cut her to the quick. "Jake's correct. I ... I could not get the words out the right way. Freya is yours. I would never dream of taking..."

"You did more than dream it, you thought it, planned it and then you spoke it," Patty replied angrily. She stood carefully enough so that she did not lose touch with the floor. "I need to do some thinking, too." She stalked to the door, her anger rising once more. "Maybe you could do some of that thinking-talking practice while I'm gone." *That was bitchy.* Patty regretted it the moment her words left her lips, but she didn't stop to take them back. She did refrain from trying to storm off down the corridor. Even with gecko-grip soles, if you stomped too hard, you lifted into the air. Frustration heaped upon frustration. There was nothing quite like a good stomp.

Patty entered her quarters and threw herself at the bed. It was impossible to miss, but it took a while to get there when you fell slowly. Low gee was not conducive to throwing your weight around. By the time the soft covers cushioned her vector Patty wanted to leap up and apologize to Lirsín, but even the one-tenth gee acceleration seemed to weigh her down.

Returning to the mothership was a suicide mission. Do I have a choice? I'm not ready for that. Jake's smile seemed to be her only light. He was always the calm voice of reason, guiding her through the dark. Could he do it again? You can't pin all your hopes on Jake. Got to check your own seals and set your own vectors. Freya has to be made flight worthy again. Patty sat up. Alan stood relaxed but on guard at the doorway. Suddenly, returning to the mothership took on another twist. Why didn't I think of Alan? Taking him on the reconnaissance mission over Darwin was one thing but taking him back to the mothership?

Wasn't leaving with The Ice Princess all about keeping him away from danger, away from the war? I can't take Alan. That would be wrong. I'm supposed to protect him, not take him on a suicide mission. Am I going to have to give Freya up? A pang resounded through Patty's heart. Alan is, for better or worse, my shadow. Where I go, he'll go, too. Or would he? We persuaded him to stay aboard Jaswinder while Cian and I tested Freya. Could I do something like that? Maybe if he thinks it is just another test? The thought she would have to lie to her brother did not sit well in her gut.

"Alan?" Patty knew she had to approach this carefully. She moved to the end of the bed and patted the embossed coverlet beside her. He glanced at the door and set the lock before sitting. Patty chuckled at the absurdity. "You know you don't have to do that. We are perfectly safe here."

Alan did not blink although his brows did tense a little as his hand spoke. "Door has lock for reason. You angry with captain. Keep safe."

"Yes. No. I'm not angry like that. Lirsín would not hurt us." *Not physically, but he packs a mean emotional left hook.* "I was wrong. I will tell him as soon as I can." Alan looked as if he didn't understand, but he accepted it with a nod. "But I wanted to talk to you about another thing, about taking Freya out on ... on a flight."

Alan smiled. It was small and somehow more in his eyes than his lips. "To the mothership, to fight!" he nodded. "Am ready. Rested."

Damn! "You understood?" Patty asked.

"USF Brigadier clear. Correct. Stop alien ship."

"You don't have to go..." Patty began.

Alan spoke before she could finish. "Must. Keep you safe." He opened his mouth, but no words spilled out. He shook his left shoulder and arm, as if to clear the pathways for speech, and raised his hand again. "You fight good. This one fights better. Keep you safe. Not your fault. Older, slower."

Old? Slow? Why you pinheaded... Patty's eyes flashed wide, her indignant reaction flooding through her, followed closely by the urge to laugh. Only her annoying little brother could get such an instantaneous response. Patty searched her brother's face for a trace of amusement but without result. Alan was as passive as ever. *Did he know he was teasing me?*

"That may be so." *Older. Slower. I'll show him. Older. Slower.* A chuckle bubbled to the surface. "But you do not need to protect me."

"Need. Need." Alan was emphatic and becoming a little agitated. "Cannot leave without this one." He loosened his blade in its scabbard. "This one needs to be with you." His pleading eyes convinced Patty more than his words.

"All right. I promise. Wherever I go, you go. I promise." Instinctively, Patty's hand crossed her heart. She did not want to be parted from him either. *Mother's gonna kill me when she finds out.* Crossing her fingers would not ward against Murphy's malign machinations, but it felt better performing the insignificant ritual than not.

"Speaking of going, if we are going to go anywhere Freya needs our attention." Alan was on his feet before Patty.

CHAPTER SIX

The Ice Princess was quiet. The First Watch was less than an hour old. Patty and Alan exited the lift and headed to the dock's internal airlock. Jake coasted around the curved passageway towards them, and a smile lit up his face. "As always, Cap'n Patty, your timing is excellent," Jake remarked and took one sliding step to stop in front of her. He bobbed to one side and smiled over her shoulder, acknowledging Alan's presence, before focusing once more on Patty. "I've been thinking about how to get in and out of the mothership in one piece. Our alien prisoner is a ... well, a diplomat for want of a better description. He didn't seem too highly regarded, but they have a protocol for just about everything. His ... clan specializes in negotiations. I want you to talk to him. He could get us in *and* out."

Patty's heart seemed to leap for joy and sink with shame within the same beat. She could imagine the negotiations. *Politics.* Patty shuddered. Sweep in amid great fanfare, mouth inanities and sweep away leaving the stinking deposit to be discovered later.

"Don't look at me like that, Patty," Jake murmured. "This is war."

"And that excuses treachery?" Patty asked.

Jake frowned. "You don't take on a stronger opponent head-to-head."

"You sidle up close, whisper sweet nothings, gain its trust then kick 'em where it hurts?" she inquired pointedly.

Jake grimaced. "If you must. They did the covert thing first. Like attracts like. Karma."

"And this alien we have..." Patty began.

"Pum," Jake interjected.

"Pum, this alien. Do you trust it? If what happened at L5 is any indication of the way they handle a sensitive negotiation, then I'm not sure we would be any safer," she noted.

Jake nodded. "Yeah. Point taken. But if there's a chance we can slip in and do the dirty without a confrontation..."

Patty had to agree. "Okay. I guess we should find out if we *can* go in through the front door." Patty stopped and looked at her friend, "We? You want to come?"

"We. Me. Yes. Hell, yes," Jake replied with a lop-sided grin. "Most of this crew would give anything for a chance to hit 'em hard. I know you. You want to go in and tackle them single-handed. It's the way you fight. Head on. I couldn't forgive myself if I let you charge off by yourself. Let's go and see Pum."

Patty felt her heart warm. "Where is he?"

Jake flicked his head back down the corridor, "Aft one deck and 'bout sixty degrees around. It's a poky little hole but sufficient." He waited for Patty's assent before leading the way.

"I suppose we shouldn't mention our real purpose," Patty inquired.

Jake chuckled, "Err ... no. Pum, he's a talker; he'd just love to be able to bring you to a negotiating table. Can't get a bead on their hooming language, but I can read him when he's excited and when he's afraid."

"But is he honest?" she asked.

"Honest enough," Jake answered nodding. "Sincere, for what it's worth. Pum would balk at anything that would hurt his race. No, we'll have to play that part close to our chests. We're going to have to give this a good spin. He may be alien, but he's not stupid."

The room was small, too small for all of them, which fretted Alan, who wanted to place himself between Patty and the twisted alien. If he did that, Patty would be out in the hallway, well almost. Patty stepped back to give the alien space for his dramatically deep bow.

"Oh, great," rumble, "queen, you," rum-rumble, "honor this

one," Pum stammered.

Patty stood and looked at it ... him. He was small - Alan was taller - and pale, with barely a warming to his grayish complexion. *Jake says it is a male, infertile but a male none the less. Did that matter?* Like all the aliens, his twisted body presented him to Patty as if he stood sideways. "Have you been well treated?" *Did that sound as stupid to the alien's ear as it did to mine?*

"Oh queen," rumble, "this one has not been mistreated," Pum stopped, and his expressive right hand stopped, silenced in mid-thought.

"You hesitate. Has someone hurt you?" Patty asked and glanced at Jake. He shrugged, bewildered.

"Only yourself, your majesty." Pum bowed nervously. *Was that nervously? Did that bobbing bow mean what I think it means?* "With your elbow, when we first met." Pum did a subtle shuffling dance, twisting as if confined. The first thing that popped into Patty's head was shame. "It is not your fault. Many mistakes can happen when negotiations begin." Pum shook his head. "There were no banners of greeting, no pipers or horners blowing the delegation's approach and no gifts." His black eyes rose, focusing on Jake perched in the doorway, "Although you could say the return of Traaaffic Control, the Jake, was a gift." There was that head shake and backward movement again. *Shame or regret?* Patty wondered.

"You still seek a negotiated peace?" she asked.

"Oh yes, your majesty!" Pum rumbled something and straightened. "The tribes will join. That is certain. There is strength in union. You will see. Strength and honor." Pum bowed, displaying a florid exaggerated dance. "There would be much honor for my clan."

For you or your clan? "But how can I trust you?" Patty asked. She leaned forward unsure if she loomed or just looked unbalanced, "Your ... your behavior was aggressive at L5. Is it customary for you to negotiate at the point of a sword?"

Pum bowed and swayed, nodding. "This one apologizes most," rumble-rum, "profusely," and then began a deep, groveling bow. *Was that really a grovel? Pretty good at faking one if it isn't.* "That was not this one's intent. Peace cannot be won with a blade, only talking binds the wounds dealt by war."

"And you would arrange this?" Patty asked. Hope blossomed in her heart.

"Oh yes, oh wise queen. It would be a meeting most," rumble, "different, be assured," Pum declared confidently.

"We would need a promise of safe passage, to come and go unmolested," Patty insisted. That was the kicker. *I'm not going to walk in there without at least a chance of walking out.*

"Without a doubt," Pum answered and bowed again. He did seem sincere. "Safe passage, this one would insist, or there could be no negotiations. It is not without," rumble-run, "precedent."

"Thank you, Pum," Patty told him. "This war is bad for both our peoples." *Did that sound pompous or regally concerned?*

"Indeed," rumble, "your majesty. Indeed."

"Your people are attempting to send another asteroid down to the surface of my world. Do they plan to destroy what we deny them? Can you live on a world so decimated?" Patty asked.

"Oh, queen," rumble-rum-rumble, "our ship has left orbit?" Pum inquired. Patty nodded. "This is sad news, but," rum-rumble, "even more it shows the need for talks. If this one could communicate with this one's," rum-rumble, "clan, matters could be," rumble, "expedited." Pum delivered another baroque bow as if to say, *let me serve you.*

"We will think about it." Patty tried to keep the turmoil boiling inside her from being evident externally and gave him a condescending nod. *If I can read Pum, then surely, he can read my body language. If I can read Pum, that is.* She turned and left the small room, Alan snapping into position on her right as she continued around the corridor, stopping only when the doorway was out of sight. Her heart pounded. Too many times, she had fought through dream-treacle to escape the mothership, and now everything pointed to her returning. Acknowledging that fear, feeling it wash over her without running to her quarters, screaming, was a small victory. She always felt better facing her problems than running from them. The worst of the wave of anxiety was over by the time Jake reappeared, rubbing his hands together.

"Oh, he's keen, all right." Jake's eyes flashed brightly. "You should have seen him after you left. He was like a puppy, almost peeing himself with worry. Had he offended you? Had he pushed too hard for a meeting? You put him off his stride asking about his welfare." Jake laughed.

"This is all on the premise we can modify Freya to carry you both." Patty did her best to resist being swept up by Jake's enthusiasm.

"The Mess." Jake checked his wrist comm. "Breakfast is still on. Best place to catch Stan at this hour." Jake pushed off down the corridor, and Patty followed. It was not like flying in zero-gee but walking with a long flat lope. Patty sent a priority ping to Madhur from her wrist comm. *She will never forgive me if I talk to Stan about modding Freya without telling her.*

CHAPTER SEVEN

The mess hall was busy. Stan sat at a table with Eg, but Cicely was not content sitting at one table, eating from only one plate. She flitted from table to table, sampling everyone's meals as she chatted amiably with the diners. No one, except Stan, seemed bothered by her predatory table manners.

"Patty!" Cicely handed a bowl back to Nanna, who sat with Myung. Both gave Patty a friendly wave as the little blond pushed between them. Cicely flung herself across the room. "Big sister!"

Patty braced herself and only just managed to avoid having her nose broken by Cicely's elbow as the energized youngster collided with her. She gave thanks to the gecko-grip people as her boots held firm.

"Wanna be my big sister? Eg an' I wanna adopt you." Cicely asked. A sloppy kiss landed on Patty's cheek. "Uncle Stan says we can, but you gotta agree first." Cicely's over-excited demeanor settled, and she looked almost solemn, except for the tiny pout. "Us orphans gotta stick together." Patty managed to swallow the lump that swelled in her throat while she gave Cicely a squeeze and peck on the cheek.

"Big sister, eh? That's a pretty big honor," Jake chuckled.

"And a big responsibility," Patty added as she felt her smile expand into a grin. Cicely's energy was infectious.

"Oh, that's okay. I'm used to looking after Eg and Kenny; you'll be no trouble at all. You and Alan. He gets to be my big brother too." Cicely twisted in Patty's arms and yelled across the room. "See. I told you she'd say yes." She wriggled, communicating her desire to free. Patty dodged Cicely's

456

swinging elbow and released her grip. Cicely pushed off, down to the deck, and then rebounded, grabbing Patty's hand as she rocketed from the floor. Only quick reflexes kept Patty's shoulder in its socket.

Stan cleared a place at the table and pulled a folded sheet of paper from his pocket as Patty settled into a seat beside him and Cicely wriggled onto her lap. "I found the little darling as she was about to scan and register this." Patty took the document from him. Stan looked secretly amused and publicly annoyed at the same time. She unfolded the page. It was a standardized legal form with blank spaces filled out in Cicely's careful round handwriting, an adoption. Two thumbprints defined the end of the legalese.

"Said she pulled your print from Freya's console." Stan's serious façade cracked, and he ruefully shook his head. "Don't know which side of the family she gets it from. I'm sorry."

Patty had to laugh and gave the little blond a squeeze. "I appreciate the intent, but it is polite to ask before signing a contract for someone."

"Yeah, I guess." Cicely pouted and her brows furrowed. "I promise I'll ask next time." She looked up, puppy-dog-hopeful. "Can I send it? Pleeaase?"

Patty looked at Stan. "Is it legal?"

"Legal enough," Stan replied with a shrug. "Cicely can't thumbprint a contract as such, but in custody matters, the courts out here take a minor's letters-of-intent quite seriously." Stan laughed and stuck out a paw. "Welcome to the family." Patty hesitated, only for a heartbeat, and shook his meaty hand firmly, squeezing Cicely as tears flooded down her cheeks. Family was so precious, and Cicely had always felt like family. *She's right. Us orphans gotta stick together.*

"What's the fuss, Patty?" Madhur asked. She yawned and leaned against the empty table beside them. "I was looking forward to at least one sleep-in now that I'm just a passenger."

Cian slipped his butt onto the edge of the table beside her, his arm around her waist. Madhur wriggled over to accommodate him. "I don't mind being woken up for a party," he said with a smile. "What are we celebrating?" He waved, and Patty glanced over her shoulder; Daichi, still in his apron, approached. "Has the watch crew left us any coffee?" Cian inquired.

"Patty's my new big sister!" Cicely snatched the adoption paper from Patty's grasp, waved it at Cian and Madhur before squeezing Patty and giving her another sloppy kiss.

"Great news. I'm happy for you both," Cian replied. His bloodshot eyes looked up at Daichi. He sighed and gave Madhur a peck as he whispered, "One double-black, coming right up."

Madhur's dreamy smile thanked Cian as he left. She blinked, and her focus snapped to Patty. "Adopted." She smiled, "Very nice I'm sure, but you mentioned modifying Freya." She gave Stan a stern look.

Stan leaned back, his hands rising defensively. "Don't look at me like that. First I've heard of this."

"USF spiked us with a comm laser at 04:30," Jake said as he propped himself beside Madhur. He leaned over and patted Stan's shoulder. "Seems they knew Patty found us."

"I guess one of the F-UNET messages I answered was a spook." Patty could not fathom the USF. Her father was proud if quiet about his time in the service, but the USF had acted like bullyboys.

"I wouldn't be surprised," Jake remarked. "They have intelligence that suggests the aliens have already picked out an asteroid. Fergus Durnin's de-mothballing as fast as he can." Stan sat up straight, going from curious to serious in an eye blink. The name, Fergus Durnin, rang a bell in the back of Patty's mind; he was someone famous from the war years. He did something notable, but Patty could not pin the memory down. Stan looked suitably impressed though. "He estimates the first squadron - as many as a dozen ships - will make contact in thirty-six hours. USF reckon the mothership will have mated to the 'roid by that time."

Cian returned carrying two steaming mugs and Daichi had bowls of porridge, thick with fruit, nuts and maple syrup. He waved Alan over and set a place for him. Cicely stole a finger full of Patty's breakfast before wriggling out of her lap. Patty ate slowly as Jake continued, comparing his impressions of the comm link to her own.

"As much as Brigadier De Cleot looks like a stuffed shirt ... anyone heard of him?" Jake glanced around and when no one ventured anything he shrugged and continued. "Me neither. Stuffed shirt or not, when he says the Belter fleet won't scratch the mothership, he's on the money. Everyone's scrambling to put together as many NNEMP warheads as they can. The electromagnetic-pulse weapons seemed to make short work of their ships over Darwin when they finally deployed them, but they won't touch the big ship."

Stan's frown hardened if that were possible. Madhur stared into her cup, then lifted her gaze. "The USF want Freya," the two engineers said as one. Patty and Jake nodded.

"Tell me you're not gonna give her up to them," Stan leaned forward and asked Patty.

"Not in a pink fit!" Patty replied. She was surprised at the venom in her voice. Stan growled his agreement and nodded as he leaned back.

"They did have a good idea, but I think we can do a bit better." Jake glanced around conspiratorially, a sly smile drifting onto his face. "They wanted Patty to fly to Sol-Earth-L1 to collect ordinance and then fly out to the mothership, board her, plant a nuke and..."

"Oh, please! Spare my aching back. What twaddle!" Stan slapped his thigh angrily. "And they expected you to buy that?"

"Seemed to," Patty answered. She took another mouthful of her breakfast and swallowed her shame. She had bought it, hook, line, and sinker. Even though the USF had treated her poorly, her first instinct was to help if she could.

"Granted. It's too big a job for one." Jake smiled at Alan. "Or one and a half."

"No job for a young girl at all," Stan harrumphed. "Don't get me wrong, my newest young niece, I think you could do anything if'n you set your heart and mind on it but," he sighed, "war or not I'd not see you used as a pawn for anyone let alone the bloody USF!"

Now, why couldn't Lirsín have said it that way? Patty wondered.

"I doubt they ever planned to let Patty and Freya out of their hands at all." Jake's frown flashed a grin. "Pum says he can get us in and out. Diplomatic negotiations. And maybe an exchange of ... gifts. Speaking of which, have you seen Lily? I need to talk to her about those Winterberg firing nodes." Jake paused to take in everyone's reactions. "We need to fit all four of us in Freya. The USF is right; she is the only ship that can get close."

"I have an aft inspection hatch from an old Junkers-Peabody that would fit quite nicely over the old exhaust port." Madhur stared at Stan expecting a hostile response. Stan just frowned, but not in a disapproving manner, nodding his head. "The plate I tacked onto Freya's hiney is not much more than a fig leaf."

"We'd have to make sure the environmental systems can handle the load," Stan's nods were positive, "but in a pinch, they could stay in their p-suits and hook up to umbilicals. Shouldn't take too long to run a couple of lines into the aft." Stan smiled. "A Junkers-Peabody eh? My grampa herded one of those for years. Last I heard she was still holding good pressure."

The two engineers looked at each other for a moment, and Jack groaned. "They're gonna go all guild on us, Patty."

"You cannae change the laws of physics." They intoned as one and then laughed.

"Sixteen hours; give or take a bit." Stan blinked erratically, his eyes darting back and forth, still calculating.

"She'll still need at least an hour for a proper pressure test," Madhur added. Her sleepy demeanor was long gone.

"We'll have to test her with the extra mass. We shaved everything we could to make sure we didn't blow the driver when we first put it in Freya," Cian added to the discussion. "If I can get your projected payload I can run it through our simulator."

"Sure, as soon as I can." Jake took an exaggerated look at his wrist comm. "Was that sixteen hours ... after you've finished breakfast?"

"Gettin' closer to eighteen now," Stan snapped back. "Unless you like your air thin ... real thin." His grin undercut his aggressive tone.

Jake chuckled and waved his hands in mock defense. "Not pushing ... just getting a timeline sorted, is all." Jake was doing his own calculating. "We're gonna have to haul ass as it is." Cian started to chuckle, but a sharp glance from Patty made him try to bury it in a cough.

"What?" Jake eyes snapped from Cian to Patty and back again.

"Jake should know what Freya can do if he is going to plan this properly," Cian said with pride.

He's right, but that fifth register still gives me a chill. "You tell him. It's your baby," Patty said and tried to face her fear, another one of her fears. They were beginning to mount up.

Cian's quick overview of the Sprocket Drive had both Stan and Jake scratching their heads. "Patty still thinks it's a glitch, but I can show you the sensor data. We were Faster-Than-Light. How much faster?" Cian shrugged. "I dunno. Have to do some more tests." He gave Patty a cheeky grin. "Scared poor Patty, it did. We've had that whole register disabled until... well, we didn't have much time to test her." His grin ebbed, and he scratched the back of his ear. "Fair call really."

"FTL," Jake sighed and shook his head as if he were trying to resettle disparate concepts. "You're right about not opening that can of worms, Patty. Not then. But if we must get out in a hurry..." He let it hang.

Patty nodded and smiled stiffly. If. If we must get out in a hurry. When would be more accurate.

Madhur made arrangements with Stan to reconvene in engineering and dragged Cian along in her wake as she swept out of the mess.

"I must talk to Pum again ... about the specific protocols, contact frequencies used, etcetera." Jake stood, looking ahead but not really seeing. His attention snapped to Patty. "I'll be back ... soon."

"I'll be with Freya, Patty replied. "I'm going to have to scrub her memory with industrial grade solvents before reloading her systems. We can't do this at all if Freya's flying blind." Patty washed the last of her breakfast down with the bulb of iced tea and turned to thank Daichi, but he was nowhere to be seen.

"We'll catch up with you a bit later." Stan glanced around trying to find Cicely.

FIRST ATTEMPT

The Badlands were not dangerous to travel through. The scorched ground struggled to sprout much more than sickly weeds, but they would not hurt you if you did not linger. Pur'unnan was almost glad the Bar'Durrunnan FirstMother had not offered to fly her to Darfelenornal, far to the north. This journey would give her plenty of time to put her thoughts in order.

The merchant train that accompanied Pur'unnan's Hel'omi entourage through the sun-struck lands was eager to continue apace, taking the quicker eastern route. But Pur'unnan had traveled that road when coming to study at the Bar'Durrunnan workshops and took the scenic western roads that wound around the diminishing edge of the inland sea. There was one place she especially wanted to visit. It was far from the sea's edge now, an isolated tor, but many GreatMothers made a pilgrimage to that place. The oldest of the memories within her happened there: Fe'ren and her parents on a picnic, her hand-woven basket full of treats fresh from the sea.

A flicker from the sky gave Pur'unnan a chill. She leaned out of the boxy litter's window and was relieved to see the trail of a meteor scorch across the sky. The bright flare of a fusion engine moved quickly towards the westerly sun as one leaped skyward from Bar'Durrunnan's landing pads to the south.

A flash in the east accompanied moments later by a rumbling boom, drew Pur'unnan's attention away from the climbing rocket. A trail of smoke from high in the atmosphere continued down to the ground. It was not uncommon for meteors to hit the ground. It had not been particularly large, but it must have had a solid core for it to survive atmospheric entry. A sickening chill enveloped her. It had not hit that far away. In fact, it looked like it came down very close to the eastern route taken by the merchants.

Although it sparked Pur'unnan's curiosity, she did not want to extend their journey and backtrack to the impact site. Something about the event scared her even as she tried to dampen the paranoia the Bar'Durrunnan FirstMother had instilled in her.

CHAPTER EIGHT

Someone, most probably Cian, had already started scrubbing her CRV's memory. Freya's console was splayed open, and the memory storage units from the comm and navigation sat on the pilot's seat, hooked to an isolated breadboard brute-force cleaning every register by repeatedly filling them with random numbers. A handwritten note tacked to the board - *definitely, Cian, bless him* - read, "Anything over 100,000 rewrites should be plenty." The meter read 230,491. Patty killed the process and began to disconnect the units.

"Thought I'd find you here." Lily's skinny frame craned over Patty's shoulder; her face creased with a wry grin. "You've sure got The Princess buzzing. Wallace was saying you're getting ready to take on the aliens single-handed." Lily laughed, and Patty tried to hide her discomfort by chuckling as she slotted the comm's memory back into place. *Which one's Wallace? I'd been contemplating going solo. At first. Maybe Lirsín wasn't acting crazy. Maybe I've been.*

"Well, maybe not single-handed." Patty reached for the second memory block.

"That's what I thought." Lily's eyes glittered.

"You're not thinking of coming, are you?" Patty asked. *Was everyone mad?*

"They'll be waiting for you this time, prepared. Guards at every entrance. We'll find another way in." Lily was deadly serious. "You might not like flying three-up, but we know Freya can do it." She squirmed a little and then pouted. "Besides, they're my firing-nodes. Ergo, I go."

"Three-up's not an issue. It's going to be a squeeze getting

Pum and Jake into..." Patty started.

"Pum *and* Jake? I'm definitely in." Lily chuckled as she gave Freya the once-over glance. "You planning on strapping them to the wings?"

"No. Stan and Madhur are opening up the aft. Going to stow them in back." Patty pointed over her shoulder. "There's room now that Freya runs on a trans-dimensional probe..."

"Yeah, Cian tried to explain it, but my head started to hurt," Lily told her. "So where is this mighty dingus that's going to put us fusion engineers out of work?"

Patty pointed to the small black box - *Are these things always black?* - ten centimeters by seven by three mounted beside the comm's innards. "Uses less energy than a desk lamp, and to tell the truth, I couldn't care if it ran on spells and pixie dust." Patty stopped to consider the tiny device. It fitted Arthur C. Clarke's description of advanced technology perfectly.

"I'd probably draw the line at sacrifice, animals, children or virgins. All equally inappropriate especially for a space drive." Lily smiled, her eyes glazed over a little as she thought. "Pum and Jake? Why Pum and Jake?" she asked.

"We're not planning on sneaking in. You're right; the aliens will be watching every entrance. Jake wants to walk in through the front door. A diplomatic mission." Patty pulled the system backup units from storage and began to copy the data to the cleaned memory units.

"Front door, eh?" Lily's eyes were thin slits, almost closed. "Front door." A smile crept across her face. "A diplomatic mission? You could make quite a song and dance of it ... draw every eye..."

"What are you thinking?" Patty inquired.

"Well, if they're so scared of you sneaking in the back door..." Lily began.

"Yes?"

"They might drop their guard if they can see you in plain sight," Lily said, rubbing her hands together. "I'm sure to be able to find another way in."

Patty shook her head in disbelief. "You really want to go."

"More than you understand." Lily's happy-go-lucky personality was discarded. "I may be a Belter, but I lost family and friends at all the LaGrange stations." Violence burned in Lily's eyes. "I gave 'em a nice hotfoot at L5, but it's not payback enough. Not near enough. Not for this girl. Belters are known for holding a grudge."

"Lily, if it was up to me..."

"You need a plan B," Lily insisted.

"I guess so." Patty checked the transfer; forty percent complete. "Truth to tell, Jake's taken over planning. I think I've been relegated to a taxi driver." *I hope.*

"Sounds fine to me. 'Bout time you made room for some other glory hounds. If Wallace has his way, the histories will only have one name in them, yours. Says he's already working with a scriptwriter on Ceres."

"Scriptwriter?" Wallace? Wallace who?

"Yeah. He says most people need their history splashed across a fifty-meter display. The more explosions, the better. The way he tells it, he's got two endings prepared: either you are the Hero that saves mankind, or the foolish girl who sentenced humanity to generations of servitude to our oh-so-benevolent Galactic Masters."

"Which one is this, Wallace? Is he from Hestia's crew? The toe of my boot's gettin' mighty itchy," Patty growled.

"No." Lily's chuckles told Patty her leg was being pulled, at least a bit. "He's with The Princess. I'm sure Lirsín will put him in his place."

Patty could not hold back the sigh at the sound of his name. Her emotions, bubbling inside, had congealed into a confusing mix of anger, frustration, and guilt. And a greasy blob of fear that seemed to taint everything. *Am I even in love anymore? Would I be feeling this bad if I wasn't in love?*

"Lirsín. I think I said ... something stupid. I got my wires crossed I think and..." Patty kept her eyes down, watching the data transfer slowly tick over.

"Was he stumbling over his tongue?" Lily asked, her warm hand settled on Patty's shoulder. "Said something inane, did he? Something insulting? Patronizing?" Her chuckle lifted Patty's eyes. "Welcome to the real world, sister. Men are so easily confused. They really are the weaker sex." Lily twisted her mouth into a rueful smile. "What are you going to do? You can only work with the material providence delivers. Don't worry, Lirsín's a good boy, you just spin him out of his standard orbit. Doesn't know if he should hold you safe in his arms or leave you flying free knowing you may never come back to him." Lily's smile eased Patty's doubts.

"You should have seen him when Jaswinder was secured to The Princess, and it was time to leave. You were out of communication, had been ever since you contacted the USF."

Really? Patty fumed at USF's perfidy.

"Fretting he was, poor dear. That's when Cicely came up with the idea of leaving you a beacon. Don't worry. I'm sure you'll work it out. He's a good boy from a good family. A good catch."

"I didn't think I was fishing," Patty muttered.

"Oh, we all are whether we realize it or not. The good ol' subconscious is sitting back there, sucking up everything we perceive. It makes the decisions; we just react or respond to its potent suggestions." Lily gave a resigned shrug.

It was true. Thinking about returning to the mothership sent a physical surge through Patty's body. Her mind seemed to pounce on the experience and give it a label, fear. That was almost too easy. Thinking about Lirsín and a completely different arrangement of feelings pulsed and flooded her body. Interpreting those feelings was the confusing part. *It was too easy just to react to the flood than make a considered response.*

"Don't worry too much. Give it time. Love's like orbital mechanics. Your flight paths will either synchronize into a stable orbit," Lily lifted one finger, "you will be flung apart," she lifted a second finger.

"Or we'll crash together." Patty could not help blushing.

"Shouldn't have to give that lesson to a hot-shot pilot." Lily chuckled and gave Patty a rough slap on the shoulder. "Right. If you can't get me on this little black tub, I better find someone who can." And then she was gone.

Patty tried to focus on getting Freya's systems into order. It helped to push all the confusing and conflicting thoughts and feelings aside for a moment. Her own systems would have to wait.

"Ahhhh! Good work," Cian said. Patty looked up at the sound of his voice. "Wasn't sure when I could get back." He leaned on the edge of Freya's cockpit and twisted around so he could get a better look at the displays. "How'd they scrub up? Looks good so far."

"Lost less than one percent in overwrite failures."

Cian shook his head and grumbled. "That's plenty of space to hide a set of rogue instructions."

"They are sandboxed off, and the sectors are de-powered," Patty added.

"Ordinarily you might be safe enough, but we are talking about the military," Cian growled. "If we had compatible memory units, I'd just swap them out, but this is all new top-of-the-line stuff."

Patty glanced down at the navigation system Giuseppe had installed at L2. She did not know how new it was, just that it worked superbly.

"Anything I can scrounge is too old, but I've got a few software workarounds that should keep the buggers out." Cian straightened, frowning. "And speaking of security, a six-year-old with a penknife could get into Freya. Ya gotta let me fix that." He gently buffed his sleeve over the panel he had leaned on. "We're not on OASIS anymore. You really want to keep anyone away from being able even to touch her. Eg and I have a few ideas about that." Cian's smile dropped into a frown.

"What?" Patty asked.

"Eg thought of it, a self-destruct routine. He's concerned about keeping the Sprocket drive out of unauthorized hands, alien or otherwise."

"Self-destruct?" *That's just wrong* Patty thought. Everything in a spaceship was built to keep the inhabitants safe. Modern fusion engines had multiple failsafe backups to prevent catastrophic failure. Wanting to develop such a feature gave Patty a chill.

"Just enough juice to fry the box, no more. Freya would still be intact," Cian added.

"Just immobilized," Patty continued the train of thought.

"Err ... That's a given. But I've had a few other ideas that don't involve killing the golden goose. Self-destruct is last resort," he reassured her.

"Thanks. I think."

"Yeah. Happy days," Cian groaned. "On a brighter note. I have The Princess's positional vector coordinates ready to download to update the navigation and the Sprocket registries. I can finish the system integrations for you if you like. Gonna need a little hacking time if I'm going to beef up Freya's security anyway."

"Okay, I guess. Thanks." Patty climbed out of Freya's cockpit as the inner airlock slid open. Nanna and another of The Ice Princess's crew were pushing a rolling workshop of tools and diagnostic equipment into the hanger. Madhur followed, pulling a small cart laden with something covered in a drop cloth, Stan ambling along beside her.

"...agree with you. There's having it on a set of plans, and then there's actually seeing it in place." Madhur moved past the portable workbench to the back wall at Freya's starboard aft.

"Patty," Stan called. "Ya got to come and have a look at this. Stark, grab the other side." Stan flipped off the drop cloth and picked up one side of the door. Stark hurried around and lifted the other, spinning it around and holding it over the black metal plate that covered Freya's stern. Patty scooted around to see what the door would look like in place. It was round, with a bubble inspection port in the center and had a simple release-and-turn locking mechanism on the lower right quadrant. It looked as though it had been built for its new home.

"I'm not sure about the green coloring," Patty joked.

"Pah! Poo. Girls and matching colors!" Stan scoffed. "She's goin' to look sweet." He already looked proud of his uncompleted work. Stan nodded to Stark, and they carefully returned the door to the cart.

"The ol' Junkers-Peabody has triple redundancy mechanical vacuum lock. Safe as. Zero failure rate." Madhur looked just as proud as Stan. "Picked it up with a bunch of odds 'n' sods at an auction last year. No idea what I was going to do with it, but she was just too good to toss."

"Anything I can do?" Patty asked. With Nanna and Stark as well as Stan and Madhur, Patty was not sure if they would let her do anything.

"Not really, lass," Stan told her. "We've pretty much got it covered. You should take the opportunity to rest up." He smiled and turned to Nanna who was laying out tools on the bench. Patty looked around the hanger. Everyone was busy.

Alan's fingers attracted Patty's attention. "Team."

"Yes, they make a good team," Patty replied.

"We team too. Not our time yet, later we work, they rest."

"When did you become so smart?" Patty asked. A momentary doubt about taking Alan flashed through Patty, but being without him was impossible to consider. "Madhur, give me a ping if you need anything."

"What? Oh sure, Patty." Madhur turned back to the monitor displaying Freya's blueprints. Patty was not hungry but returning to the mess seemed the best way of finding Jake. *And maybe I'll run into that Wallace fellow.*

CHAPTER NINE

"I still don't like it," Lirsín muttered and squirmed nervously, his eyes darting around the conference table.

Patty squeezed his hand to reassure him. "That's okay, I don't like it either, but there's a chance I'll just be the taxi driver."

Jake took a swig from his bulb of iced tea and cleared his throat. "Look, Murphy or not, I know no plan survives contact with the enemy, but with Daichi and Lily we have a second team trying for a covert entry."

Patty tried to swallow the cold lump of fear that swelled in her throat. She was going to have to fly three trips, the first with Jake and Pum. While they were negotiating for the queen-to-queen parley, Patty was to rip back to The Ice Princess for Daichi and Lily. Then back to the mothership. *Three trips. Two at FTL!* They had to keep the alien diplomat, and the covert team separate. Patty could feel her palms perspire. *I'm going to have to use the fifth register.*

The mothership was over four hundred and eighty million kilometers away, almost twenty-seven light minutes. Patty was suddenly in awe at how vast the solar system was, if the fastest thing in the universe took twenty-seven minutes to get there. And light was too slow. She had to be back with Daichi and Lily before Jake and Pum returned.

"With any luck, I'll be able to deploy, and we can all go home," Jake added. He didn't sound very hopeful despite his tone. "I know there are holes, but the basic plan has flexibility. Comments anyone?"

"Are you sure we can't stand off and lob one through the docking ports?" Lirsín asked.

Lirsín's trying to save me. It gave Patty a warm feeling now she knew what to look for.

"No," Cian said as he shook his head. "The data from Patty's last trip shows that anything fast enough to evade the mothership's defensive weapons cannot penetrate the MEM ... the mass/envelope/matrix. The interface between the external universe and the internal wraps around the ship. It's a protective bubble." Cian paused, "Anything slow enough to cross the matrix threshold can be intercepted."

"You're right, Jake," Daichi added. "Much can go wrong in any venture of this type." Daichi face was composed, his demeanor was relaxed. "But there is a good chance that one team will be successful. More would be better. There are volunteers."

"No!" Patty sighed. "There is no time for more than one trip back."

"Of course." Daichi agreed. "The ... err ... Sprocket ... yes?" He waited for Cian's nod. "The Sprocket Drive is untested at those speeds. Your concerns are completely valid, my dear."

"Anything else?" Jake sipped again and looked at his wrist comm.

"Latest from Madhur was that they were almost ready to begin the pressure tests. Preliminaries look good, so she's not expecting any problems." Cian scratched his unshaven chin. He looked tired. "I've tested Freya's new security systems."

"Yeah," Jake noted. he put a finger in his ear and gave it a vigorous shake, "my ears are still ringing."

Cian grinned. "The audio files are pumped through the MEM boundary, turning it into a really big speaker. With proper 3D targeting, we could make that into a usable weapon." He looked across the table at Patty. "Next upgrade, eh?"

"Sure." Patty shrugged. *If there was going to be a next time.*

"Okay then. Any other business?" Jake's gaze stopped at each face for a heartbeat before moving on. Lirsín squeezed Patty's hand, but he stayed quiet. "All right." Jake checked his comm once more. "Departure in two hours forty minutes on my mark ... mark."

"I still don't like it." Lirsín gripped her hand tightly, and they sat that way as everyone left the room. Patty did not mind sitting quietly with Lirsín. *He only wants to keep me safe.*

"I'm sorry, I don't want you to be angry with me, I just..." Lirsín swallowed and sighed, his eyes dewy. "I had hoped we would have more time, time for you to get to know me better, time for..." Patty stopped his rambling by leaning close and smothering his words with her lips. She needed to feel his strength and warmth, not his words.

Not enough time... I thought that it was my affliction or is it a pandemic?

Patty heard the knock, but her snooze still held her in its grip. Everyone, except for Patty, had been busy preparing for this mission, so she had come to her quarters for a snooze. She knew she had been dreaming and that it had not been particularly pleasant. There had been corridors. The scuffed pink corridors from Hestia's Hearth mingled with The Ice Princess's pale blue, Jaswinder's one central shaft, lined with pictures, and the cream passageways from the alien mothership. And they were filled with aliens, fighting. They were fighting Patty and each other and all the while she could hear her mother telling her to tidy her room, and do her homework, and to eat her peas, or she would not get any dessert. That was weird. Patty loved eating peas, especially the sweet baby peas.

There was a gentle cough, and just as Patty opened her eyes soft, slippery darkness enveloped her. Lily laughed "Come on. Wake up, sleepy head." Her voice came from beyond the layers of soft black silk. "Time for dress-ups, little sister."

Patty pushed the slippery cloth away and blinked in the light. Lily stood over her, hands on her hips, grinning like a loon. "What do you mean?" Patty asked.

"I mean you're gonna power dress for this. Jake says the more gold, the better, and nothing shows off gold better than black silk." There were two black dresses, and one pair of pajamas on one arm and Lily swirled them through the air.

"The pants, definitely," Patty told her. *Definitely.*

"I thought so too, but another layer of silk might give a little more protection." Lily tossed the pajamas to the foot of the bed. "This long-sleeved dress, I could split these seams up to the hip. Wouldn't restrict you. The gold embroidery on the hems and cuffs is a plus too." She added the elegant dress to the pajamas and discarded the strapless mini.

"Now, for a jacket." Lily held what looked like a gold and green silk smoking jacket and a black tailored coat. "I know. It's not up to par, but Lirsín said his father might have something in his wardrobe." She tossed the jackets to the bed as she crossed into the bathroom.

Patty had noticed the clothes carefully stowed in the closet but had not investigated them. She sat up and picked up the dress. She could not resist feeling its cold caress against her face. A faint floral scent permeated the elegant garment.

"Try it on." Lily was back, her arms full of black and gold. She dumped more black silk over Patty's head. "Dress ups! You should see what I've got for Alan."

"Bathroom first." Patty wriggled off the bed, both excited and full of fear. *I'm not sure I'm ready for this.*

CHAPTER TEN

Alan relented and squeezed to the side of Freya's cockpit to let Jake move forward so he could peer over Patty's seat, but he kept himself between Patty and the alien. Pum did not seem to be paying attention to the humans, his pale face and shiny black eyes pressed into the aft hatch's bubble port.

"How fast are we going now?" Jake's voice was theatrically loud and filled with wonder. He winked.

Patty silenced another annoying fake alarm. *Surely this isn't necessary.* The buffeting routine Cian had programmed into the Sprocket drive for this outward leg unnerved her, or maybe it was the subsonic pulses. It was humiliating. Freya was a trim ship that flew smoothly. Patty smiled back at Jake. *At least he looks confident.*

"I'm pushing her to her very limits, Jake." Freya gave a sickening lurch, and an array of red lights flashed across the screen. Patty sighed again and tapped one button. The alarms slowly died down, along with warning lights but the wicked shimmy took much longer to wane.

"Point zero five C, Jake! Fifteen thousand kilometers per second!" Patty exclaimed enthusiastically. *I may as well have some fun.* "Jake, we're going faster than any humans ever!" *Would Pum even hear this charade?* "And we're still going to be late." Patty killed another false alarm.

"But I thought you said the trip was only going to take seven and a half hours? The fleet won't get there for eight hours." Jake gripped her custom-formed seat as Freya dropped, or seemed to. Her flight path was straight as a die and smooth as the silk Patty wore beneath her p-suit. The shimmies, wobbles, bumps, and sways were all courtesy of Cian's malicious programming. The rapidly changing internal gravity field made them all feel that Freya was on the edge of control.

"Time dilation. Seven and a half hours for us, nearly nine for the fleet."

"Oh, I see." Jake sounded as if he did not understand. *You should have been an actor, not a pilot.* Jake's smile became genuine. "I'm still impressed." It was a real whisper, not one meant for a stage. "Well, they will just have to start without us. Protocol be damned." Patty choked down her laugh as she silenced another alarm.

Even Pum tried to see out of the canopy when they arrived at the asteroid. Patty gave Alan a firm look. He nodded and withdrew but only enough to let the alien peer forward, and he never took his hand from the hilt of his new sword. The alien squeezed in sideways beside Jake. *Could he do it any other way?*

Two burning Belter wrecks that maintained enough integrity to be still called ships drifted far to the mothership's stern. Patty logged them. The rest of the Belter squadron were fighting forward of the great ship and the 'roid. Patty could only count nine ships on the attack. *Someone is missing. There were supposed to be twelve ships.* Nine brave ships against two squadrons. A quick count tallied the aliens at twenty ships, nine in one squadron and eleven in the other. *Both flights would have started with a dozen ships. Four alien ships for three Belters.* A bright flash illuminated the asteroid's surface.

"They're attacking the asteroid?" Patty half whispered to herself.

Jake chuckled. "They're attacking the asteroid. Clever." Patty glanced over her shoulder with please-explain written across her face. "They don't have anything powerful enough to hurt the mothership, but they could break up the 'roid. If they fracture it..."

"They'll have to find another rock," Patty completed the idea. Jake nodded, his eyes darting between Freya's navigational displays and the raw pyrotechnics outside. Four alien fighters had isolated one of the Belter ships and were in hot pursuit, forcing it to arc above the lumpy asteroid. Suddenly they fell away from the chase. A powerful beam of coherent energy burst forth from the mothership, and the Belter ship vaporized. Patty blinked. Violet bars lingered in her vision. The cockpit's optics were too slow to protect them. *And then there were eight, playing tag while hiding in the 'roid's shadow.* The rest of the fleet were hours away; some would not arrive until tomorrow. *How long could they last?*

Although the asteroid belt could be hazardous to traverse in places, it was - contrary to feature presentations - mostly empty space. The chunk of frozen planetary debris the aliens had chosen was considerably smaller than Templeman-Frobisher but was potentially deadly, nonetheless. How lethal the strike was a factor of velocity. Dropped from orbit, it would make a considerable splash anywhere. If the aliens were feeling particularly nasty, they could target the Earth while traveling at or near light speed. That would smash the world into pieces. Luckily, the aliens seemed to want to live on Earth, so they were unlikely to destroy the planet.

"We have time." Jake's head was over Patty's left shoulder. From their position, it was apparent the mothership had not yet mated with the 'roid. The irregular aggregation of silicon, iron, and ice had a complex rotation that would take time to neutralize. Bright flares from tethered fusion engines worked hard to reduce the tumble to a rotation along a single axis. The 'roid would then be relatively easy to mate with then. *Are they flying manually? Ridiculous. I could write a rendezvous program for my autopilot in twenty minutes that could mate with that tumble.*

Navigation began to give an odd return. Patty rubbed her eyes to try and clear away the burning purple afterimage. Small radio sources englobed the conflict, or that was how it appeared. They were only on for a second at most, transmitting bursts; the duration varied, but navigation had identified ninety-six distinct sources.

"Jake?" Patty displayed the results.

"They used to call it Twiddling Fingers. That's the Belter's comm network. Can we tap in? They transmit at random intervals but receive constantly. Direct a transmission in the general vicinity of any one of those nodes, and it should be picked up."

Patty sent a standard login request, and almost instantly an unadorned UNET login page appeared. She verified her ID, and all her files were there, with all the new additions from F-UNET as well. A priority ping with a Belter ID demanded her attention. *That will be someone from the squadron fighting below you.* Patty plugged in a headset.

"Excuse me, Jake." Patty flicked her eyes at Pum. Jake took the hint and almost manhandled the alien aft. Patty opened the channel.

"Baby Face comm center, here. Colonel Balke, we've been expecting you. Do you need any help?" A frazzled woman in a green shipsuit was belted down and was under variable thrust conditions. Her body shook, and she thrashed back and forth within the limits of her harness as her ship maneuvered.

Colonel? Damn USF. "Err ... You seem busy enough to me. No, we don't need anything but access to your UNET server. How long is the network likely to be up?"

"Longer than we will, I reckon. Long enough. They're tough to pinpoint, and they're far enough out so that you receive an almost continuous signal. They haven't hit one yet. Help yourself. Good luck with the diplomacy thing. I'm glad someone's talking to them. Fly True. Baby Face comm, out."

"Fly True," Patty replied, but the connection had closed. Patty waved to Jake and nodded when his eyes asked about Pum. "We have near real-time access to UNET."

"Great. I've been concerned about keeping in

communication. I'll be a radio target before they see me. You can remain hidden and keep in touch. Much better than I expected." Jake turned to Pum. "You understand what this means? Her Majesty will witness the way your people treat her emissary."

Pum made a small nod. "That is," rum-rum-rumble, "understandable." He looked as though he wanted to pace. "It is always," rumble, "dangerous at moments of unexpected contact and at time of tension, war." Rumble. His left hand reached for where his weapon normally hung. "This one will defend Traaaffic Control. This one's colors will be recognized ... eventually." He shrugged and backed away.

"No worse than I expected," Jake said, and he smiled, but Patty could feel his unease. "It will be good to have *you* looking over *my* shoulder for a change. Let's do this."

Freya flew high above the fray. Patty panned her camera to the 'roid's rough horizon and tracked the pocked and broken surface until she found a fusion flare and zoomed in. It was a boxy transport constrained in some manner to the surface. With enough ships, it would not take long to tame that tumble. A brilliant flash from the surface drew Patty's eyes from the monitor.

"Did you see what that was?" she asked.

"Yeah. Direct hit on a moored ship. Knock out enough, and they'll never get that thing stabilized." Jake kept his enthusiasm in check, but his eyes shone. "Can we hold here for a sec?" Freya soared high above the gap between 'roid and mothership. "There's an installation on the nearside. Can you zoom in any closer?" Patty zoomed out and panned the camera until the equipment came into view, then zoomed in on the spidery construction. "That's a mine head. They're drilling. Do you have this speck's specs? What are they after?"

Patty had glanced at the almanac entry for (295731)2164 GY$_{19}$ during the flight and displayed it for Jake. The tumbling rock was indistinguishable from hundreds of thousands of other asteroids. "There is some tritium ice here but not in commercial quantities. Enough for them, I guess. Those fuel hog engines they use don't deserve trit. Should have had enough time to suck as much deut out of Darwin Harbor as they needed."

"Tritium. That's what they'll be after. They can power the ships that are canceling that spin with the fuel beneath their feet. Can you pan across to the mothership? The bow. The dock. It's damaged. Pum? Can you see?"

On her previous passes around the mothership, Patty noted the four brightly lit landing docks, one on each of the mothership's four sides. The dock in the center of the bow was dark. There was a melted tangle on the upper side, and scorch marks marred the mothership's broad front. Patty listened to a bout of rum-rumbling before Pum became intelligible. "It is true," rumble-rum-rum, "has been struck a fierce blow."

"Darwin." Patty could still see the echo of its flash illuminate Australia's red outback and could still feel her chill.

"Probably. Probably. If she's already damaged, it can probably afford a bit more when she's mated to that 'roid. Can you see our landing site?" Jake's matter-of-fact pronouncements calmed Patty's nerves just as he did when guiding her through her first solo rendez with OASIS.

"If you let me use the scope," Patty replied.

"Be my guest, Captain. Oh sorry, Colonel, your majesty." Jake's chuckle tickled Patty even as she cringed. She zoomed out, then panned along the mothership's gray upper surface. Pum had looked over her reconnaissance images and pointed out three or four large locks they could use on the top deck but had agreed that for maximum impact the frontal approach was best, entering via one of the four - now three - main landing docks.

Patty felt smothered by the size of the great ship. She could almost feel the claustrophobic air ducts tightening around her. *If I must go back there, I'm not crawling through any ducts.* Patty returned her concentration to the camera's display. Near the aft-starboard corner, a collection of heat-exchange fins cast impenetrable shadows across the deck. It would be a bit of a hike to the stern, but Pum assured Jake that there was access to the dock.

"Down there." Patty pointed into the blackness. She cast her eyes over the navigation display. A flight of six fighters shot away from the starboard docks and arced away to reinforce the squadron defending their installations on the 'roid on hot plasma tails.

"Please take your seats... " there were no actual seats in the aft compartment, "...places. Strap down. It could be bumpy." This too was part of their theater for Pum, but Patty was glad to have the cockpit to herself as she eased Freya closer. She gave Alan a questioning look, and he responded with a stoic thumbs-up. He was ready. Patty took them down.

CHAPTER ELEVEN

The mothership's artificial gravity had surprised Patty the first time she landed Freya on the invader's ship. Freya's sensors confirmed that the alien's mass/envelope/matrix extended a little more than twenty meters around its colossal hull. When she received confirmation from Jake, Patty sent Freya creeping across the interface and swooped down to the gray plating. Her landing gear flexed gently as they absorbed the CRV's weight and the Sprocket drive established a dynamic lock on the deck; if the ship moved, Freya would follow.

Jake set to securing the seals on Pum's Zip-Lok. It fitted the twisted alien about as well as the alien Zip-Lok had fitted Alan when she rescued him, poorly. Alan had already secured the helmet to his slightly over-sized Ice Princess branded p-suit. *C. Connaugh* - his embroidered nametag remained on the breast pocket - must have been a small man, most unusual for a Belter. His p-suit would balloon a little on Alan, but it was a marked improvement on wearing a Zip-Lok. Jake and Alan checked each other's seals before giving Patty the all clear to depressurize. Patty closed her visor and set the pumps into action.

The stars positively gleamed in the satin black expanse. *Maybe it's because Sol's so far away.* It was still the brightest star in the panoply surrounding them. Patty took a moment to take in the brilliant darkness as the canopy swung back. Her nerves quietened. Freya rocked gently as her passengers disembarked, returning Patty to the mundane. She climbed down to the gray plate and shaded her eyes from the greater part of the mothership that was in direct sunlight. Sol still had a kick.

Safety lines, as well as an umbilical, linked Jake and Pum. As

Patty expected, Alan moved through a series of exercises, his new, untested sword snapping through lethal arcs as he walked a tight path around Freya, carefully surveying their surroundings, on guard. The bright blade returned to its dark blue scabbard with a flick as Alan took his post on Patty's right. She smiled to herself. *I'd feel naked without him.*

Jake draped a black tabard over his p-suit. One golden circle surrounded by ten golden rings symbolizing the Solar system: Sol, and her ten children, Mercury, Venus, Earth, Mars, The Belt, Jupiter, Saturn, Uranus, Neptune, and The Kuiper Belt. Patty felt nervous at the thought of representing the whole solar system, but Jake was convinced it would be easier to sell a big lie than a little one. *Patty Balke, Queen of the Solar System! Huh!*

Jake reached for the controls of the holographic projector mounted to his shoulder and turned it on. A sizable holographic black and white checkered flag unfurled above their heads. It looked more suited to the finishing line at a racetrack, but Pum assured her that it would be recognized as a flag of parlay.

Jake passed the end of the umbilical to Alan who handed it on to Patty. Patty plugged herself into the closed system. Radio silence was essential. Jake bowed, and Pum followed suit, even lower, his flourishes only diminished by the unbalanced inflation in his Zip-Lok. The bright smiley-face logo did not help his dignity either; his pale blue tabard was eclipsed beneath the logo's inane grin.

"Your Majesty," Jake intoned melodramatically, "we go to lay the path to peace."

Oh, please! Patty swallowed the guffaw that threatened to overwhelm her and managed to deliver her lines. "With our blessings." *Surely, Pum could tell this was a farce.* "Pum. We will be displeased if anything should happen to our Traffic Control. Please ensure our envoy is returned to us unharmed." That still sounded strange to Patty's ears, but Jake assured her royalty always spoke of themselves in the plural. The-Royal-We, he called it. Royalty did not rule a country; they *were* the country, personified.

Pum bowed again. "There is always risk at a moment like this, oh Queen," The badly inflated Zip-Lok disguised the subtle movements of Pum's hand, and Patty felt cut off from Pum's intent. "If we survive our first contact..."

"If?" Patty interrupted, she hoped imperiously.

"Our brother soldiers can get," rumble-rum-rum, "over-enthusiastic. Deaths are common."

"The death of our most noble Traffic Control would doom these talks. We hold him in the highest esteem and would be most aggrieved if *any* harm befell him." *Was it befell or befalls? Did it matter?*

Pum bowed again. "This one will lead the way and will stand between Traaaffic Control and all others as if this one was Traaaffic Control's own pouchling." His left hand fell to the hilt of his more-than-ceremonial sword, now returned to him. *I hope he knows how to use that.* There were enough nicks in the blade to suggest it saw regular use.

"Go with our blessing." Patty disengaged the umbilical and Jake reeled it in, tucking it at his hip. They both bowed and turned away, walking out onto the bright decking. True to his word, Pum took the lead.

"Can we spar?" Alan's fingers flashed, his words apparent even with the thick gloves. Daichi had remodeled Alan's blade, and he was keen to seize every moment to practice.

"Maybe when we get back. If we have time." Patty could feel her palms begin to sweat. "Back aboard, crewman." Alan's shoulders slumped a little, but he didn't hesitate and trotted to Freya's stern. Patty followed and double-checked the new hatch was correctly sealed before climbing into the cockpit. As Freya's warm air returned, she programmed a quick flight, straight up. She wanted to get away as soon as possible.

Patty pushed up her visor and twisted around to check on Alan. "Are you ready?" He sat with his back against the quick-foam lining of the starboard panel, his feet pressed against the reclamation unit. He nodded and gave a thumbs-up. She settled back into her seat and sent Freya straight up.

Patty could only spot six Belter ships, while reinforcements had bolstered the two squadrons to full strength. Patty did not know if this mission would save the brave Belters down there. *Your sacrifice won't be for nothing. I promise.*

"I want you to keep your p-suit sealed for this trip. I'm not exactly sure what is going to happen," Patty told her brother. She felt a chill roll over her as she remembered the flash of white that had accompanied their accidental FTL trip while on Freya's one-and-only test flight. Patty swallowed the lump in her throat and tried to breathe slowly as she entered their course into the autopilot. She was not willing to navigate this trip by the seat of her pants. Her heart pounded as she sealed her visor, unlocked the fifth register and activated the autopilot.

As Freya spun on her axis, Patty could not help but grip the arms of her seat. The mothership and the chaos of battle slipped behind them as a deceptively gentle surge informed Patty they were moving. Bright flashes began to accumulate at the leading edge of Freya's MEM, and navigation's alarms began to wail. The bright sparks quickly built to a continuous flare enveloping Freya's bow. *There's nothing I can do about that.* Crashing into that drifting bulkhead gave Patty confidence that the MEM would protect them, so she turned her attention to a problem she had some hope of solving. She silenced the navigation alarms and began to trace the problem.

Before she could bring the diagnostic flowcharts to the display, the flares crashing around Freya's bow dissipated. The odd concatenation of ships that were Jaswinder and The Ice Princess was floating a kilometer away. *We're back! Already? We're here! In one piece!* Patty's heart raced. She itched to examine Freya's flight logs, but she opened a comm channel instead.

"Freya to The Ice Princess, did someone order a taxi? Over."

Stan waved her into the dock, silhouetted against the brightly lit decking. Patty slid Freya across the threshold and slowly spun her around before touching down. Too many voices burst over the comm for Patty to get a clear shot at figuring out who was asking what. It seemed like everyone was in the hanger, but Cicely was at the front, waiting to receive the first hug when Patty climbed from Freya's cockpit.

"Miss me, big sis?" she chirped.

"Kiss ya if I could." Patty returned the squeeze and bumped visors with the little blond. *Speaking of kisses...* Patty cast her eyes about for Lirsín's slim p-suit; he stood with Stan at the edge of the fray. It was not possible to kiss in p-suits, but that did not stop a girl from wanting the impossible. Patty tore her eyes away. Cicely helped her unpin the jeweled scanner from her p-suit and handed it to Jai. He grinned and dashed off to a console, eager to upload a new adventure.

"Eg, Cian, I've sent Freya's logs. Navigation. It did not seem to make any difference to our flight plan, but it lost the plot when we went FTL. I haven't had the chance to diagnose its problem. Seemed to reset when we rendezed here, and Freya's coating reacquired the target stars."

"Which targets?" Cian asked.

"As far as I could tell, anything fore and aft," Patty reported.

Cian laughed. "Don't need any help with this one, Eg." He looked a little smug as if Patty should have figured it out.

That rankled. *It's a bit different when alarms are going off, and you're going faster than ... than...* Patty did not want to think about it. Then the penny dropped, and Patty understood. "Blueshift - Redshift. Fore and aft. Gotta be." Patty tapped her helmet. Freya had traveled so quickly the light's frequencies from in front had been blueshifted up the EM spectrum and the light from aft redshifted down. Navigation logged and tracked stars by their distinctive spectrums. *No wonder the poor thing got lost.* "I'll just kill the alarms, for now."

"I'll see if I can work a patch that will allow navigation to track relativistic changes, but for now..." Cian shrugged.

"Item next. I don't think you can solve this one." Patty pushed off the deck towards the hanger doors. "Freya, or rather the MEM, is hitting a whole lot of nothing while in FTL flight." Patty pointed to a streak receding across the sky. It followed her flight path in reverse. It took a confusing moment when Freya had first arrived before she could understand what she was observing. The bright flare was traveling back toward the mothership. It was the light from her FTL flight arriving. The furthest light took longer to reach them, and so it seemed that the source retreated across the sky.

"Particles," Patty said. "The vacuum of space is not exactly empty."

Cian nodded. "Sure. And on a quantum level it's busy. I'm keen to do an analysis, but you're right, I don't think I can do anything about it. Anything smacking into a super-luminal object's gonna get obliterated."

"It's not very stealthy," Patty complained.

Cian shrugged. "Yeah. But at least it looks like whatever it is making that light is moving away."

There was that. Put it the unsolvable basket and move on. Patty left the doorway and returned to Freya. "Lily, Daichi, are you ready?" Both wore blue and white Ice Princess p-suits. Lily had a white shoulder bag with round and square shapes pushing out its soft sides. Daichi had a smaller bag and two swords in his left hand, a katana, and his shorter wakizashi.

"Ready as we'll ever be." Lily bounced a little.

"Well then, let's get aboard," Patty told her and turned to Alan. "Escort our passengers aboard and get them settled, please." Alan gave her a nod and helped Lily climb into the aft hatch. Patty searched out Lirsín and gave Cicely a quick squeeze before putting her down. A path cleared between them. Stan smiled and stepped back.

A hug would have to do. Those lips were tantalizingly close but so far away. Lirsín's arms felt wonderful wrapped tightly around her, and they switched to a private channel. "Be careful." The comm crackled unromantically, but Patty did not care. She was storing everything away for a future moment when she was lonely and needed a hug like this one.

"I promise." Patty air kissed.

"Fly true." Lirsín pulled her close and then released her. Patty was glad The Ice Princess was only boosting a one-tenth gee.

Knees! Straighten! There were more hugs and back-pats as she returned to Freya, but Patty barely noticed them.

Climbing into Freya's cockpit felt like putting on an old pair of track shoes. *We fit.* Jai reached in and pinned the scanner to her p-suit. "Can't go without it." Patty read his lips and wondered, briefly, why he was not transmitting.

"Thanks." Patty closed the canopy but did not cycle in the air. She plugged her p-suit into an umbilical instead. Lily's voice and a faint babble came through the comm. Patty blushed and reset her p-suit's comm to the general channel. The gentle chatter became a roar of well-wishing that matched the waving hands and smiling faces surrounding them.

Patty checked her passengers. They were strapped down and ready. She cycled the air. "Flight time is ... less than I think it should be."

Alan gave his usual thumbs-up.

"Let's go. Give this girl's tail a twist." Lily waved.

"I am ready when you are, Patty." Daichi nodded and sat back.

Patty gave one last wave to the crowded hanger.

"Ice Princess, this is Freya. Please advise those in the hanger to step back." Her p-suit comm was still open, so the relayed request was not necessary. Shouts of "Good Luck!" and "Hurry Back!" were overwhelmed by "Fly True!" as Patty guided Freya from the hanger.

Lirsín's whispered, "Come back to me," was as clear as if he were the only one on the channel.

CHAPTER TWELVE

"That's too weird!" Lily muttered as she stared at the apparently receding trail of Freya's flight to the 'roid and the still bright trail of Freya's earlier FTL flight.

"The light we made when we first left The Princess is going to take nearly half an hour to arrive." Patty had to admit it was a headspace twister. She looked past the awe-struck fusion engineer and locked eyes with Alan. He acknowledged her with a nod. He seemed content, focused.

"So, what would The Princess see?" Lily asked.

"I suppose they would see something similar. We outpaced the photons by quite a bit." Patty rolled Freya away from the twin trails to give Lily and Daichi a view of the situation below them. Five remaining ships from the Belter fleet fought against nineteen. Two alien craft exploded in rapid succession. Seventeen. *The aliens are going to need more reinforcements soon.* The bulk of the Belter forces were over sixteen hours away. A bright flash from the surface showed where another tethered fusion engine died. The Belters were doing more than chipping away at the alien fleet; they continued to hinder efforts with the 'roid. Patty's heart swelled with pride even though navigation showed a reduction to the 'roid's tumble since she took her first readings. At the current rate, the mothership could begin to mate in less than a day, less if they were unhampered. There was no time to waste.

Patty logged into the local net and brought Jake's video feeds to the primary display: one from his shoulder showed Pum in the ill-fitting Zip-Lok walking beneath a checkered holographic flag, and the feed from inside his helmet displayed Jake's rugged face, alert but not scared. *How does he do it?* Patty's finger trembled as she opened the mike.

"Hi, Jake," Patty said.

Lily opened her mouth to say something too, but Daichi's finger snapped to his lips, silencing the willowy Belter.

"Your Majesty, as always, your timing is excellent. I trust you have found a secure position. Pum thinks we will make contact any moment." Jake's mode of speech told Patty that the alien was on the line. "Pum thought he saw you leave, that trail." Jake slewed around and stared into the sky. "Ooh, look, there's two of them. What do you think they are?"

Pum's rumble came over the comm. "Whatever they are, they are moving very quickly, Traaaffic Control, your," rumble, "majesty. And away from us."

"Excuse us for a moment, Pum." Pum's rumbling acknowledgment cut off as Jake isolated his circuit. "We're clear. Are you back or..."

"Hi, Jake! We're here too." Lily looked relieved she was able to send her greetings.

"So that trail was you leaving and the second one?"

"That's us, coming back. Weird, eh?" Lily chuckled.

"I'll get you to tell me about it some other time. How's the battle situation?" Jake asked.

"The Belters are down to five ships, and reinforcements aren't going to arrive in time." Patty felt sick about the Belters' deaths even though she knew delaying the aliens was vital.

"Volunteers all. We will remember them." Jake's words provoked a moment's silence.

Lily was the first to notice Pum waving his arm for attention. "Looks like something's got the little fella excited."

Jake turned. Two guards in armored p-suits were charging toward them, blades drawn. Pum drew his weapon and advanced, waving Jake in behind him. The sound of Pum's rumbling voice came through as Jake reconnected the circuit. Lily glanced at Daichi and wrapped her hands over her mouth.

Patty switched off the mike. "I'll keep it off until we need to speak, okay?"

Lily sighed as she let go of her mouth. "Give us a little warning, if you can."

"I promise." Patty's eyes were glued to the monitor as Pum, and the guards came within striking distance. One of the aliens held back while the other engaged Pum with more than tentative sparring. A flurry of head cuts forced Pum to withdraw a step and then another, but there he held, all the while rumbling at the top of his voice. His right hand, a continuous blur of Sign while his left constructed an impenetrable wall with that *ceremonial* blade. Pum took a step forward.

Jake turned from the fight as two more p-suited figures approached at a run from the left and three from the right. One was smaller, mirroring the larger ones' gait. Patty held up her hand and opened the mike. "That's another Gray with two guards," she told him and dropped her hand as she muted it once more.

"Copy that," Jake replied calmly.

As reinforcements arrived, the guard on attack stepped back and saluted Pum with an elaborate bow. Pum returned the gesture. His labored breathing did not stop his rum-rumbling speech until he turned to face the approaching Gray. The left-handed alien arrived with his weapon out. Pum stepped forward. Their blades spoke and replied, a short introductory conversation that looked to be a ritualized exchange rather than a genuine contest. The Gray stepped back, sheathed his sword and bowed. Pum mirrored his actions.

"Well, this seems positive." Jake sounded relieved.

"It is, Traaaffic Control, but if this one had not held until," Pum rumbled for a bit, "arrived, it would have been," rumble, "difficult for you."

"I expect so," Jake chortled. "What now?"

"Now we will be escorted to a place where we can talk," rumble, "unencumbered." Pum waved his Zip-Lok-shrouded right arm.

Patty raised her hand. "Well done, Pum. We are grateful," and lowered it as she shut off the microphone.

"Your majesty, thanks," Pum replied. "This one is glad security is ... tight, and assistance arrived," rum-rumble, "quickly."

As Pum and Jake were led away, they walked past groups of guards heading back down their trail. Patty felt a chill. "I'm glad we're up here," she murmured.

"For now," Daichi said, watching the monitors intently. "That's a big ship down there. They have a lot of territories to defend."

"Any more thoughts on where you'll want me to drop you?" Patty asked. "It all depends on what happens with Jake, of course. You may not even need to deploy." Patty stopped herself from babbling - her nerves felt on fire - and took a slow breath.

Daichi's hand patted her shoulder reassuringly. "Jake pointed out four tertiary locks on your recon images, close to the aft starboard corner. We were going to try there first, but since I've seen that damaged dock at the bow. It looks to be a more ... attractive approach. Do you have any readings from it? How hot is it?"

Patty brought up a scan from navigation. Freya's special coating revealed the whole spectrum of emissions. Sections of the dock still glowed in the infrared, and there were enough gamma radiation emissions to kill you if you stayed long enough. The bow of the mothership was hot, hot enough to discourage habitation and maybe guards, except for a cursory glance.

"Oh, that's not too bad," Lily said as she leaned over Patty's seat and examined the display, "for a quick visit. Good idea. I don't like the idea of fighting our way through a wall of those guys."

"They have certainly increased their level of security, but we expected that." Daichi looked as passive as Alan had been when Patty first retrieved him, while he watched Jake's progress on the monitor, soaking it in. They reached the stern and began to descend a series of switch-backed stairs. At every landing, aliens in p-suits, armored, regular and in their version of the trusty Zip-Lok, gathered to watch Pum and Jake, being escorted under the billowing checkered flag.

They watched quietly as Jake stopped; he turned the last corner and caught sight of the brightly lit aft dock. Three stories of windows and balconies arched above the flight deck. Two boxy transport ships rose to the flight deck on an elevator from below. A squadron of fighters were having last minute checks carried out by teams of p-suited figures.

"Looks like we're pulling quite a crowd," Jake said, panning slowly around. The balconies were filling up with the curious, and two lines of guards formed up, hip-to-hip, with their swords drawn. "I'm glad Pum talked me out of the holographic fireworks display program. They all look a little on edge," Jake joked. He sounded amused, but Patty's stomach twisted.

Six left-handed aliens, escorted by an honor guard of twenty-four, met Jake's party at a large airlock. It looked to Patty like a prisoner exchange. The guards turned and marched away, and the new group of aliens ushered Pum and Jake inside. *Come into my parlor said the spider to the fly. This feels so wrong.* The lock closed and air began to flood the compartment. Patty could almost taste it, warm and moist.

The inner door slid open, and she saw the aliens directing Pum and Jake through into the changing room. The layout was almost identical to the smaller one Patty used when she snuck aboard the great ship. They lost one feed when Jake removed his helmet. The second cut off when Jake began to remove his p-suit, although his body's physical data still streamed in. Suddenly Jake's heart rate and blood pressure peaked. *What is happening?*

SECOND ATTEMPT

Pur'unnan did not know why she chose to dive under the assassin's blade until she was sliding across the debris-strewn floor. Jael'Dam, Bumurnam FirstSon, was already on the charge, his blade out. The rest of her Hel'omi guards were at his heels. But they were too far away to help her. If she had run towards her protectors, she would have only been able to take a step or two before the hunter would have been on her. Scrambling to her feet, Pur'unnan took off down the length of the workshop that once had been used to build great ships of the sea; a spillway still divided the space in two.

The hunter had squeezed his way out from behind an equipment locker in a way that made Pur'unnan think his carapace was collapsible. That first swing with that serrated weapon had not been directed very accurately when he sprang from his hiding place, a lethal threat that was meant to set her running. She heard him curse as he slid to a halt, and turned to begin his pursuit, but she did not look behind to confirm it.

A corroded column, one of the dozens that held up the vaulted roof, stood a few spans to her left and Pur'unnan changed course. She caught it with her left hand, and her momentum swung her around into its shelter. She only needed to fend off the hunter's attack for a few more moments. Jael'Dam was nearly there. Once he got going, the Hel'omi could move very quickly. She was a little sorry they did not share the vital spark that Little Star and Stone Son did, but Pur'unnan relied on his consistency and care.

The wicked blade, formed with serrations and little hooks, shaved brown bubbled layers of corrosion from the column, exposing a silvery center. Pur'unnan danced back and around and then back the other way as a second blade, a thin poniard coated in blue-green appeared around the other side. *Poison!* She took a hurried step back.

The assassin made one more try at reaching around the column before dashing off. Jael'Dam and the rest of the Hel'omi were too close. Pur'unnan skipped to her right, her heart pounding, and watched the hunter run towards the seaward side of the building. Three doors opened and bright yellow cloaks of Darf'ornal poured in. The hunter skidded to a halt and tried to move off to his right, but Jael'Dam's blade caught him before he could take another step. Her Hel'omi's considerable momentum added to the power of his blow, dividing the assassin in two, a hand above his waist.

"A hunter? Here?" the Darf'ornal FirstMother's voice was distinctive, high and shrill. It was usually warm and filled with good humor, but there was no mistaking it, Delad'ron was here. The Darf'ornal FirstMother was as different to the Bar'Durrunnan FirstMother as night was from day. Delad'ron had a sharp mind, or she would never have risen to the position, but she was a mother first. Pur'unnan could not believe that Nor'Harrum had ever mated, let alone birthed.

The silvery metal visible on the corroded pillar drew Pur'unnan's eye. The assassin's blade that exposed the solid core of the post had missed her, but only just. It had nearly driven her onto a poisoned dagger. The shock of her near-death experience washed over her.

"The GreatMother is unhurt?" Tor'enal, her Hel'omi SecondSon, asked. While half of her Hel'omi had continued to chase the assassin, Tor'enal and the rest of her guards had stayed with Pur'unnan. They hovered around her, skittish and alert.

"Yes, Tor'enal, we are fine," Pur'unnan gasped. "Just a little out of breath is all." The SecondSon wanted to take her somewhere safe, but here was safe enough. "We must wait for Darf'ornal FirstMother. It would be rude to leave now."

"But understandable," Tor'enal grumbled his acknowledgment and set his charges in an arc around her as the lines of Darf'ornal yellow approached. They parted to reveal the FirstMother with an array of advisers around her as well as nursemaids for her current clutch of pouchlings.

"GreatMother, are you alright?" The squat FirstMother moved forward quickly, to see for herself.

"Yes, FirstMother, quite all right. The hunter did not touch me," Pur'unnan reassured her.

"That is good to hear." Delad'ron paused and looked towards the clutch of soldiers gathered around the dead assassin. "A hunter? Who would send a hunter?" Her eyes tracked around the building, holding focus on the place where Pur'unnan had performed her most recent experiment. The apparatus, half a workbench and a circular slab of the concrete floor, sat beside a hole of equal dimensions. Sounds from the work crew clearing the debris from the space below drifted out of the circular fissure.

The expected anger at the destruction of Darf'ornal property did not come. Pur'unnan was surprised to hear a chuff of laughter. *Delad'ron is different.* "Don't worry about making a mess in here, dearest. This place has not been used for nearly twenty orbits. The GreatMother did ask for a quiet corner." She huffed again and strolled towards the apparatus, a dull gray box, unremarkable but for the array of controls that pierced its shell.

"It flies?" the FirstMother asked. "Reports were garbled."

"Yes, FirstMother, though that was not our..." Pur'unnan began.

"It flies. Bar'Durrunnan must have heard." Delad'ron stopped and shook her head. "To dispatch a hunter and set it to kill a

GreatMother, that is ... unheard of," she growled and continued forward until she stood at the edge of the circular slab of concrete. "It flies ... without great engines."

"The principles are very different FirstMother," Pur'unnan began.

"But the results are the same. She flies." The FirstMother's serious and analytical demeanor fell away as she chuffed again. "Nor'Harrum must be very upset." She glanced back to where mothers gathered around the corpse, droning the dirge for the departed. "Not that you'd be able to prove that she sent that one." Delad'ron shook, expressing her revulsion. "So, your engine..."

"It is not an engine, as such," Pur'unnan tried to correct the FirstMother.

"The apparatus," Delad'ron waved away her explanation, "will it just fly in the air, or can it achieve orbit?" Delad'ron was genuinely excited.

"Orbit and more," Pur'unnan began.

"Payload?" Delad'ron interrupted as she toed the concrete slab.

Pur'unnan wondered if the FirstMother would let her finish. "Payload, as such, is almost irrelevant. The size of the ship is not as important as the systems it would need to keep its precious cargo intact."

"How big?" The analytical part of the FirstMother's sharp mind focused.

"You could build a ship that could tuck this building into one corner, and ... and the," Pur'unnan did not have a name for the apparatus except for the description of its function, a trans-dimensional resonant probe, "the apparatus would not be under stress. With the appropriate adjustments, the mass of the ship is immaterial."

Delad'ron looked up and around. The building was not the largest Darf'ornal used; the receding seas had left it isolated. It was an impressive structure, nonetheless. After surviving over a century and two sunstrikes, it was holding up remarkably well.

"We could build a ship that big." Her voice was not much more than a whisper. Pur'unnan imagined she could see the FirstMother adding up columns of figures in her head.

"It would bankrupt Darf'ornal to build a ship like that. It would never be an economic proposition. Each seafaring ship we make must be carefully balanced against the resources needed to construct it and the value the ship will bring to our clan. Your spaceship could not, would not be used for trade but to leave this world, to try and save ... to save some of us before it is too late."

"Yes, FirstMother, I..."

"Nor'Harrum would be livid!" Delad'ron's chuff broke into a full-throated laugh that surprised Pur'unnan. "We'll build two."

CHAPTER THIRTEEN

"Jake should be back on-line by now," Lily whispered, almost to herself.

"I'm sure he is all right. Be patient." Daichi breathed slowly.

Patty chafed as the seconds slowly accumulated, ambling through thirty seconds and then a minute, a minute and a half, two minutes. Patty concentrated on Jake's heartbeat, which was dropping to a more normal rate. Suddenly Jake's drawl came over the speakers.

"...well, I should damn well think so. Are you okay, Pum?" Jake asked as a shaky picture appeared on the monitor; Jake looked into the lens. One eye was bruised, puffy and a trace of blood outlined the curve of his right nostril. The picture panned rapidly around as Jake settled the camera unit onto his shoulder. "Are you there, your majesty?"

Patty's hand snapped into the air as she opened the mike. "We most certainly are. What has happened to you?" Patty asked.

"A misunderstanding of sorts. Call it an ID check with extreme prejudice. Pum copped the worst of it. I thought they were going to take his head off." Pum turned to the lens and bowed. A cream bandage covered his throat.

"Your majesty, they needed to ascertain this one was," rumble-rum, "there is no word, this one apologizes. They," rumble, "check to see if this one has ... changed. This one," rum-rumble-rum, "is unaltered."

"Are you all right, Jake?" Patty felt frustrated; they were too far away to do any good.

"Right enough, your majesty. Caught me by surprise is all.

I'm surprised that any of us survived really. Tell Lily something failed. I think. But I am alive."

"Well, you tell them," *A failure?* Patty looked at Lily who frowned and chewed at her thumbnail. From the look in her eyes, Patty could tell Lily blamed herself. She had wired up the bomb Jake carried, and it had failed when he tried to trigger it. Plan A, executed much earlier than Patty expected, was a fail. Her heart skipped a beat at the thought that she had nearly lost Jake. *And he sounds so calm. I would have peed myself.*

"Tell them yourself," Jake said. "I'm putting you on speaker."

Patty almost gagged. "Pum!"

"Your majesty?" he replied with a bow.

"We ... are ... displeased." Patty tried to sound imperious by spacing out her words.

"Your majesty?"

"Our Traffic Control has been injured," she answered angrily.

Pum blinked and bowed, "A little."

"Have more care with my emissary. Anything done to him we consider done to ourselves," Patty instructed.

"Your majesty, it is a time of great stress," Pum tried to explain. "Allowances must be made. Things have settled already. Prince," Pum rumbled the name in a formal and long-winded fashion, his right hand carved precise swirls, "is ready to escort us within." He bowed and turned, pointing to the leader of the left-handers. All had richly embroidered tabards. The one Pum indicated who stood half a step in front of the others, had the most baroque of designs atop an embossed deep red fabric. Pum's tabard, though artful, was much less sophisticated. Pum bowed, and Jake did too, Patty guessed, as all they saw from Jake's feed was the floor.

Chills coursed through Patty as Jake left the airlock's changing room and turned right into the scuffed cream corridor. Two lines of guards held back the curious of all types. Those endless corridors had invaded her dreams too many times for Patty to be at all comfortable seeing them again. Jake and Pum followed their escort into a small bare room almost directly beside the big lock.

The high caste alien began rum-rumbling to - or rather from Patty's perspective - at Pum. Her emissary seemed outclassed by an order of magnitude by this imperious Gray, and Patty could see him buckle and bow.

"EngStand! Or nearest facsimile thereof," Jake insisted. "Stop browbeating our boy. He's here to ease the introductions. Talk to me, buddy. I know you know how." Jake stepped to Pum's side. "Our illustrious queen watches these proceedings. You guys blew your chance at earning my Queen's trust at L5 and were punished for it."

The Gray backed off and seemed confused by Jake's unbowed stance. "Traaaffic Control is known," he said, making it sound like an accusation. The hairs on the back of Patty's neck began to rise. She did not like this alien at all. He was shorter than his companions but had the posture of one that looked down on everyone. Even Pum would meet Patty's eyes; this one would not look up at Jake. "Your queen watches safely from afar." *Disdain.*

"We watch as if perched upon my emissary's shoulder!" Patty growled and watched the alien start. Her words were delayed but by less than a second. From his response, Patty guessed he thought Jake's queen was much further away. The alien re-gathered himself quickly though.

"It pleases our," rumble, "queen that you come in supplication."

"Supplication! Indeed! Leave, Jake. Leave now." Jake strode forward the moment her words arrived, much to the alien's distress. She could hear Pum's alarmed rumbling. The door began to slide open.

"Traaaffic Control! Your majesty, please excuse him," Pum called and tugged on Jake's sleeve. "His mastery of human tongue is not..." Pum rattled on.

A familiar face flashed past as Jake turned to face Pum. "Stop! Jake." Patty was not sure if she shouted or whispered.

"I see him." Jake panned a little to the left, and there stood

Christopher Balke between two minders in red; a gray tabard sporting a blue dot covered his nakedness. He looked disinterested in the activity around him, his eyes flat and unresponsive. Patty's heart sank. It was a lot to read from a wide shot, but she knew the aliens had treated her father the same way they had treated Alan, only they seemed to have completed the procedure.

"Your," rumble, "queen went to so much trouble to retrieve her younger sibling," the high caste Gray said as he emerged from the room behind Pum. "When we discovered we had another related to her line, we thought it would be an incentive for your," rum-rumble, "queen to come to us."

"Oh, I'm so sorry," Lily whispered into Patty's ear. Daichi's hand squeezed her shoulder. Patty did not know what she felt, fear, anger, surprise, love, joy, pain, all swirled around inside her. *They have Dad! They'll have Mom too, I bet.* Suddenly Pum's behavior seemed childishly naïve. This new alien's attitude was little different to the one revealed briefly at L5. *What had Jake called him? Oh yeah, Prince Rumble-Bum. A meeting to discuss peace, yeah right. With Dad dangling as a tasty inducement on the side.*

"Jake. Look after him. Wait for me. Tell them We come." Patty muted the mike. Anger burned in her gut. Her hands shook. She knew she was not thinking clearly. She remembered feeling like this when Alan had been taken from her. Patty tried to breathe through it.

"That's a bad idea." Jake's transmissions cut off; not even his life readings were being transmitted.

"We're going in," Patty growled and peeled Freya away from her holding pattern high above the conflict, spiraling down into the gap between 'roid and mothership. Her blood still boiled. All she could see was her father's wretched condition, but her heart had cooled enough for her to think a little straighter. *Jake's probably right; this is a bad idea.*

Patty tried to let go of her turbulent emotions to focus on the controls the discipline needed to fly Freya down to the battered mothership. It had seen better days. The epicenter of ruin was a crater of crushed and melted material fifteen meters below the entrance to the dock. Devastation radiated outward. Sharp lines of fire had carved cardinal points at random intervals across the blunt prow.

Freya slipped into the darkness of the damaged dock and hovered above the burnt chaos. Freya's sensitive skin soaked up the faint reflected light, the infrared, she even utilized the ionizing radiation to construct an increasingly detailed map of the space around her. Waves of heat and crushing concussive forces had spilled in here. Tornadoes of radioactive fire had scoured the dock. Not a single gantry or balcony remained fixed in its original position. The flight deck was a twisted mess. Four or five ships - there was too much damage to tell exactly how many ships were there - had been tossed around like blow-torched playthings in a child's toy box. Within a minute, Patty was able to pick out two or three possible landing sites and as much as she itched to get inside and reclaim her father - *and Mother too, please* - it was worth waiting for Freya to get a clearer picture.

"Is that movement?" Daichi pointed to the left, a corner somewhat protected by the twisted remains of a blocky transport ship. *Yes!* Patty breathed through the fright.

Lily leaned in. "Repair crew? Could mean an intact airlock. Can your scope pick them out?"

"No, too dark. But we can slip in a little closer." Patty crabbed Freya across the twisted flight deck and began to edge forward, sliding past shapes in the darkness. Freya coasted on, Patty's eyes glued to the navigation display; the view through the canopy was shadowed inky blackness.

"Bilateral," Daichi breathed as they watched the infrared blobs move about, "human." Then Patty saw it too. The aliens did not walk like that. She examined their flight path, chose a small piece of almost level decking beside the crushed starboard bow of a transport ship, and placed Freya gently down. The landing gear locked in place. *Coming, Daddy.*

"Prepare for vacuum," Patty announced as she grabbed her

helmet and carefully seated it to the rings on her p-suit. It was another discipline that calmed and cooled Patty's racing thoughts. *Racing thoughts can wait. Do this now, or you're dead.* After receiving all-clears from everyone, Patty began the cycle, and when everyone had disembarked, she armed Freya's newly installed alarms.

"Mommy'll be back soon, sweety," Patty said, priming the security routine.

"Sounds serious." Freya's new audio response made Patty smile. Using Cicely's vocal signature as a template was a perfect touch.

"It is. Lock up tight. We'll be back as soon as we can," Patty instructed Freya. That phrase set the defense system to the highest alert level.

"Roger that." A red *ARMED* light flashed in the upper right corner of the screen. Patty climbed out, closed the canopy and felt the locks *thunk* into place.

From the moment her feet hit the deck, Patty felt fear rising through her, an increasing chill as if her boots had lost their insulation. Daichi led the way. Alan wanted to advance with him, weapon drawn, but at Patty's touch, he sheathed his sword - although his hand remained on its hilt - and he assumed his usual position. Lily crowded in behind, gripping Patty's belt.

The footing was uneven as they edged around the wrecked transport and the stout truss that retained much of its integrity. *Over-engineered but strong.* Patty had seen it repeatedly in the mothership. She took a sip from her p-suit's supply to keep dryness from her mouth.

An armored shadow stepped out of the deeper darkness, toting an armful of military hardware. The shadow carried an electric gauss gun, the only projectile weapon Patty knew of that could be fired reliably in a vacuum or atmosphere. *More weapons from out of the archives.* It confused Patty to be thankful someone had stashed all these arms away, and yet chilled that populist political powers had done just that. Daichi held still, and Patty quickly reached out and clutched Alan's arm, keeping him immobile. The shadow's shoulders slumped, and the barrel dropped. Patty sighed with relief. The shade picked its way across the debris to Daichi and touched visors for a brief exchange before stepping back and taking guard. Daichi worked on his wrist comm as he turned to Patty.

The infrared comm band the heavily armed shadow used was low-res but clear enough if you had line-of-sight. Patty passed the information on to Lily and adjusted Alan's comm. "...we've cleared a space around to the left and in further. Günter will be pleased to see you." The shadow had a woman's voice. "I'll be back when I've finished this sweep." She ushered them into the dark with that monstrous gun. As Patty walked past her, the shadow took a step closer and extended an armored glove. "Glad you're with us, Colonel Balke. Gina said you'd checked in." Patty's hand was engulfed but not crushed.

"Oh, please. It's just Patty."

"Marni, Marni Shafir. Been catching your uploads. Fan-bloody-tastic. I'll be back in a bit." The shadow stepped back and gave a snappy salute before returning to the darkness.

Colonel? That felt wrong too. Everyone is here fighting a war. I'm just trying to get my parents out. What about all the other mothers, fathers, sisters and brothers in there? What about them? Who's going to save them?

Lily stumbled, and Patty snapped out of her reverie in time to save her from crashing onto the treacherous deck. "Damn, one-gee," Lily panted as she accepted Patty's assistance.

"Are you okay?" Patty asked.

"How we evolved under this load, I'll never know," Lily complained. She shrugged, took a deep breath and straightened her back.

"It's a bit more than one-gee actually," Patty informed her.

"Thanks. I really needed to hear that." Lily gripped Patty's belt again, and they moved on. Daichi led them through the burned dock until a blackened wall turned them to the right. The twisted remains of an outer airlock door stood open, and Daichi squeezed through, the rest following.

A dim light showed two space-suited figures examining the inner door. One turned and waved them closer. "Greetings, I'm Günter Drake, and this is Shun Jiang. Marni pinged us we had company." He extended his gloved hand and shook Daichi's hand and then Patty's. "We're glad you're here." He reached out and shook Lily's hand, nearly spilling her onto the ground.

"Damn it." Lily straightened slowly. "You're a Belter. How are you coping?"

Günter chuckled and slapped his armored chest. "These are powered Exo-suits. Couldn't stand up with all this gear if it wasn't." Lily cursed under her breath.

"We didn't expect to find anyone here." Patty glanced at the airlock door. It bulged outward slightly. They would never be able to get it open without causing explosive decompression inside.

"We flew over from the Bright Damsel after she was hit, using just our p-suit thrusters. We don't have much." He pointed at a bag beside the door. "Just a couple of NNEMPs. Don't know if they'll do much damage to this beast of a ship but we had to try."

"How's your progress with this lock?" Lily asked as she let go of Patty's belt and carefully stepped forward.

"Not very good, we were just thinking about trying to find another way inside." Günter shook his head. "This thing is way over-engineered. Damnably solid."

"Let's have a look." Lily mimed rolling up her sleeves and moved to the bulging door. She staggered and casually accepted Daichi's arm to balance herself, her concentration focused on the door. Lily began to walk around it, her hand tracing the straining outline. She chuckled and hummed as she examined it.

"How are the rest of the squadron doing?" Günter inquired as he glanced through the broken outer door, on guard.

"As well as you might expect," Patty replied. "Last we saw, they were down to five ships, but they were still giving the aliens what-for." Patty hoped she sounded positive. She did not feel it.

Günter leaned to one side, peering into the dark and swayed back before turning to Patty. "Good. That's better than I expected."

"You call yourselves Belters, and you didn't bring a Zip-E-Lok?" Lily stepped back and reached into her bag. Her left knee sagged.

"We grabbed what we could when we left The Damsel." Shun helped Daichi ease Lily to the airlock floor. "We have an A and B size, but the C and D were missing from the kit."

"War is hell." Lily pulled a flat package from her bag and brandished it above her head. "I'm gonna need a hand with this." She began unfolding the parcel. Patty had used a size-A Zip-E-Lok as part of her flight training but had never seen a big one deployed. The size-A was not much larger than a big sleeping bag; the size-D could hold a dozen people. Designed to aid the entry of a stricken ship, the Zip-E-Lok was an open-ended inflatable bag. Daichi helped Lily unfold the emergency airlock while Shun began spraying a layer of fast-acting foam glue around the doorway. In minutes, they had flaps from the large plastic Zip-E-Lok pressed firmly into the foam. Out-gasses from the expanding foam began to inflate tubes that ran along the seams, turning the shapeless bag into a large transparent box.

Lily stepped back proudly, her arms crossed over her chest even as she sucked in deep breaths. Patty could hardly believe Lily was enjoying herself despite having to work in high-gee. All Patty could feel was fear, as if she was treading water in it. Every so often, a cold wave of terror would smack her in the face, triggering a panicked breath. *You're going back inside there. Face it.* Patty sipped from her p-suit and took slow breaths. "It would probably be quicker if we were all inside before inflating it." She held open the sealable sleeve that served as an airlock. "Is that shadow with a big gun back yet?"

"Marni will be here any minute." Günter waved to Shun, who followed Daichi and Lily into the Zip-E-Lok. "After you, ma'am." Günter shouldered his gauss gun and glanced through the broken outer door again. Patty slipped through the Zip-E-Lok's airlock. It was nothing more than an overlap of the end wall with seals and valves at either end. There was no atmospheric recycling; gasses in the airlock were purged with every use. With a limited supply, Lily was correct to have them all in the Zip-E-Lok when she filled it.

Günter climbed into the lock as a shadow slipped through the outer door. Marni sealed up the Zip-E-Lok behind her and Lily opened the valve. "What's the internal pressure?" Lily asked. "This door should pop back into place once we're equalized."

Lily's question shook Patty from her reverie. "A bit above one atmosphere, I'd guess." *And warm and sticky but that would not matter to Lily. Breathe through this girl.*

"I'm so glad you're here," Marni's gentle slap to her shoulder startled Patty. "We never expected to see you, since The Ice Princess was so far away."

"Does that mean we have their FTL drive?" Günter asked as he stepped in front of Patty; his armored bulk was intimidating.

She patted the black gem mounted to the front of her p-suit. "I'd be silly to deny it. Yes, we've cracked most of it; there are still some ... problems about moving mass much greater than Freya but..."

Günter smacked one fist into the other, "Details! FTL! We can finally reach the stars! That's made this whole bloody mess almost worthwhile." He checked a reading on his wrist comm. "And you!" Günter's fists rested on his hips, and he let out a guffaw.

"Günter wouldn't exhale on a suffocating Earther until I made him watch your uploads," Marni chuckled.

"Colonel Balke, you made me remember that we were all Earthers not that far back in our family tree and that they can still breed 'em smart enough to get out of that gravity-well," Günter sighed. "We don't need Earth for much anymore these days, but it wouldn't be long before we would have to come cap-in-hand to those buggers. Rather do that to the damn Corporates than some interstellar bullies. If they get a foothold ... well we're here to see they don't. This is The Belt. This is *our* place, so this is our fight too."

Lily cracked open her visor and took a breath from the cold air. "Patty and her intrepid team are here to pull your nuts out of the fire," Lily chuckled.

She's actually having fun, Patty realized. Lily took a step, and shoulder charged the bowed door. She bounced, staggering back into Daichi's arms. The doors held fast. Marni and Shun took a three-count, and when their power-assisted shoulders hit the door, it clunked back into place. A blue light awoke on the panel beside the door. Lily pressed home the button below the indicator, and the doors retracted.

CHAPTER FOURTEEN

"Set that off and get back here as quickly as you can," Patty told them. "Freya can only hold two or three, but I can shuttle back and forth to ... to wherever." Patty's throat felt dry despite drinking her fill. *You're gonna need to pee soon too. Wish I had some rosin for my sweaty hands.*

"That's mighty kind of you," Günter said as he glanced at Marni and Shun. "None of us in the first squadron expected to hold out until the rest of the fleet arrived, and when we flew over from The Damsel, we didn't expect to be able to get off this ship either."

Patty's heart felt as if it broke.

"We plan to make a rumpus one way or another and that don't sit well with planting this thing and sneaking away." Günter smiled over Patty's shoulder at Daichi and Lily in their gray tabards. "We'll leave the covert stuff for your other team." He stuck out an armored paw. "I'm glad you're here. I know I wouldn't have been here if I hadn't watched you taking the fight to them." Marni and Shun nodded their agreement. Patty shook his hand and felt like a complete fraud.

"Besides," Marni extended her armored paw, "savin' the Earthers' butts will bring respect and honor to us Belters." She pulled Patty close as the handshake turned into a bruising hug. "You look fantastic!" Marni whispered before dropping her.

"Get back here if you can." It sounded empty to Patty's ears.

The internal door hissed open. One flickering light at the starboard end of the corridor shed barely enough illumination to show that the passage was empty. Patty hugged Shun before the Belters slipped into the hallway but felt nothing but guilt.

They're here because of me? They're planning to die because of me.
Cold nausea crawled around inside her belly. She watched them
disappear around the corner before looking down the dark
passage she would take with Alan. A flickering light in the
distance presaged fully lit and busy corridors.

Lily picked at a piece of lint stuck to Daichi's shoulder and
brushed the gray tabard straight. Daichi's blades were wrapped
in cardboard tubes, the bomb in a brown box at his bare feet. She
turned and stopped when she saw the expression on Patty's
face. "What's wrong?"

"What's wrong? Did you hear Günter? He's going off to die.
He's going off to die because of me." Patty wanted to sit down,
but the floor seemed too far away.

"There is a big difference between causing someone's death
and inspiring a warrior to do their best before the end." Daichi
frowned. "This must be confusing for you. While I know, you
will do your very best to get Lily and myself off this ship, I do not
expect to return either."

Patty felt her heart sag. *This was a suicide mission. Always has
been. A Hail-Mary pass.* "I feel … it feels wrong to… I want to get
my parents and scram out of here while Günter and the rest of
the Belters are sacrificing…"

"Sacrificing their lives, not because of you but because you
showed them it was necessary, that even a young woman could
tweak their enemy's nose. You made them feel guilty for being
so afraid, so cowardly." Daichi chuckled. "And I'm sure you'll
sow more than enough chaos getting your parents out to cover
both operations." Daichi glanced down the corridor where the
Belters had gone.

"Hey," Lily said in a boisterous manner. "If those guys want
to take an honor guard with them, like, I'm all for it, but I'm
planning to take you up on the offer of a ride off this fat bird."
Lily stood with her hands on her hips, grinning. "I didn't go to
the trouble of building a timer if I wanted to be at ground-zero
when it went off." She punched Patty's shoulder. "I expect we'll
be back in an hour, with a little luck. Be here, or I'll fly Freya out

myself." It felt a little better hearing the bravado in Lily's words and seeing the certainty in her eyes, but it could not lift Patty's heart.

"Patty, you are a part of a team." Daichi's eyes held her. "Your task is to distract the aliens at their highest level. If you can extract your parents, it will be a bonus that no one would deny you. I will have a sharp eye out for my niece."

"And I'll be looking for Hestia's crew," Lily added. "We'll all be looking for loved ones. Don't feel guilty about that." Lily looked Patty in the eyes and smiled warmly. "Get in there and be yourself. That'll be more than enough." Her eyes darted about, inspecting Patty from head to toe and back again. "Turn on the flag, Alan. I wanna see how you look together." Alan flicked a switch at his hip, and a projector lit on his shoulder; a checkered flag snapped in a holographic breeze above their heads. "Great. You guys look great!" Satisfied, Lily turned to Daichi, "Ready?" At Daichi's nod, she knelt and lifted the box into her arms, rising slowly but certainly to her feet. "Give 'em hell, sweetie, and we'll see you back here soon." Lily took a step back and examined Patty's black and gold tabard, a smile lighting her eyes. "Looks good on you." She staggered into the corridor with Daichi a step or two behind her.

Their momentum dragged Patty from the airlock changing room into the corridor. *Lily's right: Alan does look handsome in black.* She was not comfortable wearing the black and gold tabard, but if it did not restrict her movements, she recognized it as a significant symbol for the aliens. Someone on The Ice Princess had worked very hard assembling the images embossed into the black silk-like cloth: children's faces set before mountains, jungles, beaches, and iconic architecture of their homelands, and setting the program for the power-loom in the corner of The Ice Princess's mess. The rugs and hangings made The Ice Princess feel comfortable. She wished she had time to examine her tabard in detail but had noticed the Eiffel Tower, Uluru, as well as L4 and Tycho City amongst the images. The gold circle and the concentric rings were inscribed with greetings in every tongue and script. Such carefully detailed work had particular significance to the aliens. Pum's response to the higher ranked left-hander and his intricate tabard seemed almost instinctive. She brushed her tabard straight and glanced back into the changing room. She did not like leaving their p-suits, but they were too bulky to carry and still project a little dignity. And they *were* going to have to fight.

"Putting on a good show is half the task when dealing with these creatures." Jake's encouraging words echoed in Patty's head. "They'd make bad poker players. Couldn't bluff if their life depended on it. Watch their off hand. They talk with it."

Alan drew his newly forged weapon and swept it back and forth; the saber's stiff blade cut the air with a thin shriek. He stamped forward, practicing his own kata, his sword flashing in the intermittent light, and then he retreated to Patty's side, using precise and lightning-fast defensive strokes. His blade produced a silky sigh as he returned it to his scabbard, punctuated with a metallic click. His left hand swept into the air, his fingers flashing a message. "It is good. Balanced. Not as heavy. This one is faster now." He bounced on his toes and stretched his shoulders and neck.

Yes, it was time to go. Patty swallowed nervously, settled Lady Estelle on her hip and walked into the central corridor, into the core of the ship, her heart pounding, her thoughts whirling through her head, too fast to hold.

CHAPTER FIFTEEN

At the first cross-corridor, they surprised a single guard who immediately went on the attack. Alan bulled past Patty and dealt with the alien before she had a chance to draw Lady Estelle. *How did you miss that cross-corridor? Look where you're going, or you won't get there, girl!* Patty tried to quell the rising tide of fear inside her, but she could not stop her hands from shaking. *Focus on what's between you and your goal!* The memory of her father, standing disinterested in the bustling activity surrounding him, flashed into Patty's mind. Anger swirled inside her, displacing some of her fear. She clenched her jaw and moved past the bleeding corpse, onward to where the corridor's lighting was undamaged.

"That was a mistake, I think," Patty said. She did not expect Alan to give her a reply, but she knew he was listening. "We don't want to fight our way into this ship."

"Will be challenges." Alan's quick fingers rose in reply.

"Yes." Pum had to hold his own against a guard until another negotiator arrived. "We will have to fight, but I'm sick of killing. I don't want to do it that way. I don't think we should." She looked up at the flag. "This is supposed to be a flag of truce. We can't behave like an invading army."

"Small army," Alan signed.

Patty stopped as a chuckle bubbled in her belly. Alan's face was smooth. He was calm. *Did he mean to crack a joke?* "Nonetheless. We should try to ... to hold until someone comes."

"No kill," Alan confirmed.

"Yes. No kill."

Alan nodded, and a frown slowly creased his forehead.

"Harder."

"Yes. I guess. More like sparring practice," Patty reassured him as she led the way towards the lit corridor. Patty could see movement in the cross-corridor ahead.

Fighting the next aliens they encountered was nothing like practice and twice as hard as sparring. From the moment the guards at the next intersection saw them walking out of the gloom, the aliens linked together and charged. For the first few exchanges, it was all Patty could do to keep their bright blades away from her skin. They were not pulling their stokes. They wanted blood. And then there were the moments, the openings that would have let her finish this bout, the openings she let pass.

Two steps back became four. This is no good. They're forcing us back farther and farther away from the light of the cross-corridor. No one is going to see us back here.

"Need to change this!" Alan's left hand shouted. He was right. They could battle away in this dim corridor for hours, and no one would notice. One small nod was all it took for Alan to go onto the attack. He stepped inside his opponent's reach, turned and struck down, his heavy blade flashing. Patty stepped across, defending her brother, expecting to be covered in blood as the guard's hand was severed at the wrist. Surprisingly, only the alien's heavy blade spun to the ground.

A small opening presented itself to Patty as the line of two staggered. She lunged, piercing the guard's wrist. She did not wait for the blade to hit the floor; her blood smeared tip hovered before his eyes. The aliens staggered back against the wall groaning, separating and slumping to the floor.

"Do you know who WE are?" Patty demanded as imperiously as she could. Their shiny black eyes darted back and forth between the tip of Patty's blade, her eyes, then up at the billowing flag. First one nodded, and then the other joined in. They were afraid ... and something else. *You've seen that look before, on L2 after I defeated...* Patty's mind shied from the memory. *The aliens had all been very afraid of her that day. Even*

516

Giuseppe had looked scared. Confusion and fear. There was something else that made them bend their knees that day, something almost instinctive. The memory of Pum kowtowing to the high caste alien flashed through her mind. *Whatever it was, they did yield. Would these two do the same?* She didn't want to have to look after prisoners.

"Do you submit?" Patty asked.

Alan's fingers flashed, "Surrender!" and something else Patty could not read. The aliens flinched and dropped their gaze to the floor. They began to rumble, and Alan stepped back his left arm swinging out, moving Patty back too. The aliens regained their feet only to step into an elaborate bow that put them on their knees, their heads down and there they waited.

Patty knew she needed to do something, but what? How could she acknowledge their actions? Have they really surrendered? What did that mean anyway? Was there a Geneva Convention for interspecies war? Would she have to guard them? If I can get them to sit down and talk for a few minutes, it might be enough.

"Should not leave them behind us." Alan sheathed his blade. He flexed his shoulders and stretched his back. "They are yours now. Yes?"

"I guess, but I'm not sure what that means." Patty glanced up the corridor; their presence had not been noticed. She took an involuntary step back as Alan stepped up to the aliens. His hand flashed and lifted the lime green striped tabard from the first alien's shoulders. He tossed the fabric in his hands for a second before draping it, inside-out, over the alien's head. The tabard was not lined, and the inverted warp and weft exposed a pale reflection of its design, covered with dangling loose threads. *At least I'll be able to tell them apart.* Alan flipped over the second alien's tabard and pulled a bandage from the kit at his hip. The alien seemed surprised but did not refuse treatment. He bobbed and bowed but kept his hand still.

Patty kept watch as Alan inspected the first alien's wrist. His blow had been made with the back of his blade. The alien rumbled something and let out a small screech as Alan turned and flexed its wrist. He stepped back and collected their heavy weapons from the floor and presented them to Patty.

"Return their honor. They are ... us. Team." Alan signed.

Patty looked down at the bright-edged swords and a chill swept down her spine. *Give them back their swords? Really?* Alan seemed as confident and determined as she had ever seen him. *All right, if you think it's the right thing to do.*

She hefted the sword by the hilt and weighed it in the air for a moment. *How did Alan manage to fight with a weapon like this? It's so heavy. How am I going to do this?* And then she remembered her father. He could be all military precision when he wanted, even if he was in his bathrobe. Her present had been wrapped, hidden in her parent's wardrobe for a week before her birthday. She both had loved and hated Alan for discovering it. Knowing about her gift had been almost painful. Her parents had waited for her to unwrap the present, but her father had lifted Lady Estelle from her silk-lined case and presented the sword to her formally. *Now, what did he say?* She carefully changed her grip, holding the alien's weighty blade horizontally, one hand on the cross-guard, the other near the well-honed tip and stepped forward, presenting the hilt to the alien she'd bested only moments before.

"Arise, Sir," Patty thought quickly. *May as well start at the beginning of the alphabet,* "Sir Abe. Take this weapon and use it with honor against those who would oppress the weak and helpless." Her father had delivered a longer speech with more jokes, but that was the gist of it. Patty's throat closed, and she struggled to look the alien in the eyes as his head rose.

His eyes flashed from Patty's to the blade and back again. She saw it happen. A thought expanded behind his shiny black eyes and spread down through his body making him stand a little straighter. His head cocked before nodding, and he began a shuffling bow that ended with his chitinous right arm extended, his bandaged hand, segmented palm up. Patty laid the hilt into his hand and stepped back. She could not help but drop her hand to Lady Estelle's pommel as she retreated. *What would he do?*

Abe gazed at his blade with apparent awe and then at Patty with reverence. He bowed, not as elaborately as she had seen Pum perform but without hesitation and he sheathed his weapon. He rested, attentive to her, but his eyes darted up and down the corridor as if he stood watch. *Is he really my soldier now?*

The second alien, now dubbed Ben, tried to outdo Abe with his enthusiastic bow, nearly tripping himself over in the process. He was like a puppy, eager for her attention. Patty smiled and took a slow breath. This was much better than having to guard surly prisoners. *But if they are my soldiers, they need to know her rules. They always seem to be itching for a fight. Can they do anything else?*

"Abe, Ben, come here." Patty illustrated her words with simple gestures. If they did not understand her words, they could read her body language. She had their attention. "We are going on. We go to meet the queen." She pointed to the rippling flag. *Did they understand?* Patty continued and tried to keep it simple. "When we meet .... resistance, we fight. Surrender, yes. Submit, yes. Kill no. Do you understand?" Patty snapped her gaze between their bright eyes.

Rumble, "No," rumble, "kill." Abe's voice was very deep, and Patty had to strain to pick out the words.

"Yes. Good. No kill." Patty pointed again to the fluttering flag. "Parley. We are here for negotiations. No kill."

Abe and Ben exchanged glances and rumbles. "No kill." Rumble, "Submit, yes." Abe confirmed with a nod.

"Submit. No kill." Ben nodded enthusiastically and after glancing up at the flag, bowed deeply.

Abe took the lead, a step ahead of Ben. They paused and checked the cross-corridor they had guarded minutes before. With a nod from Alan, Abe led them into the dark corridor.

A FORMAL COMPLAINT

Pur'unnan tried to hide the elation that surged through her when she heard the Great Council deliver their findings.

"The Great Council rules that although the aforementioned apparatus has overlapping fields-of-function with Clan Bar'Durrunnan's fusion technology, the apparatus uses concepts and application sufficiently different from Clan Bar'Durrunnan. The Clan may hold domain over a specific device, not over the whole field. Fusion powered space fight is Clan Bar'Durrunnan's domain not space flight by other means. Therefore, this council rules to dismiss the complaint.

"As for the matter of so-called airlock design, Clan Darf'ornal's submitted designs, used in their underwater vehicles, show sufficient congruency with Bar'Durrunnan current usage we are surprised they have not brought a countersuit. Complaint dismissed."

Pur'unnan bowed respectfully as the Councilors retreated to their chambers. She knew she would have to work with Clan Bar'Durrunnan and did not want to antagonize them any more than she had to.

FirstMother Delad'ron had no such inhibitions and gave a full-throated cough at the retreating Bar'Durrunnan officials - the Bar'Durrunnan FirstMother had not attended the announcement of the Council's ruling. Delad'ron handed her sucking pouchling to a nurse and drew Pur'unnan with her toward their carriage.

"I'm glad that is all over, and we can get back to work," the FirstMother declared.

CHAPTER SIXTEEN

Patty was glad she had two extra blades at the next intersection; four guards held that post, and they charged out of the lit cross-corridor into the semi-darkness just as Abe and Ben had done. Patty checked with Alan who stood poised on the balls of his feet, his eyes sparkled, and a hint of a smile brushed the corners of his mouth. He was ready. Patty flexed her shoulder and wrist. *Here we go again.*

The initial exchange was brisk, and they had to retreat to absorb the energy of the guards' charge. She was pleased Abe and Ben worked well together, presenting a strong defense. Ben's broad back was a warm presence against her, and they bumped and jostled against each other as they retreated a step and then another before holding their ground.

The guards in yellow tabards worked as a well-practiced team, too well practiced. The presence of Patty, a left-hander, in the center of the line threw their routines out of kilter. It was not long before an opening presented itself. Patty lunged, taking her adversary's exposed wrist. Alan was barely a beat behind her, stepping inside and using the flat of his blade to slap his opponent about the head. The linked pair went down howling. While Alan held them in place, Patty flanked the second pair, and her attack with the flat of Lady Estelle's blade sent the duo reeling into the wall.

Abe and Ben rumbled enthusiastically at the four guards, and within moments, Alan was turning tabards, and Patty was handing back their swords, this time to Cedric, Dan, Ed, and Felix. Patty took a deep breath as she inspected her growing entourage. *Now you have six.* There were subtle differences between the striations on their smooth brows. Their engraved forearms were individual works of art. She was already having difficulty telling them apart, except for Cedric. He was the oldest of them. From what Patty could see, the engravings on his forearm extended up his arm and across his chest. He was only slightly slower than his companions, but it took more out of him to keep up. And now he was wounded. Patty took the last bandage from her belt pouch and reached for his dripping hand.

"Grrrr," he rumbled, "Mootthhh..." Cedric dropped to one knee and tried to pull his hand away. Patty had a steely expression and a good grip on one horny finger.

"Give me that." Patty pulled his hand closer. He submitted. The wound was not deep, but she could have done serious damage. He may never hold a sword again. "Who treats your wounds, normally?" The bandage would seal the wound and promote healing, but it could not reconnect severed nerves or tendons.

Rumble, "Mothers."

"Well, I guess I'm your mother now. Hold still." She sealed the bandage in place, cradling the chitinous hand in her own. "Flex your fingers." Patty gestured with her left hand, making little movements with her fingers. The three horny fingers bent, one at a time, and then his thumb. "Good, then all you need is rest." Patty stood back, and Cedric bowed low, his head touching the floor. *It's nice to be appreciated, but all this bowing is such a time waster.*

Abe paused at the next lit intersection. He looked back and signaled, two to starboard and two to port. A rumbling conversation broke out amongst her recruits. Much to Patty's surprise, her newest recruits bowed to her before heading down the lit cross-corridor, a pair going in each direction.

"What's happening, Alan?" Patty asked.

A slow rumbled gesture-filled exchange began between Alan and Abe. Alan turned back to her, his fingers danced. "They protect our rear. Bad to leave enemy behind us."

Bad to split my forces too. My forces? Patty scratched her head.

This is crazy. She looked around Abe's hulking form. The next intersection began the lit sections of the ship. There would be no skulking through darkened corridors. "Let's keep going." *How is Cedric going to cope with his injured hand?* Ben stayed in the van with Abe. Alan dropped into his usual position at Patty's hip as they marched towards the mothership's heart.

The six guards at the next junction did not charge into the dark but formed into tight ranks of three and held their position, blocking the intersection's broad entrance. Beyond them, Patty could see movement, a few females going about their business. This was a position that the guards would hold, but it was, at last, somewhere that they would be seen; help could be summoned. *Hopefully by someone that would talk rather than fight.*

A wall of three was a much harder proposition than fighting one-on-one, but Patty did not mind engaging and holding, although Ben's enthusiasm nearly split Abe's head as he dragged their line forward. *Fool!*

"Hold here!" Patty shouted above the clash of blades and Ben seemed to calm. "Back, one step!" Patty stamped back, Alan at her side. Abe and Ben followed a beat later. Their opponents did not, and the bright-edged conversation continued at arm's length, a holding pattern Patty felt they could easily maintain. They could not breach the aliens' numerical superiority or flank them in this tight corridor.

Gasps from half a dozen curious females gave Patty a heartbeat's warning. The six defenders had none. Suddenly a wave of reversed tabards poured out from the cross-corridors, and Patty quickly lost count of how many reversed-tabards there were as she stepped back from the fray. Strangely, the curious females did not flee but clustered in small groups, perhaps in readiness to perform whatever funeral rites were required. Four of the six guards received wounds before they were subdued. The females came and collected the two that did not survive the encounter. Patty could not tell what they thought, but they did not behave as if Patty and Alan were offensive or something to be feared. The four that did survive received their reversed tabards and swords with pride, and if Patty was right, more than a little wonder. *Do they expect me to slaughter the defeated? No mercy? Maybe they did.*

With his right hand in a temporary sling, Cedric stood proudly beside the company he and Dan had recruited. He made a small gesture with it as he bowed to her. Abe seemed happy or relieved to see him, and they exchanged rumbled words. It looked to Patty as though Cedric confirmed Abe's decisions as to the deployment of her forces. As they lined up, Patty did a quick headcount, eighteen! Her heart skipped a beat. *Eighteen! I'm gonna run out of names real quick.* Abe and Cedric took charge with a nod from Alan and lined them up; injuries were seen to, and water distributed. Most of her soldiers had their own supplies tucked beneath their tabards. All shared what they had.

Patty caught Abe's attention. "Should we hold here?" she asked.

He seemed to understand and rumbled something to Cedric. While he did not shake his head, Patty got the impression Cedric was against the idea. The old guard emphasized his negative rumbles, making sharp points with his left hand.

Abe turned back to Patty and bowed before rumbling; he pointed to the flag. "Need many to see." Rum-rumble, "Meeting point set," rum-rumble-rum. He twisted around and pointed down the corridor.

Meeting? Meeting with whom? "Okay, we go on then," Patty instructed. Two walls of five formed a phalanx in front of Patty with two lines of three guarding their rear. Abe and Cedric took positions in front of Patty and Alan.

The groups of females flattened themselves against the walls to make room as the company advanced. They watched Patty intently as she strode past. Patty tried to hold a female's gaze, but few held up their heads when their eyes met. On the occasion when Patty did lock eyes, she received a deep bow. She knew the whispered rumbles, and the flash of excited, left hands would spread the news faster than they could march. The females left the walls when the company past and formed tight groups that followed at a discrete distance.

As the corridor approached the next junction, it began to widen in fluted arcs. Beyond was a broad thoroughfare crowded with aliens of all castes. Suddenly Patty knew exactly where she was. She had not observed this particular corridor but knew they were approaching the central atrium, albeit from the opposite direction that her first visit had brought her.

One guard, of the eight on duty at this junction, turned and saw the phalanx approaching and staggered backward into a female guiding a group of pint-sized aliens. *Children? I didn't see children last time I was here. Of course, there would be children.* Rumbled gasps spread and a wave of collisions and chaos spread out from that first impact. Only four of the remaining seven managed to find a partner and link up by the time the tip of Patty's company pierced their position.

Suddenly a wave of retreating aliens began to pour into the already crowded thoroughfare from the cross-corridor, intensifying the tangled press of bodies. Forcing the fleeing crowds back from the left corridor were two lines of six, all wearing reversed tabards of different hues. From the right came three lines of three and two more. Patty blinked; one was smaller, left-handed, the other stood head-and-shoulders above the crowd, brandishing a blade that was longer than Alan was tall. *We're going viral! What have I started?*

Although ad hoc groups of soldiers formed lines, none had been brave enough to contact the strength and structure of Patty's company. The fleeing females and children added to the difficulty of finding appropriate caste mates. Abe and Cedric took the opportunity to reorganize the phalanx after the recruits paid obeisance to Patty. It unnerved her not being able to see over their heads, but Patty felt strangely secure behind the double line of chitinous protectors. *This could be a good place to hold. We have a clear line of sight forward and, hopefully, a clear path back to* Freya.

Patty sought Alan's eye, "We hold here." Alan relayed her wishes to Abe. He passed them on to Cedric. She felt a warm buzz when the old warrior cast a sharp eye to the forces assembled around them and a glance down the corridor behind her, before agreeing. Abe passed his approval on to Alan. *It's convoluted, but if it works for them, I'm happy.* She was glad Cedric could stay out of the fray. It was evident that everyone deferred to him although why he would be assigned to a routine security detail was beyond her understanding. Patty just counted her blessings.

Two bodies remained prostrate on the scuffed floor, one inordinately large, the other almost minute by comparison, a paler mirror image, writ small. "Up. Up." Patty stepped back to give them room.

The giant came up to one knee, his mammoth blade horizontal before him. "Yourrrrsssss..." He sounded like a purring lion with a lisp, and his eyes were big, a warm brown, and filled with intelligence. *More ritual. Their lives are full of it. How many ceremonies rule mine that I don't recognize?* Patty blinked. *No time. Focus.* Patty took his blade, the bright tip in her right hand, the hilt in her left, and was glad she had used both hands. It would have been embarrassing to drop the massive offering. *It must weigh ten kilos if it weighs a gram.* She returned it to his great hand. Beautiful etchings covered the back of his fingers. Curlicues spread up his armored forearm like a baroque tattoo. *If complexity in tabard design is echoed in body etchings, this alien was from a high caste.* She glanced at Cedric and repeated her homily about using the blade for protecting the weak while this giant's soft dark eyes seemed to drink her in. He offered no name, and none came quickly to Patty's mind except Zeus. He was as big as a mountain, his enormous presence overwhelmed her, and she tried to breathe through the intermittent waves of cold fear that flushed through her. His bow of acceptance lowered his head almost to the floor. When he rose, he took his post at her back. She felt her neck crack as she twisted around and peered up at him. *How had they suborned a giant like this? I'm not sure I want him behind me.* He gave her a slow bow but quickly returned his eyes to assessing threats from beyond the double wall surrounding them. He did, however, give off a warm presence that complemented Alan's.

CHAPTER SEVENTEEN

The pale left-handed alien remained on one knee, his blade presented to Patty. It was a small weapon, simply made, and it was not much longer than Daichi's wakizashi. She repeated the ritual and wondered if this left-handed alien could hold up his end of a conversation. Pum had been chatty. When he rose, he seemed unsure of himself, refusing to meet her eyes for more than just a glance. *Was that a tremble?* She took a moment. He was shorter than Pum, and his tabard was less ornate than some of her right-handed recruits. *Is he young?* It was hard to tell.

"Do you have a name, or do I have the honor of bestowing one upon you?" Patty asked.

"Muurrunnboobgl'dor..." was the only part of his opening salvo that Patty caught and the longer he went on, the less sure she felt she had heard that correctly. He looked like he could continue reciting his name all day.

"Will Murrun do?" Patty interrupted when he paused to take a breath.

He stopped moving for a moment, insect still, and then shook his head and bowed, "Murrun ... is," rumble, "sufficient." He bowed again, "This one is," rum-rumble, "proud to wear the," Murrun's right hand clutched at the air, "appellation?"

"Name. Your name. Murrun is your name," Patty told him.

He nodded, "This one's ... name is Murrun."

"Murrun, good. Good. We are glad you are with us. We wish to know more about you." Patty said and tried to keep a straight face as Murrun wriggled with suppressed energy. *Is that excitement?* "Tell me about yourself. You seem ... smaller than your left-handed brothers."

Murrun bowed a low shuffle, his eyes only meeting hers briefly. "This one is," rumble, "young but has," rum-rumble. He paused, his right hand reaching, "integrated, no that is not," rumble, "correct." He huffed. "It will do." Rum-rum, "This one has," rumble, "satisfactorily integrated his," rum, "initial," rumble-rum, "memories for..." he froze for a second, "the duration of most of your primary planet's orbit."

"A year. We call it a year, an Earth year," Patty helped him.

Murrun nodded, "An Eeaarrththth year." He rumbled for most of a breath, almost to himself, before he realized Patty's eyes were pinned on him. "The homeworld took more than twice as long to orbit than yours." He stood straight and tapped his chest, "This one is nearly one... one year old. Two of Earth years." He was so young and yet he was apparently competent. Not as poised or confident as Pum or Abe but that came with experience. She glanced at Cedric and hoped her inexperience was not showing too much. "Two years, is that young for your people?"

Murrun bowed and shuffled sideways, "This one has been told that," rum-rum, "he does not concentrate," his head suddenly popped up and for the first time his eyes locked to Patty's, "but this one completed all tasks assigned correctly." The flash of defiance faded quickly, and he dropped his eyes.

"We are sure you performed your tasks admirably. What were they?" Patty asked. She felt as though she were fencing with a feather, trying to tickle an opening.

A surge of excitement lifted his eyes a little, "This one served aboard," rumble-rum-rumble, "a transport ship as," rum-rum, "communication ... juncture. This one likes flying." His eyes dropped again, and he hunched in on himself.

"And?" Patty prompted him.

Once again, defiance glowed behind his dark eyes, "This would not have damaged our ship. This one was only," rumble, "investigating the flight controls. This one was sure that mastery would be possible with," rumble-rum-rum, "and a little practice." His eyes dropped along with his shoulders.

"We enjoy flying," Patty told him. "It's one of our favorite things to do. Aren't you allowed to learn?"

Murrun tugged at his predominantly blue tabard, "There is honor in being the," rumble, "binding that holds the tribes together." A disappointed sigh wracked him. "This one was told that should be enough."

"But if you really wanted to fly, couldn't you change your clan?" Patty asked. "You're now in my clan, yes?"

Too many thoughts seemed to jam Murrun's system, and he snapped into immobility for an instant. "Yes, if this one was deemed," rum-rumble-rum-rum," apologies, this one does not know if there is a word for it. Hu-umans do not," rumble-rum-rum.

"Can you explain it to me? Maybe we do something similar," she suggested.

Murrun blinked and shuffled, his right-hand flashing in tight stepped arcs, "Clans hold their knowledge sacred. To pass between tribes means the old must be," rumble, "vacated, removed. All of the old. It is to be born again with just the," rumble-rum, "simplest ... memories." The hair on the back of Patty's neck stood up, and she looked at Alan, aghast. He was relaxed but alert. Her stomach flip-flopped. *That's what they did to you, little brother; wiped you clean away.* Anger burned in her gut, overriding her nausea. *That's what they've done to Dad too.*

"Memories?" Patty asked. I'd prefer Dad with his old ones...

"Mel'andrin," Murrun said. He paused and tried to restart, "Gift-memories. Gift is ... inaccurate." Rum-rum, "Gift, donation, inheritance," his right hand darted back and forth as he shuffled on the spot, "One needs something to ... begin with, language, and," rumble, "etiquette, and depending on," rum-rum, "your clan, some rudimentary skills." Murrun looked about before returning his eyes to Patty. For the moment, he seemed to have lost his self-consciousness.

Rumble-rum, "Right-handed brothers, need few skills beyond the blade. Memories refined, distilled, gleaned," rum-rumble-rum, "passed on." *Was that how Alan knew how to fight? It seems like dangerous skills to give a slave. Maybe not if the slave didn't know they were a slave.*

Murrun snapped into immobility for a second. "This one has a gift-memory for," rum-rumble-rum, "most honorable," rum-rumble. He flowed into an elaborate bow. At its deepest point, his right hand reached into his belt pouch and withdrew a tiny silver implement. Murrun seemed to twist away as he rose, obscuring his hands. He unfolded into his final pose with his head bowed and the shiny item extended in his left hand. Patty leaned closer. An engraved spoon, no bigger than her little finger, held a glistening pearly sphere smaller than the head of a pin. An enticing aroma drifted into Patty's nostrils, something woody or maybe savory. The impulse to place it in her saliva-filled mouth was almost irresistible.

Out of the corner of her eye, Patty caught movement or rather a lack of it. Abe and Cedric watched her intently. Zeus gazed down, inscrutable as ever. She was the center of attention from all, apart from the outer line of the phalanx. *Careful, girl.* Her heart raced. *How sacred was this to these aliens? If it's not holy, they're serious about something.* Her eyes snapped back to the extended offering. *You're not going to eat that, are you? But it smells so nice. It can't really be bad for me, can it? It's so small and smells delicious.* Her mind chattered away, listing reasons why it was a bad idea to consume something that probably came from an alien's body, but in her heart, Patty knew she could not resist.

Closing her eyes made her thoughts spin faster as the savory aroma drew her closer but in doing so, they lost their grip on her and blurred into insensibility. Patty felt the cool metal of the tiny spoon with her lips. The pearly sphere slid onto her tongue, soft and resilient for a long heartbeat. Warmth flooded her mouth reminding Patty of her mother's delicious stew but with a hint of banana and maybe a touch of ... gardenia.

The bubble burst.

Suddenly the supple bead was no more. Her mouth filled with hot vapor like fine brandy. FIRE! Searing flames of ice surged through Patty's sinuses, sending waves of indescribable pain throughout her head.

And then it was gone.

The foaming wake settled. Sensory overload. Patty had felt a similar sensation the first time she went freefall. Patty began to discern an image, blurry at first but then more detail. A human face. *That's my face.* In the foreground, Patty could see Murrun's out of focus blade and could feel it's weight in her/Murrun's hand. *A memory!* It was the very moment Patty returned his small sword, yet there was more than just the point-of-view visual image. She could feel Murrun's emotions; confusion, honor, shame, confusion, and joy flooded him, but mostly he felt surrender. He was hers, lock, stock and barrel, heart and soul.

As the immediate and overwhelming impact of Murrun's gift-memory receded, waves of blurry related thoughts and memories cascaded through her, almost a snapshot of Murrun as he was at that instant, his personal history layered upon his bloodline's history layered upon his species. More than she could take in a single flash. Patty blinked and took a breath. Apart from an initial start, she felt ... okay. Her heart seemed to be loping along casually. The light was a little bright and... *Something smells.* Alan's hand was at her elbow. He looked concerned, his eyes searching hers.

Patty felt her heart blossom with love for her brave little brother. "Thank you, Alan."

"You bumped into me. Did it taste bad?" Alan's eyes darted to the silver spoon.

"No, not bad ... intense." *Intense puts it mildly.* Patty took a deep breath and a moment to settle the giddy feelings flooding her. The air smelled different, full of anticipation and excitement. She caught Cedric's eyes. Everything about him seemed poised. Concern, pride, excitement all hung in the balance waiting ... waiting upon her ... upon her reaction. Bright eyes with bright blades stared intently, all of them waiting for her.

A response bubbled up inside her, a vestige of a glimpse of a reflected memory handed down and honed, generation-by-generation. She knew her attempt at a flourishing bow was woefully below the standard she wanted to achieve; she just hoped first-left-handed-son-of-Call'uumam'oo - the rest of Murrun's name-family-caste-Clan unfolded in Patty's mind - would understand. Her bow was not formally correct, but she could already see Murrun respond to her heartfelt endeavor.

"We thank you, most deeply, for your honest and genuine gift." A joyous feedback loop locked Patty's eyes to Murrun's. She had to laugh as waves of pleasure surged through her. Her face ached as her smile threatened to overload. He loved her. The little alien loved her, although not as a human lover. *And what would it be like to share a moment like this with Lirsín?* She felt herself blush. Murrun's feelings were closer to worship than Patty felt comfortable with, but they were undeniably honest. She could trust Murrun with her life. A knot of fear unwound. Patty shook her head and shoulders to release it from her body.

A palpable wave of joy swept over the company, and unrestrained shouts broke out intermittently all around her. Patty could smell the relief and joy flowing from Abe, confidence from Cedric. The tension was gone, and eyes returned to the activity around them. Cedric passed a comment to Abe, and the shape of the phalanx tightened.

A TEST FLIGHT

Pur'unnan flew the test vehicle into position in Low Orbit and waited for sunrise. The clouded vista of their homeworld spread out before them nearly matched an ancient memory inside her. The air looked brown, thick with dust compared to the lush greens and blues that were in her memories.

"She's a beautiful world," said Delad'ron, leaning closer to the forward viewport. The other FirstMothers on the Great Council echoed Clan Darf'ornal's sentiments. The bridge of the test vehicle was not designed to hold much more than Pur'unnan and an assistant or two but the Great Council, minus the representatives from Clan Bar'Durrunnan, had squeezed in without complaint.

"But not for long," Pur'unnan told them. "There have been five sunstrikes this year already. Ten thousand lives were lost; will we even be able to save that many?"

As the Darf'ornal FirstMother stepped back from the port, her head dropped with thought. She was showing her age, yet her sharp eyes missed nothing. "The GreatMother is right. Our world is beautiful. Our thanks, GreatMother, for granting this one the opportunity to see just how beautiful she is." She turned to the other members of the council. "We will bring in more people and start a third shift, but that will not advance the launch date if Tol'edranna and Fer'entai'illy are not able to match our contribution."

The two FirstMothers exchanged looks filled with shame and grief. Tol'edranna FirstMother spoke first, "We understand the urgency of your request, but many believe the current increase in solar activity is an anomaly, that things will settle back to one or two strikes per year."

"Bar'Durrunnan has pushed that argument, but they have little or no evidence to support it. Does anyone really expect our sun to return to sedentary ways? We have known for centuries that the time we have on our homeworld is limited." Pur'unnan tried to keep the frustration-driven anger from her voice and posture, using every nuance she could muster to move their calcified attitudes.

"The GreatMother is correct," Fer'entai'illy FirstMother bowed, "but all our resources are stretched to their limits."

"We have an opportunity to save what we can. Before too long we will have neither resources nor time." Pur'unnan's anger flared, but a look from Darf'ornal stopped her from lashing out at the Clan FirstMothers. Few clans had resources and personnel to spare. The last two orbits had been hard for everyone.

CHAPTER EIGHTEEN

As Patty waited in the broad corridor for an official response to their demand for parlay, her contingent of soldiers continued to grow. They drifted in, in small groups of five or six and Patty took their obeisances and returned their weapons. All the while, from behind and above Patty, raining down in an invisible mist, came a feeling of need. Patty twisted and craned her head back. Zeus was as impassive as before but, somehow, not so inscrutable. She could see it in the subtlest of actions, the angle of his wrist, the hesitation before his in-breath; the momentary glance down filled with... hope. *Is that a glow surrounding him or am I intoxicated?* Golden shimmers of light danced around his face, all around his silhouette. So many new sensations flooded Patty, it was challenging to make sense of it all.

Zeus could read her as well as she could understand him, and he began his florid bow even as words blossomed on Patty's lips. "You have a gift-memory ... mel'andrin for me too?" She felt rather than heard a surge of joy from those now behind her and knew they all had memories for her. One glance over her shoulder confirmed it. Cedric nodded a brief bow and muttered something to Abe. They returned to managing the company; their time would come.

Zeus's offering spoon was no bigger than Murrun's although much more ornate; pierced filigree ran down the delicate handle. He held it without the slightest quiver in the tips of his enormous fingers. The pearly memory-essence seemed smaller than Murrun's but more intense, concentrated. Waves of scent surrounded it, roses and ... strawberries and freshly mown lawn.

Zeus's gift-memory surged into overload as Patty inhaled. The tiny bead popped. *Wasabi!* Patty suddenly remembered the first time she had eaten sushi garnished liberally with that fiery radish. The little sphere flared hot and then was gone. Rather than resisting the overwhelming flash, she tried to let go before the inexorable sensory flood. Sunlight where none should be. Standing high above the heads of others, Zeus could see beyond the bustling crowds. He saw Patty's face, lined with concern. His ankle still ached from the fight. Flickering pulses of humiliation receded, surprise at being taken down by an old soldier with a wooden staff. Patty, backlit by shafts of rose light. Cedric, standing before her. On the verge of kneeling in adoration, the ardent desire to be that close, to bathe in her presence. Patty's eyes were liquid pools that cooled and eased his pain. The honor of the multi-colored FirstCalled surrounding her. The combinations of colors, interlocked, were tricky to see at first let alone understand. Bright blades dancing, calling a challenge. Beams of light as if the sun had broken through storm clouds, golden light pouring down upon her.

A breath filled with complex messages stampeded though Patty's nostrils. A subtle sense of calm but dynamic stability surrounded her. She could sense Cedric and Abe, not holding the reins but overseeing the assembly, the gestalt. She opened her eyes to see Zeus's great dark eyes staring intently, centimeters from her own. Moments ago, to be so close to a giant alien would have scared Patty down to her toes but now ... Patty leaned closer, caressing his heavy brow with her left hand. A deep purr of joy rumbled through him when she rested her cheek against his. A sigh escaped her as his enormous arm carefully enfolded her.

If only you were furry. Hard edges from Zeus's natural body armor dug into her as he gave her a gentle squeeze. It's like being hugged by a giant crab. A giant warm crab that purrs.

Shouts from outside the phalanx drew her attention away from Zeus's adoring eyes. It was hardly more than a thought, but her giant guardian caught it, and he rose to his full height, lifting her smoothly into the air.

A troop of twenty or more, wearing reversed tabards, had broken out of a side corridor halfway between the junction her forces dominated and the bright light of the atrium. They hailed the phalanx with shouts that sounded more like deep-chested barks. Zeus was warm, and his large hand was softer than Patty expected. His breath rumbled through his whole body, a big crab purring. She wrapped an arm around his armored bicep for support as she looked over the heads of her men. *My men? Yes, they are my men.* She could smell it.

The newest recruits caused havoc amongst the isolated defensive lines, bulldozing two formations without pause as they charged along the thoroughfare. Some wielded swords with gusto, delivering strokes with the flat of the blades; some had bars or pipes, some waded in, with fist and boot. They seemed more like a rowdy bunch of hooligans out on the town than a dangerous fighting force. Encouraging shouts from the lines of her protectors climbed from a rumble to a triumphant roar. Arms with bright blades snapped into the air above their heads, clashing the flats of their swords together, making an awful clamor but one that set Patty's heart racing.

The bright light streaming into the far end of the thoroughfare caught Patty's eye. *Where are the intermediaries? We are highly visible. They must know we're here.* No one crossed the bright entrance, and no one entered the broad corridor except for a few mothers. There were injuries in the boisterous company's wake, but none seemed worse than a broken limb or two. Compared to the bloody conflicts she had witnessed on her previous visit, the clashes were almost polite. Clusters of females followed close behind, attending to the fallen. A fluid group of females drifted between the wounded conducting a rapid triage. Many times, heads looked up from the wounded and sought Patty out. *Sorry ladies, I hope you're not too mad at me.*

I wish I knew what was really going on here. Murrun and Zeus's gift-memories helped. At first, she had been concerned she had swept up a force around her that would be seen as aggressive, but now Murrun's and especially Zeus's gift made her feel that whatever numbers she collected it would be a drop in the bucket compared to those that could be rallied against her. Zeus would be happier with another two or three of his giant brothers and six times the numbers in her company.

Cedric glanced up at her and bowed. *He seems to know what is happening.* Through Abe, he was the linchpin that held her force together. *Why were you, an apparently high caste officer, out patrolling the darkened corridors?* Although she still felt more than a little giddy from the rush of Zeus's gift-memory, she knew she needed to taste/experience Cedric's offering.

As her clan's new members drew close, the phalanx opened and accepted them inside, the outer line rippling out as it expanded to occupy the whole intersection. Zeus stepped forward and lowered Patty until she was perched just behind Abe's right shoulder. She watched, overwhelmed by the mingling of new scents as they were incorporated into the expanded whole. Abe and Cedric took their oaths and returned their swords. A strange mix of joy and solemnity rose from them as they mingled with their new comrades, slotting into their new positions as if rehearsed.

Only one body remained prostrate. *It's almost as though Abe and Cedric are ignoring him.* Patty felt cautious about approaching. *Why is that? Who is he?* Zeus picked up on her concern and began to withdraw.

"No. Let me down. Thank you, Zeus." Her knees felt a little rubbery, and she steadied herself on Zeus's engraved wrist for a second. *Did Cedric not like this newcomer? No, that's not right. It's almost like he does not see him.* Abe seemed to have no opinion, but he stood his ground in front of Patty. Something from Zeus reinforced Patty's unease. She stepped closer to Murrun, peering around Abe to get a better look at this disruption to their wholeness.

With his head down low, Patty could not see his features, but she could see he was pale, very pale and large. He was at least as large as his RightLeading brothers. He held a wickedly contoured sword in his armored left hand, horizontal. *In supplication?* The scalloped blade was backed with serrations; it was a weapon designed to maximize damage. It gave Patty a chill and yet she could sense nothing from him. Not even patience.

"Murrun, advise us," Patty instructed.

Before the young alien had a chance to unfreeze from his momentary block, the newcomer sprang forward. Abe was caught flat-footed, and the pale LeftLeading alien's blade cut through him. Abe stiffened before falling to his knees, his breath bubbling red. The alien advanced, shouldering Cedric out of the way.

Lady Estelle flowed into Patty's hand and caught his blade. It skidded up to her bell-guard. She parried, shifting away to her left, crowding Murrun. She only needed to hold him off for a second. Alan's blade checked the stiletto in her attacker's right hand before piercing him through. Zeus took most of his head off, and Cedric's dagger emerged from his sling and took the assassin in the back of his neck, severing its spine. The attempt on her life was over in the blink of an eye.

CHAPTER NINETEEN

Heart racing, Patty stepped around the assassin's bloody carcass and sank to her knees beside Abe, holding his head in her hands. Blood bubbled from Abe's mouth, and he coughed wetly. His eyes flicked up to hers. Patty felt his body tense as he tried to bow and then he was gone. The light in his eyes faded as his body relaxed. The remnants of his essence departed with his last breath, mingling with those of his brothers.

Alan's hand on her shoulder snapped Patty out of her blank reverie. "You are needed." His eyes looked worried, and he glanced behind her at Murrun who was conferring with Cedric at the inner edge of their formation. Noticing he had her attention, Murrun's pose asked permission to come closer. He read her willingness and bowed solemnly before approaching.

"This one did not want to interrupt your time of mourning," Murrun said solemnly.

Patty could sense his confusion but wasn't sure of its source. "Murrun, if needs be, you always have permission to interrupt me. What is it?"

"Mothers have come." Murrun's rumbling words accompanied by his subtle gestures and faint woody scent brought images cascading through Patty's mind, females gathered around still bodies, mournful songs of passing, sons, and brothers gone. She had seen this for herself.

A glance from Patty, over Murrun's shoulder to Cedric, was enough and the lines opened to admit six females of various sizes in a random grouping of colored tabards. The wall sealed behind them, and they shuffled forward. Murrun moved back, but Alan stayed at her side as the mothers took kneeling positions around Abe's body. She could not understand more than every fourth or fifth word of their rumbled song; they spoke in a different dialect. What she could comprehend was the movement of their bodies. Their sense of loss was heartfelt.

Cedric, Ben, Ed, Dan, Felix and a handful more came together and began to recite Abe's name and his history, one not particularly noteworthy, but he had been a good soldier and a good companion.

"He fought courageously and guided me honestly," said Patty as tears spilled down her face. "He was my First RightLeading son." The words did not make much sense from a human point of view, but her company understood. Patty realized she still held Abe's gnarled hand and reluctantly folded it over his chest. Her knees squealed in pain, and she leaned on Alan as she rose, giving the mothers room to perform their duties. They gently but efficiently stripped Abe of his tabard and personal belongings and wrapped him in white cloth.

Zeus glanced down to check that Patty was alright but quickly returned to vigilance. Her company bristled and snarled, tense and on alert. They hummed and stamped an earnest challenge, but no one would face them. Of the pale assassin's body, there was no sign. Murrun could sense her questions, and he edged closer. So too did Cedric, perceiving her need, but they both gave way to a mother with an intricately embroidered light green tabard. She bowed, not deeply but with sincerity.

"Clan Tol'edranna TwelfthMother presents herself," she bowed again, "We give thanks, GreatMother, your," rum-rumble-rum, "was unexpected. There have been so many deaths. And thank you for allowing us," rumble, "access."

"Too many deaths. It grieves us that you were needed at all, TwelfthMother." The aliens' style of formality seemed more natural now to Patty, and she could feel the TwelfthMother respond sympathetically.

"Word had been sent but," rumble, "observing your restraint was still a surprise."

"We do not seek death," Patty insisted. "There has been too

much of it of late. We come to talk. The necessity for this," an alien gesture that described an armored cohort, and with tiny changes in emphasis, a cell, and a mathematical set, flowed through Patty's right shoulder and down her arm, "this interferes with honest discussion."

"Politics." The TwelfthMother's apologetic bow conveyed a sense of powerlessness. It-was-the-way-it-was. Patty gave her assent, and the cluster of females with Abe's body withdrew beyond her lines.

"Murrun, Cedric, what was that?" She knew they would know what she meant by the set of her shoulders and her hand resting on Lady Estelle's hilt. She did not refer to the mothers and the funeral rites but the pale, LeftLeading assassin.

Cedric paused for a second to convey something to Felix before striding over. A bloody stain marred the edge of his sling, and - now she knew what she was looking for - the outline of the dagger lying in the crook of his arm. He bowed low, shame painting his movements.

"This one abases. This one is getting too old. The hunter should not have slipped past me," he apologized.

"Stand proud, Cedric. A wall is not one paling. We could feel your unease." Patty glanced at Murrun. "Chip in if you have something to say." He froze for a second before nodding a bow. *Freezing is a bad thing, my little man. Maybe it's good they didn't let you in a pilot's chair.*

"Hunter. This one has never seen one before." Murrun's pose rippled his low caste tabard. They moved in different circles.

"Cedric?" Patty asked. He took in her gaze as she compared his simple tabard to the subtle engravings on his armored body. She felt her stance open a little, expressing her ignorance for those near enough to see her vulnerability. Alan, Murrun, and Cedric closed around her protectively. Zeus growled, towering over them all.

"Brothers," said Cedric, his clenched right fist and his left shoulder thrown back, his wide-armed gesture meant he included all his right-leading brothers, "have few words." The rest of his body said, 'unlike our honorable but too whiny/chatty LeftLeaders,' overlaid with the scent that hoped she could appreciate his humor. For a startling moment, Cedric felt like her father. *Like Dad used to be.*

His eyes lingered on the blood-stained floor, and he took on a disdainful demeanor. Honor and disgrace rippled through his posture in equal parts. "GreatMother," he rumbled, his body asking for a moment of contemplation. Cedric relaxed into a neutral stance for a breath before beginning his offertory bow. His tiny spoon was utilitarian, but the memory-essence seemed densely packed, the scent of new-mown hay, sea spray and roasting chestnuts washed over her...

Redemption. A growing realization that honor had been restored to him. It was not a single memory, bright and clear, but a series of tiny epiphanies layered one atop the other. Trust. Being sent off to gather more brothers for this strange GreatMother. Honor. Receiving Abe's request for guidance. Pride. A smile from Patty's eyes for honest service...

The light was too bright, and her head pounded as if she had spent the night celebrating at Shadrach's Bar and Grill.

Patty sat up, blinking. The world swayed around her, trying to catch up. *One mel'andrin is plenty. Three was foolish. If the rest of my company gift me like that?* No, she did not want to go there. Patty wanted to make a comic book 'hic'. *It's going to take me years to integrate all this stuff.* Cedric's life cascaded through her mind in glimpses and flashes. Honorable service and a quick mind presented him with promotions and prestige, rising to a seat on the Great Council. Cedric's fall was political, not personal. But what was a councilor's duty if not to advise? The aliens' invasion plans unfolded in Patty's mind. They long suspected one rock falling from space would not be enough. They might need three or four. They had planned for this. They had techniques to clean the skies later, but the costs. *They wanted a warmer, wetter world anyway. Wouldn't it be easier just to wipe the slate clean?* The self-serving arguments repulsed him. The RegentFirstMother's advisers vied for her approval. The announcement of the gestation of a new GreatMother was greeted as a sign. His reasoned arguments and protests, notwithstanding, the invasion was on.

Every thought brought a surge of memories, references, fields of knowledge unfolded, root, trunk, and branch. Patty reeled drunkenly back into Zeus's arms. Two lines of her men stood between her and the rest of the world, Alan at her right and Murrun at her left. Cedric stood off a little to one side making subtle alterations to the company's form. Amusement leaked from every pore. *What have you done to me, you bastard?* She chuckled and hiccupped. So many brothers, so few pale brothers. *That's what those in authority want, pale ones to compete with the other Clans' pale ones.* And to get pale ones you need lots of brothers, and if you were lucky your family could be blessed with a weak, sickly genius. *If you were fortunate.* It was amazing how the powerful had pale smart ones so regularly when the poor produced multitudes of brothers.

Patty shook her head and tried to sit up again. The world seemed more aligned. She took the offered canteen of water. It tasted flat. Murrun wanted something, but he was content to wait for her availability. *He thinks something's funny too. And not funny. Something that honors him. Something that scares him.* She wriggled and after a gentle squeeze from Zeus found her feet, somewhere below her rubbery knees. *No, I don't need Zeus.* Alan's hand on her elbow steadied her.

"What is it?" *Not another Hunter?*

Cedric had no dealings with Hunters; few did. There were not many of them. They were almost as rare as GreatMothers, loners in the extreme. Pathologically focused on a single target. Assassins. They always caused trouble, especially in close quarters. *Assassin.* Patty's blood ran cold. She had wanted to get in, get her parents and Jake and get out of here. Now she felt entangled in the generation ship's politics. *Well, you wanted to be queen. No, I didn't! All I wanted to do was get my parents out of here.* An idea began to coalesce. *Could she ask? Would they be gentle?*

Murrun took an open stance ready to receive.

"Cedric, we'll need your advice too." *If this works, it'll ease a lot of that guilt.* Murrun was ready, and Cedric approached, waiting patiently for Patty to compose her thoughts.

"You have gathered brothers to me," Patty's gesture included Zeus and little Murrun. "Valuable all."

Cedric's stance said in reply, "For strength."

"I hope you can gather ... my other people." She did not have a word for humans; none of her gift-memory contributors had much to do with the captured humans. There was a specific word/gesture set for them that would describe them exactly. Her ignorance worried her. *They'll understand.*

"My brother was the FirstReturned." Patty put her arm around his shoulder and hugged him. Alan accepted it, but the moment Patty realized he was embarrassed she let him go, secretly pleased with his response. "We came here to confront the RegentFirstMother and to find my father and mother. My family and the mothers, fathers, sisters, and sons of my people, taken and treated so, suffer grievously.

"The wiping of my peoples' minds is an abominable crime. One that you were nearly subject to." The RegentFirstMother's plan for Cedric's fall from grace went considerably further than just demotion to the lowest rank. His Clan would not hear of Cleansing him, but what could you do with a general that did not want to go to war?

"GreatMother, you consider your people still to be yours even after Cleansing?" Murrun knew she did, but the concept was foreign to him.

"They are not as a multitude of brothers," *no insult intended, Cedric.* He shrugged and nodded, not understanding. "Cleansing robs them of all their personhood with no gift-memories from their own people. To my people, Cleansing is worse than death.

To see our loved ones, so stricken, brings out powerful emotions. We fear a terrible retribution will be exacted upon you because of it."

Murrun approached speech three or four times, but each time, on the cusp, he froze as if performing a complicated calculation, and he withdrew to reformulate and reformat. "GreatMother, your people ... we are your people." He bowed, humbly including himself. "It goes against this one's understanding to retrieve those lost to the enemy, but this one is inexperienced in the ways of my GreatMother's Clan."

Much to Patty's relief, Cedric knew what she desired, and she could see him identifying individuals in his mind that would be suitable for such a mission. "They must be gentle with them," she insisted. "Do not seek their surrender by arms. My people will not resist. Is there someplace close by where they can be safely gathered?"

Murrun froze before nodding and gesturing back down the hallway. "Yes, GreatMother, two or three places suggest themselves. We would need to obtain/procure/steal portable power for lighting and supplies," he glanced at Cedric, "but that is quite achievable."

How I'm going to get them off this ship is a problem for another moment. Cedric began pulling men from the line. Ben was the first. Patty was glad to see his excitement as he bounced on his toes, waiting for the others to come forward. Murrun tried to attract her attention with a subtle fragrance - *are you ready for this one's inquiry?*

"Please Murrun, you have my permission. What is it?" she asked.

"Our GreatMother needed time," Murrun replied and bowed.

"To integrate, yes. Thank you. But you have something important too." *A burden.*

"GreatMother," he answered, "intermediaries have come."

CHAPTER TWENTY

Patty steadied herself as she stepped down from Zeus's gentle hand, squeezing his huge thumb affectionately as he withdrew and resumed his vigilance over the heads of his new clan brothers. Nothing had changed at the confluence of the two corridors except her clan had grown larger. Murrun and Cedric stood attentive but relaxed, waiting for her sign. *I need to give them more than just my reactions. If I do that, they will gut the delegation and go out hunting for more. They need a reasoned response.*

"We don't like them." *Patty paused as more inferences trickled into her mind from Cedric's gift. He coughed a chuckle. The two representatives had a dozen honor guards, well beyond the status their tabards displayed. Neither ranked sufficiently high enough to negotiate with a GreatMother. On the surface, it appeared as if the RegentFirstMother honored Patty, but to her company, it was a deliberate insult. It needed an appropriate response.*

"After sending a hunter, surely they will expect some manner of retaliation," Patty suggested. Cedric's mel'andrin held intimations of the complex rules of honor around inter-clan negotiations but nothing clear. Murrun was too lowly and too young to have any direct knowledge. Cedric had no experience negotiating at all, but he did know what happened when things went poorly, violent death.

"They are sent as a sacrifice." Patty held Cedric's eyes; he looked ready to implement what to him was the natural next move in the bloody sequence. The RegentFirstMother's offer was rejected; the clan was secure enough. There was plenty of time to wait for his GreatMother's honor to be recognized appropriately. Murrun nodded his agreement.

Time! How are Lily and Daichi doing? Patty glanced at her wrist comm; it had been over an hour since they separated. *You don't have time to wait for the slow wheel of diplomacy to grind around.* "Bring them before us." Anger boiled in her heart, but Patty tried to hold it at bay. "Scare them." *No, that's not clear enough.* "No deaths, but do not offer submission."

Cedric coughed again before bowing and turning away. Patty felt the warmth of his approval. She could already perceive a change in her company's attitude, finely balanced between aggression and control. Too much belligerence and her band would fracture into violent shards, striking out in every direction. Cedric's calm guidance was all there was between chaos and control as two wings of her company eased along the walls of the thoroughfare, flanking and then surrounding the delegation.

Murrun squirmed as if he needed to find a toilet. Patty could not stop herself from smiling. "What troubles you?"

"GreatMother," he rumbled, his bow subtly emphasized his reversed tabard. "This one has low caste..." well below the two that were being brought before her. *Like Pum, Murrun's instincts are to give obeisance to those placed above him. I'm glad my parents and teachers instilled in me a healthy sense of skepticism when it came to listening to those in positions of authority.* Her father's voice echoed through her thoughts, "Just following orders is a poor excuse for not paying attention to what you are doing." *Hang on, Dad. I'm coming.*

Giving instant obedience was convenient for those in power but not conducive to fostering self-esteem and honor. That's what Murrun needs. With a little boost, maybe he will be able to fly on his own. "Murrun, you worry about facing those born into a higher caste." Patty felt her body twist into unaccustomed poses. Mixing the words 'higher caste' with the *disdain* she felt for embedded authority was awkward. The very words were filled with honorific roots from an older tongue.

Poor Murrun shook with fear and shame interwoven with moments of frozen contemplation. Patty reached out and took his left hand in her right, her left hand resting on the little alien's shoulder. She could feel his affection, his worship of her overwhelm his fear, and his quivering settled to an occasional shake as she looked down into his eyes.

"Oh, Murrun. Our clan pays no heed to previous caste, high or low. Who your parents were is irrelevant; honor is achieved by your actions and attitude. You have great honor and status in our eyes. You are my FirstLeftLeadingSon." Patty waited for that to integrate. In frozen steps, Murrun stood taller. "No matter who birthed them," Patty glanced in the direction of the delegation, "how could you believe we would hold them in greater esteem than our FirstLeftLeadingSon?" Without turning, Patty could feel Cedric's approval. She held Murrun's eyes as his spine continued to uncurl. To Patty's surprise, he was at least as tall as Pum, nearly as tall as Alan. *That's better.* She patted his shoulder and took up her position in front of Zeus.

Murrun stepped forward and glanced at Cedric, hesitant once again. Patty's general gave him a brief but sincere bow before returning to conduct her company's movements.

Swallowing the delegation whole, they were squeezed as they were forced closer to Patty's position. The honor guard tried to form a protective shield around their two charges, but any resistance was clubbed into submission and then trampled underfoot.

Distraught and shaken, the two LeftLeading ambassadors were thrust to their knees alongside the three guards that remained bloodied but still standing. One by one, the nine others in the escort were brought forward and unceremoniously dumped on the deck. Many of the injured attendants were past the point where they would surrender. It was not offered. Their weapons and belongings were stacked in tidy piles to Patty's right.

"This is an offense to our honor that we are treated in such a manner." The senior LeftLeading legate raised his head, his chest filled with barely restrained bluster.

"You are a sacrifice!" Murrun's unexpected outburst sent the pale alien reeling. "After sending a hunter to assassinate our GreatMother, what reception did the delegate expect?"

Zeus drew his mighty blade and made to shuffle forward as if eager to do the deed himself. Patty laid a restraining hand on his arm. She could smell his fury but could feel his purr of suppressed humor.

"FirstLeftLeadingSon, perhaps they did not know of the hunter," Patty remarked as she observed the two delegates; their reactions were different. The younger one was ignorant and very afraid, the senior was also terrified, but he was conflicted. He knew things he was not supposed to share. How this was supposed to make him safe was unclear.

"GreatMother, ignorance is no excuse." Murrun's posture said he had been told that many times.

"This is just a delaying tactic. We have no desire to play another's game." Patty approached slowly and nudged one of the fallen guards with the toe of her boot. "Can they stand? We do not wish to be responsible for their care. We will return them." Patty turned her back and found herself with her nose pressed into Zeus's tabard. He shuffled back a step or two to give her space. Patty turned again and paused theatrically. "Perhaps they will be given a chance to integrate mel'andrin on honorable behavior rather than being," Patty grasped for the phrase, "Cleansed."

That hit the mark, especially with the senior legate. Patty could feel a pattern forming in her mind, fragments from all her gift-memories combining and overlaying. The political power elite held many secrets from their subjects. *Is that a species similarity or the innate nature of political power?* She was sure Cedric was not the first inconvenient opponent this RegentFirstMother had wanted to be Cleansed.

"Get them on their feet."

Cedric approached with just a nod, knowing his presence was always welcome. "GreatMother, you will go with them?" That was a question layered with more nuances than Patty could take in; uppermost was his agreement that she should go with the

RegentFirstMother's delegation. That they should give up this strategic position and move all her forces was a matter for debate. He was inclined to send a sizable escort with her. *Man of few words, indeed.*

"Yes, we will be going. We need to take the initiative and push the timetable forward. We bow to our general's experience regarding our escort."

A turn of Cedric's wrist posed another question, one that made Patty think. As much as she wanted to confront this RegentFirstMother with her strongest supporters at her side, she did not want to leave this company under the command of someone from whom she had not received mel'andrin. She could trust Cedric one hundred and fifty percent. "Will you stay and look after my people?"

"It would be this one's honor." Cedric bowed deeply. When he rose, he turned to confer with Felix. Patty could feel the company's change begin, like a cell dividing.

"GreatMother," Murrun called. He stood with a young, low caste female at his side. She bowed until her head touched the floor and stayed there. "She seeks admission."

The reason her company had no mothers flashed through Patty's mind courtesy of Cedric's gift. Mothers were non-combatants. They could not be subject to violent coercion. The concept would not parse. Mothers' allegiance to their tribe was as strong and instinctive as any of the brothers, but they could change. *Were there protocols for this?*

"Please rise, young mother," Patty instructed.

"This one gives thanks, GreatMother." The poor thing trembled. *What does she imagine I'm going to do?*

Patty tried to be as gentle as she could. She half expected the young female to shy away, skittery as a foal. "You seek admission to our clan. Why?"

She bowed again. "This one's FirstRightLeadingSon stands with you." The accompanying gesture sent Patty's attention to a brother in the second row. A tiny tilt of his head told Patty he knew his mother was there, but his focus remained on his duties. "A clan needs balance. There is honor here." The combination of words, sign, and scent confirmed this young mother's sincerity and more. There were others of like mind that waited for this moment. This one had been in contact with Clan Tol'edranna's TwelfthMother.

"We welcome our FirstMother into our family." Yes, there would be honor aplenty for this young mother, sent as a possible sacrifice. Sent to test us.

"GreatMother, this one gives thanks." From the moment she began to bow, Patty knew she was going to be offered another gift-memory. *No. Not now. You're tipsy enough as it is, girly.*

Her concern was received by Cedric and returned with a cough and a deep bow. "Integration is best done when there is time for contemplation." Felix, Ed, and Dan stood behind him, proud and happy. Cedric held a small wooden box in his steady right hand. No more than three centimeters square and two thick, the corners were rounded, softened by long years. It was old. *Maybe very old.* His fingers did something dexterous with the hidden latch and flipped open the lid. A heady aroma arose from within the box. Hundreds of tiny pearls jostled against each other. *Hundreds?* Patty glanced around. Yes, there were hundreds of soldiers around her, all with their tabards reversed. *Did they give me a memory from each of them? How will I ever know whose gift is whose? Is this pick'n'mix random-gift-memories?*

"Thank you, Cedric." Patty's hands trembled as she took the wooden box. The closer she came to the mouth-watering scents, the weaker her resolve seemed to be. *Having a chance to integrate a mother's gift-memory would give you more insight into their behavior. And balance. I have more than enough memories sloshing around inside me from all the male genders.* The idea of integrating a memory from that hunter made Patty gag. That helped to keep Patty from sipping at the offered spoon. The FirstMother did not hesitate to add her little memory-essence to those crowded together in the smooth dark-grained interior; a smaller gift than the others, a hint of gold blessed its pearly surface.

Feeling that the company was ready to divide, Patty stowed

the warm wooden box in her belt pouch. She felt subtly transferred, osmosis-like, from one secure center to another. Approximately a third of her forces wrapped around her. *Well, if that's what Cedric thinks I need.* Both cells roared a parting chant as they separated, feet stomping, bright blades clashing joyfully overhead.

DEPARTURE

Pur'unnan sat on the worn hilltop and blinked the dust from her eyes as her Hel'omi escorts turned outward in a shallow arc, warding all away. Only moments before, she'd been inside her memories, swimming and harvesting spiny green eggs with Fe'ren. The day was hot and dry; this part of the Badlands had not seen rain in many years. The dusty knoll had been flayed and burnt, and its bedrock laid bare. Gone were the lapping waters, gone the moist breezes, never to return. *It's well-past time to find a new swamp.*

Beyond the arc of her Bumurnam sons, Dre'wholla, her chief assistant and a LeftLeading brother with a particularly sharp mind, jogged up, radiating concern. All week, her chief assistant had been confident he would be able to fly Delrofenalis into orbit. He had flown her solo twice, short hops admittedly but executed flawlessly. He had an affinity with the finicky prototype. She had, on occasion, heard him coo to the probe, urging the device to perform correctly. Pur'unnan did not care how he got the job done. He could sing and dance if that did the trick.

Standing, Pur'unnan brushed off the dust and strode towards her FirstLeftLeadingSon. "Dre'wholla. What is it?" she asked.

"GreatMother. It is ... should be simple. The internal gravity aboard Delrofenalis fluctuates." His shoulders dropped. "This one has failed the GreatMother..."

"Nonsense," Pur'unnan scoffed. "We are close to launch time. Are we ready?"

"Yes, GreatMother," Dre'wholla answered.

"Then let us delay no longer." Pur'unnan took a slow breath and composed her mind while imprinting new mel'andrin.

"Dre'wholla, take this to Frel'anandis when you get to *Talefenanis*. I'll take Delrofenalis into orbit."

CHAPTER TWENTY-ONE

Lily sucked in another much-needed lungful of air as she sagged against the wall of the spiral stairwell. Her arms ached from carrying her little bomb and her thighs burned from the descent. "At least we're going down the stairs."

Daichi gave her an encouraging smile before peeking into the corridor. The sounds of feet on the treads above echoed down the shaft. "The corridor's clear. I'll try some of these doors. See if we can find a quiet place where you can get your breath back."

Despite studying Patty's previous explorations there seemed to be little in common in this quadrant. The great mothership was laid out in a convoluted organic pattern surrounding the more direct corridors that led into the central core. Keeping to the less frequented passages meant they had traipsed all over the place. Lily pushed off the wall and followed Daichi into one of the straight corridors. They moved aft with Daichi trying each of the doors as they went. There was activity further ahead; behind, the corridor's lights flickered, sending staccato images of a greater darkness beyond. The fourth door opened into a storage room stacked with anonymous brown boxes.

After carefully divesting herself of her burden, Lily slumped to the floor. She stretched her arms and neck before giving her thighs a rub. "Murphy, take this bloody gravity."

Daichi chuckled and groaned as he stretched. "I must agree. It's been nearly six months since I've been down on Earth. It does take it out of you."

"Been over two years for me." Lily flicked open her tabard, peeled a transparent soft-flask of water from the stick-em pad on her upper thigh and drank. "Didn't think we would take quite this long to find a place to plant my baby."

Nodding, Daichi pulled his comm from the stick pad in the small of his back. He frowned, turned it around and back again. "Thought as much. We're over on the starboard side, again. Hope we don't get tangled with the Belters when they start their ruckus."

"Can you get Patty's feed?" Lily asked. "What's her progress?"

"Just a sec..." Daichi tapped at the comm as he crossed the floor and sat beside her. He maximized the image. The display was tiny, but it was easy to see the alien soldiers that filled the screen. They surrounded Patty; everywhere she turned, it was aliens wall-to-wall. *At least she's not fighting.* Indecipherable rumbles dominated the audio feed. For a moment, Lily saw Alan. He had his hand on the hilt of his sword, but he looked to be his usual relaxed-but-vigilant self. Patty turned, and a pale left-handed alien dominated the image.

"She seems to be making some progress, I guess. At least they're not fighting that horde," Lily noted.

"Have you noticed their tabards?" Daichi asked.

"Huh?"

Daichi's fingers zoomed the image. "They're all different colors, all mingling together. The soldiers we've seen, always group with their colors."

"Are they inside-out?" Lily peered closer. "Weird."

"Yes, I wish I knew more about these aliens. Patty and Alan don't look like they are in any immediate danger." He zoomed the image out.

"That rumble sounds like Patty's voice," Lily said. "You don't suppose she picked up some of the local lingo, do you?"

Daichi smiled, "She's an intelligent and adaptable young woman." He chuckled and shook his head. "Her somewhat unorthodox southpaw style made mincemeat of most of the age-grade fencing teams. Patty, learning the aliens' language? It wouldn't surprise me at all."

Lily offered Daichi her water. "You know, the further we've traveled the more I think I should have made a bigger bomb."

She kicked the scuffed deck with her heel. "This place is built like the proverbial brick outhouse. Talk about over-engineered. It reminds me of a hive. The rooms are like cells. The walls and floors aren't fitted together; they blend seamlessly. This girl will absorb a huge amount a damage before she breaks."

"That means you might be able to make a big mess locally." Daichi nodded. "Then we need to make sure your device is not wasted."

"I think I've got my breath back," Lily told him. "We should make a move."

Within minutes of venturing back out into the corridor, a company of soldiers in blood red tabards charged out of a side corridor and bore down upon them. Daichi moved to the left wall with Lily on his heels. She kept her head down and took the opportunity to rest against the cream wall. It was not the first time they had witnessed a troop of soldiers marching through the twisted ways, but it was the first to come at them, charging.

"Keep still, head down. They'll pass." Daichi's calm whisper helped Lily's racing heart not one whit, and her hand clutched the remote. She did not plan to be at ground-zero, but the alternative was capture and pacification. They had seen many docile humans in their travels; the thought of that happening to her made Lily ill.

The company swept past, hardly giving the two cowering humans a second glance and turned right into the stairwell. Lily took a deep breath, released the remote, hefted the bomb in her arms and pressed on.

The passageway began to fill with busy aliens; the browner females and clumps of pale left-handed males entered the corridor from small feeder halls or rooms that opened directly into the thoroughfare. Most cubicles appeared to be meeting spaces of some description although Lily caught a glimpse of a chemistry lab in one. Soldiers stood guard at every intersection but did not interfere with the flow. Progress was slow but steady. Once again, Lily was comforted and dismayed by the sight of other humans in gray tabards. They shuffled as they carried parcels or pulled laden trolleys. Lily did not need any tips on slouching, her arms, shoulders, and back ached.

A rumbling roar preceded a change in the crowded corridor. Panicked aliens pressed out of the cross-corridor ahead, fleeing from something. A troop of soldiers pressed against the tide, hooming, and rumbling. Daichi and Lily stuck to the wall and tried not to get swept away by the press.

Suddenly the ship shook, and the ever-present lights flickered and failed. Daichi dropped to the floor, dragging Lily with him. He slapped his hands over his ears, and Lily followed suit barely in time. The pressure wave from an explosion swept over them. The corridor groaned and expanded. All along the passageway, doors snapped open to dissipate the pressure-wave. Clouds of dust and wind-blown debris surrounded them. The crowd erupted in panicked chaos.

"That would have to be the Belter's NNEMP." Lily coughed in the choking dust. The lights flickered back on at about twenty percent of their previous brightness.

"I would guess so," Daichi replied as he stood on his toes and looked out over the heads of the scrambling throng. He was back in a second and helped Lily to her feet. "This way!" he breathed into her ear. He could have shouted because no one would have been able to hear over the rumbling din of the panicked aliens.

They pressed on and crossed the congested intersection. For all their panic, the aliens were remarkably polite in close quarters, even to lowly humans. The first door they struggled past opened to an office with a desk and a view screen, but the next had a workbench and a wall with tools mounted upon it, a workshop. They ducked inside. The far end of the workshop was open; a sliding door was partially retracted. Beyond it, a series of workshop cubicles arched around a central terminus. The explosion had little effect here; dozens of left-handed technicians were servicing boxy transports and the delta-shaped fighters.

Two fusion engines on trolleys coughed and spluttered in a bay around to the right. Lily eyed the huge inefficient engines and scoffed. "What relics." Fuel lines ran back against the wall to a metered control panel. Storage tanks would not be too far away. Beside the controls, a dilapidated set of shelves slumped against the wall. They appeared to be held up by goodwill and the tattered brown boxes stuffed into their battered shelves.

"Bloody perfect." Lily's heart leaped, and adrenaline spurred her forward while Daichi kept watch. "When this little puppy lets rip, she'll take this whole garage with her." Lifting the carton now seemed effortless. "The only problem is this box looks too new," she said resting the box on a shelf and flipping it open. She quickly checked the circuits and then retested the remote while the bomb was unarmed. The burst signal leaped out from the remote into the Belter's military net and bounced back to the bomb. *Damned if I know what happened to Jake's bomb.* Lily grinned at the successful test and rearmed the bomb. A red light blinked five times. She pressed the remote back onto the stick-em under her left breast, closed the box and slid it into the shelf, pushing it as far back as she could. Her heart raced. She stood back and looked at her work. The box was the wrong shade of brown, and to her eyes, it stood out, but it was good enough.

"Let's get going," Lily told Daichi, and they slipped out into the noisy corridors.

CHAPTER TWENTY-TWO

Felix led her escort, striding confidently a few steps in front of Patty; the set of his shoulders told her that Cedric had shared mel'andrin with him before they left. A reflection of her general shone in his eyes. His nod told Patty that Felix knew what she saw and Cedric's gift-memory within him recognized a part of itself inside her too. Patty nearly tripped over her own feet, her head spinning. She steadied herself against Alan and caught sight of that checkered flag flapping heroically in a holographic breeze above their heads.

Felix should be my flag bearer. Cedric's mel'andrin agreed. *Alan won't mind.* In the meeting to come, a flag bearer would have responsibilities for her company. Alan would have to leave her side. *He won't stand for that.* It only took a few moments to transfer the projector to Felix's shoulder, and Patty took the opportunity to scale up the projection's size to suit the larger hallway. Her escort hummed with pride and stamped a cadence of approval as they marched.

As their formation approached the atrium, Patty could feel the atmosphere within the mothership respond. Tal'anis, *that's what they called their great ship.* Another name rose inside her from all three gift-memories, Li'ila'tion, the Breathing Heart. That was the atrium's name, the Breathing Heart. The scents from all quarters of the great ship mingled here. With one breath you could read the living mood of the inhabitants.

The appearance of Patty and her company on the promenade added a new note to the atmosphere. Curious mothers and LeftLeading brothers gathered in clumps. There were many conflicting scents coursing through the bright light, and the presence of a cohesive force demanded attention and respect. It was given, in between competing demands. A cohort in blood-red crossed a high arch in double time. Beneath the sound of pounding boots, Patty thought she heard fighting. *Is that Günter, Marni, and Shun?* While her company was treated with some caution, there was an air of acceptance; there was something recognizable about it. Soldiers from all the clans were drawn to the Belters, like an immune response repelling an infection.

Mothers approached at irregular intervals requesting the release of injured guards from the delegation. Patty made sure they knew they had free access to her traveling demesne. Some reversed their tabards and stayed. Her company hummed their approval as their small wholeness embraced them as their own. The RegentFirstMother's delegation was down to the five members; two of them limped as they led Patty's entourage down a curving ramp towards the plume of steam that rose from Li'ila'tion's center.

The plinth was the convergence point for the paths within the atrium and atop it was the aliens' Sprocket Drive. Six panels with their winding handles and the spherical attitude control were only a meter or two away. Billowing steam rose from behind the boards. A steam engine, driven by a tokamak, powered the handles on all but the first two of the six controls. Patty had seen it on her first visit, from across the atrium in the ventilation ducts high above. *Were they like the five registers Cian used in Freya's drive? This whole thing looks cobbled together.* The controls appeared to be set at All-Stop.

Patty couldn't keep her eyes away from the transparent box. All the gross external controls ran there, linked to slender, carefully machined probes that penetrated the case. Inside was a device; a dozen or more small metal control wheels clustered around a tiny blue-gray sphere. Small gearboxes transferred the external settings to these wheels and then into the mysterious core. *No more mysterious than Freya's new drive I suppose. Cian says I'll get the math if I study it. All Cian and Eg have to do is lick this maximum mass threshold thing. With the current civilian fleet retrofitted with new drives, the solar system would thrive and grow like never before. And then the stars. There would be nothing holding humanity back. Is that a good thing?*

The humiliated delegation shuffled on, down a curving walkway that spiraled around the central dais. Patty had not paid the walls of the plinth any attention on her previous visit. From the high ventilation shaft it had looked unremarkable, but as the ramp arced around it, she could see elaborate carvings decorating every centimeter. Much deeper than the engravings covering the corridor walls, these friezes presented many tableaux filled with intricate detail. Tiny figures with recognizable alien sideways poses stood, fought and died. If there was a narrative, it was lost on Patty, but the innate beauty and meticulous detail intrigued her.

At the bottom of the ramp, walls of soldiers held back the curious, clearing the way. LeftLeading brothers dominated the numbers on this level and one in particular caught Patty's eye. He was pressed back against the central plinth by the curious and the lines of soldiers. He held a pencil and paper and made quick sketches of their party. His tabard was pale, ice blue, although at this distance Patty could not tell how detailed it was.

Zeus knew Patty was going to stop and thus the rest of her company did too. When Patty suddenly came to a halt, her escort stopped with her. The delegation preceding her stumbled forward a step or two before they realized the company was no longer with them. The handful of aliens between Patty and the feverishly scribbling one in pale blue melted away. It was only then that the alien realized he had Patty's attention. He bowed low, with few flourishes, and remained bent over for the longest of times before returning to a slightly diminished upright stance. He wore a decorated blade at his hip, but its hilt seemed more like the handle of the tools that hung from his belt, chisels, files, and brushes.

Behind him, carved into the central column, was a fascinating tableau. A blazing angry sun, personified with six arms, each brandishing a great blade, climbed over the horizon. Exquisite detail showed the arrival of multitudes along a dozen different pathways to the foot of a rocky hill. A high wall surrounded the tor, and only a few entered. Two great spaceships stood atop the rise, taking all those that passed inspection inside their cavernous bellies.

Two ships? Patty wondered.

"Murrun, does he make these carvings?" The tools on the alien's belt suggested as much.

"Yes, GreatMother. This brother is a historian, maintaining the visual record," he informed her.

Then there were *two ships. Why haven't they brought the second craft into play? Has it been lost or was it waiting in the wings?* A half flash from Cedric's mel'andrin suggested to Patty that the second ship had been tragically lost very early on ... during liftoff. He had no gift-memory of the event but knew others who did.

"Two ships. Many come, but few are chosen," Patty remarked. *Could the picture mean anything else? Was the diorama meant to be interpreted literally? Two ships. Was that the sun, climbing over the horizon?* "The sun is fierce," murmured Patty. *Am I framing this correctly for the camera?*

"Hotter every day, this one was told, GreatMother," Murrun replied. He pointed to a lake in the foreshortened distance. A village with its dilapidated pier stood abandoned far from the water's edge. Subtle rings marked the lake's retreat. *One for every year, I'll bet.* She could see a tiny road with even tinier figures moving a little boat down an improvised slipway. Then Patty realized the street was the slipway, lengthened year after year, chasing the receding shore. *Did their sun go nova? No. This speaks of gradual change, not a sudden cataclysm. The hills look old, weathered and worn down. How old?*

Suddenly, a dull thump shook Tal'anis. The bright overhead light dimmed before flickering back to full brightness. A pressure wave blew dust and debris from the highest starboard corridors into the atrium. Patty had to swallow repeatedly to prevent her eardrums from imploding. *Was that Lily's bomb?* From the apparent lack of damage, Patty guessed it was the NNEMP device the Belters had brought. She suddenly felt naked, so far from her p-suit and then a moment later, a guilty pang hit her. *Was that the Belters last stand? Were Günter, Marni, and Shun gone? More dead.* She felt ill.

"GreatMother," Murrun bowed nervously, "can we continue this inquiry at a later date?"

"Perhaps you are correct." Patty gave the historian a small bow. "We would like to get in touch with your historians when this useless conflict is finished." The historian bowed deeply in return. "Let us continue." Patty strode forward, in step with her company.

Somewhat reluctantly, the bedraggled delegation led them on through a wide corridor lined with the RegentFirstMother's soldiers. *A mark of respect, I'm sure.* The seventy or so brothers around her did not feel quite so secure. The cream walls were covered with deep tableaux; the floors were worn and had the feeling of, if not greater age, then greater use.

CHAPTER TWENTY-THREE

The corridor opened out into an auditorium of sorts. Two levels of arched openings blended into a dome capped with a bright light. Faces from all genders and clans peered around the intricately carved balustrades and fluted pillars that ascended to the ceiling, dividing the dome into six. Glittering specks set in black covered the domed ceiling. *Constellations from their homeworld? Was Sol up there somewhere?*

A stage stood at the far end, warded by a double row of guards. Patty's heart skipped a beat as her company moved down the center of the chamber. Jake and her father were on the platform. The RegentFirstMother was there too, in a mantle of deepest red, the multicolored sash of the Great Council around her shoulders. A dozen RightLeading brothers formed a line behind her, and a gaggle of LeftLeading advisers clumped on either side of the RegentFirstMother. Of the young golden GreatMother, there was no sign.

A high caste LeftLeading brother in a rose tabard dismissed their broken escorts. Although Patty was sure punishment in some manner was due to them - that was the way the delegation behaved - the high caste brother gave no outward indication of any enmity towards them. In fact, the atmosphere in the auditorium was remarkably friendly. Once again, a flash of Cedric's gift-memory filled in some of the gaps. *GreatMothers were rare and often brought a chaotic mingling of the tribes as she established herself. It was something the alien-whole understood. A clan with an alien GreatMother was novel but not unacceptably so; alien or otherwise, GreatMothers were strange creatures.* Still, there was something about the atmosphere that tasted a little flat. It did not have the dynamic rush of scents the great atrium held.

The high caste LeftLeader strode forward and down the broad steps at the center of the stage. Felix lifted his head. The dance-proper would now begin. Murrun shook himself. As the RegentFirstMother's ambassador reached the lowest step, the twin lines of guards parted, and he walked clear and struck a relaxed pose.

"GreatMother, with your blessings." Murrun glanced at the ambassador; his left hand brushed the hilt of his ceremonial blade.

"My blessings and the goodwill of all your brothers and mothers go with you, FirstLeftLeadingSon. Be your best, Murrun," Patty said proudly.

"GreatMother," Murrun rumbled, bowing with an added flourish before turning and squeezing through the press of brothers. Felix eased his way, and the company parted around Murrun as he strode forward. Patty sat on Zeus's offered hand without thinking twice. It was difficult to feign lack of concern; Murrun's burst of self-confidence felt brittle. *I hope he gets through this exchange of honor intact.* She could feel Zeus's humorous contempt for the LeftLeaders' tiny blades. *They still have sharp edges.* Patty leaned into his self-assured purr and gave Jake a wave over the heads of her soldiers. He waved back but did not look very happy. *Where is Pum?*

The two LeftLeading brothers faced off, drawing their weapons and a formal exchange began. Murrun met the attacks in the four quadrants competently. He parried, if not quickly, then efficiently enough. Once his defenses were tested, Murrun attacked much faster than his slow defense indicated and caught the ambassador flat-footed. Zeus purred and coughed quietly. *Yes, our man's doing well.*

The next stanza was much more free-form, and the contest was even with Murrun more than holding his own. The RegentFirstMother's ambassador showed Murrun some genuine respect. Her company rumbled and stamped their feet in support as the last passages were exchanged, and the ritual concluded. Murrun rose from his bow, his confidence reinforced, although he was far from cocky.

"Yes! Well done!" Patty called. She stretched her legs, and Zeus lowered her to the ground. Her company parted; the front line withdrew until there was a clear path. Patty walked forward, Alan at her side, Zeus at her back. Felix gave a small bow as she strode past.

The RegentFirstMother's delegation began to withdraw from the left side of the stage, and as Patty stopped at Murrun's side, a line of her soldiers marched past and up the left side of the stairs, taking up positions that mirrored the RegentFirstMother's guards.

"Murrun, we are very pleased. You did well," Patty told him.

"Thank you, GreatMother." He bowed and assumed a very upright stance. *He's taller than Pum now.*

The RegentFirstMother's ambassador bowed low, lower than protocol demanded. "Be welcome, GreatMother." In sight, sound, and scent, Patty could sense no deception from him. *Why does that feel wrong?* He turned and led Patty up the stairs. She ached to rush across the stage to where Jake and her father stood, but her GreatMother persona would not allow her to more than glance at them as part of an overall assessment of the field of conflict. There were three exits from the stage, one on each side, and double doors at the rear.

The ambassador bowed to the RegentFirstMother. "It is this one's honor to present GreatMother Balke to RegentFirstMother, Leader of Great Council, Clan Bar'Durrunnan FirstMother, Harrum'Bar." *She's right-handed. She'll never be a GreatMother.* Cedric's memory said that thought should irk her, but the FirstMother showed nothing of this to Patty. Her stance, while not open, was not aggressive. She had yet to speak, but the scents, drifting across the stage, were not filled with hostility.

The ambassador stood to one side, and two clan leaders faced each other. *This is not chess.* Despite the emanations of goodwill, Patty still felt a chill of danger. *I swear, it's not more than two degrees Kelvin in here.* She kept her shallow bow a heartbeat longer than necessary and held the RegentFirstMother's eyes all the while. This was a bow of respect, not obeisance. The alien ruler returned her offering, not one whit deeper or longer.

"Greetings," Harrum'Bar's hesitation was minuscule, but Patty caught it, "GreatMother," the FirstMother said. *You didn't like saying, that did you.* But that small revelation made Patty relax a little; the Clan mother was being honest. Sight, scent and sound, she was without a glaring conflict. "While your Traaaffic Control informed us you were coming," her eyes darted to the main formation of her escort and back, "we did not realize you would subvert our sons and arrive in force." Harrum'Bar was angry, that was obvious, but she was holding it firmly in check. She took a long look at the checkered flag hanging high above them all and then down to the hologram flag waving above Patty's company.

"You come with all the formality of one of our homeworld, demanding truce-for-discussions and yet you brought soldiers-of-attack to Tal'anis." She was not referring to the company of brothers Patty had gathered around her, the RegentFirstMother's posture said *other force*, which could only mean she was talking about Günter, Marni, and Shun. Covert agents like Daichi and Lily had very different postural descriptors. "Allowances can be made," the sweep of her eyes took in Fritz and her escort, "when a GreatMother comes into her maturity, but war does not hide under a banner of truce. Which is it to be?"

At least she's not hiding behind any diplomatic double-speak. This is it, girl. I wanted the chance to talk to someone in charge. Now's my chance. Patty took a breath. "Your accusation is false, and your understanding is misguided. Those fighters boarded," the name of the great mothership rose naturally to Patty's tongue, "Tal'anis by their own means. They did not travel with us. You brought them here. The Belter clans are fiercely independent, often a bane for those from our homeworld, but your annexation of their territory and property means now we fight as brothers, side-by-side. We are surprised Tal'anis' hull is not crawling with teams of Belter saboteurs." That sent a worried shudder through the ranks of advisers.

"They are not *my* people, but their authorities are open to *our* suggestions," Patty advised the RegentFirstMother. "If you withdraw to a neutral place and cease this act of aggression and theft, we are sure we will be able to bring a halt to these wasteful hostilities."

CHAPTER TWENTY-FOUR

Harrum'Bar shook off her surprise, superior pride returning to her pose, although it took longer for her advisers, gathered on the far side of the auditorium's stage, to mimic her confidence. "The Belter ships are down to three now," Harrum'Bar said as she turned to one of her advisers, who nodded enthusiastically. *Toady.* "They have been a nuisance, nothing more. We will soon be free from their interference." The RegentFirstMother moved as if she planned to continue, but Patty cut her off.

"But they have delayed you sufficiently so that you will still be here when the rest of the fleet arrives," Patty countered A nervous twitch from one of the FirstMother's advisers told Patty her guess was correct. "You do not understand what you have done. You have awoken the sleeping giant. That annoying little squadron has hurt you and continues to hurt you. What is their kill-rate, five or six to one? You do not have the resources for a prolonged war," she lectured. "If you read our history carefully enough then you should know the Belters held Earth, with all its resources and Corporate powers, to a prolonged and expensive stalemate. The Belter Clans will bleed you dry with a thousand tiny cuts and leave you gasping for one more breath," she declared.

"Should you survive," Patty continued, "and successfully deliver this asteroid to its target on Earth, you will still be denied a foothold no matter where you try to land. You have defaced the garden of our homeworld and, as you have already experienced, we will not hesitate to despoil it further to keep you away. You will be caught between the rocks and the angry sea and torn apart. The proper course is to withdraw. Even now, there is a chance for peace. Withdraw, and now that a channel for communication has opened, you have the opportunity to turn from this path. Humanity will not love you, but our solar system is big enough for one ship of refugees," Patty offered. "Even a ship this big. And if you cannot stay, we are certain that resources can be provided for you so that you can go on your way as you search for a new homeworld. We have surveys and records of hundreds of possible worlds. Fresh new worlds."

"Worlds you have not annexed?" This seemed to strike the RegentFirstMother as nonsensical.

"Until you arrived, we did not have the means to travel so far. Once our scientists realized Tal'anis used a reactionless drive, well, the rest was just a matter of filling in the dotted lines," Patty remarked. *Well, maybe a bit more than that. Murphy must have been sleeping.*

To Patty's surprise, Harrum'Bar looked shocked and confused. "You have counterfeited Pur'unnan GreatMother's work?" And angry. "By what right do you do this? This cannot be!"

Patty felt a surge of confusion wash through her. "You don't expect to own the exclusive rights to a law of nature, do you?" Patty countered. But it seemed as though she did. Harrum'Bar stood firm. Patty's mind reeled as minor reflections from her gift-memories coalesced. That's what the Clans are. One clan controls fusion engines, one steam engines, one communication technologies, another for closed-system environmental systems. There were more. A new sect had been formed during the journey to Sol, around the invention of those white power staffs, although it was still very small and dependent on those who controlled fusion power. They're not clans; they're guilds! With all these technologies locked up behind clan/guild strictures, how did they get into orbit, let alone cross interstellar space?

"You don't seem concerned we had fusion engines when you arrived," Patty argued. "Do you expect your enemies to ignore lessons taught by such bloodshed?"

Harrum'Bar was clearly perplexed. "Our philosophers understand that for any civilization to grow there must be a certain amount of independent creation of parallel technologies, but theft? There was no indication humans possessed this technology. There can be no honor for a GreatMother in the pilfering of another's gift." There were falsehoods in her words, but Patty could not parse them correctly.

"There is no honor in death by willful ignorance either," Patty responded. "And that will be the cause of your peoples' downfall. Your ignorance of how adaptable the human species is will have wasted," there was a name in Cedric's memories, *Pur'unnan,* "wasted GreatMother Pur'unnan's precious gift. You will have wasted all that precious mel'andrin from your ancestors. They will be lost like those who remained on your homeworld. But humans won't waste GreatMother Pur'unnan's endowment. You may have won the first battle, and if you wrest this asteroid from its orbit and smash it into my home, you may win that fight too, but the secret is out. My ship Freya brought me here using her gift." The RegentFirstMother and her advisers appeared amused. *So, Pum told them about his uncomfortable journey here. Good.* "And soon there will be hundreds of ships, thousands, to harry you into submission. You cannot win this war."

The RegentFirstMother nodded solemnly, her anger and outrage packed neatly away. "You have brought eloquent and passionate arguments before our council and given us much to contemplate." The nodding heads of her sycophant advisers all agreed. "Perhaps a small recess is in order," she suggested. At her gesture, the double doors at the rear of the stage opened. "There are refreshments, a place to rest for a moment, to confer with your Traaaffic Control while we consult."

"Yes, thank you." Patty's mouth was dry, and she felt empty after disgorging all the arguments that had built inside her. *And yes, I would dearly love to get Jake's take on what was happening. How badly am I stuffing this thing up?* Patty wondered. Harrum'Bar turned and led the way, her advisers scurrying behind her. Two RightLeading brothers escorted Jake and Christopher. None of Harrum'Bar's lines of guards made any move to follow. Patty checked the atmosphere. A certain tension filled the air, but there was bound to be nervousness at a meeting like this. Everything seemed to be within expected tolerances. Felix stood proudly below their holographic banner. He was alert but not worried. She turned and followed the RegentFirstMother and her entourage with Murrun, and Alan at Patty's side, Zeus at her back.

The room was as wide as the stage it opened onto and deeper. At the far end, there was a raised platform, topped with a high-backed engraved chair. *A throne of some sort? This is where the RegentFirstMother gives judgment.* For the first time, Patty entered a space on the ship that was not dominated by the pale cream coloring; dark-grained wooden panels covered the walls, floor, and ceiling, thick beams, and columns in the corners gave the impression of strength and integrity. Bladed weapons of all shapes and sizes - from slender poniards to something Zeus would need two hands to wield - were arrayed in racks, mounted to the walls. Bright banners in the colors of all the clans hung from the joists. A table with jugs and platters of food stood along one side with benches for seating. Jake and Christopher were left at the table as Harrum'Bar, and her escort moved towards the far side of the room.

"We will find a place of honor to hang the ... colors of your clan." Harrum'Bar did not turn as she walked to the dais. *There was no honor in that statement.* Her body said she would not use Patty's black and gold colors to wipe her feet. For the first time, her comments and posture did not synchronize with her scent. Patty glanced over her shoulder as her hackles rose; two soldiers had closed the doors and stood guard within the room, and yet the atmosphere's tenor was unchanged. Patty's hands began to sweat. *We're outnumbered and cut off.* Zeus and Murrun did not seem worried. The guards stayed at their post by the door, and Harrum'Bar huddled with her advisers, but Patty could feel ice forming along her spine. *Something is seriously wrong.*

CHAPTER TWENTY-FIVE

It was easy to slip into the flow of aliens in the passageway. Dust still filled the corridor and litter tangled their feet, but Lily kept her head down and followed Daichi's back. They made slow and steady progress towards the safety of the dark abandoned corridors forward.

A pale left-handed alien in a blue-green tabard rumbled at Lily from a side corridor where many aliens were entering. The Gray harroomed a shout and waved what appeared to be a clipboard. She kept her head down and shuffled on, bumping into Daichi. He slowed and slipped to one side, allowing her to edge ahead. There were not more than five aliens between her and the flickering dark.

"Keep going. I have your back," Daichi whispered.

Lily puffed her thanks. It was not likely she would be able to forge ahead even if she had a clear path. Her shuffle was real, not assumed as part of her disguise. Her back ached, her legs burned with each step, and her neck felt as though it was going to snap under the strain of holding her head up. She breathed deep and concentrated on the next step.

At the stairwell, Daichi gave her a push in the middle of her back that sent her staggering forward. "Run!"

Lily glanced over her shoulder. The pale lefty strode purposefully along the corridor towards them, with two big right-handers backing him up. The dark was not far away. Lily leaned forward and staggered to a trot, concentrating on lifting her feet so as not to trip. Constant light gave way to blinking and then darkness. Slowing to a walk, Lily swayed and bumped into a wall. That sent her to her knees and the worn deck.

Rolling onto her side, panting desperately, Lily watched as Daichi tangled the pale administrator with the two cardboard tubes that hid his swords. He dumped the Gray onto the deck. His two blades were out in time to meet the guards as they slowed to get around the floundering alien. Daichi attacked before they could settle themselves and forced them back over the alien wailing on the floor. The sound of blades seemed to draw everyone's attention, and the two soldiers battling Daichi soon had reinforcements thundering up the corridor. Lily crawled to the wall and used it to help her stand. She was not going to waste the chance Daichi had given her.

She had only taken a few steps when she heard more feet thudding along the corridor, but this time they came from ahead, from the dark. Lily sagged to her knees and clutched the remote. They were not very far away from the blast center. A troop of aliens burst out of the dark and trotted by Lily as if she was not there. All except for one. He skidded to a halt and stood quietly beside her for a moment before lowering himself to the floor.

He rumbled, and when Lily did not respond, he rumbled again, "You surrender," rum-rumble, "take to our GreatMother." Rumble, "Safety. Our GreatMother ... your GreatMother."

Lily did not know what to think and then she noticed his inside-out tabard. "Our GreatMother?"

"She returned," rumble-rum, "took this one's," rum-rumble-rum, "submission." He nodded a bow. "This one's GreatMother now."

"You're on our side?" Lily asked.

"Our GreatMother Pa'attee" rumble, "sent us." He paused and spoke as carefully as he could, "Take my people to safety, GreatMother said. Said you would not," rumble, "resist. You surrender?" he asked.

"Yeah, I guess." Lily still held the remote close to her body, but the alien made no threatening moves. He did seem very eager, and for some reason, proud.

"Will that one," rumble, "surrender?" The alien looked down

the corridor. Lily could not see much, but Daichi had three bodies at his feet and held soldiers from both ends of the corridor at bay, his blades flashing. "He resists well."

"Help me up." Lily extended her hand, and the alien gripped her forearm, supporting her as she rose. "Daichi!" Lily shouted. "They're from Patty!" *At least I think they are.* "They say they want to help!" She could not see Daichi respond, but the aliens began a hooming rumble, as they drew their blades.

Daichi appeared, sliding along the wall, as the aliens wearing inside-out tabards took his place. He staggered and fell. Lily and her alien companion quickly crossed the corridor; Daichi was bleeding. When Lily settled at Daichi's knee, the alien produced a small med kit from his belt and a flask of water. An assistant knelt at his side with more water and bandages before dashing off.

"Daichi, are you alright?" Lily asked.

"A few nicks and scrapes," Daichi replied with a wry smile. "Nothing too serious."

"Drink, warrior." The alien held out a flask.

Daichi gave Lily a curious look as he swigged at the canteen. "I dunno what's going on," she shrugged, "Just what he said. GreatMother Patty took his surrender, he said, and sent him out to find *her people*."

The alien cleaned the wound on Daichi's shoulder, "Our GreatMother say," rumble, "Cleansing her people bad."

"Cleansing?" Daichi flinched a little but did not cry out as the alien patched a cut on his thigh.

"Cleansing." The alien paused, his smaller left hand whirling, "Cleansing ... not this cleansing," he waved a bloody cloth, "you not Cleansed." He tapped his head. "Our," rumble, "GreatMother not Cleansed. Our GreatMother's," rumble-rum, "male sibling Cleansed."

"Alan." Lily took a sip from the canteen.

"Yes, the Alaaan." The alien shook his head. "Short name." He shrugged. "Our GreatMother Pa'attee," rum-rumble, "gave this one short name, the Ben." He held his head proudly. "The Abe and the Ben, FirstCalled." He stopped, and his gaze snapped from Daichi to Lily and back again. "You in Clan, yes? Not this." His hand flicked at Daichi's tabard. "Hiding true," rumble, "loyalty."

"Yes." Daichi nodded warily.

"Time to declare." Ben brushed away imaginary dust from his inside-out tabard and set his shoulders. His assistant trotted up and rumbled. The lines across the corridor still fought but the sound seemed to be more rhythmical than the earlier chaotic clash.

"Have no fear. We," rumble, "hold. Not fight to kill. Hold easy. Our GreatMother says, no dead! We hold, easy but should go. Ready? Give help, stand, walk."

Lily groaned but got to her feet by herself. Daichi took the alien's offered hand. Ben turned and took Daichi's blades, in their scabbards, from his assistant and held them before Daichi. "Strange blades but used well." Ben bowed. Daichi bowed in return and took his swords. He gave the blades a quick check and relaxed; they had not been put away bloody. "Get belt," Ben gave a rumble, and a belt was passed from the back of the line to his assistant and then to Daichi. "Free hands, better." Rumble, "We go."

Daichi wrapped the belt around his waist and slipped the two blades beneath it. They looked as if they belonged there. He reached around and pulled out the comm stuck to his lower back and wrapped it around his wrist.

"Good thought," said Lily as she unstuck her comm and logged in. The tiny screen illuminated the dark and drew every eye.

"Human tek," Ben rumbled as he edged closer.

"Yes, it is a communication device," Lily replied and opened the feed from Patty's sensor. The image showed a group of aliens facing off against another company arrayed in front of a stage. Between the groups, two left-handed aliens sparred.

Ben rumbled excitedly, "Must go now! The Cedric needs to see this." He rumbled loudly, and the troop began to disengage from the conflict. The company divided, with troops remaining to cover their departure. Lily found herself surrounded, Daichi at her side and they began to move into the dark. She glanced over her shoulder; she could still hear the blades clash as the fight continued. They had only traveled a few steps when it was apparent she could not move fast enough to suit Ben or herself for that matter.

"Sorry guys. I should never have volunteered for this." Lily staggered, and a big hand steadied her elbow.

Rum-rumble, "Are you injured?" Ben inspected her from head to foot."

"No, I'm not used to your gravity." Lily sighed and leaned on Daichi. He did not look as though he was up for a run through the dark corridors either.

"If it gives no offense ... we give help," rumble, "lift." The alien at Lily's left gave a small bow.

"If it's okay with you, then thanks. I'm Lily." She gave a wobbly bow that made the aliens around her cough gently. Daichi stopped her from falling.

"That one is known as Da'rruman..." Ben continued rumbling for another breath introducing the alien at his side, who bowed and stepped closer. His big right arm swept around her. He waited until Lily lowered herself into his hand before lifting her. She smiled as Daichi climbed aboard another alien. Ben rumbled and the company hustled into the dark. Da'rruman rumbled at her gently as they trotted along. The alien's ridged hands did not make the ride any more comfortable, and his trot made getting a decent look at her comm-feed almost impossible.

Rum-rumble, "Hu-uman tek?" Da'rruman's voice was so deep Lily could feel it in her bones as they trotted along in the pitch black. The screen was the only thing producing light. His head hovered just over her shoulder.

"Yes, my comm is showing... this is a feed from our GreatMother. She wears the camera," Lily told him.

"So," rumble, "small. Human make many," rumble, "clever things," he replied.

The company traveled down the pitch-black corridors, up some stairs and back into the twisting hallways. A section of lit hallways appeared as they turned a corner. Temporary stands held bright lights linked by power cables that snaked across the floors. A double line of guards stood at attention across the corridor, the multiple colors of their inside-out tabards jarred Lily's dark-accustomed eyes. Behind the guards, mostly female aliens crept between rooms.

The line parted with a rumbled greeting as Ben's troop approached. Ben spoke to his men, and they peeled off, leaving him with Lily and Daichi and their mounts. "We go," rumble, "to the Cedric unless you need," rum-rumble-rum.

"No, I'm fine." Daichi checked with his alien who nodded.

"I wouldn't mind a bite of something ... something to eat?" Lily felt silly for asking, but she needed something to boost her energy. She checked her comm; Patty was face to face with aliens, mostly left-handed ones but a female dominated the screen. Lily caught sight of Jake at the edge of the frame.

Rumble, "Will have some brought." Ben nodded before he turned and jogged down the corridor. Da'rruman and Daichi's alien followed close behind. The numbers of aliens inhabiting these passages amazed Lily, and all wore inside-out tabards. *Patty's recruited more than an army!* The corridor led into a crowded thoroughfare, all in Patty's overturned tabards. Ben pressed through, and an opening was made, though how the aliens managed to do it Lily had no idea.

Suddenly Ben stopped and bowed to another, "This is the Cedric, our," rum-rumble-rum, "GreatMother's," rumble, "coordinator. If it is possible to," rumble, "show your human tek?"

Daichi was closer, so he unwrapped his comm, and he presented it to Cedric. Lily checked her comm and blinked; there was fighting! Lily could not see much as Patty was moving quickly, but she could see that she was fighting an alien.

Cedric barked, and everyone around them sprang into motion. It was all Lily could do to hang on as Da'rruman leaped forward to keep pace with Cedric. She clutched Da'rruman's scarred upper arm and brought the comm unit close. Patty was still alive.

Suddenly the signal cut off. "She's gone!" Lily cried.

SURPRISED

"The human GreatMother is here, GreatMother. Feel the air! There is a Gathering!" Genedalt cried as he burst into Er'men's bedroom, coming to a sliding halt as the antique rug from early in the Second Rising bunched up beneath his broad feet. "The human GreatMother has taken Whellanor and named him the *Ze'oos*." He shrugged, acknowledging he had no understanding of what the name meant. Er'men did not know what a *Ze'oos* was either. She had suffered the effects of her brothers' mel'andrin so she could comprehend EngStand, but many words had inaccessible cultural references, making translation difficult.

"It is said they share the Closeness." Genedalt, for the first time, seemed disappointed they did not share that special empathic link.

The Closeness. It occupied a special place in GreatMother lore. *The Human GreatMother and young Whellanor, Ze'oos, have the Closeness?* Er'men pondered, and she felt a little jealous but only a little. With Little Star nestled inside her memories, she could feel the Closeness the GreatMother shared with Stone Son. That was more than enough for Er'men. *Who is this human that can bond with Hel'omi? Is she really a GreatMother? She has something, or Tal'anis would have rejected her.*

"Whel'luminum Pum'hurnun has returned with Traaaffic Control. Pum'hurnun see and hears truthfully," Genedalt told her.

Er'men did not have to ask if he had received mel'andrin from the LeftLeading brother; that was obvious. Genedalt rarely spoke with such enthusiasm. *And running in the apartments? He will be embarrassed tomorrow.* Er'men bounced to the edge of her bed.

"The GreatMother is not as Traaaffic Control led us to believe, but she is forthright and honest and very afraid. The meeting at the human station went poorly, we knew this, but did not know why. Pum'hurnun was there." Genedalt growled. "It was disgraceful."

"If the GreatMother is aboard then we should meet her!" Er'men insisted. "Assemble an escort. And bring Pum'hurnun to me," Er'men instructed. *I must see the GreatMother while she is here. We must talk.* Genedalt gave an enthusiastic bow and nearly tripped over the lumpy rug on his way out. It chafed Er'men not to be able to experience Pum'hurnun's mel'andrin for herself - the pain and nausea were debilitating - but she would learn much from watching him talk.

As she donned her formal multicolored robes, she noticed that Genedalt had been busy while she slept; the baroque golden stitching along the edge of her robe had gained a few more flourishes. *He has such a delicate touch with a needle and thread.*

CHAPTER TWENTY-SIX

Jake looked relaxed and at ease unless you knew him. It was his eyes; they took in everything while hiding behind his lazy smile. He turned Christopher to face his daughter as Patty approached. A fading green/purple bruise marred the left side of her father's face but the injury that concerned Patty the most was in his mind, what was left of it. His eyes were flat and showed no recognition of her at all. Patty swallowed the bile that spilled into the back of her mouth as she caressed his unworried brow.

"He's responsive to simple commands, "Jake began, "but ... I'm sorry Patty, the Christopher we knew is not at home."

"He's there," Patty answered, "just buried deep." *I hope.* Although it hurt her, Patty did not expect to see any spark in her father's eyes; Alan's was only just emerging. "How have they been treating you? Have you had any word about Mother?"

"Huh?" Jake shook his head. "I mean I was surprised as all hell when you began rumbling like a native, but Patty dearest, give this ol' duffer a chance to catch up. You haven't forgotten how to speak EngStand have you?" he asked.

The world in Patty's mind spun, waves of fiery revelation exploded in her head. Murrun's gift-memory reinforced by Zeus and Cedric flared brightly, language and culture, posture and expression, sound and scent. Finding her native tongue took a second or two. "Sorry, Jake. There's a lot I need to tell you." *Did I say that right?* The EngStand words felt flat and tasteless.

"I guess so." Jake looked Zeus up and down. "Grow 'em big 'round these parts, don't they."

"Zeus, Murrun, this is Jake, my most trusted adviser," Patty spoke in EngStand augmented with sign and placed her free hand on Christopher's shoulder, "and this is my father. Both are most precious to me." Patty cast a quick look around the room; the RegentFirstMother and her advisers were huddled on the far side of the dais, the two guards at their posts on the door. There was no apparent danger, but there was a marked difference between the atmosphere in the room and what she had experienced on the stage. She felt cut off from her support.

Zeus and Murrun both bowed. "The Jake, Traaaffic Control. This one is known." Zeus's words surprised Patty; he so rarely verbalized, mostly letting his body express his opinions. The hand on the hilt of his massive sword said more than an essay; he would protect them as he protected her.

"Traaaffic Control," Murrun bowed again, "guide us."

"Thanks, son. I would if I could." Jake's concern overrode his smile. "Have you seen Pum?" Jake waited for a beat to see Patty's head shake. "Didn't think so. He ducked away not long after you announced you were coming." Jake frowned. "Bad choice, my dear. A hard choice," he glanced at Christopher, "but one I advised against if you recall, or did you cut me off before I had a chance to finish?"

"They cut you off, but they only beat me by a heartbeat." Patty could feel her face flush.

"Thought so," Jake muttered, shaking his head as he looked across the room at the RegentFirstMother and her advisers. "This place is a flamin' hotbed of political strife. You don't need the lingo to figure that one out."

Angry rumbles reverberated from around the dais. Patty could not make out the words, but Harrum'Bar's tone was unmistakable. *Now that's more like it.* Cedric had witnessed the RegentFirstMother's anger many times. The irate sounds drifting across the room fitted with his memories more than the formally polite regent that had greeted her.

"Pum said he had to get something to his mother or something and slipped away. I've been cooling my heels with Christopher until a couple of minutes ago when they hustled us here. Ol' queeny over there was in quite a tizzy. They hung that flag only seconds before you and your company marched in." Jake grinned and let out a chuckle. "You should have seen them squirming. Bounding about like you had given them all a bad case of hotfoot. And speaking of company, that's a big escort they gave you."

"There was no giving. My sons were taken." Patty reached behind her and felt Zeus's warm hand. "They are ... mine." *How can I explain this to Jake?* "It is kind of complex, but I think I've started a new clan. It's something GreatMothers do, or so I've been informed."

"GreatMothers?" Jake looked bemused.

"Think of it as a hiccup in the translation. Queen is only a rough approximation." Patty could not hear the content of the arguments coming from the other side of the room, the volume was low, but the tone and the occasional whiffs were unmistakable, fear and anger. "The little golden one, she's a GreatMother." A young mother ran from the room through a small corner doorway with the RegentFirstMother's mantle, while another hurried in with a new garment. Everything about Harrum'Bar said power. Cedric's memory suggested she was loath to give any away. "Harrum'Bar can never be a GreatMother, she's right-handed, but she holds the reins of power crafted by a GreatMother."

"And your clan?" Jake asked. "Pum was always on about the clans being united. All those? All the escort? They've what? Sworn fealty?" He looked at Murrun and Zeus's reversed tabards and chuckled. "Turncoats? Really?"

"It's in their genes, like a dog submitting to a pack's alpha male. I don't think they can help it." Patty's gift-memories told her the aliens were much more than dogs, but they had their inherited reactions just as humans did. She remembered how much the weightlessness of zero-gee scared her the first time, how it felt like so much like falling, falling, falling, falling, falling, without end. She had been caught between fight and flight. "I was sick of being a killer, war or not, and had to try something else."

"Nothing to be ashamed about," Jake reassured her. His posture reflected emotional pain, enough pain for Jake to drop his relaxed façade if only for a moment. *Why haven't I seen that in him before?* He held an old unhealed wound tightly within himself. "Killing's a hard thing to do."

"Yeah, but not-killing is a hard way to fight a war," she grumbled. Patty tried not to feel frustrated with EngStand's limitations. "The first guards Alan and I encountered would have held us in a dark corridor forever, so we pushed them until they surrendered, submitted. I think they expected me to kill or Cleanse them." Patty took her father's hand for a moment. Mind or no mind it was good to be near him; he still smelled like her father. "I gave them back their swords, and yeah, I guess you could say they swore an oath, but it's deeper than that, more like resetting a clock."

"And you fought ... all of them?" Jake looked aghast at the double doors. "What, all seventy or eighty of them?"

"No, just the first few." Patty twisted around and gazed up at the ever-alert Zeus. *Would I have been able to take him down without maiming him?* She pushed the memories of bloodshed at L5 away. "No. But they are quite evangelical."

"Huh?" Jake cautiously nibbled at what looked to be a pale-yellow plum.

"I made it clear that I did not want any killing so those I suborned went forth and gathered more." Patty shrugged. "It kinda got a bit exponential on me."

"And you trust them?" Jake asked as he pulled a face and returned the fruit to the tray, rotating the nibbled section out of sight.

"Jake! They share memories!" Patty enthused. "They secrete these little pearls packed with a moment's snapshot of who they are. Zeus and Murrun and Cedric - he's back with the rest of my people - all gave me their memories. It's fantastic! That's how I learned their language, I guess. But there's so much more."

Jake could not hide the wash of disgust that swept over his face. "You ... ate ... secreted memories?"

"Oh, it's not horrible, not at all. They're real people Jake, not some scary monsters out of a feature. They're not a hive, but they're not quite individuals either. They have lives and loves and passions and fears just like we do ... sort of." *In a limited kind of way, moods sweeping through the air-conditioning ducts could do strange things to your head. The spirit of the whole was not easily ignored, likewise the disposition of your nearby brothers.*

Jake nodded. "Know your enemy."

"They're not our enemy or shouldn't be. They're refugees." Patty felt split. "There's going to be some sort of reparation, some kind of peace agreement. They are a whole new species, far too precious to annihilate in a stupid war. They are probably the last of their kind. Refugees."

"They picked a bloody funny way of asking for help." Jake looked as though he wanted to spit.

CHAPTER TWENTY-SEVEN

"Get. Out! Of! MY! SIGHT!" Harrum'Bar's outburst reverberated around the room. Some advisers sped from her presence as quickly as their twisted bodies could propel them; others bowed low, heads to the ground, and stayed there until she stalked away in high dudgeon, flanked by two RightLeading brothers. Patty stepped away from the table to meet her, Alan snapping to his position at her right - nearly stepping on Jake's toes as he cut between them to take up his station - and Murrun at her left. Zeus had her back although he favored Murrun's side.

"After due consideration," Harrum'Bar began, "it has been decided that your so-called Clan is an abomination. You will submit. Those deceived by you will be Cleansed and reintegrated into their previous associations." If a RightLeading brother had made that statement, he would have led with the bright point of his blade. Patty had never seen such naked aggression from a mother. Her scent was as sharp as her escorts' swords; so different from the way she presented herself on the stage. So distinct and yet unified, sight, sound, and scent. And then it hit Patty.

"You use perfume..." The words tumbled out before Patty could stop them. *She was masking her scent out there on the stage! That's why something felt false.* Patty wanted to kick herself.

Harrum'Bar started in surprise. Her body language said, *yes, you are far too dangerous,* and she went on the offensive. "It offends this one to see you claim the status of GreatMother. It is a lie, most blatant. These poor sons," her eyes took in Zeus and Murrun, "have been deluded, spelled."

Patty expected the FirstMother to come out swinging and did

not flinch from the venom of her attack. "We are the emissary of the people of Earth and..."

"You are nothing, no one!" Harrum'Bar asserted. "Investigations have been made into your bloodline." She glanced over at Christopher and just held back a cynical cough. "There is no hidden aristocracy on your world or in your family, that power has slipped to the Corporate ... groupings, and you are not a part of those dynasties either. There is no human Clan for you to be a GreatMother of." Now she coughed, loud and unrestrained.

"Patty, the door." Jake's urgent whisper made Patty glance to her left; the guards approached slowly, their hands on their hilts. Ice crept up Patty's spine.

"You are no mother. A GreatMother? No, it cannot be." Harrum'Bar relaxed her aggressive pose for a moment, easing into disdain, mixed with anger. "They say you killed my captain on that listening post beyond your homeworld's moon, that you bathed in his blood." Nausea swept over Patty leaving a sickly trail of cold sweat dripping down her back. That fight and what followed was a nightmarish blur. "Fight our champion," Harrum'Bar's shoulder indicated the guard on her right, "and your people will be treated ... leniently."

"This is wrong!" Murrun blurted out, caught between his anger and his ritual deference to the high-caste FirstMother. Patty put a hand on Murrun's shoulder before he went too far.

Harrum'Bar coughed; contempt dripped from every pore. "Here is your opportunity to prove yourself. Fight but not to kill, to force submission. A secret that no enemy should know."

"Our GreatMother should not be forced to fight. This one is her champion." Alan's eloquent sign, fluent in the alien tongue, and posture should not have surprised Patty, but it did. The lack of a spoken component was inconsequential as he stepped forward, his presence as potent as Zeus's.

Instead of backing away from Alan, Harrum'Bar leaned closer, examining him. "Ahhh, the little sibling." Her head rolled to the side, and she whispered something. Alan stiffened. His body spasmed as he fell. Patty dived to her right, catching him before he hit the floor. His eyes rolled back into his head, and his jaw clenched as he shook.

"What have you done!" Patty's scream lit a fire as it ripped from her throat.

Gloating! Harrum'Bar was amused. "Some wondered how much your ... brother absorbed while he was with us. His reputed skill with a blade could only have come from us. He is how you have won your fights. You try to turn our gifts against us, but it is you who lack understanding." She rumbled something Patty's ears could not decrypt. The words were old, archaic root-words that were not in her mel'andrin vocabulary. Christopher folded, his muscles slowly losing tension. Jake was there to ease him to the floor. "That is how it should happen. Give your sibling into our care so we can complete his treatments."

Torn between holding her trembling brother and leaping up to rip Harrum'Bar's throat out, Patty had to lean back as Zeus stepped forward, his blade arcing out from its scabbard. The RegentFirstMother's flankers reciprocated, and they stood ready to fight.

Harrum'Bar shuffled back but not too far. Her unconquered pose did not shift for an instant. "Tell your boy to stand down. As yet, the one that gave birth to you ... your mother? She has not been Cleansed. She is as she was when we collected her. Mostly." The threat made Patty's head spin, and she touched Zeus's ankle. He held his ground. "This one will see the so-called GreatMother fight." Harrum'Bar turned and strode to the dais.

"What in Murphy's name is going on?" Jake's urgent whisper snapped Patty out of the grip of cold fear.

"We're in trouble," Patty told him.

"Is that so?" Jake gently opened one of Christopher's eyes. Her father appeared to be asleep rather than having a grand-mal seizure.

Taking a deep breath, Patty gave Alan's trembling body a quick hug. "She wants to see me fight."

"She wants you dead," Jake replied.

"You think?" Patty looked at the RegentFirstMother's RightLeading brother on the left. He bounced on his toes, edging sideways towards the center of the room, rolling his shoulders. The two guards from the doors looked prepared for a turn if their brother failed. Murrun's ceremonial blade would be useless against them. *You might end up fighting all of them.* The remaining guard took up a post at the foot of the dais.

Releasing her buckle, Patty pushed Lady Estelle, snug in her scabbard, to one side. She reached around her brother's quaking body and drew his unnamed sword. Reshaped from the blade that Alan claimed at Patty's first kill; it was much stronger than Lady Estelle and better suited to facing her opponent's heavy sword.

"Look after them, Jake." Patty stepped away from Alan.

"GreatMother, no!" Zeus rumbled. "This one is your champion!"

"I must do this, or she will hurt my mother. Protect my family. You are my strong ... right arm." Patty looked into his deep black eyes until he blinked and bowed. Zeus kept his heavy blade out as he stepped back. Murrun helped Jake drag Alan and Christopher under the table as Patty took a moment to get a feel for this new weapon. It weighed more but had a longer reach than Lady Estelle. For all that, it was well-balanced. One breath, two breaths; Patty tried to put aside her pain, her fears, and her anger as she stretched.

There was no referee, no timekeeper, and no rules. The RightLeading brother attacked.

TRAVELING

The ornate double-doors to the GreatMother's apartments opened onto a broad section of the passageway that was full of mothers, and Left and RightLeading sons, moving with excited purpose. Er'men had never seen Tal'anis so agitated and alive. That could be a lethal mixture. The ways swarmed chaotically in the aftermath of the human incursion. Their weapon had not done significant damage, but their very presence aboard Tal'anis put everyone on edge. Er'men was surprised and amused that the human GreatMother was so readily accepted. *She did come with recognizable communication forms, but it's more than that. Something about her must smell right.*

A full company of Hel'omi led Er'men's excursion, with her LeftLeading advisers scurrying in behind. Despite the dominating presence of her Hel'omi phalanx, they moved slowly. Clumps of Bar'Durrunnan, choking strategic intersections, did not help the press of the corridors.

The change that swept through Tal'anis when the human GreatMother appeared - if that's what she is - triggered something that was supposed to focus on me! Er'men almost laughed. Who is this human? I need to see her for myself. She twisted on Genedalt's secure hand and waved Pum'hurnun forward from the mass of the so-called advisers assigned to her by the Great Council. Were they good for anything at all?

"GreatMother," Pum'hurnun bowed as well as he was able and continued walking, "this one is at your service."

"Genedalt told me that GreatMother Pa'attee flew you to Tal'anis, herself," Er'men's statement prompted him for more information.

"Indeed, GreatMother, although it was not a smooth ride, it was fast. Faster than conventional human ships. Humans have discovered GreatMother Pur'unnan's secret ... or some aspect of it." Pum'hurnun's pose reflected his lack of knowledge of those matters.

"Humans? Not GreatMother Pa'attee, herself?" Er'men asked.

"Apparently not, GreatMother. She traveled in a bigger ship, the Jaswinder, with a larger crew. A great many contributed to getting her little ship, the Freya, ready. This one is not sure which human contributed to what areas." Pum'hurnun wriggled uncomfortably. "The Freya's modifications happened before the GreatMother joined this one, aboard The Ice Princess. There was one, aboard the Jaswinder, who engineered this device. A GreatFather?" he posed his question as one seeking enlightenment.

"Is he the one known as Traaaffic Control?" Er'men asked.

"No. Traaaffic Control was with this one, aboard The Ice Princess. He is not a ... a GreatFather."

GreatFather? Was such a thing possible? "And GreatMother Pa'attee, what of her?" Er'men asked.

"The humans aboard The Ice Princess expressed genuine love and admiration for GreatMother Pa'attee, although I do not know if they regarded her as a GreatMother, not as we do. For some, she was a sister, for others a daughter and others a mother. Some see her as a great captain, others as a courageous pilot. This one saw her as," Pum'hurnun's movements were positive and sure, precise enough for Er'men to receive a clear picture of the human, "concerned, honest and idealistic. She feels ... inadequate to the task before her, but this one sees depth and strength in GreatMother Pa'attee. *Deep water*, indeed. She is well named." There was more, but Pum'hurnun waited for permission to continue. Er'men gave it.

"GreatMother, a Gathering has crystallized around GreatMother Pa'attee. This one felt the change from the moment this one came aboard. The humans were quite unsure of our customs, and this one is," Pum'hurnun slowed, thoughtfully, "this one is both surprised and not surprised," he finished, using the human tongue, adding a contradictory twist that seemed to suit that language.

Er'men bounced with glee in Genedalt's patient and muscular arms. "Go on."

"The GreatMother Pa'attee has a reputation for unpredictability and for turning situations to her advantage. The GreatMother has acquired an understanding of *Hel'Arumpo'or* culture faster than this one anticipated. It is true that a GreatMother cannot receive mel'andrin from her sons and daughters but what of a human GreatMother?"

"Mel'andrin from her FirstCalled." Er'men whispered to herself. Now she did feel envious. The human GreatMother had *The Closeness* with her Hel'omi companion and could use her sons' *mel'andrin*. Er'men could not wait to meet her.

CHAPTER TWENTY-EIGHT

Back-peddling as fast as she could, Patty parried but still received a cut on her shoulder as she circled to her left. *This brother is good, faster than those I've faced before.* She felt and heard the silk of her tabard part but ignored the fluttering black remnant. He had practiced against left-handers and seemed to know her next move before she did. He scored another cut below her knee. *I won't win this bout defending.* For the moment, her defense was all she had. She retreated a step at a time until she felt her balance return and then pressed forward.

Trying an attack in quarte, Patty scored a hit, but her blade's finely honed edge skittered across the brother's shoulder. Patty retreated as she watched a shiny sliver of chitinous armor peel away. *That should have penetrated!* she complained.

Around and around, they turned, Patty was in retreat more often than attack. Her wrist and shoulder ached, and numerous small nicks formed a choir of pain, distracting her. She caught glimpses of Zeus, Murrun, and Jake as she fought. *Jake has Lady Estelle out of her scabbard!* Patty's heart skipped. *Put it down! You won't have a chance! Silly man's holding her with both hands. I must finish this quickly!* She feinted to the left and swung to her right with a savage head cut. The tip caught and dragged but as Patty spun away, she did not see where she hit.

The brother roared and charged, blood streaming from a deep wound above his right eye. Block, parry, block; Patty's arm ached as it held out a barrage of primitive over-arm smashes. Lady Estelle would have bent and broken under this assault, but Alan's blade held true. She wished he was fighting at her side. It felt unnatural without him beside her. *Even if the old bitch is right,* it doesn't matter that Alan helped to win my fights. *Eg and Cian built Freya's incredible new engine, Madhur and Jaswinder saved my life, as did Lily's self-sacrifice. One girl can't do everything.* Patty missed an opportunity to attack, falling back again. *Concentrate!*

"And so, we see," Harrum'Bar's voice boomed over the clash of blades, "your victory over my captain was a lie. A deception. You must have killed him dishonorably! Your blood will flow today, and this one will bathe in it!" she cried. "You killed my captain at your listening post; we know you engineered a rebellion from a hidden lair at the orbital shipyards, which cost the lives of countless brothers!" Harrum'Bar sounded deranged.

Rebellion? Shipyards? Does she mean L4? Patty did not have the time to give her rant any more consideration. Twice she had made perfect ripostes, and twice she had seen her blade turned. *Lacquered! He's lacquered his naturally armored skin.* Cedric's memories confirmed its use in ritual combat. Patty ducked, panting and felt the tip of his blade catch on a lock of her hair. She staggered back, brushing the loose hair from her eyes.

"You killed this one's FirstLeftLeadingSon! Lured into a trap, aboard that generational-ship, and then killed with all hands!" Harrum'Bar was hysterical.

Patty's heart sank. This is why she wants me here. I lured him there? You've got to be kidding! Your mind's as twisted as your body! She cursed herself for being distracted as she retreated before another attack.

"Kill them all!" Harrum'Bar screamed.

Out of the corner of Patty's eye, she caught sight of the two guards with their blades drawn, advancing on Zeus. As hard as she fought, she was forced farther and farther away from her friends by a flurry of cuts to her face. Her mind raced. *If I can get to the unguarded door controls, maybe we can get reinforcements.* Zeus held his own against the two guards even as they flanked him. Murrun had his ceremonial blade out but seemed more concerned about keeping Jake out of Zeus' way. She started a measured retreat one step at a time. There was no turning her back on her attacker.

Even now, he seemed to know what she was about and his high outside attack turned her towards the center of the room. Her quick riposte shaved another scar into the alien's forearm, but she had to fade to her right again. Again, he attacked from the outside line and turned her. She could see the door now but could not get to it.

A shout of pain, a human voice, Jake's voice, joined the stamp of feet and clash of blades behind Patty. Murrun was shouting too, but Patty could not understand him. The RegentFirstMother's full-throated cough added to Patty's fears and frustration. *What's happening back there?* But she dared not take her eyes from her opponent's bright-edged blade. Her right foot slipped as she stepped back, her ankle turned, and she felt herself falling. *This is it.* Patty's splayed right hand slid across the floor as she tried to catch herself; the air was driven from her as she hit the floor.

The brother was on her in a heartbeat. With both hands gripping the hilt, one dripping blood, it was all Patty could do to keep the rain of blows from her. There was a flurry of activity behind her. Patty paid it no attention as she wriggled across the floor. She stole a quick glance to her left. Murrun hovered over what had to be Jake's body. A rivulet of blood ran across the floor. To Patty's horror, she realized Jake's blood had brought her down. She was lying in it, struggling in it. Regret began to edge into her heart, but she stamped on it. *This is not over!* She slashed, and the brother danced away.

"STOP!" The voice was high pitched for an alien, and the phrasing struck a dominant resonating chord in Patty's gift-memories. Every muscle tensed. It took a moment to realize the brother's attack had stopped too.

"You dishonor us all with this! Withdraw!" So powerful was the command that Patty, lying on her back, felt the urge to bow. The brother, who seconds before had been howling for her blood, was on his knees; his bleeding head pressed to the floor. Patty pushed herself up on one elbow to try to see who had saved her.

A small golden figure cradled in the strong right arm of one of Zeus's cousins wriggled and was set down on the dais. The young GreatMother looked considerably bigger than the last time Patty had seen her, but she was still tiny, no taller than a meter, but perfectly formed. *For a twisted left-handed alien.* A dozen more giant brothers in the GreatMother's multi-colored tabards stood at the ready. A bevy of LeftLeading advisers edged in nervously through the rear doorway as the tiny GreatMother advanced on Harrum'Bar.

"You have dishonored us all!" she shouted.

Taking the opportunity, Patty scurried across the floor. Murrun had a blood-soaked cloth pressed against Jake's side. He looked dreadfully pale. Murrun nodded a regretful bow, "This one is sorry. This one tried to stop Traaaffic Control but..."

"It's all right, I saw you," she reassured him. Patty's heart felt as if it were about to tear. Losing her father was bad enough, she could not bear the thought of losing Jake too.

Jake's eyes fluttered open. "Sorry. I thought I saw an opening. Just tryin' to help."

"Lie still, you silly old man. You're lucky he didn't totally gut you." Patty tried to keep the quiver in her heart from reaching her throat.

"The GreatMother," Murrun acknowledged the golden child confronting Harrum'Bar, "she will travel with healers." His eyes flicked to the shuffling LeftLeading entourage. Patty was off the floor like a shot, striding across the room towards the confrontation.

"You have dishonored us all with this cowardly act." The tiny golden child danced with frustrated outrage.

"GreatMother," Patty called out, interrupting them, "Jake, my dearest Traffic Control is injured, Murrun says you have healers." Patty slid to a halt and bowed, just a little.

There was no hesitation, as you might expect from a human child; the little alien was focused and sure of herself. "GreatMother Pa'attee, it is an honor to finally meet you, but it grieves me that things have begun so badly." She bowed, deeper and longer than Patty's perfunctory effort, before turning to her entourage. "Darbapard, Pronmerd, quickly! Do your very best. We are honor bound. Quickly!" the attendants scurried, and Patty took a breath.

"GreatMother," Harrum'Bar's bow excluded Patty, "there is no dishonor in this. She is but an ordinary human. She is not a mother and certainly not a GreatMother. The flag-of-negotiation was raised under pretenses..."

"You are wrong in this," the little GreatMother cut her off and looked as if she wanted to hit the RegentFirstMother, "just as you were wrong to begin this war. Pum'hurnun, LeftLeading-Son of Clan Whel'luminum has delivered his mel'andrin. GreatMother Pa'attee deserves our thanks and praise for her courage, not this betrayal. The FirstMother does not understand." She sighed, disappointed and ashamed, and shook her tiny head in exasperation, "You may never be able to understand. She may not have been born a GreatMother, but our presence has forced it upon her. In this, Traaaffic Control was correct." The little alien's eyes were wise beyond her years, and Patty felt stripped bare as if the GreatMother knew all about her pretense. "We have been blessed with GreatMother Pa'attee's presence, her patience, and courage." She turned and almost snarled at the RegentFirstMother. "Withdraw from this place while I consider your position as our regent."

"This cannot be done," Harrum'Bar protested. "Authority cannot be passed until integration is concluded."

"Integration is complete when I say it is. Get out. Get out now. Your willful ignorance has left much for me to repair. Represent your house at the Great Council meeting tomorrow and receive our judgment. Until then, leave us."

Harrum'Bar and her remaining advisers and guards bowed deeply and began to withdraw through the rear door.

CHAPTER TWENTY-NINE

"I'm so sorry about this," Er'men apologized as she looked up at the human GreatMother. Pum'hurnun's estimation of the human was close enough to help attune her to the smaller details of human expressions. However, she was aided by the fact that the human had absorbed and integrated mel'andrin, although seeing her use a combination of the three brothers' dialect was a little disconcerting. Er'men was sure the human could see the frustration, grief, and shame she expressed.

The human GreatMother's pose showed relief and gratitude. Her head-hair was in disarray; her tabard and under-clothing were cut. *Blood!* "You are hurt!" Er'men turned to call for assistance but knew she would have to take someone from tending to the Traaaffic Control. She reached out a tiny hand in sympathy, and the human's right hand rose and took it as if compelled. "Are you alright?" she asked. The human's hand was warm and soft and conveyed all manner of subtle internal changes. *If only I could understand what the changes mean.*

"Thank you. I am alright, mostly, I guess," the GreatMother said, suppressing a groan. "It feels as if everything hurts. The cut on my shoulder has already stopped bleeding, but," she looked at the two humans lying beneath the table. "Harrum'Bar did something before the fight began. She said something that made my brother go into a seizure and put my father to sleep."

Er'men knew what the human referred to. "Language triggers." The Hel'Arumpo'or dialects were full of triggers that evoked specific responses. "Please forgive me. I never imagined this would ever happen." Er'men turned a tight circle, anger boiling from every pore. "There is much I have yet to integrate.

The trigger could be any number of words." A wave of frustration poured through her body as she sorted out the red cloak of her Bar'Durrunnan adviser, "but I think Pel'droi Bar'Durrunnan-Son can help." Er'men stomped to the edge of the dais - *I need to fix this* - and gestured towards the huddled advisers.

"Pel'droi! Attend!" Er'men leaped from the dais and bounded across the room to where the two humans lay beneath the table. One lay peacefully, the other, the smaller one, shook and twitched. His heels drummed on the floor. Er'men ducked as she ran under the table and dropped beside the smaller, twitching human. *This one must be GreatMother Pa'attee's brother, the one she retrieved when she came to Tal'anis the first time. Why is he so precious? Is he the GreatFather?* Er'men reached out and gently drew her hand across his twitching face. Pel'droi knelt beside the table as GreatMother Pa'attee, and Pum'hurnun approached. Pa'attee crawled beneath the table and sat beside her brother.

"Speak the release word, Pel'droi," Er'men commanded.

"It is not known if the human has integrated..." the clan Bar'Durrunnan adviser tried to avoid her eyes.

"Speak it! Now!" Er'men demanded and leaped to her feet. She looked ready to slap Pel'droi's face. He flinched, taking the rebuke for the act. He bowed low and stayed down.

"Po'or Reman'alt," he said.

Return to us. It was the dialect that mothers used to correct children and held some of the most influential language triggers. The quakes possessing the young human stopped. He took a ragged breath, his eyes blinked open and then closed as he relaxed. GreatMother Pa'attee pulled her brother into her arms and held him. Tears and sobs of relief came as she cradled her brother. *She would have been lost without him. Human motivations can be quite transparent.*

"Once again, I'm so sorry." Er'men knelt at Patty's side. "Our species has been confused and divided for so long; I shouldn't be surprised we made a mess of this, too."

Something she said snapped the human GreatMother out of

her fevered prayers. "I. You said I," Pa'attee spoke EngStand as if it was a foreign tongue. "Even Alan uses *this one*."

"I, yes, I, I, I, me, me, me," Er'men replied in EngStand as she gave a dainty twirl and a curtsy. There was something about the human GreatMother that had a deep effect upon her. *I want to please her. How does she do this?* A serious air fell over Er'men. "We, my people, have lost so very much. We ... they are missing a spark." Her head tilted. "Or gained one. Most of one." She dropped to the floor beside Pa'attee and ran her tiny fingers through Alan's hair. "I hope he will recover soon," she sighed, embarrassed. "This is such a mess. I don't know where to start."

"We could start with introductions. You know my name."

"Oh! Yes, of course." Er'men shook her head at her stupidity. She stopped; her head tilted fractionally to one side, before thrusting out her petite right hand. *I think this is the right way to do this.* "My name is Er'men, I'm awfully pleased to meet you," she said the words as carefully as she could. Pa'attee took her offered hand and shook it carefully as if she was breakable. "Was that right? Did I do it right?" Er'men could not help bouncing on the spot. "Is my name short enough?"

The human GreatMother laughed or did something that was the human equivalent. The sound was quite startling. "Yes, you sound the perfect little British lady. Er'men; it's a pretty name," she replied though she had difficulty rolling her tongue for the first syllable. She shook her head. *Did Pa'attee remember something?* She carefully laid her brother down, crawling to the other comatose human.

"Po'or Reman'alt." Pa'attee's pronunciation was flat and broad, but it was close enough for the human to awaken. His eyelids flickered open as he took a deep breath. A great smile lit up Pa'attee's face. The unresponsive expression that settled on him dimmed Pa'attee's energies.

"Is he alright?" Er'men's worried chirrup drew Pa'attee's attention.

"He appears uninjured," Pa'attee replied. "As well as can be expected. It's going to take more than a magic word to bring him back." The words came out stronger than GreatMother Pa'attee seemed to intend, but it was the truth.

Cringing under Pa'attee's heated gazed, Er'men bowed and shuffled on the spot. "I am so sorry. Meeting a new race, it should never have happened this way." She flopped onto the floor, head in her hands." Er'men's grief and regret were genuine. *I wish this could have happened differently.* Er'men tried to express her regret, but the GreatMother's brother woke; his eyes flickered open, and Pa'attee was at his side in a heartbeat.

"Alan!" She looked into her brother's pained eyes. Er'men sat opposite her and took Alan's warm hand in hers, as she watched the humans interact.

"What happened?" Alan's left hand signed as he groaned, his eyes snapped shut. "Head hurts. Lights bright."

"Stay still, little brother. Rest, my champion." Pa'attee stripped off her black and gold life-cloak, now torn and bloody, balled it up and placed it under his head. Her life-cloak was anonymous and bland, filled with alien symbols, presumably of great importance. *Why has she taken it off? Is placing her 'life' beneath her brother's head symbolic? If so, of what?*

Pa'attee leaned in and pressed her lips to his creased forehead. What does this mean? Is it a form of medical diagnosis? Measuring a patient's temperature? "Stay still." Pa'attee ran her fingers through her brother's hair. Does that comfort her brother or herself? Suddenly Pa'attee stiffened. She has remembered something else.

"Er'men! Harrum'Bar said she had my mother, that she was unCleansed. That was the threat she used to make me fight. She threatened to wipe her mind just as she's done to the rest of my family!"

Anger flared in Er'men's tiny body, and she leaped to her feet. *Clan Bar'Durrunnan! One day I'm going to do something about them!* GreatMother Pur'unnan had faced the most resistance from Clan Bar'Durrunnan. They were Er'men's bane too, and poor Pa'attee's. "The least I can do is try and find her before that happens. I promise, Pa'attee, I want to make everything right. I do. Pel'droi! To me!" she trotted over to her entourage and shouted commands that sent them scurrying.

"And get supplies! Human blood plasma! Bandages! Go!" Er'men pirouetted on one foot as the LeftLeading brothers hurried out the small rear door. *It seems that my advisers are good for something after all.* She danced across to Pa'attee's side and flopped down; she felt a little giddy.

"Anything else?" she asked. "There are a lot of things to set right." This was so much better than sitting in her apartments.

"Well, apart from calling in all the brothers and withdrawing from this conflict..." the human GreatMother began.

Er'men grumbled as she felt her inner light dim. "That is going to take more authority than just sending out for supplies." She sighed, "Harrum'Bar was right to expect I might require more time before integration brought me close to maturity. She holds tightly to her position." Frustration edged with despair blossomed and withdrew, displaced by her buoyant hope for renewal.

"GreatMother Pur'unnan had a plan. She had plans within plans, and if she survived liftoff, things would have been very different," Er'men told her.

"How so?" Pa'attee asked.

"There would have been a mature GreatMother directing the meeting of our two peoples. And our First Contact would not have been conducted as a surprise attack," Er'men growled. "Somehow, I must turn these events around, or I fear my people will not survive."

"I understand a little of your politics," Pa'attee encouraged her. "I know that not everyone supports Clan Bar'Durrunnan's FirstMother, that you are refugees."

"You have taken mel'andrin, gift-memories, from your sons." Er'men's use of her people's language made that statement humorously redundant. "I have GreatMother's mel'andrin, with memories from before the First Fall." Er'men began sketching out the rise and fall of her people. It was a stimulating exercise, translating memories and thoughts into symbols and stories composed as language. It was a peculiarly human mode of transferring knowledge, but it brought insight even as she spoke of successes and failures, the generations without a GreatMother to guide their species.

"We used to be bilateral like humans. There are so many gaps," Er'men said as she tapped her head. "There were plagues, viruses mutating under the increased radiation from sunstrikes. The Arumpo'or and the Hel'omi were inextricably combined into one species. A GreatMother is the closest thing to a direct throwback to the Arumpo'or, just as your Ze'oos is Hel'omi... or almost Hel'omi. Our LeftLeading brothers are close to being Arumpo'or but are missing something vital."

"Their 'I'-ness is missing," Pa'attee suggested in EngStand. That bothered the human GreatMother as much as it concerned Er'men.

"We have been in a race," Er'men continued, "to escape our increasingly hostile sun. It took GreatMother Pur'unnan's genius to develop the stardrive. She built something completely new! Everything else up to then had been a rediscovery, redeveloping old ideas, theories, and memories from long ago." Er'men bubbled. Those magnificent curves, flowed through Er'men's awareness, generating waves of joy and awe that made her giddy with delight.

"She needed the skills and technologies from all the clans to make their flight work, and somehow, she held the clans together long enough to build the ships and achieve orbit ... well almost." Er'men touched that last memory-moment within her; Pur'unnan atop the tor before take-off.

"You lost a ship? I saw two ships in a tableau carved into the central plinth," Pa'attee asked sympathetically. *Pum'hurnun is right. She is honest and genuinely concerned.*

"Yes, GreatMother Pur'unnan was aboard Delrofenalis when that ship fell." Er'men choked with grief. "I have her mel'andrin from just before take-off. She was going to be aboard Tal'anis for the launch, but something went wrong with Delrofenalis. The ship's internal gravity was fluctuating, which is crazy. That's one of the easiest settings to get right." The gaps in her knowledge gnawed at her.

"You know how the drive works?" Pa'attee asked, her eyes popping wide. Surprise again? It must be challenging to learn everything from verbal symbols.

"Oh yes. Pur'unnan's memories were the first I began integrating." Er'men held Pa'attee's hand. "Sometimes it is like she looks out from behind my eyes. But I need her willpower today rather than her intellect. She was a force of nature that hammered the Clan FirstMothers into submission." Er'men was daunted by the task. "I have precedence on my side. I am a GreatMother after all. But getting Harrum'Bar to withdraw from this room was easier than it will be to prize her grip from the Regency. Until I can do that, I cannot call off anything. I'm a passenger, a child still integrating her first mel'andrin." Er'men's temporary slump evaporated, and her natural vibrancy shone through once more. "But that's tomorrow's fight. For now, I need to make sure your injuries are treated, GreatMother Pa'attee, and that you have somewhere safe to stay."

A commotion broke out at the rear door, two LeftLeading brothers scrambled in, lamenting loudly that the way was held against them. The painfully familiar sound of blades clashing drifted in from behind them.

"Bar'Durrunnan denies our passage, GreatMother. We could get no medical supplies."

"Harrum'Bar!" Er'men stomped her tiny forefoot.

"If she's holding the back door..." GreatMother Pa'attee leaped to her feet and raced to the double door's controls. She slapped the switch, and they hissed open. Some of Pa'attee's brothers stumbled in. The roar and clash of fighting rolled in over their heads. Her company leader, beneath a projected billowing flag, was halfway up the steps, directing his clan-brothers as they regrouped on the stage. The GreatMother's sons held the platform, but that was not going to be good enough; they were vulnerable. There were Bar'Durrunnan marksmen in the balconies. Genedalt picked her up and withdrew to the dais for safety.

Harrum'Bar! How can you do this?

CHAPTER THIRTY

"Get in! Get in!" Patty waved her valiant troops into the back room, and they retreated in good order.

"GreatMother! Get behind this one." Zeus bulled his way in front of Patty, pushing her back from the threshold. "GreatMother, back. Back!" He turned and shepherded Patty to the table, lifting her off her feet as he pushed through the crowd of soldiers. There was fighting at the rear door too, and Er'men's escort seemed able to hold, but if Harrum'Bar used those white-staffs in the amphitheater, then there was no reason to believe they would not be deployed elsewhere. A shout made Patty twist in Zeus's arms. The last of her company reached safety. *Well, it's relatively safe here.* Felix, with that useless holographic flag waving above his head, breasted his way towards her. The double doors began to close, relieving pressure on those holding the threshold. The left-side door shut but the right side jammed, and the clash of arms continued in the gap.

"GreatMother! Clan Bar'Durrunnan has no honor!" Felix bowed, anger and frustration rippling through him, his red inside-out tabard swirling around him. "Twenty-three brothers fell! They attacked without warning."

An angry twitch ran across Patty's shoulders signaling to Zeus that she needed to get down. He stood, ever ready, between her and the contest at the double doors.

"There is no shame in this for you, Felix," said Patty. "We are proud of you." She leaned closer and turned off the holographic projector.

"This place can be held," Felix replied as he glanced at the rear door and the Hel'omi in charge of its security. The fight had been pushed away from the doorway and out into the corridor. Patty saw him dismiss that arena of conflict as his concern. "Messengers were sent to the Cedric but..." The set of his shoulders and the angle of his head said the rest.

"You doubt they got through. Yes, I understand." Patty's eyes dropped to the comm on her wrist. It was broken; a strike had sliced through the toughened screen and the sensitive electronics beneath. It had probably saved her wrist and her life. *When did that happen?* She glanced at her brother, still resting beneath the table. He had a comm too, but he did not use it. *He won't mind if I borrow it.* "Hold them at the door. We will find a solution." Her eyes danced around the weapon-laden walls. "Felix, if you see something you need from this stuff, take it, and use it."

"With thanks, GreatMother." Felix bowed with an excited quiver that reminded Patty of Ben. *I wonder if Ben's been successful. Oh, girl, this is a right mess.*

"With my blessings," Patty told him, but Felix was gone. Patty turned back to the table. Zeus moved with her, standing guard between her and the fighting at the door. "Murrun!" His head popped up from the group huddled over Jake. He looked confused, as if he had forgotten where he was, and then snapped into focus.

"GreatMother." He carefully extricated himself from the huddle and trotted over. "Traaaffic Control lives, though he needs blood. He is not awake. They just finished repairing his wounds." Awe seemed to envelop him; "Humans are very interesting on the insides."

"Yes, just as you are, I'm sure. Stay with Jake. If he wakes, come and get me. Okay?" she instructed him. Patty wanted to be with Jake, needed to hold her father, and there was an Alan-sized space at her side that even Zeus's overwhelming presence could not fill. She climbed under the table and checked on her brother. He looked peaceful, his breathing slow and deep. She removed the comm from his wrist. *He hasn't even turned it on.* She pressed the power button, but nothing happened; the screen remained blank. *Thanks, Murphy.*

"GreatMother! We must take you to safety!" One of Zeus's cousins was on his knee, pleading with Er'men. Anger and frustration poured from him in waves and something else too, shame. That resonated in Patty's heart. *You walked into this one girl, a den of politics. Jake warned you off, but you didn't listen, did you.*

"And how were you planning to do that Genedalt, Bumurnam FirstSon? Clan Bar'Durrunnan denies passage in the corridors. Do you think they will part and let us through?" The tilt of her head arced towards the battle at the double doors.

"GreatMother, we cannot lose a GreatMother..." The giant's head and shoulders dropped as despair leaked through his emotional control. The last word was left unsaid, even his left hand restrained from expressing it, but the subtle roll of his elbow and the aroma of regret carried its meaning.

"Again?" Er'men and Patty spoke as one.

The gigantic guard seemed to collapse in on himself in shame. "This one was but a pup, GreatMother, and does not have mel'andrin of the event but accepts the shame. A great many brothers died, their memories lost."

"And the GreatMother who died, where is her mel'andrin?" Er'men looked at her guard's drooping shoulders, and for the first time, her golden glow of self-assurance faded away. "How could this have happened?" Her eyes darted from the rear door to the fighting at the partially closed double doors and back to her guard.

"It is unknown by this one, GreatMother," he responded, taking a longer look at the well-defended doors, "But this one fears, as courageous and strong as our brothers are, without assistance, we will be overrun." His momentary lapse into despair shaken off, he appeared to solidify, anger hardening his resolve. "We will attempt another sortie through the rear door."

"No, Bumurnam FirstSon, hold this position. Just for now. We'll think of something. Just hold." Er'men seemed to take heart from her guard's courage, and her natural effervescence buoyed her up, restoring most of her radiant confidence.

"Felix has sent messengers to Cedric, my general, though I don't know if they got through," Patty said and placed Alan's comm on the table and removed the broken tech from her wrist.

"No, I don't know of a time when the corridors have been barred to anyone. Oh, is that a personal comm?" Er'men asked. "We don't have anything to match it." Er'men's posture expressed her eagerness to examine the device. Genedalt lifted the little alien so she could see the top of the table. "How do they work?"

Patty tried to express the concepts and had to dip into Murrun's subtle side-memories to find the correct terms. "The comm sends digital bursts of data to the network servers the Belters have surrounding us and then it is sent to the other distributed servers around the solar system."

Er'men interrupted, "And they pass your message to the intended recipient, clever. But who can you *talk* to?" she asked.

"At the moment, no one. If this were working, I could talk to the Belter ships out there fighting, but I don't think that would help us much." Patty tried not to even think about Lily and Daichi. She carefully opened the back seal on Alan's comm. Everything looked like everything was in order; she wriggled the battery against its contacts. *It might have taken a knock and come loose while Alan fitted.*

"Could you contact your ship?" Er'men inquired.

"Yes, but I couldn't do much," Patty shrugged. "I could send her a wake-up call to get her ready for flight. That used to take a lot longer when she was burning tritium. Now it takes only seconds."

"Can you fly her remotely?"

"No. I ... Freya had some ... security problems the last time I took her out and so I had to tighten up her access protocols. I can't even look at her flight logs without a hard-wired connection." Patty turned the comm over and turned on the power. The screen flickered to life.

Er'men sighed, disappointed. "I was hoping that we could use your ship's engine to disengage Tal'anis' drive."

"Huh?" Patty closed up the comm but when she turned it over it would not boot up. *Damn!*

"I've been trying to think of a way to get Harrum'Bar to back off. Taking control of Tal'anis' drive was my first thought, but getting to it is not possible."

What did she say? "Are you talking about using Freya to fly this huge ship? Won't happen. We've had some difficulties..." Patty opened the back again and seated the battery into place once more. The comm booted up.

"So I heard. I think I can fix that." Er'men giggled, her proximity irresistibly transmitting the GreatMother's mirth to Patty and she found herself chuckling as well. *I wish you could fix this.* "Poor Pum'hurnun was most disconcerted. It seems to me as though you've trouble with the emission harmonics. There are so many overlapping parameters it can be tricky to pin down the source of the interference but not impossible."

The comm would not work with the back on. Er'men crowded close as Patty logged in. An error message appeared declaring that the device had failed its hardware tests; they were offline. The back case held essential components for the little device's transmitters. She could, however, access the internal memory containing Alan's inertial track and the data from her previous explorations. Patty could not stop her eyes darting up to the grills covering the air ducts at the top of the room's back wall and felt her stomach flip-flop.

Er'men followed Patty's gaze. "Air ducts. Oh! That's how you moved about the first time you were here." Her finger hovered over the display. "And that's where you entered Tal'anis, through the damaged forward docks. We could use the ducts to get to your ship!"

Suddenly, Patty felt covered in dream-treacle, unable to breathe. The air ducts were the only uncontested way out of this room, but Patty had had too many nightmares about crawling, cramped and lost in the dark, to be happy with the thought of returning to them.

Er'men read her concern. "Patty, they can't be as bad as that.

It's a brilliant idea!" She jumped from Genedalt's arms and leaped across the room to her attendants, her enthusiastic glow returning to full brightness.

"Huh?" Patty felt herself stand and follow her as if caught in Er'men's wake.

"But none of us will be able to go with you, GreatMother, the opening is too small." Bumurnam FirstSon chased after her, trembling at the thought of not being there to protect Er'men. His left arm echoed a cutting blow, conveying the contempt he felt about Er'men's LeftLeading advisers. They would not be of any use if they accompanied her.

Felix stepped forward. Patty could see echoes of Cedric's bright mind in his posture. "GreatMothers," he paused for Patty to grant him permission, a formality only as Patty received him with an open stance. "GreatMothers, we can hold here but not indefinitely. It might be possible to win through, out into the auditorium, and then left, into the corridors, but they hold the high ground; the risk to yourselves is too great." Felix paused as he gathered his and Cedric's thoughts. "You must leave. By yourselves. Bumurnam FirstSon is correct; your retainers cannot accompany you. They will slow you. We will stay and fight as if you were still here, holding their focus so you can bypass them."

"If GreatMother Pa'attee's sibling was well enough..." Er'men's sincere regret harmonized with Patty's pain. It was wishful thinking even to consider taking Alan. He needed to stay quiet and heal.

"GreatMother Patty's ship is the safest place on Tal'anis. With a little tweaking, she could solve most of our problems." Er'men beamed certainty.

"Are you sure Freya can do this?" Patty found it difficult to swim against the tide of the little GreatMother's desire, but Er'men radiated confidence.

Bumurnam FirstSon bowed. "This one knows GreatMother Pa'attee's ship is difficult to find." He dropped to one knee. "GreatMother, please take our charge to safety. Take our beloved GreatMother to your ship. Keep her safe for us," he begged, his trust and confidence in her was complete. Patty's doubts and fears rose up inside her, but she could not refuse him.

The ducts aren't as bad as my nightmares paint them. The ducts aren't as bad as my nightmares paint them. The ducts aren't as bad as my nightmares paint them. Patty let the mantra roll through her as she swallowed the sour taste flowing into the back of her mouth and took a deep breath. It was not just going back into the ducts that gave Patty pause. She had come here to rescue her father, but now she knew she had to leave not only her father but her brother as well. And Jake. Murphy's really got his hooks into me. Okay. Plans change. Try and save the little alien. If what she said is correct - it was hard to imagine Er'men was lying - she's as close as it gets to being the last true representative of her species.

"Bumurnam FirstSon, I will take GreatMother Er'men to my ship. I will do my best to keep her safe." Patty's mind spun. "Zeus, my brother, my father and Traffic Control are in your charge. Care for them as you do for me." Patty echoed Zeus's grief at their parting.

CHAPTER THIRTY-ONE

Er'men had plenty of room in the duct, although her twisted body was not able to crawl with any speed. A quick glance back and she could see that Pa'attee was having difficulties. It was as if powerful memories fought within her, causing her to struggle needlessly. Light streamed in from the grate ahead accompanied by the sound of fighting in the corridor. Er'men took a quick glance but hurried on.

Thankfully, the first junction opened onto a larger duct and then to a larger one again. Patty could not stand upright, but the claustrophobic pressure receded even if they were in the dark. This section of the duct was a feeder and did not open directly to any part of the ship. Wan light pooled from the openings to smaller pipes, but it was not enough to see more than vague silhouettes - the glow from the comm display was brighter, but it ruined their night vision, making the dark darker. The sound of conflict echoed in from every direction.

"Harrum'Bar may rule Clan Bar'Durrunnan and hold the regency on the Great Council, but she does not rule all," Er'men murmured over her shoulder. "When Pum'hurnun gave his report, I had to come and see you. Li'ila'tion accepted your presence; I could feel the response from my quarters. Don't worry Pa'attee, Harrum'Bar's conduct will not be supported by the whole." Er'men looked up and down the duct. It was almost as if she had Pur'unnan's plans in front of her. "I know the way. Down here and then to our left. We need to find a vertical duct."

After locating a suitable cross duct, Er'men slowed a little and took Patty's hand. The dark made it difficult to see the subtleties of the human's body language, but her emotional emanations were clear when she touched the human. Pa'attee was worried, but that did not compare to the terror that kept intruding into Er'men's mind.

"Pa'attee, what do humans believe happens when they die?" Er'men voice was just a tiny whisper.

Pa'attee's head tilted to one side. "Oh ... um ... Human's *believe* a lot of things. Some believe an all-powerful being will sweep them to some heavenly resting place or doom them to an eternity of suffering to pay for their misdeeds."

"What do you believe?" Er'men asked as she stepped over a flange.

"Dunno really," the human GreatMother replied and shrugged. "I guess I'll just fade away, like going to sleep. I've never witnessed any all-seeing mystical power at work in my life unless you count Murphy's Law. I check my seals twice. What do you believe? None of the mel'andrin I received gave an insight into your religious beliefs. Do you have any?" Pa'attee asked as she paused for a sip of water from her canteen.

"Death comes to all creatures, but with mel'andrin there is continuity. Discovering that a GreatMother was born and lost so totally there is no mel'andrin from her scares me." Er'men squeezed Patty's hand. "Pur'unnan's mel'andrin is full of gaps, times when there was no GreatMother. I could be lost like that too."

"You won't be." Patty tried to be brave and took a deep breath as she checked the comm. They were heading in the right direction. "We'll be out of here and safe in my little ship in no time."

"I know, but that's not enough. I cannot imagine what it is like for humans. Do you have to learn everything?" *What a huge task.*

"Pretty much. Mom says that when we're born, we're a bunch of potentialities waiting to happen."

"So tiny and weak." Er'men had seen pictures of human babies.

"Look who's talking. Yeah, gestating nine months in the

womb and nine months outside, or so I'm told. Makes a stable family life important and that creates the potential for inter-family bonds of co-operation. Humans have a continuity of sorts in families and communities."

"The Arumpo'or ... we lost the ability to procreate by ourselves during the time of the First Fall when our sun began to shed its outer layers. Mel'andrin was vital to our survival. Before the First Fall, gift-memories were not as specific. A soft blurry sense of times past rather than specific memories."

"I'm not sure I understand. I've received three gift-memories today, and the memories were as clear as if I had experienced them myself." Pa'attee packed away her canteen, and they continued onward.

Er'men squeezed her hand and skipped. "I could see you had experienced something but not as many as three," she giggled, "I'm surprised you're standing." *Pum'hurnun was right again; she is strong.*

"Crouching actually." Patty chuckled as she bent lower and stepped past another thick seam in the duct.

"Originally mel'andrin was ... if you had a thousand memories of Li'ila'tion all blended. You would know the space inside and out but not as one explicit memory. Early in the Second Rising, we discovered how to create specific gift-memories."

Patty did not reply and turned her comm's display to maximum, using the soft light to check their way. Smaller offshoots branched out to either side, and a little farther on a vertical shaft appeared, cross connecting this duct.

The urge to do more than just talk overwhelmed Er'men. She could feel her mel'andrin forming in her throat sack even as she withdrew her hand from Pa'attee's. She collected her offering spoon from her belt pouch and presented the human GreatMother with her gift. "Pa'attee, I want you to have this," the silver offering spoon looked outsized in her tiny hand. The mel'andrin sparkled, a golden diamond; dazzling rays danced across its surface. The scent mixed florals, light and heady, along with deeper notes that anchored it in the real world.

"It's probably not a good idea to sample it here," Er'men said casually.

"Sample?" Patty blinked and pulled herself away from the aromatic pearl, swallowing the saliva that flooded her mouth.

"A GreatMother's mel'andrin is not as ... as volatile and will release the GreatMother's memories even with repeated use," Er'men told her. "I have, or had, mel'andrin going back to the start of the Second Rising."

"You're probably right," Pa'attee agreed. "Now is not the time to go memory tripping." Patty fumbled in her belt pouch before retrieving a small wooden box.

Er'men gasped. "Oh, it's beautiful! It's so old ... maybe from the first dynasty of the Third Rising. That's over two thousand human years ago. Where did you get it?"

"Cedric, my general, gave it to me." Patty pressed the clever catch, pushed it to one side and then in. The lid sprang open, and Er'men was immediately overwhelmed, the intoxicating aromas made her knees weak. The mel'andrin spheres flared in the reflected light of the comm, overcoming the darkness with flashes of bright color.

Er'men giggled and danced on the spot, deftly balancing the offering spoon and its precious contents as she took in the expanding fragrant cloud. "Oh, your Clan loves you, they do." She concentrated her energies and bowed formally. Upon rising, she made her offering. Her gift-memory's scent mingled and strengthened the hundreds of minor scents as the golden sphere joined the pearly gift-memories swirling around on the box's soft dark grains. GreatMother Pa'attee slowly closed the lid, taking in the heady scents.

"One day, when I have time, I would be honored to partake of your mel'andrin. I only wish I had something to give you in return," Pa'attee said as she tucked the precious box away.

"I would love to be able to make some kind of exchange. Maybe one day." Er'men reached out and embraced Pa'attee, crawling into her arms, holding her close. Pa'attee was much softer than Genedalt, and she didn't rumble softly, but for a brief moment, it felt as if all was well with the world.

CHAPTER THIRTY-TWO

Er'men surprised Patty with how well she climbed. The nimble creature scampered up the shaft as if she had done this every day and waited patiently at the first cross junction for Patty to haul herself up. There were no ladders, just the over-engineered flanges joining the ducts together.

"You mass too much." Er'men's cheeky pose was only just discernible in the dark.

"I mass just enough, thank you very much." Patty pulled herself into the cross-duct and lay back panting. She retrieved the flask from her hip and took a swig; cold water with a faint citrus-like tang. *Delicious.* Er'men declined when she offered the canteen. *Three more floors to go.*

Once again, little Er'men waited at the junction for Patty to arrive. With Er'men's joyful presence, the ducts were not as bad as her dreams had painted them although there had been moments when dream-treacle had nearly frozen her. This conduit was a major artery; big enough for Patty to stand upright and she took the opportunity to stretch once her legs had stopped quaking from the climb.

"Not far to go now. Forward some and then to starboard. We should check the vents and see if we can see anyone," Er'men suggested. Patty held in a groan as the joints in her neck and shoulders cracked. They had left the sounds of fighting behind them.

Suddenly the pressure in the duct changed. A subtle vibration beneath Patty's feet became a roar as Tal'anis bucked. Thrown from her feet and tumbled down the duct, Patty received a blow to her left shoulder and then her ribs slammed against a join in the pipe. Somewhere off to her right, she heard Er'men's scream, as potent as her own.

The darkness would have been more reassuring if each breath did not cause excruciating pain. Patty would have taken the time to take stock, but she could hear Er'men whimpering. Patty's left ankle had taken a knock, as had her shoulder but nothing felt as bad as the ribs down her right side; the bones grated together as she moved.

"Er'men? I'm coming," Patty called. The darkness was complete. The comm was lost so Patty felt her way towards the little alien.

"Patty? Oh, Patty help, oh..." Er'men tapered off into a repressed groan.

"Just stay still. I'm coming. Where does it hurt?" Patty asked. She was close.

"Oh, my head and my knee but my ... my left wrist... Oh, Patty."

"I'm here, Er'men. I'm here." As quickly and as gently as she could, Patty sidled close and traced out the little alien's limbs in the dark, leaving Er'men's forearm for last. The hard chitinous shell was fractured in several places. It oozed a warm sticky liquid that made Patty feel ill.

"Patty?"

"What is it, Er'men?"

"I'm scared, Patty," she whimpered.

"So am I, but we'll get through this." *That's the right thing to say, isn't it?* The duct was so dark Patty couldn't see her hand in front of her face, and she had no idea where she was.

"Do you think so? Really?" Er'men asked. "I can't help thinking about ... about the GreatMother before me. I don't even know her name, Pa'attee! She's lost to us. Lost to me. I don't want to..."

"You won't. Don't be silly. You've just broken your arm," Patty tried to reassure her. Cedric's memories held many instances of broken limbs, none fatal in and of themselves. They gave Patty a little confidence she would be able to bandage

Er'men's forearm without doing her any permanent damage.

"Pa'attee, will you use my mel'andrin?" Er'men pleaded. "Now?"

"Please?" Er'men's expressive right hand clutched at Patty, reinforcing her request, her need.

Even as Patty felt her mouth forming the word *no*, she could feel her fingers reaching for the dark-grained box in her pouch. *If it was a bad idea before, when we could tell where we're going, and had at least a small light, what makes it a good idea now?* But she could feel Er'men's *request* rebound through Cedric, Zeus and Murrun's experiences. A GreatMother's *request* had the force of law. *Even an immature GreatMother.* Patty could feel Er'men's emotions through her tiny hand even if she could not see her.

"From one GreatMother to another ... a request is just a request," Er'men said softly.

"Yeah, right." Patty chuckled. The GreatMother's compulsion was resistible up until the moment her thumb triggered the hidden latch, and the lid unsealed, releasing an olfactory moment that took Patty far, far away from the darkness. It did not seem possible, in that lightless duct, but Patty could see the box in her hands and sense the mel'andrin inside it. Her fingers found the offering-spoon all by themselves when Cedric's memory of its hidden trigger unfolded from a recess in her mind. *This was Abe's box.* Patty's heart skipped a delighted beat. Cedric's memories held a reflection of Abe that Patty was tempted to embrace, but Er'men's mel'andrin called to her with a bright floral insistence. The other pearls in her collection seemed to move out of the way so that Er'men's gift could glide effortlessly into the filigreed spoon.

Unlike the previous mel'andrin she had consumed, Er'men's did not explode in an overpowering wave, but there was something about it that made Patty salivate around its hardness. A warm presence rose up the back of her throat and into her sinus passages as she breathed. She rolled the spherical gem around her mouth, but it felt most comfortable beneath her tongue, and that allowed her to swallow the over-abundance of saliva that built up in her mouth. *Is it cold here?* Waves of goosebumps gave chase up her arms.

Patty felt a vague sense of disquiet - anxiety at being left out of the long chain of her own species' continuity - as she felt a familiar constriction to her breathing. The pain from her ribs seemed to reinforce the discomfort. Flashes from Er'men's short life began unfolding: the towering figures of her Hel'omi guards holding her close, Harrum'Bar bowing before her in apparent subservience and the feeling of disquiet as she sat in the RegentFirstMother's lap, while all came before her with their offerings of mel'andrin.

Suddenly, Patty became aware she was experiencing Er'men's memories; her consciousness lifted momentarily from the sensory flow. At that moment in Er'men's memory, Patty had been aboard the alien ship, watching from high above, hiding behind the air duct's grill. The duality of her own memory and Er'men's reinforced each other painfully as her point of view oscillated between her memories of looking out of the grill and Er'men's atop the RegentFirstMother's lap. Patty let go of her sense of self and fell back into the stream.

The scents, rising from the mel'andrin combined in a way Tal'anis' ducted air currents never could, overflowing the blue ceramic flask, filling her apartments. The immediate connection it brought was more important to Er'men than the ornate decorations or the historical relics filling her rooms. Although there were feelings of joy and acclaim with the arrival of their new GreatMother, currents of frustration and anger undercut what should have been a united welcome. Er'men pressed home the stopper and turned her attention to the golden mel'andrin inherited from her GreatMother antecedents, arrayed on the mottled green-blue Jahn fur pelt. It would take many years to integrate these precious memories fully. Er'men was eager to continue her education.

Patty felt herself piggybacking on Er'men's experience as the very young GreatMother dove into her inherited memories.

Pur'unnan blinked the dust from her eyes as she sat. Her Hel'omi escorts turned outward in a shallow arc, warding all away. Hot and dry. *It had not always been like this.* There had been many advantages in choosing this particular escarpment to build and launch their ships, but the lure of her oldest gift-memory drew many GreatMothers to this place; it held the memory of what had been and what could be again ... if they could find a new home.

She had confidence they would find a compatible world even if her astronomers had not yet settled on a target. Her stardrive - for a brief moment Patty caught sight of equations, and a beautiful shimmering waveform swirled around her - her stardrive would do what GreatMother Bar'enop's efforts at re-establishing a fusion-powered culture had not.

For one vertiginous moment, Patty teetered on the edge of the integrated memories of Bar'enop's short life, but Pur'unnan was not here to revisit lost chances. She breathed slowly and let the oldest memory resurface.

The colors before her changed, but the geographical features remained the same. The gray, barren hills, worn down by hot winds, sprouted life. Tall growths in deep browns and greens, interspersed with flashes of vibrant gold and purples covered the knolls. The landlocked sea refilled, drowning the long winding road until it lapped at the feet of the old township turned new again. Pleasure craft skimmed across its sparkling surface; high above, a small aircraft arced across the bright blue sky.

Patty was in awe of the dramatic changes and wondered how many thousands of years had past since this memory had formed. Even Pur'unnan did not know.

Fe'ren flexed her neck and swallowed, closing off her gills. It would not be long before they would close forever. Her parents' mel'andrin had prepared her for the changes adulthood would make to her body although she wished they were more specific. The vague knowledge that what was happening to her had been endured by millions of children frustrated Fe'ren more than it helped. She already knew that when her gills closed, she would be able to speak properly. She would not hiss and gurgle her words, relying on the gesture-language of children so she could be understood. But for now, it did not matter whether she needed help to breathe underwater like adults did or not, she wanted to swim with her father and mother as often as time would allow.

"Fe'ren?"

"Coming, Mother," Fe'ren coughed once to clear her air passages, collected the basket of whil'luw eggs and hustled up the beach.

Patty took a panicked breath and rolled the gift-memory sphere under her tongue. Pur'unnan's dive into her own integrated gift-memories faded slowly. The ancient world where Er'men's people had originated lay superimposed over Patty's senses. One part was ensconced in a dank air duct, every breath a sharp reminder of their plight, the other a cascading array of lives, back through countless years, back to this one life. And although the gift-memory had been passed through many hands and minds it was still crystal clear, from the vibrant colors to the sensations of the water on her skin.

Fe'ren's body was not twisted. While radically different from human beings, and more akin to crustaceans, she was bilaterally symmetrical, just as humans were. Somewhere in that cascading array were memories of a species changing, how they fell and rose and fell and rose again until they were able to leave their ancestral home. Their world was no longer able to sustain

627

them, stripped and baked bare by their increasingly hostile sun. The focal point of Patty's consciousness balanced on a precipice, between the air duct and a species' history, on the edge of being awake and aware and diving into a deep inner contemplation.

"How are you feeling, sister?" Er'men's hand tickled her own, bringing the presence of the duct into sharper focus. Patty rolled the gift-memory around her mouth with her tongue once more, before pressing it out between her lips. She lifted the spoon and released its precious cargo back into the ancient box.

At first, Patty had been afraid that breaking contact with the golden pearl would diminish the memories. The memory of Fe'ren, climbing out of the water, waited for her to attune her attention, paused in her life, a moment before the first fall, before their sun's old age began to destroy their world. She could feel Pur'unnan and Er'men watching, experiencing Fe'ren's memory along with the dozens and dozens of others who had passed this memory on, with all their own remembrances, side trips from this one shining hand-me-down moment.

"Are you back with us, sister?" Er'men's dialect was different, the sounds were different, and the gestures conveyed through her little hand, subtly altered. Older. Er'men. Her name, previously just a word/gesture, took on new depth in this dialect. Er'men, Star Born. Patty trembled on the edge of her memory's precipice.

"Pa'attee?" The way Er'men said her name, casting it through the lens of the GreatMother's dialect, brought to mind clear, deep, fast-running water. Her amused cough conveyed more in that dark place than Patty though possible. *Was this the kind of experience Cicely and Eg shared?* She could feel Er'men experiencing Patty's wonder as a GreatMother's perceptual patterns passed between them with touch alone; thoughts expressed without words.

CHAPTER THIRTY-THREE

Enfolded by the dark, Pa'attee could sense Er'men's presence directly - not with her eyes or ears but with her sense of smell and the subtle communication flowing between their hands. The oozing from Er'men's fractured arm smelled healthy whereas the cut on her foot needed cleaning before an infection could take hold. As much as Er'men suppressed it, the pain from her injured arm distressed her greatly. GreatMother Pa'attee could feel her hurt.

"Let me help." Pa'attee phrased it as a *request*, and painful giggles gripped them.

"Okay," Er'men responded; her trust overriding her trepidation.

It was not as bad as Pa'attee feared - Cedric had seen much worse - but even moving Er'men's arm a small amount caused the brave little alien to scream before she passed out. That, at least, gave Pa'attee time to strip off her silk shirt, using it to bandage and sling the cracked and oozing forearm. The cut on Er'men's foot would have to wait. Her breathing was regular, and Pa'attee's accumulated memories helped her find a pulse. It was a strong and regular waltz. By comparison, her own internal lub-lub felt strangely deficient.

Crawling away, Pa'attee found the nearest grill and kicked it out into the darkness. The covering did not fall too far, and from the sound, it had fallen into an enclosed space rather than an open corridor. Pa'attee carefully climbed out. Her foot found something that could hold her weight, a console similar to the one she had used to get access to the air ducts the first time she invaded the mothership. Pur'unnan's memories offered possible uses for the console if there had been power. She eased down from the duct and made it to the floor without breaking anything else, stopping to take some well-earned but slow, shallow breaths.

Gritting her teeth, Pa'attee felt around her, shelves and boxes, and then she discovered the door. Her fingers found and activated the manual release. The door relaxed back from the sill even though there was no power to operate it and Pa'attee slid it open. *Where are we?* She knew they were on the right level but as to which direction she faced, Pa'attee had no idea. *Left, or right?* As Patty's right hand slid up the leading edge of the door, her fingers traced subtle etchings unnoticed before and impossible to see in the dark. Her reinforced memories lifted her initial fears. The inscriptions were room coordinates! She knew exactly where she was, or rather Pur'unnan, Murrun, Cedric and Zeus's memories read the string of symbols under her fingertips and a location popped into Pa'attee's head. An expanded section of Pur'unnan's blueprint unfolded in her mind. She would have laughed at the sudden clarity, bright in the darkness, but for the pain she knew it would cause. *This is why Er'men knew where to go.* She looked down the corridor. *Right, then left at the next and then right. I can do this.* She turned back into the room and carefully renegotiated her way back into the ducts to recover her injured charge.

Getting Er'men down from the duct was difficult but not impossible. Patty moved the unconscious little alien to the edge of the grill and climbed down into the storeroom. It did not take long to stack enough boxes around and on top of the console, making it both manageable and safe to bring the injured GreatMother down from the air duct.

A dim intermittent flicker illuminated the corridor that Pa'attee carried Er'men down, and suddenly she knew, from her own memories, where she was. She knew this passage. Daichi and Lily had gone this way. One malfunctioning light at the far end lit the empty passageway that fronted the three airlocks. That was where Günter, Marni, and Shun had gone. *Has it all been worthwhile?*

It's not over yet. That thought held echoes from Patty's parents, and the cornucopia of experience channeled through generations of GreatMothers. The arc of a species' history beckoned with every second thought. She had never been a great fan of history, history in books, but this was different. She had real lives packed inside her head, filled with moments she could experience directly. Er'men's comment about needing time to integrate the memories rang true. *Having a few hours to myself would be a fine thing.* She instinctively glanced to where her wrist comm usually rested and felt more than a little lost without it.

The changing room was just as they had left it with human pressure suits and helmets hanging on hooks next to Hel'Arumpo'or p-suits. Pa'attee sighed with relief then regretted it as her ribs ground together. She carefully laid Er'men on a bench top and just as carefully stretched out the kinks in her shoulders. Mercifully, Er'men remained unconscious. Pa'attee rechecked her pulse. *She looks like she's sleeping. Lucky dog.*

The twisting motion needed to get into her p-suit ground her broken ribs together making Pa'attee gasp. *Slowly now.* The familiar scents of her own sweat brought a feeling of home as she sealed herself in. Being aboard Freya would be better. *I can take Er'men back to The Ice Princess and get her proper medical care.* She leaned against the door, peering out into the dark lock and the burnt debris-filled dock beyond its damaged outer doors. *Where are you Freya?* She did not have her comm. Without inertial tracking to lead her safely back to her ship, she would have to feel her way there through the impenetrable dark. It was not a pleasant thought. She might take a tumble, and that could kill them both.

Er'men looked comfortable on the bench. "I won't be long." Pa'attee stroked her tiny head, dappled in rich browns and golds. "I need to scout a path for us." *There's a torch aboard Freya.* She squeezed the little alien's good hand. Even now, the connection between them was alive; Er'men was content to wait for Pa'attee's return. She turned back to the airlock, sealing her helmet. The transparent walls of the Zip-E-Lok trembled as the doors slid open but showed no other signs of distress. Enough light spilled into the lock for Pa'attee to find the Zip-E-Lok's external access before the doors closed. She wriggled through, wincing, and stepped out into the true dark.

A wrong step could be a disaster. *A single puncture... No. Don't think about that.* Pa'attee advanced carefully, finding her way with the toe of her boot. *One step at a time. Feel for it. Good. Now the next one.* Vague shapes loomed out of the blackness as her eyes slowly adapted to the gloom. *Turn here. And again. This is where you met Marni.*

Without warning, spears of lights from behind Pa'attee lit up the burnt desolation around her. Only one object refused to be illuminated. *There's Freya!* She was only a few meters to Pa'attee's right. The beams swung away, leaving Pa'attee blinking in the impenetrable dark once more. *Er'men!* She spun on the spot and raced back to the airlock. The small windows in the airlock doors showed movement. She squeezed into the Zip-E-Lok and hurried to the door. Half a dozen soldiers in Bar'Durrunnan red clustered around Er'men. She was awake and cooperating with her captors. *She's not big enough to fight one let alone six of them.* No doubt, she was trying to charm them. Her right hand flickered almost subliminally: "Get help." *Could Er'men see her?*

Suddenly there was a pale face pressed against the airlock's window. An ashen face. He was every bit as large as the brothers around him but mirrored. *A Hunter!* Pa'attee had barely survived an assassination attempt by one of those rare Hel'Arumpo'or. *Not as rare as GreatMothers apparently.* His eyes popped wide when he saw her. Frantically, Pa'attee backed away from the door, Lady Estelle in her hand before she could even think. *Are you mad? You're not up to fighting him and six of his brothers.* Frustration and failure flayed her. The hunter reached for the airlock controls. *Don't let him open that door!* There was a correct procedure to deflating a Zip-E-Lok, but Pa'attee's method was faster. With two swift cuts, the temporary airlock emptied itself with a gust that rocked Pa'attee on her gecko-grip boots.

Well, you're safe, but you've lost everyone. What are you going to do now? This whole mission had turned inside-out, from wanting to blow the aliens up to needing to save them. *What am I really supposed to be doing here?* One thing burned brightly inside Pa'attee; she had to get back inside. She could not, would not, leave without Alan. *And Jake and Lily and Daichi and Dad. And Zeus and Er'men and ... I'm going to need a bigger ship.*

CHAPTER THIRTY-FOUR

Cold eyes stared without blinking. The hunter turned away, leading the troop of Bar'Durrunnan and their lights into the corridors. The cold dark wrapped around Pa'attee, but she did not notice it. Her mind boiled.

How can I get inside? These were not the only airlocks in the dock. Memories from both Cedric and Murrun paled beside Pur'unnan's detailed blueprints. There were many other access points. The closest was the ship elevators that brought the fighters and transport ships up from the lower decks. If that did not work, there were other ways in. She could climb out of the dock if she had to. Her suit would protect her from the lingering radiation. Pa'attee strode across the buckled deck.

The ship's elevator still seemed functional although the heat-distorted plates around it gave Pa'attee pause. *You can fit Freya in there with room to spare.* Pa'attee brushed away ash from the manual access plate. What had been alien gibberish was now plain text, *Turn to Open.* The elevator groaned, and a metallic clunk vibrated Pa'attee's bones. The deck plate dropped and withdrew as a platform rose and replaced it. It was big enough to hold two of the boxy transports. *I could fly Freya into Tal'anis.* The mothership's name slipped easily into her mind. Tal'anis was *Talefenanis*, shortened from overuse. *Talefenanis* and Delrofenalis were star-crossed lovers from deep in the Hel'Arumpo'or's mythic past. *As well-known to the Hel'Arumpo'or as Shakespeare's 'Rom and Jules' is to humans.* Hel'Arumpo'or, the Risen Ones, the Rising Ones, names that were not much more than specific rumbles, unpacked in Pa'attee's mind. Delrofenalis did not survive the flight into orbit, and Pur'unnan had been aboard her.

What had gone wrong? How different would everything be if Pur'unnan had survived?

Taking Freya into Tal'anis seemed like a crazy idea, but that came from thinking of her as a vulnerable little ship. With the Sprocket Drive tuned properly - Pur'unnan's equations flashed briefly through Pa'attee's crowded mind - Freya could be the safest place in the universe. Shaking her head - it did not help clear it - Pa'attee moved as quickly as she could to where she had parked Freya. She wanted to run, but her ribs and the loose debris lying about conspired against her. Bumping into Freya's stubby winglet made Pa'attee squeal with fright, but the relief of making it safely back made her feel faint.

Without her comm, Pa'attee could not access the new security protocols and had to resort to punching numbers into a keyboard. The eight-figure PIN-number refused to surface, and Pa'attee stamped her feet in frustration. The Hel'Arumpo'or base 12 numerical system refused to make sense of the human base-ten keyboard. *What was it?* Thinking in EngStand helped a bit. 0-9 .... 0-9-3-4-5-3-5-7. Once the first numbers came, the rest tumbled into place. Freya's internal lights glowed warmly as the canopy released. Pa'attee carefully climbed aboard, determined not to injure her ribs again.

As much as she had always preferred to fly Freya solo, Pa'attee found her little ship disappointingly empty. *Well, that'll change soon enough.* The urge to see Lily and Daichi again was nearly painful. The need to be with her brother certainly was.

But before we go, we need to reconfigure the drive. Cian would freak out at her 'unqualified' tinkering. Pa'attee tried not to laugh. She had to admit Cian wrote solid code. Navigation via the command line was one thing but reconfiguring the drive itself was another thing altogether. *Better get this right or Cian will kick your butt.*

Pa'attee's stomach rumbled, and she reached into a compartment for one of Giuseppe's goodies. A memory of his broad smile hovering over his fat belly, a glass of wine in his hand, drifted into her mind. *Thank you, Giuseppe. I don't think I could have coped without these little comforts.* She peeled back the sparkling wrapper and bit down into a chocolate-coated swirl of berries. *Heaven in a mouthful.*

Clearing the navigation display from the screen, Pa'attee loaded a copy of the Sprocket Drive's backup parameters into its specialized editor. *At least you won't have to write raw code this time.* As the GUI filled the screen, Pa'attee could almost feel Pur'unnan's attention focus and pour out of her eyes as the imaginary curves Pur'unnan held in her mind unfolded like a time-lapse blossom on the screen. Unlike the experience of the mel'andrin from Murrun, Cedric and Zeus, Pa'attee could feel Pur'unnan as an almost-presence within her, alive and curious. "Oh... that's so clever!" she seemed to say. "And the curve... it's so close. Here and here ... and here." Pur'unnan smiled inside her. Pa'attee opened the help file on a second screen.

"Oh no," the strains of Cian's voice poured from Freya's speakers, "what have you done this time, Patty?" and then a tortured sigh. "I know you'll be careful just... Be careful and good luck." The video froze on Cian's crooked smile. The desire to see all her friends again, Lirsín especially, flared in her heart. *I'll think about him when I have time and a few spare brain cells... if I have any left.*

The fact that the drive was a device that could take a ship between the stars was almost incidental. Pur'unnan's consciousness flowed into Pa'attee's mind as if it were her own; the equations sculpted such beautiful curves. *And Eg understands this? And he worked it out from first principles? The drive exists. Therefore, it must be like this. Wow.* A thrum of species-pride warmed Pa'attee's heart, knowing that humanity had someone able to match Pur'unnan's stunning vision.

It took longer than Pa'attee expected to align Eg's and Pur'unnan's equations and she heard memory-echoes of her father's frustrated voice declaring that two engineers could not design a rubber band the same way. The visions of the end-product were similar, but their approaches were totally different. She wished she had mel'andrin from Eg to help her make the transition. In the end, Pa'attee felt tired but happy that her inner vision and the newly formatted curves on the screen matched. She saved and backed up the file before loading the new parameters into Freya's drive. There was no startling transition. Freya and her precious contents remained anchored to the twisted flight deck when the drive reinitialized.

"Now, if I change this," Pa'attee's finger slid over one parameter, "and this, we can increase the boundary gradient." She could feel Pur'unnan's confirmation within her and implemented the changes. The MEM boundary was virtually airtight. *Now, what else needs tweaking? Engineers always need user feedback.* Taking a breath, Pa'attee sagged back from the controls and rolled her shoulders, easing the tension that had built while she worked. *Safest place in the known universe.* If the graphical representation was correct, they were completely safe. *If.* She did not like to hang her safety on 'if' but did not know how to test it without endangering her ship and her life. It was best to avoid relying on 'if' if at all possible.

Three red lights glowed on the comm display. Pa'attee winced. She should have noticed immediately if there were any channels open. Her head felt crammed with competing interests. All three were live feeds coming from the Belter's network. The first window showed Gina, aboard the *Baby Face*, delivering a blow-by-blow account of their fight. Pa'attee ached to be able to go out and help them. The second and third images were dark, blurry-gray. The motion was instantly recognizable to her as comms worn on a wrist. The channel IDs made Pa'attee's heart leap; they were from Lily and Daichi. Pa'attee opened the audio on Lily's feed and the cockpit filled with the sounds of shouting and the clash of arms.

"Lily! Lily, it's Pa'attee. Can you hear me? Lily!" she shouted into the microphone.

The image swirled around sickeningly before settling on Lily's face. She looked red, sweat-streaked and was panting but otherwise, her eyes shone, scared and excited both. "Patty! I knew you'd make it. You're aboard Freya, aren't you?"

"Yes," Patty confirmed.

"Cedric will be pleased to hear that. Daichi is online. He's with him," Lily told her.

"Where are you? What's happening? You've met Cedric?" Patty asked.

"Yes, a friend of yours ... goes by the name of Ben - gee, some of these aliens have funny names." Lily showed her best-cockeyed grin. "Well, Ben found us after we planted my little surprise and took us to your ... compound to meet Cedric. Patty, we were with him when I saw fighting on your comm feed and went with him to rescue you." Lily frowned.

"You're going to the amphitheater?" Patty inquired. *Maybe we should have waited.*

"We were but not now. The fighting's still pretty heavy. Daichi has all the details. I'm trying to stay out of harm's way."

"Speaking of harm's way, you set off your surprise? That was you, wasn't it?" Pa'attee winced for the camera. "Broke some ribs and Er'men's wrist."

Lily shook her head, "Who? Sorry, can't take the blame for that one. Cedric says it happened when this ship docked to the asteroid. We're heading back to Earth."

A chill flashed through Pa'attee. She lifted Freya from the deck, turning on the landing lights as she spun her around. The broad dock was sealed off. Broken rock and dirty ice lay scattered across the warped flight deck. Harrum'Bar was going to deliver another strike from above. Chilled nausea swam around in Pa'attee's belly.

"Lily, I'm coming back in. Keep safe."

CHAPTER THIRTY-FIVE

Flying Freya to starboard, Pa'attee darted to the elevator and settled her down on the platform. Using her LADAR, Pa'attee locked her drive's local offset to the platform so when it shuddered and began to withdraw below the flight deck, Freya traveled with it. Air cycled into the lock, and the inner doors peeled back. The workshop bays that surrounded the airlock were empty and dark. Two carriages sat on tracks that led deeper into Tal'anis. The only light came from blinking green panels beside the exits, left and right. Pa'attee ignored them; she would never get Freya through those doors. There was only one doorway that interested Pa'attee, and that led into the center of Tal'anis.

Releasing Freya's lock on the floor, Pa'attee flew her little ship out of the roomy airlock and across the deck. There was plenty of space. She sailed above the tracks and the carriages used to move spacecraft to and from their long-term storage bays. The tracks stopped at a pair of armored doors, wide enough to take two ships side-by-side. It was sealed and locked, but the glowing panel beside it showed that there was power. Pa'attee was glad of that; she did not fancy trying to manually open doors that weighed hundreds of tonnes. She landed Freya and climbed carefully out of the cockpit. Every movement gave her pain, every breath. *Billions of people are going to feel a lot worse if you can't stop Tal'anis.*

The control panel used Hel'Arumpo'or common-script and held a keyboard and a button to open the door. She needed the correct code to unlock the door. Cedric knew some, as did Murrun but Pur'unnan's memories held all the keys. Pa'attee used the GreatMother's access code, and the green light flickered to blue. The doors shuddered and began to withdraw. Pa'attee was tempted to leave them open. Pur'unnan's memories held details of the doors' mechanism. They would close and seal quickly if there was a pressure drop but Pa'attee still felt it inappropriate to leave them open, even if she did have to climb in and out of Freya to do it. *It's only polite.*

The broad corridor banked around to the right, but a smaller passageway led straight on. *Rank has its privileges.* Pur'unnan had built direct access to her apartments. Even if the allocated space had changed hands, it was still the most direct route to the atrium, to Li'ila'tion, the Breathing Heart. The central atrium was an impressive space, and Pa'attee had experienced its heart when she had been escorted through it on her way to meet Harrum'Bar. You could feel the emotional pulse of everyone aboard Tal'anis circulating through Li'ila'tion's air.

The passageway was smaller but only by comparison with the dimensions of the bigger corridor. There was still plenty of room for Freya. Lights flickered to brightness down the length of the tunnel. *Why did that happen?* Pur'unnan's memories did not include automatic circuits for the lights. *Someone turned on the lights.* Two Hel'omi guards struck belligerent poses outside the wide double doors that Pa'attee was sure Freya could fit between. The Hel'omi's blades were drawn. *Have to get past these guys first.*

"Who comes!" the guard on the right bellowed, and he stamped his leading foot angrily as if he was about to charge. *This place is for the GreatMother, only!*

Parking Freya a meter in front of them, Pa'attee opened the canopy and gingerly disembarked. "Gentle brothers, do you not know me?"

They did not respond verbally, but a change of weight distribution subtly indicated they had *heard* of her. That was not sufficient. Everything about them said they wanted something from her and that she had a limited time available to show them she had the right to be there.

Pur'unnan's memories provided a potential key to this door too and its attentive and aggressive guards. Pa'attee felt her body flow into the GreatMother dialect and Pur'unnan's words poured out a possible passphrase, "The great trees of the forest bow down before the fury of the north wind."

The set of their eyes and shoulders changed, and the two guards bowed with more than polite respect.

"Even as the solid ground gives way before the rushing waters, GreatMother." Rising, they kept their blades drawn but their eyes lifted to look down the corridor, alert for the approach of potential enemies.

"GreatMother Pa'attee, be welcome." The guard on Pa'attee's left rumbled.

"Err, thank you, but I can't stay. I was hoping to use the apartments to gain access to Li'ila'tion." Pa'attee rested her hand on Freya's curved prow. *I'm bringing* Freya *with me.*

The guard blinked, confused, but only for a moment. He stepped back and to the side, opening the doors, his eyes gauging Freya's wingspan. "GreatMother's will."

The other guard hesitated before stepping back. He had a question but was reluctant to ask.

"Please, ask," Pa'attee told him.

"GreatMother Pa'attee, where is GreatMother Er'men?" he asked with a hint of desperation. "There has not been a word since before the fighting started. The Great Council sent orders to remain in the barracks."

Pur'unnan bristled inside Pa'attee, "The last we saw of my sister, GreatMother Er'men, she was being held by Clan Bar'Durrunnan." Her anger, frustration, and guilt shone through, and the Hel'omi understood her pain. "She asked me to get help, and this was the fastest way." In truth, Pa'attee had given no thought to rescuing Er'men; stopping Tal'anis from delivering her load had taken precedence over everything else.

"GreatMother!" The Hel'omi snapped to attention. The guard on the right bowed, before peeling away into the apartment, breaking into a run as he bellowed to clear the way.

"GreatMother comes! Make way! GreatMother comes!"

"Thank you..." Pa'attee's posture asked for his name.

"Drallemngor, GreatMother." He shone with pride at being on duty when she called. The GreatMother's dialect unpacked his name - Staunch-as-granite. He looked it, too.

I called? Pa'attee did not need to vocalize her question.

"GreatMother Pa'attee used GreatMother Pur'unnan's codes," Drallemngor replied and glanced about the area; it obviously did not live up to his exacting standards. "It has been many years since this station has been manned." The Hel'omi felt directionless without GreatMothers to protect. *Is there anything more this one can do?*

"Gather your brothers. Protect Er'men. She is so precious." Pa'attee's ribs ground together as she reached for the edge of Freya's cockpit. Drallemngor was at her side in an instant with a helping hand. "And find Zeus for me." Pa'attee blushed with shame; she did not know Zeus's real name. "I miss him so."

"GreatMother, this one knows of that one," he coughed a chuckle, "Whellanor." The-new-boy. Zeus was young enough not to have earned his Clan name when Pa'attee co-opted him. The pitch of his shoulders asked, *what is the Zeus?*

"Zeus is the father of..." there was no Hel'Arumpo'or word in any dialect she knew of for a god or gods, "Father-of-those-that-made-us."

Drallemngor nodded, expressing his continuing ignorance. He had not understood her explanation, but that did not bother him, after all, who could understand the ways of a GreatMother.

Pa'attee settled into her seat. "Thanks again, Drallemngor." She lifted Freya from the deck as the Hel'omi stood back. She scanned the doorway with LADAR. There was enough room but only just. Pa'attee did not feel up to flying manually, so she plotted a set of waypoints and sent Freya along its path. Once she had negotiated the doorway, there was more room; Pa'attee took the joystick in her hands and gunned Freya. She had flown flight-sims that were tighter than this.

A double dozen Hel'omi, not including the panting brother

that had run all the way and had beaten Pa'attee there, held station at the GreatMother's expansive foyer. And more were assembling, Hel'omi as well as Left and RightLeading brothers in the many-colored Bumurnam tabards. Pa'attee slowed as a path opened before her. She really wanted to stop and have a look around the room. The carved decorations were exquisite, two staircases ascended from the foyer, folding doors opened into a ballroom of grand proportions. But there was no time for more than a quick glance.

The impressive ornamental doors swung slowly open revealing a double wall of Bar'Durrunnan red, barring passage. Pa'attee thumbed open Freya's external speaker,

"Follow me, sons and brothers."

CHAPTER THIRTY-SIX

With the MEM field correctly aligned and stiffened to its maximum, no one could approach Freya closer than half a meter. Pa'attee kept Freya's speed down to a slow walk at first, until the Bar'Durrunnan brothers understood what they were up against. With her landing gear up, there was enough room below Freya, and she did not feel too guilty running over the tardy.

Li'ila'tion was less than twenty meters away, and Pa'attee pressed ahead, slipping over the balcony's handrail, past the spiral ramp and out into the atrium's bright light. Almost immediately, the MEM field boundary began a dazzling display of fat sparks. *We're under fire.* Pa'attee would have laughed but for the chill that being in someone's sights gave her. *Who's shooting at me?*

Steam-powered machine gun emplacements were scattered around Li'ila'tion walkways; one sat atop the central plinth, drawing power from the great steam engine that drove Tal'anis' stardrive. It was working hard now, and plumes of waste steam filled the air with wet heat. Despite Li'ila'tion's size, Pa'attee still had to keep her speed down, or Freya might sideswipe one of the graceful ramps. Li'ila'tion was a work of art, and it offended Pa'attee - and the shade of Pur'unnan within - to see battle waging inside her.

At the narrow forward end, on the highest promenade of the atrium, brothers in Pa'attee's reversed tabards were taking a pounding from the gun at the aft end. It was not very accurate at that distance, but its huge shells did not need to be. Pa'attee spun Freya and flew her up to the apex of the dome - close enough to the bright light that her canopy dimmed - before diving down at the emplacement. She did not want to hurt anyone deliberately; her only interest was the gun. *If I can give them a warning or maybe a good fright.*

With one hand, Pa'attee reached for the audio playback controls. The first file seemed appropriate. *Security: Proximity Warning_01. That sounds about right.* She ramped the volume to maximum and hit play. Pa'attee was almost as surprised as the Hel'Arumpo'or when Cicely's voice boomed out.

"Muuummmyyyy!! There's a strange man over here. Get away from me, or I'll scream!" and then she did. Nothing could pierce Pa'attee skull like a little girl's scream. Even inside Freya's protective bubble, it was loud. She flew Freya over the handrail and along the promenade's walkway. The Hel'Arumpo'or manning the machine gun dived for cover as the MEM boundary protecting Freya's starboard wing clipped the ungainly machine gun, sending its tangled components flying. The boiler exploded most satisfactorily as Freya shot back out into the air, spiraling up towards the dome once more.

Another gun emplacement had a good line of fire on her boys, so that became the next item on Pa'attee's priority list. She circled slowly, shells sparking fire all around her. It did not feel safe, but Pa'attee trusted Pur'unnan. There was no point twisting and turning, trying to avoid their fire, the guns could not damage Freya. However, it still felt wrong taking hits and not doing anything about it. Pa'attee hit play for *Security: Proximity Warning_02.*

"Stand away from the vehicle! I am restrained from making a lethal response, but I can do this." Cicely screamed again. If anything, it was louder than before.

The Hel'Arumpo'or at the gun tried to protect their hearing as they scattered, except for the brave soul with his finger on the trigger. Pa'attee flew Freya's curved prow closer and closer until the ricocheting rounds began doing serious damage to the machine gun itself. Pa'attee held Freya still, taking the worst the machine gun could do until the gunner gave up and dived for cover. Pa'attee disabled it with a sharp smack with the MEM field protecting Freya's prow.

Security: Proximity Warning_03 was just Cicely screaming. Pa'attee looped the playback as she buzzed the plinth. One hardy soul, manning the boiler, stayed longer than the others but even he had to retreat when Pa'attee hovered two meters above him with Cicely wailing. Freya's MEM boundary still flashed occasionally, but with Pa'attee flying so close to the Drive mechanism, there was a high possibility that Harrum'Bar's forces would damage it themselves. Now that the platform was cleared of personnel, she settled Freya down on the plinth in front of the six white control boards.

The bizarre concatenation of technologies made more sense when seen through Pur'unnan's eyes. The GreatMother had bowed to the political necessities and constructed her mechanisms so the most powerful clans would have to work together. Pa'attee took a moment to fish out another of Giuseppe's snacks. The comm read 4:38 UMT. It had been a long day, and it was not finished yet.

Expanding Freya's MEM field meant opening the drive's inner workings again. *NOTE TO CIAN: Add MEM field settings to the standard UI.* A warning message dominated the screen: *Do you need to see Cian's warning again?* Pa'attee smiled, clicked *No,* and dived into the parameters. *Covering the top of the plinth should be enough.* It quickly became apparent that the steam engine would soon fill the protective bubble with waste steam. A few more tweaks made the MEM boundary gas permeable but still resistant to anything denser. Pa'attee sucked a chocolate crumb from between her teeth before opening Freya's canopy. A frenzy of sparks showed Pa'attee that someone was willing to waste ordinance. *Did the Hel'Arumpo'or exchange memories because it took them so long to learn anything?* Pa'attee gave a wicked chuckle. *No, that's being bitchy. Cedric, Zeus, and Murrun are all as smart as whips.*

Cheers from high in Li'ila'tion's upper galleries greeted Pa'attee as she carefully disembarked. "Pa'attee! Pa'attee! Pa'attee!" She could not help but give her boys up there a wave.

They should be safe enough for now. They have the high ground.

CHAPTER THIRTY-SEVEN

Tal'anis' drive still ran, and Pa'attee took a few moments to orient her headspace to the Hel'Arumpo'or controls; standing before them brought Pum'hurnun's memories bubbling to the surface. Theoretically, one person, turning the small hand-powered cranks, could operate the mechanism. The hand-driven nature of the device did not scale up to an interstellar drive particularly well. The first time Pur'unnan tested her theories she had nearly demolished her laboratory. The hair on the back of Pa'attee's neck rose. The GreatMother had survived an assassination attempt by a hunter, too.

At Tal'anis' heart, the drive was smaller and much improved compared to the prototype that had failed Delrofenalis. Neither of them had been tested on a ship of this size and only when Delrofenalis took her test flight that the drawbacks of a mechanical drive train became clear. There had been no time to change the design; there had already been too many delays. Solar flares were increasing in frequency and duration. Their sun was getting ready for another huge coronal mass ejection. It would be thousands of years, maybe hundreds of thousands of years before their sun sagged into old age as a red giant. Life on the Hel'Arumpo'or homeworld was a flickering candle in the harsh solar winds.

All the stardrive's controls were within easy reach, arrayed along one side of the drive's transparent cover, manipulators extended into the box, connecting to the multifaceted device inside. The controls were a work of art all by themselves, a combination of dark polished wood and a patinated brass-like metal. It was hand-made and hand-driven, kept in perfect shape.

It took more effort than Pa'attee thought it would, but she engaged the clutch and disengaged the steam-driven gears. The drive continued to run on the energy stored in the flywheel, humming beneath her feet. There should be plenty of power available for her to start putting things to right. The spherical control with the vector orientation indicator stood to her right, below it was a bank of electromechanical readouts. Knowing Eg's version of the Sprocket Drive gave Pa'attee a conceptual understanding that augmented Pur'unnan's. *It's like modding Freya's drive specs but backward.* Although the readouts bore no relation to Eg's coordinate system, Pa'attee knew their purpose.

Pa'attee spun the spoked control wheel that disengaged the flywheel from the drive. With no energy being transmitted through the drive shaft Tal'anis should have come to All Stop. She transferred the coordinates from the top register - the last place where Tal'anis had come to rest - to the destination register manually. That register had almost no signs of use. She knew the connections between the coordinate bank and the destination register were drawn on Pur'unnan's plans, high on her list of things to get finished. *Did the Hel'Arumpo'or fly* Tal'anis, *seat-of-the-pants style, all the way here? That's got to be difficult from here. How did they give the pilot directions? Semaphore?*

Pur'unnan's memories provided the answer even as Pa'attee's mind formed the question and she rotated a small display from its foldaway position. The resolution was extraordinary, for a pin-display. Millions of pixel-pins produced a fine image, but it took Pa'attee a few seconds to be able to understand what the picture represented. It still displayed the last function it had been used for, manipulating the size of Tal'anis' MEM field, a distended ellipse with one focal point in front of her, the other centered in the asteroid. The display had other input settings including access to radar, but Pa'attee was not too concerned about bumping into anything. Tal'anis was most certainly the biggest boat in the water. *If there's anyone out there, they had better look out for us.*

Engaging the new vector from the destination register,

Pa'attee watched the elaborate, gilded orientation control spin like a ballerina in a music box before settling into place with click-ting. She turned the wheel that reintroduced energy from the flywheel. The numbers in the Current-Offset display began ticking over. It was the only sign that Tal'anis was moving. Giving the control another spin, it locked tight to the upper stop. It would take about half an hour to return the asteroid to its previous position. *I should probably throttle the steam engine down; she's running hot with no load on her.* There was a yellow and red striped speaking-tube that linked this control area to the steam engine, but with no one there, Pa'attee would have to walk around and do it herself. Clan politics prevented Pur'unnan brothers access to Darf'ornal's control systems and vice versa. It was a miracle that the systems interfaced at all.

Pa'attee gave the autopilot a quick check. It was a Rube-Goldbergian arrangement, mechanical linkages, triggers releasing springs, moving levers, setting off new triggers connecting the destination register to the throttle. She ran it in test-mode, and everything worked beautifully, although once again, it looked to be a system that had been maintained but not used. *Have they forgotten how to use it? Maybe they never learned how in the first place?* Writing manuals for this device, while necessary, had apparently not been high on Pur'unnan's to-do list as they readied for launch.

Pa'attee's memories told her that Pur'unnan had been needed aboard Delrofenalis for lift-off. At its heart, the prototype drive was a balky, willful, recalcitrant machine, on a good day. Pur'unnan's shade idly pondered what had gone wrong, with little concern that she had not survived the event.

Scuff marks around the base of the pedestal that secured the drive to the atrium's central plinth marred the well-tended presentation of the rest of the workstation. The stand had been moved and resettled. It was not possible to do that while the drive was running. A sick chill flushed through Pa'attee's gut. Pur'unnan's memories did not include this pedestal being moved. Tal'anis' drive had failed somewhere out in the cold expanses of interstellar space. Someone had pulled the drive apart and put it back together again. Pur'unnan emanated pride that her acolytes had retained enough knowledge to do that. *I wonder how many times it took them to get the correct alignment for a restart?* That was a task that had frustrated even Pur'unnan's skills, but one that Eg and Cain had mastered before much else.

Resting her hands on the brass tube that ran above the control wheels, Pa'attee looked out across Li'ila'tion. Pur'unnan's memories filled this huge place. She had been here, on this very spot, and watched Tal'anis being built around her. Everything evoked memories and being sleep-deprived did not help. Pa'attee took a deep breath, knowing that her ribs would complain. The rattling, grinding noises from the steam engine caught Pa'attee's attention again.

Stretching her back and shoulders, Pa'attee ambled around the plinth. She caught another cheer from the cheap seats up on high and gave a tired wave in reply. The fighting seemed to have stopped and that pleased her. Clan-on-clan conflicts were common. *Necessary*, a chorus of GreatMother thoughts bubbled up. *So many RightLeading brothers are born for the chance of a successful GreatMother birth.* She was glad that was not an opinion shared by all the GreatMothers inside her. There was a solution somewhere in all that accumulated knowledge. *How could one person hope to integrate more than a tiny percentage of the many lives Er'men's mel'andrin contained?*

The fusion power plant was a pale green toroid composed of flanged sections bolted together. Fuel injection and laser pumps sat tucked up beside the steam engine's great boiler. Thankfully, a curved shell protected the controls and readouts from the boiler's heat and some of the engine's roar. An array of large circular rheostats dominated one panel. Corresponding sets of cylindrical gauges were mounted beyond the controls. The tokamak's output readings were nominal; Pa'attee tapped the output gauge's stainless-steel case with the knuckle of her index finger. The red-on-white pointer rose and fell, returning to the blue nominal-region but a degree or two lower. As she suspected, the draw on the generator was minimal.

The steam engine rattled and shook with barely restrained violence. The dual pistons labored on, pulsing gusts of waste steam as their synchronous cranks drove the engine's flywheel. A rotating drive shaft sent energy into the covered transmission system. The apparatus dripped and hissed and roared, but the control area and the boiler were centers of calm. Calm but not quiet. The controls themselves, enameled white levers with yellow trims and triggers, and hand-wrought control-wheels looked as though they could pass the most stringent white-glove test.

The one dash of color was the talking-tube that had stripes of red and purple. *Quaint. Open up the little hatch and yell.* The handle that opened and closed the tube had a whistle connected to an auxiliary tube, blow down the other end, and it would whistle here. It was the only thing about the controls that did not conform to specifications. The whistle was loose. Its pea sat in a tiny porcelain dish set in a space above and to the right of the tubes. *We are not taking calls right now.* Pa'attee chuckled as she spun down the throttle and slowly opened the release valves on both sides, venting hot white plumes. The spastic clatter and groans from beneath the transmission system's covers died down. It surprised Pa'attee how quiet Li'ila'tion was with the engine stilled. Pa'attee's ears did pick out one insistent sound: Freya's comm. She was being pinged! *'Bout time someone noticed. NOTE TO SELF: get a new wrist comm!* She gave the controls one last look - the boiler's temperature was falling, waste steam hissed out in churning clouds, and the GreatMothers within her that had aligned with Clan Darf'ornal agreed the engine was safe - before Pa'attee returned to Freya.

CHAPTER THIRTY-EIGHT

Pa'attee held her breath as she lifted herself onto the edge of Freya's cockpit. *If I knew I'd have to climb in and out of* Freya *this often, I would have put in steps.* She eased herself into her form-fit seat and gave a gentle sigh before reaching for something to drink. *Hot black coffee would be nice.* Freya's chilled drinking water would have to do. She sipped as she answered the ping.

"Daichi! How are you?"

"Good. Life is much less hazardous since you took out those machine gun emplacements." Daichi's small bow was lifted straight from Cedric, and that was when Pa'attee realized he had been speaking in the RightLeading brothers' dialect. Seeing her sudden understanding, Daichi confirmed it, "Yes, I have had the honor of sharing Cedric's mel'andrin. It is a marvelous thing, is it not?"

"Absolutely. I wish I could share something in return," Pa'attee replied.

"Indeed. Those were my thoughts," Daichi agreed.

"Was there something you wanted? Not that catching up is a bad thing. It looks like the fighting's stopped."

"It has, thanks again to you, GreatMother Pa'attee," he bowed once again, but his eyes twinkled with humor.

"What did I do? Was it Cicely's screams?" Pa'attee asked with a chuckle. "They'd have me running for cover."

Daichi coughed. *Was that a chuckle?* "We caught a little of that as you flew around - my ears are still ringing - but no, it was you taking control of Li'ila'tion. You fascinate the Hel'Arumpo'or."

I do? "Where are you?" she asked.

"Up on the top promenade, almost opposite you," Daichi told

her. Pa'attee looked up and saw an arm waving; she waved back and heard a roaring return, punctuated by stamping feet and a celebratory clash of blades. *Pa'attee! Pa'attee! Pa'attee!* A giggle bubbled up inside her.

"We've all been curious as to what you have been doing," Daichi said.

"I'm putting," Pa'attee opened the asteroid's bookmark in Freya's Almanac, "(295731)2164 GY$_{19}$ back where she belongs. After that, well, I'm sure Harrum'Bar will want to have a say about it. Is she still pulling the strings?"

"I believe so," he replied.

"Then it's her turn. I just have to hurry up and wait." Pa'attee's fingers pulled the last bonbon from the compartment on her left. *I hope it's not the last, last one.* She unwrapped it and took a nibble; chocolate covered walnut pieces and something creamy and utterly delicious. Sagging back in her seat, Pa'attee sighed and took another bite; the sensual delight brought a smile to her lips. *Music might be nice too.* She began to access the small collection of tunes she stored locally and wondered how the Hel'Arumpo'or, with their three-beat hearts, responded to four-beat music. She set a three-four filter just in case. *Maybe classical would be best, too.* She assigned the genre and reached for the play button, remembering at the last moment to drop the volume to a more sociable level. The gentle horns from Strauss' *Blue Danube* began with the strings backing up, tremulous, until they started their beautiful counterpoint, striding out to the fore.

"Can you hear that up there?" Pa'attee asked.

"Faintly. I wouldn't overdo it if I were you," Daichi advised.

"Just setting the right tone," she replied.

"Remember to keep centered, keep your guard up and don't react to Harrum'Bar's goads. Cedric has clashed with her in the Great Council," he instructed.

"Thanks, coach. I'll try." Her head rolled back against the neck seal-ring of her p-suit, never reaching the padded headrest sculpted to match her helmet. Freya was not quite as comfortable under full gravity as she was when she was flying in zero-gee. That did not stop Pa'attee from closing her eyes. *Just for a few minutes.*

"That didn't take her long. You have company," Daichi told her.

"Really?" Pa'attee asked, taking another sip of water.

"There's not many. Whel'luminum holds the honor of this moment, but I don't think that's Pum leading. Harrum'Bar's wise to use the neutral Whel'luminum as an initial probe."

"Probably scared of how I might react to see Bar'Durrunnan Red marching upon me." Reluctantly, Pa'attee opened her eyes. *I wish I had enough to splash over my face.* And then she realized she did, in the aft compartment. *It might be easier to get in and out through the aft hatch, too.* "I'll keep the line open. I'm not sure the external mike will pick up much."

"Just stay safe," Daichi encouraged her.

"You know me, coach. I'm not one to foolishly rush into a situation unprepared." The chuckle that followed stung her ribs but either it did not hurt too much, or she was becoming accustomed to it. "If you see anything out of the ordinary, send a ping."

Squeezing past her seat, Pa'attee had to grit her teeth to stop from crying out as her broken ribs flexed. *No, I'm not getting used to it.* She splashed water on her face from the temporary spigot duct-taped to the aft bulkhead, before realizing she did not have anything to dry herself with or a mirror. *I must look frightful.* The seal on the aft hatch unlocked with a satisfying clunk, and the heavy door swung open at a touch. It was easier on her ribs getting out that way. *I wonder if the music is a bit loud. Too late now. Not going to climb back in. Probably should have gotten out of this p-suit, too. Nah, better save something for the showdown.*

A bare dozen Whel'luminum, in their regimental blues, held the honor under a checked flag of truce. A small brother leading them almost had the coloration of his RightLeading brothers. *He must be quite young.* The LeftLeading brother was shorter than Murrun, and by the look of his tabard, he was a herald rather than someone with authority to deal with the crucial matters of inter-clan/inter-species negotiations. *Is he supposed to be another sacrifice?* Pa'attee wondered. *Politics.* She felt a shudder run down her spine as she waited. A glance up at the promenades showed her why the fighting had stopped; they were crowded with the curious. *Political theater in the round.*

A pair of latecomers moved as quickly as they could, without a loss of dignity, to catch up with the formation. And then another scurried down the curved ramp. *Three LeftLeading brothers from three different clans, Pur'undram purple, Darf'ornal yellow and Bar'Durrunnan red.* Pur'unnan supplied the insight: those three clans operated the equipment mounted on the plinth. Darf'ornal ran the hulking steam engine, Bar'Durrunnan the tokamak, and Pur'undram the stardrive itself. They would all want to have a voice at the table.

Waiting at the head of the plinth's stairs, Pa'attee held her ground until after the leading brother in the phalanx contacted Freya's impenetrable MEM field. The formation concertinaed a little, but they had slowed their approach considerably, and the phalanx of arms bearers recovered their poise quickly enough. She strolled casually down the stairs ignoring the formation's discomfort, as was proper. *With thousands of Hel'Arumpo'or watching, I'm going to have to rely on Pur'unnan to maintain the correct protocol, or I'm going to look a complete fool.*

As Pa'attee arrived at the MEM field boundary, the phalanx parted, delivering up the obviously nervous Whel'luminum herald. The embroidery on his tabard showed just how young he was, but it did show promise.

"The Great Council demands..."

Pur'unnan had Pa'attee turn away, disappointment dragging her shoulders down.

"Ahh... requires..."

At an internal nudge, Pa'attee began walking away.

"Um... requests?" The poor brother's voice squeaked with fear. He would be punished for his failings here. Pa'attee stopped and turned back to the now quaking emissary. "The

Great Council requests ... desires the attendance of FirstMother Pa'attee..."

Pa'attee did not need the internal guide to make her turn away once more.

"GreatMother, please."

Slowly, Pa'attee turned back.

"GreatMother, this one was given the words," he trembled as he bowed, almost prostrating himself before her, his neck outstretched as if waiting for a blow.

"We do not look kindly on Harrum'Bar's use of sacrificial offerings," Pa'attee stated. "Does she expect us to put ourselves in your hands as you have been placed in ours?" The fact there was an almost impenetrable barrier between them made no difference to the young brother. If not for the honor he held for his clan, he would have been cowering on the scuffed cream flooring.

To relieve pressure on the poor lad, Pa'attee glanced up at the limp checkered flag above his head. "Harrum'Bar has dishonored that flag." She turned away and took a single step, but that was only for effect. For the curious masses her actions could not be subtle, they had to be readable from a distance; Pur'unnan's guiding hand was ever-present at Pa'attee's tiller. "Give the Great Council our regards and apologies." She reluctantly climbed the stairs, confident that everyone watching could see she felt the meeting was an opportunity lost. The company reformed and withdrew with as much dignity as they could muster.

CHAPTER THIRTY-NINE

"GreatMother, please," a voice called, desperately.

Turning slowly, Pa'attee held tightly to her smile. The three clan-representatives clustered at the MEM boundary. She took her time returning to the meeting place. The brother that stood to the fore was as old a Hel'Arumpo'or as Pa'attee had ever seen; his skin was cracked in places and pale enough to be almost gray. The poor fellow could hardly contain his anxiety, but he held firmly to the dignity the elaborate embroidery on his tabard evoked. The second in seniority was the representative from Pur'undram who, on a second look, appeared to be at least as old as the brother from Darf'ornal, if not older. Pa'attee was perversely pleased to note that he was furious, maintaining only the thinnest veneer of formality. The Bar'Durrunnan clansman, most assuredly a Harrum'Bar plant, stood at the rear as if he remained unobserved.

"Elder brothers," Pa'attee speared the brother from Bar'Durrunnan with her eyes to make sure he understood she was not addressing him, "how may we assist you?"

"GreatMother, this one only asks permission to inspect our engine," the brother from Darf'ornal requested. "Although she sounds quiet now, she'll be like to take advantage of," he struggled to phrase it politely - beneath his anxiety burned anger just as fierce as his brother from Pur'undram, "take advantage of the inexperienced. She can be dangerous, GreatMother."

"I'm sure she can, Elder brother." Pa'attee blinked as the design on his tabard seemed to rearrange itself and reform one logical pattern placement after another. *Of course!* A tabard's design was not just an indicator of his clan; it was his life-story, his name! *Run'ned'lahl* was a strong and well-used mold, used in the casting of heavy machine parts. "Brother Run'ned'lahl, we're sure that can be arranged." She gestured towards Freya. "We will need to retire and adjust the boundary conditions. We beg your patience for a moment, please." Pa'attee bowed, noting that Run'ned'lahl was, unsuccessfully, trying to disguise his surprise she knew his name. The two elders exchanged expressions of curiosity. *I'm not what they'd been told to expect.*

"GreatMother Pa'attee?" Run'ned'lahl's bow added a formal tone to the request.

"Yes, Elder Brother Run'ned'lahl?" Pur'unnan's instincts told Pa'attee to be as formal as the person required. Using Run'ned'lahl's name without the honorific would be inappropriate.

"This one wishes to introduce this one's colleagues." He waited for Pa'attee's assent. "Elder Brother Grad'dahvro," he bowed to the Pur'undram clansman beside him. *Grad'dahvro means sure hands, or quick hands, or maybe even quick fists might fit better, judging by his demeanor.*

"And Bar'Durrunnan's ... Bel'lamado'or." *The bow was brief, perfunctory. That's interesting. Does he even know Bel'lamado'or? He's definitely been sent by Harrum'Bar. Bel'lamado'or was a sturdy plant that grew in the waterways. It bends with the prevailing current.*

"We are honored and pleased to have your acquaintance," Pa'attee replied. *What an excellent language the Hel'Arumpo'or have. I can be honest and sincere with the two elder brothers and sarcastic as all hell to the other.* Pa'attee bowed and left the senior brothers exchanging guarded comments.

Getting into Freya's aft hatch was relatively easy; being graceful, and regal while doing so was impossible. There was, however, considerably less stress on her nagging ribs. Once inside, Pa'attee ached to roll over and lie on the soft padding that lined Freya's cabin and let the gentle strains of *Norwegian Wood* wash over her, but somehow, she found herself forging through and climbing into her seat. *That's okay; this is almost as good.* Her right hand fussed about in a locker beside her feet and her fingers closed on a bonbon. There were more in there. *I always run out of things on my left side first.* Pa'attee did not bother nibbling and popped the small sphere into her mouth. *Hmm... thin, soft-toffee coating .... oh wow!* Sherbet and hard-toffee chips exploded in a shower of tingling sensations.

Opening the Sprocket Drive's parameters, Pa'attee saved the settings before softening the MEM barrier. You could walk through the interface now, but it would still refuse admittance to a high-speed round, even ones as slow as those fired by the steam-powered machine guns. There was no one close enough to rush the softened barrier, but Pa'attee still felt the chill of exposure. She saved the settings into a new preset buffer. *Better get them in here.* She stood on her seat and spoke to the small delegation. "It is done. Please come forward." As the Hel'Arumpo'or language was rooted in body gestures, if there was line-of-sight you could talk if the subject was simple enough. *And everyone's watching me. Turn. Smile. Wave.* Cheers poured down from above.

When she was sure, they had crossed the MEM threshold, Pa'attee reset the boundary's properties. *Now they're in, lock the door.* She sipped from her p-suit's supply and turned down Jimi Hendrix's *Manic Depression.* Just a bit. *Perhaps I should have shaved the genre by selecting for acoustic only. I don't have time for that now.* She clambered out of Freya's aft hatch.

Poor Run'ned'lahl had difficulty mounting the stairs, but he refused the assistance his dignified status allowed. *Are you Darf'ornal's FirstBrother?* Grad'dahvro stayed loyally at Run'ned'lahl's stately pace while Bel'lamado'or chafed at his position, bringing up the rear. He kept his head down in apparent submission, in the vain hope it would hide his intent, but his every thought announced itself in his foot placement, the roll of his shoulders and the angle of his gaze. Fear. He had a task that scared him. He wanted to get it done and get away.

"Shall we inspect your engine first, Elder Brother?" Pa'attee inquired.

"That would be most kind, GreatMother," Run'ned'lahl replied. "This one apologizes for taking so long. This old body is not as sprightly as it used to be."

"We are in no hurry, Elder Brother," the subtext Pa'attee tried to convey was that she would always have time for him. The sentiment was difficult to express without the correct olfactory component. Run'ned'lahl seemed to understand and led the way around the front of the dais and down the side, at a slow and steady pace. Grad'dahvro stopped just outside an invisible line that marked out Bar'Durrunnan's domain. Bel'lamado'or continued with them for a stride before peeling off to the left under the guise of inspecting the fusion power plant.

As if pleased to have shaken off his companions, Run'ned'lahl focused completely on his beloved engine, almost forgetting that Pa'attee was with him. She followed quietly, keeping out of his way. His whole demeanor began to change, shaking off the attributes of age, standing straighter, his eyes and hands confident. The engine was quiescent with only the occasional sound of drips splashing into strategically placed trays. He caressed the gauges and bright yellow controls as if greeting a lover. Everything was in order. Taking a mallet, an oil can, and a rag from a toolbox, he ducked away to give the engine a closer inspection. He poked, prodded and thumped the powertrain, wiping and oiling as needed. He lifted the transmission system's cover but, after giving it a brief examination, he did not continue any further.

Suddenly Run'ned'lahl seemed to become aware of Pa'attee. "She's looking in good shape," he mumbled. He was pleasantly surprised and did not mind showing it. He absentmindedly tossed the mallet, spinning it into the air; it dropped, the handle hitting his oily hand. Smack. He did it again. Smack. He was happy. "The transmission system will need to have a closer inspection," but that was a routine matter and of little concern. He packed away his tools and carefully washed his hands before giving the controls one last loving inspection. His eyes found something; or rather, they didn't find something. The pea from the talk-tubes' call-whistle was missing from the tiny temporary-turned-permanent dish. He bent over, nearly dropping to his knees, searching for the bead.

"I'm sorry, I put the pea back in the whistle. That *is* where it is supposed to be, isn't it?" Pa'attee laughed when Run'ned'lahl danced an apologetic shuffle as if he was a schoolboy caught in a silly prank. A little inter-clan niggle. *We are not listening.* Anyone who has operated a communication device, even an archaic talk-tube like this one, knew how to mute its annoying call. His apology turned into a coughing kick-step and a bow when he linked her vocal outburst - he had not heard a human laugh before - with her body's Hel'Arumpo'or expressions of mirth; a joke shared.

"We are pleased that no harm has come to your wonderful engine, Run'ned'lahl," Pa'attee told him. It did no harm to flatter him. Mel'andrin memories informed Pa'attee that the Darf'ornal clan, while technologically almost obsolete, held great influence due to the clan's longevity. They had been formed before the Second Fall and were a bastion of learning and industry during dark times. They were the sturdy rootstock from which much of the Hel'Arumpo'or species grew.

A rattling cough dismissed her flattery even as he appreciated it. "GreatMother Pa'attee," he patted the throttle, clean but patinated with age, "this one knows our engine has limits, serious limits in this modern age. We are here on sufferance, for the Darf'ornal honor."

"An honor deserved, Elder Brother. Talefenanis and Delrofenalis would never have been built without Darf'ornal's famed metallurgical skills." And Pur'unnan's designs had pressed them to their very limits.

Run'ned'lahl was again surprised that Pa'attee was even aware of the second ship. "GreatMother, this one was told you were a human impostor, not a true GreatMother, bringing only war and death."

"You were told a great many false things, I'm sure," Pa'attee reassured him. "We do not want conflict between our peoples.

This war of conquest was a serious mistake we hope to correct. There should be peace between us. Tell the truth to your brothers about me, let this moment guide them."

"GreatMother, it would be this one's honor." Run'ned'lahl bowed low and then rose, almost sprightly, seemingly eager to spread the word. "The Darf'ornal have seen many GreatMothers influence the world. There is always, war, conflict, and death, but when a GreatMother rises there is something else, something more dangerous, change," he paused gathering his thoughts, "especially when a GreatMother seeks peace. The Hel'Arumpo'or are fractious at best."

As are humans. "Fractured maybe but not broken."

"GreatMother, we should move on. This one knows that Grad'dahvro is keen to inspect the damage," cough, "that the GreatMother has inflicted upon Pur'undram's domain." Run'ned'lahl's humorous inflection was contagious, and they both took a moment to compose themselves before returning to the others.

CHAPTER FORTY

Bel'lamado'or stood quietly beside the tokamak's controls, his hands tucked beneath his tabard. Run'ned'lahl tagged along behind Pa'attee deliberately oblivious to the fact he was trespassing in Bar'Durrunnan territory; he was a member of GreatMother Pa'attee's entourage now. Bel'lamado'or was still or tried to be, his breathing was carefully controlled, feigning calm, but he was not *calm* enough to deceive Pa'attee. A part of him was relieved. Fear still drove him. He was keen to leave now that his task was complete.

You've done something. The hairs all along Pa'attee's spine sent waves of chill warning. *You don't play with a tok's settings, especially an old design like this. Once they're running, you just keep them ticking over.* The output was up by less than one percent, but it climbed further as Pa'attee watched. She tapped the gauge, and the needle rose and reset two degrees higher.

"What have you done?" Pa'attee cried, pushing Bel'lamado'or to one side. Nearly all the rheostats had been adjusted; the fuel feed was increased, and the magnetic constrictors were set to manual. *Give it twenty minutes, and she'll overload. That would be unpleasant.* Her hands wound in the automatics and dropped the fuel injection rate.

"Do you have anyone else relying on the power from this generator?" Pa'attee was sorely tempted to turn the thing off.

"Err, this one does not ... um ... this one must protest. Err." Bel'lamado'or stammered. His body-language shouted, terror. *This was not in his instruction-set.*

"Oh, it's too late for that now," Pa'attee growled. "You're obviously not an engineer. What did Harrum'Bar tell you, that the tokamak would just fizz a bit and die? Did she tell you an explosion from an overloaded reactor could make Li'ila'tion uninhabitable?" She tapped at the output gauge; it was still rising while the fusion reaction used up the excess fuel. She felt like kicking the foolish brother. Pur'unnan would have. So would Bor'enop. She was not too surprised to see that Run'ned'lahl had his blade out. Ceremonial or not she could see a sharp edge to it. Bel'lamado'or pawed at his ornate hilt but was too scared of the Elder Brother to draw his weapon.

"What would GreatMother Bor'enop have thought about your actions?" Patty asked pointedly. "How careful she was to make her rediscoveries safe, and you planned to poison your home with her gift. You disgust me. Is Harrum'Bar that desperate?" she inquired angrily. "Tell her to come and face us and stop sending sacrificial pawns. We would not sully the honor of our blade with your blood." Patty turned from him, displaying her disgust. "Run'ned'lahl, could you escort this bit-player to a safe place where he cannot injure himself or others?"

"The GreatMother's will is this one's pleasure," Run'ned'lahl rumbled and swatted the relative youngster who yelped and hopped away.

"You can't do this to me!" Smack! The flat of Run'ned'lahl's blade caught Bel'lamado'or below the hips. "Oww!"

"Complain to your mother when you get home, you loathsome pup," Run'ned'lahl growled. Swing and another miss. Bel'lamado'or moved quickly. As Run'ned'lahl strode past Grad'dahvro, his old age forgotten, he passed the Pur'undram clansman a comment, brother-to-brother. He knew Pa'attee could see the exchange but did not care. "I like her, plinth-brother. Keen eyes, she has. Harrum'Bar bends words out of true." He glanced at Pa'attee and gave a simple nod before turning back to his friend. "She's a keeper." He coughed and took off after the fleeing red tabard, waving his blade wildly.

Grad'dahvro looked bewildered; his anger set aside. Pa'attee tapped the output gauge once more. It settled back. *Output's definitely falling. The reactor's probably safe enough for now.*

"Shall we continue, Elder Brother?" Pa'attee's inflection kept her question nonchalant while posing it as a request, student-to-master. The Pur'undram Elder Brother clutched at his tabard and puffed out his chest. *You do that too often; it's worn, where he grips the cloth.*

"Oh, of course, GreatMother." *What have you done to my friend?* Grad'dahvro did at least wait until Pa'attee drew abreast before striding out.

"We shared a joke," Pa'attee confessed.

"Not that blasted whistle, was it? Harrumph." Grad'dahvro was not amused. The whistle was obviously a sore point between Grad'dahvro and his friend. Pa'attee bit down on a spicy reply. *No need to make things worse. I'm here to make friends.* They continued around to the Pur'undram workstation, Pa'attee walking in respectful silence. It did not help, but it did not hurt either.

The pace of Grad'dahvro's angry strides slowed. "What have you done? Why is the pin-display out like that?" Master-to-student he demanded answers.

I know his type, Pur'unnan's thoughts came unbidden. Keep him busy, distracted, before he can drop into his usual bluster.

Pa'attee relaxed and let Pur'unnan's voice come through, "That is the correct placement, even for Hel'Arumpo'or. You have the fine controls here under your left hand and the display selection to your right. There is no point in keeping it locked away unless you are cleaning."

"Yes, GreatMother," he answered automatically. Poor Grad'dahvro was confused; his anger was suddenly directionless. "What the GreatMother says is correct but ... it was not ... The Great Way. The plans GreatMother Pur'unnan left us describes the display in that position but..."

Pa'attee laughed with disbelief. "You mean someone has to squeeze in down there between the drive and the navigation controls and what, ask for fine tuning from someone that can't see the screen? GreatMother Pur'unnan documented as much as she could before they had to leave, but some things are just common sense." *If they had to rely on The Great Way, Pur'unnan's scant documentation, that means vital memories had been lost.* That could be fatally limiting for a young clan like Pur'unnan's. Pa'attee knelt at the coordinate registers. They were approaching the destination. The asteroid would not return to its exact position, but it would be near enough. "And here, I know she documented connecting the Coordinate Register banks here with the Destination Register there. It was high on her to-do list."

"That is true, GreatMother." Humiliation rattled Grad'dahvro. "Who are you? How have you learned these things?" he demanded.

"I know these things because Pur'unnan knew those things," Pa'attee told him. "She looks out from within us with pride, Grad'dahvro." That wasn't quite true. Pur'unnan-within wanted her to cuff the FirstBrother around the ears. While down beside the register banks, Pa'attee rubbed her fingers across the scuff marks around the drive's short rostrum. "She is especially proud of this." That was true. "You dismantled the drive and put her back together again. That must have been a frightening time."

"It was, GreatMother. It was." Grad'dahvro shuddered. "This one was but a young pup and didn't really understand the consequences." Grad'dahvro chuffed a little cough, "Us pups were having too much fun in zero-gee but when the Great Council issued its decree this one soon understood Tal'anis' peril, adrift in the great desert between stars. This one was there to witness every operation. Precious memories." Precious memories. Safe now. Passed down to a new generation of Pur'undram clansmen. "It took nearly an orbit to find the correct probe insertion settings."

"That can be tricky," Patty agreed. "Much easier with this version, though. We're not surprised Pur'unnan had to lift off with the prototype in Delrofenalis. Her loss was a tragedy that could have doomed the whole mission."

Grad'dahvro sighed as grief gripped him. "As FirstBrother, this one has mel'andrin of Delrofenalis's fall to hold and share."

Grad'dahvro looked as if he was ready to make her a copy on the spot.

"One day, I would be honored to share it," Pa'attee replied, though she did not like the thought of watching the great ship's fall to the homeworld.

Ping, ping, ping. The autopilot sounded its delicate announcement. Click, slide, snick, whir. The throttle turned, around and around from one stop to the other. Ping, ping. Ping, ping. Operation complete.

"We're here." Pa'attee climbed to her feet. "We should put a stabilizing spin on the asteroid before we let her go."

"Spin? Here? Where?" Grad'dahvro spluttered.

"I couldn't let Harrum'Bar drop this asteroid on my homeworld, so I've put it back. We should give it some spin before letting it go, to keep her stable."

"Stable. Yes." Poor Grad'dahvro was still spinning his wheels, but it looked as though his mind was getting some traction.

"Would you like to assist me?" Pa'attee changed the pin-display to show the elliptical MEM field cross-section.

"Y-y-yes, GreatMother."

"We should translate the insertion nexus to the asteroid's centroid. That will help when applying the rotations."

"Sorry, GreatMother?"

"Oh, I know it's not in the manual. Good thing too or Harrum'Bar would have had you snatch up the asteroid," Pa'attee confided. "You'd have been out of here before I could've caught up with you." Patty pointed to the pin-display. "We offset the probe's insertion point from here," Pa'attee gestured to the drive encased in its transparent box, and then to the ellipse's lesser focal point on the pin-display, "to here," her finger slid across to the greater focal point. It was near enough to the center of the oblate asteroid.

"Here, I'll show you." Pa'attee let Pum'hurnun move her hands to the right controls; it was easier than translating her memories into actions. "Now with this array selected, we apply a translation with these," her hand gently spun a control, the wood was smooth under her fingers. "We won't feel anything or shouldn't. See the crosshairs moving?" Pa'attee gave the control a harder spin, and the nexus began to move from one focal point to the other. She gave the control another turn. The nexus point picked up speed. *That's better.* As it approached the second focal point, Pa'attee used the heel of her hand to slow the control.

"Now any rotation we impart to the asteroid will be at its center, not ours."

"GreatMother Pa'attee," Grad'dahvro gasped. His anger and confusion had fled, leaving only worshipful awe. He prostrated himself before her, his head centimeters from her left foot and Pa'attee knew he would stay there until permitted to move.

"Please, Grad'dahvro, rise," Pa'attee told him. Using his name without any honorifics cut away at some of the formality his prostration imposed.

He rose but only to one knee. "GreatMother, this one has received mel'andrin from brothers watching GreatMother Pur'unnan at her work. It was not that long ago she walked among us. This one sees her in the GreatMother's sure movements, hears her in the GreatMother's voice." His head dropped.

Pa'attee felt Pur'unnan move her; her left hand fell gently to the dappled skin of Grad'dahvro's smooth skull, and Pur'unnan's benediction rolled through her throat and body. "Take these memories and treasure them. Share them so that all may know the truth."

Grad'dahvro gave the response from the oldest of his gift-memories, from the darkest of times. "GreatMother, guide us. GreatMother, keep us."

A profound stillness possessed them both.

With the hiss of steel-on-steel, Grad'dahvro presented his blade to Pa'attee. For a ceremonial sword, Pa'attee was surprised to see nicks and scars along its engraved surface. It had been some time since its edge had seen a whetstone though.

"You would pledge yourself to me, Grad'dahvro?" Pa'attee asked.

"Yes, GreatMother," his head did not rise.

"You are Pur'undram FirstBrother, are you not?" she inquired.

Pride lifted Grad'dahvro's eyes. "This one would bring all of Pur'undram. They will see what this one sees; GreatMother Pur'unnan walks amongst us once more." Like Run'ned'lahl, Grad'dahvro appeared reborn and renewed; even his faded pastel striations blossomed with color.

"GreatMother, is it true our Star-Born would have the GreatMother as her regent?" Grad'dahvro asked.

There was more than awe behind those bright eyes. "Harrum'Bar announced this?"

Grad'dahvro's cough gagged him momentarily. "No, GreatMother. It is but one of a thousand whispers that circulate." He sniffed Li'ila'tion's airs. He was almost opaque compared to Bel'lamado'or's transparency. Careful positioning.

"Politics?" she asked.

"With GreatMother as regent, Clan Pur'undram would have a voice on the Great Council again. Clan Bar'Durrunnan has led the Great Council since GreatMother Pur'unnan fell." There was that spark of anger. It had found its focus again.

Flashes of doubt swirled through Pa'attee. "Grad'dahvro, would you follow us, even if we did not take your oath? We are not GreatMother Pur'unnan. We would have other tasks if Er'men, our Star-Born, would have us as Regent." *Regent? Pa'attee Balke, Regent Queen of the aliens! Are you kidding?* But she knew she had already taken on that role, at least partially. Er'men felt as dear to her heart as Alan. *Oh, let him be safe. You can't back out now.* "If we are called to the Regency, Clan Pur'undram would have its voice on the Great Council. This, we promise. But Pur'undram FirstBrother, if that were to be so, we would have to face the humans, representing all the Clans through the difficult times ahead. We could not hold the needs of Clan Pur'undram as close to our heart as your FirstMother does."

Grad'dahvro's shoulders dropped with wry disappointment,

and he withdrew the offer of his blade. "GreatMother Pa'attee is wise. This one will share this moment with our FirstMother, with this one's Brothers Elder. They will see as this one sees, hear as this one hears. They will give whatever support the GreatMother requires." He bowed low once more before rising.

"Shall we set this asteroid rotating?" Grad'dahvro set aside the formality of the previous moment, asking Pa'attee, student-to-master. He was eager to work with her, to watch her every move, to learn, to enrich his clan.

"Okay, let's explore this a little," she said. It felt much better having Grad'dahvro as an interested work colleague than an overawed devotee. "We can attempt to set the rotation manually, like you usually do, with the manual vector control over there," Pa'attee remarked as she gestured towards the bronzed sphere with its elegant pointer aligned along the Tal'aniss long axis, their direction of travel. "But we can set up the rotations on the pin-display," she instructed. Pa'attee slipped to one side so Grad'dahvro could get a closer look, "and let the automation system implement the changes."

CHAPTER FORTY-ONE

Standing back, Pa'attee smiled and let out a careful but contented sigh. *Grad'dahvro's a quick learner.* She enjoyed working with him. He turned to her from his focused position before pin-display. *Come and see. Is this right?* The asteroid already had its slow tumble; Grad'dahvro wanted to show her his solution for detaching Tal'anis. He had set up three automated banks, two for changing the MEM boundary's permeability and shape and one to translate Tal'anis away from the asteroid, resetting the great ship's orientation relative to the solar system. His solution looked good to both Pa'attee and Pur'unnan's shade within her.

"Well done, Pur'undram FirstBrother," Pa'attee congratulated him.

"Oh, GreatMother, being able to automate this is such a boon! We would have had to crowd six brothers in here to do this in one movement." He gave a hearty cough, "and we would have messed it up!"

"Well then, make it happen, FirstBrother."

With a slight bow of thanks, Grad'dahvro threw the switch and stepped back. He was in awe again, but this time he focused on the mechanical marvel in front of him. GreatMother Pur'unnan had designed and built the automation system, and it had been under his nose and the noses of his fore-brothers unnoticed. *No, noticed, they knew it was there but without comprehension.* Ping, ping, ping. The mechanism, drawing its energy from the flywheel humming below their feet, whirled and clicked and slid and snicked. Control wheels spun; levers snapped to new detents, the controls turned to new settings and the bronzed levers reset; whiz, whir, click. The device ran through its program, whirring and clicking before sitting quietly for a moment. Ping, ping. Ping, ping. All done.

"GreatMother, this has been a pleasure unasked for." Grad'dahvro bowed, graceful but without formality. He looked satisfied, stuffed full of learning.

"Take and share what you have understood," Pur'unnan's benediction came forth naturally as Pa'attee relaxed into the GreatMother dialect.

"This one will, GreatMother!" he coughed vigorously. "Another pleasure unasked for." For the first time, he tore his attention away from the workstations, across the plinth, down to where Run'ned'lahl had Bel'lamado'or cornered, lecturing him, using his blade to add emphasis. Grad'dahvro coughed again, "Oh, he's been itching to have a go at Clan Bar'Durrunnan. The GreatMother has gifted that one with a perfect excuse."

"Has Harrum'Bar so alienated herself from the Clans?" Pa'attee asked. What is the RegentFirstMother doing? How long have I been up here performing for the audience gathered in Li'ila'tion? She should have had enough time to make a considered response by now.

"Clan Bar'Durrunnan, and from before the exodus, from before Pum'hurnun." Grad'dahvro's rumbling speech sounded more like a growl. "Bar'Durrunnan are expansionist. Our moons and the expanses of our home system were never enough for them. They gave Darf'ornal no end of trouble until GreatMother Pum'hurnun was born and grew strong enough to express her GreatMother's understanding and will. Harrum'Bar's not the first to covet the position of GreatMother."

"Politics."

"Of course, GreatMother." *As natural as breathing*, he beamed. Sure that the heart of Tal'anis was in safe hands, Grad'dahvro was keen to find his FirstMother and share the good news.

"Let me adjust Freya's boundary conditions so you can leave." Pa'attee gestured along the plinth, and they strolled towards the dark shape.

"Freya?" Grad'dahvro asked.

"My ship, Freya. She is named after a mythological mother from deep in the past, just as Talefenanis and Delrofenalis are names taken from the Hel'Arumpo'or's history."

Grad'dahvro nodded, understanding. "And she is so small." His head kept shifting from side to side as he tried to see Freya clearly, but she gave no reflections or shadings to give clues as to her real shape, just her profile. "And that," he turned his head slightly, favoring his left ear, "those sounds. It is a language unknown but known, nonetheless. It intrigues."

The second movement of Tchaikovsky's first piano concerto danced through the air; the intricate piano sent pleasurable chills through Pa'attee's mind. *Music.* The Hel'Arumpo'or culture had few referents to music. Some work-chants held a rhythmic semblance to music but little else. GreatMothers' dialect did not have a word for it although Pa'attee was sure Fe'ren, Pur'unnan's oldest gift-memory, would have known music. The Arumpo'or had a rich culture before their fall. They had lost so much.

"You are right," Pa'attee agreed. "It is a language, a language that humans use to share emotions. It is a subjective language of great subtlety. A chant, of sorts. High-chant."

"Very high, GreatMother. It makes this one's head spin."

"This piece, from a master named Tchaikovsky, is probably a bit difficult to appreciate as an introduction to music, especially this section." *That's got to be difficult to play.* "I think it is very pretty." *Isn't the second movement in six-eight? How did it get into the playlist?* Pa'attee perched on the edge of Freya's aft hatch. "I'd invite you in, but I think you'd get a better view if you went around and looked in through the cockpit." Pa'attee clambered aboard. Grad'dahvro waited patiently for her when she squeezed into her seat, as close as he could get to Freya's dark skin without touching her. Turning down the beautiful but distracting third movement, Pa'attee gave Grad'dahvro a quick rundown of Freya's controls. He was most impressed as she called up the *soft* MEM field preset.

"There is a save and retrieval system for all this?" he asked.

"These settings and more."

"GreatMother, it is all so small and elegant." Doubts about Clan Pur'undram's very analog workstation bubbled up inside him.

"Small because it has to be," Patty said. "Pur'unnan's designs say as much about her as they are about the functionality with which she imbued them. She made them with her own hands and flew Tal'anis, standing where we stood. It is perfect just as it is, a shrine to her," Pa'attee enthused. Grad'dahvro nodded, understanding. "I think we should make the links connecting the coordinate register banks with the destination register. You don't want to fly into a sun because you transferred the data incorrectly."

"Indeed, GreatMother."

Grad'dahvro met her at Freya's aft hatch, and they proceeded down the stairs to the MEM boundary where Run'ned'lahl had Bel'lamado'or bailed up against the plinth.

"Plinth-brother Run'ned'lahl speaks the truth. GreatMother Pa'attee is most definitely a *keeper*." Grad'dahvro coughed his amusement.

"Always do, brother. Always do." Run'ned'lahl poked at Bel'lamado'or who tried unsuccessfully to keep out of the blade's way. His artfully inscribed leading forearm bore the scars of the pathetic attempts of his defense. *How much worse could it have been for him to actually draw his sword?*

"Except when telling this one the whistle has not been heard," Grad'dahvro's jesting posture undercut the gravity of his words.

Many a truth spoken is in jest. At least Grad'dahvro's being light about it, Pa'attee thought.

"What was that?" Run'ned'lahl cupped one hand to his earhole in a gesture that was almost human. Pa'attee was pleased to hear Grad'dahvro's cough join with Run'ned'lahl's and her laugh.

"Brothers, take these memories with you and share them," Pa'attee intoned solemnly.

675

"GreatMother, we will." Run'ned'lahl and Grad'dahvro bowed low.

"Bel'lamado'or, take these memories and share them with Bar'Durrunnan FirstMother. Make sure Harrum'Bar knows *she* must attend *us* next time. Sacrificial offerings are not acceptable. Tell Bar'Durrunnan FirstMother to bring the Star-Born. If we are not shown GreatMother Er'men, in good health, there will be consequences."

"Consequences?" Bel'lamado'or asked, trembling.

"How long would Tal'anis last if I flew her into the sun?" Pa'attee bluffed. "Consequences. Do you understand?"

"Yes, GreatMother."

"Then be about your duty," GreatMother Pa'attee commanded. Bel'lamado'or gave a hurried bow, pressed through the MEM boundary and fled up a curving path, heading aft.

"And these plinth-brothers should attend to their duties too, GreatMother." Grad'dahvro bowed low with grace and formality, Run'ned'lahl following a heartbeat later. "Clan Pur'undram stands with GreatMother Pa'attee."

"As does Darf'ornal, GreatMother." Run'ned'lahl took a considered breath. "It is still not enough against Bar'Durrunnan. Bar'Durrunnan FirstMother holds the Great Council thus," he squeezed with his strong left hand.

"We shall see, Elder Brothers. For now, I need to see for myself that GreatMother Er'men is safe."

"Bar'Durrunnan holds her?" Run'ned'lahl asked.

"When last we saw, yes. A Bar'Durrunnan hunter and a hand of brothers had her. We fear for her safety," she told them. "We have heard she is not the first Star-Born GreatMother." It was as if Pa'attee's words darkened the great dome of Li'ila'tion brightness.

"This one remembers the events," Run'ned'lahl rumbled, and a deep sadness and pain returned to his posture.

Grad'dahvro mirrored him. "It happened so quickly. Many thought it a bad omen."

"That must not happen again," Pa'attee insisted.

"GreatMother Er'men is your most precious and delicate resource. Her wrist and forearm," *and my ribs,* "were injured when Tal'anis docked to the asteroid."

"That was a rough landing," Run'ned'lahl berated his plinth-brother, though it looked like he had enjoyed the ride.

"The Great Council's orders, brother." Grad'dahvro conceded to the poor piloting willingly. "GreatMother Pa'attee is wise to demand the Star-Born's presence."

"Come, plinth-brother," Run'ned'lahl clapped the Pur'undram FirstBrother on the shoulder, some of his youthful energies returning, "our stations are in good hands, our watch is over. Take care, GreatMother." He bowed and turned to the boundary, pushing through the thickened air.

"It has been an honor, GreatMother," Grad'dahvro bowed and left as well, quickly catching up with his plinth-brother. Pa'attee waited at the boundary as they took a ramp to a lower level. It was not long before they spiraled out of sight. A burst of fat, red sparks reminded Pa'attee that at least one sniper had a bead on her head, and she withdrew from the boundary in what she hoped was a stately and regal manner. The sensation of being in someone's sights made her neck itch.

CHAPTER FORTY-TWO

"I think you're about to receive company again." Daichi's calm tones made it sound as if she should put on the kettle. *What, no scones?* Pa'attee carefully stretched and just as carefully yawned. Her nap had not been long enough, but it had helped. *With a little extra padding, the aft section could be quite comfy. A minibar in the corner, a few throw rugs...* She felt as rumpled as her black silks, which were bloody and torn. Jake's blood. *And mine. Was he even alive? And Alan and Dad? Had Harrum'Bar acted on her threat to Cleanse her mother too? Harrum'Bar's on the way, and I don't have a tabard.* Even with her p-suit on, there were moments with the plinth-brothers when Pa'attee felt almost naked without it. It expressed a vital part of a Hel'Arumpo'or's persona. *At least I don't have a mirror. I must look a complete fright.*

"How many?" she asked.

"Can't tell yet; they're just forming up. Bar'Durrunnan and Clan Whel'luminum and Fer'entai'illy are there. It will be the Great Council then, not just the Bar'Durrunnan FirstMother. Tol'edranna banners are there. No sign of Darf'ornal yet. That weakens her but it *is* the Great Council, their banner's just been unfurled."

"Good. What of Clan Bumurnam? Even if Bar'Durrunnan or the Great Council has Er'men, they cannot deny Bumurnam access to a GreatMother." A GreatMother and her giant companion/guards were a combination reinforced again and again in the Hel'Arumpo'or culture. With only one GreatMother born at a time, she always had the Hel'omi as the basis of her support. *Zeus, I wish you were here, though I doubt you'd fit inside Freya. I really am going to have to get a bigger ship. You won't mind if*

I have to trade up will you, old girl? Freya might not mind, but Pa'attee did. With all the craziness the Hel'Arumpo'or invasion had brought, she always felt safe inside Freya and did not want to give her up for anything. *Maybe Madhur could build an extension for me?* An image of Jaswinder's gangly form surfaced in Pa'attee's mind, and she immediately began to have second thoughts about Madhur being in charge of the project.

"The escort looks bare minimum for the Great Council on the move; one hundred and forty-four I would guess. No sign of Bumurnam yet," Daichi told her.

"Do you suppose she even has Er'men?" Pa'attee asked.

"I'd give it good odds. The Great Council's standard has GreatMother attendant standards attached. Two. One on either side. One's for Er'men, one's for you, Pa'attee.

"The Regent's standard's there too," Daichi added.

"Do you think Harrum'Bar's declaring me an adolescent?"

"You aren't eighteen yet, are you?" Daichi asked with a soft laugh.

"Thanks for the support, coach," Pa'attee replied dryly. It was good hearing Daichi's unfazed descriptions even if he was not with her.

"That's all right. That's what I'm here for. How's plan B going?" he inquired.

"I'm not sure I have any position to fall back to, coach. I don't actually have to *do* anything. Without Tal'anis to drop rocks on Mother Earth, the Hel'Arumpo'or invasion is effectively over. I should be able to wait until the Belters arrive or even the USF for that matter, to make it official."

"Harrum'Bar won't make it easy for you," Daichi cautioned.

"I know. It's dodging the one you can't see that is always the most difficult."

"Well, here's one you should know about. Harrum'Bar has prisoners, from the phony meeting she had with you earlier. I did not hear, until recently, what happened there, although Cedric did. That was why he changed the focus of his assault to the Stardrive."

The pit of Pa'attee's stomach felt cold and greasy. "Do you know who was captured?"

"No. I'm afraid not. If she's smart..."

"If she's smart, she'll have Dad and Alan," Pa'attee murmured. And Zeus and Felix and... How many others held her honor today? Have I only been here one day? Did Harrum'Bar still have Mom? "Thanks for the warning."

"They're about halfway along the rampway," Daichi told her.

"Time to make an appearance?" she asked.

"Probably."

"Thanks for the help," Pa'attee said.

"You'll do well, Pa'attee, if you remember to keep your guard up and don't..."

"Don't charge in where angels fear to tread? A bit late for that don't you think?"

"The instinct does you well in a pinch," he encouraged her.

"This is definitely a pinch," she muttered.

"Good luck," Daichi remarked.

"I'd be happier to stay out of Murphy's attention thank you very much." Pa'attee scrounged for a bonbon - a cluster of chocolate covered coffee beans. *Yes!* She splashed water on her face and swirled a mouthful. *Hope I don't have any chocolate on my teeth. At least I got a chance to snooze.*

Taking a stroll around to the fusion generator, Pa'attee checked the settings. The output levels were a little low, but it didn't look like the reaction would stall. The Pur'undram workstation ticked quietly, waiting for the correct moment to turn on. Pa'attee checked on the Great Council's progress and adjusted the timer, not wanting the program to begin too early. The control wheels would turn from one stop to the other; the whole system would whir and tremble, snick-clicking as the internal mechanisms were put through their different configurations. A system check that did nothing, but it should impress the ignorant.

Taking up a position at the top of the stairs while the Great Council and their honor guard slowly approached took all of

Pa'attee's willpower. The urge to pace impatiently was almost overwhelming. The phalanx's point-guards came to a halt just outside the MEM boundary. *Someone's paying attention.* The boundary glowed with the faintest of blue shimmers and it was not too difficult to see once you knew what to look for. Pa'attee began her slow descent.

The phalanx peeled left and right, opening a path for Harrum'Bar and the Great Council to advance. GreatMother Pur'unnan's presence inside Pa'attee boiled with anger; the GreatMother's memories of the Council were filled with frustration and pain. She had battled to bring the Clans to their senses, almost resorting to physically bludgeoning the members of Great Council into submission to get her ships built. The palm of Pa'attee's left hand itched to hold Lady Estelle, but that would be a significant breach of protocols.

Strangely, the atmosphere within the Li'ila'tion, a vital changing thing, supported Pur'unnan, bringing to Pa'attee's awareness an acrid scent, anger, and resentment. She knew it was not directed at her. The Great Council, Clan Bar'Durrunnan especially, had built years of resentment during the time of the Hel'Arumpo'or's exodus.

Harrum'Bar, bedecked in her finest, stood proudly, contempt almost dripping from her. Behind her were the Clan FirstMothers, with their FirstBrothers in attendance. *Minus Clan Darf'ornal. Where are you, Run'ned'lahl? Where is Clan Darf'ornal's FirstMother? Had they been dismissed from the Great Council? Was that possible? Losing Darf'ornal's support must have upset Harrum'Bar, but you wouldn't guess it by looking at her.* The FirstMothers and their Left and RightLeading FirstBrothers looked stunned, performing a ritual ingrained into their DNA, not really aware of where they stood, their heads rose, eyes blinking, chests rising and falling. Their eyes looked flat, almost lifeless. *Cleansed? Surely not.*

"The Great Council issued a summons," Harrum'Bar's posture demanded obedience. She radiated authority almost as brightly as Er'men when she shone with excitement. *Where was the Star-*

Born? The confidence of supreme authority, tinged with condescension, exuded from her. There was something else in Harrum'Bar's belligerent pose, something off, but Pa'attee could not pin it down and was glad an impenetrable barrier stood between them.

Harrum'Bar turned and made a comment to the FirstMothers using the Mothers' dialect, "That one, alien or not, has drawn a clan around it, some respect is due but see, that one is far from a GreatMother." Her posture said she did not believe Pa'attee would understand her. It did take Pa'attee a while to filter the sounds/gestures/scents through the GreatMothers' root-language to comprehend Harrum'Bar. The mother's dialect did not come as naturally to Pa'attee as the ones she had absorbed directly from her mel'andrin gifts, but a translation came if she thought about it. The Great Council seemed to take Harrum'Bar's pronouncement as fact. *What was wrong with them? Has Harrum'Bar drugged them?*

"The summons *was* sent to me." Pa'attee did not want to exchange words with this duplicitous alien. The palm of her left hand itched. She felt out of her depth even with all those memories stacked up in her head. She understood so much about the Hel'Arumpo'or and so little. Daichi always told her to take the time to assess before launching an attack, especially when she faced opponents she had not met in a contest before. *Don't charge in.* Pa'attee sighed and leaned back a little. Harrum'Bar seemed to take her relaxed, informal posture as an affront. Pa'attee was tempted to buff her nails on her chest, but that might be pushing it a little far. "We thought it prudent to meet in a public setting this time."

Harrum'Bar stepped forward full of confidence. So strong was the FirstMother's presence Pa'attee wished she had something to sit on to keep her knees from trembling. And yet a sense of wrongness washed over her. A falseness that Pa'attee could not isolate pervaded her perceptions. Clan Bar'Durrunnan's strident FirstMother began again, her words and stance ringing with an authority that Pa'attee had to oppose. "A summons..."

Instincts had Pa'attee strike back before her mind had fully engaged. "A summons is only as good as the messenger who carries it. Did the FirstMother receive *our* summons? With *our* conditions? Where is the Star-Born? Where is GreatMother Er'men? This meeting will be over very quickly unless..."

Reeling a little, Harrum'Bar reacted, "FirstMother Pa'attee..."

It's not going to be like that again, is it? Pa'attee shifted her weight so she could look up at the Great Council's richly embroidered standard with the two GreatMother banners attached, right and left, as potent an objection as if she had spoken aloud and made to turn away. The Great Council's banner reflected the important moments in its history. This meeting would be incorporated in its evolving embroidery the next time it was presented.

"GreatMother Pa'attee," Harrum'Bar got the words out quickly, although it looked as if she had tasted something foul. *Someone had forced the dual GreatMother banners on her or had done it behind the scenes. Had she inadvertently acknowledged the fact and now couldn't take it back? Whatever the reason, it rankled Harrum'Bar.* "The Great Council has honored the request," Harrum'Bar turned and gestured to a position behind the arc of the Great Council. Two Bar'Durrunnan mothers stepped forward, one holding Er'men, wrapped in the multicolored blankets Pa'attee had first seen her in. The little alien looked pale, her eyes clouded, and her head lolled weakly to one side.

Again, Harrum'Bar made an aside to the FirstMothers sure Pa'attee could not understand. "That one may have subverted enough sons to form a Clan, of sorts, but this one will never allow an outsider to rule over the Hel'Arumpo'or." Her body and scent reinforced her words in a manner impossible in a human tongue. The Hel'Arumpo'or language, not confined to just the symbology of words, had postures and scent to reinforce emotional and contextual depth. The words she spoke produced a display of confident authority, and a corresponding reflex inside the part of her that was Hel'Arumpo'or to submit. Her use of powerful Mother dialect-sourced gestures brought instinctive reactions from Murrun and Cedric's gift-memories. The urge to bow down before Harrum'Bar was almost overwhelming. It was only the rolling boil of Pur'unnan's anger that kept Pa'attee on her feet.

"Would the GreatMother keep the Great Council waiting upon the threshold?" Harrum'Bar pressed for advantage, and Pa'attee almost responded by inviting them in.

Rather than change her lines, Pa'attee framed her response as a question, "Invite you to come closer?" and she leaned away as if the thought repulsed her. Pa'attee did not need to act. But she did want to have the opportunity to examine Er'men. *What was wrong with her?*

Er'men's expressive right hand had wormed its way from beneath her enfolding blanket, and the effort looked to have exhausted the little GreatMother; it hung limply. One finger moved, a half circle and a small flexion, extending back to its original position, the half circle again but with an extension and a flexion back to the starting position. It took several repetitions before Pa'attee realized Er'men was speaking to her using the sign language of infants. Fe'ren's memories recognized it. "Help me. Help you." Er'men's tiny gestures spun open the sparkling fractal memories inside Pa'attee's mind. Pur'unnan and all the other GreatMothers inside her held the key to surviving this moment.

CHAPTER FORTY-THREE

"Great Council, abide and listen," Pa'attee spoke the words Pur'unnan had used to the council of her day, and they seemed to reach past whatever Harrum'Bar had done to them. They did look a little more alert. "Is it a custom of the Great Council to hold a GreatMother's family hostage? Each of you, most honorable FirstMothers, has their clan and family in attendance and support. This GreatMother stands alone, and Clan Bar'Durrunnan would have us open our sanctum?" Open herself to their boots and blades? The inference was clear.

Clan Fer'entai'illy's FirstMother blinked and looked around as if discovering her position for the first time. "Regent Bar'Durrunnan FirstMother, is this so?"

Her question startled Harrum'Bar upsetting her flow, "Yes, we hold them." She floundered, diminishing as she searched for an appropriate rationalization. "They are held to ensure their own safety." That sounded so reasonable. "With so much unrest..."

Unrest you started! Pa'attee's anger synchronized with Pur'unnan's. "Return them to us!" hissed through Pa'attee's pursed lips. A painful in-breath returned Pa'attee to a semblance of rationality. She relaxed her grip on Lady Estelle's hilt. "Return our family and retainers, and we will grant the Great Council, and only the Great Council, safe passage." *No armed brothers, no advisers.*

Clan Fer'entai'illy's FirstMother found that acceptable, but her Clan had little support. Clan Fer'entai'illy, as the repository of most medical knowledge for the Hel'Arumpo'or, rarely took sides in political conflicts. Like the Whel'luminum, who willingly and safely carried messages between warring parties, they held their neutrality sacred. Fer'entai'illy FirstMother seemed more concerned with rousing her FirstBrothers.

"Does GreatMother Pa'attee fear?" Harrum'Bar was oh-so condescending.

"We are alone," stated Pa'attee. That should have been obvious.

"You have your ship with its sonic weapons," Harrum'Bar argued.

The thought of Cicely's voice described as a sonic weapon made Pa'attee want to laugh. "Unlike some, when we say safe passage, we mean safe passage."

Surprisingly, Harrum'Bar sent a quick message to a retainer. *She's prepared for this.* A signal was passed aft, and a contingent of Bar'Durrunnan brothers began to approach. Behind their double wall, someone held the holographic checkered flag aloft, for all the good that it did. Zeus's great form towered over the Bar'Durrunnan lines. Genedalt, Bumurnam FirstSon walked behind him with six more Hel'omi, but that was all Pa'attee could see of her company. Her heart leaped when Zeus lifted Alan in his great arms. Alan waved. From this distance, he looked frail, unsteady even with Zeus's support but he was alive! Alan was awake and aware; it made Pa'attee want to shout for joy and return her brother's hail. Pur'unnan's presence within restrained her, but only just.

"The Great Council is generous. We will allow them to approach." *If Alan's alive then maybe Dad and Jake are too.* "Please be patient a moment longer." *It will be good to have Zeus at my back once more.* Pa'attee's bow was directed more towards the Great Council than Harrum'Bar. It was a slight, but Pa'attee ignored Harrum'Bar's affronted reaction as she turned. Pa'attee slowly walked to the stairs and Freya's light-eating silhouette.

Rather than climbing into Freya, Pa'attee leaned in through the cockpit and hit the soft-barrier preset. By the time Pa'attee had returned to the head of the stairs, Bar'Durrunnan brothers had begun to lead the Great Council forward. Pa'attee hurried down the stairs. There was only one way to halt the rush, and that was to stop Harrum'Bar.

"We invited the Great Council. There is no requirement for added security." Pa'attee's posture brought the Bar'Durrunnan brothers to a halt; some looked ready to obey her and leave, although Harrum'Bar only slowed. Her approach became more deliberate if that were possible. Every step, every movement was driven, was informed and supported by the Mothers' dialect. *Mother is here. For your safety. Obey, child.*

While Pa'attee had not been a rebellious child, she had had more than enough conflicts with her mother to just comply. Harrum'Bar's attitude struck sparks, but before Pa'attee could respond, Harrum'Bar's pose changed again, gaining stature by the heartbeat. She even seemed taller, regal. Nausea swirled through Pa'attee's gut, and the hackles on the back of her neck rose. *Adore her? NEVER!* Thinking in EngStand made Pa'attee's head pound and her vision shift and blur. Harrum'Bar's presence was both overwhelming and yet twisted and small. *How was Harrum'Bar doing this?*

Help me, help you. The tip of Er'men's finger still traced the infant's message, throwing Pa'attee back into her GreatMother's memories. Er'men was there, but the great wealth resided in Pur'unnan's integrated memories. A moment from the Hel'Arumpo'or past surfaced, a scene from early in the First Rising when the Arumpo'or and the Hel'omi were still separate species. Mu'nruberra, working in secret in the basement of her aged parents' home, fusing the genetic material of two species together. The language-of-children was already within the genetic code. *It was not too difficult to add a few nuances of her own devising. Triggers. Triggers for obedience. The Hel'omi were good breeding stock, and with the little extra code she inserted, they would remain compliant.*

Over time, there had been significant changes. Disease and privation had altered them, twisting their bodies, mingling their DNA in ways Mu'nruberra could never have predicted. Now all were subject to those programmed reactions, and the

Bar'Durrunnan FirstMother played with those triggers as if she were a concert grandmaster. As Harrum'Bar moved into a new pose, she seemed to grow, towering beneficently over all around her. *Adore this one.*

"Learning a few words of our tongue is not enough. There is more to ruling than acquiring knowledge of a peoples' language," Harrum'Bar made a casual aside to the FirstMothers of the Great Council in what she thought of as the opaque language of Mothers. "See, that one is weak. All tremble before the Great Council." *All bow before this one!*

Although the Hel'Arumpo'or component of Pa'attee's mind felt the compulsion to bend her knee, it held no sway on the very human part of her. Acquiescence to those in authority was not built into her. If anything, she felt the reflex to rebel. *I can play the trigger game too.* She may not be as fluent as Harrum'Bar, but she had Mu'nruberra's memories, the root codes. She opened herself to them, and her stance shifted, altering the balance of power ever so slightly.

A coughed chuckle rippled through Harrum'Bar. "That one cannot even speak properly."

Speaking in the Hel'Arumpo'or dialect, she received from Murrun and Cedric would not be powerful enough to combat Harrum'Bar. Pa'attee used the old tongue Er'men had given her. The triggers were inbuilt.

"Human children learn by mimicking their parents," Pa'attee said wisely, speaking adult-to-child in a manner that even Harrum'Bar's use of the mothers' dialect could not match. Her accompanying pose cast doubt on all of Harrum'Bar ancestors. Surprise and a moment of disbelief flashed through the FirstMother, and she seemed to shrink, to contract upon herself. Letting go of who she thought she was, Pa'attee opened herself to all the memories inside her, channeling their knowledge and wisdom, supplying only her courage to power it.

"GreatMothers honor those who lead and care for their children during their absence." The change was subtle, but Pa'attee could see the Great Council respond to her. They were still blinded by Harrum'Bar's radiant proximity, but their eyes were drawn to Pa'attee.

Harrum'Bar reeled as if she had been sucker punched, diminishing rapidly. "That one cannot be trusted! That one ... that one smells ... different... smells of ... other. No one can ever really know that one or trust that one!" One hand gently stroked the embroidered edge of her tabard. *See. She has no life story. How can she be known if she has no life to read?*

And now it was Pa'attee's turn to reel back, the heel of her foot catching on the first step. *Have I retreated so far?* Without being able to produce the proper scents, Pa'attee's attempt to overpower Harrum'Bar was crippled. Without her tabard, Pa'attee felt as exposed as a newborn, inexperienced and vulnerable. *Where is Zeus?* She glanced away from Harrum'Bar's formidable presence as she took another step back. The contingent escorting her people had been stopped beyond the MEM boundary. *You're on your own.*

Ping, ping, ping! *Saved by the bell?* The ornate orientation control pointer began tracking across the surface of the bronze sphere, aligning forward. A wave of fear coursed through Harrum'Bar. "What has the GreatMother done?" she cried theatrically, playing for the wider audience. She had received Pa'attee's threat but discounted it.

She doesn't really believe I'd crash Tal'anis into the sun. "The Bar'Durrunnan FirstMother pushes beyond the bounds of her understanding." Pa'attee felt her back straighten. It was only a bluff, but it was a good one and the only trick she had left. "If the GreatMother does not control Tal'anis' stardrive, she controls nothing."

"What has GreatMother Pa'attee done?" This time Harrum'Bar address was to the ranks of advisers that clustered behind the Great Council. A purple tabard moved reluctantly to the fore. By the quality of his embroidery, he was barely within the top twenty Pur'undram LeftLeading brothers. Del'for'ren, his tabard identified him. His clan had named him Del'for'ren, shifting sands. That was almost worth a laugh. Grad'dahvro's sure hands would not have shared his memories with this one. "Go!" He had little choice and scuttled past Pa'attee as if he would receive a blow as he came within reach.

That Harrum'Bar had a pet Pur'undram brother did not surprise Pa'attee at all. In fact, she had counted on the Pur'undram workstation being examined to reinforce her bluff, although having one of Harrum'Bar's lackeys behind her eroded Pa'attee's already weakened position. She watched him avoid Freya's black presence as if it would drink him in as it did the light.

"Tal'anis goes where *we* wish it to go." Pa'attee could feel the riser for the next step behind her heels. There were only five more steps behind her. A retreat to Freya would undermine what little honor she still held. She would do it if she had to. There was another MEM field preset that would turn Freya into an impenetrable fortress at a touch, but that would give Tal'anis back into Harrum'Bar's hands. And she would have to clear Li'ila'tion with her sonic weapon again. *I hate having to do a job twice.*

"GreatMother Pa'attee has seen her FirstBrother. Would it be the last time?" Harrum'Bar held a command in abeyance, and Pa'attee knew what it was, without words.

From her position halfway up the stairs, the edge of the raised plinth masked the descending curved path; Pa'attee did not give in to the temptation of trying to look around the obstacle, concentrating solely on the RegentFirstMother. "Does the Bar'Durrunnan FirstMother think we take this position to advance ourselves?" Pa'attee's heart ached as she leaned forward. Harrum'Bar was at the bottom step, and Pa'attee towered over her even though it felt they stood eye-to-eye.

"We are but the ambassador," Pa'attee continued. "The first to breach the Hel'Arumpo'or ramparts but by no means the last. Believe me. The Hel'Arumpo'or are not ready to combat the human race. You've only awoken the sleeping giant. And when it is roused it will crush Tal'anis like a bug underfoot. The RegentFirstMother rebuts our overtures of peace at her peril and the peril of all." While she had not diminished Harrum'Bar, Pa'attee's thrust did slow her advance. She stayed below the stairs. The bluff felt paper-thin.

Ping, ping. Ping, ping. *The program stopped! How? That tears it.* Pa'attee stood her ground, but she knew her concern showed.

"RegentFirstMother!" a surprised shout came from behind the Pur'undram workstation, "The controls are free! They were doing ... doing something but now. This one has control."

Pa'attee felt sick. *It's over.* She felt her body gather itself in preparation for flight.

"Huh! This one knew! This false GreatMother is nothing!" Harrum'Bar turned to give her permission to kill the hostages, but she stopped mid-gesture. Pa'attee stepped forward and peered around the corner. Bright yellow pennants. Clan Darf'ornal's FirstMother approached with the Great Council banner adorning their own. They advanced on the same curved pathway that held the remnants of those that had supported Pa'attee's first attempt at peace talks. If Harrum'Bar let loose her soldiers, it would look as though Clan Bar'Durrunnan attacked Darf'ornal's FirstMother.

"Do not let hope cloud reality. It is but a moment's delay." Harrum'Bar's triumph was almost at its fruition, but Pa'attee could still feel there was something else up the RegentFirstMother's sleeve. *Tabards don't have sleeves.*

The sound of steel leaving its scabbard came from behind her and made Pa'attee's throat constrict. She glanced over her shoulder. The hunter stood above her! Pa'attee spun to her left, the itch in her palm finally scratched as Lady Estelle flowed into her hand. Her back pressed against the stairwell. He held a longer blade than poor Del'for'ren's ceremonial toy. The dream of a hasty retreat to the safe confines of Freya's cockpit warped into a pale nightmare with a cruel blade. *Yes, Harrum'Bar would want to see her blood. The Hunter must have climbed up the back of the plinth.* Pa'attee tried to find her center but an anguished roar - Zeus's frustrated cry - threatened to draw Pa'attee's eyes from the pale shape outlined against Freya's dark silhouette. *It's happening all over again.* Shouting filled Li'ila'tion, a roar of anger and a clash of blades.

The blade Bar'Durrunnan's hunter held before him made Pa'attee's blood run with ice. It broke with the current Hel'Arumpo'or style of an elongated dagger and was almost as narrow as Daichi's katana. It was a weapon of pain as much as it was a weapon of death. Serrations, ridges, and spurs glinted along the blade's back - sword breakers - and barbs covered the hilt. The evil weapon's tip curved back in a little hook. There was no honor in this blade or the pale creature that wielded it.

This fight's going to be over quickly. That thing's going to chew Lady Estelle up and spit out the pieces. He's got height and reach. Pa'attee took a moment to glance over her shoulder; Harrum'Bar backed away, although why she should be displaying signs of fear was a thought too far away for Pa'attee to chase. She returned her attention to the hunter's dangerous weapon and danced up two steps. *Attack low!* She dived beneath the hunter's whistling blade and felt Lady Estelle's tip score a slashing cut across the hunter's forward thigh before she hit the unforgiving steps. Her ribs screamed and so did she as her breath was driven from her.

The wicked blade glinted as it swept around and descended in a deadly arc. Without a breath in her body, Pa'attee lay there helpless, Lady Estelle held across her in a futile last defense.

Someone screamed with frustration.

A roar shook Pa'attee's bones. *Death comes.* But not for her. Pa'attee opened the eyes she did not even realize she had closed. A giant stood over her, his blade strong enough to challenge the hunter's weapon. Harrum'Bar screamed and attacked Zeus's broad back, but he ignored her. There was nothing Pa'attee could do but try and get a careful breath. Zeus roared again, feinting to the left before attacking high on the outside. Pa'attee heard the blades meet again and the sound of steel shattering. A scream of fear and the sound of running feet were overwhelmed by Zeus's triumphant bellow. He remained above her, protecting her, almost unaware of Harrum'Bar's frenzied assault.

Zeus turned, "Urgh. Stink!" He pushed Harrum'Bar back, took a fistful of her tabard and ripped it from her. He held it to his nose, flinched and tossed it away.

"No!" Harrum'Bar's scream was incensed, not because she had been stripped naked - the Hel'Arumpo'or had very little in the way of body taboos - but that anyone had laid hands upon her person at all. "That one must die!" She looked at Pa'attee, eyes aflame, drew a long thin dagger and leaped. It was smaller than a LeftLeading brother's ceremonial blade, but it seemed sharp.

Zeus caught her with the back of one hand and nonchalantly brushed her away.

Screaming, "Kill them!" Harrum'Bar sailed over the path's handrail and was caught, for a long moment, in the thickened air of Freya's MEM field boundary. "Kill them! Kill them all! Ki..." Harrum'Bar's last word cut off as she hit Li'ila'tion's floor with a sickeningly wet crunch.

CHAPTER FORTY-FOUR

"GreatMother Pa'attee, not go away again!" Zeus stood over her, gruff and insistent. "GreatMother get into trouble, and Zeus not there to save her," he coughed a chuckle, stood back and bowed. The Clan Bar'Durrunnan brothers were obviously scared of her Bumurnam caretaker and kept their distance even when they had enough numbers to form defensive lines. Zeus roared out his anger and his triumph. Genedalt and two Hel'omi charged through the Bar'Durrunnan lines as they rushed towards Er'men, brushing aside the soldiers. Clan Bar'Durrunnan cowered and scattered. Zeus chuffed his amusement before offering Pa'attee his hand, helping her to her feet. He bowed and presented her with her black and gold tabard. Someone had cleaned it and repaired the cuts with fine gold thread and the tiniest of stitches. *A careful hand is writing my life-story upon it.* Zeus huffed and fussed until it hung straight from her shoulders.

The Great Council stood about in disarray until the Darf'ornal FirstMother burst into their ragged arc. She brought with her mothers with water and cloths for cleaning faces and hands. She met with Fer'entai'illy FirstMother for a brief exchange before turning to Pa'attee. Sher'ril'lil, the life-story embroidered upon her tabard declared her name, a hardy and nourishing tuber. The plant's woody stalks had to be handled carefully, or the hidden barbs beneath the flaky bark would lodge beneath the skin and cause infection. *Beware.*

Run'ned'lahl stepped clear of the influx of yellow tabards and approached Pa'attee. He looked up, acknowledging Zeus before bowing low. "GreatMother, this one begs forgiveness. Clan

Darf'ornal's tardiness..."

"Clan Darf'ornal's arrival," Pa'attee interrupted, "turned the moment and saved us all. Our simple thanks are not sufficient." She gave, what she hoped would pass for, a grateful and relieved bow. Her whole body ached.

"We could not pass our Clan Bumurnam cousins and not set them free. It is unheard of GreatMother to keep them from their charges." Run'ned'lahl bowed in mock humility, accepting her praise.

"You allowed my Zeus to save my life," she told him plainly. If we can do anything to help Clan Darf'ornal, do not hesitate to mention it."

"A GreatMother's boon is a precious thing. We thank GreatMother Pa'attee." Run'ned'lahl bowed and rose, hugging himself as if he held Pa'attee's goodwill to his chest.

FirstMother Sher'ril'lil approached, the Fer'entai'illy FirstMother supporting her. She held Harrum'Bar's tabard as though it carried disease. They bowed low as Sher'ril'lil laid the tabard at Pa'attee's feet.

"GreatMother," Sher'ril'lil said respectfully, "Clan Bar'Durrunnan's FirstMother used special scents, impregnated into her life-cloak. We know not for how long that one used this to deceive The Great Council."

"GreatMother guide us," the Clan FirstMothers intoned together, "GreatMother, lead us." A wave of genuflection spread out from their epicenter and embraced the whole of the Breathing Heart. "GreatMother, guide us." The chant rolled around Li'ila'tion, falling slowly to silence.

A moment of doubt gave Pa'attee pause. *How could they willingly put their lives into another's hands like that?* But the memories stacked up inside her held example after example of when a GreatMother's memories were the only thing between life and death. It was in their genes.

"The paths are dark beneath the ground," Pa'attee began the benediction, then added, "and between the stars, filled with hidden falls and traps. The GreatMother's gifts light our way."

"GreatMother, guide us," the response echoed throughout Li'ila'tion.

If I wasn't a GreatMother before, I am now.

From his position, halfway down the sweeping ramp, Jake could not see anything, and his frustration boiled over. "Get us down there!" he growled. Jake had never heard Zeus roar like that. It sent a chill down his spine. *Thought the lad was a bit of a whiner. Not as bad as Genedalt, though. Talk about fret.* "They've opened the way, Felix. Get a move on!" Jake insisted and sagged back against the hard surface of the trolley, holding one hand across the throbbing pain in his gut. The memory of his intestines protruding through the opening in his belly intruded, and Jake pushed the vivid image away, again. None of that hurt as much as the thought of Patty dying out there. *Just out of sight. If these twisted bastards weren't so tall or if this damned trolley was a bit higher, I could see.*

"Can you see what's going on, Thunder Thighs?" Jake asked. The alien's name was Duntah'tis, but Jake could not help Texanizing it. He twisted around to see if the alien that pushed his trolley knew what was happening and regretted it. *Staples. They've got me held together with staples. Steady now or it will tear.*

A blood-curdling scream made Jake flinch. The wet crunch that followed it brought him a glimmer of hope. "That was the wicked witch, wasn't it?" The sound of Zeus's triumphant roar made him smile. *I'd wanna see the body to confirm it. She's just the type to rise from the dead in the last scene to seek revenge.*

"Traaaffic Control, it," rumble, "appears to be," rum-rumble, "true," Duntah'tis leaned over the railing but kept one hand on the trolley, "Bar'Durrunnan FirstMother does not move."

"That's a good thing, but what's going on down there, Thunder?" *I'm getting too old for this.*

"GreatMother Pa'attee," rumble, "moves amongst, rum-rumble-rum, "the Great Council. There is," rumble, "confusion."

Suddenly a rumble spread from the center, a shockwave that brought everyone to their knees. Finally, Jake could see down the curving walkway, down to the plinth, down to where Patty stood, her hands outstretched in benediction over the bowed heads of the Great Council, over everyone. A moment of pure stillness filled the atrium.

It took forever to finally be presented to GreatMother Pa'attee. Jake had his pronunciation corrected twice by the time they arrived. Zeus, her formidable giant companion held her in his arms as if she was a delicate bouquet. In Patty's lap was the little alien, chattering away in a manner that reminded him of a certain young blond back on The Ice Princess. *Now that'll be an interesting match-up.*

Zeus moved as if he were an extension of Patty's arm. She passed the bundle of golden energy to Genedalt who appeared beside them as Zeus lowered Patty to the ground. She moved carefully, as if in some pain, but the joy in her face overwhelmed the aches of her body. Her eyes smiled as they hovered over him for a moment before she refocused and addressed Murrun in the local lingo. The poor lad looked surprised when Patty embraced him. Jake half expected it; Patty looked filled to overflowing with excitement and relief. She looked tired too. *A young woman shouldn't have dark rings under her eyes like that.* But she carried a quiet confidence about her that he approved. He had not seen it in her except in flashes when she was not thinking too much. *You're lookin' good, kiddo.*

The trolley was not comfortable, but it was more dignified than being carried. And Jake was patient. *You're lucky you're alive.* He was happy to watch Patty pay her respects to Felix and the surviving contingent. When she turned to Jake, all trace of formality was gone from her.

"Is there another setting for that flag?" she asked with some contempt for the checkered pattern.

"You want the fireworks? I feel like a celebration." *I feel like a shot of JD. Or maybe a couple. Just to start.* Patty laughed and, for a moment, Jake saw the excited young pilot he remembered from OASIS. It had been a long time since he had seen that too.

"And you!" Patty swept her brother up in a whirling embrace. Alan was still a little weak and needed the trolley's support to stand for any length of time, but he was much improved. Before they had been brought to this big shindig, they had lain, side-by-side, recovering together. Alan was healing faster than he was. Jake could see the lad's face contort as he tried to speak. *This is going to surprise Patty.* Jake caught Alan's eyes, and he took an exaggerated deep breath. A nod from the lad told him his message had been seen and understood. Alan swallowed and took a deep breath.

"Grr ... GreatMother ... Pa'attee." Alan's face twisted into a hesitant smile that lit the touchpaper to another round of his sister's excited dance.

"Speaking! You're speaking! Alan, that's fantastic!" Patty whirled him in the tight circle of her arms, only stopping when she caught sight of her father. Christopher had been compliant, uninvolved from the strife surrounding him. Patty disentangled herself from her brother and crossed to her father. One hand rose and caressed his stubbled cheek.

"Has he been all right, Jake?" she asked.

"Unchanged, near as I can tell," Jake told her.

"He needs exercise and mental stimulation." Patty held her father's chin and looked into his eyes. She left her father and strode over to Jake's side, her eyes cold, and angry. "And you! If I ever see you pick up a blade bigger than a steak knife! So help me, I'll run you through myself."

"I'm sorry, Patty. I couldn't resist."

"Made me lose my footing at a crucial moment, and I got your blood all over my clothes." Patty gave a mock growl and hugged him tightly. "I couldn't stand to lose you and Dad too."

"You haven't lost either of us, little one. Murphy must be having an off day." Jake grinned. He had experienced some bad turns and had ridden the edge of his luck more often than was healthy.

"Don't start me. I've got a list as long as my arm of all the little stuff-ups and disasters that have happened today." Despite her complaints, Patty looked good, tired but good.

"You're breathing. Count your blessings, kiddo. They're few and far between."

CHAPTER FORTY-FIVE

"Do you understand what's going on?" Cynthia Balke asked. Her limp was not pronounced, but the walk to the central atrium was aggravating her injured leg.

"Only in broad strokes," Lily replied. As far as Lily was concerned, any walking in this portable gravity-well was aggravating. Walking anywhere felt strange, having lived most of her life floating in micro-gee environments. The alien's mothership did not interest Lily; her attraction to ship design had never extended much beyond the engine room. The etched pictures decorating the walls were nothing more than a novel texturing that relieved the beige drabness. "We're going to where they're, um, paying Patty their respects."

"Who are?" Cynthia asked nervously.

"Um, well, everyone, I think. That's right, isn't it, Ben?" Lily glanced towards the affable alien that sidled along with them. Da'rruman, the soldier who had carried her earlier in the day, followed in their wake, along with a large percentage of the aliens that had gathered around Patty. The phalanx that led the way moved with military precision but had a relaxed feeling to their actions. In fact, the whole ship seemed to have a different mood, as if someone in life-support had made changes to the atmospheric mix. The tension was gone, and this procession felt more like a carnival than a military operation. Females and clusters of young mingled with the less than military formations that rumbled a catchy three-beat chant.

"The Lily is," rumble, "correct, GreatMother's mother." Ben skipped; his excitement was barely restrained. "All go to," rumble, "Del'bidion who can." Rumble-rum, "unique moment to

700

remember and pass on when two GreatMothers," rum-rumble, "walk amongst us."

Cynthia leaned close. "Did you understand any of that?"

"Most of it." Lily had to smile, "It does take a while to get your ear in, I'll admit. He just said that everyone who can, will be going to see Patty with their own eyes so they can pass on this moment to others," she translated. Cynthia looked like she was adding columns of numbers in her head and something did not balance. "It's okay. Just ask Daichi. He'll talk you blind about the cultural goings on," Lily tried to reassure her.

"He's taken one of those bio-memory ... discharges too, hasn't he?" Cynthia's concern for her daughter was obvious.

"Yeah, but that didn't bring on his cultural interest in the aliens. His mastery of those ancient fighting skills should have tipped you to that. No, Daichi was willing to guinea pig the memory things because it gave him a chance to communicate with the aliens when we really needed it; much like Patty did, I would guess." Cynthia still looked skittery. "Are you alright?"

"Yes ... no ... yes, I guess. It's just," Cynthia looked around as if the soldiers surrounding them had their weapons drawn. Some of them did, but they were using them as a percussion instrument, supporting their chant.

"Hey Cynth, don't be scared of these guys. They're fierce in a fight, but they can be gentle too. I mean, take Ben. He found you, didn't he?"

"Yes, yes, he did. And yes, Ben was ... is polite." Cynthia nodded to their alien guide.

"He's a big puppy, ain't ya, Ben?" Lily teased.

"Pu'uppeee?" Ben's head tilted, and his left hand flicked back and forth. "Is this Pu'uppeee a good thing?" he skipped and walked and skipped again.

"Can be. Can be," Lily laughed. "Puppies can be great fun, but they're often messy."

Ben's shoulders slumped, "This one is often told it is," rumble, "messy."

"And you *are* fun," Lily encouraged him. "Maybe you are a

puppy. Do you chew shoes?" she teased.

"Shoes? Footwear?" Ben glanced down at his sandals. "Eat footwear? No. No. That would be..." Ben attempted to find the right word but could not. "No. This one is not pu'uppeee." He walked solemnly for three strides before skipping twice in a row.

A chuckle bubbled through Lily, and she turned to Cynthia. "Come on, be honest. You're not afraid of Ben, are you?"

The tiniest of smiles warmed Cynthia's bruised face, "No, you're right. Ben's a puppy."

"These aliens, they're all different, as different as you and me. It looks like the soldiers that captured you were none too gentle, but these are a very different bunch. Cedric, Patty's general, impresses me. He's fierce as a lion and as warm as my grandpa. Don't let the swords and uniforms fool you; they are people."

"The females are ... gentle," Cynthia admitted.

"And the males are bastards. Ben, were your parents married?" Lily asked.

"Married?" He considered it for a skip and a stride. "Married, no. This one does not," rumble, "know this word. Married. Is it important?"

"No. Not at all," Lily laughed.

The corridor opened onto a broad walkway that swept around the atrium. Chunks of the filigreed handrail had been chewed away by machinegun fire. The delicately embossed carvings in the walls were scarred and cracked. The curved pathways down to the central pillar were packed with aliens slowly shuffling forwards. An almost subsonic *Rumble-rum, rumble-rum*, swirled around the open space, phasing in and out of audibility.

"Is that her, down there?" Cynthia crossed to an undamaged portion of the handrail and looked down at the gathering on the central platform.

Lily tested the handrail's strength before resting her weight on it and looked across the gap. There were only a handful of humans among the aliens atop the plinth. "Yes, that's her."

"Is she sitting in that big alien's lap?" Cynthia asked.

"Looks like it to me. That's probably Zeus." Lily checked her comm; Patty was not online, but Daichi was, and she could see him down there talking to Jake. Daichi answered her ping almost immediately. "Hi, can you tell Patty we're almost there?" She waved when she saw him look up. The curving walkway between them was filled, handrail-to-handrail. "Could be a while before we can get down to you."

"I think the Hel'Arumpo'or won't mind expediting matters. See you soon." Daichi gave an enigmatic chuckle and signed off.

"What did he mean?" Cynthia sounded as though she had to prepare herself for something traumatic.

"Dunno. Maybe they have a flying fox. That could be fun." Lily held her grin while Cynthia looked around to see if any aerial rigging crossed the gap. "Cynthia, relax will you. I trust Patty, and I trust Daichi and Jake, and if they tell me the worst is over, then I gotta give them the benefit of the doubt."

"I'm sorry. You're right. Up to now, I haven't been treated … well." The poor woman looked as though she expected to be beaten by the next alien that approached her.

"By whom? These guys?" Lily asked.

"I don't know. It could have been any one of them."

"Not now though, not since Ben found you," Lily insisted.

"No. You're right, I…" Cynthia looked around as if she were lost.

"Nothing is familiar; no one has a familiar face. I'm a stranger to you. This must seem weird. You're right. It is. I have no idea what's going on, but I do know that Daichi, Jake, and Patty have made it happen. There they are. Wave. We might be marching down to our funeral, but somehow, I don't think so." Lily sighed as she rested on the handrail. "This is an enjoyable space. Feels like a sunny day." She harrumphed when her eyes settled on the mechanical contraption on the far side of the platform, "Not sure about that steam engine though."

"GreatMother's mother and the Lily," Ben rumbled, "we can go now. It would be, "rumble, "faster if we carried…"

"Oh, yes please," Lily sagged theatrically, and Da'rruman

rushed to her side. "I'm sorry." Lily stood straight, even if it took an effort. "I was playing, but thank you for your attentiveness, Da'rruman." She bowed, not too deeply or she would have fallen over.

"Da'rruman knows the Lily is special to GreatMother Pa'attee. Special to Da'rruman," he bowed deeply in return and held out his dominant right hand.

"Thank you, dear, my feet hurt something wicked," Lily said and took hold of his arm. Cynthia stood with her mouth slightly open, her eyes growing wider as Lily climbed into the alien's arms.

"What? Hitching a lift? I don't spend much time at one-gee, and they offered. They don't think it's demeaning or anything. You don't do you, Da'rruman?"

"Demean? Da'rruman has honor." Her mount managed to bow to Lily even though he held her in his hand.

"And my aching back's thanks," Lily added.

"GreatMother's Mother," Ben knelt and held out his strong right arm, the hand extended. "It would be this one's honor."

Cynthia shot Lily a pleading look. *What do I do?* "Get aboard, Cynthia. Get aboard, and we'll be down to see Patty in nothing flat. These guys can move pretty quickly when they have to."

"Okay." Cynthia turned back to Ben and gave him a stiff bow. "Umm ... thank you ... errr ... Ben," and allowed herself to be lifted.

Stiff as a board. I bet that's where Alan gets it. "Cynthia, relax." Lily leaned back in Da'rruman's arms and crossed her legs. "Oh, Ben! I just remembered. You can't be a puppy."

"This one is not sure if it should be disappointed," Ben replied.

"Oh, I wouldn't be too disappointed; you can do one thing puppies can't," Lily teased.

"Just one?" he asked innocently.

"Ben, I'll happily concede you can do much more than a puppy can, but you can do one thing a puppy definitely can't do. Cynthia, ask Ben to purr for you."

Ben and Da'rruman followed a soldier that broke from the phalanx and strode purposefully into the crush descending to the central platform. Somehow the crowd that seemed packed shoulder-to-shoulder compressed enough to make an opening for him. The opening grew wide enough for Ben and Da'rruman to follow in his wake, before closing behind them. They moved down the arched walkway as if no one else was there.

"In a ship this size, I'm surprised they don't have elevators or slideways," Lily rubbed her left foot's arch.

"I think walking makes it easier for," Cynthia glanced up to Ben's face, "it makes it easier for you to breath. Is that right, Ben?" Curiosity was sparking a light in her eyes.

"That is true, GreatMother's Mother."

"Cynthia, please. My name is Cynthia," she told him.

"This one is honored to receive it." Ben nodded a bow. "Yes, Mother Cynthia. It is easier to breathe when walking." He saw Cynthia's furrowed brow and tried to bow again. "What is it, our GreatMother's Mother?"

"What? Oh, I was just thinking. You haven't done anything wrong," Cynthia reassured him.

"What is it?" Lily sat up.

"Oh, nothing. I was thinking about a virus that produces spinal abnormalities in human babies."

Before Cynthia could continue, they were delivered to the foot of the stairs that led to the top of the platform. Aliens of all types moved with purpose up there, passing messages or holding impromptu conversations. The aliens on the walkway shuffled in a smooth stream before Patty and a beautiful red and gold glass urn. Its swirling floral shape stood about half a meter tall and was attended by one of the smaller pale aliens holding a tall staff. For an instant, Lily thought she had entered a florist's store. The aromas tantalized her senses. Lily leaned closer to the urn and let the fragrances caress her in-breath. *Delicious.*

"Mother!" Patty eased herself down from her giant protector's embrace although her hand never left his. Zeus, Alan and the little golden alien, in the arms of her giant caregiver, followed. The way Patty moved said she was sore and tired, but her face beamed joy as she climbed down the steps. Everyone took half a step back as mother and daughter embraced. "Alan," Patty reached out and dragged her little brother into the family hug as aliens moved around them, giving small bows before adding their contribution to the urn.

"Mother, I need a moment. Excuse me." Patty broke away from their hug, wiping away joy-filled tears with the back of her hand. "Ben!" Patty continued talking but in the rumbling alien language. Ben bowed, but before he could return to his feet, Patty wrapped him in an embrace and kissed the smooth, variegated skin of his forehead. Lily chuckled as Ben tried to restrain the energy that boiled in his veins and hold onto what little dignity he had left. He hopped and shuffled and tried to bow over and over again.

"Lily, it is good to see you too." Patty moved closer, and Lily met her halfway with open arms.

"In one piece I might say, though my feet are going to need major architectural reconstruction. Can you convince them to drop the artificial gravity to a more civilized one-third gee?" Lily asked.

Patty gave a small laugh. "I doubt that's going to happen anytime soon. This is their home after all."

"You look as though you're feeling a bit tender," Lily observed.

"Nothing that a trip to the emergency clinic and a good night's sleep won't cure. I hear you've been busy." Patty came to the point.

Lily tapped her wrist comm. "Been growing a database of biometrics while I was looking for familiar faces. Didn't find anyone I knew from Hestia's Hearth."

"Sorry to hear that. That database will be a great help, but there's been something else that's been nagging me."

"What can I do?" Lily asked.

"Your little presents. Now that the fighting's over, I'm concerned that someone might..."

"Stumble across them and ... yes that would put a bit of a dampener on things. And Jake's present, I should track that one down, too." Lily chided herself for not thinking about them earlier.

"Would you?" Patty asked. "I know it's been a long day."

"But it ain't over yet. Sure, I'll tidy up those loose ends, but I'm not sure exactly where I left it," Lily confessed.

"Ben found you, didn't he?" Patty asked.

"He did. He's very good at finding things." Lily enjoyed seeing Ben's excited quiver. *Purring or not, he's definitely a puppy.*

"Would you guide my friend, Ben FirstCalled?" Patty asked him.

"It would be this one's honor, GreatMother." Ben bowed as he danced an eager little jig.

Patty turned and made a subtle sign towards the aliens wearing the inside-out cloaks on the platform. Lily waved to one who stood with a dignified stance. Three soldiers peeled away from their formation and joined them at the foot of the stairs.

"Thank you, Lily. Doing this will take a weight off my mind." Patty stretched her shoulders.

"You look like you're juggling a dozen things at once. You don't have to do this all by yourself," Lily reminded her.

"Thanks. I do seem to forget that on a regular basis." Patty returned to her mother and brother.

"Ben, Da'rruman, are you ready for another jog around the ship?" Lily waited for their bows and climbed into Da'rruman's arms. "Well, let's get to it. Ping us if there's any news, Patty."

"Will do. Thanks again." Patty wrapped an arm around her mother and waved Lily off.

"Where does the Lily need us to take her?" Ben asked as they turned from the stairs.

"Remember where you found Daichi and me? Head in that direction," she suggested.

"Your will," Ben bowed and skipped before heading towards the walkway that arched down to the lower levels.

CHAPTER FORTY-SIX

The press of the Hel'Arumpo'or around Pa'attee felt comforting. The bump and slide of bodies pressed together passed subtle scents back and forth, intimate information that fed Pa'attee's maturing awareness. Li'ila'tion breathed the truth more directly than any poll. Today, now, the Hel'Arumpo'or who brought her gifts of their memories were happy, weary but hopeful as they walked to either side of the three humans, observing carefully, excited that they had a unique experience they could share.

The one burr in the smooth flow of community around her sent shivers directly into Pa'attee's body. The relaxed closeness with which the Hel'Arumpo'or moved disturbed her mother. *ANTS!* Cynthia's ankles brushed together as if tiny bodies swarmed up her legs. *She smells of fear. I don't think I've ever felt so attuned to her feelings. Have I ever bothered to consider what Mom felt?*

"Mother, come with me, up there, out of the crowd." Pa'attee took hold of Cynthia's hand and drew her to the stairs and then upward. *She's afraid, disoriented, but putting on a brave face.* With one arm around her son, Cynthia drew Alan with her. Zeus brought up the rear. That caused her mother to keep glancing over her shoulder.

She fears you, Zeus, fears your power. He read Pa'attee's thoughts, expressed in her body's attitude as if she spoke them aloud, and he slipped to the side so Cynthia could see him. It pleased the giant to be that much closer to Pa'attee. *I bet he's purring.*

The emanations coming from her mother felt as though she was wound tight. The hope, the fantasy that when she had found her parents everything would turn out all right, hurt as it peeled away. *It might've been better to keep Lily here instead of sending her off. Mom's looking at Freya as if she wants to leave right now.* The bruise on her face was a faint shadow compared to the pain and fear Pa'attee read in her mother's heart. The strong, rational woman she remembered was barely visible. Post-Traumatic Stress, she could sense it in Jake, although he was masterful at covering it up. It was something he had experienced before and had a handle on. Daichi was, as ever, calm. He dealt with stress as a reed in the wind, bending and returning. *I wish I had half his composure. Mom doesn't appear broken so much as bent, so there's hope.* She took a breath and prepared to give her mother what support she could. *Mom's looking for something. Once she gets her bearings, she'll lock on and pursue it.* The reflex to believe her mother would be able to make things better was too deeply ingrained to resist, but Pa'attee was aware she could not rely on it.

Daichi and Cedric stood at Freya's aft hatch, beside Jake's trolley, holding an animated conversation with Sher'ril'lil, Darf'ornal's FirstMother. Pa'attee's father stood passively beside them. A double wall of her sons in reversed tabards formed an arc around them from one side of the plinth to the other. *Note to self: do we need a new color scheme to reflect the human/Hel'Arumpo'or composition of the clan?* A dozen Hel'omi brothers supplemented their shorter cousins' vigilance with a central arc of their own. Most of the Great Council had returned, mingling with Er'men's LeftLeading advisers. The gathering atop the plinth almost had the feel of a cocktail party sans music and waiters with drinks. Although young mothers from Whel'luminum and Tol'edranna circulated with trays of refreshments, the effect was not quite the same.

Mom needs to be oriented, to find her feet. "I need to introduce you..." Pa'attee stopped talking because her mother's attention was not on her. She had seen something, someone. Cynthia did not let go of her daughter's hand as she set her own course across the plinth to where her husband stood. *Dad. Of course, that's who she's looking for.*

"How is he? Has his condition changed?" Cynthia asked as she caressed Christopher's stubbled cheek. She clasped his jaw and gently pulled his head down so she could look into his eyes. She watched his eyes track her finger as she moved her hand back and forth before him. The GreatMother dialect had opened a part of Pa'attee's awareness that put her mother's love, pain, and concern, her whole emotional being, on display. Opening herself to the GreatMother's support within herself, Pa'attee felt her body's posture change, her hand rising to stroke her mother's back and shoulder. Hel'Arumpo'or concepts translated into human gestures.

"He's been quiet," Pa'attee said. Her words were almost irrelevant, a carrier-wave for the emotions Pa'attee wanted to impart, strength, support, and hope. "But I haven't had any time alone with him. It looks like he's been wiped clean, but Alan was like that when I found him, and he's improved dramatically. I'm sorry, Mom." Her mother's response was subtle but noticeable; she stood a little straighter and breathed a little easier. The death-grip her mother held on the pain in her heart eased. *Let it go, Mom.*

"It's not your fault, dear. He provoked them." Cynthia ran her fingers through the short gray hair of his fringe. Christopher did not respond other than to lean against the slight pressure of her hand. Cynthia sighed, and her whole body sagged. Pa'attee thought the hand that stroked her mother's back would have to hold her up, but a sharp breath filled Cynthia, and a pain-soaked breath left her. She lifted her head again.

"He was so proud of you when they showed us pictures of you and Alan, aboard their ship," Cynthia said and glanced around, "aboard this ship. They wanted to know where you were." A smile, hindered by her heart's pain, grew slowly. "'She's got them frightened,' he said. Christopher wanted to frighten them some more. 'You had my girl but couldn't keep her!' he taunted them. 'Of course, you couldn't. Bet she tore a hole through you on her way out too,' he said. 'She'll turn up where

you least expect her to be and then you'll be in serious trouble.'
Laughed in their faces, he did and made a general nuisance of
himself." Cynthia's throat closed, tears welled and flowed down
her cheeks, but she swallowed, took a shaky breath and
continued, "That's when they took him away." Cynthia breathed
hard as she wiped at her eyes, before pulling her children to her
as if she never wanted to let them go. She released them a
heartbeat before Pa'attee felt it was time to stand apart.

Good. That's the Mom I remember. Telling her story is helping. The
catharsis was obvious to Pa'attee in the set of her mother's head
and shoulders but most noticeable in her breathing. *Prompt her
for more. It's not over yet.* "Alan and I received the two messages
you sent, although the second one was cut off."

"You received the second one?" Cynthia asked. "We weren't
sure it got through. The ship's connection to the servers failed as
I was making it."

"Alan and I had just boosted out of OASIS heading for L1
when the servers went down."

"It took us so long to get off the ground." Cynthia frowned,
anger and contempt flickering across her face. "I tell you; we're
going to get a ship that will carry us all. I know I've said that a
family ship was an extravagance, but I was wrong. I never want
to be in that situation again," Cynthia growled. Pa'attee held in a
smile; her mother hated being wrong. "And I'm sorry I was not
as supportive as I should have been when you were given Freya.
She saved the lives of my children," Cynthia said as she glanced
at the dark silhouette.

"We'd hitched a ride with Christopher's partner, Reece
Spaulding and his wife, Daisy; we made it to LEO and pressed on
to L1. When we arrived, L1 was ... it was a mess, and Reece was
intent on scattering immediately. He wanted to rendezvous
with their research facility that had left earlier. He gave us four
hours to find you. Christopher was incensed. It nearly came to
blows. I'm afraid that partnership is in tatters." Cynthia did not
appear too upset about that. "Christopher discovered a booking
for you and Alan at the Hilton." Her eyes asked Pa'attee how

that happened.

"We rendezed at the research station when we arrived at L1," Pa'attee told her. "Alan did not want to leave when the station scattered and neither did I. That was our first mistake. We should have left with them. Mister Frobisher made the Hilton booking for us, but we didn't have the opportunity to check in. We were about to enter the ingress cue when L1 was attacked. I decided to find an out-of-the-way place and headed for L2. We got your second message, or most of it, there. That's where I lost Alan." There was madness in those memories, loss and fear and blood, but the GreatMothers present inside her cooled the radiant heat of those events, the wisdom of years was a soothing balm. "I'm sorry, Mom. I was trying to get Freya ready for flight when the Hel'Arumpo'or arrived."

"It's not your fault. I know that. Your father knew that. They asked us why you came for your brother. I was surprised you dared to rescue him, but Christopher didn't doubt your courage for a second. Proud doesn't really describe him; he strutted." Cynthia caressed her husband's face once more.

"When he discovered the Hilton booking, we took what supplies we could squeeze out of the Spauldings and began searching for you. L1 was broken, but there were functional refuges. Doctors were in short supply. I don't think we would have been welcomed otherwise. I set up a clinic while Christopher searched. A few days later, the aliens arrived in force. The Hel-Ar-rum-po-or. Is that how you say it?" she asked.

"Pretty close, Mom. What Clan were they?" Pa'attee asked. "What color were their tabards?"

"Green. There were some yellow, but they were mostly green. They kept us contained but were not too aggressive about it. A few days later red-cloaked ones came and took cell samples from everyone. It wasn't long after that Christopher and I were detained along with a cousin of Christopher's. Poor woman. She was completely scared out of her wits." Cynthia paused as a stray thought caught her attention. "I couldn't find her amongst those that ... that Ben collected. Is that really his name?" an alien named Ben seemed to tickle Cynthia's sense of the absurd. Pa'attee felt a tense knot inside her unwind a little as her strong mother slowly resurfaced.

"That's the name I gave him. Abe and Ben were the first two Hel'Arumpo'or to pledge service to me." Pa'attee noted a raised eyebrow question from her mother. "Why they changed allegiance is a long story with roots in the Hel'Arumpo'or's tangled history. I hate to say I was lucky, but I was. Very lucky." *May Murphy turn a deaf ear to my praise.*

"And you trusted them? Is Abe here?" Cynthia looked at those gathered on the plinth.

Unexpected tears welled up and spilled down Pa'attee's cheeks; her throat closed as her emotions rose. *How many hours ago had it been?* They were her own emotions, real and heartfelt, but the GreatMother's dialect filtered them. A strange sense of dislocation possessed her as a rational part of her observed the emotional part. Her grief at losing Abe was something her mother needed to see, to absorb, and integrate.

"He died in my arms, mother. He died protecting me," she told her. "Do I trust them? With my life. They are my sons." Pa'attee turned to the arc of Hel'Arumpo'or in reversed tabards. "Pa'aran'noon!" *You are my sons!*

As one, they responded. STAMP, stamp, CLASH! Blades met blades. "PA'ATTEE! PA'ATTEE! PA'ATTEE!" The cry was taken up in many places around Li'ila'tion.

Awe flushed away Cynthia's initial start of surprise. "Then all these ... these Hel'Arumpo'or, the ones in the inside-out cloaks, they're your ... your soldiers and all those, back where Ben first took me? They're yours too?"

"Umm, yeah, it became what the Hel'Arumpo'or call The Gathering. That's ended, for now." Change was coming to the Hel'Arumpo'or. *Clan Bar'Durrunnan was not going to like it one little bit.* Pa'attee glanced towards the two Bar'Durrunnan FirstBrothers. They stood isolated and alone as if Harrum'Bar's absence robbed them of any motivation.

Cynthia looked at her daughter with analytical eyes,

measuring and cataloging. "You've changed."

"Not to be trite, mother, but war does that to people." Pa'attee withstood her mother's examination with ease. *I've got nothing to hide.*

"I'm sorry Patty, I didn't mean to be critical. What I see," Cynthia's smile quirked a little wryly, "human mothers call The Blossoming. I don't remember seeing you so ... so in charge of yourself." She stopped herself from continuing and began again, "No, I'm wrong. I have seen it before, that's why I recognize it now. The first time was when you took your first solo flight in a light plane. And then again when I watched you prepare and launch Freya. Some people blossom quickly; some never do. I can see what Christopher saw in you now, and it makes me proud, too." Cynthia's arm reached out and brought Pa'attee close for a brief hug. The fear that possessed her mother persisted, but the pressure had been released. She looked away from Pa'attee, taking in the bustle of the Hel'Arumpo'or parading past the foot of the stairs, the thinning lines on the walkways and the greater expanses of Li'ila'tion. The aching fear in her heart was displaced by love. There was no need for any words.

CHAPTER FORTY-SEVEN

Suddenly, Cynthia focused on the platform and those around them, specifically, the little golden alien perched in a Genedalt's arms. Pa'attee knew she could begin her introductions again. "Mom, this is Er'men. Er'men, my mother, Cynthia."

Genedalt sank to one knee, presenting the diminutive GreatMother at head height.

"I am so pleased to meet you, Cynthia," Er'men said in EngStand with a flawless, mid-western accent, "although I wish things had unfolded in a very different manner. You have been ill-treated," Er'men reached toward but did not touch Cynthia's bruised face, "and I apologize most sincerely."

"Um, thank you," Cynthia unsure of herself, of her standing. "I'm not sure what to say. I'm still catching up on events, so excuse my ignorance but, are you the ... the alien queen?"

"Don't say it like that, Mom. Er'men only drools a when she's sleeping and doesn't hiss much at all," Pa'attee didn't try very hard to keep a straight face. A very painful knot inside her gut was slowly unwinding, releasing waves of joy and relief. She wrapped an arm around her mother's waist, squeezed her - *it feels so good being with you* - and discovered that her cheeks, still wet with tears, hurt from smiling.

"I didn't think Er'men was like that..." Cynthia straightened as she began to defend herself. Her eyes darted back and forth as her thoughts whirled. She sighed, and her shoulders slumped. "I'm sorry, I did."

"I think I'm missing a cultural reference." Er'men leaned towards Pa'attee and spoke silently in the GreatMother's dialect, "Drool?"

It was not necessary to tell Er'men that she was joking, "I'm sorry, Er'men," Pa'attee continued in EngStand. "It's an old feature film reference but a potent one. I'll show you the I-mmersive remake when you're old enough." She gave Er'men a subtle cue, and the little alien sat up straight, indignant, gasping with perfect comic timing.

"Old enough!" she complained.

"Now I think I'm the one missing the reference," Cynthia said as her eyes darted back and forth, her smile lightly masked by concern.

"Er'men's only about six months old, and probably should be tucked up in bed," Pa'attee teased, *dreaming of past lives, preparing for tomorrow.*

"I've been snoozing." Er'men leaned back into Genedalt's arms.

Sleep. That would be wonderful. Pa'attee stifled a yawn with a deep breath.

"Six months? Then she's not responsible..." Cynthia began.

"Er'men was not responsible for what happened. The Great Council, some of whom are here," Pa'attee glanced around the gathering. *I should put some music on and get this party started.* A yawn cracked Pa'attee's jaw. *Maybe not.* "Excuse me."

"The Great Council was dominated by Clan Bar'Durrunnan's FirstMother, Harrum'Bar," Er'men continued for her.

"Har-rum-Bar?" Cynthia sounded the word out slowly, "he was the Big Bad?"

"*She*, mother, Harrum'Bar was FirstMother for Clan Bar'Durrunnan, the ones in red." Pa'attee corrected gently. "Politics. Harrum'Bar was a poor leader." Pa'attee yawned again, "I'm sorry. It's been a long day."

"And this Harrum'Bar's gone," Cynthia paused and almost whispered, "dead?"

"I haven't seen her body, but I have it on good authority she is." The fire she had seen behind Harrum'Bar's eyes scratched at a memory packed deep inside, but Pa'attee did not explore it.

"And that means Er'men's in charge?" Cynthia asked.

"No, the Great Council holds authority. Er'men, were she old enough, would head the Great Council. Harrum'Bar was her regent as well as leading one of the largest clans. I don't know why she thought the Hel'Arumpo'or could win in a fight with humanity." There was one way to know, but the idea of ingesting anything from Harrum'Bar made Pa'attee's throat constrict.

"So, who fills her vacancy?" The knowledge appeared in Cynthia's mind without prompting, and her head snapped around to face her daughter. "You?" Pa'attee held her stare proudly. "I think I need to sit down." Confused but not alarmed, Cynthia waited to hear more.

"It's only for a couple of years," Pa'attee explained.

"Years," her mother echoed.

"Only a few," Patty added. *Three or four.*

"Why you?" Cynthia asked. "Is it an honor you won by defeating this ... this Harrum'Bar in combat?" Cynthia's internal horizon was changing; Pa'attee could feel her shift her weight to compensate.

"No, it has nothing to do with her death. Er'men asked me to be her regent. The job doesn't particularly appeal to me, but I think I am the only one that can do it correctly."

"Because of the memory-gift things?" Cynthia's eyes took in the urn of swirled red and gold glass that held thousands of tiny pearls. Murrun stood proudly beside it. "Memories? All of them? You're not going to .... to eat, um, all of those? Are you?"

"Goodness, no!" Er'men sat up, startled. The very idea!

"That would be madness, Mother." Pa'attee took a moment to stop, close her eyes and take a slow breath. Li'ila'tion was full of life, and a concentrated component emanated from the beautiful urn, a sweet and sunny aroma.

When she opened her eyes, Pa'attee saw that her mother had discovered the delicate scent. "Is that from the..."

"Mel'andrin, yes," Patty confirmed.

"But Lily said Daichi could speak with the Hel'Arumpo'or. That he had ingested Mel-an-drin, couldn't he..."

"Daichi has agreed to stay and help me," Patty told her. "It's not just about communication, mother. Mel'andrin holds much more than language, more than vocabulary and protocol instruction sets. Daichi does not hold the memories I do." Pa'attee closed her eyes again. There would be a way to explain this if she could relax and find it. "Er'men has shared her mel'andrin with me and a GreatMother's mel'andrin is different, concentrated. It holds lives, a record stretching back thousands of years. Mother, no one can stand as a bridge between Human and Hel'Arumpo'or as I can. Er'men's closer to me than a sister. You've got a new daughter, Mom." Pa'attee thought she should tell her mother about Cicely, her other adopted daughter when there was more time.

Awe tinged with more than a little horror flashed across Cynthia's face, "How many lives?" she glanced at the urn.

"Too many," Er'men sighed.

"And not enough," Pa'attee noted dryly. "If access to the correct nutritional support had been maintained, there would not have been so many gaps between GreatMothers." She turned to her mother. "Knowing all this, how could I stand aside and let someone else appear in Er'men's stead? There is more to their story, mother, much more. The Hel'Arumpo'or need our help. They are refugees, not conquerors." Pa'attee did not plead but stood proudly.

"As I've said before," Jake's drawl cut in, "they sure picked a strange way of askin' for help." He threw Cynthia a smile and a loose salute. Daichi greeted her with a small bow.

After acknowledging their presence with a quick nod, Cynthia turned back to her daughter. *Daughters?* The question flickered behind her eyes. "Patty," she took a breath, "Patricia, it is a lot for me to take in. Please don't get me wrong; I can see your sincerity." She turned to Er'men, "and I think I can see yours too." Cynthia sighed and leaned back a little, opening her stance, vulnerable. "Two daughters; this I did not expect. I was happy to discover I still had one."

"Mom, that's all I can ask. I know it's a lot to take in." Pa'attee moved closer, and Cynthia could not resist the pleasure of having her daughter in her arms again.

CHAPTER FORTY-EIGHT

"Mother, I should make another introduction, this is Sher'ril'lil, Clan Darf'ornal's FirstMother. Clan Darf'ornal built Tal'anis." Pa'attee turned a slow circle taking in Li'ila'tion's beauty.

"I am pleased to meet you Sher-ril-lil. Did I get that right?" Cynthia added a bobbed half bow, half curtsy. She stood and examined the cabal gathered around Jake's makeshift bed.

Jake chuckled. "We were discussing the fate of the universe. Got any suggestions?"

"I'm not sure. My mind is still spinning." Cynthia looked at her daughter with awe and sympathy combined. "Does anyone know what the situation is on Earth?"

"Politically fractured at best, I'm afraid," Jake said, propped up on his trolley. His wounds had been tended to, and someone had brought him a pillow to sit on. "The USF have been overstepping their bounds, as is their want, with the Corporates at their heels looking for any advantage." Jake nursed his contempt and anger. They were old friends. "Tub-thumping fear mongers have had a field day." He shuddered.

"We were thinking of taking little steps at first," Daichi contributed. "Important though."

"Such as?" Cynthia pulled Alan closer to her.

"We thought to retrieve the Hel'Arumpo'or from their posts on the human LaGrange stations and the Moon and to retreat from Earth's airspace seemed the most obvious opening moves," Pa'attee said. She was confident that returning humans possessions was the correct first step on the path to some sort of agreement. Er'men's imperial glow supported her, buoying her positivity.

Cynthia nodded, "And then?"

"Then the negotiations can begin," Jake frowned and looked to have tasted something bad. "Then the bureaucrats and politicians wade in," he shuddered comically.

"I'm sorry, Sher'ril'lil," Cynthia began, "but your people can't possibly expect humanity to make you welcome after what has happened?" Cynthia's anger, Pa'attee was pleased to see, was restrained.

"To be honest," Sher'ril'lil replied, "this one would not blame humans if they cast us back into the deep. This one would have it known that the Great Council was deeply divided about bombarding your world from orbit. It was shameful. The Hel'Arumpo'or should know better how rare and precious a thriving green world is.

"This one has learned much in this short time conversing with the Daichi and Traaaffic Control. The Bar'Durrunnan FirstMother misled us. We would stay and right some of the wrongs," Sher'ril'lil said and bowed to Cynthia, showing contrition, "if that were possible."

"Ain't going to be easy however you split it," Jake drawled. "People are going to be deeply pissed off with the Hel'Arumpo'or. Some will be out for blood. The Corporates will be pitching for indentured servitude. Some will call for immediate exile from our solar system, but there are those that are paranoid and afraid the Hel'Arumpo'or would return, stronger."

"I think more people will understand, than you think," Daichi countered. "Humans have had some terrible leaders that left permanent scars in the populace. Are Japanese or Germans still held to account for the actions of their ancestors during World War Two? Are Mongols blamed for Genghis Khan? The Cambodians for Pol Pot? North Americans for the war crimes of Lattern or Tyler? Now that Harrum'Bar has been ... deposed," Daichi glanced beyond the plinth's edge, "I see no reason why a beneficial agreement cannot be reached between our two peoples."

"There speaks a civilized man, Sheryl." Jake mashed the FirstMother's name and winked at her. The FirstMother coughed a chuckle and patted his hand. *Was Jake flirting with her?* An incredulous smile burst across Pa'attee's face.

"The USF will come," Cynthia half muttered to herself, "and The National Federation, of course. I wonder if Freddy's still on the..." she chewed on her bottom lip as her eyes unfocused. Pa'attee smiled. Her mother's mind was engaged, and her emotions were helping rather than hindering her. *She will help us pull this together, help us set things to right. Perhaps my childish fantasy has not been too far off the mark.*

Cynthia frowned, looking at Jake and shaking her head. "But this is going to get ugly." She looked at her daughter. "And you would put yourself between these warring parties?"

"She won't be standing alone, Cynthia," Daichi argued.

"No offense, gentlemen but a washed-out war hero and a master swordsman are not going to be sufficient," Cynthia stood proudly, "to help my daughter," her eyes took in Er'men, perched in Genedalt's arms, "daughters."

"Oh, there's more than just us," Jake growled. "Thanks to that little gem, she's the toast of the Solar System." Pa'attee showed her mother Giuseppe's camera pinned to her tabard. "I don't know how much of today's exciting episode will be understood, but Patty's opinions will be listened to, and listened to by most people, directly from that camera. Without Patty, almost no one would know what was happening in this crazy conflict. Without Patty, the Belters might not have come to help out here at all."

"Historians may name this conflict any number of things," Daichi gave a wry smile, "but already it is commonly referred to as Patty's War."

Jake's right hand rose, and he stroked his lips. His eyes darted back and forth, focusing on nothing. "Patty, something you said earlier made me think. Er'men, do you have a thumbprint we can steal?"

Er'men looked at her hand and then back at Jake. "I beg your pardon?"

"Patty, I'm thinkin' you should adopt Er'men as your sister, formally." Jake pulled on his lower lip and scratched the tip of his nose.

Pa'attee enjoyed watching Jake's mind work; he always surprised her. "And that would change things, how?" she asked.

"Not sure just yet, but Cicely's a Belter, so that makes Patty a Belter too. Wouldn't it? And Er'men, if you adopted her?" Jake's face contorted. "It would be good to have a Belter representative at the table. That should muddy the waters a bit. The Corporations lost a lot at L1 and L4. They'll want to sue the Hel'Arumpo'or back into the Stone Age," Jake continued. "A place they've been more than once I believe. The Corporates can be tied up in court procedures for decades. Some are still fighting the Belter Government for war reparations. May they drown beneath a tide of lawyers' fees," Jake chuckled evilly.

Er'men leaned closer to Pa'attee and asked privately, "Is he in pain?"

Pa'attee's laugh startled Sher'ril'lil, "No, but it does look like it, doesn't it."

"The GreatMother's Traaaffic Control fashions words as we do metal," Sher'ril'lil noted. "There is much to do, but this one feels the Traaaffic Control directions are sure."

"I think they are," Pa'attee reassured her. "He has our best interests at heart." There were worries in Pa'attee's heart about the future, but for now, she felt cared for and supported by those she felt close to. They were not a family by blood, except blood spilled, but it was a family in her heart. Like all families, some members were missing. *I wonder what Lirsín's going to make of all this?* Her heart warmed, and she smiled. *He'll probably want to save me. I might let him this time.*

Cynthia frowned, her head whirling with thoughts, "Daichi, may I borrow your comm?" He nodded, unwrapped it from his wrist and passed it to her. She looked down at the screen as she logged-on. "I think I need to call our lawyers."

CHAPTER FORTY-NINE

Onlookers crowded the corridors, keen to grasp the memory as RegentGreatMother Pa'attee was escorted, with all due ceremony, to the selected reception area. It was not enough to have Alan and Zeus at her side; representatives from the Great Council and their accompanying clan guards and attendants had to tag along. Pa'attee wanted to have a simple reunion with her friends, but her newly won allies on the Great Council would not let her move anywhere in Tal'anis without a proper escort, certainly not to an important meeting like this.

And waiting for everyone to assemble seemed to take forever. There had been time for Pa'attee to be patched up, her cuts attended to, and her ribs bound; she had even had a couple of hours for a snooze. The meeting with the High Council had absorbed the rest of her morning, but she was sure she could have slept for at least an extra hour if she hadn't had to wait for her escorts to arrive. The day was only going to get busier.

Jake laughed, "Hey, you should know better. Haven't you all those memories stacked up inside you?"

"Not from the flight. It was the Bar'Durrunnan FirstMothers that used ritual and ceremony to reinforce their position," Pa'attee complained.

"And pheromones. So, change the rituals. You're the boss, aren't you?" He looked at the frustration on her face, and his grin stretched wider, "Ah, discovering the limitations of power, are we?"

"Hel'Arumpo'or are tied so strongly to their memories. I just hope they can change enough to coexist with humans. Rituals don't matter in the long run I suppose." She speared him with a gaze that made his spine chill. "I don't suppose you know who told them that Lirsín was coming?"

"I cannot tell a lie, but I didn't say he was your consort." Jake chuckled and looked up at Alan. "You didn't say something did you?"

Alan needed Jake's trolley to keep himself steady as they walked down the corridor. He did not like showing his weakness, but the option of not attending Pa'attee was unthinkable. He did not ignore Jake's jest, but his non-reaction took on a pained air.

The idea that a GreatMother could even have a consort tickled the imaginations of all the Hel'Arumpo'or, especially Er'men, and the GreatMother's memories that resided within Pa'attee's mind. The closest relationship any of them had experienced was the special connection that irregularly blossomed between a GreatMother and the Hel'omi, and there was nothing sexual about that. They had long since left thoughts of physical intimacy behind them. The concept seemed to repulse a small section of GreatMother memories. It was challenging to keep it all balanced.

Ushered into a large room, Pa'attee and her entourage were carefully arranged on a dais where Er'men, her guards, and advisers were waiting expectantly. The young GreatMother's looks were a mixture of curiosity and wisdom that Pa'attee could feel resonating inside her; GreatMothers watched from inside both of them. Pa'attee was not sure what she was going to tell Lirsín. So much had happened, it was difficult to isolate what she felt for him.

Er'men reached out and patted Pa'attee's hand. "Let it unfold, sister." *Don't let the ones inside you, tell you what to think.*

Supporting Er'men's words, Cynthia placed a hand on Pa'attee's right shoulder. She had been the one to bring her news that Jaswinder/The Ice Princess had made rendezvous with the asteroid, using a correctly balanced Sprocket Drive. Pa'attee had been in chambers with the Great Council, working with Jake and Daichi to organize the orderly withdrawal of

Hel'Arumpo'or forces. Cynthia smiled. She had had the opportunity to talk to Lirsín, and she liked him - that much was obvious - but that only made Pa'attee more apprehensive. *Have I changed too much?* Doubt gnawed at her.

A ripple of awareness preceded the doors opening. *They're here.* Pa'attee did not even know who had come aboard, apart from Lirsín. The doors swung wide and an escort of Pa'attee's soldiers, in their colorful mixture of reversed tabards, stepped inside and parted, revealing a handful of nervous humans in generic black and gold tabards. Lirsín stood nervously at the front with Stan at his right, carrying Cicely in his arms. Stan wore that iron bar tucked into his belt. Word must have spread about Stan's ferocity, and his escorts accorded him honor in their stance though he was not aware of it. Madhur and Cian followed close behind. They were both gawking around them, wide-eyed with wonder.

The blond missile exploded out of Stan's arms. "Pa'attee!" Cicely cried as she bounded across the room, breaking all formality. Taking their cue from their RegentGreatMother, not one hand reached for their weapons as the strange creature charged toward them. The wall of escorts before Pa'attee parted to allow the young girl access. "Pa'attee!" Cicely leaped into Pa'attee's arms and smothered her with kisses as her cry was taken up by Pa'attee's soldiers, and then by all the Hel'Arumpo'or gathered there.

"Pa'attee! Pa'attee! Pa'attee!" Now hands reached for weapons as feet stomped. The clash of blades, raised in praise, added to the cacophony. Cicely spun around in Pa'attee's arms, her elbow grazing Pa'attee's chin, and joined in, clapping and shouting. Stan crossed half the space, chasing his wayward niece, dragging Lirsín and the rest of them along behind him.

"Well, that's one way of breaking the ice," Jake's warm chuckle came from somewhere behind Pa'attee.

Cicely spun in her arms again. "Hi, Jake," she waved at him and then leaned back, looking up at Zeus. "Wow! Pa'attee, he's huge!" She laughed and turned again, "And you're so tiny. Hi,

I'm Cicely."

"Hello, Cicely." Er'men reached across and shook hands. "Pa'attee's told me about you and your brother. Where is Eg?"

"He didn't want to come. When the telemetry from Freya came through, Cian and Eg worked all night making the adjustments. I'm kinda surprised Cian made it. He worked just as hard." Cicely flipped in Pa'attee's arms again and looked with some curiosity at one of Er'men's Hel'omi guards. "Why is that one all glowy?" she asked in a whisper. Pa'attee recognized the Hel'omi Cicely referred to, not that she could see the glow but because of the Hel'omi's reactions. Even as he tried to remain in formation, the Hel'omi's eyes were locked on the little blond.

Er'men coughed a chuckle. "You're not left-handed, are you?" she asked.

"Me? No, I'm ambidextrous." Cicely leaped from Pa'attee's arms, into the open air. Zeus's arm whipped across, and Cicely's foot landed in his palm. She pushed off as if she expected the hand to be there from the moment she jumped. Er'men's LeftLeading advisers assisted Cicely as she clambered over them, and she scrambled across the wall of Hel'omi until she climbed into the arms of the one that interested her.

"Is she gonna be all right?" Stan rushed up, the only person in the room that seemed at all concerned.

"Stan, she's in the safest place in the world," Pa'attee reassured him as she stepped from the platform and embraced him. "And I think you might have to get used to having that Hel'omi around." Drol'lander was young but had already earned his Clan-name, Fortunate Strike. *Lucky Shot might be a better translation*, Pa'attee thought with a chuckle.

"Is that so?" Lirsín approached and stood behind Stan. Doubt and concern danced in his eyes even as he tried to hide it behind an amused mask.

Heart racing, Pa'attee felt as though her ears were tuned to a private channel, the noise in the room muted to a background hum. Time seemed to slow as her senses took in all she could about the young man in his dress uniform draped in black and gold. She could tell he was holding in his passion, his desire to embrace her and save her from the world's entanglements. He was restraining himself, and not just because of the unfamiliar surroundings, and his fear of looking foolish should he do something inappropriate. *Trust. He trusts me.* That recognition brought the room back with a crash.

Without thinking, Pa'attee slipped to one side, reached for Lirsín's collar and pulled his lips to hers. The room erupted in an excited roar of exultation, but Pa'attee hardly noticed. It was not the intimate little rendezvous Pa'attee had hoped for, but that did not matter in the least, now that Lirsín was in her arms and she was in his.

There was still a lot of work to do. Fergus Durnin, leading the bulk of the Belter Fleet would be here in a matter of hours, the *USF Cervantes* would be here in another day or so. They had to be ready, but with her family around her, Pa'attee felt that anything was possible.

"Lirsín, come and meet my mom."

THE END

Thanks for reading this far.

It would be a great help if you could leave a review.

If you'd like to hear of new releases from Craig,

sign up to receive Craig's newsletter.

.

ABOUT THE AUTHOR

Craig Miller lives on the south coast of New South Wales.
He balances his time between writing, caring for his aging
mother
– who recently turned 100 -
and watching whales migrate north and south.

He has been an eager reader of SF and Fantasy since he could
open a book.

Tina Tales

From: TinyTina@RedDust.ctznfree
To: Patty@BaSpau.com
Subject: Where R U?

Patty! Yo! Grrly. Where's your hat? On your head or on your bed?
Where's my go-to with the how-to?
I know servers are crashing, but one of these pings has gotta get
through! Had to drag out Dad's old Optical modem to get a
signal. UNET routes around the breaks but there must be F-
loads of dam. The airwaves are DEAD.
I'll keep tryin'

From: TinyTina@RedDust.ctznfree
To: Patty@BaSpau.com
Subject: Got News?

So-Cal OK? North Hem got hit hard but Links are down 'cept
local.
No news is Bad news. On a starvation diet here sis, can't feel the
pulse.
Local rumour mill is freaky. Current Top Theory: Hoons-with-
Harpoons not local boys. Got through to Hine last night but
nothing today.
More Bad Feeling.
Missing U.
Fly True

From: TinyTina@RedDust.ctznfree
To: Patty@BaSpau.com
Subject: My News 01

The Olds are in Syd or were. Last heard Syd in flames. What does that mean? Downtown? Out West? Manley? All of it? Melb and Bris too.
WTF?
Oz can be a fairly obnoxious country but orbital bombardment? Who did we offend this time?
No flights but that won't stop Dad. He'll be out on the road, even if he's on a bicycle - he's done that before. Rode from Syd to Perth via Dar. Mum'll be hating it but she won't be further than three metres from him.

From: TinyTina@RedDust.ctznfree
To: Patty@BaSpau.com
Subject: My News 03

Mighty meteor shower last night. Big piece hit down south somewhere.
Dragged out Grandpa's 8" Newtonian. Sky's busy.
I spotted the MotherShip rising out of Western sky near dawn. She's a BIG MF.
Where's OASIS? Not where she should be.
<Big Sad>.
Where are you, Patty?
Some pix getting through.
So-Cal still there. R U?
Fingers Crossed.

From: TinyTina@RedDust.ctznfree
To: Patty@BaSpau.com
Subject: My News 04

Central Server's still taking messages so I'll still send 'em. Don't know if you'll pick up but I gotta talk to someone sane. My hometown crowd have pulled their heads in. The rabbits are out there, but they're too scared to move or speak. Darwin is buckled down as if she's waiting for a Big Blow. Cyclone Phil was only a few years ago so most everyone has something put aside. You know Dad, packrat like Grandpa. Plenty of supplies, rainwater collection etc. Regular suburban survivalist, he is. Half the street has left town the rest are organising. Seeing the neighbours toting a collection of dusty hunting rifles and tasers - pretty scary. Looking again at Grandpa's pump action. Bet the shells are funky. Dad would know.

From: TinyTina@RedDust.ctznfree
To: Patty@BaSpau.com
Subject: My News 05

Half of those left on my street scrammed last night. Archer is emptying fast.
Got Dad's powerbike charged and hitched the trailer. Is there any point waiting? Where to go? Got a cousin working in Kakadu. Maybe go west and head for Broome. Dunno.
Still expect the Olds to pull up to the house and Dad to hassle me for not mowing the front yard.
Will wait for last minute, just in case.
No word from anyone!
<miffed>
Come on grrls. Ping me!
<sigh>

From: TinyTina@RedDust.ctznfree
To: Patty@BaSpau.com
Subject: My News 06

Too late to take the big bike.
The Burks, two houses up, left in their sedan and were hit before
they reached the corner.
Air cover is thick.
Downsizing survival kit. I'll hang on to dad's portable. I think
he's stashed half the UNET in it, I mean "Throat Singers of
Tibet"? No one's bothered with local storage for fifty years!
Packrats ROOL!
Will take Lady Erasmus. Seen the vids. Aliens with swords!
Freaky! She's a mite big for me but that edge is sharp and the
sabre will give me greater reach.

From: TinyTina@RedDust.ctznfree
To: Patty@BaSpau.com
Subject: My News 07

AGGRESSIVE VISITORS!
They took the airport and cut off the CBD.
Local net fractured but big battle on Stuart Hwy 10km north.
Over WAY too soon. New boys seriously kicked butt. No
prisoners.
This is FOR REAL!
Seen the vids. Big Panic!

From: TinyTina@RedDust.ctznfree
To: Patty@BaSpau.com
Subject: My News 08

Sharon, Old Ms Kitts from across the road, got her clippers out
and gave me a No 01. I'm spiky! Mum would freak to see all my
blonde locks on the floor. It's too hot to be fussing with hair.
Since I'm reduced to Shank's Pony my options are greatly
reduced but *they* say, if you can get to Humpty Doo, you can get
transport out.
Of course I ALWAYS believe *them*.
Invaders have moved down Stuart as far as Zuccoli so I'll be
heading Sth to Wickham and then west to Humpty. It's the long
route but I should be able to do it in a day or so.

From: TinyTina@RedDust.ctznfree
To: Patty@BaSpau.com
Subject: On the Road 01

Good night for it. Low cloud. Pitch black. Pack too heavy, sore
feet and just past Bellmack. Pathetic.
Have to change the setting on dad's portable played Allegri's
Miserere twice in a row and then a set of Sex Pistol's b-sides. I
know he has something from this century!

From: TinyTina@RedDust.ctznfree
To: Patty@BaSpau.com
Subject: On the Road 02

They have the Channel Island Road Bridge. Cut off. <muffle curses - very muffled> forced off road by patrol coming nth. Scout to overlooking hill.
Bridge held by 24. Saw family stopped. Father thrown from bridge. Many salties below. Very Not Good. Heading West to Mitchell. Slow going. Ground wet, soft.

From: TinyTina@RedDust.ctznfree
To: Patty@BaSpau.com
Subject: On the Road 03

Met croc crossing creek Sth of Mitchell. Too fat to bother with lil ol' me.
<shudders>

From: TinyTina@RedDust.ctznfree
To: Patty@BaSpau.com
Subject: On the Road 04

Stuck in middle of nowhere. Heavy fighting, jets et al. Once again too brief. Could see heavy firing from Coolalinga. Ground-based. Trio of alien ships silenced them < 3 mins.

From: TinyTina@RedDust.ctznfree
To: Patty@BaSpau.com
Subject: On the Road 05

No lights in Virginia.

From: TinyTina@RedDust.ctznfree
To: Patty@BaSpau.com
Subject: CONTACT 01

Still alive. Not sure why. Came face-to-face with aliens. Pix don't
do them justice, ugly.
X-ing backyards heading twds Bees Creek. Stopped x-ing street.
Couldn't help drawing Lady Erasmus. That stopped them for a
heartbeat.
Are they asthmatic? Lot of coughing. Not long enough to
escape. Lowered their white staff weapons and drew their
swords! Murphy! Bored they were. They wanted a bloody fight
for fun!
"Did huuuman fight with honour?" seemed disappointed I asked
for first-blood. Biggest one coughed a lot. Thought I would be
dead in 1st 10 secs.
Nasty dagger/sword they have. Heavy. My wrist will ache for
days.
Kept it out, circling, being faster. It was quick but blind to its
right. Scored two good hits but no blood! Made messes of fine
engraving on forearm and bicep. Got good thrust in low.
Attacking forward leg. Out-of-bounds in a comp but on the
street? Just fine.
Tina scores!
Limpy - well it is now - is escorting me back to Dar CBD. Taking a
break. I get to keep my stuff.
'YoungBreedingAgeFemaleHasHonour' apparently.
Could have told 'em if they asked.

From: TinyTina@RedDust.ctznfree
To: Patty@BaSpau.com
Subject: CONTACT 02

Limpy is slow and takes regular breaks but is alert. Have collected more prisoners as move along Stuart Hwy, women and children.
No men older than 8. Don't want to know where the rest are.
No one is taking it well. Am only one with possessions, only one Limpy will comm with.
Helped break into store for food/supplies. Seems astonished at how fragile human babies are. Treats mothers with more respect.

From: TinyTina@RedDust.ctznfree
To: Patty@BaSpau.com
Subject: CONTACT 03

MS is down! Couldn't believe peepers.
'Hanging in the air the same way bricks don't.'
Then it came down just off Bicentennial Park. Roads thick with aliens heading out of town.
Camped at Garden's Park golf course. No one was playing. Kids liked the sand traps.

From: TinyTina@RedDust.ctznfree
To: Patty@BaSpau.com
Subject: CONTACT 04

Planes from the Nth and Sth. Outnumber alien defenses. Bombs!

From: TinyTina@RedDust.ctznfree
To: Patty@BaSpau.com
Subject: RUNNING 01

Hiding in mangroves, Stuart Park.
Killed Limpy. Still shaking. Never killed anything larger than a snail underfoot. Not good. Very not good.
Bombs falling, saw my chance and took Limpy in the back.
Honour! Huh! Didn't have time to help anyone. Chaos! Was across the hwy gunning it down Duke before I knew it. Lady Erasmus, bloody, still in my hand.
More crocs and bodies.
Don't like death. Didn't think I'd like it not sure if I wanted 1st hand exp. to confirm MHO.
Don't know what happened to women and kids in park. There was bombing.
Feel bad but too scared to go back. Very Not Good. Crappy world crappy life crappy me.
Found dingy & crossed to CDNP. Dawn soon. Must find shelter.
Want to sleep but don't like ants, lil biters. No sign of aliens over here. Heading East.

From: TinyTina@RedDust.ctznfree
To: Patty@BaSpau.com
Subject: RUNNING 02

Found WW2 concrete bunker memorial. Was there for the flash. Did we lose the war?

From: TinyTina@RedDust.ctznfree
To: Patty@BaSpau.com
Subject: RUNNING 03

Heading East again.
If this keeps up, I be back in Archer before I know it.
<bangs head>
Should call in at home and see if the Olds made it back. Can't see how.
Will be able to refresh my supplies.

From: TinyTina@RedDust.ctznfree
To: Patty@BaSpau.com
Subject: Heading Home 01

Someone is following me. Only caught a glimpse.
Hope I'm not seeing things.
Seems smaller than the big brutes. Spots me without much effort.
Think my wrist comm is leaking EM.

From: TinyTina@RedDust.ctznfree
To: Patty@BaSpau.com
Subject: Heading Home 02

Left my comm at the base of a bush and circled around. My tag-along crouched close to the ground aprox 250m from my comm. Always pretty good at hide-and-seek, didn't spot me. Definitely smaller than the big ones. Don't know if it was the light but it looks greyish with red cloak.
Collected my comm once tag-along move off and headed East and turned it off. Clock function still working: off = stand-by. Moved north.

From: TinyTina@RedDust.ctznfree
To: Patty@BaSpau.com
Subject: Heading Home 03

Doubled back. Tag-along still tagging.
Wrist comm: leaks = sieve.
Power supply not easily accessible will void warrantee.
Ha!
Could leave comm but half my life stored in its tiny brain.
Cont. head east.
Short on H2O

From: TinyTina@RedDust.ctznfree
To: Patty@BaSpau.com
Subject: Heading Home 04

Comm 30 mins off.
On enough to check heading. Off again.
Keep east. Slow and steady.
Suburbs close.
Fence hopping soon methinks.

From: TinyTina@RedDust.ctznfree
To: Patty@BaSpau.com
Subject: Heading Home 05

Tag-along still there.
Watched it cross Berrimah Rd.
Moved quickly trying to catch sight of me?
Too late.

From: TinyTina@RedDust.ctznfree
To: Patty@BaSpau.com
Subject: Heading Home 06

Tag-along bloody nuisance!
Still on my heels.
Crossed East of Stuart @ Pinelands.

From: TinyTina@RedDust.ctznfree
To: Patty@BaSpau.com
Subject: Heading Home 07

Think I've lost Tag-along east of Howard Springs.
Haven't seen it all day. Heading west - home.

From: TinyTina@RedDust.ctznfree
To: Patty@BaSpau.com
Subject: Back Home 01

Home again.
They've been here.
Bright yellow tag on the front door.
Street is empty.
No Pwr from mains.
Back-ups charged 'n' ready.
Nose wet.

From: TinyTina@RedDust.ctznfree
To: Patty@BaSpau.com
Subject: Back Home 02

Well, it seems the street wasn't empty and ol' Tag-along wasn't
as lost as I thought. Didn't find out how much hot water I was in
until I was up to my chin in hot water. I just needed a bath.
Nothing else would do. Had a quick shower to scrub clean and
then climbed into the old cast-iron bath to soak.
Woke up to Tag-along pointing his white staff at me. Was sure
I'd lost it.
Spied it following my tracks with a handheld gizmo so I took to
the trees as soon as I could. Found a park with a bunch of
eucalypts and xfered to a fence, a garden shed and then
scrambled to a roof. Watched as Tag-along sniffed around the
tree I climbed, did a careful circle then headed east. I kept off the
ground as much as I could but I must have left something for it
to follow.
Patty, it had pictures of you. You and me. Wanted to know who
you were. Scared the shit out of me.
And then its head exploded!
Good ol' Ms Kitts! Gave it both barrels from a rusty old shotgun
and she was still standing! She's my new hero! Helped me clean
up the bathroom too. She's only one left in the street. She saw
me come back. Then she saw the grey one sneak in behind me.
What a courageous old girl.
We've just finished dinner and she's pouring over grandpa's
collection of vinyl. Not that I can play any of them for her, not
straight off the disk anyway. Grandpa had his own catalogue
referenced to our local database and she's racking up quite a
playlist.
It is SO good to be clean again.
I'm looking at this picture of you, Patty. The cloak doesn't do
your figure justice. What are you carrying in those boxes? You
haven't been thieving from our Galactic Overlords have you?

Whatever it is, keep up the good work. I'm just happy to know you are still in one piece. Keep 'em guessing, girl. It's what you're good at.

Then kick 'em where it hurtz

From: TinyTina@RedDust.ctznfree
To: Patty@BaSpau.com
Subject: Back Home 03

We're moving Sharon's essentials over to my place - she was down to her last candle.

Sharon's a really good cook and insists I learn.

Baked cookies this arvo. Should have seen me, flour on my face etc. Confession: It was fun.

Still starving for news.

You still kicking alien butt?

Give 'em one for me.

From: TinyTina@RedDust.ctznfree
To: Patty@BaSpau.com
Subject: Back Home 04

Been practicing with the grey alien's white staff thingy.

Limited range, not much more than Sharon's shotgun but you can dial up a shot as fine as a darning needle or something over a metre in diameter with the power of a pile driver or a feather.

No recoil no projectile.

Clever.

Don't want to use it too much. No eye deer what it runs on.

Might run out of steam - will run out of steam at worst possible moment for sure.

From: TinyTina@RedDust.ctznfree
To: Patty@BaSpau.com
Subject: Back Home 05

UNET's back!! NEWS!!
Bitrate's still tooooo ssslllooooowww for much video but Patty, you've created such a BUZZ! I had to d/l your little adventure to see for myself.
WHOA! PATTY! GRRL! Wots goin' on in yer hed, grrl?
Breakin' an' Enterin' the MS on a GRAND scale! No wonder the black-hats are out lookin' fer ya.
Thought my escapade to DAR and back was hairy but you trumped me, hands down. Sharon was impressed.
Have you caught Drang Dangle's song about you? Scuttle is that The Lerpers R composing a soundtrack to go with your vid.
Personally, I think it needs a little editing, tighten it up. Plus a few interviews to go with your Cinéma Vérité. Who should we get for the voice over?
<Grin>

From: TinyTina@RedDust.ctznfree
To: Patty@BaSpau.com
Subject: Back Home 06

Oh my! Patty! Watched your over-view of Battle of DWN.
Always knew I had an angel watchin over moi.
Found Jaswinder's yakSpace but Jai said you were not available. On a secret mission?
YOU GO AND STUFF THEM UP GOOD!
HURT 'EM BAD! REALLY BAD.
I know you can. If anyone can.
Sharon's cooler than I could believe an old girl like her could be and she did save my scrawny neck but she's not my hero.
You are, Patty.
Fly Tru

APPENDICES

CAST - HUMAN

Alan Balke -- Patty's younger brother – aged 12
Anatole LaRue -- Captain and Fencer with The Lightning Strike fencing team

Belters -- Residents of the Asteroid Belt
Biff Ramos -- Fencer with The Starlight Tigers
Brigadier De Cleot -- USF officer
Burt Hanover -- AKA Cap'n Burt - OASIS manager

Carl Hawk -- Engineer on L2
Chao Zhang -- A crewman aboard The Ice Princess
Christopher Balke -- Patty's father - CEO of Balke-Spalding Enterprises
Cian Kerr -- CRV Pilot
Cicely Underwood -- Twin Sister of Eg and Ken – aged 10
Cynthia Balke -- Patty's mother

Daichi Wakahisa -- The coach of The Lightning Strike
Daisy Spaulding -- The wife of Reece Spaulding
Damon Triggs -- Christopher Balke's personal assistant
Doctor Wentreck -- Astronomer at OASIS observatory

Egbert Underwood -- AKA Eg - Twin Brother of Cicely and Ken
Eva Trent -- A Hostess at 'Shadrak's Bar and Grill'

Fergus Durnin -- The military leader of The Belters
Francesco -- An engineer who works for Giuseppe Fermi on L2

Gale -- A medic on OASIS
Giuseppe Fermi -- AKA Slippery Joe Fermi - The owner and CEO of Fermi-Cingolani.
Günter Drake -- A crewmember from The Bright Damsel

Haruto -- Daichi's niece - A crewmember aboard Hestia's Hearth
Hine Whiniata -- A fencer with The Lightning Strike

Jaidev Sanjaya -- AKA Jai - Madhur's nephew - Strike Leader for The Starlight Tigers, Under-16s
Jake Chowdhury -- Texan - traffic control officer aboard OASIS
Jas Rightson -- A fencer with The Starlight Tigers
Jenny Northrop -- A reporter for The Times
Joshua Sanchez -- The manager of L2 Observatory

Kashi Kaur -- A Traffic Control officer on OASIS
Ken Underwood -- The older brother of Cicely and Eg - Racing CRV pilot
Kenneth Frobisher -- The brother of Phillip - manager of Balke-Spalding L1 facility

Lieutenant-Colonel Saab -- A USF officer
Lily Siskin -- A fusion engineer aboard Hestia's Hearth
Lirsín Delaney -- The young captain of The Ice Princess

Madeline Swati -- Maya's daughter – aged 14
Madhur Sanjaya -- The owner of Jaswinder
Marni Shafir -- A crewmember from The Bright Damsel
Maya Swati -- A security officer on OASIS
Missy -- a friend of Madeline - 8 or 9
Myung -- A crewman aboard The Ice Princess

Nanna -- A crewman aboard The Ice Princess

Pa'attee -- Patty's Hel'Arumpo'or name - Deep water
Patty Balke -- AKA GreatMother Pa'attee - A fencer with The Lightning Strike fencing team
Pete Rais -- The host of The Late Show
Philip Shain -- A famous actor in the feature Vegan Holiday
Phillip Frobisher -- The brother of Kenneth - Co-discoverer of Tempelman-Frobisher asteroid

Reece Spaulding -- Christopher Balke's business partner
Rogers -- A crewman aboard The Ice Princess
Security Chief Randle -- OASIS Security Chief

Shun Jiang -- A crewmember from The Bright Damsel
Stan Brennan -- The Chief Petty Officer aboard The Ice Princess

Tamir -- A crewman aboard The Ice Princess
Thrane -- A crewman aboard The Ice Princess
Tina Franks -- A fencer with The Lightning Strike fencing team
Todd Franks -- A reporter for The Interplanetary Chronicle
Traaaffic Control -- Hel'Arumpo'or title given to Jake Chowdhury

Wallace -- A crewman aboard The Ice Princess
Whetu -- Hine's niece

CAST - Hel'Arumpo'or

Abe -- First of Patty's Hel'Arumpo'or recruits – FirstSon

Bel'lamado'or -- Clan Bar'Durrunnan LeftLeading brother - A sturdy plant that grows in the waterways and bends with the prevailing current

Ben -- Hel'Arumpo'or recruit deemed not suitable for command

Bor'enop -- AKA Little Star – GreatMother

Bright Hope -- AKA GreatMother Del'armorun - Light Bringer - Young GreatMother

Byn -- Le'ealani's Hel'omi brother

Cedric -- Hel'Arumpo'or recruit - Patty's FirstRightLeadingSon

Da'rruman -- Hel'Arumpo'or recruit

Dan -- Hel'Arumpo'or recruit

Dan'thel -- Tel'sars assistant

Darbapard -- Er'men's LeftLeading attendant

Delad'ron -- Darf'ornal FirstMother during GreatMother Pur'unnan's lifetime

Del'armorun -- AKA Bright Hope - GreatMother name - Light Bringer

Dirma'don -- Nurse

Drallemngor -- Hel'omi guard - Staunch-as-granite

Dre'wholla -- Pur'unnan's LeftLeading assistant

Duntah'tis --   AKA Thunder Thighs - Jake's Texanized pronunciation - Hel'Arumpo'or assistant for Jake

Er'men -- Star Born - newborn GreatMother

Felix -- Hel'Arumpo'or recruit - Patty's SecondRightLeadingSon

Fe'ren -- Arumpo'or - Oldest of the GreatMothers' memories

Genedalt -- Clan Bumurnam FirstSon
Grad'dahvro -- Clan Pur'undram FirstLeftLeadingSon - Clan FirstBrother - Sure hands, or quick hands, or maybe even quick fists.

Harrum'Bar -- RegentFirstMother - Clan Bar'Durrunnan
Hea'rat -- Old FirstMother

Jael'Dam -- Bumurnam FirstSon for GreatMother Pur'unnan
Jar'eared -- Developer of mel'andrin production techniques that include specific memories

Le'ealani – GreatMother - metal worker
Little Star -- GreatMother Bor'enop - Rediscovers fusion technology

Mu'nruberra -- Arumpo'or - First to use Hel'omi as surrogate mothers for infertile Arumpo'or. - Engineers Hel'omi to give birth to Arumpo'or offspring if correct feeding regimen is used.
Murrun -- Patty's FirstLeftLeadingSon

Nor'Harrum -- Clan Bar'Durrunnan's FirstMother during Pur'unnan's lifetime

Pel'droi -- Er'men's Bar'Durrunnan LeftLeading attendant
Prince Rumble-bum -- Jake's name for the Bar'Durrunnan LeftLeader
Pronmerd -- Er'men's LeftLeading attendant
Pum'hurnun -- AKA Pum - LeftLeading Whel'luminum sept
Pur'unnan -- GreatMother - inventor of Hel'Arumpo'or stardrive - founder of Clan Pur'undram

Red'onothal -- Science Councilor of the Northern Science Directorate
Run'ned'lahl -- Clan Darf'ornal FirstLeftLeadingSon –

FirstBrother - A strong and well-used mold used in the casting of heavy machine parts

Sher'ril'lil -- Clan Darf'ornal FirstMother - A hardy and nourishing tuber with hidden barbs beneath the flaky bark
Stone Son -- AKA FirstSon Dangaron of Bumurnam - Little Star's childhood Hel'omi friend

Tan -- Le'ealani's Hel'omi brother
Tarrun'Bar -- Clan Durrunnan FirstMother - attended GreatMother Bor'enop
Telanor -- The Census Taker
Tel'sars -- Friend and supporter of Del'armorun
Ter'illion -- Fe'ren's lover
Tor'enal -- GreatMother Pur'unnan's Hel'omi SecondSon

Wal'dren -- Science Councilor of the Northern Science Directorate

Zeus -- AKA Whellanor - The-new-boy - AKA Ze'oos - Hel'Arumpo'or mispronunciation - Patty's FirstSon Hel'omi recruit

NOTES - HUMAN

Balke-Spalding Pty Ltd -- Manufacturers of monofilament
Broomstick -- a minimal spaceship with no life-support

CRV -- Civilian Re-Entry Vehicle

Deut -- Deuterium - stable heavy hydrogen isotope
Donegal's Suit-Sealer -- Rubberized cement for temporary
spacesuit repairs

EHF -- Extremely High Frequency - 30 to 300 gigahertz (GHz)
EngStand -- Standard English

Fermi-Cingolani -- Corporation manufacturing optical-
astronomical equipment.
F-UNET -- covert UNET access

Gecko-Grip -- Flooring and shoe sole combination used in zero-
gee
GUI -- Graphic User Interface

LADAR -- Laser Direction And Rangefinder
Lady Estelle -- Patty's replica of an eighteenth-century French
dueling sword.
Lagrange Points -- Named after Joseph-Louis Lagrange.
A Lagrange Point is an orbital position of gravitational
equilibrium created in any two-body orbital system, such as the
Earth and the sun or Earth and the moon.

There are five Lagrange points.

L1 - Between Earth and Moon - Corporate Station

L2 - Beyond the Moon - observatory

L3 - Opposite the Moon's orbit -- a collection of independent stations that grouped together during The Belter War.

L4 - 60 degrees ahead of the Moon's orbit - shipyards

L5 - 60 degrees behind the Moon's orbit - shipyard for Hestia's Hearth

LEO -- Low Earth Orbit

MEM -- Sprocket Drive's mass/envelope/matrix - The field containing the drive's effect. The field can be softened to allow crossing

Metire Universum -- Latin - measure the universe

Murphy's Law -- Whatever can go wrong, will go wrong, at the worst possible moment.

NNEMP -- Non-Nuclear Electromagnetic Pulse - a weapon-generated electromagnetic pulse without the use of nuclear technology

Pic-wall -- A large wall-sized video monitors

rendez -- An abbreviation for rendezvous

Sabre Launch engines -- Air-breathing rocket engines used by CRVs to achieve orbit - Self-landing.

SAM -- Surface-to-Air-Missile

Shadrach's Bar and Grill -- Popular restaurant on OASIS

SoCal -- Southern California

Sprocket Drive -- Cicely's name for Eg and Cicely's version of the Hel'Arumpo'or stardrive

stick-em pad -- A removable double-sided sticky surface

Tempelman-Frobisher -- An asteroid hijacked by the
Hel'Arumpo'or
The Belter War -- The Belter War began as an industrial dispute
that quickly spiraled out of control.
The Late Show -- Still running!
Trit -- Tritium - radioactive isotope of hydrogen

UNET -- Universal Internet

Whaitiri -- Māori female deity, a personification of thunder
Winterberg -- Variation of the ORION atomic drive - Creates
thrust by exploding one-kiloton nuclear bombs beneath it.

Zip-E-Lok -- An emergency access inflatable airlock
Zip-Lok -- Manufacturers of emergency pressure suits and
emergency access inflatable airlocks

NOTES - Hel'Arumpo'or

Cleansing -- The technique of erasing personality and memories. It is initially used to transfer Hel'Arumpo'or between Clans - Used for political enemies and employed to wipe the memories of human captives.

Closeness -- Deep emotional and empathic bond between a GreatMother and their Hel'omi FirstSon

Darfelenornal -- A city with steam-powered technology - Origins of the Clan Darf'ornal

Del'bidion -- to be presented before a GreatMother - a gift of mel'andrin is given

Doronem -- Small moon orbiting the Hel'Arumpo'or homeworld

Gathering -- A call from a GreatMother when she recruits members for a new clan - A Gathering is aided by scents given off by a GreatMother's Hel'omi

GreatMother -- Rare LeftLeading female. Currently, only one is produced every three or four generations - They are a near throwback to how the Arumpo'or used to be before their genes were mixed with the Hel'omi.

Hel'omi -- The Hel'omi were once a species related to the Arumpo'or in a similar way that gorillas are related to humans. Because their fertility was unaffected by their sun's activity they were used to help the Arumpo'or survive. They are now more intelligent than they used to be and share a close bond with GreatMothers and serve only her.

Hel'Arumpo'or -- A blend of Hel'omi and Arumpo'or species. The Hel'Arumpo'or differentiate into five types:

RightLeading Males - common Light brown striated with deep green, mottled into darker and lighter patches

RightLeading Females - common
deeper saturation of colors

LeftLeading Males - rare - pale almost
gray version of Males - throwback to Arumpo'or

LeftLeading Females - extremely rare -
throwback to Arumpo'or - supersaturated brown colors from
the female side become golden

Hel'omi -- a throwback to the original
species
Hunters -- Hel'Arumpo'or extremely rare genetic sports -
LeftLeading but the same body size as RightLeading
Hel'Arumpo'or - used as assassins - Almost no scent

Jahn -- A large ocean-going mammal harvested for its soft
dappled pelts

Li'ila'tion -- The Breathing Heart - the great central space within
Tal'anis crisscrossed with walkways - Contains a central plinth
where the stardrive is mounted.

mel'andrin -- RNA memory-transfer spheres secreted by
Hel'Arumpo'or
Pearl - RightLeading male and Hel'omi
Pale gold - RightLeading female
Golden - GreatMothers

Ninkers -- small rodents

Pa'aran'noon -- You are my sons
Po'or Reman'alt -- return to us - Release word for the Cleansed

Returned -- Cleansed humans recruited and Returned to
GreatMother Patty

sunstrike -- when a Coronal Mass Ejection (CME) hit the

planetary surface

Thang berries -- sweet fruits
The Fire -- Planetary Magnetic Field collapse allowing the CME to touch the surface
The First Fall -- The collapse of Arumpo'or society when their sun began a period of instability before changing into a Red Giant
The Lights -- Aurora from initial effect of Coronal Mass Ejections preceding The First Fall

whil'luw eggs -- large fish eggs collected from the shallows before The First Fall

Hel'Arumpo'or CLANS

The Hel'Arumpo'or Clans were formed around technologies rediscovered by GreatMothers.

Clan Bar'Durrunnan -- Fusion power
Medical - developed
Cleansing
previously Durrunnan
until the takeover of Little Star's newly formed clan
Color - Red

Clan Darf'ornal -- Metallurgical and Steam technologies
Color - Yellow

Clan Fer'entai'illy -- general medicine
Color - Green   -Blue

Clan Pur'undram -- Stardrive operations
Color - Purple

Clan Tol'edranna -- Life support - recycling
Color - Green

Clan Whel'luminum -- Communications
Color - Blue

HUMAN- SHIPS

Baby Face -- Belter ship - comm center for Belter attack wing

Freya -- Patty's red and gold striped CRV
Mercurio Cuore - MC-250T worked out to a 310
                        Call sign DH-1031C

Griffin -- G.A.V. racing team's CRV piloted by Ken Underwood

Hestia's Hearth -- First generational starship – under construction at L5

Hunter -- CRV - Cian Kerr's old Singer

Jaswinder -- Madhur's ship - a strange old bus, part Winnebago, part umbrella

Mercurio Cuore -- Mercury's Heart! She won the inaugural Trans-Lunar race in '27

OASIS -- Open Access Science Industrial Station - space station in LEO

The Bus -- Public transport to LEO

The Ice Princess -- An Ice tug - catches and delivers Mylar covered tritium ice comets sent from the Belt - Captained by Lirsín Delaney

Hel'Arumpo'or - SHIPS

Delrofenalis -- Tal'anis' sister ship that crashed during take-off
Tal'anis -- Aka Talefenanis - shortened from overuse -
Hel'Arumpo'or mothership

BOOKS BY THIS AUTHOR

Talismans

To free his beloved, Ross must master skills he's been told don't exist.

Ross Cambridge, a young artificer, was arrow-shot and left for dead by a sorcerer from the cold southern lands who quested north for a long-lost artifact. Although helpless to stop Salena, his betrothed, from being dragged away and Bound to the sorcerer, Ross held to a glimmer of hope. What could be done, could be undone.

The Quathiels, ancient elemental beings, had a plan. Steps were laid before Ross's feet, and the cadence set. To save the woman he loved, Ross must learn this new dance—and risk becoming the very thing the world feared.

Craig P Miller